Marg...

ACT OF
VIOLENCE

ADMIT TO
MURDER

A CASE TO
ANSWER

By the same author
SUMMER FLIGHT
PRAY LOVE REMEMBER
CHRISTOPHER
DECEIVING MIRROR
THE CHINA DOLL
ONCE A STRANGER
THE BIRTHDAY
FULL CIRCLE
NO FURY
THE APRICOT BED
THE LIMBO LADIES
NO MEDALS FOR THE MAJOR
THE SMALL HOURS OF THE MORNING
THE COST OF SILENCE
THE POINT OF MURDER
DEATH ON ACCOUNT
THE SCENT OF FEAR
THE HAND OF DEATH
DEVIL'S WORK
FIND ME A VILLAIN
THE SMOOTH FACE OF EVIL
INTIMATE KILL
SAFELY TO THE GRAVE
EVIDENCE TO DESTROY
SPEAK FOR THE DEAD
CRIME IN QUESTION
A SMALL DECEIT
CRIMINAL DAMAGE
DANGEROUS TO KNOW
ALMOST THE TRUTH
SERIOUS INTENT
A QUESTION OF BELIEF
FALSE PRETENCES
CAUSE FOR CONCERN

Featuring Patrick Grant
DEAD IN THE MORNING
SILENT WITNESS
GRAVEL MATTERS
MORTAL REMAINS
CAST FOR DEATH

Collected short stories
PIECES OF JUSTICE

Margaret Yorke Omnibus

ACT OF VIOLENCE

ADMIT TO MURDER

A CASE TO ANSWER

MARGARET YORKE

timewarner
paperbacks

A *Time Warner* Paperback

This omnibus edition first published in Great Britain by
Time Warner Paperbacks in 2003
Margaret Yorke Omnibus Copyright © Margaret Yorke 2003

Previously published separately:
Act of Violence first published in Great Britain in 1997 by
Little, Brown and Company
Published by Warner Books in 1998
Reprinted 1998, 1999
Copyright © Margaret Yorke 1997

Admit to Murder first published in Great Britain in 1990 by
Mysterious Press in association with Century Hutchinson Ltd
Published by Arrow in 1991
Published by Time Warner Paperbacks in 2002
Copyright © Margaret Yorke 1990

A Case to Answer first published in Great Britain in 2000 by
Little, Brown and Company
Published by Warner Books in 2002
Copyright © Margaret Yorke 2000

The moral right of the author has been asserted.

*All characters in this publication are fictitious and any
resemblance to real persons, living or dead, is purely coincidental.*

All rights reserved.
No part of this publication may be reproduced, stored in a retrieval system,
or transmitted, in any form or by any means, without the prior permission in
writing of the publisher, nor be otherwise circulated in any form of binding or
cover other than that in which it is published and without a similar condition
including this condition being imposed on the subsequent purchaser.

A CIP catalogue record for this book is
available from the British Library.

ISBN 0 7515 3505 2

Printed and bound in Great Britain by
Mackays of Chatham plc, Chatham, Kent

Time Warner Paperbacks
An imprint of
Time Warner Books UK
Brettenham House
Lancaster Place
London WC2E 7EN

www.TimeWarnerBooks.co.uk

ACT OF
VIOLENCE

1

In prison, people don't talk about their crimes, unless to say they are innocent. Oh, you get to hear why some are inside – drugs, maybe, or debt. And you know about those who've made headlines in the papers. When they arrive after sentencing, everyone feels the tension. Lifers are put in the hospital wing at first, in case they top themselves. Some try it; some regret what they've done and want to atone. If they don't, or don't profess to, they won't be paroled. Most are released, eventually. After all, they've served their time and paid their debt to society. Like me.

Meanwhile, survival is the name of the game: getting through your time as best you can; keeping out of trouble.

Oliver Foxton glanced at his wife, who was looking through some papers, frowning. Recently she had been prescribed spectacles for reading, but rarely wore them. Was it vanity? Didn't executive women regard them almost as accessories essential to their image? He sighed. She was an executive now, but she seemed no happier than before she embarked on her career.

He felt responsible for her discontent. Ever since they met, his main aim had been to make her happy, but he had not suceeded. He was too old: that was one reason for his failure, but when they first married the age difference had been what had drawn her to him. She had dropped out of university after a damaging love affair about which he never learned the details. He had met her on a skiing holiday; he was staying with a group of friends in a chalet, and she was in another, with her brother and his wife, who had taken her along to cheer her up. Oliver was a competent skier, not fast, but neat. Not very tall, thickset, already secure in his position as a solicitor in Mickleburgh, he was the complete opposite of her discarded lover. That, and the rebound factor, accounted for Sarah's interest in him; it was easy to understand why he had fallen in love with her. He was ready to settle down, and she came along: young, pretty, bright and, at the time, rather brittle. The brittleness which he had hoped to smooth away had never wholly disappeared.

Like accidents, marriages result because those involved happen to arrive at what might be the wrong place, at the same time.

But it wasn't wrong for him. He wouldn't change that part of the story, only his own performance.

Back from the French Alps, he had immediately pursued her, and they were married in the summer. It had been hasty, he acknowledged now, but things had gone well at first; in fact, people thought they had an ideal marriage, and in many ways it was. They had a son and daughter, both now adult – Tim at medical school and Judy at university reading law. Oliver allowed himself to dream that Judy might one day join the practice.

The Foxtons lived in Winbury, a village three miles from Mickleburgh; they gave and attended small dinner parties, and Sarah undertook various voluntary activities, extending their range as the children grew older. For a while she helped a friend run a curtain-making business, soon acquiring expertise. Commissions fell away during the recession, and then the friend moved from the district. Sarah took a business course and now worked for a management consultancy, analysing statistics and advising on the reorganisation of small companies. Oliver wanted her career to succeed; if it did, she might find contentment, but so far this had eluded her.

They'd never had the struggle experienced by many newly married couples; he was already established in his family's firm, and money, though limited, had not been really short. They'd had holidays abroad, and had recently had a new kitchen fitted when Sarah had complained that theirs was out of date and shabby. If she wanted something for the house, she could have it; Oliver was generous, but she, in turn, was not extravagant. Their partnership excluded conflict, but nothing seemed to cure her perpetual unspecified dissatisfaction.

She was so cold.

That was it: she was distantly affectionate, dutifully so, but she was cold, and it must be his fault.

'How was your day?' he had asked her when she arrived home an hour after he had returned from the office. She had been to London.

'Busy,' she'd replied.

'Did the meeting go well?' He wished she'd tell him about it, describe what it was about, share it with him. Apart from wanting to meet her on her own ground, he would have been interested.

'I suppose so. We got our message across,' she said flatly. 'I have to go up again next week.'

Well, at least she'd told him that. She enjoyed her London trips, which had become more frequent lately. He must not ask her if she had had a pleasant lunch; he'd done this before and had been accused of prying.

He'd cooked the supper, something she rarely let him do. She'd seemed to enjoy the meal and even dropped a kiss on his head as she passed his chair; it was the sort of kiss a father might receive, he thought sadly.

He'd try no more this evening. Oliver rose quietly and left the room, going to his study where he put on a tape of *Don Giovanni*. Then he went over to the big square work-table he had recently installed near the window; on it stood the subject of his new interest: a Victorian dolls' house, which he was restoring.

Sarah was not so immersed in her papers that she failed to notice Oliver's departure. He'd be playing with that dolls' house again: what a puerile pastime for a grown man, she had thought, when he first brought it home, but now, as it was gradually returned to life, she saw how delicately he worked, how neat his big fingers were, how intriguing the result would be. She would not admit it, however; not to him, and not even to herself. She preferred to nurse her resentment.

In the train from London, she had run over in her mind the events of the day, the eager anticipation with which she had arrived at her meeting, a seminar with delegates from several consultancies and businesses. Clive Barry, from her own firm, had been there, and during the lunch break she had heard him in discussion with the managing director of a company for which they had aready done some costings. A new post was to be created within their organisation, covering much of the work for which they now employed an outside adviser. She'd apply. It would offer her a daily escape to London, and who could tell what she might yet accomplish, given such a chance? She might even have to spend occasional nights in town. Visions of her own tiny flat swam into her mind.

Of course, she told herself, she was always glad to return to Winbury in the evenings; she loved her pretty, comfortable house, but she would be happier if it were in some agreeable part of London. This was impossible, so working there would be the next best thing. Meanwhile, in a few weeks' time, she was going to a conference in Kent, and that would mean staying away overnight, the first time since starting work that she had done so.

Challenged, she would have said that she was fond of Oliver; it was simply that he had become dull: old and dull. After all, he was fifty-five. Clive Barry, for instance, was her own age, and many of the people with whom she worked were younger, like Daisy, the secretary she shared with several other senior staff members, who was only twenty.

For the first years of her marriage, Sarah had been too busy to indulge in regrets and had basked in being a youthful, pretty mother. Tim was born eleven months after the wedding, a plump, docile baby. Sarah ran things smoothly and was unaware that other new mothers among her acquaintance found her intolerably smug. Everything went well for her: the babies appeared as if to order, first a boy and then a girl, who both proceeded through infancy and childhood to satisfactory teenage years, causing only minor alarms. Sarah was a good cook and manager, and she always had reliable help, a woman from the village who came daily and did whatever was required, including looking after the children when necessary. Though past sixty now, she still came twice a week, and extra if required. This had made Sarah's career debut easy. No one suffered at home.

She had been charged with energy while she did her business course, and Oliver, aware that trying to restrain her would only make her more determined to go her own way, encouraged her to spread her wings, all the time fearful that, one day, she might fly right away.

Before he finished work that evening, Oliver, on impulse, had walked up the High Street to the market square, turned left by the church, and entered a narrow street where once there had been a butcher's; this had been replaced by a dolls' house shop, selling kits to build them, miniature furniture and artefacts, and books and magazines about their restoration and construction. He was looking for a replica stove to put in the kitchen of the house he was restoring. He spent ten minutes browsing without finding what he sought, but he bought a tiny plate of artificial fruit to set on the dresser. They knew him now, in the shop. The manageress gave him a limpid smile as she attended to an elderly couple who were disagreeing about how best to equip the thatched farmhouse they were building.

They were arguing, not discussing, Oliver decided, hearing bitter tones. The distinction made so much difference. The manageress excused herself from them, took his money, and he left, somewhat depressed. Returning to the office, he saw Miss Ellis's car parked in the yard behind his Rover. She was back early today. She worked in Fettleton, a market town ten miles away, but he was not sure what she did. She was a remote, withdrawn woman; they exchanged greetings if they met but never more. One of his partners dealt with her lease; there had never been complaints on either side. The new couple in the other flat were not home yet; their windows were dark. Perhaps they should consider fitting time-switches, he reflected, although with direct access only through the courtyard, the flats, which had been converted from the stable block of the house where the offices of Foxton and Smythe were situated, were relatively protected. Miss Ellis had not needed that advice; her lights came on automatically.

Oliver had lived in the area for most of his life, joining his father in the firm as a young man. Bill Smythe had died fifteen years ago, but Oliver had kept the name; the firm had had expanded, acquiring partners specialising in divorce, which formed a large part of their business these days. Litigation, wills and conveyancing still went on; people would always need lawyers. At the moment one of his clients had been accused of fraud and another of embezzlement. Foxton and Smythe did not handle many criminal cases, apart from motoring offences, so these made a change.

We haven't had a murder yet, Oliver found himself thinking.

He had driven home wondering what sort of mood Sarah would be in after her day in London. Perhaps he should have bought her some flowers instead of pottering about in the dolls' house shop. But she would only have said, 'What are these in aid of? It's not my birthday,' and assume he wanted sex.

He did, but only if allied to love. Flowers and presents could not win that; it had to come from the heart.

Rosemary Ellis had planned to rent a flat in Fettleton, where she worked, but when she saw that one was available behind the Georgian building which housed the offices of Foxton and Smythe, at the end of Mickleburgh High Street, she was immediately drawn to it, chiefly because of its seclusion. It was near the church, and not far away was a footpath along which one could walk to the river and across the fields. She had new neighbours now, a young couple who had taken the downstairs flat where previously a frail elderly couple had lived. They had moved to a bungalow; she had not fraternised with them.

From across the yard, if she were at home when he was there, she could see into Oliver Foxton's office. She liked watching him at his desk, shirt-sleeved in summer except when clients came in. They and his secretary would sometimes mar her view on the rare occasions when she had the chance to watch him from her hall window. It was enough; she did not ask for more, although if they met in the yard, where their cars were parked, that was a bonus.

She knew where he lived. She'd driven past his house, The Barn House, Winbury, a long low building made of the local stone, set back from the road at the end of a short drive. Beside it was a barn from which it must derive its name. She'd seen his wife – a pretty, smart woman, always in a hurry when occasionally she called at the office, but then Rosemary herself was rarely in the flat in working hours.

The new couple in the flat below, Ginny and Bob, had invited her to their house-warming party soon after they moved in. She was surprised and touched, though at first she was inclined to refuse, but she accepted, to be neighbourly; however, she would keep her distance. She bought them a plant in a pot, which they accepted with apparent pleasure.

The party was noisy; many of the guests were staff members from Mickleburgh Comprehensive, where Ginny and Bob taught, and some were the parents of pupils. Rosemary was handed a glass of white wine and introduced to someone called Guy, who asked her what she did, and without waiting for an answer, told her all about himself. He was an accountant, recently divorced, with two children at the school. Rosemary listened to his monologue, letting it wash over her. Of course he was not interested in her, but nor was she in him. She could not move away for she was hemmed into a corner and the room was crowded. At last Bob, circulating with the wine, rescued her.

'Sorry you got stuck,' he beamed at her. 'Guy's a bit of a pain when he starts talking about his obsessions. Have you met Kate?' and he left her with a thin young woman in black leggings and a short black skirt who turned out to be the head of drama at the school. Rosemary had no interest in the theatre; their conversation stumbled along as they failed to find common ground, and eventually, when Kate drifted away, Rosemary returned to her own flat without saying goodbye, her departure unnoticed. She heard the noise of the party throbbing on below until nearly midnight. Then there were farewells, the sound of car doors being slammed, and, at last, blessed silence.

The next day, a note thanking her for the plant and apologising for the noise, adding that that they did not often have late parties, was pushed through her door. She had not invited Bob and Ginny back.

Kate, however, she met again, a few weeks later, one Saturday. She was in the town bookshop collecting a book she had ordered when she saw the other woman in conversation with a boy who must be, Rosemary supposed, one of her pupils.

'Hallo,' she said. 'We met at Bob and Ginny's party. You're their new neighbour, aren't you? This is Jamie, my son.'

Jamie mumbled some sort of greeting.

'I'll be off, then,' he said, and slouched away, large and uncoordinated, in a big fleece jacket and grubby trainers. His feet were enormous.

'He's tall,' Rosemary managed. Kate did not look old enough to have a son older than a toddler.

'Yes, isn't he?' Kate looked proud. 'He's brilliant at music,' she said. 'He plays the cello.'

'Oh,' said Rosemary, at a loss for the right response. She was not musical. 'How nice.'

'Well, I mustn't hold you up,' said Kate, turning towards the door.

'Goodbye,' said Rosemary, glad to be released. On her own ground, she was fluent, but in a social context she was inept. Intimacy alarmed her and she avoided it.

2

The scene is as familiar to me now as it was when it happened. Shots of it were shown to the jury: the long winding path through the forest where she walked her dogs, the beeches in their summer leaf spreading out among the scrub, and, further on, glades of larches with their spiky foliage. There were places where the cover was dense, and patches where coppicing would clear out saplings.

I'd picked the spot, and waited for her, trusting that no one else would walk that way that day. I'd followed her before, looking for a likely place where I could lurk, observing her, planning it. We'd even walked there together, more than once, for we were friends. That was mentioned at the trial, blackening my character. If the dogs turned on me, I'd have to kill them, too, but they knew me. They would not recognise me as an enemy.

I was often at their house. I'd made love there, in her bed, while she was visiting her parents. Of course he felt he must be loyal to her, must stay with her, because there were the children. Choosing between us was too difficult for him, but whenever he told me that we must part, that I must stay away from him, all I had to do was press myself against him – I was tall, unlike her; we were physically matched – start kissing him, and he would respond. With her gone, the way for us was clear. That was how I saw it then. It seemed so simple. And it wasn't as if the children did not know me. I had often babysat for them.

No one would suspect me. I'd have an alibi and I'd express horror when I heard that she'd been the random victim of a prowler in the forest. It was unwise to walk alone down those dark rides and bridleways; anyone could be hidden there, among the trees, vandals on motorbikes at the very least.

She hadn't heard a thing, had suspected nothing until, in my strong boots, I came right up behind her and plunged the knife into her back. Then she had turned startled eyes towards me, and, in the instant, as I'd hoped, she recognised me, perhaps guessed the reason for the deed, uttered a faint gurgle, and collapsed. On the ground, she writhed, and so, to make quite sure, I withdrew the knife and stabbed her again, several times, until she lay still, blood pumping out. I hadn't expected that, imagining one thrust would be enough, but then a frenzy overtook me, lest she should survive. One of the dogs, Hector, uttered a bark and stared at me in puzzlement, and I got him, too, in case he started howling before I could escape. The terrier had run off and disappeared, and it was his barking outside their house, disturbing neighbours, that caused alarm, so that she was found within hours. I'd hoped she'd lie undiscovered for a long time. After all, the house was empty – he was at work, not due back until the evening, and the children were at their school, where I was working at the time, which was how I had met the family and obtained my babysitting post.

I'd expected the children to go home, find their mother missing and be alarmed. Then a search would begin.

I'd planned to drag her off the track, into the long grass and scrub, to keep her hidden for as long as possible, but when I realised that I would be covered in her blood if I carried out this scheme, I changed my mind. I stepped carefully away from her, and walked back the way I had come, not wanting to create a trail leading from the main track.

I met no one.

Then I went to see my mother. I knew she would be out that day, doing voluntary work she regularly undertook. I told her I'd arrived an hour before in fact I got there. She believed me. Why not?

Later, in court, her evidence helped to convict me.

I dropped the knife in a ditch on the way home, but the police found it. There were no prints on it. I'd worn gloves. They discovered who had bought it; the shopkeeper had thought it an unusual purchase for a young woman, though I had said it was for my father, a keen fisherman. Surely there were women anglers, too? The conversation had caused him to remember me: unfortunate.

In the end, I confessed, because she was pregnant. He'd cheated on me. I admitted manslaughter due to diminished responsibility, but my plea was not accepted. I received a life sentence, but at last I was released.

The boy with the knife in his bag walked down the road to school. Now he could prove he was a hard man. If anyone threatened him, he could win in a struggle. They'd back off as soon as they saw his weapon. If he wanted another boy's trainers, or his dinner money, he could get them, and no one would dare tell.

A knife meant power. You didn't have to use it, but knowing you had it gave you control.

The first tenant of the upper flat behind Foxton and Smythe's office had been Prudence Wilmot. When she was unable to decide where to live after the sale of her house in Wiltshire, the estate agent who had acted for her mentioned it as a possible temporary measure; its lease was handled by another branch of his firm. Prudence, whose husband had recently died, found the prospect of living in a small country town appealing; she could try it, and if she liked it, would look for a house nearby. This she had done, and now she lived in the High Street, near the market square, in a small terraced house.

Her husband had been in the diplomatic service and they had spent many years abroad in different postings; then, when they were enjoying their retirement, living in what had been her parents' house, the collapse of Lloyd's had brought financial catastrophe. Prudence's husband had had a stroke and died. Prudence, however, owned the house, and thus was saved from penury. While she was living in the flat she had time on her hands, and wrote an historical novel set in Athens, where she and her husband had spent some years. After several rejections, she found an agent and then a publisher; a second novel had followed, and a third; she was now writing one set in Florence. The income brought in by her books, though not large, was a welcome supplement to her budget, and she enjoyed the research. She worked on an old typewriter at a desk overlooking her small garden, easily distracted when unusual birds arrived on her lawn, and often going to check on her plants' growth. She lived there contentedly, without an intimate circle of friends because writing took up most of her time. Oliver Foxton had grown fond of her while she was living in the flat, and his firm had done the legal work involved in the purchase of her new house. When she moved from the flat, she had shown him the old, grimy and damaged dolls' house she had kept back when much of her furniture was sold; it had been in her family since her own childhood.

'It's silly to hang on to it,' she had said. 'Look at the state it's in. It's only fit for a jumble sale.'

'It's not,' said Oliver. 'It could be restored. It could be quite valuable, it's so old. Let me renovate it for you.'

'But I can't ask you to do that,' she'd exclaimed.

'You're not. I'm asking you,' he said. 'Indulge me.'

You can invent your life – your history. Who is to know if what you tell them is the truth? You're stating your version of the past, and it may be false, as in my case.

I have a new name, a whole new identity, and though it was all in the papers, sensationally described, it was nearly thirty years ago. I have been living as another person for a long time, moving around, it is true, but now settled here indefinitely.

After my release, I went to live in Wales and found employment as a post office clerk. Those connected with what they called my rehabilitation arranged this, and I stayed for eight years, doing charitable work in my spare time. I led – and lead – a blameless life and am of benefit to the community, not a danger. I have paid my debt to society.

There are others still inside who should be freed. Why not, when they have served long sentences? Some, like me, committed their crimes when very young, and as the result of passion; after years of incarceration they are new people, wholly altered. Confining them is most unjust.

My days are spent aiding others. I work conscientiously, discharging all my duties, more than fulfilling my obligations. I never talk about my crime, and rarely think of it.

It's better so.

Oliver had decided to furnish the dolls' house in the same style as when Prudence had played with it. Some dolls remained inside it: a father and mother, two girls and a boy, and several items of furniture which he cleaned up and mended. The house, Prudence said, was a replica of her childhood home. In those days her father owned a carpet factory and was prosperous. He had had the dolls' house built by a craftsman he knew and equipped it to mirror their surroundings, even to supplying their correct family, with her, her much younger sister and her older brother, who had been killed in the Second World War.

After his difficult evening with Sarah, Oliver spent nearly an hour working on the dolls' house. At the end of that time he had decided that he must devise a way to give her a treat – dinner somewhere, or a theatre. They could invite friends along, if she would be bored with only him.

He had not heard her go to bed. She was asleep, or seemed to be, when he went up.

It wasn't difficult to become a counsellor. All I did was advertise in the paper and put a brass plate on my gate, then wait. I'd done it elsewhere, before I rented a consulting room in Fettleton. I'd joined an association which required no qualifications, simply some statements as to education and intent; I was entitled, then, to proclaim myself a member.

I had the money to do it; having served my sentence, I'd built up funds in my various posts. I'd driven taxis, and worked in hotels, always keeping remote from other people. I never sought affection; it brought problems. Then my parents died – first my mother, of an illness, then my father. According to the lawyer who eventually traced me, people said he perished of a broken heart, because of what I'd done. How sentimental. I'd kept away from them after my release. Ever loyal, they had visited me in prison, but with little to say, though assuring me that they would always support me; after a while their visits grew fewer and fewer, and when I took on a new identity, we severed ties. It was not discussed; it just happened. However, they left me adequate funds to enable me to escape from office drudgery. Conscience money, I decided.

Enough counselling went on in prison for me to pick up much of the jargon, and I learned in the raw from those around me. I read various books to reinforce what I already knew; then

I was ready. It's easy to advise my clients; much of the art of counselling is simply listening, which isn't difficult though it can be excessively dull. Then I suggest ways in which they can confront their problems; common sense is often all that is necessary.

I don't like to think about the reasoning that motivated me all those years ago. What I did was wrong; I've admitted it often enough, and I had to show remorse in order to obtain parole. There was grief at the time, mostly his, and that of the children left without their mother – a role I had expected to assume. Mine was the sorrow of betrayal. There was the unborn infant, too; the papers made a meal of that.

He abandoned me, saying that he had never loved me. He took the two children overseas and, after a while, married someone else. Like me, he started again. Now it's as if he'd died, as though it had never happened. In fact he did die, not long ago. It was reported in the papers, with a reference to the case. I suppose these things never cease to haunt. He had manipulated me because he wanted me, perhaps as a boost to his ego, as I was so young, or perhaps he was simply a lecherous man who needed more than one woman.

Now I manipulate others, sometimes gaining considerable control. In addition to my straightforward consultations and on the strength of my professional reputation, I write an advice column in a trade magazine. I get satisfaction from what I do. I am an influence for good, and the past is expunged.

3

How was she to occupy Saturday?

Sarah, waking, saw that Oliver was already up. He'd be out gardening, she thought, or maybe working on that silly house. She supposed it was a good thing to have a hobby. People said so, and if you had one, you met others who shared your interest, possibly even life partners. There were amateur dramatics, for instance, and badminton or tennis. Sarah was not attracted to any of these activities; as a girl, she had not been good at games; nor was she musical, but she had been willing to fall in with the plans of others, one who was led, rather than a trail blazer. She embarked on an affair during her first year at university partly because the idea of romance was already in her mind, and she thought it was essential to acquire a boyfriend. When she was singled out by a young man who had a beaten-up old MG, and who was a rugger enthusiast, she was ecstatic. An emotional path had been mapped out for her, and with dedication she learned the rules of rugby, standing on the touchline, shivering in spite of her thick coat and woolly hat, cheering Harry on. She endured long draughty drives in his car, and his clumsy sexual fumblings, and, regarding her cooperation as compulsory, hoped that these would become more tolerable in time.

In the summer, when Harry took off for a backpacking holiday with a girl called Amanda, she was mortified. It seemed that everyone but Sarah knew of their romance; however, Harry had decided not to have it out with her but to slide away.

'What a heel,' said another girl, attempting consolation, but Sarah was too far gone to benefit from her words. 'You'll soon find someone else,' the girl encouraged. But Sarah did not want anyone else; she wanted Harry, the rugby hero, whom her parents had met when they came to see her one weekend. She was too keen too soon, thought her friend. But Harry had given Sarah status; his defection was, to her, a major humiliation.

Then she met Oliver, who offered her an escape which salvaged her pride.

Being in love with him, as she eventually decided she was – he was certainly in love with her – was much less upsetting than being in love with Harry. For one thing, she didn't have to watch rugger, or cricket, which in the summer had taken over as Harry's main interest. Nor did she have to drink too much, which she'd done to keep up with Harry and to help with sex. Oliver did not expect her to go to bed with him until after they were married; before then, he kissed her rather nicely and sometimes caressed her intimately, but he never attempted more. Once, when she had had a few drinks at a dance – dances didn't seem to exist now – and she had twined herself around him as Harry had liked her to do, he unwound her and said that it was time to say good night.

Sex with Oliver had not been a gymnastic contest, nor a power struggle. Slowly it became rewarding, and was so still, though now it had become a habit. She was bored with him. Perhaps, as time passed, everyone grew bored with their husband or wife. Verbal communication between them seemed to be dwindling away; Oliver would tinker with his dolls' house, or deal with the papers for the various charities with which he was concerned, and she would watch television and then go to bed. Lately, it hadn't mattered. She had her own papers to work on now. She'd found a new role, and she was meeting different sorts of people all the time, clients and colleagues.

Oliver was in the kitchen when she went downstairs. He had made coffee, and, after pouring her some, he suggested they might have dinner that night at a riverside restaurant they liked. Sarah was pleased, and she agreed to his proposal that they should invite the Stewarts to join them. The two couples had been friends for years; their children were much of an age. The parents met less often now that their families had dispersed; it would be a chance to pick up the threads. Daniel Stewart had been made redundant five years ago, and after being rejected by numerous firms to whom he applied for a job, had opened a second-hand furniture business in a former corn merchant's just off Mickleburgh High Street. Sarah called it a junk shop; very little of what he sold could be termed antique. He cleaned, repaired, stripped and polished, and sometimes painted, the things he bought up cheaply, often at sales. Midge, his wife, had started picture-framing in part of the premises and Oliver suspected that hers was the more profitable operation. The Stewarts, however, remained cheerful if impecunious; they were delighted at the prospect of dining out, and conversation was lively during the meal, with Sarah deploring the hours worked by young doctors – Tim was worn out, she said, and they seldom saw him. Midge enquired about Oliver's dolls' house, which had fascinated her when she saw it. Sarah thought this a pointless topic and began discussing a local road-widening scheme which was attracting protest.

The Foxtons had picked up the Stewarts from Deerton, the small village a few miles away where they lived in a slightly crumbling house built thirty or so years before in what had been the orchard of the rectory. After dinner, they drove them back, and Daniel invited them in for coffee. Sarah accepted, and Oliver assented; a delayed return home would postpone a post mortem on the evening, with accompanying criticism.

Midge led the way indoors, flipping on lights as she went. There was an air of shabby scruffiness about the interior; surfaces were dusty, and there was a pile of letters, some unopened, on the table. Bills, Oliver guessed. They went through to the sitting room at the rear of the house, where in daylight there was a view across the garden which was mostly apple trees, rough grass, and, in spring, hundreds of daffodils. Now, faded apricot velvet curtains were drawn across the windows. The room was chilly.

'Sorry,' apologised Midge. 'We didn't light the fire before we went out. We were at the shop till late.' The shop was open on Saturdays, and she had had several pictures to frame, promised for the afternoon.

Daniel offered brandy, and had one himself, but Oliver, who was driving, had had a glass of wine with dinner and would not risk going over the limit.

'Just coffee, please,' he said. 'Shall I make it?' He knew where most things were in this shabby, comfortable house.

'Would you? You are a dear,' said Midge. 'I'll light the fire. You'll have a brandy, won't you, Sarah?'

Sarah, suppressing a shiver, said she would.

Midge was on hands and knees busy with twigs and firelighters. The grate, which was not the open-hearth kind, as in the Foxtons' house, where ash intentionally accumulated, hadn't even been cleaned, Sarah noticed. Midge was such a sloven. It was surprising that Daniel didn't appear to mind. Oliver shouldn't be drinking coffee so late, she thought; it would keep him awake. Except that nothing seemed to do that.

'How many coffees?' asked Oliver, putting his head round the door.

'I'll come and help,' said Midge. 'The fire's going now and Dan will keep an eye on it. Won't you?' she added.

'Of course,' he said, smiling at her, sorry the Foxtons had decided to come in, but after all, they had paid for the dinner, refusing his attempts to split the bill.

In the kitchen, Midge and Oliver soon brewed the coffee in the cafetière which Midge said Mark and Jonathan, her sons, one an engineer in Scotland, the other at university, had given her for her birthday. They found cups and saucers, Midge scuffling past the mugs she and Daniel always used. You didn't serve coffee to Sarah in a mug, not unless it was elevenses in the kitchen.

'Sorry about the mess,' said Midge.

'I see no mess,' said Oliver, although by comparison with Sarah's, the kitchen was untidy, with crockery on the drainer and a tin of biscuits on the table.

'I'm a bit of a muddler,' said Midge.

'I don't think you are,' said Oliver, pouring boiling water into the pot. He gave it a stir. 'I always do that,' he said. 'I'm not sure if you're meant to. Stir it, I mean.'

'So do I,' said Midge. She smiled at him, then gave him a quick peck on the cheek. 'You're a saint,' she said.

Oliver looked startled, but he beamed at her.

'You're a corker,' he said.

'What a strange expression. I hope it's a compliment,' Midge replied.

'Oh yes,' said Oliver. 'It's meant to be.'

When they returned to the others, Midge bustled about, wondering aloud how long to wait before plunging the filter down on the coffee. Sarah was sipping her brandy. Her hair, which she had grown recently, and wore loose tonight, fell on to the shoulders of her scarlet coat.

She looked very beautiful, thought both the men.

And I'm the one who goes home with her, Oliver reflected. He had never stopped marvelling about this, blaming himself for any disappointments.

They had already brought each other up to date on their children's progress, and talk died away as they finished their drinks. Driving home, Sarah commented on Orchard House.

'What a mess the place is,' she said. 'Midge is a real slut.'

Oliver had feared this sort of conversation might develop.

'She works hard, and she hasn't got anyone to help in the house,' he said.

'She could find someone. She used to have a cleaner.'

'I don't suppose they can afford it,' said Oliver. 'Times aren't easy and they've still got Jonathan to subsidise.'

'Oh,' said Sarah. 'Are they really so hard up?'

'I think so,' said Oliver. He knew that Daniel owed money.

Sarah was silent. She was lucky to be able to afford to dress well and have more or less whatever she wanted. She did not say this aloud; nor, as they prepared for bed, did she mention any pleasure she might have derived from the evening.

'That sauce on the duck was far too sweet,' she said, as she turned off her bedside light.

Oliver, still cheered by his moment with Midge in the kitchen, had planned to slip his arm round Sarah tonight, testing her mood. This remark instantly cooled his ardour.

'I thought it was delicious,' he said. 'I'm sorry it didn't please you.' By his standards, this was a waspish remark. He leaned over to deliver a good-night kiss on whatever surface of Sarah he could easily locate. It proved to be her hair, and she did not feel it.

She wouldn't have minded an approach tonight, she thought, rolling over, her back to him. Of course, he never sensed how she felt. Unable to count her blessings, Sarah slept, while a few miles away their dinner guests lay linked together, mutually comforted, like nesting spoons.

4

Jamie Preston was spending Saturday night at his friend Barry Noakes's house in Deerton. Barry lived in Orchard Close, a group of seven modern houses in a cul de sac opposite the Stewarts. His parents had gone to a wedding in Sheffield and would not be back until late, so Jamie was keeping Barry company. Two of their friends, Peter Grant, who also lived in the close, and Greg Morris, whose shortest route home was through the Noakeses' garden, over the fence and across a field, had come to spend the evening. No girls were present; that was a restriction imposed by Barry's parents; there was to be no opportunity for licentious conduct. Barry and his friends, however, were content; they talked about girls and scuffled with them when they got the chance, but none was yet ready for a no-holds-barred session. They had hired three videos and settled down to enjoy pizzas cooked in the microwave and cans of Coca-Cola.

They were sprawled in the living room, watching a horror film which they were too young to rent legally, when the doorbell rang.

Barry opened the door, and saw four boys from the year above them at their school. They crowded into the doorway and before he could prevent them, they had pushed him out of the way and burst into the house, surging on into the room where the others sat in front of the television, empty Coca-Cola cans stacked neatly on the hearth at the side of the electric fire, their pizza plates piled on a coffee table.

The intruding boys had already been drinking. One of them, Wayne, had bought a six-pack of beer.

Their escapade had started as a dare, after they met at Trevor's house. He had been boasting that he could drive and would take them for a spin in his mother's car, which he could borrow without her ever knowing. She and his father had gone for their usual Saturday night out. They went clubbing and were always late home. The car would be back in its place when they returned. The whole evening stretched ahead of the bored boys, and here was a challenge. The four of them had piled into the Lada and their first stop was to buy another six-pack. Then they drove through the town and into the country, the passengers all drinking while Trevor displayed his skills.

Seeing Deerton indicated on a signpost, one of the others, who knew that Barry Noakes lived there and had heard his plans for the evening being discussed at school, told Trevor to turn off.

'There's a few having a party there,' he said. 'Let's join in.'

The others were pleased with this suggestion; it was much too early to go home. They urged Trevor on, though they were vague about finding the close and Trevor overshot the turning, stopping beyond it. They piled out of the car, giggling. There was a short argument about which was the right house; Peter Grant lived here too, and there were seven houses.

'We'll try them all till we find them,' said Paul.

This seemed a good idea. They started at the first house, on the corner, and Barry answered the bell.

Led by Wayne, the four boys pushed past him. Wayne had

a can of beer in his hand and he pulled it open, putting it to his mouth, staring at what the others were watching.

At first it was all right. The intruders stood for a few minutes, gaping at the television. Then Kevin spoke.

'What a load of shit,' he said, and began picking up cushions and throwing them at the screen.

'Wouldn't mind some food,' said Wayne. He looked at the soiled plates. 'Got any more of that? Had a takeaway, did you?'

'Sorry, no,' said Barry nervously. 'My mum left pizzas for us.'

'Your mum left pizzas, did she?' Wayne mimicked Barry's half-broken voice. 'Well, let's see what else she's left,' and, followed by Paul, he went through to the kitchen, where they opened the fridge. Paul took out a bottle of milk and drank some, then, looking at Wayne to make sure his action was observed, poured the rest on the floor and dropped the bottle, which rolled over under the table. Hearing their excited cries, Kevin and Trevor followed them into the kitchen and began emptying the fridge, throwing margarine on to the floor and standing on the packet. They found Lily Noakes's store cupboard and began spilling rice and flour around them.

'Hey, stop it,' Barry, following them, protested, trying to bar the way to other cupboards while Peter dragged at the invaders' jackets to pull them back. Wayne turned on the taps at the sink and began splashing water about, and then Kevin and Paul broke away, going upstairs, their feet covered in the sticky mess from the kitchen floor.

Jamie ran after them, shouting at them to stop, but they took no notice, pulling the beds apart, flinging duvets and pillows around. Then Paul leaped up on to Barry's parents' large bed, undid his zip, and urinated in a wide arc over the duvet.

Jamie was still yelling at them to stop, tugging at any part of their clothing he could reach, but, intent on their wanton destruction, Paul and Kevin ignored him, pausing only long enough for Kevin to hit out at him, sending him off balance, but he recovered and caught Paul round the legs as he zipped up his fly, bringing him down on the bed so that his face made contact with the sodden duvet. At this, Kevin rounded on Jamie, who presented a vulnerable target as he bent over, grasping Paul. Kevin pulled his hair and dragged him to the ground, where he kicked his head. Somehow Jamie managed to wriggle free, and, realising he could not defeat the two boys, he ran downstairs, but Paul and Kevin, their blood up now, went after him. As he fled, sounds of battle came from the living room. Jamie dragged open the front door and ran into the road, shouting for help.

He did not turn into the close but dashed across the road to a house whose porch light was on, Daniel and Midge having failed to turn it out after Oliver and Sarah left. Jamie ran up the path to the front door and rang the bell, then thumped the tarnished brass knocker, yelling as loudly as he could.

To him, it seemed like hours before Daniel Stewart opened the door and saw a blood-stained, frightened youth who gasped something incoherent about boys trashing a house in the close.

'Calm down. Tell me what's going on,' said Daniel, and the boy said a gang had gatecrashed Barry's house.

'They're wrecking it,' he said. 'They're fighting.'

'I'll come. Just a tick while I put on some clothes,' said Daniel, who had dragged on a towelling robe before answering the door. He raced upstairs, where he put on tracksuit trousers and top while Midge, woken too, sat up in bed asking what was going on.

'There's a fight in the close. Ring the police,' called Daniel. 'There's a young lad with a bloody nose outside.'

Jamie had not waited for him. Recovering his breath, thinking of Barry and the others, he ran back across the road to help his friends.

Daniel, following at a trot, saw that the trouble was at the first house, for the front door was open and he could hear cries. As he reached the scene a jumble of boys spilled out into the road, all fighting and punching one another. He couldn't see the one who had come to ask for help; in the dark – there were no street-lights in Deerton – they were just a mass of thrashing limbs. He reached into the scrum and grabbed a boy, dragging him back just as another adult male arrived from a neighbouring house and cuffed one of the boys around the head. It was impossible to tell who was on whose side, and the men tried simply to separate the youths. Two of them peeled away and ran back into the house from which all of them had erupted. Now Daniel and the other man had become the enemy, and as the attack turned towards them, even Barry shrank away, leaving only Jamie to oppose the other four. His blows seemed futile as he pummelled the backs presented to him, then tried to pull the boys away from the men. One of the men caught hold of Paul and held him in an armlock, and at this Kevin pulled a flick knife from his pocket. He thrust it into the midriff of the man, Daniel Stewart. The second man, punched in the guts by Wayne, was winded and had turned away. Kevin's victim released his hold on Paul, sinking to the ground, and Paul and Kevin started kicking him as he lay curled up, emitting wailing cries. Jamie did not realise that he was crying himself as he went on trying to drag Paul and Kevin away from the injured man. Then Kevin turned and stabbed him in the arm. The others had got the second man on the ground by this time and were kicking him, but then the doors of other houses in the close opened and lights came on.

'Beat it,' Kevin cried, and they sped back to the Lada.

They had gone before the police arrived.

The boys had disappeared so rapidly. One minute there had been the flailing limbs and tangled bodies, then the groans, and as the stabbed man collapsed, the other man, doubled over, had been brought down and was a target for the blows and kicks that followed. Moments later, as several neighbours appeared, there was the sound of the Lada being driven off with the engine revving loudly. The only youth remaining on the scene was Jamie, clutching his wounded arm. It was bleeding freely, and, without a jacket, suffering from shock, he was shivering. The gathering group of adults did not, however, see the blood, which his dark shirt was absorbing. Some turned threateningly towards him while others bent over the two men. The second one was soon on his feet and someone went to call an ambulance. Jamie retreated towards Barry's house, where Barry, horrified at what was happening but not brave enough to rejoin the fray, stood in the doorway.

'Friends gone without you, have they?' said one man, advancing upon Jamie, who, very frightened, backed into the house.

Hands dragged him inside and closed the door, and then the boys in the house saw that he was hurt. It was Peter Grant who fetched a towel and wrapped it round Jamie's soaking sleeve, making Jamie bend his arm against his chest.

Midge had not followed Daniel immediately. After she had telephoned the police, she had pulled on a sweater and trousers and gone downstairs. She put the kettle on. That was what you did in an emergency. Then she opened the front door. Strangely, as she realised later, the fight had not been noisy; there were no shouts or cries, but slowly a sense of foreboding filled her. She pulled the kettle to the side of the Aga, found a coat and a torch, and as she left the house a car tore past, travelling fast out of the village. She ran then, suddenly extremely frightened, yet expecting to see Daniel coming towards her, the louts having been despatched.

A man who she realised only later was Ted Grant was

standing, bent over, hugging his arms across his body. Someone else was stooping over a figure on the ground, who lay motionless, curled up in the foetal position. Then the police arrived. They had been very quick, someone later commented.

They took her to the hospital in their car, saying it was better so, for Daniel was dead. They were very kind. She noted that.

At the hospital, when they asked her who to telephone, she thought of Oliver at once. Only a few hours before, they had been laughing in the kitchen at Orchard House, brewing coffee, and now there was no Daniel.

With the front door closed upon the suddenly quiet scene outside, and unaware that Daniel Stewart was dead, Barry and Greg emphasised that they must give the police no names. Peter was less certain but he was busy administering first aid to Jamie.

'Kevin will murder us, if we do,' said Greg. 'And Paul. He was wild tonight.'

'He was on something,' Barry said.

'It'll clean up. The house, I mean,' said Peter, an anxious, rather studious boy. He was not yet aware that his father had been involved in the affray.

'But what about my arm?' said Jamie. 'Kevin had a knife.' He was feeling rather faint, more from shock than loss of blood, and though back in the warm house, he was still shivering. 'I can say it was an accident,' he added quickly.

At this point there was the sound of a siren outside and the ambulance arrived.

'You'd better go out there. Get the medics to see to you,' said Peter. 'I'll take you.' The towel he had wrapped round Jamie's arm was now soaked in blood. 'You'll need stitching,' he declared.

He put an arm round Jamie and led him out to where a group of adults surrounded the figure on the ground, screening it from both the boys. A police officer detached himself and came towards the pair. There was no need for Jamie to explain that he was injured; it was obvious.

'Come with me, son,' said the officer. 'Here's one you can help,' he told one of the green-overalled ambulance attendants.

Jamie, by then, was only too thankful to be told what to do and taken care of. In the ambulance, however, the man who had been attacked lay very still, his face covered.

'Is he dead?' asked Jamie. Surely people didn't die like that, in seconds?

One of the police officers was travelling with them in the ambulance.

'Yes,' he said. 'I'm afraid so. Stabbed. Like you, Jamie, but you'll get over it.'

He'd asked Jamie his name immediately and had been kind, but he knew that though wounded, Jamie might be an assailant, his own knife in some way turned against him.

When the telephone call from the hospital woke him, Oliver found the message incredible.

Sarah heard him say, 'Oh no! No!' and then, more calmly, 'Very well. I understand. I'll come at once.' As he spoke, he was getting out of bed.

Sarah was instantly alert.

'What's happened? Is it Tim?' she cried.

'No – no, it's not Tim, nor Judy,' Oliver said, already pulling on some clothes. 'It's Daniel. That was the hospital. He's been stabbed.'

'Stabbed? How? Do you mean they had a break-in after we left?'

'No. There was some sort of brawl in the village and

he went to investigate. I'm not too clear about the details but Midge isn't hurt. She's at the hospital. She asked them to ring us.' Oliver paused, and added heavily, 'He's dead, Sarah.'

'Oh, Oliver, no! Oh, he can't be!' Sarah gulped and her eyes filled with tears, which she blinked away. Sarah never wept. 'Oh, poor Midge! You'd better bring her here,' she said, immediately practical. 'I'll put the electric blanket on in the spare room.'

'Yes – do that,' said Oliver.

'What about Mark and Jonathan? Do they know?'

'The police will be dealing with telling them,' said Oliver. 'They're at the hospital – the police, I mean. I'll sort things out with them.'

'Shall I come with you?' Sarah asked. She did not want to; proximity to suffering was so upsetting. But poor silly, clueless Midge might need her. Sarah shuddered. In a flash, Midge had become a widow.

'It would be better if you got things ready for her here,' said Oliver. 'The business at the hospital may take some time. Formalities and so on. You're absolutely right. She can't go home on her own.'

'She'll be so shocked,' said Sarah.

'Yes.' No words were adequate. 'I'm off. I'll ring if we're going to be ages.'

'Right,' said Sarah, already planning sandwiches and coffee. Or maybe Horlicks. Coffee kept you awake.

Oliver bent to give Sarah a quick kiss and was gone before she could kiss him back.

What if Oliver, driving through the night, were in an accident? What if she never saw him alive again? He might have a heart attack – anything could happen. For the last twenty-three years he had been a steady fixture in her life. How would she feel if all at once he wasn't there? Frightened by these intimations of mortality, Sarah braced herself and banished them from her mind.

She put on trousers and a sweater, brushed her hair and tied it back, then went to find a new toothbrush and a nightdress for Midge, although by the time Oliver brought her back, it would scarcely be worth anybody's while to go to bed. Still, it was Sunday. No one had to work. Sarah could meet Mark at Heathrow, for surely he would fly back from Scotland. Turning her thoughts towards practicalities, she went to the kitchen.

Oliver, driving towards Fettleton, reflected that a police officer, possibly someone younger than Mark himself, might be knocking on Mark's door even now.

5

Kate Preston's was the third door to receive a pounding in the night.

She and Jamie lived in a small house behind Mickleburgh Sports Ground, where Jamie was a member of the junior rugby club.

Who on earth could be making such a racket in the middle of the night? She put her head out of the bedroom window and saw, illumined by the security light which had come on at their approach, two uniformed police officers, a man and a woman. What now, she thought, putting on her dressing gown and slippers, never for a moment connecting their visit with her son, who she believed was safely in Deerton with his friend, and, at this hour, sound asleep.

When the officers asked if they could come in she was alarmed. Had something happened to her parents, who lived in Devon?

They made her sit down before they told her that Jamie had been wounded in a fight.

'But that's impossible. He's at Deerton with his friend,' she said.

'That's where the fight was,' said the male officer, PC Roberts.

'He's not badly hurt,' said WPC Tracy Dale. 'It's just a flesh wound in the upper arm. He was lucky.'

While Kate tried to take this in, they told her that they needed to talk to Jamie, who was too young to be interviewed without a parent or a guardian present.

'Some lads came to the Noakeses' house and there was trouble,' Tracy Dale told her.

'Jamie wouldn't start a fight,' said Kate.

'Someone else got badly hurt,' said Roberts. 'We want Jamie to tell us what occurred.'

'I'm sure he will,' said Kate. 'I'll go straight to the hospital.'

'We'll take you,' said the officers.

Kate, feeling frantic, took two minutes to throw on some clothes. The police might not be telling her the truth about how badly Jamie was hurt. How could such a thing have happened?

'Are Barry's parents back yet?' she asked. 'They went to Sheffield, to a wedding.' Jamie and Barry were sensible boys; leaving them together for the evening, with Barry's parents due home that night, had seemed a reasonable plan. She should have had both boys over to her house, Kate thought, but, a lone mother, she encouraged Jamie to be independent.

'I couldn't tell you,' Roberts said. 'We've simply come to take you to your boy.'

'Was Barry hurt too?'

'I don't think so. Just the house,' said Tracy Dale. 'The other boys trashed it.'

Kate was silent as they drove on towards Fettleton. How could this be? Deerton, with a church and one pub, had a population of only about three hundred people. The village shop had closed some years ago; it was a backwater, with very few new houses. Other pupils from the school lived there; had some of them joined Barry and Jamie, maybe high on drugs or something?

'Jamie wouldn't start anything,' she repeated. 'He'd help a friend, though. Are you sure he isn't badly hurt?'

'That's what the man said,' Roberts told her. 'We haven't seen him. We've come for you.'

While Roberts and Tracy Dale were dealing with this aspect of the incident, other officers were in Deerton, seeking witnesses. The Scenes of Crime Officer and his team would be searching for forensic evidence from the site. They needed to find the weapon used; this was a murder enquiry.

Jamie, his wound stitched and dressed, had been pronounced fit enough to leave hospital and he was waiting for his mother to arrive. He was very white, trying to control his trembling when Kate rushed to him and hugged him, gently, because his right arm was in a sling.

'Whatever happened, Jamie?' she asked him, but he could only shake his head.

They were taken to a room near the casualty area, a place where bad news was broken, Kate decided. There, Roberts and Tracy Dale asked Jamie the same question.

He saw that he had to give some sort of explanation, but he told them very little. He and Barry, with Peter and Greg, had been watching a video when some other boys arrived, forced their way in and started wrecking the place.

'It got a bit rough,' Jamie said. 'This man came to sort things out. The fight was in the road by now.' He didn't want to say that his three friends had gone inside the house and left him to it. 'The man got in the way of the knife and so did I.' He did not mention that he had fetched the man. He looked at his mother. 'He died,' he said. 'The man.'

'Oh God!' It could have been Jamie who was killed.

'Have you got a knife, Jamie?' asked Roberts.

'It wasn't my knife. I didn't do it,' Jamie said, and the trembling began again.

'So you have got a knife. Where is it?'

'In my jacket. It's a penknife,' Jamie said.

'You can't think Jamie killed the man! Why, he's been hurt himself,' said Kate angrily.

'That could have happened in the tussle,' Roberts said.

'It did,' said Jamie. 'I told you, I got in the way.'

'You must know who the other boys were. The ones who broke in,' said Roberts.

'They didn't break in. They banged on the door and when Barry opened it they rushed past him.'

'If you won't tell us who they are, we've only got your word for it that they existed,' Roberts said. He spoke quietly.

Kate stared at him. She could not believe what she was hearing.

Nor could Jamie.

'Barry wasn't going to trash his own house,' he said fiercely.

'There were two other boys in the house with you,' said Roberts. 'Friends of yours and Barry?'

'Yes. They'll tell you what happened,' said Jamie.

'Had any of you been doing drugs?'

'No – of course not. That's sick,' said Jamie.

'You say so. What about the others?' Roberts persisted. Jamie might have had a blood test at the hospital; if so, it would show whether he was drugged up or not.

'My son isn't a liar. Why don't you listen to him?' Kate was furious.

'Please don't interrupt, Mrs Preston,' Roberts said curtly.

'I tell you, we'd just had some pizzas and were watching the video,' said Jamie. 'Then these other guys arrived.'

'If you tell us who they are, then we can talk to them,' said Roberts.

Jamie wavered. Then he set his mouth in a determined line. The others would have told their tale by now.

'I can't,' he said.

Kate understood. She was a teacher. She knew the code.

'Jamie's been badly hurt and he's shocked,' she said. 'Let us go now and you can talk to him tomorrow, when he's had some rest. He's not fit for this,' she added, 'and I'll soon find a doctor to say so.'

She was wondering if they needed a solicitor. Surely not! When she had a chance to talk to Jamie, she'd find out what had really happened.

'Very well.' Roberts knew he had pushed it as it was, but either Jamie was involved or he knew who was. 'We'll run you back,' he said. Roberts had considered taking Jamie to the police station to be interviewed in depth, even to be charged, but he'd get bail as soon as a solicitor was called. Besides, the boy did look ill. Innocent or guilty, he would not be judged fit for questioning.

In the car, Kate pressed Jamie's hand, urging silence. He was only too keen to keep quiet, and she felt him quivering with nerves beside her. Tears came to her eyes. Jamie, wounded, was the victim of some thugs, and this rude, callous policeman did not believe him.

When they were back in Mickleburgh, Roberts wanted to follow them into the house, but Tracy Dale stopped him.

'We'll see you in the morning, James,' she said. 'Get some sleep.'

Kate got him up to bed, tucking him in with a hot water bottle and a milky drink. Should she try to get the story out of him now, while it was all fresh in his mind? Would his resolution to stay silent strengthen if she left it?

'I tried to get him off that man, Mum,' said Jamie.

Get who, she thought, but did not ask. It might emerge.

'Did you tell the police that?'

'Not really. They were telling me what happened, sort of. By the time I'd been stitched up, they'd decided.'

And tried to stitch you into it, thought Kate.

They'd sort it out in the morning. She wondered about telephoning the Noakeses, who might know what had really happened, but realised that their house would be full of policemen. She would leave it till later.

She hoped Jamie would sleep. The hospital had provided a sedative and he had washed it down with his drink. She didn't expect to sleep again herself, but she went back to bed, managing to doze from time to time, while images of the past, her brief marriage, and her own childhood, spent in the Devonshire countryside where knife attacks and muggings were, at that time – and on the whole, now – rare, kept flickering across her mind.

Progress, she thought. Internet and schoolboys armed with knives.

Who was the man who had died? No one had supplied a name.

Jamie, surrendering to exhaustion and the tablet he had taken, had time to think that if he had not gone to fetch the man, he would still be alive.

'You were a bit hard on that poor lad,' said Tracy Dale as she and Roberts drove away.

'If his hand didn't hold the knife, he knows whose did,' said Roberts, unmoved.

'He'll tell. His mother'll get it out of him, when he's had some sleep,' said Tracy.

'We should have got his knife,' said Roberts.

'He said it was in his jacket. He wasn't wearing one,' Tracy said. The hospital had sent him home wrapped in a blanket, which Kate was to return.

'Hm. Wonder why that was,' said Roberts.

'Because he dashed out of the house, as he said he did, to lend a hand to the man who was killed, of course,' said Tracy.

'He knows more than he's saying,' was Roberts' reply, and Tracy knew it was the truth.

'I expect he left the jacket at his friend's house. He wouldn't have been wearing it watching videos, would he?' she said.

6

Trevor lay in bed listening for his parents' return from their night out, his duvet, in its red and black cover, pulled up to his ears. He tried not to think about what had happened in Deerton. It hadn't been his idea to go there; he'd simply accepted the dare to take the car. It was Kevin who had started the rampage, though Wayne and Paul had soon joined in. They'd somehow caught the mood from one another.

It was Kevin who had pulled the knife.

Trevor had one, a large one with a serrated edge. It was in his school bag and he felt good, knowing it was there, just as he'd felt good tonight, driving off, showing the others what he could do.

That guy they'd gone for would be all right. Kevin hadn't hurt him badly, and it was his fault for interfering. Trevor had punched him, but he hadn't touched the second man, nor kicked either of them hard. He'd thrown some stuff around at Barry's house but he hadn't seriously wrecked the place, and he hadn't gone upstairs. He didn't know what had happened there; he was in the kitchen at the time. If they were caught, though, he'd be in as much trouble as the others – more, maybe, because of driving without a licence, and not insured.

Would Barry and his mates blab on them? What about that

kid, Jamie Preston, who'd gone running off, squealing for help? He'd been in the fight and seen it all, even though the others had gone back into the house. They all knew one another; there was no chance of not being recognised. What had started as a bit of a laugh had ended up as big trouble. Trevor had meant only to show off and get respect, but Kevin had gone crazy, and Paul had taken something, silly sod.

If they all kept quiet, if Jamie Preston shut his face, it might just go away. Trevor guessed that Kevin and Paul, and maybe Wayne, would sort Jamie Preston, go round to his place and scare him shitless. He'd get the message. Everyone knew they were hard men.

He couldn't get warm, and as for sleep, he'd never felt more wakeful in his life. Trevor's mind kept replaying scenes from the night's events. There were questions, too: where had that man come from, the one Kevin knifed? They were on their way out, chasing after Jamie – Kevin had yelled, 'Let's get him,' but Trevor did not want to remember that – when the man arrived. If he hadn't interfered, they'd have gone with no harm done except a bit of mess in the house, which Barry and his mates could soon clean up.

Like many guilty people, Trevor sought to appoint blame anywhere but where it belonged. Those two men had brought all this on themselves. They'd not poke their noses in again in a hurry.

Could anyone have taken down the number of the Lada? It had been parked beyond the turning, so it couldn't have been seen except by someone standing in the road. That thought consoled him, but there weren't too many Ladas about; he hoped no one had had a good look at it. He'd got it back and parked it in the exact spot where his mother always left it, and it was totally undamaged.

He was still awake when his parents returned. Neither of them touched the bonnet of the Lada, which might have been still warm. They went up to bed, confident that he was in, for his trainers, which he was not allowed to wear indoors, were standing neatly in the hall.

I heard about it on the news on Sunday morning, and felt a frisson of recognition, then a thrill which I suppressed because, undeniably, a wicked act had been committed. The radio report was sketchy: a man had been killed in Deerton, stabbed to death while trying to separate some brawling teenagers. A second man had been attacked but had not needed hospital treatment. A youth, slightly wounded in the struggle, was helping police with their enquiries. No more details were given in the broadcast.

I could imagine it: the strange ease with which the knife sank in, the sudden feeling of elation. This boy's experience would have been the same as mine, even though his action had not been premeditated, but if he had not been prepared to use his knife, why carry it? My crime was different: mine was planned, but it had not brought the result I had expected and desired. It had not beaten her; in the end, dying, she beat me.

This boy, the guilty one: he'll be scared. If caught and charged, he may be too young to be named. Perhaps he meant to use his knife to wield power, impress his friends. Image has always been important to young people; that's what much of commerce is about. Very few youngsters come to me for counselling; I prefer them to go to specialists in their particular problems, but their parents are among my patients, desperate because they can't control or understand their children. It's no wonder, when they won't take time to listen to them.

I'm consulted about office power struggles and the sexual tensions that develop. People spend more time with their work colleagues than with their families, or 'loved ones', as it is the vogue to call them.

Often they are not loved at all.

This dead man, this victim, may have had some loved ones; we'll soon hear all too much about them. Maybe they'll be exhibited on television, weeping and appealing for 'someone who must know something' to disclose the killer's name. Perhaps those exposures do shame relatives or so-called friends to name suspects.

This boy must be taught that he can't go about stabbing people just for kicks. He must pay his debt to society, but when he emerges after whatever sentence he receives, will he be redeemed, or merely hardened, ready for a life of crime?

I've never done it again. There has been no need. Since my release, I've avoided close emotional encounters. I can live without them, and vicariously, through the lives of my patients, I experience many things. They tell me their most intimate fears and secrets, and reveal their cravings. I simply guide their reasoning until they devise ways of dealing with what is causing them to lead unhappy lives, damaging to themselves, if not to others. I am powerful.

Sensational murder cases interest me. I'm sometimes tempted to attend trials of particular appeal, but I never give in to this impulse. It could be morbid, have a bad effect on me. Most of the time, I don't think about it. I can almost say it is forgotten.

The four boys involved in the attack, scattering afterwards, had not arranged to meet next day. Sunday mornings were usually spent in bed, though Trevor was reasonably conscientious about his homework. All four would normally arrive downstairs in time for whatever meal was going. In Trevor's house it was conventional, a roast, eaten at around two o'clock. More flexible arrangements operated for the others.

This Sunday, all four woke early. Trevor contemplated contacting Wayne, who had been less involved in the attack on the men than Paul and Kevin. He wouldn't mind a chat about it. Wayne would soon say there was nothing to worry about; it was just a breeze and no harm done. If they hadn't gone to Deerton, they'd have done something else and he might have been persuaded to drive to Fettleton, or even further, where the police could have stopped them and then he'd have been in real trouble. After consuming a large bowl of cornflakes, he walked across the town to Wayne's house, only to find that he had already gone out.

He did not know that Daniel Stewart was dead. None of the four learned that until much later in the day.

Midge, sedated, had eventually fallen asleep in the Foxtons' spare bedroom. Oliver persuaded Sarah to return to bed, where she drowsed, the upstairs telephone turned off, while he, in his study, was ready to answer calls if Mark or Jonathan rang after hearing of their father's death. The police, who would break the news to each of them, had been asked to tell them that their mother was spending the night in Winbury. There was no more to be done at present. Oliver could not believe that this dreadful thing had happened less than two hours after he and Sarah had left Daniel and Midge. It seemed to have been established that hooligan boys were responsible for the murder. This was not an inner-city area where difficult living conditions and rival gangs exacerbated crime; it had happened in a quiet village where episodes of drunk and disorderly conduct and minor theft were the usual reported offences.

Despair filled him as he thought about this manifestation of current youthful mores, and he reminded himself that such incidents were isolated: one did not hear about the law-abiding youngsters who were not part of this aggressive culture. But example was a strong factor; children aped their elders and if discussion was turned into confrontation, as happened in public interviews, while newspaper reports described objectors to anything as 'hitting out' at whatever it was they took exception to, it was hardly surprising that the pattern was absorbed and followed. A peaceable man, Oliver knew that some things must be fought for; he would stop at nothing to protect Sarah and their children, and there were plenty of public issues on which he held strong views, but he deplored the cut and thrust of public argument which seemed to have replaced debate.

He sat down on the small stool he had placed in front of the dolls' house. The downstairs rooms and four of the bedrooms were almost finished now. He had found a tiny scrap of sample carpet for the stairs and he would use straightened paperclips for stair rods. The original dolls had been wrapped in a soft cloth, and this had protected them; perhaps they were a little grubby, but he was fond of them and did not want to replace them with modern replicas. Midge had christened them the Wilberforces – Mr and Mrs Wilberforce and their children, Joe, Phoebe and Maud. He smiled as he took them from the drawer where he kept them while he was working on the house. Carefully, he put the father and the mother doll in the sitting room, and Joe and Phoebe in their respective bedrooms. Maud's room was not quite ready yet. He looked at them: Daniel and Midge, he thought, and their children, except that one of the boys had turned into a girl. Sighing, he removed the father doll and replaced him in the drawer.

Playing like this, he felt a sudden chill. What would Sarah say if she caught him? Besides, his analogy was morbid. He bundled up the other dolls and stowed them away. Then he began trimming the carpet to size, but his thoughts returned to Daniel, his friend, whom he would miss.

The police would want to speak to Midge in the morning. They hadn't really questioned her properly yet, but there was little she could tell them as she had arrived in the close after the boys had fled, and Daniel was already dead. They had had no chance to say goodbye, he thought. The post mortem was probably in progress now, but it might have been delayed until the morning as there was no real doubt about the cause of death. The inquest was likely to be opened on Monday or Tuesday but no funeral plans could be made because the defence, when someone was accused of being responsible, was entitled to a second post mortem. Poor Daniel, subjected to this indignity.

Unaware of Jamie Preston's role in the night's events, Oliver reflected that the rampage in Orchard Close must have been noisy to have woken the Stewarts, but their house was only just across the road. Midge might not be able to remain there. Oliver wondered what sort of insurance Daniel had carried; just enough to clear the mortgage, he suspected.

He went to the window and drew the curtains back. It was still dark, but dawn was not far off. Down there, beyond the garden, was the river. It was quiet in the house; he hoped the two women were asleep. Sarah had been splendid when he brought Midge home; she had not been over-fussy, nor sentimental. She'd given Midge a hug – a brisk one, not an all-enfolding one, but still a hug – and said, 'I'm so sad for you. Poor Midge,' which was just right. Then she'd bundled her upstairs and Midge had gone obediently while Sarah told her, 'You'll have things to do in the morning – horrid business things, and Mark and Jonathan will be arriving. You must get some rest. You won't want to make it harder for them.'

No, she wouldn't, and Sarah wouldn't let her. Midge, who still felt numb and stunned, allowed herself to be taken care of, just as if she were a child. There would be plenty of time to think about it all when she had to do so.

Two detectives in plain clothes, and driving an unmarked car, called at Kate's house at nine o'clock on Sunday morning. They had come to take Jamie, who was in the kitchen toying with some breakfast, to the police station for questioning. Kate must come too, they said, and they wanted Jamie's clothes from the night before. Silently, Kate found them and they dropped the garments into plastic bags which they sealed and labelled.

'We'll give you a receipt,' said Detective Sergeant Shaw. 'Where's his coat, then?'

'I don't know,' said Kate. 'And he didn't stab that man. He told those other officers, last night. He only had a penknife and he said it was in his jacket.'

'My jacket's at Barry's,' Jamie said. 'I rushed out without it when—' He was going to say 'when I went to fetch the man', but he didn't want to mention that.

'When what?' encouraged Shaw.

'When it all started,' Jamie said. 'When they trashed the place.'

'Want to tell us about it?' tried Detective Constable Benton, but Jamie shook his head.

'Hasn't Barry Noakes told you what happened?' Kate asked. These two were very different from the uniformed pair who had brought them back from the hospital the night before; the man had been a bastard, intent on bullying Jamie and pinning the blame on him.

'Not so far,' said Shaw, a stocky man with very short red hair. 'He's keeping stumm, like young Jamie here.'

Kate sighed. Jamie was frightened, and small wonder, but if Barry had said something, he would have opened up, she felt. She'd rung the Noakeses' house that morning, before Jamie woke, but could get only the engaged signal. She told Shaw, who said the receiver must have been taken off the hook.

'They aren't there,' he said. 'They're at a neighbour's house. Our forensic people have been going over it for evidence, and the Noakeses won't be let back till that's done. And then the clearing up will be quite a business, I can tell you.'

'Maybe Jamie's jacket's been found, then,' said Kate. 'And his knife. It won't have blood on it, I can tell you.'

Kevin and Wayne, passing Jamie's house, saw him and his

mother leaving in a car with two men who had to be policemen. Was he going to take the rap for what had happened, or would he split on them? And if he did, would he be believed? Everyone knew the police got things wrong and once they'd made their minds up, wouldn't shift.

Seeing him watching them from the car's rear window, they gestured threateningly.

7

On Sundays Rosemary Ellis went to church. This was habit, based not on conviction, nor on duty. It gave shape to her week and she liked to sit, respectably clad as ever, in a pew near the rear, where she would be inconspicuous and safe. Life had not always been safe. She had known fear and passion, but she wanted no more of either and so she sought to live at a distance from emotion.

It was a bright, cold day. After the long dry summer, when the trees had borne parched leaves which looked as though they would soon drop, at last rain had fallen and the autumnal colours glowed. Rosemary, letting the words of the service wash over her, contemplated driving into the country in the afternoon. Most historic houses open to the public were now closed until the following spring; she often visited such places at weekends and would imagine living in a mansion, one well endowed, with no need to entice paying visitors to troop round. She would cast herself back in time and become a wealthy Victorian matriarch or early feminist who had inherited these acres and this fine building. Servants, in these images, flitted past: maids in white caps and aprons, maybe a dignified butler with side-whiskers. It was a secure life, free from financial, emotional and physical anxiety. No one, in these dreams, died untimely of illnesses then fatal but now curable; no one starved or froze to death; no one went off to any war.

Sometimes, in these fantasies, the vague figure of Oliver Foxton hovered; he seemed so benign and reassuring, appropriate in such a setting, never a disturber of the peace she had designed. She did not picture an intimate encounter; everything was at a remove, as a pop star or a sporting hero or an actor might be idolised. Surrounding herself with phantom company did no harm and had no effect on her efficiency for she yielded to it only rarely, when she gave herself permission.

In church this morning, though, her musings were interrupted when shocking news was given of the local murder in the night. Some people, and she was one of them, had already heard it on the radio, but now it was brought closer as the vicar prayed for those affected: the bereaved family, and others who were concerned.

'Sadly, it seems evident that juveniles from the community were involved,' he said.

Rosemary joined sincerely in the prayers.

Jonathan Stewart, arriving in Deerton in his elderly Escort, had had to explain who he was before he was allowed to enter, for the area around Orchard Close was cordoned off and police officers were painstakingly examining the ground. With horror, he realised that they were searching for evidence connected with his father's death. The knowledge sickened him, and bile rose in his throat as he drove slowly through the gates and parked his car. He had often been alone here when his parents were out or away, but they had always returned, still solidly affectionate towards each other, partners in a successful marriage. Now all that was over. His poor mother! How must she be feeling? Jonathan himself felt dreadful and in dire need of comfort. He reminded himself that he must be the comforter now, at least until Mark arrived when they could share the task.

Act of Violence

His mother might return from the Foxtons' at any minute. He'd tidy the place up a bit, light the fire, put the kettle on. First, he went upstairs to his own room which was heavily adorned with a variety of posters. His school trophies were arranged on shelves his father had put up. He flung down the bag into which he had thrown his razor and a few other things; he'd manage otherwise with what was here. His parents' bedroom door was open, and though the curtains were still drawn, he saw the unmade bed, his mother's nightdress and his father's pyjamas cast aside where they had shed them last night. The sight brought tears to his eyes. He went into the room, pulled back the curtains, and made the bed, tucking his mother's nightdress under the pillow on her side. Not knowing what else to do with them, he put his father's faded green Marks and Spencer pyjamas in the laundry basket. Still in the bathroom, he looked at his father's shaving tackle and toothbrush, and the aftershave he used, all on their usual shelf. Should he get rid of them before his mother returned? Would seeing them upset her?

Throwing them away would upset him; that was certain. Jonathan closed the door upon his dilemma and went downstairs. He'd ring Oliver, let him know he'd arrived.

On the telephone, Oliver spoke calmly, telling him that Midge was still asleep but that she would have to be woken as soon as the police wanted to talk to her. Detective Superintendent Fisher, who was in charge of the investigation, had already rung him and had agreed to come to Orchard House at half-past nine. He had told Oliver that the police had so far found no trace of the car in which the boys had driven off.

'Have some breakfast,' Oliver advised. He knew from experience that if you went without sleep, you could not function adequately if you also fasted, and pouring out cornflakes or making toast or whatever Jonathan might do now would provide him with an occupation and distract him from the police activity which must be going on outside the house.

He explained that Sarah was already on her way to meet Mark at Heathrow and would bring him straight to Deerton. Then he went to see if Midge was stirring. Though asleep, she sensed his presence in the room and opened her eyes.

'Oh, Oliver,' she said, blinking at him drowsily, still affected by the sedative. 'So it wasn't all a hideous nightmare, then.'

'I'm afraid not, Midge,' Oliver replied. He picked up the dressing-gown which Sarah had left for her. Sarah thought of everything. 'Jonathan's rung,' he said. 'He's at the house, having breakfast. I expect you'd like to get there pretty quickly, wouldn't you?'

Most of all, Midge wanted to burst into tears and be comforted by Oliver, who reminded her of a gentle bear, with his broad build and short button nose. She looked sadly up at him. His once brown hair was turning white. A grey bear, she thought. She mustn't give way now, though, if ever; Jonathan needed her, and soon Mark would be arriving home. Home. Home without Daniel, but still their home.

Oliver could see confusion on her face and he felt like wrapping his arms round her and holding her close to comfort her, but it wouldn't do to get emotional. Midge could do that later, with her sons.

'There's coffee on,' he said. 'I'll make some toast. You must have something.'

'Can I have a bath?' asked Midge.

'Of course. I'll ring Jonathan and say that's what you're doing, and to expect us in under the hour,' said Oliver.

'Oh, thank you, Oliver,' Midge said. 'If I talk to him, I'll only start to cry and that will upset him.'

No doubt it was the truth.

'I'll turn the water on,' said Oliver, and he did so, pouring in some of Sarah's bath oil.

He delayed making the call until Midge had been in the bathroom for a few minutes, and Jonathan's voice now sounded steadier. He said he had opened the windows and aired the house, and that the police were crawling about on hands and knees in the garden near the road, and opposite.

That must mean they hadn't found the weapon yet. It might have been thrown over the stone wall which fenced off the Stewarts' garden from the road. It could be anywhere. Young lads rampaging wouldn't be thinking about fingerprints and might have left some in the house they had wrecked. Eventually there would be a line to follow; a neighbour might have identified the car they used. One or more of the boys would, in time, supply names, when they knew that Daniel was dead. The wounded lad had been aware of that, last night, but the police seemed to think that he could have been responsible. If so, the weapon, when discovered, might confirm his guilt.

Midge wouldn't be much help to the police. She hadn't seen a thing.

Kate said, 'Jamie, you must know who was involved in this. You must know who those boys are.'

They were alone in an interview room at Fettleton police station, given a final chance to sort this out between them.

'I can't say,' Jamie insisted. He didn't add, they'll kill me if I do, but he had seen Kevin and Wayne earlier, gesturing as he was driven off. Jamie's mother, who would have recognised them, had not noticed them. They could take revenge on her, if not on him. He'd tell if all the others did: not on his own. He needed to talk to them but how could he, shut up here at the police station?

'Jamie, a man who came to break the fight up was killed,' said Kate. 'This is very serious. You must tell what you know.' She did not add, if you don't, you may be blamed. Surely the police couldn't really suspect him? It was only their alarming way of trying to make him to tell them what he knew.

He did not answer, and she told herself to keep calm. There would be fingerprints on the murder weapon, when they found it, and Jamie's penknife would be in his fleece jacket, as he'd said. Their detective powers must have led them to that, in the Noakeses' house. Barry would have described what had happened; with his parents there, he would have told the truth.

Mother and son both had a sense of unreality, and Kate, who loved him, wanted to shake Jamie to rid him of his stubbornness. The stalemate was broken when DS Shaw and DC Benton returned to see what headway had been made. But they could get no further though they questioned Jamie patiently. He related how the marauding boys had entered the house and begun throwing things around, milk and stores from the cupboard, and he told how two had gone upstairs and started on the bedroom. He even said what one of them had done there, mentioning no name, and that he had followed because he was trying to stop them. But he would not say who they were.

Kate said, despairingly, 'He doesn't want to tell on schoolmates. That's it, isn't it, Jamie?'

'Sort of,' he said, studying the table top in front of him.

Kate saw that they would get no further now. She asked to speak privately to Shaw, who left the room with her while Benton stayed with Jamie.

'You don't really think Jamie stabbed that poor man, do you?' she asked Shaw, who didn't, but there was no other suspect. 'Surely Barry has given some information by this time?'

'Not so far. They're all banding together. As you've said, kids do,' said Shaw. 'It's early yet. The man hasn't even been dead twelve hours. One of them will crack, or we'll get a lead from something the forensic chaps dig up. The boy whose father came to help may weaken. His dad was winded and he's cracked a rib or two, though he said last night he was just bruised. He was kicked in the genitals, as well. That was what laid him out, I expect. But two grown men can't beat four lads armed with knives.'

Shaw knew that Jamie's penknife had been found inside his jacket, with nothing more incriminating on it than traces of pencil sharpening, and the blade that had killed Daniel Stewart was a long slim one; however, a lad could carry two knives, and if Jamie had another it might have been turned upon himself, but he was not one of the vandals; that had been established. As far as Shaw was concerned, Jamie was in the clear, although he had said nothing to prove that he had not been somehow responsible, however accidentally, for the killing.

'We'll talk to Barry's other friends,' said Shaw. 'And we're questioning all the neighbours, but so far nothing useful has come up. It doesn't seem to have been a noisy incident. They'd all got their tellies on, and such. Gate-crashing parties often happens, and that's when alcohol gets brought in. There were empty beer cans in the house and I don't think Barry and his friends were responsible for them. There will be prints on the cans and the innocent boys can be eliminated. Unless they moved the cans, clearing up, or trying to. Barry and his mates had begun that before we got there.'

'The other man – the one who came to help – he may have seen some of them,' Kate said.

'We'll hope so,' Shaw replied. 'But he's said they all had baseball caps on, and it was dark, with no street lighting. By the time he got there they were already in a sort of scrum.'

'And no one lost his cap?'

'Maybe he did, but as far as I know, it hasn't been found,' said Shaw. 'We'll be talking to the man again. Someone may be with him now. And Superintendent Fisher is meeting Mrs

Stewart this morning. Not that she'll have seen them. She arrived when it was all over, poor soul.'

'Just as well,' said Kate flatly.

She felt better after this conversation, but not much. Weren't you supposed to be innocent until proved guilty? That constable the night before had, she thought, been on the point of charging Jamie.

Rosemary learned who the suspect was from Bob and Ginny. They were about to set off on their bicycles when she returned from church. Both were keen cyclists and on fine weekends went for long rides into the country, stopping for lunch at various pubs. They were late leaving today, delayed by the dreadful news, as several other teachers, hearing what had happened and that some of their pupils had been involved, had been on the telephone. Wearing fluorescent jackets, they were pumping up their tyres when she walked across the yard.

'Good morning,' she said, formally. 'Off to the country, then?'

'Yes,' said Bob. 'We're later than we meant to be. You've heard what happened in Deerton last night?'

'Yes. It was mentioned in church,' said Rosemary. 'I believe the victim was trying to separate some fighting boys.'

The congregation, leaving church, had been discussing nothing else.

'Yes – and someone thinks they've arrested Jamie Preston,' said Ginny. 'You met his mother at our party. Kate. Very small, with short dark hair.'

'Oh, surely not?' Rosemary could not believe that the pleasant, gangling boy she had seen in the bookshop had been an aggressor in a brawl.

'He can't have done it,' Bob said. 'It's not possible, or if he did, it was a complete accident. I'm not sure he's really been arrested,' he added. 'But he was involved and he's been taken in for questioning.' Hearing this rumour, they had telephoned Kate but got no reply; then they had rung up one of her neighbours whom they knew, who had seen two men who looked as if they could be CID officers in plain clothes driving off with Kate and Jamie.

'Oh dear,' said Rosemary. 'I'm sorry.'

She hurried into her flat, and Bob and Ginny, who had wondered whether to cancel their outing in case Kate needed help, went on their way. If Kate was not at home, they could do nothing for her. They had made sure their answerphone was on. If Jamie was charged, they would soon hear about it.

Prudence Wilmot had also heard the news and was shocked and saddened. She had met the Stewarts briefly at the Foxtons' when they had a summer party, and she had had some pictures framed by Midge. She would send flowers to her tomorrow: flowers for the living; she never sent flowers to funerals.

Depressed, she had two dry sherries before her Sunday lunch instead of the usual single one. Then she cooked her solitary chop.

8

Barry Noakes's parents, returning from their wedding party, were astonished when they were confronted by a police road block outside Deerton. Guilty calculations about how much he had drunk sprang into Cliff's head, and he expected to be breathalysed. However, when they had supplied their names, they were allowed to pass, and one of the officers on duty spoke into his radio. They were stopped again outside the close, which was cordoned off, and a uniformed officer came towards them.

'What's going on? What's happened? It's Barry – is he all right?' Frightened now, Lily Noakes, a pretty woman with rich copper-coloured hair, who had once won a beauty contest and maintained her glamour, sprang from the car, subconsciously aware that no fire engine nor ambulance was visible and that her house still stood.

'He's all right,' the constable assured her. 'But there's been trouble here. Barry's with a neighbour.'

'But—?' What about Jamie Preston? He was supposed to be staying over. A primeval cautious instinct stopped her asking more questions. Barry was safe, but something serious had happened here to account for the police presence. She could see that the place was swarming with uniformed officers, and the one who had spoken to her was now talking on his radio.

He turned to her.

'Detective Superintendent Fisher will be with you in a minute or two,' he said. 'He'll put you in the picture,' and soon a tall thin man whose pale grey suit hung loosely around his angular frame came towards them.

'What's going on?' Cliff was now as alarmed as his wife. 'Where's our boy?'

Fisher took them into their own house, where the forensic scientists had finished examining the sitting room. He would not let them go further.

'I'm sorry – you can see what's happened here,' he said, as Lily gasped and put a hand to her mouth. Her prized neat room was wrecked, and precious ornaments were missing. Barry and Jamie had never done this. 'I'm afraid the rest of the house is in a worse state,' said Fisher. 'Your boy and the friends he had visiting cleared up a bit in here before we arrived.' He told them that a group of young vandals, bent on trouble, had invaded their house, and that two local men had intervened and been attacked. 'There was a fight in the road. One of the men was stabbed,' he said. 'I'm sorry to say he died.'

'Jesus!' Cliff exclaimed.

'Who were they? Who was it died?' asked Lily in a whisper. She felt dizzy with shock.

Fisher related what was known: that Daniel Stewart had been killed, and Ted Grant slightly injured. 'One of the boys was stabbed, too,' he said. 'Jamie Preston. He was stopping over with Barry, I believe.'

'That's right. Oh dear! Does Kate know? Jamie's mother?' Lily asked.

'Yes. She's with him at the hospital. It's not serious,' said Fisher.

The man looked ill himself, thought Lily inconsequentially.

His face was pale and there were deep hollows under his eyes, but Neil Fisher had looked like this for years and was perfectly fit.

'Who did it? Who were these boys?' Cliff Noakes demanded.

'I wish we knew,' said Fisher. 'Barry isn't saying, but we can't interview him properly without you. None of the others will tell us anything. Perhaps they'll change their minds by morning. I certainly hope so.'

'But Mr Stewart! Oh, that's terrible,' said Lily. Poor Mrs Stewart, she was thinking: such a nice woman. At least she had those two sons; she wouldn't be on her own, poor soul. 'And Ted's all right?' she asked. 'Is he in hospital?'

'No. He wouldn't go, but I think he'll see the doctor today,' said Fisher. Ted Grant had admitted that his ribs were very sore; evidence of his injuries would be needed for the prosecution when whoever did this was in court.

'He was a good bloke, Mr Stewart was,' said Cliff, who was a plumber. He had done work for the Stewarts and was always paid on time. Some customers who lived in larger houses, with a grander life style, often kept him waiting.

Fisher had now been joined by a woman officer whom Fisher introduced as Detective Inspector Flower. Her colleagues called her Poppy and the pair, who frequently worked together, were known irreverently as the two Fs.

'We've found various sets of fingerprints,' she said. 'Barry and his friends, and you, of course, can be eliminated when we have all your prints for comparison. There were at least nine sets in the house and some of them will be alien.'

Alien prints. It sounded as if the place had been invaded by monsters from outer space.

'I want to see Barry,' said Lily. It seemed he'd had several friends round. She'd wondered about leaving him for so long on his own with only Jamie Preston for company, but she and Cliff were coming home, after all – here they were –

and the house wasn't isolated. Kate Preston hadn't seemed concerned.

'Of course, but he may be asleep by this time,' Poppy Flower said.

'When did all this happen?' asked Cliff Noakes.

'Before midnight. We got the call about ten to,' said Poppy. 'I don't know how long the lads were here. Barry and his friends weren't certain. They'd been watching videos.'

'Why did no one help them? she asked.

'They did. Mr Stewart and Mr Grant,' said Poppy. 'The fight was all over very quickly, Mr Grant said. The four boys ran off after he and Mr Stewart were hurt. By that time, several other people had come out to see what was happening. Three of the boys were quite large, they said, and one was smaller.'

'They left in a car,' said Fisher. 'Unfortunately no one saw what make it was, nor got the number.'

'Then they weren't from Deerton,' Lily said.

'It seems unlikely.'

'We'll talk to Barry. We'll see what he can tell us,' Cliff promised.

'They don't like what they see as telling tales, Mr Noakes,' said Poppy. 'That's the trouble. None of them's wanting to drop a mate in it.'

'Funny sort of mates, doing all this and killing someone,' Lily said. She was almost in tears, just holding on wondering what other damage had been done to the house. She could hear the forensic scientists moving around upstairs.

'Why do they do it?' Cliff wanted to know. 'Carry knives and that.'

'I wish I could answer you,' said Fisher. 'They think it's macho. They catch a sort of fever from one another and make each other worse.'

'Were they on drugs?' asked Lily.

'It's possible. Not necessarily,' said Fisher, thinking of the beer cans. 'More probably it's lads with too much time and energy and not enough to do, looking for excitement or making their own on a Saturday night. Maybe they were looking for a party to gatecrash and couldn't find one, so they hit on coming here.'

'Lads' stuff, eh?' said Cliff. 'No girls. Pathetic.'

'That lot probably can't make it with girls,' said Poppy. 'It's why they do this sort of thing. After all, the girls can choose, and decent girls aren't going to want to have much to do with lads who go in for rampaging.'

'It's sad,' said Lily, though she hoped Barry would leave girls until later.

Cliff and Lily got nowhere with Barry that night; he was still awake when they went round to the Grants to talk to him and kept saying he was sorry that he couldn't prevent the damage being done, but his real concern was for Jamie.

'He was trying to help the men,' he said. 'He was alone out there with Peter's dad and Mr Stewart. Only I didn't know then that it was Mr Stewart.' In the end they'd all left Jamie on his own.

Fisher had been listening to the conversation and had prompted its direction with an occasional question. At least he had now learned that Jamie Preston had been trying to help the men.

Barry might reveal more when he made an official statement later on, but it was a pity he hadn't told them that before. Not that Fisher was suspecting Jamie of being the perpetrator, however accidentally, but others did. Fisher, however, was the boss.

After Trevor dropped them off the night before, the other boys had separated, going to their own homes. Paul, still on a high, took some time to come down and then he told himself that he was safe. He hadn't stabbed that man; it was Kevin. Anyway, the old git was probably back home again by now; he couldn't have been badly hurt. Besides, it was his own fault. It would show him what was what, who was in charge, that Paul and Kevin and their mates weren't going to stand for being messed about. Kevin had a bit of a temper when he got excited, and he had had a knife. Paul had one too, but it was in his school bag, in case it might be needed. They must all just carry on as normal.

He felt better still when he heard from Wayne that he and Kevin had seen Jamie Preston being taken off for questioning. Wayne had come round to see him after parting from Kevin and he'd found Paul up surprisingly early for a Sunday morning, sitting in the kitchen with his headphones on, eating a thick piece of toast spread with jam and butter. They'd gone straight out into the back yard to talk. Kevin had said they'd better keep away from Trevor for the moment, since he'd been the driver. He wouldn't tell on them if he was caught, nor would they dob him in, and Jamie had better keep his mouth shut or they would shut it for him.

It was not until after midday that they learned that, between them, they were responsible for a man's death.

When Oliver took Midge home, he hung back while she went into the house and was embraced by Jonathan. The police had waved them past their cordon as soon as Oliver had told them who his passenger was, and identified himself.

The kettle was simmering on the Aga, and although she had only just had coffee at The Barn House, after their long hug and subdued murmurings, Midge, inconsolable, accepted more, and mother and son busied themselves with brewing it and pouring.

Only a few short hours ago, he and Midge had made coffee here together, Oliver recalled. He wondered whether to fade away and leave them on their own, but soon Sarah would arrive with Mark, and Superintendent Fisher was almost due. He could be useful, and it was soon clear that Midge and Jonathan needed him. Neither knew how to comfort the other and wanted to postpone the moment when they must.

'There'll be things to do. The police, you said.' Jonathan looked at him in desperation as they sat round the kitchen table.

'Yes. They'll want to know how Daniel got involved. I suppose you heard the racket those boys were making?' Oliver turned to Midge with the question.

'No. We didn't. We were asleep,' she said. After making love, a quick, tender session because both of them were tired. They would never do that again. It was over. Tears suddenly rolled down her face, and Jonathan clasped her while Oliver pulled tissues from a box on the dresser.

'Why did he go out, then?' Jonathan asked, when she was calmer. 'If it wasn't because of the noise?'

'Someone banged on the door and rang the bell. A boy. He wanted help,' said Midge. 'Dan put some clothes on and followed him over the road and I rang the police. I didn't follow straight away.' After saying this, more tears fell. Had she gone over sooner, she might have been with Daniel when he died, perhaps even, she thought unrealistically, have managed to save him.

When Fisher arrived, with Detective Inspector Flower, Oliver had to remind her to tell them about the boy who had come to the house. She couldn't describe him as she hadn't seen him, but Dan had said he had a bloody nose.

Fisher was gentle with her, and she had little to add to what they already knew.

'Did you see the lads drive away?' he asked.

'No. I heard the car roar off,' she said. It had been driven towards the centre of the village, where the road looped round and joined crossroads; it was not possible to say where it was heading.

'What about the boy who fetched your husband? Did he go with them?'

'No, he couldn't have. He wasn't part of the gang – he came for help,' said Midge. 'A boy got hurt. He went in the ambulance.' With Dan. She hadn't even shared that last ride with him. 'All the boys had vanished when I got there, and then this boy came out of one of the houses. He had a towel round his arm. I didn't know him. Another boy was with him – it might have been the Grant boy. His father tried to help Dan.'

All this was helpful in that it let young Jamie Preston off any hook PC Roberts had attempted to impale him on, but it brought them no nearer tracking down the guilty group. Poppy Flower had made notes of their conversation. To spare Midge, she said she would get them typed up and bring them out for Midge to read and sign. They were not going to make her go to Fettleton police station: not yet, at least.

The two officers had just left when Sarah arrived with Mark. She had food in the car, a cool box containing a pack full of chicken casserole, complete with vegetables, for the Stewarts' lunch. She knew Midge would have nothing suitable in her ill-stocked freezer, and those poor boys must be fed.

Oliver watched her proudly as she decanted the block and put it in a saucepan on the top of the stove, where it could begin to thaw. She put some other smaller packs in the freezer, so that they had more prepared food to fall back on. She was so capable, and she thought of everything in times of crisis, as was being proved at this moment, Oliver reflected. It was just as well that she was emotionally cool during this dreadful time when even he felt like weeping.

'We'd better leave you to it,' he told the family. 'We'll come back later if you want us. We'll ring up.'

'We will want you,' said Mark, a dark, stocky young man. He tried to smile. 'Thank you both so much,' he said.

On the short flight, he had had time to gain some control, and Sarah, at the airport, had been brisk and businesslike, giving him a hug and immediately telling him that his mother was all right and had had some sleep, and that Jonathan had arrived.

In the car, driving back, she told him what she knew.

'It must all have been very quick,' she said. 'I mean, there wasn't really time for Dan to know what was happening. He was stabbed and that was it.' But he had been kicked and punched. Oliver had told her that his injuries had been horrific. There was no need, however, for Mark to hear this now, even if he had to later.

'I'd like to kill whoever did it,' Mark said fiercely. 'Dad never harmed a soul.'

'No.' He was a bit of a wimp, Sarah had sometimes thought, but he hadn't been wimpish at the end. 'He was very brave,' she said. 'Going to the rescue.'

'Yes, but boys! You don't expect kids in Deerton to turn on you with a knife if you go to sort them out, do you?' said Mark.

'No. It's shocking,' Sarah said.

They had driven on in silence. What else was there to say?

9

From Deerton, Detective Superintendent Fisher went to see the Prestons while Poppy Flower dealt with Midge's informal statement. Kate, not long back from Fettleton police station herself, had begun cooking spaghetti bolognese for lunch.

Fisher introduced himself, producing his warrant card. So this was the man in charge, thought Kate; what now?

'I'd like a brief word with you and Jamie, if you don't mind,' he said, and added, seeing the despairing expression on her face, 'Don't worry. I suspect young Jamie's really quite the hero, if only he wasn't also such a clam.'

As he followed Kate into the sitting room, he caught a whiff of an enticing smell coming from the kitchen and it reminded him that he had had no breakfast. Jamie was half watching an old film on television. He started to get to his feet but Fisher told him to sit down again and asked after his arm.

'It's OK,' said Jamie.

Kate had sped out to turn down the gas, and Fisher waited till she returned before he said, 'Why didn't you say it was you who went to get help from Mr Stewart?' Peter Grant's father had now confirmed that Jamie had been trying to drag the attacking boys off the two men.

'No one asked me,' Jamie said. 'And if I hadn't, he wouldn't have been killed.'

Oh, poor Jamie, Kate thought: he was blaming himself for Daniel Stewart's death.

'Hm. Well, I don't think anyone else sees it quite like that, Jamie,' said Fisher. 'You weren't to know those lads had knives, were you?'

'S'pose not,' said Jamie.

'I'd imagine you'd want whoever did it to be punished,' Fisher suggested.

'Yeah,' said Jamie.

'So why won't you tell us who it was?'

No reply.

'It's because you don't want to drop your friends in it, isn't it?' said Fisher.

'They're not my friends,' Jamie growled.

'But you still won't name them?'

Jamie shook his head.

'If only you'd change your mind, you'd save us hours of work,' Fisher told him. 'We'll get them in the end.' He turned to Kate. 'Mrs Stewart told us that a boy came to the house asking for help, but she didn't see him. Her husband, though, said he had a bloody nose. Your nose bled last night, didn't it, Jamie? You got a punch on it. What a pity we didn't find this out sooner.'

Kate thought so, too. Immense relief flooded over her and she beamed at this bearer of good news, whilst wanting to shake Jamie for his folly and praise him for his valour.

Unable to persuade Jamie to say more, Fisher left, to try to piece together what information they had so far managed to retrieve.

Jamie, the prospect of arrest retreating, found he had an appetite.

'Smells good, Mum,' he said eagerly, as the door closed behind the departing officer.

The copper had said they'd get Kevin in the end. His nerve might fail, or Paul's. But they were iron men who wouldn't weaken easily. If he had told, they'd have found out and goodness knows what revenge they'd take, or get their mates to take. He had to protect his mother. His father's last instruction before he left to fight in the Gulf War, where he was killed, had been to look after her.

I went to church today. I got into the habit of attending services in prison. It looked good to the board of visitors and to the staff, and it helped to pass the time tranquilly, away from conflict, though most of the women inside revered me for the magnitude of my offence. Sometimes I'd talk to them about him – usually the younger ones – telling them about our hours together. I invented most of it, culling the romantic details from books and magazines which described all the things we might have done, but didn't. They believed everything. People will, if you speak with conviction. If the truth were known, we'd had so few times together. He was always afraid of being caught, but I grew skilled at tempting him when we had a chance, if she was out somewhere with the children. I needed only to touch him on a certain spot, on the back of his neck just below the hairline; an erogenous zone, it was – I learned that term later. It was amazing how fast I learned. I hadn't had another lover – something that astounded him and he said (but insincerely, as I discovered) made me mean so much to him. It all came naturally to me. I've never had a male lover since; it makes one much too vulnerable. Instead, I watch people, and I use power, carefully and selectively applied.

That woman – the new widow. There will be pictures of her in the morning papers. I expect she'll look pathetic – well, you would, after such an experience. I wonder if she's well insured. There are two adult sons, it seems, so she won't be alone.

His children will be long grown up by now. Sometimes I wonder about them. It was a late summer's day when it happened, the leaves still thick on the trees. Someone – a walker – had seen two figures walking in the woods. I had thought us quite alone. My shoes had mud on them but that proved nothing, as my counsel said; it could have come from anywhere at any time. She'd bled more than I expected. I'd read that if you struck a certain spot, in the back, the lungs would bleed internally. They said I stabbed her fifteen times. I don't remember that, so perhaps my mind really was disturbed, as I maintained to minimise my sentence. That was how the blood got on my clothes. I washed them, but it didn't all come out. It was long ago, before DNA testing was developed, and they could prove only that stains on my jacket, which I tried to burn, might have come from her. I didn't succeed in burning it completely, and the police found fragments in the grate at my bedsit.

He was in a dreadful state after she was discovered. He wouldn't let me near him to comfort him, though I went round to see the children. I used to like children: some children. I don't know what made the police suspect me. Maybe it was footmarks. It had rained recently and they made casts and matched them to my shoes. I'd worn heavy ones, suitable for walking. It wasn't wet enough for boots. Then letters were found. He'd kept notes I'd written him. You'd have expected him to get rid of them to protect me, but he didn't. He said I'd had a crush on him and pestered him, not confessing, for a long time, that we were lovers. The police took days to get him to admit that, and only succeeded after I kept insisting that it was true. I was proud of it. He'd wanted me, found me utterly desirable. He'd said so. He'd said she hadn't wanted sex for years, and that turned out to be a lie. What a two-faced bastard he turned out to be. I was glad I'd wrecked his life, because he had deceived me and destroyed mine.

It's hardened me. You don't survive so many years in prison without becoming tough and learning strategies to minimise the hardship. I took courses, passed exams, got in with a few women of a better type than the tarts and drug users. I had a woman lover for a while. She admired me because I was so strong. In the end I broke with her; she was too feeble, too demanding, and sex was not what I needed.

Before I found out he was dead, I used to think of tracing him, confronting him, seeing how he would react, but as he'd gone half across the world it seemed pointless. I'd expose myself, my past would be revealed and the respect I've earned through the effective practice of my work would be forfeit.

Inside, I learned the value of routine, and now I live my life by regulation. Up at seven o'clock, ten minutes' exercise to clear my mind, then fruit and muesli for breakfast, taken with herbal tea; caffeine is so bad for one, though I do enjoy a cup of coffee as a treat. I keep those hours even when I have no early consultation and need not hurry to leave my flat. My parents blamed themselves for what they called my fall from grace; they'd brought me up strictly and I'd done well at school, but I hadn't gone to college. Tertiary education was less universal then. I'd had various jobs and was working as a temporary secretary at the primary school where his children went when we met. It was a part-time post and so I could meet him when he snatched time off from his office. He worked locally. I was waiting to take up a purser's job aboard a cruise ship. It semed a good way to travel and capable women could do well, working for a shipping line.

I might have done it later, after my release, but by then I knew that I could no longer live close to other people, in a crowd. I needed space. I followed various other career lines before I chose to set up on my own as a counsellor, a decision I have never had occasion to regret.

'I didn't realise we had gang warfare in this area,' Sarah said on Sunday evening. The whole episode had jolted her out of kilter. So swiftly could death come, in hidden guise, in the shape of a lad who had not, that morning, planned that by nightfall he would be a killer. She could not explain her inner panic to Oliver; all she could express was shock, and pity for the Stewarts.

'On this scale, there isn't too much of it,' said Oliver. 'Gangs, yes, and punch-ups, and muggings, too. But not a lot of this.' He wanted to reassure her, but these were facts. 'Boys have attacked men who've tried to break up their hooliganism. That's not uncommon, and people have been injured. We don't hear about those incidents unless we know someone who's involved.'

'It's dreadful.' Sarah did not like to think about violent conduct. Suddenly her world seemed unsafe.

'Things have changed,' said Oliver. 'Some youngsters don't learn to respect anything, these days.'

'And none of those boys will talk? None of the decent boys?'

'Seems not. It's still early days. One will crack, or the culprits' parents will get suspicious.'

'Would a parent turn them in?'

'Who knows? It would be a difficult decision,' Oliver said.

'What's going to happen to poor Midge? Will she have to sell the house?'

'I don't know. I haven't got Dan's will. I hope he made one,' said Oliver. 'They'll have to have a hunt through all his papers.'

'And the funeral? When will that be? Next week some time?'

'Most unlikely,' said Oliver. 'The coroner will adjourn the inquest, even if by then someone's been charged, while the police complete their investigation, and the defence will be able to ask for a second post mortem. They may want to try to prove that Dan had a heart attack, and then it wouldn't be murder, or even manslaughter.'

'So will the funeral have to wait till then? What if they don't catch whoever did it?' Sarah was aghast at this; poor Dan doomed to lie indefinitely in the refrigerator at the mortuary.

'The family will have the right to ask for a second post mortem, so that they can arrange the funeral,' said Oliver. 'If it drags on, I'll talk to Midge and the boys about that. Much better get it over.'

'I should say so,' Sarah agreed.

They were spending the evening by the fire together. It had taken the murder of their friend to keep Oliver from returning to his dolls' house restoration after dinner.

10

Oliver went to the office early on Monday morning, anxious to deal quickly with the post, and, by cancelling appointments, win time to help Midge and her sons if they needed support. At the moment, with detectives still busy in Deerton, the press had been kept at bay and the Stewarts were not answering the telephone. Mark had brought his mobile, and this was their means of communication.

The inquest was to be opened the next day, Tuesday. The coroner would keep it as brief as possible, and then adjourn it, to let the police get on with their investigation, but Midge would have to be a witness. He wondered if they would call the boy, Jamie Preston, who had summoned Dan to the close.

The Times had reported the murder on an inside page. Oliver could only imagine what the tabloids would do with the grim story and hoped Midge would see none of them. They'd send reporters to the inquest, for sure, and plaster her photograph, with imaginative captions, all over the front pages unless some sleazy scandal or other murder was thought more titillating.

At breakfast Sarah, who had an appointment in Birmingham that day, wondered aloud if she should cancel it; might she be of use to Midge if she cried off?

'You go,' said Oliver. 'It might be more important for you

to be free another day, if something crops up.' He thought that Midge, whilst grateful, might find her role as victim in receipt of Sarah's kindness too demanding; even in woe, Sarah would be critical. Yet she had been very upset the night before, reminding him of the vulnerable, wounded girl she had been when they first met.

He wasn't quite sure what she had to do in Birmingham. However, she was developing latent business abilities and he did not begrudge her the freedom to grow; in his view, that, not possessiveness and the exertion of control, was what constituted love.

He parked the Rover and walked across the yard to the office. As he did so, Rosemary Ellis came down the steps from her flat and went over to her car. He turned and gave her his usual pleasant smile, saying, 'Good morning.'

Rosemary's heart never leaped, but its beat quickened. What a fortunate piece of timing: what a bonus for her day! Her own smile transformed her square features, softening her face.

He forgot about her the moment he entered his office, but Rosemary's mind dwelt on him for several minutes. He was in very early today, she thought, not connecting him yet with the crime in Deerton.

Sarah, in the train, was relieved to escape from the sorrows of the weekend. She still felt stunned, unable to believe that she would never see Daniel again: his funny smile, his thinning faded hair and his lean shape. He was not a big robust man, like Oliver, who was so solid. Oliver would have been a match for a lad with or without a knife, she thought, and then she knew he wouldn't. Burly policemen, trained in combat, had been stabbed to death by villains. She shuddered, and she grieved for Midge who would find coping alone well-nigh impossible. She would have to train for some career, thought Sarah. At least she could help there, having done it herself, not that Midge would be capable of achieving as much. Resolved on this, she opened a file and scanned it. She liked to look important in the train and never read a novel. She seldom read novels anyway, unless they were being much discussed, preferring to browse through books on interior decorating or home management, even house design.

When she reached Birmingham, a short walk took her to the restaurant where she met Charles and Hugh, who wanted her advice on how to reduce staff without incurring lawsuits or losing efficiency, and at the same time increase their seating capacity. She inspected their premises, where lunch preparations were under way, and saw that the layout could be streamlined by minor structural alterations. The initial outlay would, in the long run, cut the wages bill. She made notes, took measurements, and said she would produce a scheme and cost it, and after lunching with her clients, suggested that the extensive menu could be reduced; a smaller choice, while maintaining their high standards, would reduce waste. Diners, she said, could sometimes be overwhelmed by too wide a selection. Charles and Hugh found her ideas stimulating and planned another meeting.

At the station, before catching her train home, Sarah bought an evening paper. *Quiet, have-a-go hero built life anew after redundancy*, she read. How did they get hold of such stuff? From some chatty neighbour, she supposed. Perhaps Daniel was a hero. How astonishing to think of him like that. She'd always found him rather dull: good, but dull.

She'd met a lot of men through her new career, a few of them moderately exciting, and whose conversation, when they discussed business, was interesting. Some were arrogant and pushy, and she had been propositioned, not always subtly, several times. She dealt with these suggestions by ignoring them, since administering a snub would, in her view, be an over-reaction.

Act of Violence

Sitting in the train, in her scarlet coat and black skirt, a scarf at her throat and a gold bracelet on her wrist, Sarah knew that she looked good. What would she do if Oliver dropped dead?

Pick herself up and get on with things, of course.

All the boys involved in Saturday night's affray had gone to school as usual, even Jamie, his arm still in a sling but more to protect it than from medical necessity. His mother was thankful he was well enough; she had classes she must teach and to be left alone at home all day, after such an experience, would be bleak. Barry, Peter and Greg would be there, too; resuming normal life, as nearly as was possible, must be best for everyone.

Kate's path at school did not cross Jamie's; he did not take her subjects. Both liked it this way; it wasn't always easy if your parents were on the staff, but Kate was popular and made her classes lively, so no one had a down on him simply by association. Some people didn't even know they were related.

He wondered if those four would turn up: Kevin, Wayne, Paul and Trevor. Surely they wouldn't have the nerve to show their faces, but then, if they stayed away, would they be suspected?

In the reports about the stabbing, which mentioned an injured boy, no name had been given because he was protected by the law for minors. When other pupils asked what he had done to his arm, Jamie simply said he'd cut it in an accident. His three friends kept quiet, too, but the staff, who knew the truth, speculated endlessly about which boys could have been responsible. Bob and Ginny, returning from their cycle ride the day before, had called in at Kate's and heard the welcome news that Jamie was in the clear.

'I've said nothing,' Jamie told his three friends when they met at break.

Nor had they, but they were all in trouble with their parents for failing to supply the names of the guilty.

'You were great,' Peter told Jamie. 'My dad knew a boy was trying to help but he didn't realise it was you, in the scrum. He says we're committing a crime by not helping the police.'

Jamie remembered the threatening gestures made by Kevin and Wayne the day before.

'They'll get us if we do,' he said.

'Not if they're arrested,' Peter said.

'They'd get bail,' said Jamie.

'Would they? After killing someone?'

'They didn't all kill him,' Greg pointed out. 'They'd let the others out, most likely.'

All agreed that this was probable. They knew of other youngsters who had got into quite serious trouble for thieving, even breaking and entering, and who had been swaggering around without a care in no time, after not even being cautioned.

'The police will catch them in the end,' Peter said. 'They've been searching the road outside our house, looking at every blade of grass by the hedge and so on. They'll find something. Or someone will have seen the car.'

'It was probably stolen,' said Barry. 'You bet they nicked it.'

Peter's father had done what he could to describe the miscreants, but they were already attacking Daniel Stewart when he arrived, and he did not see their faces. One was shorter than the rest, and all were wearing jackets. Only one boy, and that was Jamie, had had no jacket on; if he had, his arm might have been protected. It was dark in the road; the porch lights from Barry's house and his own were the only illumination on the scene. As far as he could tell, all the boys wore some form of headgear: baseball caps, he thought.

'The police will talk to every boy in the school. You'll see,' said Greg.

And they set out to do so, starting with those in the same year as the four boys whose names they knew.

Kevin and Paul met, as they did most mornings, on the way to school. Walking slowly along, they agreed that to have stayed away might draw attention to them, but that they would keep apart during the day, and avoid Trevor and Wayne. Usually all four spent some part of the day together, but to do so now would emphasise the fact that they were a quartet. It seemed that Trevor and Wayne had the same idea, for they, though they did not avoid each other, kept their distance from the other two.

'It didn't happen,' Trevor told Wayne. 'If we keep our heads down, it will go away.' Neither of them had used the knife. Neither had anything to fear unless that berk Jamie Preston talked.

'He won't,' said Wayne. 'Me and Kev saw him going off with the cops yesterday. We let him know he'd better watch his step.'

All four had rationalised the night's events. They hadn't set out to fight, only to have a bit of fun at Barry's, knowing he and some of his mates were on their own, and it was Saturday. That old guy had come round poking his nose in and had got in the way of Kev's knife, which was in his hand because he might need to protect himself against the interference. Not one admitted any shame to another; to do so would be weak. None admitted to the surge of excitement he had felt when the violence escalated and they were all in there, punching and kicking. It had been a stupid accident; that was all.

None of their parents suspected anything, but all were surprised when their boys stayed in that night, each upstairs in his room, allegedly busy with his homework.

11

By Monday night the police were no further forward with their investigation. Almost every boy in the same year as Barry and Jamie had been traced and interviewed, but though some were unable to explain their movements on Saturday in an altogether satisfactory manner, so far there was nothing to connect them with the crime in Deerton. More checking would be done, and Detective Superintendent Fisher had arranged with the headmaster that he would address the school assembly in the morning. Several known troublemakers were questioned, but none of their prints matched those found in the ransacked house.

And there was no sign of the knife.

'We need one of the four musketeers to weaken,' said Fisher, who had thus christened Barry and his friends, as they were all for one and one for all. 'If young Jamie Preston's wound had been more serious, they might have been scared enough to talk, although God knows one wouldn't wish that on the lad.'

'He certainly knows who stabbed him,' said DS Shaw. 'He may let something slip to his mother.'

The dead man's clothes might yield traces from his killer, whose own clothes would be stained with blood. Find a suspect and you would find the evidence, Fisher thought, but a likely candidate had to be in the frame before such proof could be established. Ted Grant thought all the boys were wearing poplin type jackets, which did not readily leave fibres, nor attract them, but they would mop up blood. However, there were plenty of traces at the Noakeses' house, including urine-soaked bedding.

So much detection involved slow, careful checking; flights of fancy rarely led to arrests.

Mark Stewart left Deerton early on Monday morning to drive up to the Lake District, where his paternal grandparents lived, to tell them what he could about Daniel's death. They had wanted to come down to Deerton, but had been persuaded to remain at home because they could not help at present, and they would provide fresh targets for the media. Midge's parents lived in Spain, where money went further and the sun shone much of the time. Midge had telephoned them on Sunday afternoon, catching them after their siesta, and they had volunteered to fly back at once, but she urged them to stay where they were.

'Or you come here, pet,' said her father, a former market gardener who now grew fruit and vegetables in his sunny garden, and sold some of them.

'Later,' she said. 'In the spring, maybe, when this is over.' She might be strong enough to face their kindness then; not yet. She promised to let them know as soon as there was any news and explained that much of the time they were leaving the telephone off the hook as they were receiving so many calls from reporters. They'd understand that; they'd see the English papers when they went into town; her father often bought one. Now he'd make a special trip, most likely.

Poppy Flower came to see her after Mark had gone, to report progress – none – and to explain about the inquest the next day. She was sure a boy would talk eventually, but that could mean a day or two, and meanwhile they hoped the knife would turn up, or some mother would discover blood-stained garments being washed in secret.

But Kevin had slipped out on Sunday night and dumped his jacket, wrapped in two dustbin liners, in a bin outside a row of shops. It would be cleared away on Monday morning.

Midge and Jonathan went to the workshop after Poppy Flower's visit. There was no queue of irate customers lined up outside, wanting to know why it was not open, but fresh bills had landed on the mat. Jonathan retrieved them. He and Mark had had a brief discussion in which they shared concern about the business and its solvency, recognising that they must discover the true position in the next few days. More unpaid bills were stashed in the desk. There were also outstanding debts from customers who owed money.

'Things aren't too good in here,' said Midge. 'No one wants to buy our stuff though Dad did a lot of repairing.'

'Is there much of that waiting to be done?' asked Jonathan, who might be able to do the simpler jobs. His father had become extremely skilled.

'Not really. Dad was pretty much up to date, I think,' said Midge. 'There's some framing. Nothing that must be done today. I can manage the repairs, you know. Maybe not to Dad's standards, but I've helped him. I'll only take on easy things in future.'

'Mm.' Jonathan didn't know how to say it. She couldn't manage on her own.

'I'll see how it goes,' she said. 'I've coped when he had flu.'

'Let's put a notice on the door saying we'll be closed tomorrow, anyway,' said Jonathan. 'We'll have to sort all the papers and stuff. We can do a bit of that now, and maybe pick out anything that's promised, so we can tell the customers, if necessary.' It was too soon to make decisions. His mother

Act of Violence

hadn't really taken in the finality of his father's death, and nor had he. Then there would be the funeral and all that. Oliver had quietly explained the situation and they had agreed, if no one was arrested, to ask for the second post mortem to be done as soon as possible. Poor Dan must not be left where he was longer than was unavoidable.

Those little shits. If Jonathan could get his hands on who had done it, he would willingly strangle them with his own bare hands.

'Maybe we can sort things out at Christmas,' he said. 'Mark'll be back for a bit, and Judy will be around.' He paused. 'I could skip the rest of term,' he said. 'You shouldn't be all on your own.'

'You mustn't do that,' she said. 'I'll manage.' At the moment she couldn't imagine it, but she would have to do it.

'Pity Sarah's got a job now. She'd have helped – kept you company,' he said.

'Yes, but she makes me feel incompetent,' said his mother.

'How silly. You're marvellous,' said Jonathan, and gave her a hug which nearly made her crumple. 'You're just as capable as she is, if not more so, only you don't make a meal of it, like she does, for all to admire.'

Midge had to laugh at this shrewd assessment.

'She's never satisfied,' Jonathan went on. 'Not even with Saint Oliver.'

'Maybe she'd like the challenge of a devil,' said Midge, surprising him. Perhaps she would; it was a novel thought.

Kevin hadn't meant to kill that man. Or had he?

He thought about it briefly, walking away from school. He'd got a knife, and so, when he was thwarted, he had used it. He was a hard man. Pity only a few guys knew that, but it couldn't be made public as the stupid git had snuffed it. Kevin felt not one speck of remorse or shame for what he had done, nor any pity for the suffering he was causing. He didn't give the aftermath a thought. He swaggered on down the road. That man in charge, Superintendent Fisher or some such, had addressed the school that morning, describing what had happened and asking anyone with information to come forward. It would be in strict confidence, he said; Detective Inspector Flower would be in the headmaster's office, waiting. She stood beside him, Detective Inspector fucking Flower. Seeing her, Kevin had adopted a serious expression; she might be seeking signs of guilt but she wouldn't find them on his face. He could trust his own mates to fake innocence, but what about those others, those four who knew the truth?

On the whole, it had seemed wise to bunk off as soon as he got a chance to slide away from school unseen. The police couldn't interview you without a parent or guardian there if you were under sixteen, and he was, for a few more weeks. Perhaps teachers counted as guardians. He wasn't sure about that, and he didn't mean to find out now, as everyone knew the police could put words in your mouth and make you admit to things you hadn't done.

If that silly old fool hadn't come interfering, they'd have driven off and no harm done. Those kids would have had some explaining to do about the mess in the house but they could have cleaned up most of it in no time. He hoped Jamie Preston had taken note of the warning he and Wayne had signalled on Sunday morning. They'd been cautious, making sure the two police officers were looking ahead and that only Jamie, staring at them from the window, had seen them. It was lucky they had had the chance to warn him. He was a kid without a dad, no one to stick up for him; he'd take heed.

Kevin was a bit bothered about the knife. What could have happened to it? He'd thought he'd shoved it back in his pocket, but it must have dropped out. He hadn't worn gloves, so if it was found and had some blood on it, he could be in big trouble, but he'd never been fingerprinted; the police didn't know about Kevin Parker. They couldn't trace the knife to him.

It had all got a bit heavy, out in the road, but Kevin wasn't going to let it get to him. He'd act normal – not too angelic or folk would wonder – but he'd keep within bounds for a bit. He'd liked being the leader; he'd shown the others what he could do. He'd had power. He hadn't meant to cut the kid: of course not. Jamie Preston had just got in the way.

It did not occur to him that if luck had been against his second victim, he could have been responsible for two murders, not just one. And he didn't think of it as murder. It was an accident.

This morning a woman came to talk to me about her husband. She suspected that he had a mistress, and I coaxed her to talk about the reasons for her fears, and to consider what separation, which she was contemplating, would mean in practice. She cried a great deal, which irritated me, and I told her she was weeping for her father, who had died when she was ten, and that she was seeking to transmute her youthful unresolved grief into current anxieties. I didn't suggest that she had been abused in childhood; many counsellors go down that road and it's too easy a way out. All most of my patients need is a listening ear, because friends don't have the time these days, and nor do doctors, and few priests or parsons are pastorally oriented. I give my patients value for their money as I sit facing them in my consulting room with its plain white walls and leather chairs. I gaze at them, maintaining steady eye contact, and I have a box of tissues handy, even coffee keeping warm.

They feel better when they leave, after paying my fee of forty pounds a session. They've had my undivided attention for the period of their appointment, and often their problems can be dealt with by the sort of advice given in the agony columns of magazines. Sometimes I make notes on a pad placed on the desk in front of me. I keep a file on every one of them, and I know many secrets. I've got plenty of scope for blackmail.

It's doubtless true that this woman's husband has found someone else; who can wonder at it, looking at her? I'll foster her suspicions, nourishing her flickering desire to declare the marriage over, but I'll make her understand the economic disadvantages for her, and the inevitable difficulties for the children – there are two teenage girls. I'll point out that as she is still mourning her own father, so will they mourn theirs if he leaves, and that they may decide to lay the blame on her. It will take us many expensive sessions to reach this conclusion. By then the husband may have acted independently and the choice will not be hers. Whatever the result, she'll need support through the period that follows, and she'll pay me for providing it. I will need to calculate what she can afford; those unable to pay my fees can go to the Citizens' Advice Bureau for practical advice, at no cost to themselves. My patients must pay for the indulgence which I offer.

I have male clients, men who are impotent, or gay – what a misnomer when often they are seriously sad – and can't accept it, or can, and are wondering what society will say. Some men who consult me have wives obsessed with becoming pregnant when the very thought of having an infant to complicate an already difficult or over-intense relationship terrifies them. Sometimes I want to shake them, tell them to face up to their obligations, be men, as they sit before me, whimpering, pale caricatures of masculinity, wanting mothers. Don't men ever grow up?

Some men have paranoid delusions that the whole world is against them, and I direct them to list the good things in their lives, and then the bad, and weigh them up. Often I can see how those in a failed relationship will refuse to take responsibility for any part in the breakdown, when both parties are obviously to blame. Lack of communication is frequently the real trouble, but at least one partner is trying to communicate with me. By using the correct language, the appropriate terminology, I render them more articulate.

I don't want to lose the easy patients; they, after all, pay my bills. I don't refer on the more difficult ones unless I think they are unstable, deranged enough to harm physically themselves or others; these are outside my remit and I urge them to consult their doctors and seek psychiatric help. Such people rarely come to me because they are reluctant to admit they have a problem. The ones I see are those who could redeem themselves. Some have lives which are extremely drab; some stories are pathetic; and there are tragedies: women who think they will lose their husbands' love if they cannot reproduce, and, occasionally, the bereaved.

Treatment can become addictive. Patients return because they see me as their friend, perhaps their only one.

Prudence Wilmot had recently installed a fax machine. It was still a novelty to her, but it was useful when communicating with her American publisher and her family and friends who were overseas, most of whom had access to this rapid means of communication. Oliver had told her that she should link herself to the Internet, where e-mail would open up a whole new world to her. Prudence was not sure she needed a whole new world; the one around her was enough.

'Have you done that?' she asked.

Foxton and Smythe had not.

'I often hanker for the old world,' Prudence had confessed. 'Where people had good manners and life did not rush past so rapidly.' She had sighed. 'In my parents' generation, it was travel that developed at amazing speed. The first car took the road in their infancy, and they lived to see men land on the moon. In my generation, it's the revolution in communication that's so difficult to keep up with. What do we do with all this time we've saved? And do we really communicate, if it's all done by electronics?'

Oliver had agreed that she had a point.

On Monday morning, she walked along the street to the florist's and ordered white and yellow flowers to be sent to Midge. Why was she called that, she wondered; some childhood nickname carried on, she supposed. Emphasising that she wanted no heavy purples, no russet shades, she paid and left, and when she reached home she wrote Oliver a message which she faxed. He could attend to it or not, as he liked; telephoning would be a definite interruption.

VERY MUCH REGRET THE TRAGEDY YOUR FRIENDS HAVE SUFFERED, she wrote, in bold block letters so that they would transmit clearly. LET ME KNOW IF I CAN HELP. BROAD SHOULDER, TIME AVAILABLE, ALSO BEDS IF RELATIVES NEED THEM. ASSUME GUILT NOT YET ASSIGNED. It was like a telegram of old, she thought, feeding it into her machine.

Oliver smiled when he received this missive. He had brewed himself a strong cup of coffee, earning a reproof from his secretary who said she would have gladly done it for him, and took time off from going through the pile of mail to reply.

MANY THANKS, he faxed back. ASSUMPTION CORRECT, BLIND ALLEY. MIDGE AND SONS STUNNED BUT COPING. DITTO FOXTONS. MIGHT CALL UPON SHOULDER LATER.

Prudence had once told him that one of the consolations of age was the acquisition of new friends across the generations, and the freedom to enjoy the company of men to whom, twenty years before, if one was of the same generation, one might have been attracted.

'With,' she said, 'devastating problems and possibly dire consequences.'

Oliver understood. He could chat to Prudence to his heart's

content without Sarah raising any objection. She wasn't even his mother, whom until her death Sarah had resented, though she never interfered and had been very generous to them.

When he had taken on the restoration of the dolls' house, Prudence had been touched. As a child, she had loved playing with it; it had stood on a cupboard at a level with her face, and she had spent hours arranging the family of dolls inside, putting them to bed and getting them up, sending the father doll off to work, just as her father had departed daily, and the small boy to school. When her sister was born, a baby doll had appeared, representing Emily, who later had taken the house over. Embarking on his self-imposed task, Oliver had revealed unexpected talents and a dextrous touch. She knew that he enjoyed it. All that would be on hold, now, she thought, while he helped the Stewarts through their crisis. As, of course, he would.

12

Sarah walked across Fettleton station yard to her car, which she had parked near one of the pay machines, beneath a light, obedient to advice about avoiding vulnerable situations. She had never felt at risk in Fettleton, but after Saturday night's events, she knew that danger could lurk anywhere, and cars had been broken into here, their radios stolen and any articles left visible to thieves. The station itself closed down at five o'clock; after that you had to buy your ticket from a machine, and if you needed help or information, there was no guard or ticket collector to approach. Oliver had insisted that she carry a mobile phone, now that she was travelling around, and she was amenable; she did not want to be stranded with a puncture or a car that wouldn't start.

There were no problems tonight. The car started and she drove off through a mist of gently falling rain which had replaced the earlier frost. What would it be like to make a train trip every day to work? She must pursue the possibility of the job she had heard discussed in London last week, just a day before Daniel was murdered. It seemed an age ago.

The house was empty when she reached home. She had expected Oliver to be there and because he was not, she felt aggrieved. There was one message on the answerphone:

Judy, deeply upset by what had happened to the Stewarts, was coming home, and Oliver had left a note to say he had gone to meet her at the station.

Shedding her smart coat and skirt, putting on slacks and a big sweater, Sarah decided that this was confirmation of her theory that there was an interest between Mark and Judy that went beyond the scope of their childhood friendship. Oliver had not agreed. It would be difficult to nurture a romance when they were separated by several hundred miles, he suggested, though of course it was quite possible. He suspected that it was Jonathan with whom Judy had a strong bond. They were close in age, and had always been great friends. He said nothing of this to Sarah; he knew she had ambitions for her daughter, whom she pictured, if she completed her law degree, marrying a barrister who would become a silk, perhaps a judge, not a mere provincial solicitor like Oliver.

Sarah poured herself a glass of wine and went into the kitchen, where she began putting together a pasta meal, enough for three. Judy would be hungry.

But only Oliver returned. He had left Judy at Deerton. He invented placatory messages from Judy to her mother, and ate his portion of the pasta with appreciation. Sarah had had a lavish lunch in Birmingham; he had had sandwiches in the office. During dinner, he asked about her day and listened while she told him a little about it, refusing to let his mind stray towards the Stewarts and their plight. But Sarah's basic soundness soon surfaced, and she asked how things were with the stricken family.

'They're all still stunned,' said Oliver. Midge had looked like a little ghost, and both the boys, a sturdy pair, had pale drawn faces. Judy had burst into tears as soon as she saw them, and there had been hugs all round, and tears from everyone, though Oliver had turned away to hide his, which he blinked away, unnoticed.

He told Sarah that Midge and Jonathan had been to the workshop and discovered that the business was in deep financial trouble. Daniel had managed to hide the full gravity of the situation from Midge, although she knew that things were tight. A copy of his will, dating from when the couple married nearly twenty-five years ago, had been found at the house, and the solicitor who made it had been traced. Oliver had spoken to him; the will was valid. Everything was left to Midge and, if she predeceased him, in equal parts to any future surviving children. It was straightforward. The question was, had he anything, except debts, to bequeath? There were other papers to be gone through. Mark, back from his lightning trip to see his grandparents, said he would get on with this as soon as possible, but there was the inquest the next morning.

It was all very depressing, but at least there would be no legal complications about settling the estate. A partner in the firm which made the will was named as executor; he was dead now, but a colleague had taken on his clients. The firm would communicate with Oliver, who would, he had told them, act for the family in any way that would be helpful. In view of what had happened, the other solicitor, based in Norwich, where Daniel hailed from, was only too thankful for this offer.

There might be some delay with probate due to the manner of Daniel's death, but at the moment all such questions were purely academic.

Oliver told Sarah some of this.

'Couldn't he have managed things better?' she asked.

'He couldn't foresee that he would lose his job at the age of forty-four,' said Oliver. 'He kept working. He worked bloody hard.'

It was rare for Oliver to swear. Sarah felt surprise.

'What will Midge do?' she asked.

'It's too soon to make plans,' said Oliver. 'We'll have to see how things work out.' He thought she might have some

Peter knew that this was very likely true. He stared at his feet, not answering.

'I wish you'd say, Peter,' said his mother, who had been listening to them both in anguish. She understood Peter's curious warped loyalty, and she understood, too, that he was frightened of reprisals. These boys, whoever they were, were capable of anything, as had been proved. She could scarcely believe that all this had happened while she and Ted were watching television, with Peter, as they thought, safely in their neighbours' house three doors away.

'You may think you're brave, keeping stumm,' said Ted, who was an electrician, working on his own. 'There's other sorts of courage, like doing the right thing when it isn't easy.'

He couldn't believe that this had happened on his own doorstep. Boys could be wild, and high spirits could lead to recklessness, but this was vicious, mindless violence. Leaving out the fact of murder, and the attack on him, what had happened in the Noakeses' house was horrible.

Greg's mother took the same line. She had two daughters as well as Greg, and was divorced from Greg's father, but she had a boyfriend who stayed overnight in Deerton when he could. He was a long-distance lorry driver and was often on the road. He'd been at their house on Saturday and that was one reason why Greg had gone out. He didn't like to think of Rick in bed with his mother and found it difficult to be civil to the man, though Rick was always pleasant enough to Greg and his sisters, and generous to their mother. Greg suspected that he had another family in Leeds, which was where he was based, and he was perfectly correct.

The parents of the miscreant boys had no suspicion that their sons were involved. The murder was discussed in each household. It was the sort of shocking crime you didn't expect in a small village. Stabbings happened outside pubs and clubs when people were drunk and got into fights. In Kevin's house on Sunday, over the meal the family had together after the pubs closed – his parents liked to go down to the local around one o'clock on Sundays – it was the main topic while they ate the pie his mother had made. She was a dinner lady at a local primary school. After saying that he hoped Kevin would have nothing to do with lads like that, his father, a telephone engineer, wondered aloud if he would finish a job he was doing in the allotted time. He'd run into problems with the installation.

Except for Paul's mother, the parents of all the boys had jobs; none was neglected. They only rarely played truant. None of the four fitted the profile of a shiftless, deprived adolescent who was programmed to commit crimes. Wayne and Trevor, though doing better at school than Paul and Kevin, had not achieved enough to give them confidence, and both found it difficult to handle teasing and practical jokes. Neither had any major interests or enthusiasms. They would join others in looking for a laugh, but a laugh might be an act of petty vandalism. Until now, none of the four had been involved in anything serious; on Saturday, very briefly, all had found being on top exhilarating.

On Tuesday morning the inquest was opened and, as expected, adjourned after evidence of identification had been given and the circumstances of Daniel's death outlined. The knife had pierced his heart. As no one had yet been charged with the crime, the family had to understand that the body could not yet be released. It was so cruel. Midge, horrified at the prospect of further assaults upon it in another post mortem, agreed that they should wait for a few days, at least, before insisting that it be carried out.

'People don't think about these things when they go around stabbing people,' Midge sobbed, collapsing.

'People don't think about others at all when they use knives. They are governed by their violence,' Neil Fisher told her. And, at times, a prior plan; sometimes aggressive self-defence was their only instinct.

Oliver, needed in court by a client who had been charged with dangerous driving, had had to leave them after the inquest. Judy had gone back to Deerton with the Stewarts, and, once home again, Midge succumbed to a storm of noisy grief triggered off by the bureaucratic red tape. Judy sat her down in front of the fire with a box of tissues while Jonathan went to make some tea. Mark had another thought and rummaged in the sideboard in the dining room. Surely Dad had some brandy somewhere? He found a bottle, nearly full, and poured them all, including Judy, a tot. The girl sat awkwardly beside Midge, wondering how to comfort her. She patted her hand.

'He was great, Dan was,' she said. 'He's always been there, in my life. I won't ever forget him. He was fun. He made us laugh. Remember the firework parties when we were young? How we used to sing, dancing round the bonfire? It was Dan who started all that.' He had been more lively than her own father; quick-witted and amusing. 'He was so alive,' she said, and she too began to cry.

This enabled Midge to regain control. She blew her nose on a tissue, then sat up straight and told them all that they must resume their own lives.

'We'll finish sorting out Dad's papers and things,' she said. 'We'll decide what bills to pay and all that, and I must carry on with the business. We can't make any proper plans until the police catch that wicked boy. I'll need you then – all of you,' she said, including Judy, who would be hurt if she were left out, and who anyway was dear to Jonathan, as was obvious. And to Midge. She was not at all like Sarah. 'I've got to get used to being on my own,' Midge continued. 'I can do more framing and cut down on the furniture part. I won't buy in any more at present. We'll see how things go. Oliver will have some ideas about the best way forward.' That was the phrase. Politicians used it all the time. Sometimes, though, the road wound and twisted; you could not always forge straight ahead.

At the moment, all she wanted was to be alone, to weep and wail and spill out her anguish without having to exert control. But Mark and Jonathan had also been bereaved; they had their own loss to deal with. Sudden death, if not murder, happened all the time and people survived, and so would she, if only the agonising ache which filled her chest would dissolve. The pain was so intense that she wondered if she was having a heart attack, and then she understood that this was what was meant by heartbreak.

In the kitchen, finding lunch from among the frozen items Sarah had provided, Judy told Mark and Jonathan that she was sure her parents would gladly have Midge to stay indefinitely, but they all agreed that this would be only a temporary solution. Daniel's parents might come down, but that would mean more work for her. It would be different if there was any practical way to help; at the moment, with the police investigation apparently achieving nothing, it seemed that there was deadlock everywhere.

Midge had gone upstairs to wash her face. Returning, she realised they were discussing her and went to tell them that they must stop worrying. She was afraid that, to fill their time, they would start wondering what to do with Dan's clothes, and at the moment she could not bear the thought of discarding so much as a pair of his socks.

'You must all resume your lives as soon as possible,' she repeated. 'Now, what have you found for us for lunch?'

Sarah was right. Food was essential and the need to eat it filled the time as another hour of the unending day dragged by.

* * *

Act of Violence

Later, when Jonathan drove Judy back to Winbury, there was no one at home. Sarah was at her office and Oliver was still dealing with his recalcitrant motorist.

'Your mother enjoys her job, doesn't she?' said Jonathan, kissing Judy in the hall.

She put her arms round him. Funny that Midge and Daniel, both willowy, had two such sturdy sons.

'She certainly does. She's good at it. She's quite ambitious,' she said.

'How does Oliver feel about it? She'd never worked before, had she?'

'He's pretty proud of her, I'd say. I think he's sometimes felt guilty about snapping her up almost straight from school, before she'd had time to turn into her real self,' said Judy.

'She seems real enough to me,' said Jonathan, who admired Sarah without ever feeling drawn to her. She was a very confident woman, he thought, unlike his own diffident mother.

'She was only nineteen when they got married,' Judy said.

'Things were different in those days,' said Jonathan. 'And there wouldn't have been you and Tim if they hadn't.'

'No – funny, isn't it?' said Judy. 'We'd have been other people. Or not existed. Weird.'

'Unimaginable,' said Jonathan. He loved Judy and when they were apart he missed her, but he knew they might end up with other partners. On the other hand, they might separate and, eventually, come together again, like streams of mercury. Neither would put chains upon the other; not now, not ever.

'I wonder how Dad's getting on with his house,' said Judy. 'Have you seen it?'

'What house? Has he bought a seaside bolthole?'

'It's in the study,' Judy said. She led him there, and Jonathan saw the old dolls' house on its table. She opened it to reveal its three storeys, the staircase, now neatly carpeted, the various bedrooms, the bathroom with its old-fashioned fitments. 'He hasn't fixed the lights yet,' Judy said. 'But he's done a lot this term.'

The dolls were arranged in different rooms, the children in bed, the father in his study, the mother in the kitchen. Until recently, the house, in human terms, had been unfurnished; now, much of it was fit for habitation.

'Good heavens!' Jonathan exclaimed. 'Where did he find it?'

'It was Prudence Wilmot's. It turned up when the stuff at her old house was sold. She couldn't bear to part with it,' said Judy. 'Dad's fixing it.'

'Prudence Wilmot – that's who sent the flowers?'

'Right. Prudence used to live in one of the flats behind the office. She and Dad are great mates,' she said. 'It's nice for them. She's at least seventy,' Judy added, seeing his expression. She took the child dolls out of their beds and arranged them downstairs, appropriately, and put the mother in the drawing room. 'They must be up by now. It's tea-time,' she declared, and closed the house.

13

'We may have to fingerprint every teenage boy in the area,' said Fisher, when by Tuesday evening they were no nearer lining up a likely suspect. 'I wonder if we'd be able to set that up at the school or will we have the parents shouting about their kids' rights?'

He pondered to himself. The headmaster had been very helpful, but had been unable to name possible tearaways. He had suggested the offending boys might have come from Fettleton, where there were several notorious gangs. Fisher had discounted this idea. The boys were known to the four he called the musketeers; that meant that they were local.

'The innocent lads will cooperate, whatever we set up,' Shaw remarked. 'It's only the guilty who'll give trouble.'

After the Noakeses' prints and those of the three visiting boys had been identified among the rest found at the ransacked house, four unidentified sets had been discovered. One set had been on a discarded beer can; four clear fingers and a thumb; others were less distinct, but sharp enough, on items thrown about the rooms, particularly the kitchen. There was plenty of proof, once they knew who to test, and they would find all four boys in time; Fisher had said so on television, asking for those who knew anything to come forward. There would have been some blood-stained clothes, for instance. All this delay, and stress, not to mention cost, could have been avoided if only the four musketeers would talk.

It was decided that if they were no further forward by the morning, as was most probable, they would seek to set up the mass fingerprinting operation on Thursday, obtaining whatever clearances were necessary. But not every boy would be in school. The guilty might bunk off; still, a list of absentees could be useful. Because the boys they sought, or some of them, were almost certainly under sixteen, the police must be meticulous in what they did to apprehend them. The smallest technical oversight could lead to the acquittal of a guilty individual.

After this depressing conference, Fisher left his subordinates to continue the door-to-door interviewing of every boy qualifying as a possible suspect. Many pupils, like Barry Noakes, lived in villages around Mickleburgh. It was a slow and tedious job, and irritating when the lad to be questioned was not at home. Most seemed to have busy social lives and their parents did not always know where they were, or how they had spent Saturday evening.

Fisher went to see Kate and Jamie Preston. Jamie was the most promising prospective source of information.

Opening the door, Kate was not too dismayed to see him. She did not find this thin man with the lined face intimidating, but she did not underestimate his intelligence. He was alone, which reassured her.

'Come in,' she said. 'Jamie's upstairs, doing his homework.'

'How's his arm?'

'He says it itches. I suppose that means it's healing,' she said.

She led him into the sitting room and gestured to a chair, then sat down facing him. The room was small and pretty; like her, he thought, fancifully. Fisher lived among severe, functional furnishings in a modern flat in Fettleton. Framed prints of various theatrical productions adorned Kate's walls; there were flowers on a table, and a pile of books on the floor.

'Has he said anything?' asked Fisher.

'About who did it, you mean? No.' Kate shook her head.

'It's possible they've been threatened. Jamie and the other three,' said Fisher. 'Those young villains won't hesitate to beat up these other lads if they split.'

'I know,' said Kate. 'The kids at school won't ever tell, if there's bullying or some trouble of that kind. Not that there's a lot at our place. It's pretty good, on the whole, but you always get the bad apples.' She hesitated. 'I told him they'd all be safe if whoever did this was arrested and locked up, but he said they'd get bail.'

'It's not very likely,' Fisher said. 'But on the other hand, only one boy stuck the knife in. Whoever else was involved might get bail, depending on his luck. I'd oppose it very strongly, for their own protection as much as anyone else's. People would find out who they were and the lynch-law factor has to be considered.'

'I'm so angry about it,' Kate said. 'I'm in a real rage. Jamie might so easily have been killed, like that poor man.'

'I'm angry, too,' Fisher told her. 'Why should decent boys get dragged into this sort of thing because of some evil little toe-rags who don't give a shit about anyone except themselves?'

Kate stared at him, astonished.

'You really do care, don't you?' she said.

'Of course I do. All coppers do. Well,' he qualified, 'most of us. We care about innocent bystanders getting killed.' And all too often, police officers were the victims.

'Shall I get Jamie down to talk to you?' Kate asked. 'Or would you like to go and talk to him?'

'I can't legally interview him without you there,' said Fisher.

'You can go and talk to him, though, can't you? Like a friend?' she suggested. 'He means to go into the army, like his father,' she added. 'He's interested in tanks. And he plays the cello.'

'I don't know a lot about tanks,' said Fisher. 'But my father was in the army in the war. In the infantry.' He'd lost a leg, but Fisher did not tell her that.

'Then you've got a bond,' said Kate. 'Try it.' She smiled at him. 'I'll put the kettle on,' she added. 'For when you're done.'

Jamie might make some casual remark that would give Fisher a lead, but it was unlikely; the boy would be on his guard. However, if he didn't resent the superintendent's presence, he might let something slip to his mother later.

But he didn't. Fisher spent only a short time upstairs, and when the two came down together, Jamie had a Pepsi while Fisher drank a cup of coffee with Kate.

Fisher had given him his personal card, with the telephone number of the direct line to his office. Jamie had accepted it and put it in a drawer in his room.

It was a long shot, Fisher thought, but it might yield something, if the weight of Jamie's knowledge grew too heavy for him.

After Fisher left, Jamie was tempted. He felt terrible about the man who had been killed. If he, Jamie, hadn't chosen that door to bang on – had gone to a nearer house, even Peter's across the road – that man would be alive. But Peter's father might be dead instead. And would Kevin have pulled the knife if the man had not arrived? It might have been Jamie himself who was the target, he knew; they had left the house to come after him. The more he mulled it over in his mind, the more confused he became. Kevin ought to be punished for what he'd done, but then there was the question of revenge. The gesture he and Wayne had made on Sunday was explicit. It was lucky the police officers hadn't seen them; they might have gone and asked what they were doing, and the boys would have thought Jamie had named them.

Jamie knew that witnesses could be frightened off from giving evidence; it had happened at school on a minor scale over some thieving, which had gone unpunished because no one would speak up for fear of reprisals, and no one split on those who used or dealt in drugs. Like many others, Jamie didn't want to know; he walked away.

That copper, Fisher, had been cool. He'd glanced round Jamie's room and talked about football, seeing a poster on Jamie's wall, but said he liked cricket himself, though that was less popular with his colleagues. He said it was sometimes difficult to take a line that wasn't the same as your friends'. Jamie heard the hidden message, but Fisher didn't keep on about it. He'd seen Jamie's cello standing in the corner and said he used to play the saxophone. Then he'd handed Jamie his card.

'We'll get those lads in the end,' he said. 'But you and your mates could make it easier for us. Point us in the right direction.' He'd paused, and added, 'Your mum's got the kettle on. I'd quite like a coffee. How about you?'

Jamie had followed him down the stairs and had listened while Fisher and his mother drank their coffee and talked about plans for Christmas. Fisher said that crime was sure to flourish over the holiday period.

'Unless it snows,' he said. 'That keeps thieves indoors. And if they do come out, sometimes they leave footprints we can follow.'

Kate had laughed. She said that she and Jamie might go down to stay with her parents this year, instead of inviting them to come to Mickleburgh.

While she was seeing Fisher off, Jamie returned to his room.

He closed the door and lay on his bed, eyes shut, while the horror of Saturday night washed over him. Why had he run to that particular house? Because he saw its porch light shining, and it was away from the close, where he would be penned in if Kevin and his gang came after him. He'd wanted to put space between them. How could he know that they would turn on that man and pull a knife on him? Kevin hadn't taken his knife out in Barry's house. Thank goodness! In that small space, he'd have done dreadful damage, waving it around. All Jamie had wanted was to stop them destroying the Noakeses' house; he'd seen fights enough at school, but he hadn't understood that vandalism could whirl up into a real battle, as it had in the road. His memory of pitching in himself was vague; he'd tugged at a boy's sleeve and he had pummelled Kevin's back. Then there had been the sharp stinging pain in his arm as Kevin had swung round.

Jamie could see them all: he could hear the laughs and jeers while the four boys set about their destruction of the Noakeses' house; he could see the scowls and hatred in their faces, and then there was their united attack on that one man, and he remembered Wayne punching Peter's father in the stomach, and when he was on the ground, kicking him in the ribs and in the balls. Peter's father – a broad, burly man, much bigger than the one who died – had groaned. He must have seen their faces, but then it was so dark and all the boys were in similar clothes – jeans and black or navy anoraks.

He'd almost told Fisher who they were. The man was decent; he didn't question him, or threaten. He hadn't come on all kind and sentimental, and then turned hard, which was what was supposed to happen when you got arrested. He wasn't like that other man, the night it happened, PC Roberts, who was sure that Jamie was the murderer. If he told anyone, it would be Fisher.

Later, his mother tapped on his door and, at his murmur, entered. Jamie was still lying on his bed.

'How about getting undressed?' she said. He looked very white. Was he having an attack of conscience, or was it delayed shock? Maybe a bit of both.

Meekly, Jamie let her help him take off his shirt; then he went to the bathroom where somehow he got into his pyjamas, one-handed.

'Forget it all for tonight,' was all she said, as he turned on his radio with its snooze button.

'At least that man didn't have any little kids,' said Jamie.

'No. His children are grown up,' said Kate. But there is a widow, she reflected. 'Good night, Jamie. See you in the morning.'

'See you in the morning.'

People said that with confidence, trustingly, or 'see you', meaning 'see you soon', but fate could intervene to render it impossible. There was no 'soon' or 'in the morning' for Daniel Stewart. Kate knew what sudden bereavement was; when Jamie's father was killed, it had happened to her, and at a distance, and sometimes she thought she had still not accepted it, but on occasions, hearing of broken marriages, she had asked herself if theirs would have lasted. Could it have survived the stress of his career?

She thought so. She had known, in theory anyway, what she was taking on when they married; she was aware that there would be separations, frequent moves, and that his life would often be at risk. But when they were together their closeness grew, and now Jamie was beginning to look so like his father, much more than when he was a little boy. Since being widowed, she had not wanted a relationship that might harm her bond with Jamie and bring difficulties to their lives. Failure could threaten their security, and as it was, they managed very well. She was a teacher before she married, and a brief retraining course equipped her to resume her career. At first they had lived in Devon near her parents, who had been a great support during the early years. Without them, things would have been much harder, and her parents, elderly now, were still glad to have her and Jamie visiting at any time.

They would be shocked and anxious when they knew their grandson was involved in Saturday's act of violence. Though the names of none of the boys were mentioned in reports about the murder, there were photographs of Barry's parents outside their vandalised house. It would not need much sleuthing skill to identify that family, and, by connection, others. So much for privacy. At least no reporters had lined up at Kate's door. Jamie had not yet been flushed by a brash journalist who would want to talk to Kate and quote her, or offer huge sums of money for her story.

A neighbour in Deerton had been found to pay tribute to Daniel Stewart, describing him as a quiet man, always ready to help with village events and who worked long hours at his business in Mickleburgh. Someone knew that several years ago he had been made redundant from a position with a furniture factory which was taken over. He and other staff were disposable as the new owners brought in fresh faces; he had started his own repair workshop, funding it, it was hazarded, with his redundancy payment.

Poor man. A nice man. Kate sighed, reading this. Tomorrow she would try to talk it through with Jamie again.

In the morning, after a restless night, she woke with an aching head, and to a silent son.

On Wednesday, at midday, Peter and Jamie walked into town together to buy chips.

Each evening, Peter's father had lectured him, to be told that you didn't grass on your mates.

'Funny sort of mates,' said Ted Grant, 'gate-crashing the Noakeses' house and breaking the place up.'

'They didn't mean to kill Mr Stewart,' Peter said. 'It was an accident. He happened to be there.'

'Like I did,' said his father. 'Trying to help.'

'Yes – well—' Peter could not look his father in the eye.

'He had a knife,' said Ted. 'A flick knife. I saw it in his hand. Not a penknife.'

Peter did not answer. He knew that other boys at school had knives.

'Think about it, Peter,' said his father.

While they ate their chips, Peter and Jamie discussed the situation, and Jamie reported Fisher's visit of the previous evening.

'He's all right,' he said. 'He didn't hassle me. I feel bad about it.'

'So do I,' said Peter.

'He gave me his phone number,' said Jamie. 'I suppose he meant so that I could ring him privately.'

'Will you?' Peter wished he would, and take the load off him.

'I'm afraid of them getting at us – and at my Mum,' said Jamie. 'She's on her own.'

So were lots of other mums, thought Peter, Greg's for one, though she had that Rick bloke.

'I could do it,' he said, reluctantly. 'I could disguise my voice and say I wasn't you.'

'They'd trace the call,' said Jamie.

'I could use a phone box. One near the school. Then they'd know it was a pupil, but not who.'

'You'd have to wipe the telephone, to get rid of fingerprints,' said Jamie, for the police had all theirs, the four of them.

'No wonder criminals get caught,' said Peter. 'There's such a lot to think of.'

'They don't all,' said Jamie. 'The police need tip-offs and stuff.'

'Let's give it another day. Maybe two,' said Peter. 'And if the police haven't managed it by then, we'll think about it seriously.'

Having reached this compromise, both boys felt happier.

14

Violent crime fascinates me. I buy, as well as The Guardian, a tabloid paper which reports, in lurid terms, the most horrific crimes. Perhaps, in the way that I help my patients transpose their troubling impulses and emotions into acceptable channels – gardening, tapestry, charity work, even sport or jogging – I am vicariously laying ghosts.

I have dreamt about it, seen her trusting back turned towards me, the little dog running at her heels, the larger one ahead, and the appalled expression on her face as she stared at me, understanding my action and that she would die.

It was wrong. I know that. I've said so often enough, but it's difficult to feel regret. If my efforts to deflect suspicion had been more successful, the killing would have been blamed on some itinerant mugger and, in time, when he had recovered from his guilt, we would have married. Although her being pregnant put a different slant on things; he had deceived me most dreadfully. As it was, if he had not gone overseas, I would not have been able to keep away from him. I would have traced him – that would not have been difficult – and I would have watched him, tried to infiltrate his life, been what is these days called a stalker. Once someone has been as important as he was to me, they cannot be forgotten, even if what I felt for him afterwards was contempt.

I might have sought to punish him. Perhaps I did it anyway.

I'm accustomed, now, to being close to no one. Perhaps I never was; the only deeply serious relationship I ever had, and that proved false, was with him. I was an adopted child, something I did not know until my adoptive brother – I thought he was my real brother – told me when I was thirteen. He'd heard an aunt and uncle talking about it, though to be fair to them, they were not aware that he was within earshot. He'd challenged them, asked for the truth, been told it and been sworn to secrecy. Of course, the next time we quarrelled – this often happened – he broke the news to me, mocking me, taunting.

Then my parents – as, for want of a better term, I still called them, and sometimes think of them, even today – told me a charming tale of how they chose me – ME – this particular infant – from among a dozen others. In those days, before the advent of effective contraception for unmarried girls and legalised abortion, babies for adoption were readily available. Their family unit enlarged by my arrival, they promptly produced their own natural son, followed by a daughter. They assured me that they loved me just as much as this younger pair, my mother – a secretary before her marriage – gazing at me solemnly, holding my unresponsive hand, while my father, managing director of a prosperous manufacturing business, remained silent, falsely smiling, nodding now and then to endorse her words.

I felt differently towards him after that. If he tried to hug or kiss me, I saw it as a sexual threat – though I understood my revulsion only later, when I studied psychotherapy in prison, reading it up compulsively, not realising then that I could turn it into a career.

It helped me to understand my actions. I was not to blame. I had been betrayed, first by my natural mother who had abandoned me, then by my adoptive parents who went on to have their own children, and finally by Lionel.

He was the one I should have killed. He destroyed me; but I destroyed him too: I must remember that.

I have rebuilt my life. I'm a respected member of society, practising an honourable profession, doing good. I keep a low public profile, not anxious to become too notable in the area in case I am asked about my life, although I have a blameless history since my release, and one that can be verified.

When it became possible to trace one's real mother, I set the operation in train. It took time, but I located her some years ago. She's still alive, and now a wealthy widow. I've written to her, giving no address, posting my letter in London, wanting to disturb her. How shaken she would be to learn what I had done. Her respectability would be shattered. I enjoy knowing that I have the power to do it. Though I have assumed a new identity, it could all be proved; DNA testing would confirm our relationship beyond all doubt.

I feel remarkably incurious about my natural father. Strange.

Now I'm wondering about the widow of the man stabbed in Deerton. What are her thoughts? How is she feeling? Bereft, yes – but what does that mean? Abandoned, rejected? If she consulted me, I would suggest she feels resentment because he left her alone, late at night, to intervene in a dispute between some loutish boys. According to reports, that seems to have been what happened. He could have stayed at home with her, letting the boys sort out their own quarrels. Is she angry because he chose to interfere, and was killed for his pains? If not, she should be; it would be a natural reaction but she would think that it was wrong. Exploring her guilty feelings would be good for weeks of sessions.

Deerton is not far away. I might post my card through her door.

I'll wait for a while and see what happens. It won't be difficult to discover some background so that I can amaze her with my insight. I already know that she has two adult sons and they will be affected, too; they will feel increased responsibility for her. She and the dead husband had a business in Mickleburgh, selling antique furniture or something of the kind. I will look into that. It will be months before there is a trial, if the boys responsible are ever traced. Probably they will be: one of them will give himself away. The stabbed boy would make an interesting study, but though he may have nightmares, and conflicts of conscience over giving information about other boys to the police, the authorities will elect to counsel him; he will not come my way, however badly he is troubled as a result of the incident.

I could teach that woman, Marjorie Stewart, known as Midge, how to be strong. What a silly name. Is she like a gnat, darting about? Probably I'll get in touch with her, but not yet.

This afternoon I have a male patient whose problem is a failing relationship. He's been married once, and was divorced; then, too quickly, he entered into this new partnership with a woman with three small children. He sees himself as their saviour, and perhaps he is, moving in with them, providing money, a stepfather figure. He had no children from his marriage, and I asked him why this was. Had he been against having a family, or had his wife? I was curious to know. It just hadn't happened, he had said, though his wife had undergone fertility treatment – drugs to boost ovulation, he had explained, looking embarrassed; they hadn't got as far as attempted test-tube conception. When I think of my own unwanted birth, I feel disgust; nature loads the scales so unfairly. I feel disgust, too, when I hear of temperature-taking, charts, the obsession that makes begetting a child the sole reason for intercourse – though some churches tell us this is what it should be. I told my patient that it was no wonder his marriage foundered under such a strain. Now I see clearly that he cast himself in the paternal role that nature denied him, living out his fantasies through this other woman's children, but she resents him disciplining them and the eldest, a boy of seven, is openly rebellious. My patient wants to have a child with her, but she won't agree; she isn't confident that they will stay together.

Nor am I. I must decide this afternoon whether to point out ways in which he can improve things, by making concessions to her wishes and by ceasing his stern reprimands to the children. After all, it is her house, and he is the interloper. He's tried showering the children with gifts and treats, and seems to see-saw between extremes in his attitude towards them. He hasn't explored his own essence adequately, his inner core; he doesn't know what sort of man he really is. Shall I help him to find out, effect a positive result, or shall I introduce him to a construct, to an artificial concept of what he wants to be, teach him to adopt that role, and plan his future going on from there? He's already had four sessions during which I've tediously noted down his history and listened to his self-pitying monologues. What has he done to deserve these two raw deals, he enquires, when others can be happy? I've asked him if they really are. All life is compromise, I say, and one has to decide how much of it to practise. His current relationship is surely doomed, but it could be prolonged for some weeks, if not months. He says it's difficult to meet potential partners, and I'm sure that's true. Various newspapers run Lonely Hearts sections, but I hesitate to recommend answering those advertisements. You never know who will reply. After all, I could insert one and no respondent would know that I have served a prison sentence on a charge of murder, and am still on licence. A woman making an appointment to meet a man this way might be entering a danger zone. On the other hand, two lonely people who might be compatible could meet by such a means. It is a gamble.

Having to miss the inquest irritated Sarah but there was no need for her to go; she had not been present when Daniel died, was not involved except as a friend, and had no excuse for missing work that day.

'It won't take long,' Oliver had told her, when she expressed doubts as to where her duty lay. Today was a normal one, in the office; there was no outside commitment. Even so, she telephoned Orchard House, offering to cancel everything and come, to be reassured by Mark.

'It'd be better if you can keep in touch with Mum after we've left – Jonathan and me,' he told her. 'That would be a big relief to us.'

'Of course I will, Mark. You can rely on me,' she said.

Mark knew he could; her job meant that she was probably too busy now to try to take his mother over, which might have been a risk. In fairness, Sarah wasn't a monster and she could be very kind, as long as what she did was recognised; her kindness did not operate invisibly. He didn't know how long he and Jonathan should stay. Sooner or later, their mother must be left, but their father had been dead for only three days. How was he getting on? Was he used to it by now? Was he truly at peace and sleeping, as Mark hoped? Surely he couldn't be in purgatory, or limbo, as some religions would insist? Troubled by the prospect of eternity, Mark settled for oblivion.

He wondered what his mother believed about all this. If she broached the subject, he'd pick her up, develop a discussion, but he wouldn't start one.

Would the police ever catch those guilty boys? Surely the other lads would tell, the Noakes boy and his friend Peter Grant? Mark was not too old to have forgotten schoolboy ethics, but this was serious stuff. He accepted that the boy who stabbed his father might not have had the intention of killing him, and Oliver had warned that a plea of self-defence might be entered and sustainable. It would be alleged that Daniel had over-reacted and misjudged the degree of the affray in progress. But he'd had no weapon. He hadn't taken a shotgun with him; he didn't own one. There had been cases where householders protecting their property with guns were accused by apprehended burglars of assault, if not actual bodily harm, and convicted.

He decided to talk to the two boys who lived in Orchard Close, Barry Noakes and Peter Grant, and see if he could persuade them to reveal a name. They'd be back from school around four-fifteen; the bus would drop them at the crossroads and they'd walk home from there. He'd waylay them, invite them in, and lure confidences out of them through a softening process. That would be a better tactic than going to one of their houses and having to get past the parents. Ted Grant, who had given evidence at the inquest, might still be at home, nursing his injured ribs, but Barry's father and mother wouldn't be back from work until much later. Mark knew the form; he and Jonathan had attended the same school.

Accordingly, he prepared to meet the boys that afternoon. After the inquest they had all come home and had a quick lunch; then Jonathan and Midge had gone into Mickleburgh to look through the workshop books in detail. Mark's task was to bring order to the papers in his father's desk at home. Apart from the copy of his will, unearthed from a faded folder, they had already discovered outstanding domestic bills, some of which must be paid at once or Midge would find herself without electricity or the telephone; Daniel had been staving off disaster by instalments. With the consent of the solicitor in Norwich, Oliver had arranged to open a client's account for Midge to deal with any outstanding payments which the bank would not honour while Daniel's affairs were sorted out. Mark suspected that Oliver was guaranteeing this account himself; he must find out for certain, for he, Mark, could put some money into it. They could not be under an obligation to Oliver for long. Jonathan might be able to do something about the money owed to the workshop by chasing up the customers who had not paid their bills. Mark sighed. There was a lot to do, and yet not enough. They could not draw a line beneath their father's death: mourn, and hold the funeral. All depended on the police discovering who had used that knife.

He sauntered up the road, a sturdy young man with brown hair and a small scar on his cheek from a fall from a tree when he was ten; he had broken his collar bone at the same time. He felt totally exhausted, physically and emotionally, after the long drive to Kendal and back the day before, and two near sleepless nights filled with anxiety and grief. Soon he saw, coming towards him, two boys. They were talking together, quietly, not joshing each other, or kicking stones, like boys on their way back from school so often do: they were holding a serious conversation.

Peter and Barry had parted from Greg and several other schoolmates further along the road, where their ways divided. They did not immediately recognise Mark; he was just someone in jeans and a dark fleece jacket. They were walking slowly, reluctant, in Peter's case, to go home, where his father might be waiting to have words with him. Both knew their parents would be pressing them to talk to the police. They were planning to go to Barry's house, where there would be no parents yet.

'Well – Barry – Peter,' said Mark confidently, coming up to them and addressing them collectively, for he was uncertain which was which. Except for university vacations, and short visits, he had not lived in Deerton for years, and could not safely identify youngsters who had turned from children into adolescents in that time. On the other hand, it was reasonable to suppose that they might know who he was, but he took no chances. 'Maybe you don't remember me,' he said. 'I'm Mark Stewart and it was my father who was killed on Saturday. I'm wondering if I could have a word with you. Both of you,' he added.

The boys exchanged glances. They could refuse, could run home; he couldn't force them. But they were both unhappy about their ethical dilemma and he might devise an escape route for them. He was closer to them in age than their parents, and he was looking at them in a friendly way. He wasn't angry.

'Can't do any harm, I suppose,' said Peter. 'I'm sorry about your dad.'

'So'm I,' said Barry, who felt responsible for the whole tragic business because it had begun in his house. 'He was all right.'

Mark wanted to ask how Peter's father was. He hadn't had a chance to speak to him at the inquest as Ted Grant had gone off with the police, who were going to show him numerous school photographs to see if he could pick out any of the offenders. Unsure as to which boy to address, he turned to walk with them to Orchard House and, gazing ahead, said, 'Your father tried to help, Peter. He got hurt, I know. How is he?'

One of the boys, the slightly taller one, replied.

'Says his ribs still hurt. Says he'll be all right, though,' he answered. Ted had displayed his bruises to his son, wanting to break his silence, and very nearly succeeding.

They had reached Mark's gate, and he led the way up the short path to the front door, which was unlocked. He opened it and ushered them ahead of him.

'There's no one here, only me,' he said. 'Go on in.'

To both boys the house, though larger than theirs, seemed very shabby. The window paint was peeling; the striped paper on the walls in the hall had faded; the carpets were worn. Their own modern homes were kept in spanking repair and, except for their rooms, which were often untidy, were spotless. Both fathers redecorated at least one room every year. The two boys stood awkwardly together, waiting for what was to follow. Mark said that he was going to have a cup of tea, and would they like one, or would they rather have coffee, hot chocolate, or fruit juice? He didn't think there was any Coca-Cola. Both said they'd love a cup of tea, which quite surprised him. He thought few youngsters drank it, these days.

'Let's go into the kitchen, then,' he said. 'I'll put the kettle on.' Before he went to meet them, he had brought it to the boil. Now, telling them to sit at the table, he raised the lid on the Aga and moved the kettle on to the hot slab. 'There are some biscuits in that tin,' he said. 'And a cake in the other one. Help yourselves. Knives are in the drawer there.'

The cake was courtesy of Sarah: a gooey chocolate sponge, with butter icing. The boys were unable to resist it, and Peter cut them each a slice.

'Some for you?' he asked Mark, knife poised.

'Yes, please,' said Mark, and while the tea brewed, he found plates for everyone.

The boys were relaxing. Put food in a boy's stomach and, if flagging, he would revive. It was one of Mark's grandmother's dictums and she had followed the prescription when he arrived in Kendal the day before, to good effect.

There was silence for a few minutes while the tea was poured and the cake consumed. Mark, who wasn't hungry, sociably ate his piece and felt better straight away. He poured himself a second cup of tea, and cut another slice of cake for each boy.

'It must have been horrible that night,' he said. 'Those boys just barged in, didn't they, Barry?' He addressed the shorter, tubbier boy, who had a snub nose and freckles and a rather trusting face.

'Yeah,' he agreed, cautiously.

'You weren't expecting them?'

'No.' These admissions had already been made to the police, so repeating them could do no harm.

'There were four of them?' This was the number estimated by Peter's father and the forensic experts. Mark didn't know if the boys had confirmed that to the police, so it might be useful to hear them do so now.

'Yeah,' Barry repeated.

'And they started wrecking the place straight away?'

'Yeah.'

'They pissed on Barry's mum and dad's bed,' Peter burst out. 'Scumbags.'

'Was that what made the other boy – Jamie – go for help?'

'We couldn't get them out,' said Peter. 'We tried. Honest, we did.'

'I believe you,' Mark said. They'd been taken by surprise – almost ambushed – by tougher, if not older boys; Mark concluded that as soon as they realised that Jamie had gone for help, the cowards had fled, and met his father as they left. He had been in their flight path, like the victim of a bee sting.

'They go to your school, don't they? The other boys?'

Peter and Barry did not answer.

'I take it that means yes, or you'd have said no,' said Mark, who, not being a policeman, was bound by no rules as he conducted his interview.

'Did you see the make of car they drove?' he asked.

'No,' the two boys said in unison.

'We were in the house,' said Barry sheepishly.

'Jamie came back after fetching your dad,' said Peter. 'He needn't have. They went for him while my dad was still running across the road.'

This was a full sentence. Mark, encouraged, asked another question.

'Your dad might have been killed, like mine,' he said. 'And

so might the boy who was hurt. Jamie. He's a friend of yours, isn't he?'

'Yes.'

'Those boys might do it again, and someone else might get killed, if they're not caught,' said Mark. 'The police haven't found the knife. That means whoever used it's probably still got it.'

'He could get another one, if he hasn't,' Peter pointed out. 'That's easy.'

'Yes – well—' This was off the point. 'He's used it once. He could do it again,' said Mark. 'How are you going to feel if he does, knowing you could name him now and he'd be arrested?'

Neither boy replied.

'You'll feel you were to blame,' Mark told them roundly. 'And you would be. You could mention a name to me, and I could pass it on, not saying where I'd heard it. Then the police could question that boy and they might find the knife. And they could take his fingerprints. There were plenty in your house, Barry. When they know who to talk to, they'll find proof.'

'They'd guess it was us. They'd know. The others would get us – not – not—' Barry pulled himself up short. 'Not the one with the knife. The others. 'Cause in the end, they'd go down too, if he got caught. But not at first.'

'You think he'd drop them in it?'

'He wouldn't want to take all the blame,' said Barry.

'One of them must have stolen the car they came in,' Mark said. 'Isn't that right?'

Neither Barry nor Peter knew who the driver was, or that the car was not exactly stolen.

'Maybe,' said Barry.

Mark knew that the police were checking up on cars stolen in the area that night. One might be found which would yield helpful evidence. How could he trap these confused, decent boys into making a slip, giving the tiniest hint? He racked his brains.

'I suppose lots of people at school have got knives,' he said. 'Serious knives, I mean.'

No reply.

'As I've said, if they do hurt someone else, or kill someone, you're going to feel pretty bad about it, aren't you? I think you feel quite bad already. You'd better go home now and think about it. You can give a name to me, as I've said, and I'll tell the police if that makes it easier,' he told them. 'But you might have to have the guts to stand by that later.' Then he added, 'Jamie had a lot of guts that night. So did your dad, Peter, and mine. Where's yours, now? All you have to do is give me a name. They'll be arrested if you do. Just one name.' For one would lead to the others.

Neither boy spoke. Mark escorted them to the door. He had given them the message; now their consciences must do the rest. Silently, they trudged away, Peter turning at the gate to say, 'Thanks for the cake.'

If either was going to crack, it would be Peter, Mark decided, going in to clear up the used crockery before his mother came home and found out what he had been doing. If she looked in the cake tin, she would marvel at his greed.

15

Oliver, having pleaded what mitigation he could devise for his unhappy client, though there was very little, and managed to placate him in the matter of his fine and suspension, returned to the office by way of Daniel and Midge's workshop. He knew that she and Jonathan had planned to go there this afternoon, but they might have lost the impetus when they went home after the inquest. However, they were there, Midge putting tacks into a picture frame, Jonathan sitting at the desk, confronting piles of paper. His attitude was one of despondency; as far as he could tell, the financial position of the business was disastrous; trying to stay solvent, his father had been juggling funds but several balls he had had in the air were about to crash, and the bank might get restive. The recession had affected the business, which was overstocked because Daniel had bought up items at various sales, hoping to make a good profit when they had been repaired and smartened up; what he had not considered adequately was the inevitable slow turnover. Until a year ago he had employed an accountant but had ended that to reduce outgoings. Jonathan had been forced to conclude that this might have been a mistake, especially as the cost could have been offset against tax, and he was in despair about how to put things right. His father hadn't even got his records on computer, a matter Jonathan, a modern young man, found extraordinary. All this mess, he thought, looking at the various heaps of bills and peevish letters, could have disappeared. This wasn't strictly true: the bills would still arrive, but Daniel could have filed everything away on disk with memos to himself.

Oliver's arrival was a big relief. Perhaps he would break the bad news to his mother. Jonathan looked up at him.

'It'll take days to sort things out,' he said. 'Just look at this,' and he showed Oliver a sheet of paper on which he had listed the sums his father owed.

'I can't guess what the stock is worth,' he continued. 'Though it will be possible to calculate what was paid for it.' He had a feeling that Mark's labours at Orchard House were going to produce a similarly dismal catalogue. The only part of the business which showed a healthy profit was Midge's framing, but its scope was limited because of the prohibitive cost of more advanced equipment and a wider range of styles.

After looking up to greet him, Midge had carried on with her work. Oliver cast a glance in her direction and raised an eyebrow at Jonathan, who shrugged.

'Still dazed,' said Jonathan. 'We all are.'

Oliver, who had helped Daniel with the acquisition of the workshop premises, knew that the lease ran out at the end of March. It was renewed quarterly, in advance, but it seemed safe to assume, from Jonathan's gloomy demeanour, that the rent was not paid up. Midge couldn't possibly carry on, but it was much too soon to force her into that conclusion. If time allowed, she would have to reach it by herself. But would it be good for her to be here alone, among these stacks of cupboards, tables, chairs and chests? Maybe he could find someone to lend her a hand until Christmas, although it would be for company more than anything. Adopting an optimistic expression, Oliver watched as she cut a new mount, using the big guillotine.

'It's too soon to make any decisions,' he said. 'We'll have to have a holding operation for the moment.' He'd try to pacify the bank. 'I'll be in touch,' he added, and left them to it.

Soon afterwards, Jonathan decided that he could face no more of this today, and he urged his mother to call a halt. They closed up, set the security alarm, and as they were were walking back to Jonathan's car, an elderly woman, on foot, noticed them and hesitated, then advanced.

'Marjorie – my dear – and it's Jonathan, isn't it?' said Prudence Wilmot, who was walking home after collecting some books she had ordered from Mickleburgh's small branch library, whose staff were very helpful, though sometimes she had to go to Fettleton, where there was a large reference section which she consulted on the spot. 'I'm so very sorry,' she said. Aware of Midge's real name, she thought the diminutive might be reserved for intimates and had not liked to use it on so slight an acquaintance. Leaning forward, she gave Midge a big, maternal hug, managing not to hit her with the bag of books.

'The flowers. You sent the flowers,' said Midge. Her eyes filled with tears. 'Thank you. They're lovely. I'm sorry I haven't written.'

'Oh – for goodness' sake – there's no need for that,' said Prudence.

'They are lovely,' Jonathan echoed, shuffling his feet, afraid his mother might disintegrate out here in the street.

'Where are you off to now?' Prudence asked them. 'Would you like to come home with me and have a cup of tea? I live just round the corner, in the High Street.'

Jonathan thought this was an excellent idea. His mother needed what he and Mark could not provide, but which Judy, for a while, had given: female support. He took Prudence's bag from her and they walked together to the end of the road, turned into the High Street, and went down it to Prudence's pretty house in its terraced row opposite the market square where, except on market day, cars were parked. She found her key and let them in, shedding her coat and taking Midge's.

'I'll just put the kettle on,' she said. 'It won't take long.' Tea, the remedy for pain and shock, and for social unease, as now, where all three were shy, and Midge and Jonathan embarrassed. Why should bereavement make the afflicted feel like that? It happened, Prudence knew. You were a worry to your friends, and maybe all you wanted to do was go into a wide open space and scream.

Unlike Mark, at this moment entertaining his schoolboy guests in Deerton, Prudence could offer hers no chocolate cake, but there were rich tea biscuits and a few custard creams, which her cleaner liked.

At the back of her sitting room, which overlooked the garden, Prudence had added a circular conservatory, where she worked; they could see her desk, and an old manual typewriter. She sat them down in front of the coal-effect gas fire and, in a very few minutes, returned with the tea. She poured it out. Jonathan took sugar.

'Sudden death is always shocking,' Prudence said firmly, not pussy-footing round the subject. 'And murder is much worse than death from natural causes, because it need not have happened.' On various postings, her husband had had to deal with the aftermath of both. 'I suppose the police haven't arrested anyone yet.'

'No,' said Jonathan, while his mother, at the moment incapable of uttering, gulped down her tea like someone parched. 'And we can't make plans – the funeral – all that. There may have to be another post mortem.'

'Oh – of course. For the defence, when there is a suspect,' Prudence said.

And there would be the trial, the newspaper reports, the reliving of it all.

'Oliver is being marvellous,' said Midge, speaking at last.

'And Sarah, too,' she added hastily. 'They rescued me that night – Saturday – and put me up. It's only Tuesday now,' she went on. 'It feels like months.'

'Oliver called in at the workshop this afternoon,' said Jonathan. It would not do to discuss their financial problems with this comparative stranger, however nice she was, but he could not avoid saying, 'There's quite a bit of paperwork to sort out.'

'I expect there is,' said Prudence. He'd mentioned plans. This pleasant young man and his brother might be full of notions that their mother should be plucked out of her surroundings and popped into a flat. Was she as much as fifty? Hard to tell in her present state, but Prudence didn't think so: quite a long way off, more Sarah's age, she decided. 'I do hope you won't have to sell your house,' she said. 'At least, not yet. Give yourself time if you can.'

Midge believed she could not bear to leave Orchard House, where Daniel's presence lurked round every corner and all his clothes still hung. When she had taken her own coat from the cloakroom that morning, there was his waxed jacket on its hook. She had buried her face in its fleecy lining, smelling him in the fabric.

After two cups of tea, her colour was returning, and she was able to look past Prudence, through the conservatory to the garden.

'That must be lovely in the summer – your conservatory,' she said. 'We've got a sort of utilitarian one, square, with garden chairs and stuff in it. We haven't had much time to sit there lately. I use it for cuttings and things.'

'I've got a tiny greenhouse,' Prudence said. 'I grow tomatoes and a few plants in pots.'

They discussed gardening for a while, and despite her shaky state, most of Midge's remarks made sense. At length she and Jonathan rose to leave.

'Come in any time if you're in Mickleburgh,' Prudence told her. 'I'm usually here.' She hesitated. She scarcely knew the younger woman. Then she added, 'My husband died four years ago. I still miss him.'

She saw her visitors to the door and watched them walk away, then turned back into the house, closing the door. In the sitting room she collected up the tea things and was about to carry the tray into the kitchen when she saw Midge's handbag on the floor, beside the chair where she had been sitting, and almost out of sight.

Prudence picked it up and rushed out of the house, pausing to pull on her coat which lay where she had left it, draped over the banisters. It was cold, and it was getting dark. She hurried up the road towards the Stewarts' workshop, where she knew that Jonathan had left his car. If Midge had not already missed her bag and turned back, she might just catch them before they drove off.

As, panting slightly, she reached the side road, Jonathan's Escort edged forwards to enter the High Street, and Prudence waved the bag. He braked, and amid explanations and apologies, it was transferred to its owner. Jonathan offered to run Prudence the short distance back to her house, but she said it wasn't necessary; it was so close, and his route to Deerton lay in the opposite direction.

She walked rapidly back, and as she drew near her own door, a woman came towards her on the inside of the pavement. Prudence had to pause to let her pass before she could enter. The woman was middle-aged, wearing a black and white flecked tweed coat, her dark hair pulled back from a pale angular face and secured in a French pleat, once so fashionable. Prudence could see her plainly in the light from the nearby street lamp, and knew that they had met before. For a few seconds they stared at one another as, incredulously, Prudence recognised her, even after nearly thirty years.

The woman gave her a cold glance and walked on as Prudence, chilled right through, entered her own house.

She had very good reason to remember her, although it was so long ago. Prudence had seen her across a law court, daily, throughout the trial. She'd worn her hair – fairer then – in that same pleat, though months earlier, at the time of her arrest, it had hung in a long bob below her ears.

She had committed murder, but she had not got away with it. She must have been released years ago, for a life sentence no longer meant just that.

What was she doing here in Mickleburgh? And had she recognised Prudence, who since then had tried, with some success, to forget her existence? Did it matter if she had?

The evil that men do lives after them, Prudence thought. The consequences of that woman's evil deed were terrible, and she could never atone, no matter how many years she spent incarcerated.

Prudence felt quite shaken. Here was, indeed, a spectre from the past. Just as an unknown boy had killed Daniel Stewart and destroyed the lives of those who loved him, so had Wendy Tyler, with a knife, snuffed out another life and wrecked a family, but in her case she had not killed a stranger.

She had murdered Prudence's younger sister, Emily, in a premeditated, shocking way. The evidence had been conclusive: the knife was found, and blood-stains on the accused girl's clothes. There was a motive: not love, but lust. In France it would have been labelled a *crime passionel* and the sentence would have been a light one. It wasn't so here; Wendy Tyler had been found guilty of murder.

If you behaved well in prison, and expressed regret for your offence, you were freed after a period of years. It was alleged by some, and especially the guilty, that by then you had paid your debt to society. As if such a debt – the taking of a life –

could ever be repaid. Wendy Tyler might be unlikely to kill again; perhaps she had genuinely repented, although she had shown no sign of remorse at the time. The newspapers had remarked on it, and it had been palpable in court. Lionel, her lover, stunned, horrified and subsumed by grief and guilt, had rejected her immediately. He had not seen her after her arrest until they met in court, and then he had not glanced at her once. Prudence, seeing this, had felt a sharp stab of pity until a different expression had crossed Wendy Tyler's ashen face, a look of utter hatred. After that, she had revealed no emotion throughout the trial, even after she was sentenced.

Emily had been ten weeks pregnant when she died and the affair between Lionel and Wendy had lasted for five months.

Lionel, attempting to restore his own life, and his children's, emigrated. Wendy would come out of prison one day, he declared, and unless there were oceans and many miles between them, he would not trust himself not to seek revenge.

Or she might, Prudence had thought, remembering that savage face. In this case, love – obsession – lust – whatever it was – had turned to bitter hatred. Prudence and her husband had approved of Lionel's decision and, through various connections, had helped him to find a position with a firm in Toronto. Later, he had moved west, to Vancouver; the whole family had taken out Canadian citizenship and he had met the woman who became his second wife.

Instead of returning to her typewriter, or even consulting the books she had collected from the library, Prudence sat by the fire remembering that dreadful time. Her husband was at the Foreign Office then, so that they were both at hand to offer help to Lionel and the children, who were too young to understand the full scandal of their father's conduct. They were what mattered, not him, but he had to be forgiven, for their sakes. Those were terrible weeks, with the press trying to waylay the children, who were five and seven years old;

they had to be removed from school and went to stay with their maternal grandparents in the Wiltshire house where later Prudence and her husband had spent their retirement. She remembered Lally playing with the dolls' house which Oliver was now restoring. Lally had moved the family of dolls around, hiding the mother doll and using the girl doll as a small adult, which she christened Wendy. One day Lally's grandmother had found the doll Wendy in bed with the father doll, and the mother doll lay in the bath, with a tiny knife from the kitchen poised above her china form.

So the children had understood. Had they seen their father and the girl in bed together? No one knew for sure. In those days counselling, often routine now, was for the disturbed few. Though she accepted that there were crises and tragedies too difficult to face unsupported, and not everyone had wise and patient friends or spouses to share their problems, Prudence considered it had gone too far today; people were not encouraged to brace up and display courage but to crumple. Lionel had been abruptly forced to acknowledge what he had done, and had accepted his own disgrace and responsibility. His second wife, a calm woman, had nurtured him and the children but the marriage had not lasted. Lally was now a television reporter, and her brother Charles was a marine biologist.

Prudence rose and picked up the telephone directory, checking through the Tylers. There was no Tyler, W. in Mickleburgh. That proved nothing. Sickened, she closed the book. Even if she had been listed, exposing Wendy would help no one and would cause fresh pain by resurrecting the old story. All the same, it was wise to know your enemy, and Prudence was very sure that her feelings towards Wendy were still extremely hostile. She would be alert, ready to recognise her promptly if their paths crossed again, and she would, in that case, try to track her down and find out where she lived. She felt sickened. She did not want her peaceful new life contaminated by this presence from the past.

Rapists and child molesters were released into the area where they lived before they were arrested, and this meant many of them were in proximity to their victims, who might pass them in the street. Prudence shuddered at the thought of it. Later, when the Stewart tragedy was resolved and its immediate impact was fading, she might tell Oliver the story, and of her sighting of her sister's murderer. He had been only a young man when it happened, about the same age as Jonathan was now; he might remember the case because, at the time, it was notorious.

Wendy would not have recognised her. They had never met, and Prudence had played no part in the trial, though her photograph as the bereaved sister had appeared in some newspapers. Ten years older than Emily, she did not resemble her at all, even before her hair went white.

Feeling old and sad, Prudence sat by the flickering flames, which never altered their pattern, unlike those in a real fire, but nevertheless they gave out a comforting glow as she recalled those tragic months. Somewhere, there were newspaper cuttings which she had preserved. When she began writing, she had thought she might use the triangular theme for a novel set in Edwardian times. Maybe writing a fictionalised version of the truth would lay some ghosts. Was there, however, another chapter of the real history waiting to be written?

16

It was dusk when the woman nearly knocked into me as I walked along the street. I was walking on the inside of the pavement and she stopped in front of me, so that I, too, hesitated, and she stared at me. Street lighting lit us both, and I saw an old, white-haired woman, neither short nor tall, completely unremarkable, wearing a dark coat. Pausing only for an instant, for I give way to no one, I walked on, but briefly we had exchanged glances and she looked at me with what, if it had not been impossible, I would have said was recognition. Then the moment passed, I went by, and she let herself into the house outside which we had met. Next door, attached, was a large house with a bow window. I would remember it as a landmark.

Because of the intent look she had bent on me, I wondered if she might have been a patient. I put them from my mind as soon as their treatment ends, though I keep their details in my files in case they return; however, I would know them in the street, perhaps not immediately by name, but I would recollect that I had treated them. Some can't exist without an injection of sympathy and interest, and mine is not wholly insincere, because, living vicariously, I like to know about their lives and I enjoy the power I wield, changing their circumstances, often for good, but not always. Some recommend me; if I make them feel better about themselves, they are grateful, even if that has meant a change of job or a broken marriage. Most make up their own minds, which is right; my role is to help them discover what they really want to do, how they wish the situation to resolve.

Jealousy is a powerful emotion. It was jealousy, so people said, that turned me into a murderer; others said it was infatuation, even lust. I saw it differently. I had acted out of love, to open up his way to freedom. By removing her – the obstacle – our path ahead was cleared, uncomplicated. But already he'd betrayed me and what followed was his fault. He led me on – I was young and inexperienced – and he took advantage of me, flattered me, made me feel special, then seduced me.

I was a virgin until then, and they say you always remember your first. It's true for me, at any rate. There have been no others: no more men.

We'd lie in bed – her bed – and plan how we'd run away together, leave her, go abroad and start a new life. It was all just a dream to him, a sort of 'let's pretend' such as you play with children; he was always playing games like that with them. 'Let's pretend we're pirates. Let's pretend we're in a train going to London. Let's pretend we're soldiers.' His ideas were so childish, but they liked the games, Lally and Charles, and I went along with them. I didn't realise that the game he played with me was the biggest fantasy of all. In the end, he did go overseas – to Canada, I found out, after my release. In fact, that silly Emily was an unnecessary sacrifice; my valour was quite wasted. But I have paid for what I did. Now I owe nothing.

After meeting the strange, hostile woman – she was hostile; I sensed it – I went home and put on Bartok. I don't like soothing melodies. Then I thought about those boys and their crime, and the new widow. Would the guilty boy break and confess? I would not have done so. It was more likely that another boy would grass him up. I learnt all the jargon while I was inside, and I still think in those harsh terms. As well as reading murder reports in the papers, I watch television documentaries about prison reform, false imprisonment, and detection. Some of them make me angry; others are simply amusing. None reveal what it's really like to be banged up, forced to socialise, as they put it, with people you would ordinarily go out of your way to avoid. Some inmates form deep friendships which last after their release: not me. I'm a survivor, and I don't need other people; they need me. I'm acquiring plenty who can't do without my cool room and my quiet presence as, with just a word here or there, I direct their thoughts, often their destiny.

I've helped mend several marriages. What's the use in encouraging a plain, dull woman to give up on a philanderer who, in other ways, is an adequate husband, meeting his financial obligations and functioning effectively as a father? She won't meet anyone better, and she'll lose out materially. I help such women, when they consult me in despair – and when they write to my advice column – to accept the limitations of their lives and adopt a hobby. Often it works. To those trapped in violent marriages, however, I advise action, calling the police, who are better than they were at dealing with such cases, with Domestic Violence units deployed in many forces. If such a husband or partner doesn't reform, I counsel leaving him. It's not the fault of the woman, though she often thinks it is. He, by eating away at her confidence, has been the cause of her disintegration. I advise attending a course in assertiveness. People are so polarised; there are those who blame themselves for every misfortune that comes their way, shouldering all responsibility, and others who will never admit that they have brought about their own disasters. Some people are always finding fault with themselves; others perpetually look for it elsewhere and become paranoid, taking offence at the least thing.

The boy who stabbed that man will blame him for interfering in the affray. To blame himself would be too diffcult. He must convince himself that no fault lies with him; he was provoked. The widow will blame herself for not following her husband to the spot in time to save him.

The law will blame the boy, but his background may explain or excuse his violent nature. As we don't know his identity, we don't know if he has already been in trouble with the police, or whether he has been reared in a disadvantaged home, or felt rejected, needing to strike out at someone.

I can't get that old woman encountered in the street out of my mind. I'm curious enough to want to know her name.

Kevin was beginning to feel safe. His friends wouldn't tell on him, because they'd all been in on it with him, and they'd be for it, too. Those other boys wouldn't dare say a word.

He hadn't read the papers or seen any news bulletins about the case; he didn't want to know. He just wanted it all to go away, and it would.

In his hearing, his parents discussed appropriate punishment for lads who were violent. Kevin's father thought a short sharp shock, army-like, would be the answer. He'd always been strict. Kevin's sister, who was older, had had a difficult time when she acquired a boyfriend, with their dad wanting her in by half-past ten and warning her about rape and pregnancy. In the end, she'd gone off with a man who ran a travelling fish van, and now she lived with him near Birmingham, but they weren't married. Their parents thought this disgraceful, so Kevin knew they wouldn't be well pleased if they learned what he had done, even though he wasn't to blame.

His dad would kill him.

If there was nothing for them to go on, the police investigation would slow down. He did wonder about the knife. He'd thought of going back to look for it in Deerton, but if the police hadn't found it, would he? Where else could it be?

He slept soundly on Tuesday night, untroubled by guilty dreams, and in the morning set off to school in a defiant mood. He'd tough this out. He was important, a person to be reckoned with: why, the whole of the local CID were out there looking for him, if the truth were known. Too bad it had to be kept quiet.

On Wednesday morning in Assembly, however, the headmaster had some words to say. He referred to Detective Superintendent Fisher's visit on Monday, and the fact that it had yielded no information despite his appeal. It seemed certain that boys from the school were involved, and there were times when loyalty to the community was more important than loyalty to individuals. If whoever was responsible came forward, his confession might earn him later leniency, and equally, if any other students knew who had carried out the attack – the headmaster tried to avoid emotive terms – they should pass on what they knew. It could be done in confidence, he ended. Two police officers were available, in the building.

The officers were in the hall. One of them, Shaw, though he thought the appeal worth making because it would put pressure on the boys who knew the truth, said it wouldn't work. No matter whereabouts in the school he or DC Benton chose to wait, any pupil approaching them with information would be observed.

The tactic, however, had some effect on Peter Grant and Jamie Preston.

'They think we'll tell in the end,' said Peter, and he wanted to, so badly.

If Kevin and the rest were caught, what would happen to them? Neither Peter nor Jamie knew much about institutions for young offenders. They'd get bail, Peter was sure, and they'd clobber him and Jamie, maybe kill them.

All the same, it might be worth finding out what would be done with them. Who would know, apart from the two officers waiting patiently for information which did not arrive?

After school that afternoon, Jamie asked his mother. She was unsure, but when he had gone upstairs to do his homework, she rang Fisher to enquire.

He came round later.

'If I go up and tell Jamie what you've just told me, he'll know I rang you,' Kate had said on the telephone.

Fisher had suggested coming round on the pretext of asking about Jamie's arm, and somehow turning the conversation towards the subject. So they set it up, and when he called, Jamie and Kate were having supper at the kitchen table. It was shepherd's pie, one of Jamie's favourites, and easy to eat with his left hand, with peas and carrots. His mother protested if he took his injured one out of the sling and used it.

'Will you join us?' Kate invited, after Fisher had apologised for interrupting their meal. 'There's enough.' She had cooked some extra vegetables in case he called while they were eating.

'Oh – thanks,' said Fisher. 'Are you sure? Well, why not?'

While they ate, they talked about the chances for various teams in the forthcoming football season, and England's dismal showing in the Test Match series. Jamie wondered why there were no Test Matches involving Scotland and Wales, and why cricket was so peculiarly English. No one really knew the answer.

Helping them to apple pie from Sainsbury's, Kate said casually that the police had been at the school that morning asking for help with the enquiry, but that it was a wasted effort as no one would come forward publicly.

'I know, but it was worth a try,' said Fisher, accepting his plate of pie.

'If you find out who did it, what will happen to them?' Kate asked, offering Fisher crème fraîche.

'Well, if they're charged, they'll be sent to a young offenders' detention centre,' he said. 'Somewhere very secure, where they'll be locked up. They won't get bail, if that's what you mean. They'll be remanded for trial, and that will give us time to assemble our evidence.'

'All of them?' asked Jamie. 'The ones who were there but didn't do it?'

'They were all accessories,' said Fisher. 'One used the knife, but if we knew who they all were, they'd all be locked up, partly for their own protection but also to prevent witnesses from being intimidated. None of them would get bail.'

'I see,' said Kate, and changed the subject.

It was Peter, however, who telephoned. He did it early the next morning, using a kiosk in the centre of Mickleburgh, and wrapping a J-cloth he had taken from his mother's cupboard round his hand. Jamie would not be in school that morning as he had to go to Fettleton Hospital to have his wound examined and the stitches removed.

His efforts, though, bore no fruit, because all he did was dial 999, ask for the police, and then mutter Kevin's name with no explanation.

The civilian clerk who took the call merely logged it, deciding it was a nuisance call. Her request for the caller's name and more details had gone unanswered as Peter had hung up. He spent the day in a nervous sweat, expecting cars with flashing lights and wailing sirens to collect Kevin from his chemistry lesson or his maths class, but nothing happened.

Jamie returned in the afternoon and the two conferred.

'What did you tell them?' asked Jamie, and Peter told him what he had done and how his call had produced no result.

Peter, who had made an enormous effort, felt deflated.

'Maybe it's a good thing,' he said. 'We don't want trouble.'

'No, we don't,' Jamie agreed. Then he said, 'How can they walk about like that as if nothing had happened? Heck – they killed a man. Or Kevin did. They'd all be locked up,' he added. 'The super – Fisher – he was at our house last night and he said so.'

'They'd get out again,' said Peter gloomily.

'Not for years and years,' said Jamie.

'They might get off,' said Peter. He had heard his parents endlessly discussing the failure of the police to make an arrest and the lack of clues. 'If they kept denying it, the police might not be able to prove that they'd done it.'

'Not if we gave evidence,' said Jamie.

They looked at one another in desperation.

'Well, I have told them,' Peter pointed out. 'If they're too dumb to do anything about it, that's their fault.'

Further action was postponed.

Fisher, too, had delayed the plan to fingerprint the school. It was not a popular idea, and subtler methods might be equally productive.

17

The police had started to trace the movements of the boys in the year above Barry and his friends, but the process was proving slow and unsatisfactory. Not all were in when the police called, and often there was only the parents' word that they had been at home on Saturday night. Some boys had been at clubs or discos where their presence was vouched for by other boys, all dependent on one another's confirmation.

Kevin and Paul had both dodged direct questioning by managing to be out of the house when the police called. Trevor and Wayne, also, individually saw them arrive, and departed through the back doors of their respective houses. The police had a list of boys who must be located to give an account of their whereabouts when the crime was committed.

Trevor's mother was sure her son could not possibly have been involved. True, while she and his father were out on Saturday night, Trevor might well have been seeing one of his friends. When asked who they were, for connecting boys with others could help collate information, she said he had a lot of friends, too numerous to mention. Much the same response came from Wayne's father; his mother, who was a waitress in a local hotel, was working when the police called, and she had been working on Saturday night. His father had been out then, too, with a young woman he had met while doing door-to-door deliveries.

Appointments would have to be made to see the remaining boys, either at home, with a parent there, or at the police station. Each one would eventually be found and questioned.

Fisher and his Detective Chief Superintendent discussed the advantages of an appeal on television by the dead man's family. Such a tactic sometimes paid off, when bare-faced grief was publicly displayed, but Fisher was against it.

'It's too emotional a stunt for Mrs Stewart,' he insisted. 'She's stressed enough, poor woman, and the guilty kids won't be watching.'

'Their parents may be,' was the response.

'If any parent suspects that their boy is involved, no amount of appealing is going to make them turn him in,' said Fisher. 'It takes a bit of doing, when it's murder.'

Rosemary Ellis, seeing Bob and Ginny returning home from school on Wednesday, opened her door and walked halfway down the outside staircase to enquire if there was any news about the case. Were the police near making an arrest?

They had no inside knowledge, they declared. No boys, so far, had come forward.

'Can't they all be interviewed at school?' Rosemary asked.

'Not exactly. It's private premises. A parent or a guardian must be present,' Ginny said. 'I believe there are plans to change this, and the police were hoping to make some special arrangement, but it hasn't happened yet. They've been there appealing to the students.'

'Oh,' said Rosemary. 'Can't you search for knives? Do many of them carry knives?'

'I wouldn't like to say,' said Ginny.

'But why do they do it?'

'It's about looking good,' Bob said.

He had come to this school from an inner city area where many of the pupils he taught lived in rundown flats with fathers who, if they lived at home, had never worked and where there was a serious drugs problem. Drugs were freely available in Mickleburgh, but less openly.

'Society is decaying all around us,' Rosemary declared. 'What has happened to the virtues?' After this remark, she walked back upstairs and went into her flat.

What indeed, thought Ginny.

'Bit intense, isn't she?' said Bob. 'Bit holier than thou.'

'She's quite concerned,' said Ginny. 'After all, she has met Kate, and Jamie was lucky not to be badly hurt.'

'True enough,' said Bob. 'But I wish the little blighter or his mates would spill the beans so that this could be cleared up.'

By Friday night, when there were still no arrests, Peter and Jamie were at a loss, and very worried. After all, Peter had rung up the police the day before, though he hadn't used Fisher's number.

Jamie turned over in his pocket the card Fisher had given him. He could try again. Perhaps he should. If Kevin was arrested, he couldn't attack anyone, and if Paul and the others chose to have a go, well, Jamie and his mates would be ready for them. His arm was much better now and he'd be able to protect himself. He was going to enrol in some type of martial arts activity as soon as he was better – kung fu, or karate. Even so, if he'd already trained in one of those disciplines, could he have saved either Mr Stewart or himself last Saturday?

He might have brought Kevin down, put him on the ground so that Peter's father could get hold of him, but there had been all the others – Paul, small and wiry, and Wayne and Trevor. There had been so many arms and legs flailing about in that struggle, and it had all been over so quickly. His mother said she was proud of him; he'd shown courage, trying to help. Was he showing courage now, wondered Jamie, afraid of what he was beginning to see was his duty. He knew he was keeping silent because he was frightened of the consequences, not because it was dobbing someone in. None of the boys was a friend of his. No way.

Like many an older, more experienced person faced with a moral dilemma, Jamie was bewildered and almost felt like tossing a coin to decide what he should do. In the end, he made a telephone call, like Peter from a public call box, which was easy since he lived in Mickleburgh and could walk to one – in fact, the same one that Peter had used. But he dialled Fisher's number, and he got the superintendent himself.

Jamie spoke gruffly, to disguise his voice.

'Someone rang saying a name but nothing's happened,' was his message. 'From this box, I think.' Then he added, in something more like his usual voice, 'Another person. Not me,' and he gave Kevin's name. Then, heart thumping, he rang off and hurried home.

Fisher, hearing the line go dead, sprang into action, checking all recorded calls. He traced it, in the end, the call that had not been reported.

Only Kevin was, at first, arrested. His was the only name Fisher had been given.

In the presence of his father his fingerprints were taken, but he refused to speak.

His father asserted angrily that the charge could not be justified. Kevin – so far not interviewed as he had been out each time an officer had called round – would account for his movements at the relevant time, and there would need to be an apology of some magnitude for this mistake. Where was the proof?

Kevin thought they must have found the knife, and inwardly he cursed. Why hadn't he made sure it was disposed of? Where had he dropped it? It was still in his hand when they ran away from the scene. But it was fingerprint evidence from the Noakeses' house that the police mentioned. He'd been there, they alleged, causing damage. After a while it emerged that they could prove he was involved in the rampage, but this did not mean that he had stabbed Daniel Stewart. His father demanded to know where was the evidence? Where was the knife?

Fisher and his team would also like the answer. They asked Kevin where it was and now, encouraged by his father's attitude, he said he'd never had one. He tried saying that of course his fingerprints were in Barry's house; they were friends and he often visited.

'Oh yes?' Detective Sergeant Shaw was assisting with the interview. 'That's why they were on a broken vase in Mrs Noakes's bedroom, and a beer can in the lounge?' he said. 'I'm quite sure Mrs Noakes hadn't gone out leaving empty cans from a previous visit of yours in the grate.'

Now Kevin was afraid. His father, sure of his innocence, had refused the offer of a solicitor, and the questions went on and on as Fisher and Shaw described the wrecking of the house, the damage in the bedroom, and said they would ask for samples for DNA matching. Paul had pissed on the bed. Could they prove that?

Kevin had had enough.

'Yeah, well I was there,' he at last conceded. 'It was just for a laugh. We chucked a few things around, cushions and that, but I mostly watched.'

He thought of naming Paul as the killer, to get the police off his back, but he didn't want to cause him grief; besides, if he did, wouldn't Paul – to save himself – say that Kevin had the knife? It seemed they hadn't found it, and unless they did, they couldn't prove anything more than trashing the house. There were the other two, however, Wayne and Trevor. Trevor had come along because borrowing his mother's car was a dare, but if Kevin named him, he'd tell it all to save himself. So why not name Wayne? Wayne was tougher than Trevor, and likely to be more loyal to Kevin. In despair, he named Paul.

'Are you saying he stabbed Mr Stewart?'

Wearily, Kevin looked at the brawny man facing him across the table; he couldn't meet the gaze of the leaner, darker one, the detective superintendent.

'Best ask him,' he drawled. He hadn't really dropped him in it.

But he wasn't released, and now his father did demand a solicitor, who took some time to arrive; when he did, he looked very serious and failed to get bail for Kevin. There was enough evidence to charge him with criminal damage, just to start with, and more serious charges were probable.

His father, baffled, all his bluster gone, said, 'How did you get to Deerton, anyway? You never walked.'

'I'd like to know the answer to that one, Kevin,' said Fisher mildly. No local car theft on the night in question – and there were some – had so far revealed any connection with the crime.

Kevin did not answer.

'Nicked one, I suppose,' said Shaw.

'I didn't,' Kevin said.

'One of the others did, then?'

No reply.

'Are you going to tell us who it was?'

Silence.

'What happened to it later?' Shaw tried.

'Took it back where he found it, didn't he?' said Kevin.

'Who did?'

But Kevin had told them enough. He closed his lips firmly and looked down at the table.

The solicitor suggested that his client needed a rest, and

Shaw took him away to have it in a cell while Fisher turned to the boy's father.

'Thank you for coming in, Mr Parker,' he said. 'I'm sorry Kevin wouldn't open up a bit more. It might have helped him in the long run.'

'He didn't do it. He didn't do the stabbing,' said Joe Parker. His anger was returning, but now it was directed towards Kevin, for having been one of the young hooligans wreaking havoc.

'Well, we'll get to the bottom of that eventually,' said Fisher. 'Now, I'm sending you home with an officer, and we'll be wanting Kevin's clothes. The ones he wore on Saturday night. We'll need to examine them.'

'You can't have them without a warrant,' Parker protested.

'I can very soon get one,' Fisher said. 'Do you want to do this the hard way? What about Kevin's mother? What's she going to say about all this? Have you thought of that?'

He had, with dread. She'd have to know how serious it was, and she'd have to find Kevin's clothes, but with any luck, knowing her, everything he'd had on that night would be washed and ironed by now.

Fisher had the same thought as Shaw and Tracy Dale set off back to Mickleburgh with Joe Parker, who sat seething in the car, his big hands clenched on his knees, his thick thighs tense, filling out his worn but spotless jeans. This couldn't be happening. A bit of horseplay, some laddish pranks that went a bit far – that was one thing, and it was bad if there was damage, but stabbing someone – being mixed up in a murder – no! He couldn't believe it of his boy.

All too soon they reached the Parkers' house in its quiet, respectable street. The police rarely called in this neighbourhood, though there had been an occasional burglary. Joe Parker walked up the path, his gait lumbering, his breathing heavy, and let himself in through the front door. His wife was in the lounge, trying to watch television but she couldn't settle, fretting all the time about Kevin.

Joe glanced at her and said, 'They want Kevin's clothes. What he had on on Saturday.'

She stared at him. She knew what it was all about for the police had cautioned Kevin when they took him in for questioning.

'I've washed them,' was her answer, as Joe had anticipated. She rose, and though she was a thin woman, her tread had become almost as weighty as her husband's as she went upstairs with Shaw and Tracy Dale. The basket in the bathroom was empty. She washed every day, she told them, but there was some ironing not yet done. Several of Kevin's shirts would be among those garments, but by now she would have dealt with whichever one he wore last Saturday and it would have been put back in his cupboard.

'What about a coat? A jacket?' Shaw asked.

'Well, he's got several,' Amy Parker replied. 'He's got one with him now.' Then she hesitated. He'd not been wearing his black jacket with the tartan lining and the inside pockets when he went off earlier. He'd had on an old fawn anorak which normally he shunned. Come to think of it, she hadn't seen him in the black one all week, and it was almost new, bought with some of his birthday money in September.

An innate sense of danger made her keep quiet about it. Kevin would have done nothing worse than cause some mess in the Noakeses' house while his companions did real damage; she wouldn't start the police hunting for a missing jacket. There was probably some simple explanation for its absence, like he'd lent it to a friend. Not his new jacket, though; he wouldn't lend that out. She pulled a green anorak from among his clothes.

'He may have worn that,' she said. 'I don't know. I didn't see him go out.'

Tracy took it from her and put it in a plastic bag, which

she sealed. They bagged up his shoes and two pairs of jeans. Downstairs, they went through the washing but everything was as pristine as in a detergent advertisement; there was not a sign of blood-stains anywhere.

'When are you letting him come home?' she asked.

'Not yet, Mrs Parker,' Shaw answered. 'He still has some explaining to do and we have to make more enquiries.'

'He's not a bad boy,' she said, entreatingly, as they left, with Joe following in his own car. He had to be present while his son was interviewed.

'They all think that,' said Shaw, as they drove away. 'It's not their precious lamb who's deep in shit.'

'They're decent folk,' said Tracy. 'They don't need this.'

'Who does?'

Other officers went to arrest Paul, who lived with his mother and stepfather and two younger half-brothers on an estate where several problem families were housed and where the police had already checked on some lads known to them. None had been involved in the Deerton murder. Paul had not been in trouble before, but he was a boy who, like Kevin Parker, had been out each time an officer called to question him.

His wardrobe was not as extensive as Kevin's, and his mother was behind with her laundry, so that a soiled sweatshirt and several pairs of Paul's dirty socks were available, not that the socks were likely to be useful. His mother knew he'd had on his dark jacket – almost black – which she'd picked up at a jumble sale. He wore it now, and at the police station was asked to take it off.

His mother found a neighbour to mind her younger children while she went with him to the police station.

'He'd not do anything like that,' she told the police. 'Not Paul.'

She was afraid he might be into drugs. Not hard stuff, mind, or she'd have done her nut – but a bit of pot and maybe a few pills. She'd never mentioned these worries to her husband, who was down on Paul as it was. She'd hoped that she was mistaken, or, if she was not, that he'd soon chuck it on his own. After all, they got taught a lot about drugs at school.

But the police found amphetamines and two tablets of Ecstasy in Paul's drawer. They told her so.

They'd pin that killing on him. She knew they would. What would his stepfather have to say about that? Luckily he was out just now; she had no idea where he was, but it meant that she'd have time to invent an explanation for Paul's absence. Though if he was charged and went to court, everyone would know, and his brothers and the neighbour had already seen him driven off by the police.

18

The period that followed the arrests was difficult for everyone connected with the case. There was relief over the breakthrough, but detailed information and evidence still had to be gathered. Fortunately, because the boys' identities were protected, there was a media clampdown and even the most tenacious reporter's revelations were limited, but gossip was rife, and the names of the boys concerned were known generally in Mickleburgh.

So far, they had been charged with assault and criminal damage while the police continued to investigate. Murder charges had not followed because there was no evidence firm enough to bring before the court. Fisher and his team were patiently seeking scientific proof as to who had wielded the knife. Kevin was insisting that Paul had done it, while Paul, suspecting but not sure that it was Kevin who had grassed him, declared that it was Kevin. After all, it was the truth.

Blood-stains on Paul's jeans and shoes were eventually proved to match Daniel's blood, and a faint stain had been found on a shoelace of Kevin's, but there was nothing that a competent defence lawyer could not shred in minutes, probably reducing any conviction to GBH. It wasn't enough. Remanded into secure accommodation, the boys were sent to different centres.

Sarah found that time now went so slowly. Though it was not much discussed, thoughts were centred on the trial which lay ahead, and it was so depressing. She had failed to get the job in London and had applied for another, but she had not been short-listed. This was a serious disappointment, though a private one as she had kept quiet about it. She was glad when her routine was broken by a conference in Kent, and went off eagerly to stay in a luxurious hotel at the company's expense. Jonathan and Mark had left Deerton, and Daniel's parents had stayed with Midge, his father helping to repair some of the workshop stock, and his mother giving the kitchen cupboards a much-needed clear out, so that later Midge could not find things where she expected them to be. She was grateful, though; the couple were as sorrowful as she was, and they understood her determination to keep the workshop open while there were still goods to sell and she had framing orders.

While they were in Deerton, Daniel's funeral took place, the coroner having allowed his body to be released after resuming the inquest and pronouncing him the victim of unlawful killing. On a bleak day, he was cremated at an early hour, to avoid possible media harassment and in the presence of just his family and the Foxtons. Tim managed to take time off, and Judy came. It was a very sad little ceremony; poor Daniel's body had lain in the morgue for weeks, frozen, as Midge said bitterly and inaccurately, like a leg of lamb. She could not face a decision about disposing of his ashes, and agreed that his parents should take them home when they went back to Kendal, and scatter them in some lovely spot that they were fond of. Mark drove down to join them for the melancholy ritual, which made him feel much better than the brief, respectful service in the crematorium.

It was Sarah who suggested planting a tree or shrub in the

garden at Orchard House, as a memorial. She went with Midge to buy one, and they chose a rose, Nevada, vigorous and showy, which would grow to a great height and cheer Midge up in the early summer, and she helped Midge plant it. Sarah didn't garden much; she left most of that to Oliver, and the man who came for several hours a week, but she liked to have flowers in the house and, Midge discovered with surprise, seemed to know quite a lot about growing them.

At Christmas, Sarah had again proved her worth. Mark and Jonathan had both come home, but Daniel's parents, though invited, decided that it was better not to travel when they might not be able to return if it were to snow. Often they were cut off in the winter. Sarah and Oliver invited the Stewarts to spend the day in Winbury, and they were grateful. Now there would be no need to keep thinking that the year before, Daniel had been with them, carving the turkey and beating them all at Scrabble. They didn't want to forget, but they did not want to be forced into remembering. Midge thought about him constantly.

She and Prudence Wilmot had become friendly. Prudence had taken to calling in at the workshop now and then, and had helped with paperwork occasionally. Knowing this, and because she was alone and Oliver was fond of her, the Foxtons asked her too. She would help to dilute the Stewarts.

They'd had a very late lunch, after champagne and smoked salmon while everyone opened their presents. It was a bright, cold, invigorating day, and Prudence had decided to walk across the fields to Winbury. She wrapped up well, wearing black trousers and warm boots, carrying a pair of pumps in a plastic bag. She'd made the plan with Oliver the day before, delivering to his office a small pile of gifts for those expected at The Barn House. He'd fetch her if the weather was bad, he said, and drive her back in any case. Her way led beside the river past bare willows which bordered the black water flowing between rimed banks. The air was crisp and clear; it was a day when it was good to be alive.

Winbury was a small village lying in a hollow, with a church, a pub and a post office which sold groceries. There was no school; local children attended a primary school in a nearby village, and the older ones went to Mickleburgh. Prudence often walked this way; she liked to stride about, mulling over the development of her plot or characters as she went, glad that she had such an absorbing and rewarding, though demanding, occupation.

Today, though, she was preoccupied with thoughts of Midge, whose courageous attempts to disguise her misery did not deceive Prudence, who knew she was near breaking-point. It was clear that the business was foundering and she might soon go bankrupt, though no doubt Oliver was keeping an eye on the situation. It was a monument to Daniel's failure, and Midge was unable, on her own, to put it right. Until the case was resolved and the guilty boys sentenced, Midge would know no peace, and what if they were not charged with murder, or, literally, got away with it? It could happen. Prudence knew from Oliver that the police case against the two arrested youths was not strong, and it could be that one of the other two, as yet unnamed, had used the knife, not either of those now on remand.

Wendy Tyler had been on remand for months before her trial. It had been a dreadful time for all of them – Prudence and Emily's parents, and Lionel, not that they had felt much sympathy for him then. Prudence had not seen the woman she was sure was Wendy again. Perhaps she had been only passing through Mickleburgh that day.

Banishing her morbid thoughts, Prudence climbed the final stile by the church and took the footpath leading to the main street. It passed between the churchyard wall and a field where two horses, rugged up against the winter, were eating hay, one of them tossing it up and snorting as he munched. The service was over, but Prudence saw a tall woman walking along the road some way ahead of her. She wore a camel coat and an enveloping type of hat, pulled low over her ears. A dark brown shawl was thrown over her shoulders, muffling her. Prudence slowed her steps as the other woman turned down a side road and went past The Barn House, pausing briefly at the gate and looking up the short drive. Then, not glancing back, or she would have seen Prudence, she walked on.

Rosemary Ellis, attending the service in Winbury church, had hoped that Oliver would be among the congregation. She allowed herself to create a scene wherein, recognising her, he invited her to his house for a Christmas drink. But it was not to be.

She moved away after shaking the vicar's hand and prowled around the graveyard, looking at tombstones, until everyone had gone, including the vicar, who hastened back to his home in another village, for he ministered to three parishes. Then, with no one in sight, she strolled along the road and turned down the lane in which, as she knew, stood The Barn House. She had often walked past it, admiring its old mellow stone and the neat shrubs beside the gravelled approach. Now, she saw a shabby Ford Escort parked outside the door. Perhaps the son's? He was a doctor. Inside, there would be a blazing fire, holly, a Christmas tree hung with baubles, piles of expensive gifts for everyone. Sarah Foxton, a lucky woman who had had it easy all along the line, would be presiding over everything with grace and competence. Conscious of a movement behind her, Rosemary realised that her curiosity might be noticed by anyone approaching and walked on, not glancing back. She had learned to practise iron self-control.

Prudence found the day poignant, and painfully illuminating. Midge and her sons did their best to be cheerful and to help with what was going on, but Sarah was so well organised that she needed little assistance except to carry in the dishes and set them on the long refectory table in the dining room – a low-ceilinged room which faced north and was rather dark, but with lighted candles on the table, it looked festive.

When she arrived, a glass of mulled wine with a kick in it was put into her hand; after her trudge, it was very welcome. Jonathan and Judy were out walking, she was told, but as she had not met them, they must have gone another way. Mark and Midge arrived soon after she did, driving up in the Volvo, Mark looking strained and Midge with bright patches of false colour on her cheekbones, and dark stains beneath her eyes. She had spent a wakeful, weepy night, taking a pill at three in the morning and then lapsing into a torpor. Her sons had tiptoed in, and finding her asleep, had left her to wake naturally; Jonathan, eager to see Judy, had gone ahead to the Foxtons, leaving Mark to follow with their mother.

Even after several cups of strong coffee and a bath, Midge still felt like a zombie, and Mark, anxious and alarmed, saw her gradually adopt a brittle animation which he found as dreadful as it was artificial. She smiled and prattled when they reached The Barn House, almost as if she were drunk. What had she been taking? Mark had seen her with some pills. Surely the doctor hadn't given her anything like speed? Could she have bought something at the chemist's? She was, he realised, very near hysteria.

Some time after the two youths were arrested, Ted Grant had come to see her. He had told her that someone tipped the police off and he would like to think it was Peter, but nobody was saying. He'd touched lightly on his son's expressed fear of revenge. Two other boys had been involved and they had not been traced. Although Kevin and Paul were both locked up in a secure unit, messages could be got out by the determined and if they were allowed to use the telephone, they would be able to organise intimidation.

Midge, required to assuage this decent man's sense of guilt, had done her best.

Gwen Grant, too, had come across to see how Mrs Stewart was getting on. She had brought over freshly baked scones and flowers in an effort to console, and Midge, deeply touched, had wanted to hurl herself into the arms of this kindly woman and sob her heart out. Instead, she strove to be contained, thanked her, and offered tea, which Gwen accepted and then somehow contrived to make, mildly clearing up some of the clutter in the kitchen while she did so.

Now Midge pecked at her helping of turkey with its trimmings. She had drunk her champagne with alacrity, hoping it would put new life into her, and had eaten several wedges of smoked salmon perched on brown bread in an attempt to stop her head from spinning. She felt that she was on the verge of losing all control and it was terrifying. Oliver cast anxious glances at her and was sparing as he refilled her glass. Prudence was shocked at her appearance; it was only a week since she had last seen her and she seemed to have lost several pounds in weight since then. She was much jumpier, more on edge. Perhaps it was the strain of having to face this long holiday, with all its emphasis on family solidarity, often such a myth. Determined not to sit silent, Midge was asking everyone what they were planning to do in the next few days, who was going to the cinema and what would they see, questioning Judy about her course, wondering how Tim was; he was on duty over Christmas but would be home for a brief visit soon. He telephoned during the meal, and had a short conversation with his parents and his sister, and sent his regards to all the others. Sarah said what a pity it was that he couldn't be with them.

'Then we'd all be here,' she said, and Judy kicked her hard under the table, for Daniel wasn't.

Prudence leapt in with a diversion, asking Oliver how the dolls' house was getting on, and he said that it was almost finished. He would give it back to her quite soon, he told her. They talked about it, spinning the subject out for a while, letting the charged atmosphere subside. There were no crackers. Oliver, who rarely insisted on anything with which Sarah did not agree, had decreed that pulling them and wearing paper hats would be too much to expect of the Stewarts. As soon as they left the table, Prudence asked to see the dolls' house, and went with Oliver to his study. Midge followed them.

'I want to see it, too,' she said. 'I think it's wonderful. It was yours, wasn't it?' she asked Prudence.

'Yes. I loved it. I made up stories about the people in it,' Prudence said. 'And my niece played with it when she was little.'

Midge had not heard Prudence mention a niece before. She knew Prudence had a son who held some diplomatic post in Moscow.

'Where does she live?' she asked, and did not listen to the answer as she looked inside at the family of dolls. 'Oh, poor Mr Wilberforce,' she said. 'Whatever has happened to you?'

Sarah, in a fit of malice, had removed him from his position at the table, where Oliver had left him, and had laid him prostrate on the floor.

19

Christmas has always been a lonely time for me, but I am far from unique, and social isolation is surely preferable to the charged atmosphere that can prevail when families, confined together, are forced into false jollity, compelled to co-exist for hours, even days, eating and drinking too much, envying and resenting those they think more fortunate than themselves. However, afterwards, it brings me new patients, those who have found the strain too much and snapped, or almost lost control. I resume consultations the day after Boxing Day, when present and prospective patients are still on holiday and have time to attend; people even come in off the street, with no appointment, hoping I will have the time to see them. The Samaritans and I, and others of my colleagues, are the ones who pick up the post-festive pieces and either put them together again or make the fractured victims understand that their case is hopeless – not that the Samaritans do that: they never give up hope, and actively discourage suicide.

In prison, attempts were made to mark the season. Paper chains were hung, and turkey featured on the menu. I, being one of the religious group, spent hours in church. I sang carols, took my part in anthems, even read the lesson. Soberly, I stood and knelt, appeared to pray, to be devout. It was easy and became a habit, so that I still adhere to it today. It punctuates my calendar. I went to Midnight Mass this Christmas Eve and sang carols. My voice is good, a light contralto.

On Boxing Day I posted my professional card through various letter-boxes, some in the town, but I went out to Deerton, too, and put one through Mrs Stewart's door. There was no mistaking Orchard House; the name was on the gate. It looked deserted. My card bears, in bold type, my initials and my name, with the prefix Dr, to which I am not entitled, but, with the name of the professional association I joined so easily, it inspires confidence.

On my card – postcard size – is printed in italic script my message:

> *DEPRESSED? TIRED? LONELY?*
> *CHRISTMAS IS FOR FAMILIES. IS YOURS DYSFUNCTIONAL?*
> *DO YOU FEEL ISOLATED? UNABLE TO COPE?*
> *Consult a trained and confidential counsellor.*
> *Fees moderate.*

I knew my delivery drop would have some results. Even so, I was surprised when, a week later, Mrs Stewart telephoned.

Kate Preston and Jamie had spent Christmas with her parents, in Devonshire. Kate wanted to escape from the aftermath of the murder and the arrest of the two boys.

After they were charged, Jamie had not wanted to discuss it.

'They were there,' he finally admitted to Fisher, when he was asked for corroboration.

'Aren't you going to say which one of them stabbed you, Jamie?' Fisher had asked him. 'We had a tip-off, you know. Two, in fact, but the first message didn't get through. Both anonymous.' He was steadily regarding Jamie, who looked sheepish.

Fisher had explained that, for want of direct evidence, so far the boys had not been charged with murder.

'They're both guilty, though. The one who stabbed Mr Stewart and the one who aided and abetted him. He's an accessory to murder, and so are the other two, whose names we don't yet know, but we'll trace them now. Guilt by association. You know what that is, Jamie. I don't have to spell it out for you,' he said.

Fisher, who had come to talk to Jamie at home and off the record, deplored the prospect of youths who had hitherto kept out of serious trouble being given long sentences and then, when too old to remain in young offenders' institutions, being sent to adult prisons where they would meet real vice and violence. When finally released, as they would be, whatever the verdict and the punishment, they might emerge as confirmed villains. He wanted to see such youngsters being helped to straighten themselves out, as happened already in some centres; the good work could, however, be undone. Violent youths and children who killed – there were a few – should never, he maintained, be transferred to adult prisons.

He said some of this to Kate, in Jamie's hearing. Kate, in the calm of her parents' cottage overlooking the sea, meditated on his words and whether to open the subject with Jamie. Maybe it was better left, to be faced when they went home.

His grandparents, horrified by the whole business, had understood his dilemma. While he was out kicking a football around with some local boys, they discussed it with Kate.

She told them about the two calls the police had received. Fisher, loyal to Jamie, had not revealed his suspicions about the callers' identities, but Kate shared them.

'Jamie was very brave the night it happened,' Kate said. 'But not quite brave enough to tell the whole story. Neil Fisher – that's the detective in charge of the case – hopes they'll get enough evidence from the forensic scientists to convict the boys they've arrested, but there were two more, and someone stole the car they used. That hasn't been traced.'

'And the whole thing was a sort of gate-crash which went out of control?' asked her father.

'Yes. Mind you, they were bent on mischief – must have been. They took beer with them – there were several empty cans in the Grants' house. By the time they got there, they were probably drunk. Jamie has said he thought Paul – one of them – might have been high on something. Some drug,' she added, in case they hadn't understood.

'And it's a misplaced schoolboy code of honour that's stopping the law-abiding boys from saying enough to convict the others?' asked her father, wanting to be certain.

'Not just that. The two others – the ones still at large – could get at Jamie and his friends,' said Kate. She wondered why the police had not carried out a mass fingerprinting operation to find those boys. Perhaps they still hoped that the arrested pair or the innocent quartet would soon name them.

'Savages,' said Kate's father, a retired merchant seaman.

Jamie succeeded in putting the whole thing out of his mind while he was away. He enjoyed being with boys who knew nothing about it. He slept and ate well, played Scrabble and Monopoly with his mother and his grandparents in the evenings, and went out sailing, well wrapped up, in a boat owned by his uncle, who ran a chandler's shop at a marina not far away.

After they returned to Mickleburgh, just before the new school term began, Peter telephoned when Jamie was alone at home. For a while they talked about what they had been doing during the holiday, and then Jamie asked if there was any more news.

'Can you come over?' Peter said. 'Greg's coming, and Barry. We fancied a chat.'

'All right. Mum's out seeing about something to do with timetables at school. I'll bike over,' said Jamie. 'See you.'

He left a note for his mother, and set off before she could return and tell him he was not to go to Deerton. But she wouldn't do that, he thought; she might have driven him there, though.

He pedalled off. It was very cold, and he wore the knitted cap that had been so useful out sailing, pulled well down over his ears. Usually he scorned gloves, but not today. The exercise soon warmed him up as he tucked his nose inside the zipped-up neck of his fleece jacket, the same one that he had worn that night. It hadn't seemed as cold as this on his uncle's boat, but sea air was somehow different. He enjoyed cycling, and rode fast; he had a good mountain bike which his mother had helped him pay for two years ago. On the journey, he thought of nothing except the speed at which he was travelling and the miles he was clocking up.

It was good to see his friends again. He parked his bike round the back of Peter's house and went in. Peter's parents were both out at work. Ted had plenty to do and not enough time to fit in everything; Gwen, who was a hairdresser, had clients wanting to look glamorous as they celebrated the New Year.

Barry had been glad to get out of his house, where his father, who did not really want to take time off, was restricted because builders' and plumbers' suppliers had all closed down and he could not get materials he needed. He was dealing with emergencies, but, apart from that, was continuing the refurbishment of the house. The atmosphere at home was not altogether friendly, though, as Barry's mother pointed out, all he had done was open the front door to the invaders.

Barry's own desire now was to punch the heads of those responsible. He said so to his friends.

'Well, we can't punch Paul or Kevin,' Greg, who arrived

just after Jamie, declared. 'But maybe we should have told, right away.'

'And got beaten up ourselves? Maybe killed?' asked Barry.

'They'd already done Mr Stewart,' Jamie said. 'They might as well do us too. They'd get no worse punishment. The police did nick them, after all.' He glanced at Peter; neither of them was going to tell the other two what part they had played in this. 'And they'll get more proof,' he added, hopefully.

'But what about Wayne and Trevor?' said Greg, who was having bad dreams about that dreadful night. In these nightmares he was always running home across the garden at the back of Barry's house and then over the allotments that separated his house from Orchard Close, but instead of managing to escape, he was pursued by the four troublemakers, all of them brandishing knives, until eventually he could not run fast enough and they caught up with him and plunged their knives into his body. At that point he would wake up, sometimes, to his mother's dismay, screaming.

'Kevin and Paul will split on them,' said Barry sagely. 'Once they're committed for trial. My dad says they'll know then that it's no good keeping quiet, and if they talk, they may get shorter sentences.'

'But it was Kevin that did it,' said Jamie. 'He was the one with the knife. He stabbed me. I should know.' More and more, he was feeling he should tell Fisher the whole story. He knew he was likely to be called as a witness and that he could not refuse to testify; Fisher had already made that clear. If he did, he might be guilty of contempt of court. 'I thought about it on the way back from Devon,' he said, and, looking abashed, added, 'My granddad got a medal in the war. He was in the merchant navy bringing stuff across the Atlantic. He was pretty brave, I'd say. And then my dad was in the army.' He paused. The others knew his father had been killed on active service. 'He was brave, too,' he went on. 'I can't be a coward. It's just

– if I tell Fisher all about it, it's my mum I'm worried about. If they did me – Trevor and Wayne – would you lot see she was OK?'

The others shuffled their feet in embarrassment and mumbled that they would, and Peter added, 'I can't see that they'd get you, because by then they'd be locked up, too.'

'There'd be their mates. They've got other mates,' said Greg, but he was wondering whether, if Trevor and Wayne were arrested, his bad dreams would stop.

'They wouldn't go for any of us after that,' said Peter. 'It's too serious, this one is. They'll be inside for years and years and we'll all have left school and even college by the time they're out again, if they ever are.'

'My dad said they oughtn't ever be let out,' said Barry. 'Throw away the key, he said. A few years ago they'd have been hanged, he said.'

'Not kids. They didn't hang kids,' said Greg.

'A hundred years ago they got sent to Australia,' Jamie said. 'Even for stealing sheep, or bread, you got transported.'

'Stealing sheep?' This from Barry.

'For food, it would be,' Jamie said. 'They do it still in Wales and places. Sheep rustling. I suppose they get fined now if they get caught.'

'Well, Kevin and Paul won't get hanged and they will be let out one day,' said Peter. 'Not for ages, though.'

'Suppose they get off?' asked Greg. Then they might come after him in real life, not just in dreams. 'People do. Lawyers get them off.'

'Not for killing people,' Peter said.

'It depends on the evidence,' said Jamie. 'They need solid evidence to make it stick. That superintendent – Fisher – said so.'

'And us telling would be it – the evidence,' said Peter, not asking; stating it as fact.

Act of Violence

'If we all do it together, we'll be all right,' said Barry. 'They'll believe us, too. We were there, after all.'

They looked round at one another, four adolescent boys, two tall and thin and somewhat uncoordinated, growing fast, one – Barry – short and stocky with a round determined face, and Greg, whose acne was a problem.

'Shall we?' asked Jamie. 'I've got Fisher's number. It's his direct line. Shall we do it now?' He hoped they would say yes, so that he could stop wondering about it and take action. Then it wouldn't be their worry any longer.

Trevor's mother had put her Lada up for sale. She'd advertised it in the *Mickleburgh Herald*, a local paper funded mainly by advertisements, and was now cleaning it out, ready for the prospective buyers she hoped would soon flock to inspect it. She'd use the money for a holiday to celebrate Fred's fiftieth birthday. She had changed her job after Christmas and now worked in a newsagent's in Mickleburgh, where extra staff were needed to sell lottery tickets, and she could walk to work.

She attached a long hose to her vacuum cleaner and plugged it in, then set it to devour the dust, sweet papers and general mess that had accumulated in the car in recent weeks. It had never been a treasured possession, more a convenience to take her to her former job in Fettleton. Some kid might buy it, Trevor had said, though not one who valued his image.

'A girl might. Someone sensible,' his mother had responded sharply. Image, indeed. 'You might help me,' she'd suggested, but there was no sign of him so far.

He emerged while she was scrabbling under the driver's seat, pulling out tissues and a long-lost glove.

And a knife.

She wasn't sure what she'd grasped at first, as she looked down at it, holding it inside a tattered piece of paper – an advertising flyer – which had covered it among the other rubbish. It wasn't an ordinary knife, nor a penknife, but one that disappeared inside its handle: a flick knife. She stood up and stared at it, slowly realising what it was as Trevor, carrying a bucket which he had filled with water and detergent, came to lend her a hand. Seeing what she held, he dropped the bucket.

'Trevor,' she said, very calmly, 'what do you know about this?'

20

She came to see me a few days after Christmas, in the long fallow period before the world started back to life again. I had had several urgent callers seeking emergency appointments and she, it seemed, was one of them. From the window, I saw her park an old Volvo in the road outside; my consulting room is in a quiet residential area where it is easy to park in the daytime, though when I see patients in the evening the residents' cars tend to fill most spaces.

I waited for her to ring the bell, then pressed the automatic door release so that she entered my small hall, where three tweed-seated chairs indicated that each patient was only one among many wanting my attention. Arranged on a low table were some magazines – all recent editions, none tatty as in other waiting-rooms – Good Housekeeping, Country Life, The Lady, even some motoring magazines: nothing flash or tasteless. I buy them in a casual manner; I subscribe to none.

She was early, so I made her wait, though I had no patient with me. From the start, I have to establish my authority. After a few minutes – not long – I opened the door of my consulting room and asked her to come in. Conscientiously, I smiled down at her: she is very small, five foot two, perhaps, and extremely thin. I imagine she has lost weight since the murder. It's understandable. She has a raggedy crop of ill-cut dull brown hair.

She was trembling, so I poured water for her, and she sipped it, spilling some before setting the glass down on a Crown Derby saucer placed for the purpose on the corner of my desk.

'Now, Mrs Stewart, tell me how I may help you,' I invited.

She found it difficult to speak.

'My husband died. Suddenly. It was violent. He was stabbed,' she said, speaking in jerky sentences, twisting her hands together. 'You probably heard about it. Some boys did it,' she continued. 'In November.'

'How terrible,' was my soothing murmur. 'I'm so sorry. Tell me how it happened. Were you there?' I was not sure if she had witnessed the incident.

'No. He went to intervene – some boys were vandalising a house opposite ours, in Deerton, and one boy – not one of the hooligans – came to us for help. Dan went, and the boys turned on him and stabbed him.'

'I read what was reported in the papers,' I encouraged her. 'It was dreadful for you. Shocking.'

'Yes, and I'm not dealing with it very well,' she said. 'I'm trying to pull myself together and put a good face on things, but I'm not succeeding. I keep on crying and I can't concentrate. I don't want to worry my sons or my friends. I found your card and wondered if perhaps you could help.'

'That's my job,' I told her. 'To guide people towards managing their lives.'

A regular consultation twice a week would be a useful contribution towards my rent, and I would feel good about assisting her, since she was clearly in a state of utter despair. I wanted to be involved in this: I wanted to know as much I could learn of the story, how her circle of friends was reacting, what part that old woman I had seen in Mickleburgh was playing in her life. I had seen this pathetic woman, Mrs Stewart, entering her house more than once when, hoping to learn something about the occupant, I was passing. I hadn't recognised her then, this tiny woman; the newspaper shots of her had been indistinct.

I still didn't know the older woman's name.

She told me the story, more or less coherently, her thin body shaking and her hands tearing at one another. I remember how one shakes like that, in deep stress. I had done it, too. I asked if she was eating, and could she sleep, and she said she had no appetite but tried to force food down. She was sleeping badly, waking up remembering what had happened, reaching out to touch only the empty bed.

I understood her deprivation. I, too, in different circumstances, had lost my lover, my sustainer, but mine betrayed me. Hers was taken from her by a violent hand.

'How do you feel towards the arrested boys?' I asked, genuinely interested.

'I don't know. They're youngsters – fifteen, sixteen – it wasn't personal. They were lashing out – hitting at authority, perhaps,' she said. 'Sometimes I hate them. Sometimes I think they are victims too.'

She told me about the funeral, how it had to be delayed and then how sad and bleak it had been. Emily's had not been delayed long; my defence, content with the official post mortem, had not wanted a second one. She had received hundreds of letters, she revealed, offering condolences, but had not replied to any of them, hiding them in a drawer where her sons would not find them.

'Why don't you let your sons deal with them for you?' I suggested. 'They could send a small printed slip mentioning that you received too many to acknowledge individually.'

She liked this idea, but thought that her sons would be

shocked that she had left them unacknowledged for so long. They'd read some of them, she said, those that came soon after the event, when both young men were still staying with her.

'*Perhaps some friend?*' *I proposed, and she said that she would think about it.*

Something positive had been achieved. I asked her then about her friends. Was she receiving adequate support from them?

'*Oh yes. My friends have been wonderful,*' *she enthused.* '*Oliver and Sarah Foxton in particular. We'd all had dinner together that night, the night Dan was killed. They helped me then. We went to them on Christmas Day, my sons and I. Oliver is a solicitor. He says I can't keep our business going. It was losing money even before – before—*' *Her voice trailed away.*

'*Can you sell it? Do something else?*' *A pragmatic person myself, I can often direct others into practical channels.*

'*I could sell the lease if anyone wanted to buy it,*' *she said.* '*But who would? It's not really central and it's not in good repair.*'

'*A new venture would require its own layout,*' *I explained.* '*It might not suit everyone, but there could be a use for it. Now,*' *I added, for I was wearying of her, and I had given her several excellent suggestions to consider, surely good value for her forty pounds,* '*Your real need is for sleep. When you are more rested, some of these difficulties will not seem so immense and you will have more energy to deal with them, and, of course, my support, if, as I hope you will, you continue with these sessions. One is not enough, Mrs Stewart,*' *I added.* '*Not when you are the victim of such trauma. I'm going to give you some herbal remedies which will help you, and I want you to return in three days' time.*'

She took the little bottles: floral essences I buy and repack myself. Some people find them beneficial, and placebos have their uses.

She paid in cash, trying to laugh it off, saying the bank might not like her cheque.

I was pleased. I need not put this consultation through my books. It had been an interesting session.

Trevor's mother saw shock and guilt, in equal measure, on her son's face as she held the knife towards him, still resting on the scruffy piece of paper.

'What's the explanation for this?' she asked, her voice icy. Then her hand began to shake and she closed it gently round the knife, still protectively surrounded by the paper. She was remembering that after the shocking murder, Trevor had been out each time the police had called to see him. She had mentioned their visits to him, and he had said they were talking to every boy about the Deerton stabbing. Of course they were; it made sense. 'Come inside, Trevor,' she said.

'It's not mine,' Trevor began, and he turned away, ready to flee from the scene.

'You're not going anywhere,' his mother stated. 'Go into the house. Go on. Now.'

He hesitated, but only for a moment, his stomach churning as, in panic, he obeyed, sliding through the door into the kitchen. She followed him, and laid the knife down on a plate, which she lifted from the drainer.

'It's not mine,' Trevor repeated. 'I don't know how it got there.'

'I think you do,' his mother said. 'You'd better tell me, before I ring your dad.'

His father, a storekeeper in a discount warehouse, had no long Christmas break.

'I didn't touch him. It was Kevin,' Trevor burst out. 'They got the right one.'

'They've got that other boy, too. That Paul,' said his mother.

'It was Kevin had the knife,' Trevor insisted.

'And what had you to do with it?'

'I don't know anything about it,' Trevor blustered, but his mother would have none of that.

'You were there. You said it was Kevin had the knife. You saw what happened. You helped those others trash that house,' she accused. 'How did that knife get into my car?'

'It was an accident – it was just a joke – then this old guy came along,' said Trevor, whining now.

'Some joke,' said his mother. 'I suppose you drove them there. Those others, Kevin and Paul, and there was another, wasn't there?'

She remembered which night it was. She and Trevor's father had made an evening of it, and the news had broken in the morning, but the Lada was in its place when they came home. Trevor had been a bit quiet the next day, she recollected.

Trevor did not answer. He sat facing her, looking sullen, shifting his feet to and fro beneath the table. Then he reached out a hand towards the knife, and she knocked his arm aside with a sharp blow.

'Don't you touch it,' she ordered him. 'Have you handled it before? The truth, now, mind.'

'No,' he said, and added, in a growl, 'Kevin must have dropped it.'

'So you did take it? The Lada?'

Mutely, miserable, he nodded.

'I'm calling the police. Then your dad,' she said, picking up the plate on which the knife rested and taking it with her to the telephone. 'I think you'd rather talk to the police about this than your dad.'

His dad would belt him, and he'd deserve it. Shaking now, partly from shock and fear, but also with suppressed rage, Trevor's mother dialled 999, and when Trevor, desperate now, pushed past her, making for the door, she called him back. 'You're not going anywhere,' she said. 'You'll answer for your part in this.' But he'd named the boy who had used the knife.

The knife was carefully bagged and sealed. Possibly its blade would bear stains of Daniel Stewart's blood, or Jamie's, or even, if they were lucky, identifiable amounts from both victims, but it might also yield a fingerprint. When Trevor's father arrived, not long after the police, Trevor finally accepted defeat and told his story, limiting his own role to that of providing the car and acting as the driver.

'I didn't nick it. I just borrowed it,' he muttered.

'Driving without a licence and insurance,' said Detective Sergeant Shaw, who had arrived to reinforce the uniformed officers who had answered the call.

His father could not believe what he was hearing. His face turned purple, and Trevor's mother's decision to get the police there first, if possible, was justified. He'd have lammed into the boy for his part in this, even if all he did was, as he maintained, take and drive the car.

The police knew, however, from Ted Grant that all four boys had attacked him and Daniel Stewart, though only one had produced a knife. All four had kicked and punched both men as they lay on the ground, and at least one of them had gone for Jamie before he was stabbed by another. They were all accessories. All would face serious charges.

Trevor was taken to the police station for further questioning and, at last, to be fingerprinted. The results of that would put him in the Noakeses' house at the relevant time. Both his parents went with him, while the uniformed officers guarded the Lada until the transporter arrived to take it away for scientific testing. It might retain traces of its passengers on that fatal night, even after such an interval, for the knife had been there, probably dropped by its user in the confusion as they fled, and kicked under the driver's seat. Trevor's mother seldom had a passenger; not much had been disturbed for weeks.

Trevor named Wayne in his statement, and he was arrested later in the day. Neither boy was granted bail, and when Trevor's mother protested, she was told she could be thankful that he would be safe in custody, out of reach of any lynch mob who might want to get their hands on him.

Next day, both boys were remanded to secure accommodation for a week. Like Kevin and Paul, they would be inside until the trial.

Sarah's office had closed down over Christmas but she had brought home with her details of a project for a firm in Swindon which required the reorganisation of its management systems and office layout. Working on it, she grew bored and felt like throwing all her ideas into the wastepaper basket. She'd played about on her computer, drawing shapes and forms, studying the time and motion aspects of various proposals, then costing them as far as she could while unable to contact suppliers who were also closed.

Oliver had not taken the week off. Solicitors were still required to deal with urgent matters, and it was a chance to clear backlogs in the office. While he was there, Fisher, aware that he was supervising the interests of the Stewart family, rang him to tell him about the two new arrests. Now the case was firing up.

Fisher said he planned to break the news to Midge himself, and Oliver decided that he had better be there, too. He wondered if Midge would be at home. She might be at the workshop, although there could be scarcely any business for her to attend to. In order to find out, he rang the premises, but there was no reply. It was safe to assume she was at Orchard House. She would be on her own. Mark had gone back to Scotland for a few days' skiing in the Cairngorms before returning to work, and Jonathan and Judy were also skiing, in Austria, with a university party. Midge had persuaded both her sons to take this break. She said she would need them more when it came to the trial.

Before going over to Deerton, Oliver rang Sarah to explain.

'Shall I come?' Sarah volunteered immediately, glad to have an excuse to interrupt a task she was finding tedious. Since the conference in Kent, she had lost much of her enthusiasm for her work.

'I'll ring you if it seems a good idea,' he hedged. 'Maybe later, if she goes to pieces.'

She might. He had not seen her for several days but she had been so tense and febrile at Christmas, it had seemed as if she might suddenly flare up and fizzle out, like a firework.

Driving over, he remembered finding the father doll, Mr Wilberforce as Midge had named him, lying on the dolls' house floor. What on earth had made Sarah move him? Was she giving him, Oliver, a message? No one else could have done it, but it was unlike Sarah to be fanciful, let alone malicious.

He reached Deerton before Fisher. Midge, who had been warned by a telephone call from Poppy Flower that they were on their way, heard his car and had opened the front door before he reached it. She put a hand on his shoulder and reached up to kiss him. He felt her cool lips on his cheek and hoped it wasn't bristly.

'I miss kisses,' she said, turning back into the house.

'Poor Midge. I expect you do,' he said.

'What's happened, Oliver?' she asked, going ahead of him into the sitting room. 'Did Fisher tell you?'

The fire was low. She poked it ineffectually, and Oliver took the poker from her and added some logs.

'Are you all right for logs and coal?' he asked. The next thing would be that she would succumb to hypothermia; there was no flesh on her bones to keep her warm.

'Yes,' she said. 'Well, tell me, Oliver.'

He put on two more logs. Well dried out, they crackled cheerfully. Apple, he thought; had Daniel cut down an apple tree for fuel?

'He said they'd arrested two more boys. I don't know any more than that,' he answered.

'Oh, I see. Well, that's good. That means there will be a stronger case. They'll know it all now, with all the boys caught,' she said. 'Dan's parents will be pleased.'

'Aren't you?' he asked her curiously.

'Oh yes. Yes, of course I am. I wonder what happened.'

'I expect he'll tell us,' said Oliver. 'Probably one of those decent lads spilled a few more beans. It was bound to happen. They couldn't go on saying almost nothing.'

'Poor kids. How's this going to affect them?' Midge wondered. 'Is it going to blight their lives?'

'I doubt it. Young people are more resilient than we remember,' said Oliver.

What a funny way to put it, Midge thought. He meant, than we remember being. Perhaps she had been resilient years ago, or perhaps your resilience was a finite store and if you dipped into it too often, it ran out. She might ask that counsellor woman what she thought of such a theory.

Fisher soon arrived, and he told them about the discovery of the knife and how this had cleared up the mystery of the car the youths had used. Oliver asked a few questions. The evidence which it was hoped the knife would yield would greatly aid the prosecution, and would mean the four could be charged with murder.

'But they still won't be tried for months, will they?' Midge asked, when Fisher had gone.

'No, I'm afraid not,' said Oliver. 'There will be a preliminary hearing – that might take place fairly soon, as some of the preparation will already have been done –

that's just to commit them for trial. To decide there is a case to try.'

'I see.'

Midge hadn't cried. She seemed almost catatonic, which in a way was more alarming than her feverish gaiety on Christmas Day. Oliver suddenly had an almost overwhelming desire to pick her up and carry her upstairs, and try to comfort her by making tender love to her, but he knew better than to attempt it. To kill a friendship with sexual intimacy would be another murder, and besides, she would be horrified. He knew she felt no reciprocal desire for him; he was good, safe Oliver, her and Daniel's trusted friend.

'I don't think you'd better be here on your own tonight,' he said. 'Will you come back to Winbury with me?'

'What will Sarah say?'

'She'll be delighted. She offered to come over with me just now. I said we'd ring her if you went to pieces,' he said, with a wry expression.

Midge actually laughed.

'I haven't, have I?' she remarked.

'No,' he said. 'Well done. Pack a few things and we'll get going, and while you're doing that I'll dismantle this lovely fire so that we leave it in a safe condition.'

'What a waste,' she said.

'Never mind.'

That night, Oliver took another female doll from his small store, one he had bought the day before. He put her in the dolls' house, hesitating over where to place her. Finally, he arranged her in the armchair in the second largest bedroom, put the child dolls in their respective beds, the mother doll in the drawing room, and the father in his study.

Let Sarah make of that what she would, if she looked inside, he thought. He wasn't sure what he made of it himself.

21

Jamie soon heard about the arrests. Someone had seen the police car at Trevor's house; someone else had seen Wayne being driven off, and outside the chip shop, where the youngsters often gathered, the word had spread.

After making their big decision in Peter's house, Jamie had undertaken the task of telephoning the police, for none of the Deerton boys wanted the call to register on their parents' bills. He would do it when he reached home.

Pedalling back before it grew dark, he passed Oliver in his Rover on the way to Orchard House, but he missed Fisher, whose route from Fettleton did not overlap with Jamie's journey back to Mickleburgh.

While he was out, his mother had come in and had gone out again. She'd left him a note saying that she was going round to Bob and Ginny's, and would be home by six o'clock. If she was later than that, would he turn the oven on. He looked inside and saw a chicken with some foil across it, waiting to be roasted. Jamie pottered about for a while, hanging up his jacket, washing, brushing his hair. Sometimes he wished his mother would find a good bloke and get married again, as parents who split up often seemed to do, he'd noticed, but perhaps it was different if you were a widow. It would be nice for her, he thought, but if the new bloke didn't take to him, it could be tricky. He might have kids of his own who Jamie would have to accept as brothers and sisters. What if they didn't get on? On the whole, he was glad he didn't have to share her with anyone else; they'd been on their own a long time now, and he was old enough to be a help to her, and not a drag. Except for this Deerton business.

He couldn't get out of his head the fact that poor Mr Stewart would still be alive if he had not gone for help, but then Kevin and his mates might have done worse damage to Barry's house – might even have set it on fire. Jamie wouldn't have put it past them. Paul was a really crazy oddball who had boasted that he had done stuff like that – torched a car and got away with it, and other things. Of course, he might have been just talking big; you couldn't always believe what he said. He'd get into real trouble one day, Jamie knew, and then remembered that he had.

He could put it off no longer. Slowly, Jamie went to the telephone. Even more slowly, he dialled Fisher's number.

A woman answered. She said she was Detective Inspector Flower. Superintendent Fisher was out just now, but she would give him a message the moment he returned, or perhaps she could help. Jamie wouldn't tell her why he had rung, nor would he give his name.

Poppy Flower quickly traced the call. She did not ring back. She knew whose that number was; it was written on a pad on Fisher's desk, but though Jamie would be required as a witness, his help in identifying the other two boys involved in the murder was no longer needed for they had already been arrested.

When Fisher returned to the station after his visit to Midge Stewart, he did not call back either; he decided he would go round and tell Kate and Jamie what had happened. It would let the poor kid off the immediate hook. Much would depend now on what the forensic scientists could learn from their examination of the weapon and the car.

By the time he had finished in the Incident Room, it was after seven. Fisher reached Kate's house just as she and Jamie were about to start their meal, and a tempting smell of roasting chicken wafted towards him when she opened the front door. Fisher, a divorced father like those Jamie had been contemplating earlier, who would have collected a pizza on his way back to Fettleton, needed no urging to accept a second invitation to join them. He apologised again for disturbing their evening, but Kate said Jamie would be glad to see him; he had told her what he and his three friends had decided, and she had been relieved and thankful. He had said that he'd already rung Fisher, who was out. They'd agreed that he would try again after supper; Kate had Fisher's home number.

Now he could speak directly to the man.

'Jamie rang you today. You were out,' she said.

'Is that right, Jamie?' Fisher asked. Pre-empted, he thought fast. Should he let the boy give his information or should he, as he had intended, get in first and tell him what had happened earlier that day? He knew immediately that he must retain the boy's trust; if Jamie revealed the full story of that fatal night and then learned that Fisher already knew and had made two more arrests, he might feel betrayed.

'We all decided—' Jamie began, and Fisher interrupted him.

'You and your three friends? Well, before you tell me what your decision was, let me tell you what I came round here to say. We've arrested two more boys. We've found the knife – it's almost certainly the one that was used – and the car they borrowed. It wasn't exactly stolen, as we'd believed.'

'You caught them?' Jamie's face had split into a huge, relieved grin. 'Really?'

'Really,' Fisher confirmed.

'That was pretty cool detecting,' said Jamie.

'Sort of,' Fisher said. 'I can't tell you any more just

now, but let's just say we had a bit of luck when the knife turned up.'

'Oh, great,' said Jamie, still beaming. 'Wow!'

'Wow, indeed,' said Fisher, and he smiled at Kate, who had risen to take a bottle of supermarket Riesling from the fridge.

'Let's have some of this,' she suggested. 'Jamie, you can have some too, or would you rather have a beer? It's a celebration.'

And it was, and he would, and he did.

When Oliver returned with Midge that evening, Sarah felt a mixture of exasperated pity and impatience. Was she going to hang about their necks for ever, like the albatross in the poem?

Forgetting that she had not been enjoying the work she had been doing, Sarah now resented the interruption, sighing as she shut down her computer and put on a smile of welcome.

For the first time in their long marriage, Oliver felt like shaking her. She had everything; Midge had lost the person she most loved in the world, apart from her sons, and had been left financially strapped, whereas if he were to die, Sarah would be well provided for, and, an attractive widow, could have a pleasant life.

She wouldn't miss him all that much, he thought; it was what he represented that she valued.

Speaking sternly, he explained what had happened.

'Well, thank goodness. Now perhaps the police will get on with things and we can put all this behind us,' Sarah said. 'Or you can,' she told Midge. Sarah had already done so, but, as now, it kept being resurrected by events.

'I'm sorry, descending on you again like this,' said Midge. 'Oliver insisted,' she basely added, but she didn't want Sarah to think it was her idea.

She looked like a bedraggled little girl, thought Sarah,

irritated by her forlorn, waiflike appearance, which only too clearly appealed to Oliver's chivalrous nature. She was so small. Bulky men like Oliver felt sorry for her and wanted to protect her while Sarah, though acknowledging that what Midge had suffered was horrific, wished she would get her act together. And how like reckless, foolhardy Daniel to dash straight out into the affray without waiting for the police to arrive. Didn't they always say you shouldn't 'have a go'? He'd been brave, she conceded, but rash, and now Midge was faced with the consequences.

Oliver had had to return to the office. After he had gone, Sarah made an effort, asking Midge to explain what the new arrests would mean, and then, settling her down by the fire with some magazines, she went off to find extra food for dinner, not that Midge looked as if she was eating at all. She might tempt her with something succulent, Sarah thought, as ever stimulated by a challenge, however minor, to her domestic competence. She put a container of frozen homemade carrot and orange soup on the top of the Aga, where it would thaw, and also took some sole fillets from the freezer. While she was peeling and thinly slicing potatoes, she had an idea which would solve her dilemma as well as Midge's. She mulled it over while she decided spinach would go well with the fish. Then she returned to Midge, who had an open magazine on her lap but was not looking at it, staring instead at the fire.

'You can plan your future now,' said Sarah briskly. She sat down opposite Midge, leaning forward, intent on gaining Midge's attention. She'd take this one by stages, weed out the other options first.

'How?' Midge asked, her tone bleak. The magazine slid from her knees to the floor, and as she appeared not to have noticed, Sarah rose, picked it up and closed it, then put it on a table.

'You'll have to sell the business. The lease – whatever. Oliver says it's in a hopeless state.' The soul of discretion, he had not, in fact, gone so far, but by inference Sarah had understood the extent of its liability. 'You'll have to get yourself a job,' she said.

'But I've got a job,' said Midge.

'A proper job,' said Sarah. 'What can you do, besides frame pictures? Can you type?'

'A bit,' said Midge. 'I'm not bad at accounts, though Dan did most of the book-keeping. I'm not into computers. I suppose I could learn.'

'Perhaps you could.' Not in her present state, thought Sarah, who had been thinking that, through her connections, she might find Midge an office post, but just look at her! No employer would consider her. She was a mess; she'd have to smarten up a lot. And she was skeletal. Sarah was at last aware that Midge was almost past being able to help herself.

'When did you last have a decent meal?' she asked.

'I suppose I had some breakfast,' Midge replied. Had she had lunch? She'd been to the shop, she remembered, but there had been no customers. Her novelty value as the victim of a serious crime had worn off, and in the post-Christmas period, people were not thinking of framing pictures or buying cheap second-hand furniture. She had some memory of a banana she had taken with her. She hadn't eaten it. It must be sitting on the desk. She'd gone home and then Fisher and Oliver had come. 'I know I'm a problem to everyone,' she said. 'It seems I may go bankrupt. You can start again if you do that. But I don't like that idea. I must pay what we owe. Some of our troubles came from people who owe us.'

This was doubtless true. Sarah knew about business practice. This was the moment to make her proposition.

'Why don't you turn the business into something else?' she asked. 'Use the premises for a new enterprise?'

'What sort of enterprise?'

'Something necessary. A secretarial bureau, incorporating

a staff agency, for instance,' Sarah said. 'You could offer copying facilities, word-processing and printing documents, desk-top publishing, flyers and so on for individuals and small businesses who can't afford the time or staff to do these things themselves. You could supply temps and part-timers, too – full-timers, even. There's no agency of that kind in Mickleburgh. There must be an opening for one.'

'I'd never manage all that,' Midge said despairingly. 'I don't know anything about it.'

'Maybe not, but I do. We could be partners,' said Sarah said, eyes shining. 'I'd get the bank to back us. We might need a loan to get us started. I'd be the more active partner,' she emphasised. 'Just while you get over all this trouble and find your feet. You could be in charge of background matters. Interviewing staff. Working the copier. That sort of thing. You'd soon pick up the rest.'

Midge stared at her. Sarah was away on a wave of enthusiasm.

'But your job. You've got a job. A very good one,' she said.

'I'm getting no further with it,' Sarah said. 'I'd like to work for myself now. I've got a lot of experience. It'd be good. I could go round the local companies, tendering for pamphlets and so on. I'm sure it's a viable idea.' Not often impulsive, Sarah grew more determined with each minute.

'I don't know,' Midge temporised. Could she work with Sarah? 'We'd need to ask Oliver,' she said. Whatever else, it would be better than going bankrupt. That would be letting Daniel down.

Sarah, reinvigorated by her scheme, was not going to let it rest. In her mind, she refurbished the place, knocking down walls, putting up new ones and creating small sub-sections. Leasing arrangements could be made for computers and the other equipment they would need. When she heard Oliver's key in the door, she was ready.

As usual when he came home, Oliver's first action, after hanging up his coat, was to greet her. She was in the kitchen, making a sauce for the sole, and he dropped a light kiss on her cheek. This was ritual. She accepted it without turning her face to his; that was normal, too, but tonight she went straight into a litany about her inspiration.

Oliver was startled. He knew she had applied for a job in London which had not materialised for reasons he had not been given, but he had not imagined she would want to set up on her own. Why not, though? And it would be a bonus if it would help Midge. He instantly foresaw snags in a partnership between them, but if they were anticipated, they might be avoided. He could see that the project might be feasible.

'It's well worth thinking about,' he said. 'How does Midge feel about it?'

Midge, Midge: it was always Midge these days, Sarah thought crossly.

'Is she in any position to turn it down?' she asked. 'It will be the saving of her.'

That could be true. Oliver knew that if he showed too much enthusiasm for the idea, Sarah might lose hers; tactically, and also because it was his duty, he should pick holes in it, point out disadvantages. There might be quite a few. He asked her if she was prepared to leave her current job and risk investment in the new venture.

If she went ahead, and he could find no great objections, he would have to underwrite her, but he must not be influenced by his desire to help Midge. The proposition would have to be thoroughly researched. Sarah could not be allowed to back a failure.

Before he could suggest it, she explained that she would conduct a survey of the likely demand for what she would offer. Of course she knew what she was doing, he admitted; she had been very successful in the last few years and now she would have an outlet for her energy and experience, and be working for herself. He had to give the scheme his blessing.

'How's Midge?' he asked, when it seemed that there was no more to discuss until she produced some facts and figures.

'Shattered, poor thing,' said Sarah, briefly forgiving her. 'I gave her a stiff drink and left her by the fire. Maybe she's gone to sleep. She looks exhausted.'

'I'll go and see,' said Oliver.

Midge wasn't in the sitting room. Perhaps she had gone up to her bedroom; if so, she had taken her drink with her: no glass stood on any surface. Oliver crossed the hall and went to his study. The door was not quite closed, and when he pushed it wide, he saw Midge kneeling in front of the open dolls' house. She was crooning to herself, rocking to and fro, holding close to her the mother doll and the other female doll which Oliver had added to the household.

She heard him, and looked round. Her eyes glittered in her pale face.

'I'm playing houses,' she said. 'You've got a new doll, another woman. Which is the right wife for Mr Wilberforce?'

'It doesn't matter,' Oliver replied. 'You can take your choice.'

His heart was thumping. What spirit of mischief had prompted him to buy the new doll?

Midge put both of them carefully in the drawing room, at either end of the tiny sofa.

'Mr Wilberforce will have to choose,' she said. Then, after a pause, she added, 'I wonder if Prudence had names for them. She's lonely, isn't she? Though she has the people in her books for company. Still, she has to invent all their conversations.' Idly, she picked up Mr Wilberforce and stood him in front of the fireplace from where he could contemplate both female dolls.

Oliver was surprised by her remark about Prudence. Was it true? He watched her as she crouched down, like a child, with the dolls. She did not seem to want an answer, asking him if Judy had played with a dolls' house as a child.

'No,' said Oliver. He had wanted to get her one when she was five or six, but Sarah had rejected the idea, saying that even if she liked it for a while, she would soon be bored with it.

'As we only had boys, it didn't arise in our house,' Midge said. 'I had one, though. Not such a fine one as this, more a modern villa, but I loved it.'

'I'll find another old one and do it up for you, if you'd like it,' said Oliver, astonishing himself. 'I'm going to give this one back to Prudence when it's finished. It's almost done.' He crossed over, reached behind the structure and moved a switch. 'There,' he said. 'The fire is alight now,' and sure enough, in the hearth, warm coals seemed to glow, warming up Mr Wilberforce and his ladies.

'You are clever,' said Midge. 'It's lovely. But do you really want to mend another?'

'Yes,' said Oliver, who knew that when he passed this one on, he was going to miss the interest. 'It's a soothing occupation, and keeps me at home, unlike golf and such. So Sarah won't object.' Though she might, if she knew it was for Midge.

'Did she tell you about her big idea?' asked Midge, who had heard him go into the kitchen. 'She wants to transform the business.'

'So she said,' he replied. 'How do you feel about it?'

'It sounds possible,' said Midge. 'I'm not sure how she'd feel with me as her partner. She'd have to be the boss.'

'As long as you see it that way, it should work,' said Oliver.

'What can I do, if I don't do this?' she said. 'I know you've been trying to postpone the moment when I have to face facts, but it's here now. There's no way I could expand the framing. I'd need a heat sealer, for starters, which would cost a bomb, and it would be very expensive to stock enough mouldings to provide a big choice. You have to buy a huge length when you only want a foot or so. That's why I stick to just a few popular lines.'

'You'd have to have an agreement,' he said. 'A way for each of you to get out, if either of you wanted to. If it did well, you might be able to sell out your part very profitably.'

'Might I? So it wouldn't be like marriage, for better or worse, till death—' here Midge's thin, pretty face, which had briefly worn an animated expression, crumpled.

'Not at all,' said Oliver. 'A divorce could be arranged. Now, let's put the idea on hold and see if dinner's ready. Sarah wants to feed you up. I'll see what she's done about some wine.' Knowing her, a bottle of something white, light and dry would be chilling in the fridge.

'I think I'm a bit tiddly already,' said Midge. 'Sarah gave me an enormous gin and tonic.'

'Don't feel guilty because you can sometimes laugh again,' said Oliver. 'You will heal.'

'Will I? I think I'm getting worse.'

'That's because of the circumstances. Because it's all still going on. You'll get better very slowly. It's like having an amputation and learning to accept an artificial limb. The stump will always be prone to pain, but you'll manage.'

'Dan wouldn't like to be called a stump,' said Midge.

'I don't know. He was thin, but solid. Not a weeping willow sort of chap,' said Oliver. 'Come on, Midge. You need feeding,' and he took her hand and pulled her to her feet.

He was smiling, and Midge was flushed when they entered the kitchen. Sarah, noticing, wondered why.

Oliver did not mention his plans for restoring another doll's house, but he turned over in his mind how to find one which would be a challenge. It must be a period house, elaborate, needing a lot of work so that it would absorb him. He still had connections with the estate agent who had sold Prudence's Wiltshire house; he might know of another dolls' house coming up for sale. It would be worth asking him, before adopting other methods, such as advertising.

Midge's thoughts, however, were more concerned with Sarah's ideas for their joint future than with what she felt was Oliver's sudden whim.

22

Midge had two people with whom she might discuss Sarah's plans, but would it be disloyal to consult Prudence, who had known Sarah for much longer than she had known Midge? Uncertain, she decided that her professional counsellor would be the better, more impartial adviser. Midge could state her fears plainly: worries lest the business relationship damage the friendship between the two families and in particular the closeness between Jonathan and Judy. These anxieties could be dismissed or endorsed, and she might see other possible disadvantages that had not occurred to Midge.

She had slept surprisingly well in the comfortable spare bedroom at The Barn House. Perhaps it was because she was not alone. Sarah and Oliver were just along the passage in their large room with its pale cream carpet and vast bed. You could be two islands in it, Midge thought. She'd even eaten well; the sole was delicious and had seemed to melt in the mouth. Sarah could always run a restaurant, Midge had told her, if their communications centre, as Sarah was already calling it, did not succeed.

A curious calm came over her the next day. Sarah, her office still closed, ran Midge back to Deerton after breakfast, dropping her at the gate and saying she would be starting on the research for their project right away.

Midge went indoors, unpacked her few things, and then rang up the counsellor to bring forward her appointment if it were possible.

She had done nothing about those letters yet, the sympathetic messages of condolence. They were still arriving, now singly and at intervals, from people who had only just heard of Daniel's death.

Sarah would have dealt with them immediately, she thought. She might yet do it, if Midge told her of the problem. On her computer, she'd soon whip up a response and print it off in dozens.

The counsellor allotted her an appointment for the following day.

She came to see me soon after the second pair of delinquent youths had been arrested, seeming relieved that things could move forward now. Like their friends, they had been remanded in custody. As it was all sub judice not much had been mentioned in the media reports, but there was the suggestion that the weapon had been found and I felt sure that each of the four boys would now be blaming the others in order to save his own skin. General complicity was certain to be proved, and they would all go down for some years, even if only one of them was convicted of the murder. A manslaughter verdict was quite possible. After all, it had started as merely a rampage.

She accepted that it had begun that way and that there was no personal grudge against her husband. She was trying to modify her feelings towards the boys in the light of this knowledge, but I told her not to suppress her anger.

'*You should release it,*' *I told her.* '*You've a right to hate them, to demand punishment for what they did. There was no excusable provocation.*'

'*Some would say I should forgive them,*' *she said.*

'*Others would suggest that you forgive the sinner, not the* sin,' I answered, always ready with a platitude. 'And no one has the right to forgive on your behalf.'

'Getting angry won't bring Daniel back,' she said. 'Besides, how can I release it? I can't go round hitting people.'

'It's too cold to dig the garden,' I pronounced. 'Manual work releases tension. You could knead bread.'

'I scarcely eat any bread,' she said, taking me literally when I had been speaking metaphorically. 'And I should be working. Only there isn't much for me to do just now. Except the letters. I haven't tackled them.'

Nor would she. I could see her leaving them stuffed in a drawer, to be discovered after her own demise.

Then she told me about Sarah Foxton's plan for a joint operation in the premises now occupied by the almost defunct business she and her husband had run.

'The Foxtons are old friends,' she said. 'He's a solicitor. We had dinner with them the night Daniel died. They've been wonderful to me.'

She was able to say it now. That was an improvement.

'And how do you feel about it?' I asked.

It might be her salvation; a feeble individual to begin with, she had been deeply traumatised by her bereavement. Her husband's attitude appeared to have been paternalistic, protecting her from the full knowledge of their financial difficulties, though she was aware that the business was not thriving. The weak do not survive without support and this project, if it succeeded, could set her on her feet again in so far as that was possible.

'I'm quite intrigued,' she said. 'It would be a fresh start, and we've got the space. If we could get funds. Sarah thinks the bank might help.'

I'd been past her premises, partly curious to see them, partly when I was wondering about that old woman I had seen, whose face keeps coming into my mind. I'd looked up the Stewarts' *workplace address in the telephone directory. They hadn't run to the Yellow Pages, only the ordinary local one; an oversight, if they wanted customers. I'd wondered if the old woman could have been on the jury which convicted me, but there were only two women on it, one who was quite young and who would now be middle-aged; the older one had had red hair and freckles; she had looked like a barmaid and perhaps that was what she was. I'd had plenty of time to study their faces during the trial. Neither could have turned into this elegant person. She was always well turned out; I had seen her several times now, though at a distance as I wasn't keen to meet her again face to face.*

I decided to encourage Mrs Stewart in this new venture and claim credit if it succeeded, but, were it to fail, I needed to offer some caution to emphasise that she must make the choice, not I.

'Her husband is a solicitor, you said.' A professional man was not likely to encourage a questionable venture.

'Yes. They've been so kind to me,' she repeated. She had told me about them in previous consultations.

'If problems arise, I will be able to help you resolve them,' I reminded her. I should enjoy that; supervising her enterprise would provide me with an interest in the coming months.

'You think I should go ahead?'

'It's your decision. I think you've already made it,' I said, to push her into it.

I wondered if she was at all drawn towards Oliver Foxton. She was vulnerable and he had been kind: a recipe for some sort of sequel.

'Perhaps,' she said, still not convinced. I felt impatient.

'Is there anyone else whom you could consult?' I asked. 'A friend of all three of you, who knows your personalities?'

'Well – yes,' she hesitated. 'I had thought of asking her. She's known the Foxtons for some time, but though I'd met

her a few times, I've only got to know her since Dan died. She's been very understanding. She's a widow, too. Older than me, quite a bit.'

'Oh?'

'She's a Mrs Wilmot. Prudence Wilmot. She lives in Mickleburgh High Street not far from our workshop.'

Was this the mystery woman? Could Mrs Stewart have given me my answer? I asked her no more questions then. Besides, she'd had her allotted time. I'd find out more about this Prudence Wilmot during my patient's next appointment.

Midge felt guilty as she paid out another forty pounds. This was costing her a lot of money, and she had none to spare, yet it was such a relief to be able to reveal her worries to someone who was listening not from kindness, but because it was her professional duty, and who was not swayed by sentiment or pity.

Driving home, she saw that although she had supposed she was being encouraged to accept Sarah's suggestion, she had been given no firm advice, merely guided towards making up her own mind, but that was what counselling was about: helping you to work through your problems and confront your fears and doubts.

Prudence had told her that she would have to learn to let go of Daniel.

'But it won't happen for a long time,' she said. 'Maybe years. You don't want to, do you? You want to feel he's still with you.'

Midge did. She still expected to see him in the house or garden and sometimes spoke to him, surprised when he did not answer.

She would have to go in with Sarah, she concluded, turning off the main road into the lesser road for Deerton. What was in it, though, for Sarah? Surely she would earn more in her present job, where she was secure? She stood to lose money over this, whether her own or Oliver's. Midge was sure some capital would have to be produced up front to enable the business to be launched. A quarter's rent would have to be paid, for starters, and there would be the cost of adapting the workshop into the smart commercial premises Sarah had in mind.

Had something gone wrong at her own job? Did she want to leave it for some reason of her own? She couldn't possibly have been sacked; she was much too efficient. But if staff were being pruned, no one was safe, as Daniel had discovered.

Baffled, Midge turned in at her gate and had just put the car away when footsteps approached and she saw Peter's mother standing in the drive.

'I hope I didn't startle you, Mrs Stewart,' said Gwen Grant. 'I came to see how you are. You'll have heard about those other arrests.'

'Oh, Mrs Grant – how nice of you – do come in,' said Midge, suddenly glad of the presence of this kind woman, with whom she was linked irrevocably by a violent event. 'Come and have a cup of tea,' she added. She could do with one herself, she who had, for weeks, seldom thought about sustenance of any kind, drinking water if she felt thirsty.

She unlocked the back door with a key she took from a nail banged into the wall of the house and covered with ivy. They had almost always used the back door when going out in the car, as it was so much closer to the garage.

'I hope you watch who sees you with that key, Mrs Stewart,' said Gwen.

'Oh yes,' said Midge airily. She was going to add that strict vigilance wasn't essential here in Deerton when she swallowed the remark. It simply wasn't true.

Gwen followed her into the house and once again put the kettle on while Midge took off her coat, washed her hands and pulled a hasty comb through her hair. There was no fire in the sitting room; ashes lay in the hearth, and it was very cold. To save fuel, Midge had been running the heating very sparingly, but this meant that the house took a long time to warm up.

'Let's stay in the kitchen,' she said. 'It's the warmest room. The Aga's wonderful and keeps the whole house warm.' This was not strictly true, though there was a warm core where the flue ascended.

Gwen Grant's own much smaller, more modern house, less solidly built than this, was nevertheless well insulated by the efforts of her husband and it was snug, with electric heating throughout, expensive but effective. There was no mains gas in Deerton.

'I came to see how you felt. After those arrests,' she repeated as they sat at the table, the brown teapot before them.

'How do you feel?' Midge parried.

'Ever so relieved,' said her guest. 'And for my boy. What a load off his mind. He wouldn't blab, you see. Even though his dad was hurt – and look at what happened to Mr Stewart. He still wasn't going to tell. Kids are strange, aren't they? They won't tell on their friends even if it's something serious, like this. Not that them boys are friends of Peter's. Were your lads like that?' They'd been nice boys, she remembered, and were now agreeable young men. They'd be a great help to their mother, but then they were both away. They had their lives.

'They were never put in such a spot,' said Midge. 'None of their friends ever did anything nearly on a par with this.'

She suddenly felt that she could eat a biscuit. Midge rose and fetched the tin in which there were a few tired Hobnobs. Mark liked them. Mrs Grant accepted one and they both nibbled while they continued their conversation.

'Parents don't always drop their children in it, either, do they? Even when they know they've done something dreadful,' said Gwen. 'Trevor's mother was brave – hard, even – ringing up the police when she found the knife in her car.'

'Is that what happened?'

'Yes. Didn't you know?'

'The police weren't saying much,' said Midge. 'They came to see me – the superintendent did – Mr Fisher. He just said they'd found the weapon and made two more arrests. He did mention the car – said something about them having sorted out what had happened.'

'Well, I can tell you, she was cleaning her car ready to sell it – it's advertised this weekend – but she can't sell it now, of course, because the police have got it. Testing it. She found the knife under the driver's seat. It wasn't her Trevor as used it; we know that. It was one of them first two that got arrested – that Kevin, Peter's saying now – but Trevor took the car. Her Lada. They didn't steal one, like the police thought. She was out – his mum, and his dad – and he borrowed it, he said. Right nerve, he had. Some sort of dare, he told her. She's a nice woman, Trevor's mother. I know her. She doesn't deserve this.'

'No. Poor woman. Her son probably only meant to swank around a bit in the car with his mates,' said Midge.

'That's what she said. And now look at the trouble he's in.'

'Were they drunk?' Midge asked.

'Well, there were those empty beer cans left in the Noakeses' house,' said Gwen. 'It's likely.'

The two women looked at one another across the table – the slightly younger one whose husband, with his own successful business, had not been badly hurt and whose son had been involved on the side of the angels, and the other, now bereft, and barely coping.

'I'm ever so sorry, Mrs Stewart,' said Gwen. 'I feel so bad that we've been lucky over this, and you haven't.' She'd had another bit of private luck, too, which it would be wrong to mention in these circumstances.

'Don't feel bad,' said Midge. 'None of this is your fault, and it must have been very hard for Peter. At least there aren't two new widows in the village. And my sons are grown up. Mark's working, and Jonathan is in his second year at university.'

'He will stay there, won't he?' Gwen asked.

'Oh, he must,' said Midge. 'We'll manage that.' There was his grant, after all.

'What about the business?' This was delicate territory. Ted and Gwen knew the workshop; they had pottered in there and found nothing that they wanted, but Gwen had had a picture framed, a flower print she had bought at a car boot sale; Midge had done it nicely and she didn't charge a lot. Not enough, probably, thought Gwen now.

'Well, it's not going too well,' Midge admitted. 'It wasn't even before – before.'

'I see,' said Gwen.

'I'm going to have to give it up,' said Midge.

'Oh dear,' said Gwen. 'Still, it'd be a lot for you to manage on your own.'

'Well – yes. But I'll need another job. I'm thinking about it,' Midge told her. Then, wanting to get away from the subject, she said, 'That woman – Trevor's mother – must have had an awful shock. She did the right thing, of course, but it was brave.'

'I suppose she did,' said Gwen, who was not certain.

After Mrs Stewart left me, I had another bereaved patient, a man who was plunged into despair by the death of his dog, which at the time was fourteen years of age. They'd been mutually devoted, said my patient. The dog was obedient to his least command, welcomed him, made no demands, gave him more affection than he received from his family.

I nodded as he told me this, his hands twisting in his lap, his voice unsteady, so like Mrs Stewart.

This was his first consultation and when I asked him why he had come to me, he said his wife was unsympathetic about his loss and at last had told him to get his head sorted out. Then he'd seen my advertisement in a local paper.

'Would you grieve like this if it was your wife who had died?' I asked him, and he looked astonished.

'I haven't thought about it,' he replied.

'Think about it now,' I suggested, and after a short pause, out came a tale of resentment towards his wife and how his love had been diverted to the dog which never questioned him or went against his wishes.

I asked about his wife. She worked for a local firm, keeping the books, I gathered; he seemed vague about her actual duties; and she performed with an amateur dramatic society. Their daughter was at college, with her own interests. The son was still at school.

'You feel that none of them have time for you. Is that right?' I asked.

He agreed, but said that he brought in the income and they should be grateful.

'Your wife seems to contribute,' I pointed out, and he had to admit that this was true. They ran a joint account. Foolish woman, I thought; she should preserve her independence.

'You want to control her and she won't allow it,' was my diagnosis.

'That isn't true,' he indignantly denied.

'She's doing her own thing, and you don't like it,' I insisted. 'Your dog was happy to obey you. Your wife is not.'

I discovered that the dog was an Alsatian, a sizeable dog to have about the place, whether you are a dog-lover or not. I'm not.

'He was your wife's dog too? The family pet?'

'No. He was mine – a one-man dog.'

'Who fed him? Prepared his bowls of Chappie, or whatever you gave him?'

'She did. My wife.' When I did not reply he added, *'She doesn't like me in her kitchen.'*

'Who took him for walks? You?'

'When I was at home. I have to travel for my work and can be away for several days.'

'So your wife, who didn't want the dog in the first place, unless I have misunderstood you, had to assume responsibility for it in your absence, and look after it? A large, strong dog, which she had to take for walks?'

'Yes.'

'I see.'

I longed to tell him what a selfish monster he was, but I had to master my desire. This was a patient whose treatment could be made to run and run, if I controlled the hostility he aroused in me.

'Have you no other friends? Only the dog?' I asked him.

'Work colleagues. I have no need of others. I have my family,' he said.

But he hadn't: not really. Odd how so many men lack real friends. Perhaps, in the power struggle, women are easier to subdue than men and so they keep a female at home to dominate. And, in his case, for company, a dog.

I sent the man away with a string of appointments booked for when he can fit them in among the other demands upon his time.

'Are you going to get another one?' I asked.

'Another what?'

Stupid man.

'Another dog,' I said. *'Why not?'*

'She says she'll leave me if I do,' he answered. *'My wife.'*

'We'll take it from there next time,' I promised him.

It could be interesting. Had he thought of acquiring another wife instead of the one he'd got? I'd ask him, in due course.

I wondered why the wife had not sought another husband.

23

Oliver had decided that he must return the dolls' house to Prudence as soon as possible. The temptation to play games with its inhabitants was becoming dangerous, and now he was not the only player. When he found another one to renovate, it would have no occupants; Midge could select some at her leisure.

Returning from the office on the day that Midge had entertained Mrs Grant to tea, he found Sarah home early. She had been to Birmingham again, where her work had been over sooner than she had expected. Everything was going well for Charles and Hugh in their restaurant. Her task there was completed.

'Looks good,' he said, seeing diced chicken, strips of carrots, and chopped herbs all waiting to be assembled. 'There's no need to take so much trouble just for me. I'd be happy with a simple meal and I'll gladly help you with the cooking.'

'It's my job,' said Sarah stiffly. 'Aren't you satisfied?'

'Of course I am. You're a wonderful cook,' he said. 'But you're out all day too, and you have a longer journey than I have, and today I know you've had a train trip.'

'So what?' said Sarah. 'I won't be travelling much when I'm in partnership with Midge.'

She'd already sent in a letter of resignation. Doing so had given her great deal of satisfaction. Would she be entreated to withdraw it?

'Are you sure about that?' he asked her. 'Do you think it will work? Won't you find coping with her in her present nervous state difficult? I don't imagine she's going to improve much until the trial is over, and even then it may take months for her to adjust.' Or years, he thought.

'I thought you wanted everyone to help her,' Sarah said. 'You didn't oppose the idea when we were discussing it. Why change your mind now?'

'I haven't changed it. Not if it's what you really want and if it will make you happy, and providing we establish that it is likely to be profitable. But you can't build your future on a wish to help Midge. There are other solutions for her problems.'

'Yes, and she's looking for them,' said Sarah. She finished laying chicken slices in a dish and added a mixture from a waiting bowl. Then she put it in the oven, closing the door firmly. 'She's seeing a shrink of sorts,' she said. 'When I got back from Birmingham, a road was up near the station and I had to take a diversion. Who should I see coming out of a house ahead of me but Midge? I recognised her at once, and slowed down, but she got into the Volvo without noticing me, and drove off.' Sarah paused. 'I parked in the slot she'd just left and took a look. There was this brass plate on the front door.'

'You went right up to it? Through the gate and up the path?' He could not believe what he was hearing.

'There wasn't a path or a gate. The front door was only a few feet from the pavement, with just a low wall along either side of it. I could read it easily without going too near. I wrote it down,' said Sarah. 'Counsellor, it said, and some initials after it. Some qualification, I suppose. All tasteful. Brass, shiny, well polished, and a glossy front door. Looked all right, if you want to judge by appearances.'

'Oh dear,' said Oliver. 'I wonder if the doctor referred her to this person?'

'Who knows? She never mentioned it to me, if so, but then why would she?' Sarah said.

'What made you stop and investigate?' Oliver asked. It seemed an extraordinary thing for her to do. She was usually too wrapped up in her own affairs to have much time for those of others.

Sarah did not want to answer this. She was astonished at herself. She had, in fact, wondered if Midge had been meeting some man there, though it seemed unlikely, but you could never tell. She couldn't admit this to Oliver. He would be horrified.

'I don't know,' she said. 'I suppose I was just curious. She's seemed so hopeless. At least she's trying to do something about it, which is good.'

Was it, though?

'If she was sent there by the doctor, then that's fine – probably a good idea. But if it's some quack—' His voice trailed off. 'There are some unqualified people about,' he said.

'Well, there were these initials,' Sarah reminded him. 'And it said "doctor". I noticed that. Perhaps we could check in some register.'

'Yes. That's a good idea.'

'I'll do it,' Sarah said. 'The name and address are in my diary, in my bag.'

But she forgot about it.

After dinner, Oliver put the finishing touches to the dolls' house, and the next morning he loaded it into the car before leaving for the office. He'd take it round to Prudence in the evening, and while he was there, he'd tell her about Midge seeing the counsellor, and about Sarah's plans for their partnership. Her views would be worth hearing.

During the day, when he had to deal with two feuding neighbours arguing over a boundary and the trespassing of the bull terrier of one party into the garden of the other, draw up two wills, act for the vendor of one house and the buyer of another, and advise a client who faced a slander allegation, Oliver had allowed himself, at intervals, to anticipate the attractions of a civilised half hour in Prudence's small sitting room. Not wanting to disturb her if she was working on her book, he faxed her to see if his visit would be convenient and soon had an answer, saying she would be delighted to see him. Later, anxious about Midge, he telephoned her at the workshop where she was sorting things out. She didn't intend to stay long. She had no framing orders, and had thought it might be a good idea to list her stock. As she would be closing the business, she would have to sell it for whatever she could get.

This was practical. She was accepting the inevitable and was doing something positive about it. Maybe the counselling had already done her good.

Prudence was pleased to see him, and she was delighted with the dolls' house. At her direction, Oliver put it on a table by the window, and she spent some time admiring it, inspecting all the rooms and rearranging the furniture in accordance with what she remembered from her childhood.

'Emily may have fixed it up differently,' she said. 'She was my younger sister – I was much older – and she played with it, and then her daughter did. My niece.'

'You don't talk about her. Where is she? Your sister?'

'She's dead. She was murdered,' Prudence said. 'It was years ago.'

'Murdered?'

'You'll remember it, perhaps, although you must have been a very young man at the time. It was notorious. A woman – well, she was little more than a girl – who was having an affair with my brother-in-law stabbed her to get her out of the way.

She thought that he would marry her. Of course, he loved my sister, really.' Prudence had had to keep assuring herself of this, in order to be able to speak to Lionel civilly, and help him with the children. She told Oliver a few more details and he recalled the case. 'As we were both married, we had different surnames, so you wouldn't have connected it,' she said.

'Do you know if she's been released? Wendy Tyler?' he asked. She must have been after all this time, unless she had been troublesome in prison.

'Yes, I'm sure she has,' said Prudence. 'She wouldn't have served more than about ten years, if she behaved well, and I expect she did, in order to get out. In fact, Oliver, I think I've seen her. Oh, it's such a relief to tell you! I think I saw her in Mickleburgh just after Daniel was killed. I passed her in the street. I'm certain it was her. I saw that face every day in court, at her trial. Hard, showing no remorse, even making out that Lionel had suggested she do it, which was never wholly disproved though there was no evidence to support it. He denied it, naturally, and I believed him. He never got over his feeling of guilt. Emily was pregnant at the time. It was terrible.'

'How dreadful,' said Oliver. He was horrified. 'Where's he now? Lionel, is it?'

'He took the children to Canada. He became an alcoholic and he died about eighteen months ago. Suicide,' she told him.

'And this Wendy Tyler? Are you saying she's living here now? In Mickleburgh?'

'I don't know. I looked her up in the telephone directory but there's no W. Tyler. She's probably changed her name.'

'Perhaps she was only passing through,' said Oliver.

'I've thought of that,' said Prudence. 'And if it was her, she wouldn't recognise me. I've changed more than she has – white hair and wrinkles – and she wouldn't have noticed me in court. We'd never met. I wasn't a witness.'

'To set your mind at rest, I could try to find out what's happened to her,' said Oliver. 'She's on licence, after all. She's only got to slip up and she'll be locked up again. If she has got a new name, someone must know what she's calling herself.' But she would not be listed in a register of past offenders. There was no such simple record. She was free to move about at will.

'Could you? Without being morbid about it, I think I'd like to know. But really I'm trying to forget about her. I'm not expecting to see her whenever I go out.' She was still standing looking at the dolls' house, noticing the new adult woman doll, wondering why Oliver had added it to the family. She decided not to ask him. 'This smaller girl was meant to be Emily,' she said.

They sat down by the fire and talked about the horror of murder, and the evilness of jealousy, and then Oliver told her about Midge consulting a counsellor. He said that Sarah had discovered it by accident, which was the truth.

'Maybe it's not a bad idea,' said Prudence. 'It depends on the skill and training of whoever she's seeing. But some are so intrusive, and not trained at all.'

'That's what I'm afraid of,' Oliver declared.

24

The full statements which the four victimised boys had now given, together with the scientific evidence – the knife had yielded a clear thumbprint from Kevin and blood-stains found on Paul's clothing matched Daniel Stewart's blood – put both those boys at the murder scene and could prove that Kevin was his killer. Trevor's evidence, admitting that he took the car but denying any part in the violence, contributed. Each guilty youth condemned the others, providing enough corroboration for the Crown Prosecution Service to proceed with murder charges, and after the preliminary hearing, they were committed for trial at the Crown Court.

This was a happier time for Jamie and his friends, now freed from their moral dilemma. They did not talk about the case at school, and even avoided mentioning it among themselves, postponing, in their minds, the knowledge that they must give evidence in court. In case any of them thought of dodging this, Fisher had explained about subpoenas and how they must attend. Kate had suggested to Jamie that, independently of the statement he had made to the police, he should write down what he remembered of that fatal night, because it would be months before the case came up, and his memory might fade. Then he could forget it till just before the trial. He did this, hating the task, but once it was done he felt liberated. Among the innocent boys, his evidence was the most important, because he had summoned Daniel, was at the scene throughout apart from those few minutes, and had been wounded. The others could testify accurately only about the vandalism and the general assault outside.

There was talk of counselling, but it could interfere with their memories of the event and might have to wait; however, the parents all rejected the idea. Their boys could face up to what had happened, Ted Grant robustly declared, and so could he. The headmaster, at the start of the new term, had spoken about the crime in general terms, naming none of the boys concerned but deploring the alleged involvement of pupils from the school in such a dreadful incident. He touched on the importance of being a good neighbour, as the dead man had proved to be, and on the folly of mindless vandalism which could escalate so tragically.

Most of the staff, and particularly Kate, were pleased that he had said so much. The feeling was that once the boys had been convicted, he might go further, but until they had been proved guilty, he must be careful not to seem to prejudge the outcome of the trial. A verdict of manslaughter for all of them was foretold, even for the one who had used the knife.

'If they hadn't had the knife, they might have thumped the two men and Jamie, but no one would have been killed,' said someone.

There were problems in the school with disruptive pupils, but control was generally maintained. What happened outside school hours was outside staff jurisdiction.

'It's frightening,' said Ginny. 'Some of these kids have no respect for other people.'

'There's respect for animals,' said Kate. 'Those same boys might have gone bananas over a puppy.'

'You're not necessarily right about that,' said Bob. 'Some kids enjoy tormenting animals.'

'Some,' agreed Ginny, emphasising the word. 'Do we know if any of these charming adolescents kept hamsters or rabbits?'

No one did.

'I feel sorry for Trevor's mother,' Ginny said. 'She'll be getting hell from those who think she shouldn't have turned him in.'

'She gets my admiration,' Bob said firmly.

Ginny's remark had been apt. Those who knew who the four boys were – families who lived near them and their contemporaries at school – soon spread the word, and the parents had received hate mail. Slogans had been sprayed on the walls of their houses, and Trevor's mother had been jeered and mocked by two factions: those who deplored the crime and those who called her unnatural because she had surrendered her son to the cause of justice. If adults behaved like this, was it surprising that youngsters were so turbulent?

Some time after she took possession of the dolls' house, Prudence, who had not seen Midge recently, rang her at the workshop and invited her to call in on her way home and stay to supper, if she didn't mind the dark drive back to Deerton.

'I've got something to show you,' she said.

Midge, who had been continuing the dreary task of making an inventory of her stock, with, when she could find the relevant receipt, what had been paid for each acquisition, and whose only relief had been an occasional framing commission, accepted with pleasure, tinged with diffidence.

'Please don't go to any trouble,' she said, not adding that she still had no appetite.

'We'll eat early,' Prudence said. 'Then you won't be too

late getting back.' And she could spend some time on the set of proofs which had come that morning.

When Midge arrived, Prudence took her coat and led her straight to the sitting room where the dolls' house stood on a table in the window.

'Look!' she said. 'Oliver has finished restoring it and given it to me. I know you've watched its progress while he's been working on it. I'm so delighted with it.'

'I'm sure you are. It's lovely,' said Midge. 'Can't you just imagine their lives – the people in the house, I mean. How's Mr Wilberforce?' At Christmas, when Mr Wilberforce had been laid out on the floor – perhaps having supped too much of the Christmas claret, Prudence had suggested at the time – Midge had explained how, on a whim, she had christened him. 'Ah – there he is,' she said, and she beamed as she saw the father doll in the armchair by the fire. 'He's relaxing after his day in the city,' she declared. 'He's a financial magnate, isn't he?'

Prudence was enchanted by this sudden burst from Midge, and, as if her guest were a child with whom she was colluding in a game, she said, 'I think he's an industrialist who makes carpets.'

'Was that what your father did? Did you pretend it was him?' asked Midge, turning to face her, a rush of sudden colour in her cheeks.

'Yes,' said Prudence. 'And we were the family. My brother and my sister.'

'You said you had a niece who played with the house. Will she be coming to see you? Will she see it again? Won't she be thrilled with it?'

'I hope she will come over one day,' Prudence said. 'She lives in Canada.' She hesitated, and then said, 'When she was five years old, her mother was murdered. She was my younger sister. She was stabbed to death.'

Was it right to tell Midge this? Prudence waited for her reaction.

'Oh! Oh, how terrible!' Midge had now turned pale and sought about for a chair, into which she almost collapsed. 'Oh – I didn't know.'

'How could you? It was a very long time ago.'

'Who killed her? Was it like Daniel?'

'No. It was a premeditated crime. My sister's husband had been having an affair and the woman – his mistress—' She paused. That word was seldom used these days. 'She thought he would marry her if my sister was removed.'

'Oh no! Oh, that's much worse than how Daniel died,' said Midge. 'His death was a random accident. That boy hadn't set out to kill him. But to hate someone enough to want to murder them – oh!' She put her head in her hands and rocked to and fro in distress.

Prudence watched her. Was this a wise way to be proceeding? Would this be damaging to Midge, or would it help her to accept her own grief?

'It was dreadful,' she said. 'My brother-in-law never got over it – never forgave himself.'

'He couldn't have known such a fearful thing would happen,' said Midge. 'Plenty of people have affairs without them ending in murder.'

But some affairs do end in violence, Prudence reflected, and some lead to divorce, and many involve pain and misery.

'He went to Canada,' she said. 'He married again, but that didn't last. He's dead now.'

She would not tell Midge that Lionel had taken his own life. That was too much to expect her to absorb.

'Oh – that's terrible! And what about your niece? Were there other children?'

'Yes. There was an older boy. And Emily was pregnant when she died,' said Prudence.

'Oh, the poor woman! What a shocking thing! She was the innocent one,' said Midge.

'Isn't the victim almost always innocent? Except when it's gangs and drugs?' Prudence said, and added, 'The children are all right – they are survivors. My niece is a television reporter and my nephew is a marine biologist.' She remembered how Lally had called one of the dolls Wendy, and the game she had played with her, and suppressed a shiver.

'And what about the one who did it? The murderer?'

'She was eventually released,' said Prudence. 'I expect she's leading a normal life now. She may have married – had a family. Who knows? She'll probably have changed her name.'

'That's not right,' said Midge. 'Not when she caused so much anguish.'

Anguish: yes, that was the *mot juste*, thought Prudence.

'I rather tend to agree,' said Prudence. 'The argument is that although sentenced to life imprisonment, serving a number of years in prison wipes the slate clean.'

'But you can't cancel that sort of debt. That doesn't bring back your sister or give those children their mother.'

'No. I agree,' said Prudence.

'And those boys who killed Daniel will get out, too, one day,' Midge said. 'They may get married and their wives won't know what they've done.'

'It's possible.'

'Forgive and forget, eh?'

'It won't hurt so much after a while,' said Prudence. 'After quite a long while.'

'Oddly enough, I don't feel bitter towards the boys,' said Midge. 'I blame myself for not going with Daniel and in a way I blame him for being so bloody brave and reckless.' Saying that, she burst into tears.

Prudence produced a box of tissues, and Midge took a bundle from it, blowing her nose and dabbing at her eyes.

'I mustn't keep on crying like this,' she apologised. 'She says I'll have to stop some time. Maybe that should be today.'

'Who says?' asked Prudence carefully. She had set the whole evening up with the intention of trying to prod Midge into revealing that she was seeing a counsellor. Here was the opportunity, arrived at not by her guile but by Midge's own disclosure, for surely this must be the 'she' to whom she had referred.

'Oh—' Midge crumpled up her sodden tissues and took some new ones from the box. Prudence rose to put the wastepaper basket near her, in case she threw the wet mess into the realistic coal-effect gas fire. 'I've been to see this woman. A counsellor.' Midge looked sheepish. 'You may think it's weak and silly of me, but I was weary of boring Oliver and Sarah and everyone, and I thought she might help me sort myself out.'

'And is she helping?' Prudence asked.

'I don't know. I talk about it, and what to do. I suppose mostly she just listens,' Midge declared. 'She thinks it was a dreadful thing to happen, but everyone's agreed on that. None of it brings Daniel back.'

'No – well, nothing can. That is the tragedy. It's so final,' Prudence said. 'And not having had the chance to say goodbye must be so hard. It must seem unendurable, but in the end it is bearable. You've lasted this long, and I think you've been most courageous. The trial will be an ordeal, but you needn't go to it, except if you're needed as a witness, unless you want to. Once it's over, you must try to rule a line under that part of your life and move on to a new chapter.'

'I'll have to go to court. I'll have to see it through to the end. For Daniel,' said Midge.

She might change her mind by the time the case was heard, reflected Prudence. Midge had reached the point of wanting to help herself: indeed, she had never left that position and much of her current agony was due to her own high expectations of herself.

'Be content to make haste slowly,' Prudence advised. 'You can't leap up, miraculously healed and consoled, overnight. Tell me about this counsellor. It's a woman – you mentioned "she" – did the doctor send you to her?'

'No. I found her card pushed through my door one day,' said Midge. 'So when I was feeling pretty desperate, I made an appointment. I've been several times. I'm going next week. Look – I've got her card here.' She fumbled in her handbag, pulled out a battered purse, and took the card from a collection wedged into a small inner pocket. 'She thinks I should go ahead with the partnership with Sarah,' she added, and then, more honestly, 'Well – not exactly – she didn't say, one way or another. She told me I must make up my own mind.' She handed the card to Prudence.

Prudence looked at the card, did her best to memorise the name and the address, returned it, and, on the pretext of getting both of them a drink and out of sight of Midge, wrote the details down. What was all this about a partnership with Sarah? Over their drinks, she asked Midge, who explained, her anxieties obvious as she spoke, although she seemed to consider that the scheme would be her economic salvation. Prudence shared her apprehension. The enterprise might turn out to be a commercial success, but how long would it be before Sarah grew tired of it and pulled out?

'I don't think I've got a choice,' Midge was saying. 'It's this or go bust.'

'You could sell out your part, once it's got going. Someone will want to buy it then,' said Prudence, echoing Oliver.

'Yes,' said Midge. 'I suppose so.' She sounded doubtful.

'Is this counsellor really doing you good?' asked Prudence.

'I don't know. How can I tell? I still can't sleep, and I weep buckets.'

'Why didn't you go to Cruse?' asked Prudence. Cruse specialised in bereavement counselling and did valuable work.

'I never thought of it. I went to her because her card arrived like a sign,' said Midge. 'But you make me feel much better than she does. You understand.'

'I don't suppose she's done you any harm,' said Prudence. 'Let's see if I can coax you into eating something.' She had put a fish pie – light and tasty – in the oven earlier and hoped it would not have dried up by now.

Driving home, after a meal during which Prudence had regaled her with a rundown of the book she was working on, Midge felt comforted. For a wonder, she had actually enjoyed the food. Prudence had given her small helpings and she had eaten everything. Prudence Wilmot was a kind, wise woman and, amazingly, she too had met murder at close quarters. What had she meant when she said that the professional counsellor had done Midge no harm? Did she consider that the sessions had also done no good?

Had they? Midge couldn't say for certain, and they were very expensive.

She hadn't told Prudence about Oliver's plan to renovate another dolls' house; he couldn't have really meant it, and it wouldn't happen.

25

When Mrs Stewart kept her next appointment, I expected to hear her say that plans were under way for her joint venture with Sarah Foxton, but she came in looking subdued.

'This must be my last appointment,' she announced, astonishingly.

My previous patient was a teenage girl who had read about bulimia and had decided that she had it, and must effect a cure. I told her the truth – that the remedy lay with herself and she must cultivate self-discipline, which would lead her to develop self-respect, both of which I would help her to acquire. In my opinion, she is merely suffering from adolescent gluttony. Like many of my patients, she paid me in cash, and I wondered where she'd got it from, but did not ask. That was not my business. I was still musing on my plans to aid the girl when Mrs Stewart, early, rang the bell.

'Why have you decided to discontinue treatment?' I asked her. 'You need a long course – three or four months, at least.'

'I agree with you that I won't be back to normal in five minutes,' she replied. 'I'm sure you've helped me a great deal, and now I must begin to help myself.' Just what I had told my last patient she must do. 'And I can't afford any more sessions.'

'But I've pencilled you in twice weekly for the coming month,' I objected. She was a weak woman; it would be easy to make her change her mind.

'I didn't make any more appointments,' she declared with, for her, surprising firmness. 'As I've said, this must be the last.'

'I can see that it's the cost,' I said coldly. 'You can resume when you are in funds.' I would have liked to show her out immediately, but she had forty pounds for me in her purse, and I would part with her in a professional manner. 'Now, how have you been since your last visit?' I tried to smile, to reassure her lest she think I was offended. 'Have you firmed up your business plans?'

'No,' she said. 'And I'm not going to. It's all off.' Then, clearly relieved at having surmounted the difficult hurdle of telling me she was dispensing with my services, she said in a rush, 'I have a friend who has been very helpful – a Mrs Wilmot – I'm not sure if I have mentioned her to you before. I'm sorry to say I lost control the last time I went to see her, and made an idiot of myself, crying and so on.'

While she spoke, she gazed at me quite steadily, no sign of tears forming in those large blue eyes.

'And?' I prompted, bored now, but I must see the session through.

'She told me about the dolls' house,' she said, as it seemed inconsequentially, but patients do have trouble keeping to the point. I steer them back discreetly, as the need arises. Mrs Stewart did not wait for me to give her this guidance but forged on. 'It's a lovely old one. A model of a large house, which belonged to her and her sister when they were young. Oliver Foxton restored it and returned it to her. She told me about her sister, then.'

'What about her sister?' Where was this taking us?

'How she was murdered. It's so dreadful. Her husband had

a lover – a mistress – and she killed her. The mistress killed the sister. Stabbed her. She thought her lover would marry her if he was free.'

I was silent, but the pounding of the blood in my veins seemed so loud that I thought Mrs Stewart would hear it.

'What was her name?' I asked at last.

'Whose name?'

'The woman who was killed,' I almost screamed. 'Who was she?'

'I don't know,' she answered. 'I don't know what Mrs Wilmot's name was before she was married, and they would have had different names anyway. What does it matter?'

'I was just curious,' I said, trying to speak calmly. 'A counsellor is interested in everything.' What had got into this meek, depressed creature to make her show this unusual spirit?

'She was called Emily. I remember Mrs Wilmot saying that,' she said. 'The husband is dead, now, too.'

I heard this in silence. This must be the woman who had stared at me so intently in the street in Mickleburgh. I had my explanation. She must have been in court, and she would know my face although hers had made no impact on me.

'Presumably she was arrested and imprisoned,' I said coldly.

'Oh yes. But she would be out by now, walking around, as if nothing had happened,' Mrs Stewart said.

'She would have paid her debt to society,' I stated.

'That's a debt that can't be paid,' she said. 'Money embezzled or goods stolen can be returned but you can't return a life.'

'Loss of liberty is punishment,' I told her.

'It doesn't cancel the crime,' was her answer. She seemed to shake herself, then continued. 'When I heard about this – about Mrs Wilmot's niece who'd played with the house and lost her mother – my own tragedy seemed to diminish. My children are grown up and I had a long and happy marriage, with no other *person intervening. There is nothing to regret, only blessings to remember. I don't need any more counselling.'*

She rose to her feet and fumbled in her shabby bag, the usual preliminary to pulling out my fee.

'You haven't had your full time,' I said, but I was shaking. I wanted her to leave.

'I know. But of course I'll pay,' she said, and laid two scruffy twenty-pound notes on my desk. 'Thank you for your help.'

I did not show her out. It was all I could do not to lean forward and bang my head against the surface of my desk. I hadn't expected anything like this; I'd imagined that I'd met this woman – Mrs Wilmot – in some professional capacity – perhaps as a patient, or she could have been a doctor, or someone I had encountered in the normal run of life. She might even have run an exclusive dress shop. I don't buy cheap clothes. Being tall, I have difficulty in finding garments that are long enough.

I sat there, stunned. It had to be the same Emily, the one that I had sent on her last journey. A trick of fate had led me to the same area as that stupid bitch's sister. She may not have recognised me – may have thought she had just seen me somewhere – it's often difficult to recognise people seen out of context – but she could do so if we were to come face to face again. And to think I had walked round Mickleburgh and past her house, on the off chance of seeing her again. No wonder I had been haunted by her stare. But, aware now, I could avoid her. If I were to be exposed, I would lose everything I have built up over the years, my list of patients and my steady income.

What should I do? Should I move away and start yet again? I was in a district hundreds of miles from where it happened, yet this freak coincidence had occurred.

That silly little cow, Mrs Stewart: why did she have to upset me like this, after all I've done for her? Look how much I have helped her! And because she has been offered a business opportunity, even though it's been withdrawn, she thinks she is strong enough to stand alone, but I'm the one who's put her on her feet. Murder and bereavement brought her low, and I have raised her up. How grateful she should be, and she should have told me so in fulsome terms instead of those few perfunctory words uttered before leaving so abruptly.

I went out to the washroom, splashed my face in cold water and made a determined effort to regain command of myself for I had another patient needing me. Mr Leonard, the man mourning his dog, had the next appointment. Because stupid Mrs Stewart had left early, I had an interval in which to compose myself before his arrival, and, never one to waste time or give way to my emotions, I made up my accounts and checked my diary. I had a lot of bookings; there are plenty of isolated people reaching out for understanding. I've even got a Roman Catholic priest, who arrives dressed in jeans and a leather jacket. He is having problems over celibacy and chose to consult me rather than his superiors. Because of my regular church attendance, I am familiar with the scriptures and can discuss his predicament in an informed manner. I see he has an appointment in the week ahead. I shall have to devise a structure for the consultation. Simple lust is his dilemma. At first it was erotic dreams, he told me. Now his base thoughts and yearnings, as he sees them, have focused on a young woman in his congregation. He hasn't spoken to her outside the church; it's all in his head, a fantasy.

Why don't you get on with it, I long to say; talk to her, ask her out, become acquainted? But if he does, he thinks he will be tempted by the devil – in the guise, one imagines, of this blameless girl – and have an urge to make a physical approach. It's all so adolescent, but I must treat him seriously. I made notes on how to channel his vapid musings into more positive action, then brewed some coffee, which I needed now, drinking it down while still pensive about Mrs Wilmot.

Act of Violence

When the dog mourner, Mr Leonard, arrived, it was clear that he was very angry.

'Why, Mr Leonard, what has happened?' I asked, seeing his evident rage. This could be healthy; it could indicate that his mourning had advanced.

'She's left me,' he declared, his voice loud. 'She's gone – packed everything she thinks is hers, though much of it is mine, and moved out to a flat, taking my son with her.'

'What brought this about?' I asked, thinking, good for her, as he is a dreary, unattractive man. I looked at his puffy face, sulky mouth, and small, accusing eyes, and knew that whatever she was like, she was better off without him. I was her benefactor.

'I bought another dog,' he said. 'A new Alsatian with a pedigree.'

'So? She wasn't pleased?'

'It bit her,' he acknowledged. 'But it's only a puppy. It will learn.'

'A dog?' I asked, idly. 'Or a bitch?' I did not care which it was.

'A bitch.'

'Ah.' I made a note. 'And did you leave it in the house when you went to work?' He'd done that with the other dog, my notes reminded me.

'I couldn't take her with me,' he said. 'I had to leave her.' He'd started to refer to the dog by her gender, I observed.

'And what about your wife's work? She couldn't take the dog, either.'

'No, but she has a shorter day than I do, and she doesn't travel. I had to go to Brussels soon after I bought Phoebe – that's the dog – and when I returned, my wife had put her in kennels and had gone.'

I felt like saying, 'I hope you and Phoebe will be very happy together,' but restrained myself.

'And?' I prompted.

'Well – how am I to manage? I'm left doing all the housework and my own cooking, and there's Phoebe to be considered,' he said, almost ranting.

'You chose the dog in preference to your wife, Mr Leonard,' I pointed out. 'She told you what would happen if you went ahead.'

'I didn't think she meant it,' he replied, almost in a growl, like the dog. 'I thought it was an empty threat.'

'Do you want her back?'

'I don't want to be alone,' he said.

'But you're not alone. You've got Phoebe. You got along better with your other dog than with your wife. You've mentioned no friends, no social life. You have problems with relationships, Mr Leonard,' I told him, speaking sternly because after all, he had come to me for help and it was my task to guide him towards coming to terms with himself and his own nature.

'My dog wasn't so difficult – so demanding,' he complained.

'You took no trouble to please your wife. You don't need to think about a dog's emotions; all it needs is food,' I said.

He was thoughtful after I'd said that. I felt sorry for the wife – a most unusual experience as I try to be detached, and normally do not find it difficult, but it is by no means rare for me to dislike a patient. I like very few people, as it happens.

'Do you think I should go after her?' he asked. 'My wife?'

'That's up to you. Do you want her back, or do you want to keep the dog? You can always hire a cleaner for the housework.' He could afford my fees. He could pay for a cleaner and a laundry service.

I did not point out that, if necessary, he could pay for sex. That could be the subject of a further session.

He left at last, having written out his cheque, still consumed with self-pity, but less angry. As he walked towards the door I heard him mutter, 'You said I should get another dog.'

Perhaps I did.

26

As suddenly as she had decided to end her counselling sessions, Midge had made up her mind not to fall in with Sarah's plans. The resolution, reached on the way to keep her appointment, rocked her almost more than relinquishing her consultations in that plain white room with the plain, pale woman sitting across the desk from her, listening impassively to her disconnected ramblings. But like a revelation, Midge had realised that she must not jeopardise her friendship with the Foxtons by submitting to Sarah's brisk dominance. It could never be an equal partnership.

She'd have to get out of the lease in the least damaging way possible, but for that she would need Oliver's help. She'd have to give a reason for her change of mind that would not wound him, or hurt Sarah, and then stick to it. Sarah could still pursue the same scheme, in the same premises, but with another partner; with all her business contacts, surely she would find one?

With that all put in train, Midge would find what work she could. There must be something she was equipped to do.

Driving back to Deerton, her bridges burned, she felt as though a huge weight had been lifted from the top of her head. The dull ache in her chest remained, but perhaps she would get used to it and cease to be aware of it. Once home, she put the car away and then walked round the garden in the glow from the security light over the back door. Mark and Jonathan had decided that as she was on her own, she must have this extra protection, and they had got Ted Grant to fit lights at appropriate spots so that as you walked round the house they came on in sequence. That morning, she had noticed that the small spikes of bulbs, stiff as spears, were already pushing through the frozen ground. They'd bloom eventually; the daffodils would be bright beneath the apple trees, and the cherry would be smothered in pink blossom, but Daniel would see none of this. Last spring had been beautiful; he hadn't known that he would never see another.

Thinking this, Midge felt the warm tears pour down her face again. Where did they all come from, this unending stream? Half blind, she stumbled towards the house to be met by Gwen Grant, who had seen the lights come on and was walking round the side of the house in search of her.

Gwen's bountiful bleached hair stood out round her head in an aureole. She was teetering along in her fashion boots and shiny gold raincoat.

'Oh, Mrs Stewart – dear – Midge, isn't it? Don't cry, love,' pleaded Gwen. 'Come along in and let me make you some tea,' and she put an arm round Midge, leading her in though the back door, this time reaching out to unhook the hidden key herself.

This was the third time Mrs Grant had come round and plied her with tea, thought Midge, stifling an almost hysterical giggle as she allowed herself to be swept inside and guided to one of her own chairs while Gwen put the kettle on.

'My name's Gwen,' Mrs Grant reminded her. 'Now, weak and with sugar, isn't it?'

'No sugar,' Midge managed to reply.

'Well, a biscuit then. You need something sweet, blood sugar, you see,' said Gwen.

Without Midge explaining where they were, she found the tin, with still a few stale Hobnobs left. She'd get some more and pop them round, thought Gwen. She felt quite at home now in this kitchen. In search of milk, she opened the fridge; it was almost empty, and she clicked her tongue. The poor dear was skin and bone and here was proof that she wasn't eating properly.

After they'd had their tea, and Midge's tears had ceased to flow, Gwen explained the reason for her visit.

'We've got a plan, you see. Me and Ted. About the business. Your place. We wondered if you'd be interested, seeing as how Mr Stewart isn't here to do the furniture. We thought, if you were free tomorrow night, maybe you'd come with us to The Bridge for a meal, and then Ted'll put it to you, like.'

Midge stared at her. A plan?

'It's about a job,' said Gwen. 'And about your workshop.' She paused. This was very difficult. She'd told Ted they must give Mrs Stewart some clue about the reason for their invitation or she would be much too embarrassed to accept. 'I told Ted we must explain a bit first. Then you can think about it.'

'Explain what?' Midge was mystified.

'Explain as how Ted wants to expand and have a proper workshop, and he'll need some office help, which I can't give as I've got my own business, you see, and the books have got too much for me now that our Josie's married and gone away – well – we'll explain, if you'll come out with us. We thought we could talk it over during the meal. Our treat, of course,' she ended.

Midge couldn't believe what she was hearing. Miracles did happen, after all.

'You mean you want to take the workshop off my hands and offer me a job?' she said.

'That's it,' said Gwen, beaming at her. 'I think we'd all get along just fine. Details to be arranged.' Gwen intended to move her own hairdressing business into part of the premises, and branch out later into beauty treatment.

Midge managed not to say she would give the workshop away.

'Oh,' she said. 'My goodness.'

'You don't have to decide anything now,' Gwen told her. 'We'll tell you what we're thinking of, and then you can take your time making up your mind. What about if we pick you up at seven?'

'I'll be ready,' Midge said, still amazed. Ted hadn't yet sent in the bill for fitting the lights. What about that, now? She knew it would not come. At least Mark had bought the lights themselves at Argos, so there was no debt for them.

'See, there is light at the end of the tunnel,' Gwen couldn't resist saying.

After she had gone, Midge thought that maybe there was also life after death.

During the night, she wondered if they had devised this plan from pity, and the knowledge that Dan had died and Ted had not. But it was going to cost them. Had they had a sudden windfall?

She was waiting at the gate as they pulled out of Orchard Close. She wore her good coat over a black velvet skirt and waistcoat and a peasant blouse bought years ago on some holiday. She had lost so much weight that her clothes hung loosely on her, but she had washed her hair and put on make-up, adding mascara and brushing blusher on her cheeks.

Gwen was sitting in the back of the Vauxhall, and Ted leaped out to open the passenger door for Midge. She felt reckless and light-headed. No one except her hosts knew where she was going, and it was the first time she had visited a restaurant since the night Daniel died. Well, she had to do it sometime.

I mustn't drink too much, she told herself, and I mustn't cry. I must be calm and level-headed.

She'd been to The Bridge with Dan, but she wouldn't let herself remember that. Not tonight.

'We like this place,' said Gwen as Ted drove into the car park behind The Bridge. 'Our Josie used to work in the bar, when she was studying.'

Now Midge learned that Josie was expecting a baby in the summer. That topic kept them going for a while; Midge sensed that Gwen was anxious, conscious that their social circles did not overlap, but that soon passed as she and Midge drank white wine and Ted had a beer before they ordered. They sat by the log fire in the bar, studying the menu, and Midge let herself be guided into having casseroled pheasant, which Gwen had never tried and also chose, wishing to sample it. Ted, who had ordered steak, related how he had hit a pheasant on the road not many days before.

'Shame. It was a lovely bird but it didn't stand a chance – came out of nowhere,' he declared. He'd got out of the car to make sure it was dead, but had left it on the verge.

'What a waste,' said Gwen. 'It'd have made a nice supper for us.'

'I couldn't have fancied it. Not after that,' said Ted.

He had a tender heart, thought Midge. After a suitable pause to show respect for the slaughtered pheasant, she asked how Peter was, and heard that he was spending the evening with Jamie Preston. They were to do their homework together. Kate would see to it, said Gwen.

'Have they – the boys – got over it?' Midge asked. 'It must have been awful for them.'

'Yes, it was. Funny, weren't they, not speaking up? And just when they'd decided to, the knife turned up,' said Gwen. Neither Peter nor Barry had mentioned Mark's talk with them to their parents. 'But you can understand it in a way. At that age, they can't always see things straight, but it wasn't as if those four were their friends.'

'I expect they were confused,' said Midge. That was the word to use: she was confused, her counsellor had told her.

Further talk about the subject was interrupted by the approaching waitress.

'Here's the girl to say our meal's ready,' Gwen said. 'Come along, Midge. Is that really your name?'

Midge laughed.

'No. It's Marjorie, but I hated it when I was small and I didn't like Marge, and somehow it got turned into Midge and stuck. Not very dignified, but I'm used to it.'

'I'll stick to it then, if that's all right,' said Gwen firmly. 'But in the business, if you agree to our idea, you'll be Mrs Stewart. It's more respectful.'

'If you think so,' Midge said faintly.

'I do. There'll be young girls about, and they must mind their manners,' Gwen said. 'Now, we'll not talk about all that till we've eaten. We want you to enjoy your meal.'

Midge managed to consume the consommé she had asked for, deciding it was the lightest starter on the menu, and she ate some of the pheasant, hiding the rest under the bones. She quite enjoyed the ice cream she had for pudding; Ted had apple pie and Gwen chose chocolate mousse.

Afterwards, while they had coffee, Ted was frank.

'We had a bit of luck,' he said. 'It was just after all that business. Gwen had a win on the lottery – not the jackpot, mind. She and the friend she runs the salon with in Fettleton shared their stakes, and they won a tidy bit between them. They didn't want any publicity, so no one knows about it. Gwen's friend is going to live in Spain, but Gwen wants to keep the salon on, only its lease is up in March and she'd like new premises in a better area. Your place would be ideal – not central, but near enough, and with parking handy. I reckon I could open up the back to get the van in.' He was surprised Daniel Stewart hadn't done that; it would have made loading and unloading much easier. 'If I go in with her, using some of the space for spares and that, we can expand in both directions. Of course, we might need planning permission for a change of use, but they're already commercial premises. I don't think there'll be a problem.' He didn't tell her that a friend of his, a chartered surveyor, masquerading as a customer, had had a good look round and had deplored the misuse of space. The place had a high vaulted ceiling and he thought they could install an upper storey. 'There's a lot of work for a good electrician locally. I get contracts from builders and there's plenty of ordinary jobs, too. I'd hope to get a young lad in as an apprentice, until Peter's old enough, if he wants to join me.'

He beamed at Midge across the table, a confident man, very masculine, sure of his own skill and ability. There was no indecision here.

'How wonderful about the lottery,' she said. 'You did well to keep it quiet. I'll have to ask Oliver Foxton about the lease but I want to get rid of it. I'm sure that part will be all right. He's a solicitor – you know that.'

'We'll need a lawyer,' said Gwen. 'Maybe he'll look after us.' At the moment their winnings were sitting in a building society high interest account growing all the while. 'Then there's your little niche,' Gwen went on. Midge was wondering when they would come to that. 'I mentioned the books earlier. I'm not wonderful at that, so we thought you might take it on. You've been doing some of it, haven't you?' Midge had, until Daniel had tried to stop her discovering the extent of their losses. 'Then, if you fancied the idea, there's a need for a receptionist at the salon.' She'd add style and class, once Gwen had tactfully smartened her up a bit, and she would attract a certain type of customer. 'Some of my ladies will follow me from Fettleton,' Gwen said. 'They're used to me.'

They'd got it all worked out, and Midge could see it shaping up, the place gutted and refitted, with enough capital available to do it properly. There would be room to expand into light fittings and so on, if Ted wanted to. She pictured Gwen's part of the operation, with the row of basins and the overalled figures ministering to the needy heads.

'I think you'd better give me a new haircut,' she said, smiling. 'At the moment I'm not a very good advertisement for the new venture.'

27

'Has she made up her mind yet?'

Sarah looked at Oliver across the breakfast table. It was Saturday morning, and neither was going to work that day, so there was no easy separation. Oliver was planning on working outside, cold though it was. The shed needed clearing out and he could prepare the greenhouse for the tomatoes he would grow there later. Soon he'd have another dolls' house to restore; his estate agent contact knew of one a woman who had bought a house from him wanted to sell privately. Oliver had made an appointment to see it next weekend.

He knew at once what Sarah's abrupt question meant. She was frowning with impatience as she waited for his answer.

'I don't know,' he said. 'You must give her time, Sarah.'

'I don't know why she didn't jump at it,' Sarah complained. 'What choice has she, after all?'

'Several. She could sell the house, get rid of her lease, and move to France. Or Spain or Turkey,' said Oliver, plucking countries from his mind at random.

'Whatever for?'

'She could live more cheaply. Or marry a Turkish waiter,' said Oliver. 'Or both.'

'Now you're being ridiculous,' said Sarah. 'What's got

into you? You don't fancy her, do you?' She said this in so scornful a voice, deriding Midge's appeal as she had done before, that Oliver was incensed. 'You can't,' she answered her own question. 'She's a mess.'

In his head, Oliver counted to ten but reached only six. What if he were to say he lusted madly after Midge? What if it were true?

'You're the one who's talking nonsense,' he retorted sharply. 'It's Midge's future that's at stake, and her income. And her friendship with us. If anything were to go wrong – if you found you couldn't work together or the project failed – all these things would be jeopardised,' he said.

'It's my future and my income, too,' said Sarah.

'You won't starve if it flops,' he answered. 'And what if you get tired of it – or her? You do get tired and bored with things, Sarah. You know you do. Have you got bored with your job? Is that why you want a change?'

'I want to help her,' she declared.

'And yourself. You want someone you can push around, who won't stand up to you,' said Oliver, his tone still heated. 'You've never really been put to the test, Sarah. Even Judy, at her age, knows more about life's difficulties than you do.'

'Oliver! Whatever has got into you? Calm down. You'll have a heart attack if you go on like that,' said Sarah. 'You must be feeling ill, to speak to me in that unkind way.

Oliver took a deep breath and made an effort to compose himself. He did not approve of lost tempers.

'Not at all,' he said, more temperately. 'But I want you to understand that this is a very serious step you plan to take, and you won't be able to throw it away for some whim, if you don't enjoy it later. You have enough business experience to know that.' He paused; then, as she seemed about to speak, he went on, 'My life has been spent trying to make you happy and to please you, and I know I haven't always succeeded, but I'm not going to let you manipulate other people's lives just so that you can feel good.'

'Oliver!'

He turned away, afraid he might dredge up from his subconscious some observation which would do untold harm. Words uttered could not be revoked.

'I'm going to sort out the garden shed,' he said, and left, aware, with alarm, that he had parted from her feeling deeply hostile.

Going to the back lobby to put on his old gardening jacket and his rubber boots, Oliver was dismayed. He and Sarah were almost quarrelling; this was their second sharp exchange and each time it had been because of Midge. Whilst part of him was shocked and startled, he also felt a sense of freedom such as he had not known for years; it was as though he had pulled the stopper from a bottle, let out the genie of his repressed feelings, waved restraint and caution away. This might not be the end of it: Sarah might create a scene when he returned to the house, or she might pursue him down the garden, demanding his apology, though brooding silence and a sulky face were more her line.

Sarah, however, was not prepared to wait. She loaded the dishwasher with her breakfast things – Oliver had already stowed his away – and then went into his study. She'd wreck that dolls' house he had spent such hours on; pull the doors off, dismember the doll family and stamp on the furniture. That would really hurt him.

But it had gone. Preoccupied with her own plans, the cleaning taken care of, she had not been in his study since he took it back to Prudence.

She stared about her, her vengeful impulse thwarted. What had he made of her earlier subversive actions? Had he even noticed? Why should he take so much trouble over repairing a battered toy for an old woman? He'd never made anything for her.

Now it was Midge, Midge, Midge, the whole time. Midge, who was a weak, silly woman who had gone to pieces after Daniel's death. Sarah worked hard at whipping herself up into a mood of jealous resentment. She felt injured and neglected.

Against her will, she remembered the conference she had been to in Kent, not long after Daniel's death. She'd looked forward to it, the first one that involved a night away. The day's meetings had gone well and she had made a presentation which had been commended, but after dinner, when the evening ended, Clive Berry, her immediate superior, had come to her room. He seemed to think he had received an invitation. Sarah had been shocked and frightened as he closed the bedroom door behind him – she had opened it quite innocently when he knocked, thinking he had some message for her for the morning – but he had walked past her, carrying a bottle of champagne, set it down, and moved in on her. That was the wording Sarah's secretary, Daisy, used when describing a sexual approach. It was accurate. Clamped by two powerful arms, a sweating face looming over her, hard, slobbery wet lips pressed against her mouth while a huge tongue probed her lips apart and was thrust down her throat, she had understood that rape was easy because he was so strong. He pushed her against the bed and she fell back upon it, only then somehow managing to bring up her knee and kick him in the genitals.

He had let her go at once, doubling up in agony, and Sarah had made a dash for the door, hesitating there, reluctant to run into the corridor and shout for help. It would be so undignified. She opened it and managed to say, 'Please leave,' standing against it so that she could flee if he refused, but as soon as he could move, he went, picking up the bottle as he did so.

Sarah knew that if her kick had missed its target, the incident could have ended very differently. As it was, he had merely muttered, 'Bloody stuck-up bitch,' and a few more choice epithets. If it had been Midge, who was so small and slight, she might have been overpowered. Rape wasn't always committed by a stranger in an alley.

She had not told Oliver. After all, she had survived without more damage than some bruises on her upper arms, which he hadn't noticed as afterwards she had worn a nightdress with loose sleeves which hid them. However, she had felt humiliated. It had been so degrading; how could Clive have interpreted her friendly manner as an invitation? Since then he had picked on her, going out of his way to find fault with her work. He wanted her to leave, but of her own volition. Well, she was going to do so, and had handed in her resignation letter, saying that she intended to form her own company.

It was rather a pity she wasn't doing that, she thought: she should be setting up her own consultancy, not going in with Midge. Perhaps she had been hasty in proposing that idea, though she thought it was a good one. She might undo it; it wasn't too late. Oliver had just said so, more or less. If she started her own consultancy, she could work from home. She already had a computer; a fax could soon be installed, even a separate telephone line. The outlay would be minimal, and she could take some clients away from Clive.

She'd tell Oliver she had changed her mind, but not today. He must suffer first, repent his cruel words, apologise, and then she might forgive him, but she would not forget his unkindness.

Her morale restored, Sarah set about her Saturday morning chores, which were not demanding. She had just finished when she heard a car outside.

It was Midge.

There was a short ring and a tap of the heavy knocker, Midge's signal. It irritated Sarah that she advertised her presence in this individual way, since a glance from the hall window would reveal her car. Cross, she opened the door.

Midge, heavy with resolution, her courage screwed up tight,

did not notice Sarah's tension as she was admitted, and she did not act with her normal diffidence, starting her set speech at once.

Sarah, giving the door an extra push – it sometimes stuck, Oliver would have to see to it – heard with disbelief what she was saying.

'Sarah – sorry to barge in like this, but in fairness I must tell you straight away, and I didn't want to phone about something so important. Our business deal – your kind idea – it's off. I'm doing something else with the workshop.'

There! It was out; she'd said it. Relief poured over her.

But Sarah's reflexes were swift. She rallied. Frustration would not defeat her fighting spirit, and she said, 'I'd changed my plans, too.'

'Oh?' That did startle Midge. 'So I'm not letting you down, then,' she said. 'That's wonderful.'

The two were still standing in the hall. Pale winter sunlight filtered through the window, casting brilliant slats across the oak table in the centre, on which stood a brass bowl containing daffodil bulbs almost in bloom. Midge smiled nervously. There was no thought in her head that the reverse might apply; that Sarah was reneging on her offer.

'What are you going to do?' she asked, genuinely curious.

Sarah launched into an eloquent explanation of her plans. Midge listened carefully.

'Sounds good,' she said. 'No overheads, and you won't be depending on someone scatty like me. But won't you be lonely?'

'I'll probably need an assistant fairly soon,' said Sarah.

Midge had put her finger on the sole snag. Sarah needed someone to react against, not as company, but as an audience, though she did not think of it in those terms. At work, Daisy, who admired her greatly, fulfilled that role. Still, she'd discomfited Midge, kept the upper hand.

They had never moved from the hall. Sarah opened the door again to let Midge out, and did not stay to witness Oliver, who had seen the Volvo arrive, come round the side of the house and whisk her off to the garden shed, where he had been tinkering with the rotary mower.

There, Midge told him of her plans, and as long as they were subject to various safety clauses and considerations, and an appropriate contract, he applauded them.

Sarah, in a rage, never noticed that the Volvo had not been promptly driven off.

'It's that counsellor woman! She's made Midge change her mind,' stormed Sarah when, towards the end of the morning, by which time the shed was immaculate and the greenhouse ready for spring planting, Oliver returned to the house. Midge had not stayed long. She had a date to show Gwen and Ted Grant round the workshop.

'Midge told me that you said you were pulling out,' Oliver stated. He was calm now; the morning's labours, and Midge's news, had restored his good humour. He was relieved at Midge's decision not to collaborate with Sarah; she had told him she had made up her mind before she heard the Grants' proposal. The opportunity they offered was at least as good a prospect as Sarah's scheme, and she would be under much less strain as a paid member of the staff than as a committed partner. It wasn't always wise to go into partnership with a friend.

'Yes – well, it's true, but she wasn't to know that, coming round and springing it on me,' said Sarah. However, as she had not let Midge give her any details, she was in the dark about her plans.

'I imagine you're thankful,' said Oliver. 'Now you won't be leaving her in the lurch.'

'That counsellor person has a lot to answer for,' said Sarah, keen to milk the subject dry of every drop of disapproval she could squeeze from it.

'How do you know they discussed it?' Oliver asked her. 'I understand the Grants invited Midge out last night and put the idea to her then. She hasn't had time to consult the woman since.'

Who were the Grants? What was the idea? Sarah did not know, and she did not connect the Grants with Daniel's murder as she had paid scant attention to the identities of the various boys, the good ones or the bad.

'I see you've heard all about it,' she said.

'Yes. I saw Midge's car and came up just as she was leaving,' he replied.

'Trust you. You wouldn't let her go without talking to her,' said Sarah.

'No, I wouldn't, Sarah. Not if I saw her, and I'm surprised you didn't call me when she arrived.'

'There wasn't time. She was in and out of the house in seconds,' said Sarah sulkily.

That, at least, was true.

'Well, anyway,' said Oliver pacifically, 'it's all good news. Neither of you is abandoning the other. Let it rest.'

But Sarah couldn't. She was frightened. She had backed off from a plan that could have been successful, and which Oliver would have kept an eye on in the background. Now she had committed herself to a venture on her own, and if it failed, there would be no one else to blame, only circumstances, if they filled the bill.

'She told you what I intend to do, I suppose,' she said. 'Work from home?'

'It sounds a good scheme,' said Oliver. 'There's plenty of room. Later, when you're established, you might do better placed more centrally. You could look into renting an office when you've got going.'

He wasn't even going to disapprove, so giving her grounds for further argument.

'Maybe,' she said. She still didn't know what Midge's fine new plans were, but she was not going demean herself by asking.

Their light lunch was consumed in frosty silence. A telephone call from Judy, now back at university, was an interruption greeted with relief; she rang simply for a chat. Then Tim called to say he had exchanged duties with a colleague and was coming down that night.

'He needs sleep,' said Sarah, putting down the telephone. 'He's exhausted. Their hours are horrendous.'

'Yes,' agreed Oliver. At least she was briefly thinking of someone other than herself.

Tim's rare visits were undemanding as he was always so tired that he spent most of his time sleeping, while Sarah washed and ironed his clothes and cooked his favourite food.

She should have had more children. Then, as Oliver had failed to satisfy her, she might have been fulfilled, with younger ones coming on, needing her expert domestic skills.

He might have liked it, too.

Tim's presence helped them through the rest of the weekend. Though he was tired, he seemed happy and was enjoying his work. Oliver was proud of him, and Sarah's admiration shone from her; here was someone she really loved, thought Oliver, and spared a moment to reflect that it was lucky Tim hadn't brought a girl with him this time. None was mentioned during his brief visit; perhaps he was between women, or he might be seriously involved and not keen to expose a relationship he valued to Sarah's critical inspection.

He left early on Monday morning, and his parents later departed for their own concerns. Sarah, in the office, grimly working out her notice, was sorting through some files when, halfway through the morning, Clive entered, crossed over to her and, leaning close, told her that he wished she was not leaving and couldn't they be friends?

In the open-plan office, in front of other staff, Sarah did not wish to make a scene.

'I'm leaving. That's decided,' she replied.

'Have lunch with me,' he said. 'I'll be in The Verandah at one o'clock.'

The Verandah was in Mickleburgh, not far from the offices of Foxton and Smythe. What a place to choose, if he meant to set up an intimate encounter. But he might not know what her husband did; she had never told him. Coldly, she refused, and said she would stand by her resignation letter. At last he left, and she sent Daisy out for sandwiches. Sarah spent her lunch hour calculating what she must spend on setting herself up in Winbury and how long it would be before she could expect to see a profit. Midge had precipitated her into acting out her bluff, if bluff it was. She was restless and had applied for other jobs, but would she have left without one if Clive had not assaulted her? She could have reported him, made a fearful fuss, but an inner voice questioned whether, although she had certainly given him no encouragement, by not actively distancing herself, she might have seemed to signal green.

She was drinking her coffee when Daisy came rushing in, eager to impart some news startling enough to confound even Sarah. One of the juniors had accused Clive of sexual harassment. She had complained to the managing director himself, and was prepared to sue. What about that? Daisy's blue eyes were enormous in her cheerful face.

'What did he do?' asked Sarah.

So that was why he had invited her out to lunch. He wanted to make sure she didn't support the girl's allegations. If they had a social meal together subsequently, she would lose credibility. What a creep he was.

'Pressed against her by the copier. Touched her up. Made personal comments and improper suggestions,' said Daisy primly. 'He's a sleaze-bag, Sarah. You don't like him, do you?' Just recently, that had been obvious, though they had seemed to get along all right until that conference in Kent, which Daisy had not been to as it was for senior staff.

'I can't say he's my favourite person,' Sarah answered rather curtly.

'He gave me a lift home once, and groped me in the car. I soon hopped out,' said Daisy. 'He said she could leave. Jenny, I mean. Told her she was insolent.'

Sarah, to her own astonishment, for she thought she was never impulsive, heard herself saying, 'I'll back up her story. He harassed me at the Kent conference.'

'No!' Daisy's eyes grew even rounder and still larger.

'Yes.' She felt a glow of righteousness surge over her. 'I'll talk to Jenny. We'd better make a plan.'

She wouldn't involve Oliver in this, and she wouldn't describe the lengths to which Clive had gone; that scene was not for public edification. But if she and Daisy endorsed Jenny's complaint, the management would have to take it seriously and Clive, at the very least, would have to mind his step and grovel.

28

It transpires that one cannot escape one's past. Sooner or later, it rises up, however well it has been buried, however many precautions against exposure have been taken, however much may seem to be forgotten.

I find this in my work. I have been consulted by an elderly woman whose husband, after years of quiet retirement, is visited by dreams of his wartime experiences. His ship was sunk; men drowned around him. He was rescued but he could not save his greatest friend. Guilt and remorse now plague him. I told her that after living through the horror again, his haunting dreams might eventually disappear, be exorcised. If not, he should seek medical aid. It was a sad case, but she said that talking about it had done her good. She came in several times, to report no real improvement in her husband.

Is this happening to me? I find myself thinking about the past more frequently than for many years. It must be because Mrs Wilmot has threatened my security. I risk discovery. That woman is a danger to me. What can I do about it? Wait for nemesis to defeat me? Not without a struggle.

I wrote a letter just the other day, one that should arouse alarm.

*   *   *

Prudence was in Fettleton library when she saw the woman she had recognised as Wendy Tyler again. She had gone there to check some details about Florence in the nineteenth century, where her heroine was a governess whose path had crossed that of the Brownings. She had finished the proofs which had interrupted the flow of the new book and was glad to return to it; Midge's enthusiasm, hearing the outline of the plot, had encouraged her. She still marvelled that people enjoyed reading what she had spent months constructing; they did, for with every book her sales went up, and one had been broadcast as a radio serial.

Wendy Tyler was collecting some books she had evidently ordered. She had not seen Prudence, who was sitting at a table by the radiator, where it was warm. Having accepted the books from the hand of the librarian, Wendy paused at the notice board and studied it; then she left the building.

Prudence did not hesitate. She abandoned the book she had been consulting and followed her, leaving a surprised librarian to come upon it later. Mrs Wilmot was normally punctilious about replacing books or handing them across the counter.

What am I doing, Prudence asked herself, following her quarry into the road. She should have asked the librarian who she was; Prudence was well known in the library, where they were aware that she was a novelist, and the information might have been supplied. She hurried on, following the tall figure who today wore a camel coat, her hair in the same severe swept-back style.

Wendy strode on, past Boots and a delicatessen. Had she more shopping to do, or was she returning to her car? Prudence's was in Safeway's car park; she disliked multi-storey parks and there was always something she needed at the supermarket, entitling her to use its space.

What would she do if she caught up with Wendy? Challenge her? But she wasn't going to overtake; it was all she could do to keep pace with her long strides. Wendy marched ahead through groups of shoppers which parted before her, then closed up in front of Prudence, who marvelled at what confidence she had, arrogantly going through them like a ploughshare. She turned into an arcade which opened between Dixons and a dry cleaner's, and when Prudence went the same way, she had vanished.

Prudence walked the length of the arcade in vain. There was no sign of her. She might be in one of the shops but it was not feasible to enter all of them in search of her. Prudence abandoned the trail and went back to her car.

The woman she knew as Wendy Tyler had seen Prudence reflected in a plate-glass window, and had ducked into the first crowded shop in the arcade while she passed.

It had happened once; it could happen again. Mrs Wilmot would see her and an encounter might be unavoidable.

Seeing her like that, coming up behind me in the street, unnerved me. She might not have noticed me; it could have been chance, but I would not risk finding out if she was following me. I did not want a challenge, or, if one had to come, I would have it in a place and at a time of my own choosing. If she thought she recognised me, she could find out my new name if she set her mind to it; a private detective would, for a price, be able to accomplish that feat. If she does that, I'll have no option but to move on, and to float a new identity.

It's so unfair.

I doubled back after she had passed and returned to my car, driving swiftly away to my consulting-room where Mr Leonard was due in his lunch hour. He had rung me up requesting an emergency appointment.

I calmed myself down, breathing deeply, sniffing some herbs I keep arranged in water on my desk to inspire confidence in my patients. In a short time I was myself again — like Macbeth.

Now why did I think of Macbeth?

I made a mental switch and turned my mind towards Mr Leonard and his canine problems. Or his marital problems. The two were intertwined. He was early, and I pressed the buzzer to open the front door when he rang the bell.

Things started to go wrong immediately. Instead of waiting meekly until I bade him enter, Mr Leonard stormed straight into my consulting room, and he had his large Alsatian dog with him. He had said it was a puppy, but it was enormous and looked more than mature, snarling at me, the hairs on its neck bristling. I'd seen enough of Alsatians in my years in prison to last a lifetime. I was about to ask Mr Leonard to remove the dog and tie it up outside when I saw that he was snarling, too, glaring at me with a maniacal expression on his ugly face.

The desk was between us. I stood behind it, my left hand resting on it, my right hand in my pocket as he began to speak. I was ready if the dog should pounce. I hate all dogs.

'You told me I had to choose. I chose the dog and she left me. My wife left me.' He almost shouted the words in my face, standing up, leaning towards me.

'I know she's left you. You've already told me,' I said steadily. 'You chose the dog.'

I sat down, to indicate that I, at least, was calm. The dog was growling softly, but now, as if to mimic me, it crouched on its haunches, presenting a less menacing appearance.

'Sit down, Mr Leonard,' I commanded. 'Let us talk this through.'

He sat, winding the leash round his wrist, and the dog slumped down, mercifully out of my sight, but I could hear its noisy breathing, punctuated by low, sullen growls.

'There's nothing to discuss. She's gone and it's your fault,' he said.

'It was your choice. You chose the dog,' I repeated. *'Why is your situation worse today than at our last consultation?'*

'She went off with Frank Hines. A man she works with. I've only just discovered that,' he said.

'Perhaps Frank Hines prefers her to a dog,' I said.

It was a reasonable and obvious observation, but he seemed to go completely mad, springing to his feet and cursing, blaming me for the misfortunes of the forty-odd years of his life. It is strange how reluctant people are to shoulder the blame for their own mistakes; it's more comfortable to place it elsewhere.

The dog stood up and started barking, and for the first time in my life as a free woman, I felt physically threatened. That could not be permitted.

I reached into my pocket and removed my knife. I am never without it.

'Mr Leonard, if you don't control your dog, I shall take drastic action,' I said.

Rosemary Ellis was very tired that night. She had had a gruelling day, concerned with the difficulties of other people, and for once she thought it would be agreeable if someone were to be concerned with her. But she had never let anyone come close to enough to do so, not for a long time.

Driving home later than usual, suddenly the prospect of another meal alone, and a solitary evening before she could reasonably go to bed, was unappealing. She would break her routine and eat out. She could go somewhere unpretentious. What if she called in at The Verandah for dinner?

Why not? Wasn't it time she had a treat?

Oliver Foxton would have gone home by now. There would be no chance of seeing him if she went straight back to the flat. It was strange how each small sighting of him seemed to keep her content until the next one. Crumbs, she thought: food for fantasy. She was not coveting him; she did not desire him physically; she feasted only on her glimpses of him.

She was able to park in the market square, not far from the restaurant, and, after locking her car, walked there. Several tables were vacant and she was escorted to a corner, which suited her as she had no wish to be islanded in the centre of the dining area. Asked if she would care for a drink, she ordered a glass of white wine, and when it came, the first sip seemed to rush straight to her head, but it relieved any awkwardness she felt at being there alone, the only solitary diner. She ordered a fish dish; salmon in a sauce which the waiter said was interesting.

While she was waiting for the soup which she had chosen to begin her meal, another woman entered, on her own, and was shown to a table on the far side of the room. Rosemary did not look at her; she lowered her gaze, and waited for her plate to be removed.

Oliver had suggested that Sarah should go with him to inspect the dolls' house he had arranged to see. They could make a day of it, have lunch somewhere, visit a garden centre or go shopping, whatever she would like to do. The dolls' house owner lived in a village not far from Bath.

But Sarah said she was too busy setting up a mailing list for her prospective business and analysing surveys regarding its potential which she had already carried out.

'Can I help?' he offered. The dolls' house could wait. But no, there was nothing he could usefully do.

Except keep out of her hair, he thought.

'Suppose I take Midge, then?' he asked. 'Would that be all right with you? She was so taken with Prudence's that I said I'd find one for her. It might give her an interest. She could look out for the bits and pieces.'

'All right. Take her. Though will she have time for this interest, with her wonderful new career?' asked Sarah, who still did not know what Midge's plans were.

'She may not want to come,' said Oliver. 'I'll ask Prudence too,' he added. Surely Sarah could not be jealous of Midge? The idea was laughable.

But was it? he wondered, as he dialled Midge's number.

He did not tell her the reason for his trip, merely that he had an appointment. She accepted eagerly, and then said, 'Sarah will be coming too, of course.'

'She hasn't time,' he answered. 'But I've asked Prudence.'

'Oh – that's lovely,' Midge said. 'What fun.'

And it would be, he resolved.

29

Saturday was a cold, clear day, the frost that had hung about for weeks still lingering. Midge planned that she and Prudence would amuse themselves in Bath while Oliver kept his appointment. Prudence was already in the car when he called for Midge, and they set off in high feather, with Oliver feeling as if he were playing truant. Perhaps he was. Prudence had thought him wise to include her on the expedition; however innocently undertaken, if he and Midge were seen setting off together, mischief could be made, tongues could wag, and two and two could so easily be wrongly added up.

'Who's this demanding client who requires your presence on a Saturday?' asked Midge, who, without a pang, had closed the shop to go with him.

Oliver had explained the reason for their trip to Prudence. Now he confessed to Midge.

'Oh, Oliver!' Midge knew he'd never say anything he didn't mean. Even so, she protested. 'I can't let you do that for me,' she said.

'He's doing it for himself, Midge,' said Prudence. 'He's lost without his hobby. You're only his excuse. When he's done yours, he'll be hunting about for someone else to mend one for. Let him do it.'

No one mentioned Sarah. All of them knew that she was not the least bit interested in this diversion he had found, but only Oliver knew how bitterly she resented it. He put the matter from his mind. Today was a fiesta.

There was some talk about their destination. They discussed a likely spot for lunch. Prudence consulted various guides Oliver kept in the car, and after a while, looking in the driving mirror, Oliver saw that Midge had fallen asleep.

Lady Fortescue opened the door to them herself.

Her house was beautiful. Oliver had stopped the car outside the gates so that they could admire the pale stone of its construction, and the soft grey tiles on the roof. Then he drove slowly down a straight avenue between two lines of trees, careful not to send gravel scudding over the frosted grass at either side.

'What a gorgeous place,' said Midge.

Its owner must have heard them, or been watching for them, for she was standing at the top of the short flight of steps leading to the entrance as they got out of the Rover and walked towards her.

She was of medium height, plump, with white hair and a lined face; a woman in her later seventies, thought Oliver, who had looked her up in *Who's Who* but had not found an entry for her. He introduced his companions, and she looked sharply at Midge, so that he sensed she might have recognised her. It would not be surprising; after Daniel's death, and again after the later arrests and the committal of the four youths, her photograph had been in many of the newspapers.

'I'm moving from this lovely house,' Lady Fortescue explained. 'My husband died last year and it's much too big for me to stay in alone. I've bought a small house three miles away, as I have friends here and don't want to leave the district. Sadly, I have to dispose of a great deal of furniture.

And the dolls' house, which has been in the attic for more years than I care to think about.'

She led them through the large square hall from which rose a central staircase which divided into two upper flights, and into a small sitting room furnished with two deep sofas and some armchairs covered in rose linen; there was a television set in a corner, but the tables – a mahogany sofa table and two tripod tables – were obviously good. Decanters and glasses stood on a tray on a Georgian pier table against the wall.

'How sad for you to have to move,' said Midge. 'My husband died last year, too, but luckily I can stay in my house, anyway for now. It's not like this, of course.' She spoke quite naturally, without embarrassment. Oliver and Prudence exchanged a glance. A week ago she could not have managed this.

'Ah – I'm sorry. You're young,' said Lady Fortescue. 'Your husband should have had a longer life. Mine was old – over eighty.' She smiled at Midge. 'Sherry?' she suggested.

How civilised, thought Prudence. It was half-past eleven. Several miles away, they had stopped for coffee and what Oliver called a comfort halt, so sherry now was just the thing.

'The house is for Mrs Stewart,' said Oliver, who had introduced them formally.

'Oh?' Lady Fortescue poured sherry into fine glasses and put a small table close to Midge.

'Oliver has just restored one that has been in my family for generations,' said Prudence. 'Midge – Mrs Stewart – has admired it, and he badly needs the occupation as an interest, so here we are.'

'Oliver painted a tiny portrait, smaller than a postage stamp, for one wall in Prudence's house,' said Midge. 'And he's made or mended lots of bits of furniture.'

'Mine will need that,' said Lady Fortescue. Then she continued, 'The furniture I don't need is being auctioned, but I didn't want the dolls' house to go to just anyone. You may think that's silly, but it's the truth.'

'I don't think it's silly at all,' said Midge stoutly. 'You're fond of it. You want it to go to a good home.'

'That's it, exactly,' said Lady Fortescue. 'Have you a daughter?'

'No,' said Midge. 'But I have two sons.'

'And what are they doing?' Lady Fortescue asked.

Midge told her, her colour rising, due partly to the sherry, while Prudence and Oliver sat back, like proud parents pleased to see their offspring performing well.

Lady Fortescue then answered the question none of her visitors had liked to ask.

'We had no children, unfortunately,' she said. 'It was a disappointment.' She set her glass down. 'Shall we go and look at the dolls' house now? It's upstairs in a cupboard. I hid it from the auctioneers who came to catalogue what I want to sell. I didn't want them telling me I could get a fortune for it. I don't want a fortune,' she added hastily.

Oliver intervened.

'May I look at it with you on my own, as this is my little enterprise?' he asked. 'Prudence and Midge just came to keep me company.'

'Certainly,' said Lady Fortescue. 'Help yourselves to more sherry, do,' she added to the two women, and led the way from the room.

The dolls' house was in what must have been her husband's dressing-room. She opened an enormous dark oak wardrobe, almost an armoire, and there it was, resting on a shelf inside, a miniature replica of an eighteenth-century house, shabby and grimed, the wallpaper hanging from the walls of the rooms, and with some woodworm damage, which its owner pointed out.

'How can you bear to part with it?' said Oliver, gazing at it, rapt. Love at first sight, thought Lady Fortescue, touched.

'It's been in the attic ever since I've lived here,' she said. 'It was in my husband's family, handed down – too good for children, in a way, and they weren't originally children's toys, as you know, I'm sure. I was shown it as a bride and told by my mother-in-law that I should have it when I had a daughter old enough to appreciate it. When we came to live here, the right time had somehow passed, and I left it in the attic. It was already decaying.'

'What a pity.'

'Yes. Your friend – forgive me, but she is the woman whose husband was murdered by some schoolboys a few months ago, isn't she?'

'Yes. You recognised her, did you, from the papers?'

'I wasn't sure. But you live near Fettleton, don't you? Where the boys were charged? I noted that crime particularly, because it was so horrific.'

'Yes, it was,' said Oliver. 'Your dolls' house is worth a great deal of money, even in this state,' he went on. 'I couldn't make you a fair offer – it would have to be valued by an expert.'

'And then, if you were to buy it for your friend, she would be embarrassed by the cost of your kindness.'

This was patently true.

'She needn't know that part of it,' he said.

'She'll find out. Someone will let the cat out of the bag. No, the money isn't important. I have more than enough, and there is a buyer in the wings for the house,' said Lady Fortescue. 'He's made a fortune from a microchip device, and he is pleasant. He has a nice wife and some children who will like living here. He can afford to keep it all up and I expect he'll put in a hard tennis court, and a swimming pool. I would, if I were him.' She smiled. 'The surplus furniture will fetch a great deal, too. As I have no children, I don't have to consider anyone except myself.'

She said it sadly. Who would see about arrangements if

she became too frail to manage on her own? A solicitor like himself, he thought; he had carried out the same function for several clients.

'It's very generous of you,' he said.

'It's not. It's selfish. I will get pleasure from knowing you and that poor woman are enjoying it.'

Oliver thought of suggesting that she should come and see the work in progress, or at least the finished article, but refrained. That could wait. He thanked her once again.

'It will please me to think it may help your friend to have the interest,' she said.

'I'm hoping that it will,' said Oliver. 'The trial is still to come, and that will be a hard time for her, I'm afraid.'

'They've got them all, have they? The guilty boys?'

'Yes,' said Oliver. 'After a long stalemate. She stayed with us – my wife and me – after Daniel was killed.' Oliver thought he had better convey to Lady Fortescue the fact that he was married. 'The house I was repairing then intrigued her. She named its occupants. It diverted her.'

'There are no occupants for mine, alas,' said Lady Fortescue.

Oliver was relieved to hear it.

'What's your favourite charity?' he asked her.

She told him. It was a charity for children.

'I'll send them a cheque,' he said.

'Very well. That would be nice. But not more than you can afford. The dolls' house will cost a bit to put in order, after all.'

She opened doors for him as he carried the dolls' house carefully along the corridor and down the wide staircase to the hall, where, on her instructions, he set it on the table in the centre. Lady Fortescue went off, saying she thought she could find a box large enough to hold it.

While she was gone, Oliver called Midge and Prudence to look at his acquisition. Both thought it was wonderful, though they exclaimed about its condition, and Prudence said it would provide inspiration for her next book. One family of participants could live in a house like her own, and another in one like this.

'You've already got the Wilberforces,' Midge declared. 'Now you'll have to give them all real lives.'

'So I will,' said Prudence, eyes lighting up at the prospect. 'That's good. An idea before I'm finished with the current one.' And a rebirth.

They were discussing Mr Wilberforce's family when Lady Fortescue appeared with a large cardboard carton behind which she was almost invisible. When she learned Prudence's profession, she was intrigued. Prudence, who wrote as Prudence Dane, partly to conceal her own identity and partly as a tactic to use a name better placed in the alphabet to catch the eye of a browsing reader, discovered that Lady Fortescue, who admitted that her chosen reading was biography, had read her last book when staying with a friend and had, she said, enjoyed it very much. She went off again, to fetch newspaper to wrap round the house and stop it moving in the box. Prudence followed, to offer help. While they were absent, Midge expressed anxiety about what the house had cost, and Oliver told her what had happened.

'Don't cry,' he warned, as her eyes filled with grateful tears. 'You can later,' he said, and she laughed.

At last it was all packed up and safely in the car. They said farewell, and left, driving slowly down the drive. Lady Fortescue stood watching them till they were out of sight.

'Does she live there all on her own?' Midge asked.

Prudence had learned the answer while they found the newspapers.

'She has a daily housekeeper from the village who doesn't come at weekends unless Lady Fortescue is having guests,' she said. 'It must be very lonely, on her own.'

Going back into the house, Lady Fortescue thought, as she did every day, of the daughter she had borne, and what had happened to her. It was ten years since she had learned the answer.

HOW DOES IT FEEL TO KNOW THAT YOUR BETRAYAL LED TO THIS? a typed message, in an envelope delivered by the morning post and enclosing a faded newspaper cutting, had demanded. Below the headline, the murder by Wendy Tyler of her lover's wife was related, and the fact that Wendy Tyler had been adopted as an infant. I MAY COME AND SEE YOU, the letter ended.

Mary Fortescue had checked the details instantly, obtaining copies of further newspaper reports of the crime, eventually employing a private detective to confirm the facts. It was true. Wendy was her daughter, conceived during the war when she, already married, was serving with the WRNS in Ceylon. Mary's husband had been captured after the fall of Singapore; at the time, she did not know if he was still alive. Her brief, ecstatic romance ended when her lover, a naval officer, also married, had been posted away, and then she had discovered that she was pregnant. She had managed to get herself sent back to England and discreetly discharged, saying she had been invalided out, which was true, and implied anaemia and the need for convalescence. She had gone to a remote part of Yorkshire, where she had had the baby, which was adopted after only a few days. It was all over before the war ended and her husband's eventual return. He had never learned her secret, but after it became possible for adopted children to seek out their natural parents, she had grown anxious, and when the letter came, she had feared an overt, determined approach which would destroy not only her life, but her husband's, too. Her daughter would now be fifty-two years old.

There had been no good reason why she did not conceive again; perhaps the problem was with her husband, but they had never enquired. In those days, people did not question fate, as happened nowadays; nor did they believe it was the right of everyone to have exactly what they wanted.

Occasionally, further missives, which she had managed to keep from her husband, had arrived, with messages such as I HAVE NOT FORGOTTEN, and just a week ago Mary Fortescue had received one which said, I MAY COME TO SEE YOU VERY SOON. The earlier ones had borne London postmarks. This one's mark had been Swindon. That was close to home.

Well, she could come now. It didn't matter. Her natural father, who was not named on her birth certificate, had been killed when his ship was torpedoed and he never knew about her birth. There was no one left alive who could be hurt.

Mary found it hard to think of her as Wendy; she had named her Philippa, because her father's name was Philip, and in the newspaper photographs, in spite of the girl's angry, bitter expression, there had been a likeness.

Last night, or rather, in the small hours of the morning, the moment she had dreaded had arrived.

She had been asleep when she heard the noise – the echo of the doorbell being held down with persistence, shrilling through the house, and a loud thumping as the heavy knocker was banged over and over again. An earlier sound had already disturbed her, penetrating her consciousness but not really waking her. The nights were peaceful here, the dawn noises normal country ones: birds, and an occasional bark from a dog. Cars did not race up the drive during the hours of darkness. Even the milkman, in his electric float, did not come until nine o'clock and the postman was still later. Startled, but not afraid – burglars did not advertise their presence in such a manner – she switched on her bedside light, found her slippers and her dressing-gown – a warm woollen one, pale blue – and turned on the main light in her room. All the while the ringing and the hammering continued, not stopping when Mary put on more lights before she came downstairs.

It could be someone who had had an accident, or witnessed one, in the road, and needed to telephone for help, she thought, descending. Hers might be the nearest house. She had convinced herself that this was the reason for the tumult outside before she opened the door and saw the woman on the step.

Mary knew who she was at once.

'There's no need for all that noise,' she said. 'Come in, Philippa.'

30

'That's not my name,' the woman had said, her tone petulant, accusatory.

'No – not now,' Mary had agreed. 'You've had several, I believe. Would you prefer me to call you Wendy? I've always thought of you as Philippa.'

'Thought of me? You never thought of me at all. You gave me away,' she said.

They were still standing in the hall.

'Come along to the kitchen, where it's warm, and I can make you a hot drink,' said Mary, and she led the way, turning her back upon the woman, fighting to breathe evenly and retain the composure she had learned throughout a long life married to an ambitious man. To compensate for his years of lost youth, once he had regained his health, her husband had developed the business which his father had started and had then gone into politics. The fear through all those years that her own secret might be exposed and ruin him had never left her, and it had increased when the first unsigned communication had arrived. Even after he retired from public life he had been active until shortly before his death, and it could have wrecked his final years. Now that danger was past.

'Sit down,' said Mary, indicating a chair at the large pine

table which stood before the Aga. She did not invite her caller to remove her coat, for she did not want her to stay; this morning a man was coming to inspect the dolls' house. She might have to put him off if this woman refused to leave.

This woman. It was odd to think of her like that. This tall woman with the ravaged face, looking older than her years, her hair smoothly coiled back, was once the tiny, red-faced infant for whom Mary had felt a visceral, primitive love transcending any emotion she had ever felt before, the memory of which had never left her. Now, she saw someone she would not have recognised if she had sat opposite her in a train.

Did Philippa feel equally remote from her? Had she an image of her natural mother that conflicted with reality? Philippa was tall, like her father, and her resemblance to him was marked, although he had been only thirty when they met, and she was now much older. Philippa, it was obvious from her expression, hated the world and everybody in it; her father, when Mary knew him, had loved life and humanity.

Philippa, or Wendy, would not sit. Mary, her hand on the kettle waiting for it to boil, watched her pacing up and down the large room with its quarry tiled floor, staring not at Mary but at her own feet: pacing, pacing, thought Mary, as if she were in a prison cell.

'What is wrong?' she asked at last, as she poured water into a teapot. Tea, not coffee, she had decided: it was less stimulating, more soothing; this woman was already tautly strung, at snapping point.

She carried the pot to the table, and set out cups and saucers and the sugar bowl; odd not to know if your daughter took sugar in her tea. She went to the tall refrigerator for the milk, almost crossing the other woman's path as she still paced.

'Do sit down,' Mary repeated, and, ungraciously, her visitor subsided on to one of the chairs. Mary poured the tea with a steady hand.

'Milk?' she asked, the small jug poised above one cup, and, when there was no response, she poured some into both filled tea cups.

'You would add it last,' her daughter growled at last. 'Where I grew up, it went in first.'

'Many people prefer it like that,' said Mary calmly. 'Some think it mixes better. It's a matter of taste.'

'Yes, and it's a matter of taste that you live here in this – this mansion, and I grew up in a suburban street in Birmingham.'

'You were brought up in a good area and your adoptive father was a successful man who prospered after the war,' said Mary. 'Your adoptive parents stood by you when you really needed them.' All this she had discovered, even to the eventual legacy they left her.

'But you weren't there. My real mother. You didn't rescue me.' The tone of this remark was flat, as if the speaker was in a trance.

'I had no idea you were Wendy Tyler,' Mary said. 'And do you really hold me responsible for what you did?'

'You rejected me. You made me search desperately for love,' the other woman said. 'And you made it impossible for me to find it.'

Poor tragic soul, caught in a labyrinth of excuses for her conduct, thought Mary.

'I made the best arrangements I could at the time – more than fifty years ago – to place you in a family who craved a child,' she said. 'Your adoptive father had not been called up for war service, and he was financially secure. I knew that they would love you. If I had kept you, I would have been ostracised – especially as my husband was a prisoner of war in the Far East at the time.' Mary saw her daughter make a sudden rapid movement as she said this. 'Oh yes. I was married but I could not pass you off as my husband's child – something that has happened throughout history in such cases.

And your real father was also married.' She did not mention his children, this woman's half siblings; no good could come of that. 'He was killed before you were born and he did not know I was pregnant.' It was clear that although Philippa/Wendy had done enough research to track her down, there were limits to what she had discovered.

'Who was he?' The words seemed to come out reluctantly.

'He was a naval officer I met on an overseas posting. I'm not going to excuse our behaviour, but it was wartime and people were under strain. You were conceived as the result of a great passion,' Mary said. It would not do to call it love. 'Contraception in those days was less dependable than it is now. Nor was abortion legal then. You look like him,' she added. 'Except that when I knew him, he was good-humoured and happy. Clearly, you are not.'

'Would you be, with my history?' the younger woman demanded, more animated now.

'You loved a married man,' Mary replied. 'You killed his wife, hoping that he would marry you. That is my understanding of what happened. I, also, had a love affair with a married man, but I did not wish his wife dead, though I feared my own husband might be.' She looked at the woman it was so difficult to regard as her flesh and blood. 'I don't think you were pregnant, when you did what you did.'

'His wife was,' said the visitor, in a hiss.

'Ah,' said Mary. 'But he took care that you were not.'

'How did you know that?' The question was snapped back at her.

'I'm guessing. I think you might have wished to trap him.'

Saying this, Mary Fortescue felt a great weariness. She was responsible for the birth of this bitter woman, yet in her she could recognise no trace of her own or Philip's character – but how well had she known him? Theirs had been a two months' interlude while he was based near her, before he went to sea again. It had happened all the time during the war, often resulting in hasty marriages which had not always worked out well.

'I hate you,' said Mary's daughter. 'I hate you! Oh, I hate you!'

'And you've come here to tell me so,' said Mary. 'Perhaps you plan to kill me.' The woman did; she knew it in her bones. She began refilling both their cups. Almost without noticing it, the visitor had drunk her tea. Mary had only sipped at hers. Now she took a good gulp, swallowing carefully, anxious not to choke, before continuing, 'If you do, I shan't mind too much, though I should not care for suffering great pain, if you mean to inflict it on me. I am old, and no one depends on me. But I am expecting visitors this morning, and they will be concerned if I do not greet them. By now you will have left traces of your presence in the house. You are not wearing gloves, and I am sure your fingerprints are held on some file. People may have seen your car, and the milkman will be calling soon. The postman, too, will come to the house. I have letters almost every day. I rather think you are on licence and would be locked up again immediately if I died violently and your visit here was discovered.'

The younger woman's stare was glassy now. Suddenly her body slumped, so that it was all Mary Fortescue could do not to rise and go to her, embrace this desperate, angry stranger who was her daughter. But she would not show weakness.

'Why now?' she asked. 'Why have you waited so long to confront me, when I know you traced me many years ago? Are you in trouble? Real trouble? Have you—' she hesitated, wanting to wrap her question in some diplomatic circumlocution. 'Have you made a serious mistake?'

'No,' was the answer, for Wendy Tyler had not stabbed either Mr Leonard or his dog, but both had fled from her presence, Mr Leonard saying she was a danger and ought to be locked up. He might go to the police, though even then it would only be his word against hers.

'Then you are unhappy, and you have made yourself ill by blaming me for what has not worked out for you, instead of examining your own actions.' For the woman was unwell; there was no doubt of it. Mary stood up. 'You must leave now,' she said. 'It's for your own sake, as much as mine. I imagine you have made a place for yourself in society, with a new identity. Go back to it. Don't throw away what you have achieved because you are so full of hatred and resentment.' She moved towards the door. 'As I said, the milkman will be here quite soon, and after him the postman.' Had her visitor called on Sunday, she would have had neither of these excuses to press her to go, nor would she, this weekend, have been expecting guests. 'And my other visitors are due a little later. I must prepare for them,' she ended.

She did not look back to see if the other woman was following her, but walked out of the room, along the passage and into the hall. For want of an audience, her poor, sad daughter must follow, or else perform some melodramatic action. She opened the front door and a blast of icy air blew in.

The tactic worked. Mary saw her daughter walk down the few steps to cross the gravel to her car, a blue Renault, she noticed absently. Mary closed the door at once, and, listening, she heard the car start up. It did not leave immediately, but after a few moments she heard its engine roar and it was driven away very fast.

I offered her no money, she thought, leaning against the door. That, at least, I could have given her, but she was driving a good car, and she was wearing an expensive coat.

She went slowly back to the kitchen and cleared away the tea things, washing them carefully, wiping them, removing all traces of the visit. While she was doing this, the milkman called, much earlier than usual. He could have passed the Renault in the road.

Lady Fortescue had some time to compose herself and rest a little, before preparing for Mr Foxton's arrival. She would not put him off. He would give her a focus, help her to get over this intrusion. For that was what it had been, a terrible and terrifying invasion.

I had no choice but to turn to her, the wealthy, privileged woman who is my natural mother. After I produced the knife, Mr Leonard had left, threatening to inform the police that I had attacked him, but I had not touched him, nor his vile dog. At the sight of the knife he had moved swiftly, got control of the dog and backed off, swearing at me.

Prison habits die hard, and I can swear, too. I did so, more colourfully than he, and told him assaults from patients were not uncommon and that professional people have to protect themselves. I pointed out that his dog had growled at me, and had slavered on the floor.

'Don't call again,' I told him. 'All I did was point out your options. You made the wrong choice, if you wanted your wife to stay with you.' But of course it was the fact that she had a lover which had tipped him over.

After he had gone, I realised that he had not paid for this session.

I tidied up, cleaned the dog's mess away, vacuumed round and wiped the surfaces. Then I took his card from the file and scored it off with a big red line. Discharged himself, I wrote. I made out his account and put it ready to drop in the postbox on my way home.

The incident was unsettling. I felt restless. Ever since I saw that woman, Mrs Wilmot, and met her unrelenting stare, I have not been myself, and when silly Mrs Stewart revealed her background I knew my unease was justified. She threatened my security. Now, two patients had defied me: Mrs Stewart, persuaded, I was sure, by Mrs Foxton, her reneging business partner, to give up her treatment, and Mr Leonard.

I left my consulting room, posted Mr Leonard's account, and drove to Mickleburgh, parking not far from Mrs Wilmot's house. It was in darkness, the curtains drawn. No chink of light was visible as I walked past. Of course, she had money. I had enough independent income to live on, but I had never owned a house. I had always rented. I deserved better. I'd been denied a normal life because I had received such unfair treatment – farmed out as an infant, then betrayed.

Walking along, wondering whether to turn back and ring Mrs Wilmot's bell, confront her, ask her if she had recognised me and if so, what she meant to do, I felt the knife's reassuring hardness in my pocket. Then I noticed The Verandah restaurant. Its softly lighted windows lured me towards them. It would be warm inside. Why should I not have a treat tonight? I needed a pleasant experience after my fracas with Mr Leonard, and, even more, his dog. I went in.

With my meal I ordered wine, and enjoyed it. I seldom drink; it makes me nostalgic. Tonight, though, was different, and it relaxed me. Leaving the restaurant, going out into the night air, I felt a sudden anger because I had been denied so much. It should have been my right to visit pleasant places, to be cherished, nurtured.

She had made it impossible, the woman who had borne me but had surrendered me without a qualm.

I knew where to find her. I would go there now.

On the way, driving through the night, I almost fell asleep, so I turned off the main road into a side lane and found a layby where I pulled in, and slept. With all the car doors locked, no sense of danger came to me, and I had the knife.

I woke feeling frowsty and unclean. A bath or shower would have been welcome. I've appreciated easy cleanliness ever since my time inside. I'd stop when I came to a service area and freshen up, then consult the map. It might be that the motorway, which I had chosen, was not the best route to the village near Bath where she had lived for years in the manor house. Lady Fortescue. A titled woman is my mother. Her husband had been knighted for some service, reference books had told me when, years ago, I traced her. He's dead now. I know that, so I would find her alone, unless she had staff in her large house. She'd played false, I was the result, and she'd got rid of me so that she could continue with her lavish life. Long gone was the childhood dream I'd had of a weeping mother forced to abandon me lest both of us starve.

Leaving the main road, I had some trouble finding the way, but when I reached her village, there was no doubt about which was the manor house. I drove past darkened cottages and a few modern houses. Then I came to huge wrought-iron gates, which were open.

There was no lodge. That surprised me. If she had resident staff I should just have to get past them. I had every right to see my own mother.

The house was in darkness but it must be nearly morning. I drove fast up the drive, my headlights picking out pale tree trunks on either side. A small animal scurried across in front of me, and I pulled up sharp on a wide gravel sweep before the imposing façade which, at my approach, was illuminated by some automatic system. I doused my car's lights, walked towards the door, and rang the bell. A house like this would be alarmed, I thought, and rang again.

No one came. Was she away? Taking the sun in some expensive resort?

I pressed the bell again, then leaned on it, and banged the heavy knocker, up and down, over and over, thumping it.

To me, it seemed like hours before I heard bolts being

drawn. My hand was still raised as the door was opened. She stood there – unless this old woman was the housekeeper – unprotected, no chain holding the door. She stared at me, and knew me instantly.

'There's no need for all that noise,' she said. 'Come in, Philippa.'

She was so small. That was a surprise. She was plump, too, a short, stocky figure in a blue woollen dressing-gown, walking ahead of me towards the back of the house.

I could have struck her then, stabbed her as I had stabbed Emily so many years ago. She, too, would have time to be aware that I had done it. Emily had gurgled, stared at me in shock, then died. She – my mother – would know, too. My fingers, in my coat pocket, clutched the knife. I looked at her grey head – the hair curly, almost white – no rinse, unlike mine which I began to tint as soon as I saw the first grey strands. It would have been so easy.

But I didn't do it.

We went into the kitchen where a green Aga, with four ovens, dominated the room. She put the kettle on as if I was just any caller dropping in. I paced about, wanting to shout at her, to damage her as she had wounded me, but she moved calmly on, setting out pretty china cups and saucers, and a large brown teapot – not a silver one. She used teabags, too, and that almost made me laugh and want to ridicule her: Lady Fortescue using common teabags and a cheap brown pot.

I don't quite know how I came to be sitting down, even drinking tea; it was as though a few minutes had been blotted out, as in an amnesiac fugue. It came to me that I was very thirsty. I drank with eagerness.

I didn't frighten her at all. She wasn't even slightly scared as she told me some romantic tale about my father and their love, and how he had been killed without knowing she was pregnant with me. She said I looked like him.

Suddenly I didn't want to learn any more, and then she was talking about fingerprints and people coming to the house – tradesmen, and visitors – and she was showing me the door.

She called me Philippa.

Before I got into my car, she had closed the door, not even waiting to see me drive away. My mother.

I passed the milk float in the village. My car had been seen, but I had done nothing wrong. It isn't wrong to go and see your mother.

31

Sarah was disappointed and annoyed when Oliver went off with Midge and Prudence, leaving her behind alone. She knew this was unreasonable; he had explained his mission and asked her to go with him, but nothing would induce her to go seeking a silly toy for him to play with, and all as a treat for Midge. She would have been bored to tears while he chatted up some dull woman in an unknown village. She had expected him to cancel his arrangements, and stay to keep her company, but it was true she had pleaded work as an excuse for staying behind. It was also true that she had refused his offer to help her, but she conveniently banished that reflection.

She had gained a weird pleasure from moving the dolls about in the house that was now, thank goodness, no longer in the study. Midge had christened them the Wilberforces; how childish. Well, she'd put Mr Wilberforce out for the count, at least, and she could play games with the next lot of people Oliver installed in the new house, if he bought it. As he would, unless it was a hopeless proposition.

She could always destroy it, as she had contemplated doing to the last one, if she found it all too irksome.

At this thought, Sarah pulled herself up short. Why did such an idea even enter her head? Oliver might be unexciting, but he was reliable and kind, and he had never behaved in the way that Clive had done that night in Kent, when she had been really frightened.

Sarah took her files and went to her computer. She'd concentrate on making her new business a success, and that would show them all, including Clive, just what she could do. And he had a few shocks coming to him, if Jenny went ahead with her complaint.

She was absorbed in her calculations when the doorbell rang – not one sharp ping but a sustained summons, piercing through the house.

Making an impatient sound, Sarah left her desk and went to the front door.

'Yes?' she enquired of the woman she saw standing there, a tall woman in a camel coat, with hair swept round her head in a coil. Had they met? Sarah couldn't place her.

'You're Sarah Foxton,' stated the woman, and before Sarah had realised what was happening, she had pushed past her into the hall.

'I am Sarah Foxton,' she agreed, put out by the woman's tactics, for she was used to holding itinerant vendors at bay, but the woman looked respectable and seemed well spoken. She was annoyed, not alarmed. 'Who are you?' she asked.

'I am Mrs Stewart's counsellor, and you have seriously upset her treatment by cancelling your business project with her,' said the visitor.

She had pushed the front door to behind her, but it had not latched, and now cold air was whistling through the gap. Sarah could not get past her to close it properly, but at the same time, the woman was not welcome, so she made no move to do so.

'Mrs Stewart made the decision herself,' said Sarah firmly. 'And I don't see what it has to do with you.'

'It's very much my concern, if my patient's equilibrium is

likely to be disturbed by outside actions,' was the answer. 'She has ceased her treatment.'

'Obviously that's because she's so much better,' Sarah said. 'I expect you've done her lots of good. Look, I'm very busy now. If you really want to discuss this, can't we do it some other time?' Like when Oliver is here, she thought. Surely it was most unprofessional to discuss a patient with someone else? Wasn't what was said in counselling sessions confidential?

'No, we could not,' said the woman, now advancing towards Sarah, who was suddenly alarmed.

The woman's eyes were glossy bright under the well-defined brows. Her gaze bored into Sarah's, who under the intent stare found herself retreating across the hall. The tall woman continued to move forward until Sarah, at a loss, turned and walked into the sitting room. She told herself to keep calm; this was just a nuisance visitor. A short placatory conversation should be enough to reassure her and she would go.

'Well, let's sit down and discuss it calmly,' Sarah said, and crossed to a wing armchair, not her usual seat but one in which she would be positioned to regain control of the proceedings. Her visitor, however, remained standing. She loomed over Sarah, who gripped the arms of her chair, reminding herself that this person was a specialist who listened to people's problems, not the avenging angel – or devil – she seemed to be at present. 'Mrs Stewart was free to discontinue treatment when she chose,' she said. 'If there's a matter of outstanding fees, I'm sure they can be settled.' Maybe Midge had cried off in mid-course, having pledged to pay for a set number of consultations; it would be just like her to enter into some such foolish agreement.

'Her condition is serious. She is most unstable at the moment,' said the woman.

'She's been depressed. It's not surprising, and it's why she came to you in the first place,' said Sarah. If anyone's unstable, she was thinking, it's you, her so-called counsellor. She decided to attack. 'How is that you know what's best for her?' she challenged. 'Why shouldn't she decide for herself, and ask advice of those who have known her for years, like my husband, who is a solicitor.'

'Oh, I know who he is,' said the woman. 'I've heard about you from my patient. You've had it easy, haven't you? This lovely house. Your high income. Mrs Stewart is the friend you like to patronise, isn't she? To pick up and condescend to when it suits you, and to cast aside when you have other plans. She's had a hard time in recent years, with her husband's business failing, and their debts, and then his death. And when she was counting on you, you threw her over.'

'It wasn't like that,' Sarah said, but was interrupted before she could explain.

'You're a spoiled, ungrateful woman,' said the visitor. 'You have a complaisant husband and you don't deserve him. If he was free, he'd find someone else who would appreciate him – Mrs Stewart, it might be. I'd be doing him a kindness if I did away with you, like that other one. Only I was wrong that time.' She frowned, thinking about it.

'What other one? What are you talking about?' Sarah, until now only puzzled and uneasy, became frightened. She sprang from her chair and moved behind it, and as she did so, she saw a knife appear in the woman's hand. 'Now wait a minute,' Sarah said, and she gripped the back of the chair, holding it before her as a shield. Things like this, women pulling knives, didn't happen in places like Winbury.

But they did. Daniel had been stabbed to death not many miles away, in an even smaller village. He was killed by wicked boys, but she was being threatened by a woman.

A mad woman.

Oliver would not be back for hours. It was no good, this time, expecting him to rescue her, and no one else would do it. She must save herself. She must calm this woman down, make a friendly overture.

'Would you like some tea?' she asked. 'Or coffee?'

'Tea. Coffee. That's what people always give you. She did, too, that other one, this morning. Tea, that was. With sugar. Milk in last. Silly old bat.'

She'd already referred to 'the other one', saying she had done away with her. Had she killed someone earlier today? Some old woman?

'Who do you mean?' asked Sarah, thinking she must keep the woman talking.

'That old bat this morning. My mother,' said the woman.

'Your mother? Would you like to ring her up?' Sarah offered. She could escape and go for help, if the woman used the telephone. But hadn't she implied the other one was dead? Her mother?

'She doesn't want to know,' said the woman.

That was scarcely surprising, if this was her daughter's normal mood; she must be a schizophrenic who had flipped. She was still standing in front of the fireplace, between Sarah and the door, which was ajar. The knife was in her hand, but it was not extended, and she had moved no nearer. She might throw it, like a dart, thought Sarah, ready to duck behind the chair.

'You find that upsetting, then,' said Sarah. 'About your mother.'

'Wouldn't you? To have a child, then give her up and wash your hands of her?'

What could she mean? Had she had a child and had it adopted?

'Have you no patients waiting?' Sarah tried, as a diversion, but she wouldn't have on Saturday, would she?

'Waiting for what?'

'For your advice.'

'Oh. I didn't understand you,' said the woman. 'Patience, I thought you meant.'

It took Sarah a second or two to realise what she meant, but then she felt encouraged. The woman was losing the initiative.

At that moment the doorbell rang again.

'Who's that?' demanded the woman, and she waved the knife around.

'I've no idea,' said Sarah. 'I'd better go and see.'

'Stay where you are,' the woman ordered. 'If you don't answer, they'll go away.'

That was all too likely, but then Sarah remembered that the door, on its sticky latch, had not shut properly. She took a chance and called out very loudly, almost shouting.

'Do come in. Come right in,' she instructed, gripping the chair hard. 'Into the sitting room,' she added, her voice shrill.

Would whoever it was hear her, and obey? If they pushed on the door, it would open easily. She called again, ready to welcome Jehovah's Witnesses, knife sharpeners, dubious pedlars, boys touting for odd jobs. Anyone arriving in the room would break the spell gripping this crazed creature. She listened, her senses sharp, and thought she heard the faint squeak as the heavy old door moved on its iron hinges.

'Come in,' she called again. 'In the sitting room. Please come in.'

She was watching the door of the room, and after what seemed like hours but was, in fact, less than a minute, she saw it open fully and another woman stood there, again tall, but this one was wearing a sober felt hat. It was Rosemary Ellis, the tenant of the upstairs flat behind the offices of Foxton and Smythe. She worked for some welfare organisation based in Fettleton, and was, according to Oliver, painfully shy and awkward but respected in her job. She had a tragic background of some sort – she had been badly beaten up by a lover or a husband, something dreadful, which the charity had hinted at when he checked her reference. Sarah had never been so thankful to see anyone in her life.

'Rosemary,' she cried warmly. 'Come in,' and she emerged from behind her barrier, moving towards Rosemary, hand extended welcomingly. 'Do you know Dr Warwick?' Miraculously, the woman's name had come to her. 'This is Miss Ellis,' she told the counsellor, who had taken her adopted name from the county she had lived in during her childhood years. 'Dr Warwick is just leaving,' she went on. 'Let me see you out, Dr Warwick. What an interesting chat we had. Goodbye,' and in moments Dr Warwick had been ushered out of the house. Sarah pushed the front door firmly to behind her, then leaned her back against it, and slid down, putting her head on her knees. 'Sorry, Rosemary. I'm feeling a bit dizzy. I'll be all right in a minute. Thank goodness you arrived when you did.'

Rosemary gazed down at her. She had been startled when instructed to walk in, and had only faintly heard Sarah's call as the sitting room was right across the hall, but because the door was on the latch, she had obeyed. When she entered the room, the tension between the two women had been almost palpable. She had not seen the knife; it had been pocketed as her foot crossed the threshold.

She had walked to Winbury that morning because the day was fine, and she had decided that she would allow herself to pass The Barn House in case Oliver could be seen working in the garden. Perhaps they might exchange a word across the fence, which in one spot bordered the footpath; she had seen his grey head there one summer's day, when he was cutting the grass.

She knew what she was doing would be seen as ridiculous by any ordinary person; it was a melancholy fixation, but it harmed no one. The exercise she took was beneficial, and she had grown bold enough to have a sandwich in the pub on one occasion. Last night she had dined out; that was a tiny triumph, too. Nothing had gone wrong; no one had snubbed her; the waiter had been polite and helpful. She must do these things which other people found so simple more often.

Oliver was not in his garden, or not where she could see him from the path. She continued past the church and down the street, recalling how, the last time she had done this, on Christmas Day, someone else on foot had approached behind her, and could have seen her pause to look through the gates at the house. No one did this now, but, halting, she saw the garage doors were open and the Rover was not there. So he was out. Probably Sarah was with him, but would they then have left the garage open, with her white Nissan in full view? Perhaps it was safe to do so here in Winbury; it was not a chance she would take. However, a blue car was parked on the gravel where the shabby Escort had been at Christmas.

Last night, the other woman who had dined alone at The Verandah had drunk a whole bottle of red wine. Rosemary, across the room and growing bolder, had seen her speak imperiously to the waiter as she ordered. She had not eaten much; Rosemary had seen her summon him to take away a plate of some barely touched first course. After that she had toyed with whatever she had chosen next, and then she had gone out, only moments before Rosemary received the change from her bill and also left. Walking back to her car, Rosemary had seen her standing still, staring at the attractive house where the Foxtons' friend, Mrs Wilmot, lived. When she saw Rosemary approaching, she had moved on, and had got into a blue Renault car and driven off, passing Rosemary who stood watching her go by.

She wasn't fit to drive after all that wine, and judging by the way she had treated the waiter in the restaurant, she was in a filthy temper. Rosemary had memorised the registration number of her car and had written it down as soon as she reached home. She was good at numbers; she did the accounts for the association which employed her and she lodged it firmly in her mind. When she saw the blue car, which looked so similar, drawn up outside the Foxtons' house, some impulse made her walk up to it and check the number. It was the same car.

The woman, angry and the worse for drink last night, was probably a close friend of the Foxtons, or a weekend guest, but her behaviour had been strange. The way she had stared at Mrs Wilmot's house was peculiar. Rosemary had had the feeling that she might break a window, which was a ridiculous idea. No doubt it was her imagination which was running away with her; she lived too much in her head, and not enough in the real world.

I'll pretend I'm appealing for the association, she told herself as she tried to think of a feasible excuse for ringing the doorbell. There was to be a raffle soon; I'll ask them for a prize, brazen it out, she thought, with unusual courage. As she waited for the door to be opened, she expected to see Sarah Foxton appear, politely masking her annoyance at being interrupted when she was entertaining a friend. Instead, she had clearly broken up an altercation.

'I don't know why I did it,' she kept saying later, while they made a fuss of her.

As soon as the so-called Dr Warwick had departed – they heard her drive away – and Sarah had recovered from what was almost a faint, she had declared that Rosemary had saved her life, and that the woman had been threatening her with a knife. It was all, somehow, connected with Midge Stewart and her plans.

Sarah had telephoned the police and Rosemary had given them the make and registration number of the car. She was still in the house, plying Sarah with strong coffee, which they had made together in the kitchen, when the police arrived.

They caught 'Dr' Warwick fairly quickly. She had the knife in her pocket. They were already looking for her because a patient she was treating had complained that she had threatened him.

She was very soon in prison, with her licence revoked, and facing fresh charges.

And Rosemary had been to Sunday lunch at The Barn House, where Midge Stewart and Mrs Wilmot were both present; she had been shown the dolls' house they had bought while 'Dr' Warwick had been threatening Sarah.

Oliver had said he could never thank her enough for listening to her inner warning instinct. 'Dr' Warwick had, it seemed, blamed Sarah for Midge Stewart's cancellation of her treatment, but this was just the trigger which had sent her into a form of mental breakdown. It was a very complex, tragic story, he declared. The enquiries he had initiated into the whereabouts of Wendy Tyler had filled in various gaps, but her connection with Lady Fortescue had not been revealed.

No one knew when, if ever, she would be free again.

She comes to see me regularly. I'm in a hospital now, not prison. I don't know why. They say I need treatment, and she agrees. How foolish.

She sits across the table from me, asking how I am, and if there is anything I need which she may be allowed to send me. She has supplied books and tapes, expensive soap, even clothes. There is no warmth between us, no affection

She's looking older, and seems to have lost weight. I've noticed that. She's moved, she's told me, into a smaller house quite near that mansion which I visited. She never told anyone about that; not wanting, even after all this time, to claim connection with me.

I punish her by sitting silent, never speaking. Once I refused to see her after she had driven all that way, but I like watching her suffer, so I may not do that again. I'll see. It's nice to have that weapon up my sleeve.

Maybe she'll give up – the visiting I mean. Although I didn't touch another person, wounded no one, I shall be here for a long time. It isn't fair.

I've never told anyone who she is, though she says such a revelation can't hurt her now. Maybe that's true. Maybe that's why I haven't made it. She's just a friend, I say. She talks. I listen. After all, I am a counsellor.

If she didn't come, no one would.

ADMIT TO MURDER

All the world's a stage,
And all the men and women merely players;
They have their exits and their entrances;
and one man in his time plays many parts . . .

As You Like It, Shakespeare.

PART ONE

1

Prologue: 1976

She disappeared on a Wednesday night after the weekly practice of the Feringham Choral Society.

Norah Tyler, in her Pimlico flatlet, heard the news on the radio the following morning. The announcement was brief, merely stating that Louise Vaughan, aged twenty-four, had last been seen getting into her dark red Mini after the singers had ended their rehearsal of Fauré's *Requiem*, which they were to perform at Easter. She had not returned to the village of Selbury, five miles away, where she lived with her parents.

Tutting under her breath, Norah made her tea in the Crown Derby pot she always used. Two slices of bread already lay under the grill, and automatically she turned them at the precise moment when they were toasted just as she liked them. Butter, in a glass dish with its own silver knife, stood on the small table beneath the window. The morning sun made a pool of gold light across the pale linen cloth which was laid with delicate porcelain: cup, saucer and plate. Honey this morning, thought Norah, taking a pot from the cupboard, her movements precise. She liked things to be neat and orderly, and, when it lay in her power, they were. For ten years now she had been personal assistant to the managing director of an electronics factory which, with the development of new technology, was rapidly expanding. Norah's job had developed with it, and her salary had increased to match her responsibilities. She earned a good income and could afford to indulge her taste for modest luxuries.

As she made her small, routine movements, she allowed herself to absorb the shocking news she had heard. Louise was not an irresponsible girl. If her car had broken down or she had been delayed in some other fashion, she would telephone so that her parents did not become anxious. She must have had an accident, Norah decided, putting the toast in a small silver rack which old Mrs Warrington had given her one Christmas.

She sat down to eat her breakfast.

Wouldn't the police have traced her to a hospital by now, if that was the answer? Had something really dreadful occurred? Surely not. There would be a simple explanation.

She would telephone later from the office.

Norah first obtained permission from Mr Barratt. She never took advantage of her trusted position.

'I'm an old friend of the family,' she explained. 'It's most worrying.'

'Of course you must telephone, Miss Tyler,' Mr Barratt urged. He never called her anything else; both of them understood these subtleties, not like the young girls in the outer office where everyone was called by their first name as soon as they were engaged. Sometimes Mr Barratt thought it would be agreeable to have a voluptuous assistant wearing tight skirts and high heels and with long red hair, called Valerie, instead of Miss Tyler with her greying perm and her thin figure in the plain suits or skirts and shirts she always wore as she efficiently managed his affairs. But Valerie might not be able to spell and Miss Tyler could, and Valerie might marry or leave, and Miss Tyler had done neither. She was, in fact, the perfect secretary.

He never wondered about her private life and she never mentioned it; this would not have been suitable, in her view. But she knew a great deal about his, his wife and three daughters, their A levels and boyfriends, and the Corfu villa the Barratts annually rented, Miss Tyler making all the arrangements.

This was the first time she had mentioned anything remotely personal, and during the afternoon he remembered to ask her if she had made her call.

'I haven't been able to get through,' she replied. 'The line's been engaged each time I've tried.'

'The girl will be all right,' he assured her, but he knew that if one of his daughters had vanished, he would have been nearly out of his mind.

'They'll find her car, if it was an accident,' Norah reasoned aloud. 'That is, if she was taken to hospital unconscious and unable to give her name. But of course, she'd have her bag with her – her driving licence and so on.'

'She might not,' said Mr Barratt, whose own daughters had large sacks they slung over their shoulders in which all sorts of things were kept but not papers denoting identity.

They returned to Mr Barratt's programme for briefing the next board meeting, and Norah put the Vaughans out of her mind until it was time to go home.

The thick black headlines screamed at her from the evening paper on the news-stand by the tube station.

HEIRESS GOES MISSING, she read, and there was a blurred photograph of Louise, enlarged from a snapshot and unrecognisable, her fair hair blown across her face. She bought a copy.

Pressed among a mass of humanity strap-hanging homewards, Norah could not read the paper in the tube. She kept it until she was back in the flat, and broke with routine enough to sit down before taking off her good black coat.

Pretty fair-headed Louise Vaughan, 24, went missing after choir practice, Norah read. MOTHER'S VIGIL, announced a line in thick type above a paragraph revealing that Louise should have been home by half-past ten, eleven at the latest, after the weekly rehearsal for the Easter concert to be given in Feringham Town Hall. *Her mother Susan Vaughan, 57, waited up in the large secluded mansion where Louise had her own flat in the west wing,* the report went on, and Norah learned that occasionally after a rehearsal Louise would go with friends for a drink but was never later than eleven. She might, it was hinted, have gone home with someone.

'Hmph!' Norah snorted aloud. Not Louise, not when

her parents expected her. And flat in the west wing, indeed: what next? The house was certainly large, but scarcely a mansion, and Louise occupied the room which had been hers from childhood. It overlooked a rough patch of orchard where now the daffodils must be out, a mass of yellow under the apple trees which soon would be laden with blossom. Old Mr Warrington had kept bees there during the war and one had got tangled in Norah's hair. Mr Warrington had gently removed it and she had not been stung, but he had, and his hand had swelled up enormously. Some people did react like that, he told her, and warned her not to get between bees harvesting honey and their direct flight home to their hives.

She had never seen bees in hives, nor apple blossom, until she went to Selbury during the war as an evacuee and her life became linked with the family in the big house.

She took off her coat, hung it up, then tried the telephone again. This time, George Vaughan answered. Louise had not been found, he said; she had not been admitted to any hospital. Her car had turned up, however; it was parked in a side road on the new industrial estate in Feringham, with the keys in the dash. Her handbag was on the rear seat. They must be prepared for the worst, he told her, but of course there was hope. She might have been kidnapped, for instance, and this call must be kept short in case Louise, or her abductor, rang.

'That was Norah.'

George Vaughan returned to the drawing-room, where

Susan was sitting by the fire. The day was fresh and bright, not cold, but she felt chilled through. Neither of them had slept, though in the end they had undressed and tried to relax in the silent darkness of their room, separated by the narrow gap between their twin beds. Both were thinking that this could not be real, it could not be happening, but Susan knew that tragedy could strike without warning. Hadn't she already had her share of it, she thought, staring at the lightening sky showing behind the curtains as dawn broke. Her first husband had been killed during the war, and their child, a boy, had died before he was one, a victim of what was now called cot-death syndrome. It had been a terrible time; the police had behaved as if she had killed him herself, even though she lived in Selbury House, her parents' home, and all agreed she had adored the baby.

Now the police were back, because another child had vanished. But she wasn't dead; Louise couldn't be dead. Susan shut her mind to the possibility.

'Norah?' Detective Inspector Scott, sitting on the other side of the hearth, looked up. The call would have been recorded; by this time the telephone had been tapped in case there was a ransom demand, although Scott and his chief superintendent thought it most unlikely. The parents, though comfortably off, were not in the really rich league, but kidnappers – and newspaper reporters – might think otherwise.

'Norah Tyler,' George explained. 'She's someone we've known for years.' It was always difficult to explain Norah's role in their lives. 'She'd heard, of course, and wondered if there was any news.'

'If she's been kidnapped, how soon will we know?' asked Susan. Her voice was steady but her expression was strained and she mashed a handkerchief between her bony fingers.

'It's hard to say.' Scott had never been directly involved with a kidnapping. 'They might wait for a while to – er—' he sought the appropriate expression, not wanting to raise false hopes but feeling that it was too soon to admit to the worst.

'To soften us up?' George suggested.

'Exactly,' said Scott.

'We're not rich enough,' Susan said.

'You live in a large house and you run an expensive car,' said Scott. George Vaughan drove a Rover 3500. 'Some people would consider you good for a touch.' He looked round the room. There were various pieces of furniture that were worth a bob or two: that bureau, for instance, with all the inlay; he didn't know what it was, Sheraton maybe, something like that, and those chairs were antique; you got an eye for that sort of thing, in his job. The sofa he sat in, however, needed re-springing and the chintz which covered it was faded. The house was not all that old; it had been built in the late 1920s by Mrs Vaughan's father, a prosperous manufacturer, something to do with biscuits, Scott believed. Her mother still lived here, in the lodge at the gates. At the moment she was on holiday in Madeira, where by now the news of her granddaughter's disappearance would have been broken to her. It had been decided that she could not be left exposed to the risk of discovering it herself from a newspaper or radio broadcast, and George had telephoned her companion, another elderly widow with whom she often went away. George had urged her to change no plans, for Louise might soon be found and the old ladies could do nothing if they returned; in fact she was better out of the way, one less person to worry about. He had promised to telephone as soon as there was anything to report.

While Scott sat with the parents, asking them about their daughter, Detective Sergeant Marsh and a woman officer were up in Louise's bedroom, seeking any clue to what might have happened. It was routine; they did not expect to find anything helpful, except perhaps an address book with details of friends not already mentioned by her parents.

The two officers appeared now, with tea on a tray.

'Thought you could do with a cup, Mrs Vaughan,' said Marsh, a sturdy young man with brown hair and a pair of shrewd blue eyes.

'Oh, how kind,' said Susan vaguely. Surely tea was over long ago? Someone had given her a biscuit. She hadn't wanted it but had tried to nibble some crumbs.

The woman officer could see that Mrs Vaughan was far too shaky to handle the teapot, so she picked it up.

'Shall I be mother?' she said, and began pouring.

Scott was glad of the intervention by the two younger officers. There was no right way of dealing with this type of case; days of suspense lay ahead, but he was certain that Louise was dead.

All day officers had been making inquiries around Feringham and in the village; Louise's Mini had been taken off to the laboratory for testing; searches had begun in the fields round the town and it might be decided to drag Feringham canal. The parents hadn't known much about their daughter's private life. They said she had no special boyfriend at present, though she occasionally spent the night in London, where she had once shared a flat with two other girls. She worked for a small publisher who specialised in books on art and natural history, and was an editor producing a series about alpine plants and the wild flowers of various areas. She had returned to live at home a year ago; it was easy to travel back and forth from Feringham station.

Her colleagues at work would have to be interviewed; the Met must be asked to help with that task. Scott didn't think the answer lay there unless someone obsessed with her had followed her and observed her habits. More important would be a close study of interviews with the rest of the Feringham Choral Society. By now most of them had been contacted and he would concentrate on the men; if she had given one of them a lift home, he might have tried something on and met resistance. Such things could escalate and end badly. If this were the answer, her car should provide some clues.

Much later that night, when reports had been collated and the chief superintendent had been brought up to date on what was so far known, which amounted to very little, Tom Francis, who had a pleasant baritone voice, received a visit from the police.

He lived in a four-year-old house in Coverton Park, a still-developing estate on the edge of Feringham. He was a computer programmer and had a wife, Anna, and two small children, a boy and a girl. He had been visited earlier, as soon as he returned from work, by a constable who had taken a statement confirming that he had attended the choral rehearsal the evening before, and volunteering the information that he and several others, including Louise, had walked together to where their cars were parked in the market square. A visit to The Swan had been discussed; they often called in there for a drink and a chat before going home.

'To wind down,' Tom said now, when Detective Inspector Scott and Detective Sergeant Marsh called to ask him about his movements.

'Wind down?'

'The singing is stirring,' Tom answered. 'Gets the pulse going and all that. You know.'

Scott didn't: not really; but he nodded.

'So you went to The Swan last night?' That had not appeared in his statement.

'No, I didn't. Jennifer's got tonsillitis and I wanted to get back,' he said. 'My wife's a bit ragged round the edges after being up with her most of the night.'

'Did Louise go to The Swan?' No one had said that she did.

'No. She drove off alone,' Tom said.

'That's unusual? She normally joined in?'

'Oh yes.' She'd been very quiet, Tom had noticed, and hadn't looked very well, now he came to think about it. Still, that was irrelevant to the present inquiry.

'What's she like?' Scott sounded as if he really wanted to know.

'Very friendly,' said Tom. 'But not pushy. Shy, really, I suppose, until you get to know her.'

'Attractive?'

'Yes – yes, very,' Tom answered.

'So you found her attractive,' noted Scott, nodding to Marsh to make sure he was writing this down.

'Yes.' Tom sounded puzzled now.

'If you weren't married, would you have wanted to date her?'

'What a strange question!' Tom's bewilderment was obvious. 'I am married. It didn't arise.'

'But supposing?' Scott persisted.

'Well, maybe. Probably,' Tom decided.

'But you hadn't?'

'No.'

Scott kept at him, going over the time the rehearsal ended and discovering that once, when his car was out of action, Louise had given Tom a lift home.

They knew this already. One of the other choir members had remembered the occasion and mentioned it in his own statement. He'd added that she'd done the same for him, another time.

The difference was that he had volunteered the information and Tom had not.

Tom Francis was taken back to the police station and questioned for as long as the law would allow, without being charged. This was years before the Police and Criminal Evidence Act imposed stricter limitations on such detention. The clothes he had worn on the night Louise disappeared were removed and sent for testing, and visible even to the naked eye were traces of blue wool that could have come from the sweater Louise had, allegedly, been wearing that night.

'How can you tell, since you haven't found her?' Tom demanded. 'It might just as well have come from Jennifer's dressing-gown. That's made of blue wool. Why don't you try testing that?'

The police declined this invitation. Tom had said that he went straight home but his wife, interviewed while he was being questioned, had told them that he did not return until eleven o'clock. She had not been alarmed because she thought he had gone, as usual after the practice, to The Swan, though he had said he would come home promptly. It seemed that twenty minutes to half an hour of his time was not accounted for, and he grew angry when asked to explain the discrepancy. He said he had filled the car up with petrol at the one garage which stayed open late, not wanting to be delayed in the morning, but inquiries failed to confirm this since he had paid cash and the duty cashier could not remember whether or not he had been a customer. The place was self-service and the staff barely looked up as they took the money.

After a few days, when Louise had still not been found and there were no more clues as to her fate, Tom was taken in again. Pushed hard enough, he might crack and admit to murder; then, once he'd confessed, he would reveal what he had done with his victim. Any further evidence needed for his conviction would soon be found when the body was examined. For by now everyone, even Louise's parents, was sure that this was a murder case.

But he did not confess.

They took his Cortina away for testing, but without

Louise herself, it was impossible to prove that any traces found in the car were hers. They found what must be assumed to be her fingerprints in her room at Selbury House, on folders to do with her work, and her hairbrush and other possessions, but no matching prints were found in Tom's car. Blond hairs discovered on the upholstery probably came from the heads of his children.

As he had not been in The Swan and yet was late home, Tom's wife was curious about where he had been during the unexplained period of time that Wednesday evening.

'Getting petrol,' said Tom. 'I told the police that and I'm telling you. I didn't want to stop on the way in to work in the morning.'

But apart from the fact that filling the tank would not take more than ten minutes, Anna knew that it had been almost full that evening. She had used the car after Tom had come home from the office to go to the surgery to collect a prescription for Jennifer, nipping out while Tom had a quick meal before the choral society's meeting.

He couldn't have been having an affair with Louise, could he? Or wanting to, and she wouldn't? Or wanting out, and she wouldn't let him go? All these possibilities ran through Anna's mind. Her own life was so taken up with the children, and his day at the office was so long except on singing nights when he always managed to get home earlier, that they seemed to have little chance to talk together. Louise, unattached and attractive, might have presented some sort of temptation. But Tom would never have killed her. That was impossible, unless there had been a quarrel followed by some dreadful sort of accident.

Anna took to watching Tom, speculatively, wondering how many secrets he had. After all, she had a few herself; innocent ones, such as how she enjoyed her chats with the milkman when he called for the money. He was a cheery man who told her about his racing pigeons, which wouldn't have interested Tom; and there was the bank teller who always looked at her as if she were still available and worth more than a glance when he cashed her cheques.

Tom became very silent in the days that followed, during which no trace of Louise was found. She seemed to have totally vanished, although there were reports that she had been seen in Glasgow and in Liverpool, and even in Penzance. All these rumours had to be investigated; all led nowhere. There were the usual crank telephone calls from people alleging that they had killed her and dumped her body in various sites ranging from silos to reservoirs. Some of these allegations were explored; others were not. Meanwhile, anonymous letters arrived at the house, accusing Tom of murder. Although he had not been named in reports that a man was helping with inquiries, his identity had been discovered because of the frequent calls at his house by police and because of his absence from home. The letters were all local; no one outside the area could know who he was. Tom threw them away, but Anna rescued them from the wastepaper basket and brooded over them. She knew they came from evil or, at best, unbalanced people, but they had an effect on her. So did the sly looks and muttered comments of several neighbours.

★ ★ ★

Louise's grandmother returned from Madeira and resumed residence at the Lodge House, as it was now called. Re-wired, re-plumbed, and slightly extended, it had become a comfortable small house easily maintained by Mrs Gibson who came in daily from the village and, besides doing the cleaning, cooked lunch for herself and her employer and left something ready for supper. Mrs Warrington did very little for herself.

Her companion in Madeira had been Dorothy Spencer, the widow of a former Member of Parliament who had been knighted when he gave up his safe Conservative seat to make way for a younger and promising candidate. Lady Spencer had worked with Mrs Warrington in the WVS during the war and they were old sparring partners as well as friends. Though both were now in their eighties, they travelled up to London to matinées or exhibitions once or twice a month, lunching at Fortnum's or, occasionally, Brown's Hotel. During the weeks after Louise disappeared Lady Spencer telephoned daily, and often came over to keep her friend company. Both old ladies were filled with angry frustration because, powerful though each had been in her time, there was nothing that they could do either to make possible Louise's return or to discover what had happened to her. When search parties combed the fields round Feringham and later a wider area reaching a radius of ten or more miles, her father joined in, raking the hedgerows with sticks, stirring up heaps of dead leaves in the woods, prodding streams and culverts, coming home wet and exhausted but feeling that he was doing something active to help. Malcolm, Louise's older adopted brother, named after his uncle who was killed in the war, went out with them too. He lived thirty miles away in Corton, where until he could find more lucrative work he drove a minicab, and he often spent the night at Selbury House, but when she disappeared he was driving a fare to Heathrow.

While the men were out, Susan stayed by the telephone in case there was news, occasionally reinforcing with tea and sandwiches the catering laid on by the police. She never went out without leaving someone else in the house to answer the telephone.

Soon, Norah was there to take over.

She took unpaid leave.

Louise's disappearance was still holding the interest of the major crime reporters, who conjectured about her fate and compared her case with that of other young women who were missing. With every day that passed, the chance of finding her alive diminished.

Norah had gone down to Selbury the first weekend, leaving the office early and getting off the train at Feringham station just as Louise had done for so long.

George met her.

'I'm glad you've come,' he told her. 'You'll be company for Susan while we wait. I'm going out with the police, searching, whenever they'll let me. It's better than sitting about.'

He would have to go back to work soon, Norah thought. He was a director of Warrington's and still very active on the production side of the business.

They drove through the town and George took a

detour to show her where Louise's car had been found, outside a factory that packaged toilet goods. The wide new street on the outskirts of Feringham was surfaced with shining macadam. Tall lamps were bright sentinels punctuating the pavement. At this hour of the evening, with all the works shut, there was no one about and no other car to be seen.

'I ask you, what was she doing down here?' George demanded. 'She'd no call whatever to come this way.'

'But wasn't the car dumped here? By whoever—?' Norah let her question die.

'I suppose so.' George sighed and scraped the gears, making Norah wince, as he changed down to turn by the bus-stop. He was normally a very good driver who never abused any part of the machine. They drove back towards the centre of town, passing the new comprehensive school formed by the marriage of a grammar and a secondary modern school years before, and past rows of shops to the market square and the town hall, where the practices were held and where the concert would eventually take place. 'You see, it was nowhere near her way home,' George said.

'Haven't the police got any ideas about it?'

'They've been interviewing a man called Tom Francis,' said George. 'He sings with the choir. I suppose they're all suspect – all the men, that is. It must have been someone she knew, after all. She must have given a lift to someone who turned – well—' He sighed. 'She wouldn't have picked up a stranger.'

'But someone she knew – she would have talked herself out of trouble,' said Norah. 'She's very sensible.'

'She's not very big,' said George. 'And a man's strength – she wouldn't be a match for it, if he was determined.'

'She'd have scratched him, though. Fought him off,' said Norah. 'He'd have scars.'

'I suppose the police have thought of that,' said George. He wrenched the steering-wheel viciously as they rounded a bend on the long winding road that led to Selbury.

'How's Mrs Warrington taking it?' Norah asked.

'She's only just got back from Madeira,' said George. 'We telephoned her to let her know what had happened, but we insisted she stayed the fortnight. She was there with Dorothy Spencer. She's much calmer than I am.'

'She's seen it all before,' said Norah.

'Not murder,' said George, at last using the word everyone had so far been avoiding.

'Murder of a sort, surely?' said Norah. 'Both her sons killed. And her son-in-law.'

'Ah, but their deaths were a glorious sacrifice,' said George bitterly. 'Or so she can tell herself. Killed for King and country. She's had her share of sorrow, poor old lady. She shouldn't have to lose her granddaughter too.'

And why should I lose my lovely daughter, he was screaming inside his head.

They were entering Selbury, passing a few outlying cottages which had once stood in isolation on the fringe of the village, but now the gaps between them were filled with modern houses. The village had grown to accommodate commuters and people who worked in local industries. George slowed at the speed restriction sign on the rise leading into the village. It was awkwardly placed and for years he had been trying to persuade the council to move it, giving motorists more warning that the village lay beyond their horizon. There had been a bad accident when a car sped over the brow of the hill and knocked down a child running across the road. He had sustained various fractures and cuts. The inference was that unless someone were to be killed, the council would not shift the sign.

Now, Norah saw a raw gap gouged out of a bank at the side of the road; a skip stood there, and a pile of bricks.

'What's happening at Mrs Benham's house?' she asked.

'It's been sold and pulled down so that the site can be developed,' said George. 'Thirteen rabbit hutches are to go up instead.'

'Oh dear! What would she have said?' Mrs Benham had died two years before.

George made a sound which was an attempt at a laugh.

'She thought one of the family would live there,' he said. 'Didn't realise the commercial potential, I suppose.'

Mrs Benham had been a magistrate and had run the Girl Guides. Her large Edwardian house had stood in nearly two acres of garden where the Guides had camped and cooked sausages over fires, and where her own sons and daughters had played as children themselves.

'There's another colony springing up behind the Post Office,' said George.

'But that's agricultural land, isn't it? I thought you couldn't build on that.'

'It depends where you're standing when you look at it,' George replied. 'It can be called in-filling, and it's very profitable if you have land to sell. Feringham is growing all the time and people have to live somewhere, of course. Villages seem to have the choice of expanding or of dying – losing their school and their post offices and shops. We've got a new butcher in the village now, and Dobbs' Stores has changed hands and is on the up-and-up.'

Dobbs was the village grocery, which sold everything from cheese to shoelaces. Norah had spent her sweet coupons there during the war. Every time she returned to Selbury she remembered the first time she had seen it, brought in a bus to the village hall as a girl of thirteen, sent out of London for safety in 1939. The children had been as much selected by their future hosts as allocated by the billeting officer, and Norah was a better bet than most. She was picked by the gardener's wife from the lodge at Selbury House, earmarked already as a bigger girl useful for duties about the place. She was soon helping wash up at weekends and in the evenings, when the Warringtons' maids had gone to work in munitions factories. Susan was young then, and newly married. Norah thought she and her handsome husband in his army uniform were like people in the films. It was even quite film-like when Hugh Graham was killed at Dunkirk, before the birth of his son, though it was dreadfully sad.

She still felt some of that magic.

It was the waiting that was so hard.

'If only we knew,' said Susan, on the Sunday afternoon. 'If only we knew what we had to face.'

When Hugh was killed, she had known very soon that

there was no hope; for her, there had been no weeks or months while he was posted officially missing before his death was confirmed. But there had been no body then, either: no funeral rites to observe. In time there had been a memorial service in the village church, attended by some of his surviving fellow officers, and later she had married one of them.

A body was found in a river in Wales but it wasn't Louise. George was taken there in a police car to make sure. He looked at the pitiful collection of flesh and bones on the mortuary table and shook his head. This was someone else's tragedy.

Louise could be hundreds of miles away. Whoever had killed her could have taken her off in his own car, or one he had stolen, and dumped her anywhere in the country. While the search was centred around Feringham, he would have had plenty of time to find a good hiding-place elsewhere.

'We may not get a lead until some other young woman goes missing,' said Detective Inspector Scott on one of his visits to the house.

'Goes missing,' snorted Mrs Warrington. 'What an expression. Girls don't go missing, they disappear.'

She hid her grief under a fierce, autocratic manner. This time there had been no warning, no premonition, no awareness of particular risk. During the war she had been prepared, braced to face disaster, with mental plans about how to behave when it happened, and although part of her had died with each of her sons, on the surface life continued as usual. She had continued with her voluntary war work and had set an example of fortitude.

Susan was living at Selbury House when Hugh was killed. During the few weeks of their marriage, while he was with his Territorial regiment training on Salisbury Plain, they had rented a cottage near Warminster. As soon as he was posted abroad, she had gone home to wait for her baby. At that time life was still comfortable in the big house, even without the two maids. Mrs Johnson, the cook, who was in her fifties, remained; and Ford, the gardener, who had flat feet and poor sight, would not be passed fit for active service, so he continued to dig for victory in the large garden where fruit and vegetables already flourished. Mrs Ford undertook most of the cleaning and it was natural for Norah to help her. She was nearly fifteen when Hugh was killed and would soon be leaving school. Mrs Warrington had decided that she would shape into a useful little nursemaid for the coming baby. She was a biddable girl, not pretty, but pleasant-looking, with alert brown eyes and shining dark hair. Since living in Selbury she had grown and put on weight, and her face had a healthy glow; she had settled well and seemed to like the country, cheerfully helping a local farmer with the harvest in the long summer holiday that marked the Battle of Britain. The Fords had been lucky securing such a child; the Warringtons themselves took in two small boys, one of whom wet his bed and constantly cried for his mother. It was Norah who, discovering their misery on the way to school, consoled them and helped them adjust until, after a few weeks of the phoney war, they both went back to London.

One of them was later killed in a bombing raid, and so were Norah's parents and her elder sister. After that there seemed nothing else for her to do but remain in Selbury until she was old enough to be called up.

After baby Harry died, Mr Warrington had advised Norah to stay on at school for another year. Since Mrs Ford would no longer be paid for her board, she could have one of the attic rooms in Selbury House and, in return, could make herself useful about the place in her spare time.

It had become a habit.

PART TWO

1

Norah

The radio alarm woke Norah at seven o'clock. Normally she slept well, but for the last weeks she had woken in the small hours and had lain in the darkness listening to the World Service, with the automatic cutout adjusted so that it went off after an hour by which time, with luck, she would have fallen asleep again. Sometimes she started awake when a burst of music interrupted the even tones of the announcer relating news of famine, earthquake or terrorism, or analysing political events in some remote part of the globe. She let the sound wash over her, the volume low; if you listened too intently, interest kept you awake.

Susan had given her the radio for Christmas the year they moved into the Lodge House, after old Mrs Warrington's death at the age of ninety-one. Selbury House was put on the market and once again the Lodge House was refurbished. A second bathroom was installed above a study built on for George, who had now retired, and the kitchen, drawing-room and main bedroom were extended, turning it into a spacious house with three large bedrooms and a small one, and a quarter of an acre of garden.

Susan, who loved her garden, had taken to working in it obsessively after Louise's disappearance, clipping and pruning, planting and hoeing, until she was exhausted, reluctant, it seemed, to be in the house at all. One reason behind the move was George's hope that with less land around her, she would begin to spare herself, but Selbury House had become too large for them. Besides, they needed money; so much had been spent on Malcolm, settling his debts and saving him from bankruptcy when various ventures he started went wrong. After paying off his creditors when the house was sold, George had told him that this was the final reckoning and now he must take the consequences of any further folly.

Selbury House had been sold to a couple with two children. The husband worked in the City and the wife, alone while the children were away at school, had become bored and lonely. Village gossip said that one reason they had moved into the country was to steady her down as she had been having affairs in London; whatever the truth of that, they separated after less than two years and she demanded a generous settlement. Selbury House had been sold to provide it, and went to the highest bidder who gazumped a private buyer. The new owner was a property speculator who had hoped to build eighty houses in the grounds, but the planners permitted him to put up only ten. This he had done, and retained the land against a change of heart by the council. The house itself had been divided into two large flats and a small one in the main building, with another flat over what had been stables and were now extra garages for all the new inhabitants.

When the Vaughans realised what was happening to the place they were dismayed, and almost regretted what they had done, though there had really been little choice unless they let Malcolm go bankrupt and, as they saw it, defraud those to whom he owed money. It wasn't as if they had grandchildren to fill up the big house on regular visits; however, they had hoped that it would continue to be a family home.

Norah had pointed out that there might be grandchildren one day. Malcolm might yet have a family.

'Well, that doesn't look much like happening,' said Susan. 'Sad though it is to admit it.' As she spoke her thin face, with the fair skin etched by a network of broken veins, took on a forlorn expression. 'And anyway, if he does, I'll be too old to help take care of them.'

'Norah won't,' said George.

I won't be here, Norah said to herself. But four years later, here she still was and it was time to get up and tidy downstairs before breakfast, which democratically they all ate together in the kitchen. Norah, quick and neat in all she did, would clear away her own cup and saucer and plate as soon as she had finished her toast and marmalade, and leave husband and wife with the percolator and the newspapers while she went upstairs to make the beds in their two bedrooms, for since the move they no longer slept together.

Once I was personal assistant to a managing director,

Norah thought to herself as she shook duvets – she had managed to modernise Susan and George that far – and plumped up pillows. Now I'm simply a housekeeper, a grand title, really, for what I do and no disgrace in itself, but I had risen in the world and now you could say that I'm back to my origins. Though not really; not when I'm on such intimate terms with my employers. The thought made her smile.

She had slid into it. Five years after Louise disappeared, Norah's firm was taken over by a large consortium and she was made redundant. Her compensation was generous and she was in no hurry to make plans. She went down to Selbury for a visit and had stayed there ever since.

She had fully intended to find another job or, because at her age good openings were limited, to set up on her own, but at Selbury House there was always plenty to do. Then old Mrs Warrington fell and broke her hip. After she came out of hospital, Norah moved into the Lodge House to look after her. Why engage a stranger when she was available, said the old lady, propped up in bed discussing what must be done. Besides, a woman from one of those agencies would be very expensive.

'Norah must be paid,' said George, who had been meaning to offer her something for doing his typing.

'Why?' Mrs Warrington saw no reason for such a step. 'She's part of the family now and one doesn't pay family members for their help. Besides, she gets her keep. And she had a pay-off, didn't she, when she stopped work? Anyway, she'll soon be eligible for her pension. She can't need much spending money.'

Susan was less shocked by these reactionary remarks than George, but she agreed that Norah must be recompensed to some extent. It was decided that they would stamp her insurance card for the remaining years when this would be necessary, and that she should be paid thirty pounds a week.

'There's no point in her having to pay tax,' Susan pointed out. 'And she'll get lots of perks.'

When Norah, who had been earning an excellent salary, was told of these decisions, she remembered the hours she had spent as a girl helping Mrs Ford wash up, polish floors, clean silver. She had peeled mounds of potatoes and had put eggs in waterglass for Mrs Johnson, the cook. She had bottled plums and dried apple slices, and she had, incidentally, become a very good cook herself, helping out when the family came home on leave and special celebratory meals were prepared.

Old Mrs Warrington had left her a thousand pounds in her will, and her garnet brooch as a keepsake. Norah had bought a car with the money, adding to it some of her own. Malcolm had found her a low-mileage secondhand VW Golf, economical to run and easy to park. It enabled her to achieve some freedom and she went away for occasional weekends at country hotels, something she had begun to enjoy in the last years of her time with Mr Barratt.

While she lived at the Lodge House there was no room for Malcolm, as he would never settle for the small room above the hall, where there was just space for a single bed and a chest of drawers. The Vaughans never had overnight guests now; indeed, they had rarely done so before the move, though occasionally Louise had had friends to stay. Their social life had dwindled since her disappearance. Susan's closest friend was Helen Cartwright, Lady Spencer's daughter, who had married a merchant banker and lived fifteen miles away, between Feringham and Malchester. The two had been at school together and were godmothers to each other's children.

Susan had expected to rebuild the family after she had married George. She had replaced her husband and she would have other children, lots of them, and in time would forget that one small baby who had been so smiling and happy and then was so suddenly dead. How could the police imagine she might have had something to do with that? In those days there had been a constable in the village and he had been very embarrassed at the implications of his visit, with a sergeant from Feringham, and the nature of their questions. It was impossible for Mrs Vaughan to have done such a thing, he had insisted. The sergeant had pointed out that she might have been in a state of distress because she was now a widow, and the constable had opined that this was very likely, but she would be comforted by having her baby. He knew this was the truth; he knew that Susan was devastated. In the end the coroner agreed with this view and the sorry inquiry was over. Susan was left with her grief and a tiny grave in the churchyard.

After her marriage to George, no new baby had arrived and so, eventually, they adopted one. Before the advent of the contraceptive pill and legal abortion there was no shortage of babies for adoption and they were considered a highly suitable couple. Malcolm was two weeks old when he came to them, and two years later Louise, their natural daughter, was born, but there were no other children after her.

Susan was disappointed. Four would have been nice, she thought; she had had easy pregnancies and gave birth without complications. They did not, however, adopt other children, for already Malcolm was proving to be a handful. At five years old, fully aware of the consequences of his action, he deliberately threw a stone through the drawing-room window when his grandmother was sitting at her desk writing letters. Mrs Warrington was cut, though not badly, by splintered glass. She would not believe that the child had deliberately aimed at her, but he was quite old enough to know that what he was doing was wrong. George would not spank him, but she did, until bright red marks showed on his plump white buttocks. Susan had been upset by her mother's action and had comforted Malcolm with kisses and cuddles.

Norah had not been at Selbury then, but she heard what had happened, just as she heard about everything of importance that went on, for Susan wrote to her at least once a month.

It was Susan who had helped her to advance herself in the world, and it was because of Susan that she had again become the family's prisoner.

Since Louise's disappearance, the population in Selbury had almost doubled, swollen by the arrival of young families in the smart new houses which had sprung up wherever a clutch could be inserted. There were some bungalows to attract the retired, but most of the newcomers were on their way up in the world of commerce – computer programmers, accountants, executives in companies either local or at some distance. The village lay six miles from a motorway junction and commuting was easy, making it an attractive area. The schools were good and there was a large branch of Sainsbury's in Feringham, but there was scant provision for young couples marrying within the parish; they were forced by high prices to move away.

Walking around the village with Bertie, the Vaughans' black Labrador, Norah would recall the days, not so long ago, when doors had been left unlocked because no opportunist thief could possibly be wandering about during the daylight hours, and she could remember when the telephone exchange was manually operated by Jessie Brown who would tell you that so-and-so, whom you wished to call, had just gone out and could be found at such-and-such a house up the road.

'Do you remember?' she used to say to Mrs Warrington, during their evening games of Scrabble; but it was she who indulged nostalgia, not the old lady. The past, which held Norah's days of innocence, was too painful for Mrs Warrington.

Louise's body had never been found, and after a while interest in the case died down. Other people vanished, were found or not, and horrible crimes were committed, taking the headlines. Sometimes, if an unidentified body were discovered in some remote area, there was speculation about Louise, and until dental records or other evidence proved that it was somebody else, the mystery would be resurrected. As the years passed it was accepted that she was dead, and the truth about what had happened would never be known unless the perpetrator were to commit another crime and be caught, when he might confess. Susan was torn between longing for this to happen, to put an end to her imaginings, and dread that another victim would succumb to the same assailant.

In the first weeks after it happened, Norah spent a lot of time at Selbury House doing what she could to help, which meant making sure that Susan and George, and Mrs Warrington at the Lodge House, were fed, and that someone was always there to answer the telephone. Later, when she returned to work, she came down every weekend and helped to answer the scores of letters the Vaughans received. Most were sympathetic; some were from clairvoyants and people who said they had dreamed about Louise and her fate. A few were damaging, vicious documents which accused the Vaughans of being heedless parents or, worse, alleged that Louise had had a secret life devoted to sexual promiscuity or drug-taking. After a time, George sorted the mail and left any envelopes which might contain such communications for Norah to weed out. Norah would cart them to the end of the garden to burn, enjoying stirring the angry words into cleansing flame. What made people write such vile accusations? The same sort of motives that spurred others to physical violence, perhaps.

Things had gradually died down. George took early retirement so that Susan was less alone. He stood for the district council, seeing it as his duty to put something into the life of the area, but he found the work wearing and often grew discouraged, though he fought hard to retain school dinners and prevent over-urbanisation. Susan spent more and more time in the garden; she would dig up huge areas and plant them with shrubs, then change her plans and root them all out, grassing them over again. She made ponds and a connecting stream, George helping her when he could in an attempt to prevent her from exhausting herself, but it was her way of coping with what had happened and when she was physically worn out she did not think about Louise. Later, encouraged by her friend Helen Cartwright, who thought such activities more appropriate than excessive manual labour, she joined a fine arts group and, apart from attending their lectures, went to exhibitions and visited galleries in London. She also helped raise funds for various charities.

Susan was out a great deal, and the housework was done by two visiting daily women who each came for three mornings a week, overlapping on one day to combine for major tasks. There was still fruit to be picked and made into jam, vegetables to be frozen, and the cooking to be done. Once a keen cook who had enjoyed running her home efficiently, Susan had lost interest in anything to do with it. She ate very little herself, and became very thin. Life, for her, had become something to be endured and had lost all its pleasure.

After her enforced retirement, Norah gradually took over what was being neglected, and more. She typed George's council correspondence. When repairs were necessary, she obtained estimates and supervised the resulting work. She painted several rooms herself and she found someone to mend frayed curtains and make new chair covers. She sorted Louise's clothes, which was something neither parent could face because to get rid of them was so final; Norah packed them in polythene bags and labelled them clearly. One day they could be sent to Oxfam.

As a girl, Norah had worked hard in Selbury House, eager to pay for her food and her keep, but she had never resented it for she loved to look in at the window of life in the big house.

'Norah will do that,' people said when an errand had to be run or some extra job done. Mr Warrington, who went daily to the works, where output now had to conform with food rationing and its limitations, sometimes gave her a ten-shilling note as a bonus.

Things hadn't changed a great deal, Norah thought, as she accepted the terms she was offered many years later, well aware that by working for one of the agencies to which Mrs Warrington would have had to turn if she had refused, she could have earned a great deal more.

'You must have plenty of time off,' Mrs Warrington had told her. 'And use the car whenever you want to go out.'

She thinks she's being generous, Norah thought. She considers me lucky to live here, in this house that is really rather inconvenient with its coke-fired Aga and ancient Hoover. She thinks being at her beck and call is a privilege.

'You'll have a little income, won't you, from your

golden handshake,' Mrs Warrington had added. 'And if you sell your flat, you can invest that money.'

It was true. Norah had seen that if she gave up her home she was, in effect, surrendering, but she did it all the same. It was not practical to leave the place empty and if she sub-let she might have difficulty getting tenants out. She could always buy her way back into the property market again.

But after she sold the flat, prices soared, and unless she moved to Scotland or the remotest tip of Cornwall, she could not rehouse herself for the same amount.

She had settled down, devising little routines to give herself comfort and maintain a degree of independence. She insisted on having the big spare bedroom at the lodge, not the tiny boxroom Mrs Warrington thought would do, and she used some of her own furniture in it; her china and other possessions were packed in tea-chests in the loft against the time when she made her escape at last. Before long it seemed obvious that this would be only when Mrs Warrington died, for with every year that passed it became less possible to abandon her. Norah would take her on little drives in the car and to lunch with Lady Spencer, going off on her own to the local pub and collecting her later. Unlike Mrs Warrington, Lady Spencer had learned to cook and was a dab hand at omelettes and chicken *suprême*. Mrs Warrington had discovered that if you were unable to do something, such as cooking, for yourself, there would always be someone else to do it for you; and now she had Norah, with Mrs Gibson still coming in to do most of the cleaning but reduced in her weekly hours.

Sometimes Lady Spencer came to lunch at the Lodge

House, and Norah would give the old ladies chops and creamed spinach and Duchesse potatoes, followed by *crème brulée* or strawberry fool. They liked grilled trout, or sole *Véronique*, if such occasions coincided with the weekly visit of the fishmonger's van to the village square. She enjoyed preparing these feasts and had heard Lady Spencer tell her friend how lucky she was to have such a treasure.

'Well, she owes us a lot, you know,' Mrs Warrington said. 'But for our family, she would still be living in the East End of London and would probably have married some oaf who would have beaten her black and blue and given her eight children.'

Lady Spencer had laughed at this and told her old friend she was a disgraceful snob. Why shouldn't Norah have married a kindly tradesman who would have looked after her well?

'No reason at all, I suppose, except that she had a nose for trouble when she was young,' said Mrs Warrington.

'It takes two, you know,' Lady Spencer had remarked.

Norah herself sometimes played the 'What if I'd done something else?' game. What if she had remained in London, never set off on that September morning with her bag of emergency rations and one change of clothes, her gas-mask over her shoulder?

She'd be dead, of course. She would have been killed with the rest of her family when a bomb wiped out their house. Instead of this, she had had a rewarding career and subsequently had been usefully occupied in such ways as driving old Mrs Warrington's elderly Maxi to collect the groceries and visit the chemist. After lunch she would take the old lady out for a drive, and if it was warm enough they would park the car and stroll on the common above Feringham, looking down at the growing town, the outcrop of factories, the place where Louise had met her death. Norah felt herself to be no longer personally vulnerable, unlike Mrs Warrington and her family who had been stalked by tragedy over the years.

One day, there would be serious trouble with Malcolm. Only influence had kept him out of court when he had picked a fight in The Grapes in Feringham soon after Louise had vanished. He had laid out a youth who had, he alleged, provoked him. Money had passed then, Norah knew, and it had smoothed his path many times since, though, as far as she was aware, violence had not been involved again.

As a small boy, he had been fearless and bold, and charming to look at, with dark curls and pale blue eyes. He had grown into a big, handsome man with a highly aggressive nature but without the intelligence to direct his energy into profitable directions. He had one broken marriage behind him, for which failure Susan blamed his pale, shy ex-wife Gwynneth. Luckily there had been no children to have their lives torn apart by the separation.

When Louise disappeared he had just returned from four years in Australia, but he was not officially living at home though he frequently arrived without warning, even quite late at night, announcing that he wanted to stay. This continued through the following years and sometimes he stayed for weeks at a time, when he had been turned out of lodgings for non-payment of rent or had broken with the current girlfriend. He moved in with various young women who had their own flats or houses, and sooner or later he moved out again. Norah marvelled that there always seemed to be someone new who would take him in, but surely the supply of gullible females must one day run out? Susan lamented over him, consumed with guilt because she felt his failures reflected on her and his upbringing, convinced that if he could only find the elusive Miss Right who would understand him, he would gain confidence in himself and find the proper direction for the ability she felt he must have.

He had always been jealous of Louise, imagining that she had replaced him in their parents' affections and, when he understood the difference between them – that he was adopted and she was not – resenting it even more.

'But we chose you,' Susan would say, hugging him as he wriggled on her lap, not wanting to attend to some story she had been reading. 'Louise just arrived.'

Louise, however, did well at school; she was small, fair and pretty, everyone's idea of a dream daughter, and George adored her. Malcolm seized every chance he could find, when no adult was about, to torment her, pulling her hair, teasing her, hiding and even breaking her toys. Once, Norah saw him lift her, struggling and screaming, out of a window above the stables and deposit her on the flat roof over the garage outside. He closed the window so that she could not climb back. Norah rescued her and told George what had happened. George did not believe in beating children but he was so angry with Malcolm that he could think of no other appropriate punishment and the boy was still young enough to be laid over his knee and thrashed with his hand. Two days later Malcolm shut Louise in an outhouse and she was there for half an hour before Ford, the gardener, heard her cries and released her.

This time, Malcolm's punishment was to dig a large patch of vegetable garden instead of going on a long-planned seaside picnic with some other children.

'I didn't want to go on the silly picnic anyway,' said Malcolm. Physically strong, he dug up the patch of ground very rapidly and afterwards went off to the shed in the paddock to smoke, something he had lately taken to doing. He threw his cigarette end into some hay in the corner and burnt the place down.

George could not prove he had caused the fire, but he knew. So did Norah, who had been staying for a few days during these events. She sometimes came down in the school holidays, helping Susan buy clothes the children needed for the next term and stitching on name tapes, even taking them to the dentist. Susan found it hard to believe that Malcolm had been so naughty, and though she did not excuse him for what he had done to Louise, she told George that Louise must in some way have provoked him. But even she was relieved when the new term began and he went back to his boarding-school. Louise did not go away until much later when she was sent to her mother's old school in Surrey, where she acquired seven O-levels and two modest As. Then she went to stay with a family in France, on and off for over a year. She had always been good at languages and she ended up speaking excellent if not totally fluent French.

Malcolm survived his prep school, but he was asked to leave his public school after a year. It seemed that he had started a fire in the games pavilion. The evidence, circumstantial though it was, convinced George, though not Susan, of his guilt. Shortly before the blaze was discovered, Malcolm was seen leaving the building and, when he was later questioned, there were matches in his pocket. After this he was sent to a school with less ambitious academic aims and a wide curriculum combined with a loose system of discipline. He and another boy got drunk one night on beer they had bought unchallenged on a trip to the nearby town. They became involved in a fight with some local youths, one of whom had been badly cut and bruised. The police were called to the affray, but all the boys escaped with a caution.

George decided that this school was too lax in its approach to be right for Malcolm, even if they agreed to keep him after this episode. Desperate, he made extensive inquiries and discovered a place in Yorkshire which catered for difficult boys and concentrated on physically demanding activities. Here Malcolm learned rock-climbing, canoeing and sailing, and worked on the farm attached to the place. George began to hope that he could be sent to an agricultural college and in due course, perhaps, be set up with a smallholding or even a farm of his own. He also learned motor mechanics, at which he was brilliant, and there was scope to drive old bangers restored by the boys around the large grounds.

He was often in trouble even here, provoking fights, but there were other large and aggressive boys, and nothing happened which could not be handled by them or the staff. If this place couldn't sort Malcolm out, George decided, then nowhere could. In the past, wild boys like him had made excellent fighting soldiers, but there was now no war for him to take part in. Perhaps he would join the army, however.

Malcolm did not do that. He did not care for regimentation.

He had brought little joy to his parents, thought Norah. She knew he resented her position in the Lodge House and her occupation of what he thought should be kept as his room for his various homeless spells between girlfriends. He had attended his grandmother's funeral looking very correct in his dark suit with his black tie, his springy curls brushed down, and he played the part of the grieving grandson to perfection. Mrs Warrington had left him her books, hoping, she said in her will, that he would profit by reading them.

What good were sets of Dickens and Scott and the Georgian poets to Malcolm? He read the sports columns of newspapers, and the racing news to decide how to place the bets with which at intervals he sought to restore his fortunes, but little else. Even so, he took the trouble to consult several second-hand booksellers in order to obtain the best possible price when he sold them. He did not realise enough from his inheritance even to take his current girlfriend to the Bahamas.

What a chance he had had in life, Norah thought, and how he had messed it up. He had cost George and Susan a fortune in getting him out of trouble.

How much was due to heredity and how much to environment? What had his true parents been like? Norah knew that her own were hard-working and honest; her father had been a baker's roundsman and her mother, once in service – they met when he called at the house where she worked – had later had a job as an office cleaner. The two of them had dove-tailed their hours so that there was always someone at home for their daughters, who had been much loved. Susan and her brothers, though, had been packed off to boarding-school and had grown up with a number of inhibitions quite foreign to Norah. The educational pattern had been followed with Malcolm and Louise.

Norah had kept a keen eye on the conversion of Selbury House and at first she had entertained a fantasy of buying the smallest flat for herself, thus regaining her independence whilst still being close to Susan and George. But if she staked herself to that out of her small capital, with a mortgage, she would no longer be able to run a car or take her annual foreign holidays, for she was realistic enough to know that at her age she was unlikely to find a well-paid job in the area. She was trapped in a gentle web of mutual dependence, for without Susan and George she would be quite alone.

She made friends with the builders, walking up to the house with Bertie, the Labrador, and introducing herself to the foreman.

The earth gaped raw where a giant grab had torn out a track to form a side entrance away from the Lodge House. Huge tyre marks dented the loamy soil and uprooted shrubs lay on their sides, their leaves dropping. Here were the laurestinus and lilac, the syringa and mahonia, the various berberis plants with their spectacular foliage and prickly stems that had grown undisturbed for years, shielding the garden which they enclosed from the weather and from the curious gaze of passers-by. Here, Norah had helped to cut holly boughs to deck the house at Christmas. There, beyond the site of Susan's water garden, now demolished, lay the orchard, most of it to be preserved as the property of one of the new occupiers, but the mistletoe-bearing apple tree that had so amazed her when she first came to the place had been cut down. A huge JCB was parked near where there had been a small pond with goldfish lurking beneath the water-lilies. In the bitterly cold first winter of the war they had been frozen into blocks of ice, but two of them had miraculously revived when Mrs Warrington had chipped them out, brought them into the house and thawed them. Tough little creatures, they had later repopulated the pond. No trace of this remained.

Heaps of scooped-up soil lay in mounds at the side of the fresh approach to where the new houses would be built after the main conversion was done, and several workmen stood about while a man holding a large plan discussed it with one of them. The site manager, Norah decided, and so it turned out.

She walked past them and gazed at the house where it stood in the bright spring sunshine, its brickwork looking raw because plants that had covered it had been pulled out to allow for new external doors. The big wisteria had gone. Norah felt a pang; Susan had cherished it over the years. Perhaps it would rise again from the roots. She had not inspected the plans at the county offices, and nor had Susan, unable to bear the thought of what was to be done to the place, but George had, in case there was anything to which they should object. He was in an awkward position about this, since he was now on the council and as a close neighbour had an interest, and was relieved to find that the details were not unpleasing, though it was a pity that so much of the mature garden would be lost. The new houses were to be set some distance from the original building and were not being packed densely together; each would have a reasonable plot of its own. The high-density building would follow when the rest of the land was developed, as must inevitably happen in time.

One of the workmen saw Norah and made a move towards her.

She immediately addressed the man holding the plan.

'I hope I'm not trespassing,' she said. 'I was interested in what you are doing here. I used to live in the house.'

'Oh, good morning,' said the man, who wore a Barbour jacket above corduroy trousers and mud-encrusted wellington boots. 'You'll be Mrs Vaughan.'

'No. My name's Norah Tyler. I'm Mrs Vaughan's housekeeper,' said Norah. 'I've known this place since I was thirteen years old.'

'Have you really? This must be a shock to you, then,' said the man. 'Seeing the mess we're making, I mean. But when it's finished it will be quite attractive, you'll find, and bang up to date. Everything of the best. Go in and have a look round, if you like. Now's your chance, before anyone moves in.'

'Are some of them sold yet, then?'

'They all are,' said the man. 'They're so convenient, you see.'

Norah had not been into the house during the interval when the couple from London had lived in it, so she had not seen the alterations they had made, but Susan had described the purple walls in the study, the bilious ochre oval bath in what had been the main bathroom. The kitchen had been stripped of its Aga and turned into something starkly white which had made her think of a hospital operating theatre.

Now Norah discovered that in place of that former kitchen and the scullery where as a girl she had so often washed up in a papier-mâché bowl in the large porcelain sink, there were a bathroom, bedroom and living-room. A space where the coal had been kept had become a small kitchen. The rest of the house had been similarly transformed and some of the apartments were quite large; all were equipped with top quality fittings, as the site manager had told her.

Who would move in? Would they be happy? Were there ghosts here who needed to be exorcised? Did Louise's spirit come back, looking for sanctuary, and what would such a sad spectre think about all the changes?

Norah shivered, as if a goose had walked over her own grave. So many people had died.

Old Mrs Warrington had grown physically frail in the last years of her life but her mind had been alert to the end. As her sight began to fail, she had liked Norah to read to her and even after so many years would correct what she heard as a slovenly vowel sound. George had bought her a Walkman and the tapes of several classics but she preferred to hear Norah, liking the company, and pretended she could not work the set, which was quite untrue.

'It takes up a lot of your time,' George grumbled to Norah.

'I don't mind,' Norah replied. 'It's quite restful, though I get a bit croaky after an hour or so. After all, she has more or less educated me and I owe her something.'

'That's been paid back long ago,' said George.

Ah, thought Norah, but there's more to it than you know. Mostly, now, she was able to shut her mind to that dreadful time, but its consequences had shaped the rest of her life. It was Susan who had insisted that she must get away and make a fresh start, helping her leave the factory and join the ATS. Norah had remained in the service for five years, during which time she had acquired secretarial and accounting skills, risen to sergeant, and finally had been offered a commission.

Susan had urged her to take the opportunity. It would give her a chance to see the world. If she'd done so, she might have ended up with high rank and a generous pension, but she had decided that she wanted to put down roots.

Her training had helped her to a good secretarial post in London, and, changing jobs several times before settling with Mr Barratt, she had gradually acquired some possessions along with her mortgage. She had had only one serious love affair after that bitter experience when she became pregnant at the age of seventeen.

She was doing the ironing in the kitchen of the Lodge House when the doorbell rang one afternoon. She had appropriated Mrs Warrington's Walkman and tapes and was tuned in to *Our Mutual Friend,* so that she did not hear the bell, and the caller had come round to the back door before she realised that there was a visitor.

She looked up from the ironing-board as a shadow fell across the kitchen window, and unplugged herself to see who was there.

A large man in his forties stood bulkily filling up most of the door-frame.

'I rang the front doorbell but could get no answer,' he said.

'Well?' Primed by tales of con men disguised as officials to prey on the elderly, Norah squared up to him, working out that she was unlikely to win in a test of strength over closing the door.

'You don't remember me, Miss Tyler, I can see,' said the visitor. 'Marsh is my name. I'm a Detective Superintendent now and just back in this division.' He took a police warrant card from his pocket and showed it to her.

'Oh – Sergeant – no, Mr Marsh – I'm sorry. I remember you, of course, but I didn't recognise you,' Norah said, her mind flitting back to the dark-haired sergeant who had spent months investigating Louise's disappearance. The man in front of her was balding, thickset but not paunchy, with deep lines on his rather pale face. 'You've changed,' she said, and added, 'So have I, I expect. Won't you come in?'

Detective Superintendent Marsh came into the large kitchen with its wide windows, oak fitments, geranium cuttings on the sills and green oil-fired Aga.

'Changed a bit, hasn't it? The kitchen wasn't as big as

this in the old lady's time, if I remember correctly.'

'No. It was all enlarged after she died,' Norah explained.

'Ah. When was that, now?' asked Marsh.

'Four years ago,' said Norah, switching off the iron. A sweet smell of freshly pressed linen gently rose to meet Marsh's nose as he entered. His sense of smell had sharpened since he gave up smoking.

'She must have been getting on.'

'Ninety-one,' said Norah.

'A remarkable old lady,' said Marsh. 'She took all that amazingly well.'

'Her generation was brought up not to show emotion,' said Norah, who had found some of that training brushing off on herself. 'It doesn't mean that she felt it any the less. Would you like some tea, Mr Marsh?'

Why had he come? Was there news after all this time? Was there another poor, decayed body to go and inspect? Surely a superintendent wouldn't call in person about that? It would be a telephone call first, then a sergeant, or at most an inspector. Wouldn't it? Or perhaps this time they were sure it was Louise, and Marsh, having worked on the case before, wanted to break the news himself. She remained outwardly calm. The man would explain when he was ready.

'Thank you,' said Marsh, accepting the offer of tea.

'Do sit down,' said Norah, adding, 'I hope you don't mind the kitchen. It's warmer in here than in the sitting-room. The fire's not lit yet in there.'

'The kitchen's the heart of the house, I always say,' said Marsh, lowering his bulk on to one of the oak-framed chairs by the big square table and watching while Norah put the kettle on and found cups and saucers. She was still a slim woman, in her dark pleated skirt and maroon sweater. She wore low-heeled black pumps and pale ribbed tights. He recalled that she had always been bandbox neat. When he had returned to take charge of the CID in the area, one of his first actions had been to ask what had been happening to the Vaughans, but now there were not many officers left in Feringham who remembered the case, as the senior detectives involved had retired and others had moved to different divisions. This afternoon, with for once some time to spare, he had decided to go to Selbury and find out for himself how the family had survived the years. 'I went up to the big house,' he went on. 'I expected to find Mr and Mrs Vaughan still living there.'

'You had a surprise, then,' Norah stated, pouring water into the teapot to warm it.

'Yes. Well, I suppose it was a big place for just the two of them. There's quite a colony up there now, I discovered. There were some children tearing about on cycles having a great time. There was a son, though, I remember. Still, he'd be married and gone. He lived at Cornton then, didn't he? Came out on some of the searches.'

'That's right,' Norah said. 'He's living in Malchester now but he isn't married.'

'And you're visiting again?'

'No. I'm here permanently now,' said Norah. 'Or sort of. I was made redundant and came for a visit, and stayed on.'

'I see.'

Marsh had not taken a great deal of notice of her, years ago. She had clearly had nothing to do with the girl's disappearance and he had thought her some sort of distant relative until, from the case reports, he had learned otherwise.

'Is there news, Mr Marsh? Is that why you're here?' Norah briskly poured boiling water into the pot as she spoke.

'No, I'm afraid not. I've just come back to the district and thought I'd take a look round the village,' Marsh explained. 'I've often thought about that poor girl and wished we'd managed to find her.'

'There have been many more disappearances since then,' said Norah. She opened a decorative jar and put biscuits from it on to a plate.

'Ah,' said Marsh. 'This is nice.' The china was good, there was a tiny pot of winter jasmine on the table, and Norah had put a silver teaspoon in his saucer. 'It's a lot more elegant than what we get at the station. Two sugars, please.'

Norah poured out.

'Do help yourself to a biscuit,' she said.

They were custard creams, which George adored.

'My favourites,' said Marsh. 'Thanks.' He seemed to remember her producing tea at intervals during the investigation, always in a quiet, self-effacing way, yet somehow exuding efficiency. She was, he realised, a confident woman. 'What do you think about it all now?' he asked. 'Have the parents adjusted?'

He did not ask if they had got over it. No one could get over a daughter's violent death.

'They've survived,' she replied. 'Her mother has changed completely. She spends very little time in the house. She works in the garden or goes to art exhibitions or lectures.'

'And has nightmares,' said Marsh.

'Yes, sometimes,' said Norah. 'She's never stopped blaming herself for what happened, though how she could have prevented it, I don't know. You can't chain up an adult young woman.'

'No. I was surprised she was still living at home,' said Marsh.

'Well, she had shared a flat with some friends for a while, but she got rather tired and thin and I think her parents persuaded her to come home again. I used to see her in London sometimes – I lived there then – and she didn't really enjoy the social life her flatmates liked.'

'There was no special boyfriend, I recollect.'

'No.'

'Poor girl. She was in the wrong place at the wrong time,' said Marsh. 'Maybe someone asked her the way and got fresh and took it from there.'

'You gave that young Tom Francis a grilling,' Norah reminded him.

'Well, he was a likely suspect. It's usually someone known to a victim who kills her, and he did have some time unaccounted for that evening.'

'You remember the case very well,' said Norah.

'I do, because it was so frustrating,' said Marsh.

'Poor Tom had been seeing someone else. Someone in the choir, as it turned out, but they'd been very discreet. She was married, too. They'd met that night to end their affair. His wife found out, of course, after he'd been questioned so much. It broke up their marriage.'

'Oh dear. I'm sorry about that,' said Marsh.

'Yes. If she hadn't, it might have all blown over and they'd still be together, not adding to the divorce statistics,' said Norah, who blamed the police for what had happened.

'There were children,' said Marsh.

'Yes. One was only a baby then,' said Norah. 'I don't condone what he did,' she added. 'But their whole world broke up.'

'You never married, Miss Tyler?' asked Marsh.

'No.' Norah pressed her lips together. There was no need to tell him about the long liaison she had had with a man she had met through her work, who at first had said he would leave his wife and marry her. After some years, she had realised that the time would never be right for the break to be made and it would not happen. Later, growing bored with each other, they had ended the affair by mutual consent. She had never regretted the experience, and she was glad, now, that his children had been spared the pain of their parents separating. Two years ago, on a trip to London, she had seen him, quite by chance, with his wife; they were going into Fortnum and Mason as she went past on her way to Hatchards to buy a book for George's birthday. Out of curiosity, she had followed them into the store and had seen them discussing some purchase in the grocery department. They had looked rather old, but sleek and content, and she assumed that they were. They never saw her, and she looked rather old, too, she had decided, going back into the street without any regrets. 'A lot of men have patches in their lives when they seem to need two women,' she said. 'One for excitement, and a workaday model for domesticity.'

'That's true,' said Marsh.

'Are you married?' she asked him.

'Not any more,' he said. 'It's difficult for wives, with the job. I've got two children, though,' he added. 'A girl and a boy, ten and eight. I see them whenever I can. It's all quite amiable, really.' Sometimes he thought it would be easier if it were not: if he and Lynn could be so friendly now, why couldn't they have got over their troubles and stayed together? She'd been lonely, of course. She'd got some fellow in tow, a furniture salesman, but he hadn't moved in with her and there was no talk of marriage. Marsh didn't know what the children would make of having a stepfather, and he wasn't at all keen on the idea himself except that it would mean he could stop paying her maintenance.

'I'm sorry things didn't work out,' she said. 'Are you going to reopen the file on Louise?'

'It's never been really closed,' he replied. 'Just left in a sort of pending file. We won't be doing anything unless some fresh evidence turns up.'

'Like a body, you mean,' Norah said.

'That's right.'

'There have been one or two,' she said. 'Mr Vaughan has gone to look at them. It's been horrible for him.'

'I'm sure. He's retired, then? They told me that at the big house.'

'Yes, but he keeps very busy with village affairs,' said

Norah. 'And he's on the county council.'

'The brother thought Louise would come back, didn't he?' Marsh said, taking another biscuit. It was nice sitting here in the warm and chatting as if they were old friends. In a way you could say that they were. 'He thought she'd had a row with someone and would turn up again when she'd cooled down.'

'Yes, he did, but that was a silly idea,' said Norah. 'Louise wasn't like that. Besides, how could she have managed without any money? The police never seriously considered it, I believe.'

'Not on the evidence,' said Marsh. 'And who was the quarrel with, anyway? She got on well with everyone in the choir who knew her, and all the singers were checked out.'

'The one person she might have wanted to get away from was Malcolm,' said Norah. 'He hadn't been back from Australia long, and they'd never got on together, but he wasn't living at home and she seldom saw him, so that couldn't have been a serious problem.'

'No. Well, I'm afraid we're unlikely to find the answer now,' said Marsh. 'Unless whoever did it is arrested for something else and confesses. That's about the only hope.'

'That will be too late to help her parents,' said Norah.

'If it happens at all,' agreed Marsh. 'I'd like to know who it was, all the same, and see that he got put away. He was a tall chap. We know because he'd put the seat of her car right back.'

'I hadn't heard that,' said Norah, surprised. Louise's parents had kept the car for two years, but at last they had sold it and given the money to a children's charity.

'There's no secret about it,' said Marsh. 'It was all in the reports, though perhaps it didn't get into the papers. Would you give me Mr Malcolm Vaughan's address? You said he's living in Malchester. I might have a word with him in case at this distance in time he remembers something that didn't seem important then.'

'I doubt if he will,' said Norah. 'He's running a second-hand car business in Sebastopol Road, called Vaughan's Reliable Cars, and he's living with a young woman. I can't remember the address but I'll just look it up.' She rose and left the room, soon returning with a piece of paper on which the name and address were neatly printed. She gave it to Marsh. 'I don't suppose he'll be very pleased to see you,' she added. 'He's put all the past behind him.'

2

Malcolm

Malcolm Vaughan had always known he was special. His mother had often told him so as she tried to teach him to read or helped him assemble his model train. He enjoyed playing with that, especially when it crashed going too fast round a bend. She bought him Dinky toys which she allowed him to park all round the drawing-room fireplace on the carpet. She told him the pattern on the Persian rug by the hearth was marked into roads and towns, but he could never see it himself. Her brothers had arranged their toy cars on it, using it as landscape, she had explained, and seemed disappointed when he did not understand. To him the lines were like a series of car parks.

Later, when he overheard his grandmother talking to Lady Spencer, he learned he was not so special.

'How does one know what characteristics they've inherited?' Mrs Warrington asked. 'It might be just the shape of a nose or the colour of their hair, but what about other things, other tendencies? Adoption's a risky business.'

'It was a wonderful chance for the boy, though,' said Lady Spencer. 'Coming into a family like this should be the making of him. I admire Susan for taking it on.'

'What's adoption?' Malcolm had asked a teacher at the small private kindergarten he was then attending, and she, unaware of the significance of the question, had explained.

It was months before he asked Susan if she had gone to the same hospital to adopt him as when she had collected Louise. He remembered that; she had been in bed for a while and he had been taken to see her and the small, pretty baby who had looked like a doll.

'But Louise isn't adopted, darling,' said Susan, and then realised what the question implied. She had turned quite pale but had grasped the nettle. 'You're very special. I've always told you that and I would have explained it properly when you were a little older. I can see I shall have to try to explain it now.' She took a deep breath and plunged. 'No baby came along after Daddy and I were married, and we wanted a boy so much. Sometimes babies come to people who can't look after them, and they go to live with families who want them a great deal. We chose you from among lots of other babies.' She cuddled his sturdy body close and kissed his springy dark curls, so unlike her own fine, straight hair which she had lightly permed to give it some body, and different, too, from George's black thatch. She began to tell it like a story, how the day was fine and sunny, and they had gone in Daddy's big car because it was more comfortable than her small one, and there he had lain in his cot looking appealingly up at them, only two weeks old. The sun had been shining when they left with him, all wrapped up in a very soft shawl, and they had been so happy.

Malcolm wriggled about as she related this tale; it seemed to apply to somebody else, and years passed before he understood the difference between him and Louise. Susan could not think how he had learned about himself, and supposed there might have been talk in the village which had somehow got back to him. She had always been resolved that he should never have cause to feel inferior to Louise, and she spent a great deal of effort and energy attempting to compensate for failing to be his natural mother.

A year later Malcolm joined together the long hair of two girls who sat in front of him at school. The teacher found it impossible to undo the knot he had somehow managed to tie before one of the girls felt what was happening and jerked her head away, pulling the connection tight. Scissors were required to separate the pair. For this offence, Malcolm was kept in at playtime and made to write lines.

He enjoyed the attention he attracted by this piece of mischief. Some of the little boys thought he had been funny and bold, and the small girls began to avoid him, whispering behind their hands and shrinking away whenever he came near them. Never good at his lessons, he devised ways of avoiding boredom by carving his initials on his desk, reading comics, and, when detected, swaggering up to receive his punishment which, as time went on, involved being kept in after school so that his mother knew what was going on. Susan pleaded with him to work harder and at home tried hard to help him learn his tables and read.

His misdeeds were undetected at the prep school where he was sent as a boarder at the age of eight. Tall for his age, and solidly built, he was good at football and the other physical activities which the school encouraged. He joined the Cubs, and when a tent went on fire one afternoon, was never suspected of being responsible. He had earlier found a master's cigarette lighter lying in the grass, where it had been accidentally dropped, and thought it would be fun to make a blaze and see the other boys run. No one was hurt, and Malcolm hid the lighter in a hole in a tree in the copse; it might come in useful again. The episode was written off as a freak accident, and when the term ended Malcolm retrieved the lighter and took it home. He sold it to a boy in Selbury village for a pound, a great deal of money then.

When a very small boy fell into the swimming-pool and alleged that he had been pushed, since Malcolm, the only other boy about, had leaped in after him and hauled him out, the victim was assumed to be romancing. Both were rebuked for being near the pool at an unsupervised time, but Malcolm was praised for his presence of mind.

Other things happened. A master walking in the copse received a crack on the head from a stone. It knocked him out for a few moments, long enough for Malcolm, perched up a neighbouring tree armed with a catapult – strictly forbidden – to escape without being seen. Then he began gambling, taking bets on whether he could climb out of the dormitory window and walk all round the roof and back, a feat another boy had attempted the previous term, ending up being caught by the headmaster. Years before, went the legend, a boy had fallen from the roof and been killed, trying the same thing. Malcolm succeeded and won a shilling from every boy who was part of the dare.

Other bets followed, involving less risk: whether a certain boy would win a particular prize; how many times the vicar would say 'And now finally' in his sermon on Sunday; who would win various matches with other schools. Sometimes he won and sometimes he lost, but he was elated when his bets came off; it was money for nothing.

His first sexual experience was with a girl who worked as a maid at his final school, where he had learned so much about cars, and that came about as a result of a bet that he would produce her panties, sure proof of conquest. He won the bet but did not reveal that the girl had not been compliant; she had struggled and had been left weeping and bruised but intact. She had allowed various boys certain liberties in return for rewards of a financial nature but had permitted nothing below the belt. When Malcolm, now a big, strong boy, offered her five pounds for the trophy – he would clear a good profit with what had been staked and had no need to achieve anything more – she agreed only when he caught her by the wrist and twisted her arm. To the girl, surrendering the panties seemed the easiest way to escape and she would avoid him in future, but, with the prize in his hand and titillated by the look of fear on her sharp, pertly pretty face, Malcolm sought more. It was only his lack of expertise and her agility that saved her from actual rape. She did not report the incident because she should not have been taking money for such favours as she had hitherto granted, but after that she gave in her notice and left the school.

Malcolm made a good tale out of the event but what he had most enjoyed was his sense of power. Later, he found prostitutes, and then, working on a farm in Wales where he had gone at George's insistence after other career ideas had failed, he had met a meek, pretty girl who kept him at arm's length and it seemed to him that the best plan now was to marry. At that time the age of majority was twenty-one, and as soon as he reached it they went off to the registrar's office together. Gwynneth's parents had, at first, protested, advising the couple to wait, but their objections collapsed when Malcolm subjected them to the full battery of his charm. It was clear, too, that he came from a moneyed background and had an assured future. He made out that he was gaining experience from a variety of jobs before joining the family firm, though the truth was that no family member would be employed there unless he or she were of outstanding ability.

Gwynneth spent a good deal of her honeymoon in tears while Malcolm was drinking too much in the bar of the hotel in Corfu where they were staying. She lay on the beach in her bikini while he went swimming, and her fair skin soon grew red and sore. Sometimes she splashed in the shallows, but she could barely swim and Malcolm made no effort to help her become more confident although the clear, calm water was ideal for such practice. He talked to other people he met on the beach or in the hotel, mostly men; she pretended to read a paperback novel she had found on a shelf in the foyer, but she was too wretched to take in much of the story. He seemed entirely different from the person she had known – or thought she knew – before they came away, and in bed he was rough and demanding; none of this was what she had expected, and they had nothing to say to one another. Perhaps things would improve when they went home and perhaps she would get used to what must be endured. She could not understand why people raved about sex when to her it was painful.

They settled down to raise chickens on a smallholding near Hereford financed by Malcolm's parents, to whom he had presented his bride with some pride; an acquisition he had obtained without their aid. Susan and George had liked Gwynneth, although they thought her excessively timid and later admitted to one another that perhaps a wiser choice would have been a girl with more self-possession. Still, that might come with time. Gwynneth had at first been frightened of them and of the style in which, as it seemed to her, they lived. She was afraid, too, that they would be angry about the secret wedding, which they were told of only weeks later. But they had been kind and friendly, and Malcolm had been on his best behaviour during the visit, drinking moderately and finishing with her very quickly in bed. That haste was the one thing that made it bearable; she gritted her teeth and lay rigid until it was over.

The marriage lasted for less than two years, during which time the poultry farm lost money and the couple ran into debt. Malcolm would go off on drinking bouts and would place bets on horses in the hope of putting things right. When he came home, angry and frustrated, Gwynneth was at his mercy. The farm was isolated, and when Malcolm had taken the Land Rover, she was marooned. Then one day an old school friend came to see her, found her moving about the kitchen as stiffly as an old woman and noticed a bruise on her arm. Out came the whole story and when Malcolm returned that evening, Gwynneth had gone.

He went home to give his version of events before Gwynneth had a chance to spread hers. He alleged that she was unfaithful and did nothing to help with the chickens. At that time divorce was not possible until after three years of marriage, but Gwynneth immediately sought a judicial separation and a financial settlement, charging Malcolm with physical and mental cruelty. The Vaughans paid her off with the farm and a capital sum on the understanding that later she would sue for divorce on other grounds. There had been a distressing interview at her parents' house, where she was living, when George and Susan had driven over in an attempt to bring about a reconciliation.

Gwynneth was waiting for them with a solicitor at her side, a short, middle-aged man with steel-rimmed spectacles, determined to do well for his client. It was made very clear that at the first hint of opposition to Gwynneth's demands, the fact that Malcolm had knocked her about causing bruises noticed by neighbours, had been before magistrates on a charge of drunken driving for which he had been lucky not to lose his licence, and was in debt, would become public knowledge. Indeed, it was possible that she might be given special permission for an early divorce before three years were up, said the solicitor, chancing his arm.

George and Susan had been routed. They drove home in silent despair, until at last Susan spoke.

'Of course she drove him to it,' she said. 'She's such a milksop. Those great spaniel eyes and all that sad hair hanging down her back.'

Gwynneth had had a different effect on George. He had shared the sentiments clearly felt by the solicitor, wanting to wrap her, figuratively speaking, in blankets, tell her not to worry and he would see that Malcolm never hurt her again. She was no sophisticated actress assuming a wounded little girl role; she had been genuinely hurt, both mentally and physically. He had known, when Malcolm brought her to Selbury, that she would never be able to deal with him.

'The boy's a bully,' he had answered. 'He bullied small girls at school, he bullied Louise, and he bullied Gwynneth. If he'd picked a big, robust girl who would swear at him and give as good as he handed out, it might have been different.'

'But he'd never be drawn to a girl like that,' said Susan. 'I expect he lost patience with Gwynneth's whingeing.'

It was as close as she would come to criticising Malcolm. Both snatched at the idea of a trip to Australia as a remedy, and George had arranged an introduction to a sheep farmer who might give Malcolm work. With any luck he would like the life enough to stay there, George had thought. While he was away life at home had been much easier, though Susan had fretted because Malcolm wrote so seldom. George remarked that no news was good news, and earned a reproof for being callous. During Malcolm's absence, Gwynneth's uncontested divorce petition on the grounds of desertion was granted.

'Why can't he take himself to Leeds or preferably John

O'Groats?' George had remarked to Norah soon after Malcolm's return. They were having dinner together in London, something they did from time to time, very discreetly.

'It's Susan who draws him back. He's as besotted with her as she is with him,' said Norah.

'Besotted? Is that what you think?' George asked.

'Well, obsessed, if you prefer,' Norah said.

'I think that's a truer description,' said George. 'Poor Susan. She still thinks he'll settle down one day, but how much longer do we have to wait?'

When George was Malcolm's age, he was commanding a company in France, following D-Day.

Norah shared George's concern, and she understood Susan's feelings of guilt because Malcolm had turned out so unsatisfactorily. Susan was sure that his upbringing must be somehow to blame; perhaps, when sent away to boarding-school, he had felt rejected. Norah did not think it was as simple as that; traits ran in families and little was known about Malcolm's antecedents; he might have rogue genes.

Some months after Louise's disappearance he found a job as sales manager in a garage. This lasted until there was trouble over money paid as deposits on new cars and never received by the company. Unknown to George, Susan bailed him out to prevent him being charged with embezzling the firm's funds. Then she helped him to open a motor accessory shop, which was not the career she would have chosen for him but seemed suited to his abilities; it was clear that he was unlikely to succeed while working for somebody else. Grateful, he promised never to cause her another day's anxiety.

At the time, George told Norah that he was sure the venture would fail and regretted that remittance men were a thing of the past.

'You can't just write him off, George, like a bad debt,' Norah protested. 'After all, he is your son.'

'But he's not,' said George, and added, 'Thank God.'

The accessory shop lasted three years before it went under, leaving Malcolm on the verge of bankruptcy. Once again, Susan saved him and paid off his creditors.

Now he was running a second-hand car business in Malchester. Nobody dared to ask how it was doing. Between times he had tried other things, including selling double-glazing, but nothing had lasted. He worked on cars he bought, and sold them in good condition; there was some visible turnover, and if he had asked for money recently, Susan had never told either George or Norah.

More than two weeks after his visit to Selbury, Detective Superintendent Marsh went to see Malcolm. He had had no time to spare before for a case which was inactive and might never be officially investigated again.

He drove past Vaughan's Reliable Cars in the dusk of early evening. Three vehicles – a Porsche Carrera, an old Jaguar XJ6 and a Maestro saloon with a D registration number – were parked on the forecourt outside a large barn-like building. The Jaguar and the Maestro had price labels attached to their windscreens, and invitations to pay in easy stages were written below the totals. Lights were on in the building, and Marsh, after parking alongside the Maestro, pulled open the sliding door to enter.

Inside, he saw a blue Metro elevated on a mechanical hoist and an elderly Triumph Vitesse, with its bonnet raised, beside the lift. A big man in green overalls was adjusting something on the engine of the Vitesse. Pop music played loudly.

'Mr Vaughan?' Marsh inquired.

'Right.' Malcolm extracted his upper torso from the car's vitals and turned to switch off the portable radio which stood nearby. He turned upon Marsh a smile which someone less cynical than the superintendent might have found disarming. He had pale blue eyes in a rather florid face that was already puffy round the jowls. How old was he? About thirty-eight? He looked more. A drinker's face, Marsh decided. 'This old girl will soon be ready for sale.' Malcolm indicated the engine he had been working on. 'She'll be good for many more miles when I've finished with her.'

'Do them all up, do you, before selling?' asked Marsh.

'Too right,' said Malcolm, who sometimes affected an Australian accent, and indeed other accents from time to time when attempting to make some sort of impact on a new acquaintance. 'What can I do for you? Are you interested in something I've got on show or do you want to sell? Part exchange can be arranged.'

'No.' Marsh was not tempted to feign interest in one of the cars. He produced his warrant card. 'My name's Marsh. Detective Superintendent Marsh,' he said. 'Twelve years ago, when I was a detective sergeant, I was on the investigation after your sister went missing, and now that I'm back in the area I'm making a few checks on those involved.'

'Oh, are you?' Malcolm was not able to mask his surprise. 'I thought all that was over now,' he said.

'No case is ever over until it's solved, Mr Vaughan,' said Marsh.

'Isn't it? Well, you'd better come into the office,' said Malcolm. 'Though there's nothing I can add to what I said at the time. I wasn't living in Selbury then. I had my own place at Cornton.'

He picked up the handset of a cordless telephone which lay on the workbench beside him and led the way into a small room opening off the workshop. Marsh had expected a shabby cubicle with tatty filing-cabinets and a scratched desk, but the area was classily furnished with a desk whose melamine top resembled mahogany and was only slightly dusty. Behind it was a padded revolving chair and there was a comfortable, if small, upright armchair facing it, for a client.

'Tea?' offered Malcolm. 'Or coffee? I'd better not suggest anything stronger,' he added as he replaced the telephone on its base.

'Coffee, please,' said Marsh. 'Milk, if you have it, but no sugar.' He did not really want it, but was curious to see how Malcolm would prepare it. There was no equipment in sight.

Malcolm opened a door at the rear of the office. It led into a lobby where there was a sink and worktop along one wall. Marsh saw an electric jug-type kettle. Malcolm opened a cupboard and took out two mugs, a jar of instant coffee and a carton of milk.

'I've got no fridge here,' he said. 'But I've got other things – there's a shower beyond that door.' He nodded towards the rear of the area. 'I get pretty grubby working and need to clean up,' he explained.

'Ah,' said Marsh. 'Very convenient.'

'Yes,' agreed Malcolm, returning with the coffee. He set one mug down opposite Marsh and took a gulp from the other before seating himself in his swivel chair. 'And what is it you want to know?' he asked. His manner was easy and as assured as though he had just poured Marsh a Scotch in a well-ordered drawing-room.

'I'd like to know how you've spent the years since Louise went missing,' said Marsh. 'And whether there's anything about her disappearance which, with hindsight, you think might be helpful in finding out what happened to her.'

'Does that mean you're opening the case again?'

'No. As I said, I'm just bringing myself up to date because I've returned to the area,' said Marsh. 'There could be some trivial detail – possibly the name of a friend who wasn't mentioned before – a remark she'd made – just a little thing, perhaps, but significant and overlooked at the time.'

'You can't expect me to remember everything that happened so long ago,' said Malcolm. 'As I said in my statement, I'd last seen her the weekend before, when I was at the house. She seemed all right then.'

'She was all right until she went missing,' said Marsh drily. 'You were not living at Selbury then.'

'No. I'd come back from Australia a couple of months earlier and hadn't found work that really suited me,' said Malcolm. He fixed Marsh with a frank, honest gaze as he spoke.

Marsh gazed steadily back, unimpressed.

'You were driving a taxi,' he stated. 'Is that correct?'

'More a mini-cab, really,' said Malcolm. 'Just helping a friend who was short-staffed. My father wasn't too keen, to tell you the truth. He thought it rather down-market for me, but I was providing a service. What's wrong with that?'

'What indeed?' Marsh concurred. 'You had a fare that night?'

'Yes. I told the police at the time. I had a run out to Heathrow,' said Malcolm.

'And you were living in Cornton, in a flat in Thames Road?'

'Right.'

'Where are you living now, Mr Vaughan?' Marsh had the address because Norah had given it to him, and he knew, because he had asked his department to check, that the householder was a Mrs Brenda Carter, who ran an employment bureau from a small office in a narrow street behind the abbey.

Malcolm glibly gave the address.

'And do you own the house, Mr Vaughan?'

'I pay the mortgage,' Malcolm replied. 'It's my girlfriend's place. She's divorced – no kids. I met her when she needed a car.' He wore on his face the smile that had charmed Brenda then.

'And the lady's name?' asked Marsh.

'None of this has got anything to do with her,' Malcolm protested.

'Of course not,' said Marsh. 'Still, I need to keep records up to date. It's no secret, is it, if you're living there openly? She's not on social security, is she?'

'Certainly not,' said Malcolm. 'She runs her own business.' He supplied Brenda's name.

'And you've no theories about what happened to your sister?'

'No. She must have been stopped by someone who attacked her,' said Malcolm. 'That's what everyone thought, isn't it?'

'Would she have stopped for a stranger?'

'I don't suppose so, but he might have got into the car at the traffic lights,' Malcolm suggested. 'She wouldn't have locked it.'

'Hm.' Marsh could not remember discussing this possibility. 'But there were no signs of struggle in the car,' he said.

'Well, maybe they got out to argue,' said Malcolm. 'How should I know?'

'You were fond of your sister?'

'Of course I was. Well, we had the odd row – brothers and sisters do quarrel, don't they?' Malcolm said. 'She could be obstinate at times.' He stood up and took his empty mug through to the sink where he rinsed it and set it on the drainer to dry. How pernickety he was, clearing it away so promptly, thought Marsh.

'What did you and Louise quarrel about?' he asked, when Malcolm returned.

'Oh, I don't know. It's so long ago,' said Malcolm. 'She thought our mother favoured me and was jealous,' he said. 'Of course, I was the son, you see. Mothers like their sons.'

'Did she get on with your wife?' inquired Marsh.

'My wife? God, that's going back a bit,' said Malcolm.

He had almost forgotten Gwynneth's existence. 'I don't know if they met. Louise was living in London then.'

'What's your view on why she returned to live at home?'

Malcolm shrugged.

'George kept nagging at her to come back. Thought she wasn't safe in London, with dozens of lecherous blokes after her,' he said.

'And were there dozens?'

'I doubt it.'

'What about her mother?'

'Oh, Susan thought she should stay in town. Thought it was the best place to find some nob to marry,' said Malcolm. 'It was top priority, that, with Susan. Getting her married. That was the pattern, you see. She'd done it – married when she was very young, and found another husband fast enough after the first one died. It was what happened then. Girls had to find some guy to take them on, provide a meal ticket for life and get them off their father's hands.'

'Did Louise go along with that?'

'No. She wanted something romantic,' said Malcolm. 'Well, girls do, don't they? Till they get some sense and learn what it's all about.'

'And what is it all about?' asked Marsh with interest.

'Bed, of course. Sex, if you'd rather call it that,' said Malcolm. 'That's what makes the world go round, and some of them aren't too keen.'

'Do you think Louise was one who wasn't?'

'How should I know? She was supposed to be a virgin, wasn't she?'

'And you don't think she was?'

'No. She'd been having it off with a bloke for years,' said Malcolm.

Marsh tried not to show his excitement at this revelation. Here was what he was hoping for: a new observation.

'Was she?' he asked. 'Who with? Do you know?'

'His name was Richard Blacker,' said Malcolm.

'Really? You didn't mention this at the time,' Marsh pointed out.

'No. Well, he couldn't have had anything to do with it, and there was no point in spreading scandal about her if she was dead,' said Malcolm. 'He was married, you see.'

'How can you be so sure he wasn't involved?'

'They'd broken up. That was why she came back to live at home,' said Malcolm. 'Susan and George didn't know about it. It would have fairly cracked up George if he'd found out.'

'Ah. What did he do, this Richard Blacker?' asked Marsh.

'Something in advertising, I think,' said Malcolm.

You don't just think: you damn well know, Marsh reflected.

'She told you about it, did she?' he asked.

'Of course. What are brothers for?' answered Malcolm.

But that was not how he had learned about the affair.

He escorted Marsh to the forecourt, saw him into his Cavalier, remarked that it was a useful car and offered to find him something with a little more dash any time he felt like a change, then sketched a waving salute as the superintendent drove off. Traffic was building up towards the rush hour now as people started to leave their offices and the shops closed. It was a fine evening, though windy; November had been unusually dry this year, with bright, sunny days and skies massed with huge, billowing shadowy clouds.

Back in his office, Malcolm found he was sweating. He had not expected interest in Louise to resurface after so long, not unless she were to be found. He mopped his face with a piece torn from a roll of paper towel and threw the crumpled stuff into the waste-bin beside his desk. His hands were shaking and he needed a drink. He took a bottle of Scotch out of the kitchen cupboard and poured himself a stiff tot. He wouldn't go back to the workshop now, except to lock up; what he needed was Brenda. He'd take her somewhere special tonight, treat them both to an extra good meal. She was no cook and nor was he, so they often ate out, and he enjoyed being seen with an attractive woman as much as eating a gourmet meal. Brenda always looked smart; she said it was important in her job, and he agreed. If you didn't look good, people didn't respect you.

Brenda was tough. She'd had a struggle, setting up the business, and she was hard enough to take a high fee for what she did. She was physically strong, too, and played badminton twice a week. She didn't go weepy over a bit of rough stuff when that happened but gave as good as she got, and he had found that a turn-on at first. Now it was more of a challenge. He'd liked being able to make that stupid Gwynneth cry, and other girls he'd been with, but he had never seen Brenda shed a tear.

He took off his overalls and had a quick shower. Brenda hated the smell of engine oil, which she said clung to him if he came home without showering, so he had had the fitment installed. It was useful, making it easy, when he was taking cars to prospective buyers, to freshen up first. Dressed in a dark suit, with an expensive shirt and a silk tie, he made a favourable impression on those he was meeting for the first time. The cars he sold were in good condition. Sometimes he cannibalised two to make one vehicle out of the best parts of both, and he enjoyed working on really old cars, almost veterans; there was satisfaction in making an engine run sweetly and cogs mesh smoothly together. The trouble was that it took time, while the bills piled up; his desk was full of them, and his rent was owing.

Brenda had been surprised to discover how tidy he was and wondered where he had learned his neat ways. His memory took him back to when he was five or six, and for some reason Norah Tyler was staying at Selbury House. She came for occasional weekends and would sometimes stay with the children while George and Susan went out. In those days they frequently went to lunch parties or to play tennis, and in winter George would go shooting; Susan used to accompany the guns, enjoying the day in the open air.

They had treated Norah as an unpaid mother's help, he thought, looking back, and wondered why she let them make use of her like that. Probably she enjoyed being able to say that she was going to visit her smart friends in the country and liked showing off photographs of the large house. He and Louise behaved well in her care; she had a knack of promoting harmony between them and could interest them in various ways which both enjoyed. She played games with them and, when they were old enough, took them on bicycle rides round the lanes; there was much less traffic then than now. But she had been extremely tidy and had made them fold their clothes and put their toys away after use. He remembered her making him clean up the sandpit. It was full of old patty-tins, buried wooden spades and discarded cars. She had provided him with a large-meshed garden sieve obtained from Ford, the gardener, to go through the pile of sand, rescuing buried treasure. Louise had not had to help.

Malcolm forgot that she was only three or four at the time, and that he had, when Norah was not in sight, thrown sand at his sister and been given the task as a punishment. Later, at school, being tidy had been a way of safeguarding his possessions: knowing just where he had put them meant that he was on sure ground if another boy borrowed something and deserved a bloody nose. Perhaps he owed some of this to Norah, but later, in prison in Sydney, he had had to be tidy, though no one over here knew about that.

'Aren't you curious about your real parents?'

Brenda had asked Malcolm that after she had been taken to Selbury Lodge for lunch one Sunday. Until then, she had not known that he was adopted, but afterwards she had commented that he was not very like either of his parents.

Malcolm had found that telling people he was adopted worked to his advantage with women. They were filled with pity at the notion of his being abandoned as an infant; one of his girlfriends had devised a script with his desperate mother seeking a safe place for her infant and dumping it on a hospital doorstep, with a note attached to its hand-knitted shawl praying that the child might prove to be the answer to an unhappy couple's prayers. Malcolm could not believe that the scenario attached to his birth was like that; he remembered Susan's tale of their selection of him, implying that it was made from among a wide choice of babies. He decided, however, not to reveal this conviction.

'They could be anyone, you know,' Brenda said. 'You can find out, Malcolm.'

'What difference does it make?' Malcolm said. 'They didn't want me. Susan did. That's all that counts. She'd had this other kid that died, from her first husband. I suppose she thought I'd look like him. Maybe I do look like her first husband. Hugh, his name was.' He had never thought of this before.

Brenda liked the idea of romance attached to his origins, and the mystery explained things that didn't quite fit together. His manners in public were everything you would expect from someone with his background, but he could lose his temper and his control in seconds, and he was happiest among people who did little talking but engaged in some shared activity like drinking, playing darts or gambling. A lot of people, she thought, and especially men, were like that, while most women enjoyed a good natter.

'I know a girl who traced her real mother,' she told him. 'She – the mother – had married and got other children. My friend didn't just barge in. She rang up and made a date to meet at a café. This old lady came in. Well, she seemed old. But she was nice – said she'd always wondered about my friend and thought of her on her birthday. She'd told her husband about it and it was all right and now my friend has a whole new family. Your real mother probably thinks of you on your birthday.'

'Well, she'll have to get on with it, then, won't she?' said Malcolm. 'She can find me, if she wants.'

'She can't. It's the other way round – the children trace the parents. They gave up all their rights at the time of the adoption.'

'Oh.'

'It could be hard for the adoptive parents, having the real ones muscling in when they've done all the work of rearing the kid,' Brenda said. 'What about Norah? Do you fancy her as your mother?'

'Norah? Don't make me laugh,' said Malcolm, not looking the least bit amused. 'She's never had any kids.'

'How can you be sure about that? She's not married, it's true, and single parents were bad news in her day. Wouldn't it be quite likely she'd give her baby to friends to adopt, if she had one? You could do that sort of thing then. Nowadays there are all sorts of rules.'

'It's a theory, but it didn't happen like that,' said Malcolm. The idea was repellent. He remembered Norah's stern words to him when, as a child, he had transgressed, and she was less than warm to him when they met now.

'What do you know about her? How did she get in with your parents?'

'Oh, she's always been around,' said Malcolm. 'She came to the village during the war to get away from the bombs. She was only a kid then – an evacuee. Her parents were killed in a bombing raid and she more or less stayed on. Later she went into the army and after that she had a job in London.'

'So why did she give it up?'

'It gave her up,' said Malcolm. 'Booted her out. So she came running back to the Vaughans expecting to be rescued.'

'Well, maybe they rescued her before,' said Brenda, though she had formed the opinion that any rescuing at the Lodge was being done by, and not to Norah.

'They certainly taught her to drop her Cockney accent and all that sort of thing,' said Malcolm. 'She's on to a good racket now, living free and all that.' And occupying the room that should rightfully be his.

'If you want to stay in Selbury, you can buy a place of your own,' George had said when the big house was sold.

'Where do I get the money?' Malcolm had asked, and George had replied that he hoped Malcolm would not apply to Susan.

Not normally perceptive, Malcolm had noticed that latterly George had stopped referring to Susan as 'your mother' when mentioning her to him.

They had sounded surprised when he had telephoned to say he would be bringing Brenda over, and they had said that he could not do so on the first date he suggested because they were going out themselves. He had been quite annoyed by this rebuff. However, they had been friendly to Brenda when the occasion finally arrived. Norah, who had sat at the table with them unlike a real housekeeper who would, in Malcolm's opinion, have known her place, had shown interest in the employment agency, asking about temporary positions and wages, so much so that George had said, 'Are you going to look for a job, Norah?'

She had laughed and said, 'You never know.'

She had cooked the lunch, of course: roast lamb with peas and new potatoes and treacle pudding, his favourite, with fruit salad for those who preferred something less substantial. Brenda had been amused to learn that Malcolm liked steamed puddings. They were never available at any of the restaurants where the couple ate; on the rare occasions when they ate at home it was usually convenience food from Marks and Spencer, cooked in the microwave.

Since this conversation Malcolm had begun to wonder about his real mother, but not enough to want to trace her. After all, she'd given him away, hadn't she? Could she really have been Norah?

Brenda had enjoyed her day at Selbury and felt she understood Malcolm better now. It wasn't easy, past forty as she was, to find an unattached man, and she did not like living without one. Malcolm was presentable and she was not dependent on him in any way, which kept him guessing and meant she could turn him out of her house if she tired of him. So far, whenever he had lost his temper, she had been able to bring him to heel.

She would get rid of him when she found someone interesting enough or attractive enough to take his place. Meanwhile, it would be amusing if he could be persuaded to trace his real parents. In his place, she couldn't have borne not to know.

Malcolm hated being alone, unless he was working on a car when he became absorbed in what he was doing. Even then, except when he was tuning an engine and needed to listen to what it was doing, he liked a background of pop music.

When he went home after Marsh's visit to the workshop, Brenda was out. He was annoyed. She had said nothing this morning about being late. If he'd known, he'd have gone somewhere himself instead of coming straight back. Malcolm never admitted a need for reassurance, for to do so was to be weak, and he was strong. He did not understand that his talk with Marsh had unsettled him, just that the silence in the empty house was oppressive. He turned on the radio while he looked in the fridge for something to eat. The freezer section held various processed meals but he had an urge for a steak, large, red and juicy. He would go out and get one.

He had already showered and had run a razor over his face; Brenda didn't like even a hint of stubble, which she said scratched her skin and gave her a rash. Now he took time to change his shirt, slick down his dark curls and select a new silk tie before he went out to look for company, drink and food, in that order.

At The Bull he found some acquaintances in the bar.

If asked, he would have described them as his friends, but he knew very little about any of them though they often met in various bars, especially this one. Some were, like him, displaced persons with difficult or broken marriages; others were sales representatives working away from home. The few who had merely looked in for a drink on the way home or to complete some business discussion soon left. Malcolm, his craving for steak alleviated by alcohol, continued with the rest to drink and tell tall tales to impress one another. Malcolm did his share, enlarging on his experiences in Australia where he made out that he had been very successful and ignoring any questioner who wondered aloud why, in that case, he had returned to England. He had some good stories about sheep that went down well with an uncritical audience. Four of the group at last moved on from the bar into the restaurant and Malcolm went with them. They were all noisy and spuriously cheery. One man tried chatting up the waitress and another told her not to believe a word he said. She took no notice of either; she was used to all sorts and there was help at hand if things went too far. They all had prawn cocktails and large sirloin steaks, and four bottles of burgundy between the five of them, followed by brandy.

Three of the men proclaimed their need to relieve themselves and went out to the washroom from which they failed to return. When the bill came, the fourth man followed and Malcolm was left to pay.

He decided to treat it as a joke. He'd get even another time, do the same thing when he got the chance. In a way it was his own fault; he liked to make expansive gestures and imply that money flowed from his fingertips, often buying rounds of drinks outside his turn and saying just leave it to him about meals. It made him feel good. But at the moment he owed money all round and could get no more credit. Two cars he had recently sold had not yet been fully paid for and he had bought the Vitesse to keep stock turning over. In an attempt to clear some of his debts, he had staked three hundred pounds on a bet on an outside chance two days before and it had not come off. He was in debt to the tune of over forty thousand pounds, and now he was adding two hundred more to the total as he wrote a cheque against non-existent funds.

The best thing would be to go bankrupt. Then he could write everything off. Too bad about those to whom he owed money. He could start again, float a new business in someone else's name – Brenda's, for instance. He took a bottle of whisky home with him.

Brenda had not returned, so he opened it and turned on the television. A film was showing. Cars screeched round corners, and palm trees bordered a brilliant blue sea in the distance. Malcolm sprawled in an armchair gazing at the screen, not taking in what he saw. He needed it to deaden the silence and give him the illusion of company.

Suppose he found his real mother? Would she help him now? Would things suddenly go right for him if they met? Not if Brenda was right and it was Norah. He thrust the distasteful idea away. Anyway, none of this was his fault; it was all down to the failure that Susan and George had made of his education and training. Why hadn't he been sent to an engineering college, for instance?

He remembered the day he went to his preparatory school, in his grey shorts and maroon blazer and cap, delivered by Susan at a large building bigger even than Selbury House and where every boy was a stranger. She had gone off without saying goodbye while he was being shown the train room where there was a huge electric lay-out. It was an hour before he discovered that she had abandoned him.

He decided not to cry. Two other new boys had lapsed into tears and had been regarded with scorn by others. Instead, he fostered an inner truculence and the following day had a fight with the boy meant to be his 'shepherd', which meant teaching him the rules and how to find his way about. There had been no provocation; Malcolm just turned on the other boy and punched him, taking him completely by surprise and giving him a bloody nose.

A different shepherd was appointed after this incident, a bigger one. The headmaster had not known what to make of the episode since the original shepherd had shielded his charge from blame, alleging that he had bumped his nose on a door, but there had been an independent witness, an under-matron walking across the playing-field some distance away, too far to see more than that Malcolm had struck the first blow. Provocative words might have been uttered first, though it seemed unlikely since the shepherd was of a placid disposition.

Malcolm soon established a reputation among the boys as one not to be crossed because he struck at once, and he was bigger and stronger than most of his contemporaries.

He had lost none of his aggression, and his impulse, still, was to strike out at anyone who used words or anything else to attack or taunt him.

Norah had always been somewhere about in the background, perhaps not seen for months but turning up after Christmas or at Easter and often staying as much as a week in the summer.

'She's like a poor relation,' he had once heard old Mrs Warrington, his grandmother, say when she and her friend Lady Spencer were watching Louise and a friend play tennis. Malcolm, lying in the long grass beyond the shrubs bordering the tennis court, had been smoking, the light wind taking the fumes away from the two old ladies. Then Lady Spencer lit up, saying that the smoke would keep the midges off. This was to counter Mrs Warrington's disapproval, for Lady Spencer had a persistent cough and frequent attacks of bronchitis but would not give up what she called her one vice. 'She's always with us but in her case useful,' Mrs Warrington had added, referring to Norah.

'Where would she be without you all?' murmured Lady Spencer.

'She's certainly done well. She's got a very good job,' said his grandmother.

'Yes. Considering that unfortunate business, it's all worked out for the best,' agreed Lady Spencer.

'I sometimes wonder if we did the right thing,' Malcolm had heard his grandmother remark.

What about, Malcolm had wondered, eyeing the girls

in their short pleated skirts and little white pants. Louise's legs were thin; the other girl was plumper, with a round behind revealed when she spun about.

'Well, she couldn't keep it,' Lady Spencer said. 'A girl of her age with an illegitimate baby and no means of support.'

'She never married,' his grandmother said.

'No, but nowadays marriage isn't everything. A girl can be independent and have a career and she has done that. It wasn't the same in our day.'

Years later, sitting alone by the television set in Brenda's small house, Malcolm suddenly remembered that afternoon and what he had overheard. At the time he had been more interested in peeping than listening. He would have been about fifteen years old.

'Adoption was the right answer,' his grandmother said, and then Lady Spencer began coughing, obscuring any subsequent comment. When her attack was over they started to talk about something else.

Why hadn't he thought more about what they were saying? Why hadn't the meaning of it sunk in? Well, he was remembering it now, all right, and the blood began to pound in his head as he saw what it could imply: just what Brenda had idly suggested. Without her words he might have never cottoned on to the truth.

For it must be that: it made sense of so many things.

What was he going to do about it, now that he knew?

3
Susan

She would lie in her small bed, which had half sides to prevent her rolling out on to the floor in her sleep, and watch the shadows cast by the dying fire. There would be fearsome shapes on the cornice and ceiling, the pointed hats of witches and the gnarled noses of gnomes, but the glowing caverns among the coals were more friendly, with warm grottoes full of gold or hidden treasure or peopled by happy pixies. Every morning Mabel, the under-housemaid, lit the fire before Susan got up, coming in with bucket and brushes to sweep out the dead ash from the night before and kindle new flames which soon crackled up the chimney. Susan would sit up in bed with the thick eiderdown pulled close against the cold, watching her, and they would chat. Mabel told tales of a fox with an earth in Selbury Copse and how he had crept out at night to kill Mrs Betts' chickens, leaving only feathers and bits of bone behind him. Or she would recount the latest adventures of her own brother who had run away to sea and sent postcards from places like Buenos Aires and Panama, making his life sound unbelievably romantic. These interludes would be ended by Nanny, who would come into the room briskly clapping her hands and saying, 'Now come along, Mabel, you haven't all day to waste chattering. Joyce is looking for you downstairs.' Joyce was the head housemaid under whose instructions Mabel carried out the more menial household tasks such as doing the grates, polishing brasses and cleaning shoes. She would carry the brass cans of hot water up to the bedrooms, and Joyce herself would take one into mother in the big bedroom overlooking the gardens. Father's dressing-room was next door and he had his own brass can. Mabel brought the nursery hot water, and later, breakfast to the day nursery.

Looking back, Susan would marvel, half ashamed, at all the chores undertaken by Mabel, and her myriad laden journeys up and down stairs, but the large house could not have been run without the help of its staff. That was before central heating was installed and when there were only two bathrooms, one upstairs for the family, and another with a bath covered with a board when not in use in a small room opening off the scullery for the use of the servants. Later, that had become a laundry room equipped with washing-machine and iron; now it was part of Myra Slavosky's flat. In those days before the war, when Susan was a child, Selbury House had been full of activity and housed at least ten people. She and her brothers, and their parents, were dependent on others to keep things running smoothly and themselves fed and warm.

Her mother never even made up the drawing-room fire herself; Mabel would enter at intervals during the day to add coal. The washing had all been done by hand with a scrubbing board and large blocks of yellow soap, then put through a mangle to wring out the excess water. She had enjoyed watching this being done; the rollers would flatten the linen, part-ironing it in the process. She couldn't remember when Joyce got her first Hoover but she had not forgotten the machine itself, made of dull chrome with a black bag. Presumably before its arrival Joyce had used brush and dustpan to clean the carpets, or more likely it was Mabel who went down on hands and knees. Susan had an impression that used tea-leaves were scattered first to bring up the dust. All this work was done before the family came down for breakfast, an array of kedgeree, scrambled egg and bacon, arranged on hot plates kept warm by heaters running on methylated spirits, and served in silver dishes. Nowadays it was generally thought that Joyce and Mabel and their fellows had been grossly exploited, and in some households that was certainly true; their pay was low and the hours long. But in other families they were happy, well fed, and surrounded by friends. Good employers felt responsible for their staff, looked after them, saw that they were cared for if they were ill and finally gave them pensions. Paternalism was considered a dirty word today, but it had not been entirely a bad thing; it involved thinking of other people as a duty.

How they worked, though. If mother and father went out to dinner, Joyce or the parlourmaid waited up for their return, no matter how late that might be. Mabel's lot was improved when a bootboy was taken on; he fetched coals for the fires and did other odd jobs besides cleaning the shoes. Susan and her brothers saw very little of their father, who went up to town every day on the train from Feringham, returning in the evening just before Nanny came to take them up to bed after their time with Mother in the drawing-room. Later, Malcolm stayed downstairs for an extra half hour, and in the final term before he went off to prep school he had dinner in the dining room twice a week.

Malcolm was the eldest. Then came Susan, and finally David. She remembered being pushed out in the big pram with him. David, in woollen jacket and bonnet, sat up beneath the hood, and if her legs grew tired after walking, she would be lifted into the pram to sit facing him, with her feet in a well in the centre. If you stamped, it gave out a hollow sound. Life was cosy and safe. Nanny would take them to look for primroses and to see young lambs at the farm where Joe Simpson, with his dog, would come and talk and would show them new calves and piglets. Nanny always lingered when Joe was around. He was a widower whose wife had died when their third child was born; later he married Nanny and they had two more children. Visiting them was, after that, a rare but wonderful treat; Susan loved sitting in the large kitchen drinking milk fresh from the cow and eating scones or biscuits Nanny had baked.

Mother had been seriously displeased when Nanny departed.

'What does she want to get married for now?' she had grumbled. 'She's too old. She was settled here.'

'She's only thirty-one,' Father had said from behind his paper.

Susan, playing with her Noah's ark on the floor, went on pairing the model animals ready to parade them to safety. She liked the zebras best, with their smart stripes. All the animals were made of real skin, soft to the touch, the hairs silky.

'Well, she should have more sense,' said Mother.

'Don't you recommend matrimony, my dear?' Father asked.

'For some, yes, and younger women,' said Mother. 'But she'll regret it. She'll have to work very hard.'

'And I suppose she didn't do that here?' Father was smiling, teasing Mother. 'You're just cross at losing an excellent nanny.'

'I'll never find another as good,' Mother had lamented, and it was true. David was still only four, and he and the new nanny got on well enough, but Susan did not care for her ways, which involved having bows in her hair which were pulled so tight that they hurt, and curling-rags at night. She couldn't sleep, tied up like Ameliaranne Stiggins. Luckily Father made some observation about her surprising new curls and the rags were abandoned.

Curling-irons came next. Bidden to a party, she would be put into her white organdie dress with the pink satin sash, white socks, and her bronze pumps held on by elastic crossed over her insteps, and Nanny would crimp her hair with tongs. There would be a singeing smell as the ends were twisted into ringlets.

Malcolm used to laugh at this process but he was sympathetic.

'I should cut it off,' he advised one day. 'If it was short she couldn't do it to you.' He had a running feud with Nanny, who administered Californian Syrup of Figs once a week. Malcolm, back from prep school for the holidays, found the stuff nauseating and refused to submit, skilfully sicking it up all over Nanny's clean uniform dress, after which she contented herself with painfully scrubbing behind his ears and putting him on the rule of silence at meals whenever she had the least excuse.

He had enthusiastically helped Susan cut off her hair, finding a pair of sharp scissors and holding the strands so that she could do the actual hacking herself. Susan snipped a fringe across her forehead, like the pages in fairy tale illustrations, and Malcolm neatened its jagged edge so that it ended up very short, well above her eyebrows.

That night they were both sent to bed with no supper and Nanny beat Malcolm with the back of a hairbrush on his bare buttocks, finding the strength to hold down his wriggling, protesting form. She was just about to beat Susan too when Father walked into the nursery. He so rarely did this that it came as a total shock to all the occupants, including David, who was standing with his thumb in his mouth wondering if he would be next.

Nanny was sent out of the room and they never saw her again. Mabel, deputed to get them up the next day, reported that she had been despatched with her trunk and her bags.

'Sent off, bag and baggage,' she told them with glee. 'Gave herself airs, she did. Been in a lord's family, or so she said, and thought trade a come-down. Well, she'll not get into any other lord's place after this.'

Susan thought Mabel meant something to do with Our Lord in Heaven and was mystified.

'Never mind, dears. Forget the silly old thing,' Mabel advised. 'I'm going to be looking after you until they find someone else.'

Halcyon days now began, for Mabel, who by this time was nineteen, proved so good at her job that she slid into being their permanent nanny and a new under-housemaid was taken on in her place. Mabel worked harder than Nanny had done, still carrying their meals upstairs and doing the nursery fires as well as the washing, ironing and mending, but she found time to play with them and tell them stories, and it was she who took them to visit their old nanny, now Mrs Simpson, at the farm. She left in the end to marry the Spencers' chauffeur and after that there were no more nannies. A nursery governess arrived and some other children joined them for lessons until David went off to school. After that Susan and the Spencer girls shared a different governess who came daily to the Spencers' house; the boot boy, Alfred Ford, now a man, had been taught to drive and he took her over in the Austin. Later still, after central heating and a new plumbing system had been installed, with two more bathrooms upstairs and basins in the bedrooms, he became the under-gardener until finally, when the war began, he was the head gardener with a boy under him who cleaned the shoes and washed the cars.

Susan herself went off to boarding-school in the end, with the Spencer girls. There were only a hundred pupils, who lived in a large house on the South Downs overlooking the Channel. The air was bracing, the food plain but nourishing, and the tuition moderate, with an emphasis on equipping the girls for life as the wives of successful men. Few girls achieved academic distinction, but most were happy enough at the school.

As they grew older, Susan and her brothers had ridden their bicycles for miles round the country lanes near Selbury. They were allowed a lot of freedom. The boys would cycle to Feringham to buy parts for their bikes, or sweets, and to go to the cinema. She rode her pony over the fields alone. Neither of the boys had liked riding and Father was no horseman.

'I wasn't born to it,' he would say, with a smile, but he offered his children the opportunity to try a variety of sporting activities.

Susan and Dapple used to canter along the headlands of ploughed fields, jump the stooks of corn after the harvest, wander down woodland paths. She loved the golden late summer days with the stubble pale against the brown earth when ploughing began. In spring the woods would be full of primroses and bluebells, with the fluff of catkin and pussy willow softening the brown of the hedgerows. Sometimes Susan would meet the Spencer girls, all of them with sandwiches in their pockets, and they would have a picnic lunch before riding home. The worst calamity that ever befell them was when Helen Spencer's pony stumbled one day, tipping Helen over his ears so that she hit her head on the ground and sustained mild concussion, sitting up and talking nonsense afterwards. Pamela Spencer had stayed with her sister, and their two ponies, reins looped over a handy tree, had stood docilely by while Susan rode dramatically off to the nearest house to telephone for help. Not a serious mishap, and an innocent adventure: nowadays few householders would welcome someone wanting to telephone in an emergency, fearing confidence tricksters seeking to steal from them. You still saw children out riding alone, but all in hard hats essential with so much traffic about; that had not been a hazard before the war.

Louise had had a pony too, and had enjoyed riding until she was about fifteen, when she had gradually lost interest; but Malcolm, like his uncles, had never been keen.

When her thoughts turned to Malcolm, Susan always felt as if a great weight sat on her chest. He had been such a lovely little boy, lively and physically strong, and not really naughty, she still excused, until he began pulling Louise's hair and hiding her toys to tease her and make her cry. Even that was just what boys did; Susan's brothers had teased her too, but never with malice. Louise had always been better with words than Malcolm, and Susan suspected that as she grew older she had verbally provoked his attacks.

Now only Malcolm was left. Her brothers, and Hugh and her first little baby had all gone, then Louise. Susan felt that her earlier bereavements had made it easier for her to accept Louise's death, though not its manner, than it had been for George. What she found hard was to be in the house where she kept expecting to see Louise, just as for years she had expected one or other of her brothers to come walking in or to be sitting in the drawing-room, or striding about in the garden. This was what people meant when they said they saw ghosts, she decided, and she could cope with it out of doors, so gardening became her solace. This helped life with George, too; they did not have to spend long hours together if she kept active with other things. A gulf had opened between them as they found they could not discuss what might have happened to Louise, for her fate was too terrible to imagine. George could not bring himself to talk about it, while Susan, at first, wanted to pour out her theories and fears.

Norah had been wonderful then. She had known just what to say and when to let her weep. Susan believed that without her support, she would have gone out of her mind. Norah had been there at all the other bad times, too, though she was still at school when Hugh was killed. Her being made redundant had, in the end, worked out well for them all. True, she had had ideas about setting up in some way on her own, but Mother's accident had put paid to that.

'Of course Norah will look after me,' Mother had said. 'Look at what we've done for her. She'll be glad to, and it will be doing her a kindness. Where else would she go, after all? Whom has she to turn to but us?'

Mother had still equated putting a roof over someone's head in return for long hours of work with doing them a favour. She herself had been careful never to learn to cook, though she could heat up the dishes Mrs Gibson left ready for supper and had been known to make tea and to open packets of biscuits. She had always been able to find someone to look after her.

Susan, grown old herself, with fine wrinkles lining her

thin skin and with her faded, almost white hair once again cropped short though now in a neat cap close to her skull, could remember Norah arriving to live with the Fords, and the two little boys who had been sent to Selbury House. The boys, six and four years old, brothers, had not wanted to be parted and her mother had handed them over to Joyce to be housed in an attic and cared for by the maids. Norah had taken a sisterly interest in them and often came up to the house to play with them and see that they were behaving themselves, as she put it. The three children had all found country life very strange, and the boys had been awed by the size of the house they were living in. Norah, though, had been fascinated by it, by the life and the people within.

'It's so quiet,' one of the boys had said, missing the daily sound of traffic, the big red buses passing by, but he had liked seeing cows in the fields and had been amazed to learn that milk had a source other than bottles. Norah, older and more experienced, had been to the country before, on day trips with her parents and sister. Her mother had come down to see her whenever she could afford the fare, and had been ambitious for her daughters. Susan's mother, losing Joyce and the under-housemaid to war work, never, as it turned out, to be replaced, and left with only Mrs Johnson the cook, had offered Norah's sister a place in the house, but she had already found a job as an office girl in the City.

Then she was killed, and her parents, too.

Norah, hitherto a bright, funny girl who made shrewd, forthright remarks, became silent and withdrawn. Mrs Ford kept her busy after school, work being the best remedy for grief. She had begun to read a great deal, borrowing books from the public library in Feringham, and she had worked hard at school. In the few short weeks of his life, she had helped Susan with baby Harry and had several times wheeled him out in his pram. Then, all at once, that had ended.

Susan had been working for some months as a VAD nurse at Feringham Hospital, where there were now whole wards full of wounded servicemen as well as civilian patients, by the time Norah left school and started at the factory. Sometimes, depending on their shifts, they travelled in together. Norah, just sixteen, was a pleasant concerned companion for Susan who still felt stunned by her double loss. Norah was bereft too; her whole family had been killed, though at the time Susan forgot that. She remembered it now, looking back.

From time to time Susan's brothers came home on snatched leaves. Often they would bring a girlfriend down or go off to a party somewhere; both had sports cars and carefully hoarded petrol coupons. It was odd to reflect that both Father and Mother were relatively young then. Father, only fifty-two, was asked to advise a government department on fuel economy in factories and said he had become an honorary civil servant. He often stayed overnight in town and firewatched for incendiary bombs, sometimes extinguishing them with a stirrup-pump. Mother presided over the village First Aid Post, for which a room in the house was set aside, and she helped with the WVS, directing the rehousing of bombed-out people, and she gave first aid lectures to groups of women. Everyone was busy.

Bombs fell on Selbury.

Susan was in the garden one day, before Harry was born. She was mourning his father, unable to believe that her handsome young husband would never return, but she was sustained by the young life within her, nature asserting its claims. There was a droning sound overhead at a little distance and, hearing faint bangs, she looked up to see several planes flying quite low. The small white cotton-wool puffs of anti-aircraft fire around them told her that they were enemy bombers, but she felt entirely calm, watching them with interest, not fear. Months later a stick of three bombs unloaded at random by a Heinkel or Junkers unable to reach its target fell in the village. One landed on a cowshed, which was empty, one in the road at the top of the hill entering the village, and the third in a field. All left craters in the ground to be marvelled at until filled in. The village had been very lucky to escape without real damage or death.

People tended to think that quiet places like Selbury had escaped the worst of the war, and in many ways so they had, not exposed to direct intensive bombing and with gardens in which to grow vegetables and keep chickens to bolster the rations; but the war memorial in the square bore a long list of names of the dead, including Malcolm and David Warrington, Susan's two brothers, and Hugh, who by marrying her became an honorary resident.

Susan had lived in Selbury nearly all her life, apart from the time spent away at school and the year in Switzerland where she had skied, learned some French, a little cooking and dressmaking, and had passed the time pleasantly until she was old enough to be launched into society with a view to getting married as soon as possible.

It was all we thought of then, she remembered, and to be single at twenty-two was to be on the shelf. She and the other girls would discuss their ideal men, how many children they would have, where they would live, and so on. Some were to be presented at court, with three feathers attached to their heads and long satin dresses with trains. Susan had had no wish to be among them although Lady Spencer, it seemed, had offered to present her with Helen, Pamela having made her curtsey the previous year. Mother had not been presented herself and privately agreed with Father that it was all a lot of humbug. Susan had had a dance, however: a fine affair at the house, with a band, and even Father, writing the cheque, had said that it hadn't been a bad evening at all.

We were indeed born with silver spoons in our mouths, Susan thought, and she had continued to live a quietly comfortable life with kind George, adapting to the changing conditions without any great hardship, becoming a good cook herself as help grew more difficult to find but never left coping alone. She had enjoyed entertaining for Malcolm, named after his dead uncle, and Louise when they were children, giving parties with conjurors or film shows, and later there had been modest dances, the big house once again fully used. Did people still have dances or was it all discos now?

If only Malcolm would marry again, have children and settle down. This girl – well, woman – he was living with seemed nice enough, pretty and bright and efficient, and obviously older than Malcolm. She had arrived to lunch dressed smartly in a black skirt and long scarlet jacket, with an emerald silk blouse, and she wore very high-heeled shoes which Susan had been brought up to think was not done in the country; it had made showing her round the garden a hazard. Some of Selbury's new residents could be seen teetering along in spike heels under slacks, propelling their children in plastic cocoons inside pushchairs, often with enormous dogs in tow. Times had certainly changed. Brenda must have found the Lodge House ordinary enough; doubtless her parents lived in something similar. She would have been impressed by Selbury House, however, Susan was sure. It had taken her some time to get used to less space.

In the big house, there was plenty of room to get away from people if you had quarrelled or felt unsociable. How dreadful it must be to live in a tiny house with two or three children always on top of you, thought Susan, stretching out in her single bed at the Lodge. It was a relief to be alone at night. Some people never slept alone in their lives, sharing with siblings as children, then marrying, and perhaps only on their own when widowed. George had had his dressing-room at Selbury House and had slept in it more and more often after Louise disappeared.

They lived a very quiet life now. Newcomers to the village gave drinks parties and invited each other to dinner, and there were a number of widows who entertained one another to luncheon, but the Vaughans kept apart from this although, had Susan wished to take part in the cutlet-for-cutlet routine, the food would have been Norah's responsibility. But Norah would have thought it a waste of time and money, except on special occasions, and might have rebelled. She seemed content enough, going once a week in the winter to learn French at adult education classes in Feringham and playing her language tapes on the headset that had been Mrs Warrington's, and spending time at Selbury House with Myra Slavosky and some of the other residents. Myra had escaped from Estonia ahead of the Russian advance, had married twice and made money from buying old houses, renovating them and then moving on, finally opening a dress shop in Feringham where occasionally, when other staff failed, Norah helped out on odd days. Susan was not sure if the husbands had died or were merely discarded. She found Myra rather noisy and foreign; she spoke fluent English with an accent which George thought attractive. Norah had met her when out walking Bertie and had managed to track down someone to clean the flat which Myra, as a working woman, said she had no time to do. Myra occasionally came in for a drink in the evening, more as Norah's guest than theirs; George enjoyed hearing her tales of her youth on a vast estate with two lakes and a small forest.

Susan had feared, when her mother died, that Norah would leave. She was only fifty-eight then, fit and slim, though she was plumper now. She had been quite a plump schoolgirl, with shining eyes and a lot of vitality. Susan could remember her running across the big garden, laughing for the sheer joy of being alive. They had been stupid not to see how attractive she was as she grew older, and of course she was always about, part of the scenery. No wonder David had lost his foolish young head over her and of course she responded.

At the time, Mother, in her anguish because David had already been reported missing, believed killed, had angrily alleged that Norah had deceitfully trapped him, but Susan and Father had known that this was not true. Poor Norah had been devastated and had quickly begun to look very ill. She had truly loved David, with all the devotion of a very young girl in her first romance, and had thought that he loved her. To do him justice, he probably said that he did and may have believed what he said, though how could such an unsuitable attachment have lasted? It would have been difficult for any susceptible girl to resist him once he turned his blandishments in her direction. He had been so handsome and full of laughter, blue-eyed and fairhaired, with a cleft in his chin, a Flight Lieutenant in Bomber Command.

It was Susan who had taken care of Norah when it was all over, advising her and finally helping her to join the ATS and get right away to make a new life. It was Susan, too, who had kept in touch and who, after quite a few years had passed, had suggested a visit. By then she had made her mother concede that David had been as much to blame as Norah.

Father, even while shocked by his new bereavement, had been angry because David had been so careless.

'Getting her in pod – wholly irresponsible,' he had said, with touching faith in the contraceptive arrangements then available.

Susan had wondered if perhaps Father had someone in London during those war years when he so often spent the night in town, or wasn't there time amid all the bombs? She, a chaste widow living at home, could presumably have lived differently if she had wanted to do so, with opportunities at the hospital if she had sought them, but she had never felt such an urge. Sex had not been important to her, even in the first happy weeks of her marriage to Hugh when they made love in the thatched cottage near Warminster where Harry was conceived. If Hugh had not died, how would they have got on, living together for over forty years? She sometimes wondered if he would have been as kind and as gentle as George had turned out to be. A woman, even one with money, needed a partner, for life was geared to people in pairs.

Louise would have accepted the conventions and married some nice man, a barrister or a merchant banker, perhaps, if no suitor with land and a fortune came along. She would have seen the advantages of family life over a career spent doing the bidding of some testy employer in the name of independence. She would have had money of her own when Susan herself died, even after the depletions on her capital made by inflation and Malcolm's demands. Indeed, if she had lived and had children, Susan might not have felt obliged to help him so much in recent years. As her will stood at present, he would inherit whatever was left, though the house and the income from the remaining capital would be George's during his lifetime, if he survived her.

She should look at her will again.

She was going to London soon; perhaps she should see her solicitor then.

4

George

Not a day went past without George thinking of Louise. He treasured photographs of her at every stage in her life from an infant a few days old to one taken in the garden at Selbury House the summer before she disappeared. The sun had been in her eyes and she had her hand up, shading them, laughing at him. Every year on her birthday he remembered how old she would have been and wondered how her life would have developed, had she been spared to enjoy it. It was hard to imagine her at thirty-six, which by this time would have been her age. Probably she would be married with two or three children. He knew she had had some sort of unhappy romantic experience while she was living in London but she had, he believed, recovered from that and eventually would have met someone who would have been able to make her happy. With luck they might be living not too far away and would often come over at weekends. Susan would have enjoyed a grandmother's role; in his opinion she had been a perfect mother, endlessly patient and good at playing imaginative games, though Malcolm hadn't been able to make much of them apart from being a fearsome pirate with a bandana round his head and a patch over one eye. Malcolm had liked the tree house, built in an oak tree and reached by a rope ladder, but if Louise was up there he would twist the ladder round the tree so that she could not come down and go off, marooning her, or he would not let her climb up if he was aloft. Once he had made her walk the plank. He had taken a board up and balanced it across the platform forming the house, wedging it under a strut. Then he had forced Louise, trembling with fright and crying, to walk along it towards the end which extended over the long grass below. The height was not great, perhaps ten feet, but even so, if she had fallen she could have been badly hurt.

Ford had heard her screams, hurried up the rope ladder, plucked her to safety and given Malcolm a clip round the ear which had made his head ring. The boy had protested that he was only testing her and of course he would have allowed her to walk back to safety.

'It was like in *Peter Pan*,' he said. The children had been taken to see the play at Christmas. 'She's a silly coward to cry.'

Ford, reporting the incident to George, confessed to hitting Malcolm. George said they would keep that fact to themselves since, with such a witness, Malcolm was unlikely to complain to Susan.

After that, Louise never went up to the tree house again and Malcolm, sole possessor of the territory, was very pleased with himself. He kept a store of fruit there, and if she passed within range he would bombard her, calling her an enemy alien. She soon learned to keep away and Malcolm discovered the power that grew from creating fear.

When he went away to school, Louise's life became easier, but it was clear that the boy resented her being at home when he was absent. He was very jealous when Susan gave her attention to anyone else. Trying to find excuses for him, George recognised that he felt he was a second-best, a substitute son. Other adopting families might have met the same problem, George supposed, but he knew that very often the arrangement worked most happily. Perhaps it was simply in Malcolm's nature to seek causes for resentment. George might as well have been jealous of Susan's first husband, but he wasn't; he had liked Hugh, a cheerful man with an extrovert personality who had died bravely fighting a rearguard action and had been awarded a posthumous Military Cross for his courage. George had visited the cottage near Warminster where Hugh and Susan had spent their short married life and had thought, even then, that they were playing at keeping house; it was all a sort of tender game, snatched at before disaster overtook them. Like Norah, he saw them as a fairy-tale couple, a handsome prince and a beautiful princess who had not anticipated a dark side to life. Susan should not have had to face so much tragedy; she needed love and protection and that was really all he had to offer her when she agreed to marry him. He was fourteen months younger than she was and had left school only a year before the war began. He had spent the interval teaching in a school near his home in Somerset and was planning to take it up as a career. After he was demobilised, he was offered a job by his new father-in-law and he flung himself conscientiously into learning the business from the bottom up. In time, as a director, he earned a good salary, but he had no capital of his own. With hindsight, he could see that Susan, after her comfortable upbringing, might not have appreciated life on a schoolmaster's salary, but he had not thought about that at the time, nor of the problems that could come from a wife having a higher income, whatever its source, than her husband.

After the war housing was scarce, and while George was still in the Army, stationed at Catterick during the last months of his service, they rented a cottage on the edge of the moors. For Susan it was a reincarnation of her first marriage, but the pregnancy she had longed for did not follow. George sometimes wondered if she had married him merely as a means of replacing her lost child, although he knew she was fond of him. She would make love with muted passion, affectionately, but he could never really arouse her. Her deepest feelings were stirred by Malcolm and Louise, an entirely different sort of emotion.

George would not allow disappointment a place in his thoughts. He put a great deal of effort into his job, working very hard to justify his appointment which could have been classified as nepotism. By this time they were living in a small house in Woking, from which he commuted by train. George had bought it on a mortgage and with two thousand pounds he had recently inherited from his grandfather. When Mr Warrington died and Susan's mother suggested that they return to Selbury House, George, whilst not eager to live under the same roof as his mother-in-law, saw that this was what Susan wanted and agreed. He spent the money raised from the sale of the Woking house on modernisation. It was several years before Ford retired and it became Mrs Warrington's own idea that she should remove herself to the Lodge.

George had married a wife with money but he had kept his pride and his self-esteem and had, on the whole, lived a happy life. He and Susan never quarrelled. Since his retirement, on a generous pension, George had become treasurer of the Parochial Church Council and had eventually felt obliged, for want of other promising candidates, to stand for the District Council. He needed to be busy and he had time for the work required, although he deplored the intrusion of party politics into local government. He scored a personal success by winning, although standing as an Independent. The few original village families remaining in Selbury trusted him, and he convinced enough newcomers of his suitability for election. Since then he had worked conscientiously to improve what he could and protest at what he could not alter, but he was often depressed when cuts were imposed where, in his opinion, more money should be allotted, and he fought a vigorous though unsuccessful battle for the retention of school meals in the district. Children who had started out for the day on only cereal, if that, needed a hot meal with meat and vegetables at midday, he said. Normally mild and calm, he raged when a child who lived one hundred yards inside the boundary imposed for free bussing to school was denied a seat though the coach daily passed and had space inside.

It was Norah who listened to these tales of frustration and those that ended more satisfactorily, and who helped him arrange meetings with planning officers and collect grievances and complaints.

They had been occasional lovers for years.

Louise's disappearance had been a dreadful watershed in George's life and he would have traded everything for her safe return. He had worried about her when she lived in London, where she had shared a flat with a Spencer granddaughter and another girl with whom she had been at school. She became very thin and had lost her characteristic giggle, which he supposed were the consequences of growing up, but both manifestations saddened him. After her year in France she had been to a secretarial college and at first did temporary work until she got a post with a literary agent. She found this interesting, and when an opportunity arose, had moved on to a small, specialist publishing house where she eventually became an assistant editor. The books they produced about wildlife and country lore, all beautifully illustrated, appealed to her, for she had always enjoyed being out of doors. The firm had subsidised these publications by producing a range of definitive textbooks, but some years after her disappearance it had been taken over by a bigger firm and although the series she had been editing was completed, the list was now less esoteric.

Though George kept urging her to live at home, for it was perfectly easy to travel up daily, as he did, and she had friends with whom she could stay the night if there was a late party, she resisted, and when she changed her mind it seemed a sudden decision. If he had let her be, encouraged her to stay in London, she might still be alive for she would not have become a member of the Feringham Choral Society. She would have travelled on the tube, or walked from her car to her flat along an ill-lit street with muggers in the shadows, but she might not have been in the wrong place at the wrong time, which was the only explanation for her fate.

She had talked a lot about her work, enthusing over some of the books she worked on, lamenting that she had also to read unsolicited submissions which were usually useless. The firm commissioned much of its work and she found working with authors rewarding as she watched the projects grow. She had to find artists to illustrate particular books and she began to have a feeling for the fine arts which she had lacked before, much as her mother had done more recently, though Mrs Warrington, daughter of a prosperous industrialist and married to another, had been a great haunter of antique shops and had acquired some beautiful and valuable pieces to replace the unexciting, functional furniture with which Selbury House was originally equipped.

George himself, son of a country parson, had grown up with good solid Victorian woodwork around him, large, sagging chairs covered in faded floral linen, and a study full of books. His father, an impoverished younger son, had been a kindly scholar steeped in ancient history which he spent as much time studying as he could possibly spare from the supervision of his flock.

Your environment shaped you. George had learned certain values from his own. Why had this not worked with Malcolm? All his life, the boy had been nothing but a worry. George could admit this to himself, and to Norah too, though never to Susan. He suspected that she was still helping him financially, even after they had agreed never to do so again. There had been reason behind paying his creditors; George, too, did not want them to be ruined simply because Malcolm was, at best, feckless. George knew from their tax returns that Susan's investments had decreased, but he never questioned her about them. It was her business, and she had a stockbroker to guide her. She had mentioned that she had given money to the charities in which she took an interest, and that was her affair as well.

The girl, Brenda, who was living with Malcolm at the moment – or rather, with whom he was living, which was a different matter altogether – would tire of him in time. She was too bright to put up with his drinking and his improvidence, although it was a fact that many otherwise sensible women made endless excuses for wastrel men and inexplicably tolerated their behaviour.

One thing that had improved with time was Malcolm's attitude to Louise. His childish jealousy of her had been obvious, but later he had seemed eager for her company. When they were young adults he had asked her to go with him to various parties and had been genuinely disappointed when, after agreeing several times, she refused further invitations. As a young man he had run with a wild crowd. They had torn about the countryside in fast cars on scavenging and treasure hunts and other chases, ending in some pub or other where they drank too much. Sometimes they had patronised dinner dances at hotels. The company was too rowdy for Louise; this was not her scene, and Susan was right when she insisted that marriage and a family would have made her happy.

All that was required was that she should meet someone worthy of her, perhaps even agreeable enough for George to approve. He knew that he was biased; perhaps fathers always were.

He could not bear to think of what must have happened in her final hours and prayed that it had been quickly over. He would always wonder, and he was never going to know.

When George returned from a discussion in the graveyard about removing the tombstones to make mowing easier – George was against it, though he favoured levelling the graves – he found an unknown man in the kitchen with Norah. Learning that it was Detective Superintendent Marsh, he was taken by surprise.

He remembered the younger Marsh. Heart thumping, he took a deep breath to steady himself as Norah said, 'There's no news, George. Mr Marsh has come back to Feringham and called just to make contact.'

'I'm sorry if my presence is disturbing,' said Marsh, who could see very well that it was. He repeated what he had told Norah – that he had never forgotten the case and his regret that it had gone unsolved.

'You did all you could,' said George, sure that this was true. He would never forget the searches, the broadcasts, the newspaper appeals. 'Of course, that was before *Crime Watch* and *Police Five*, all the things on television that can help you now.'

'They're good ways of alerting the public,' Marsh responded. 'Sometimes they shock other villains into shopping those they know about. Then there are all the new scientific developments, like DNA fingerprinting. That makes it much harder for—' he had been going to say rapists, but it would be crude to be so blunt to this man. 'For villains to get off,' he ended.

'If you ever find Louise, it will be too late for that,' said George, understanding perfectly.

'I'm afraid so, sir.'

'You'll see a lot of changes here,' said George, taking another chair at the table. Norah had made fresh tea when he came in and now poured him out a cup which she put beside him silently. 'Thank you,' he said to her. She had never seen his perfect manners fail.

'Yes. Selbury has grown,' agreed Marsh.

'It'll join Feringham if the developers have their way,' said George.

'And how is Mrs Vaughan?' asked Marsh.

'Very busy,' George replied. 'She does charity work and attends art lectures, and she's always been a most enthusiastic gardener.' He looked at the policeman. 'It stops her thinking, or that's how I understand it,' he added.

'Well, it's hard to come to terms with things,' said Marsh. 'But what about your son?'

'Yes – well, a son moves away, doesn't he? Makes his own life.' George could find little to say about Malcolm.

'You had a dog,' said Marsh.

'Yes. A black Labrador. We had another – his son – until a few weeks ago. He was run over in the village and we've decided not to replace him,' George replied. 'There's a lot of traffic in the lane and Bertie had managed to escape.' He'd been in pursuit of a bitch at one of the new houses up the road, his ardour leading him to snatch his chance when Susan was in the garden, planting bulbs. She had not seen him slinking off. George missed him, but Susan had not seemed particularly affected. After all, what was a dog, after losing a daughter?

'I see.'

'You don't need to speak to my wife, do you? She's in London at an exhibition, and I'm not sure which train she's catching back.' George spoke defensively; he did not want Marsh upsetting Susan.

'No. This is an unofficial visit – almost social, you might say,' said Marsh, who had learned all he needed to know from Norah.

'I'm glad you called, Superintendent,' said George. 'I'm glad you remember Louise.'

When Marsh had gone, George sat on at the table. Norah poured him another cup of tea and he absent-mindedly helped himself to a biscuit.

'Perhaps I drove her into the clutches of whoever that scoundrel was,' he said.

'Whatever do you mean?' demanded Norah, pausing as she bent to put the superintendent's cup and saucer in the dishwasher.

'I loved her almost too much,' George said. 'Just to see her every day – to see her growing up so pretty and so clever – she meant the world to me.'

'There's nothing wrong in that,' said Norah. 'Most fathers feel the same about their daughters.'

'I'd have cheerfully killed that man – the one who did it,' George declared. 'I'd rend him limb from limb if I could find him.'

'Mr Warrington felt like that about Susan,' said Norah. 'He hated Hitler for making her a widow. Other women lost their husbands and it was sad, but for his daughter it was something else. He was pleased about you, though,' she recalled. 'Thought you were kind and would treat her well.'

George had to laugh at this, and the way she spoke, looking at him speculatively, smiling.

'What a lot you know about us all,' he said.

'Too much, I sometimes think,' she said, and sighed.

'What was David really like?' he asked her. 'Susan seems to think he was just a happy-go-lucky boy.'

Norah found it easy to answer calmly.

'That was how he seemed,' she said. 'Living to the full while he could. How else could they cope, those boys? They were like undertakers, making jokes all the time because their days were so fraught.'

'Do undertakers do that?'

'I believe so,' Norah said. 'My uncle worked for one and that was his opinion. The other brother was different,' she went on. 'Malcolm was the first. He was more serious – his mother's prop and stay. David was her baby.' She was silent for a moment and then added, 'I never saw her shed a tear, not in all the years I knew her. I suppose she wept in private.'

Norah had cried.

When Susan had told Mrs Warrington what had happened to her, Norah was sent for and, terrified and heartbroken, she had sobbed resoundingly. Mrs Warrington had steepled her fingers together and decided what should be done. Norah was too sick in heart and sick in body to do other than submit.

'I'll light the fire,' she said now. 'It'll soon warm up in there. Go and do the crossword until it's time for the news. I've got stuck with it.'

'You bully me,' he told her, smiling, a balding man with strands of greying hair brushed across his pale scalp, blue eyes and a strong, straight nose, still handsome. Norah knew that he wouldn't have stood a chance with Susan unless he had been good-looking.

5

Susan

Susan went to the Henry Moore exhibition at the Royal Academy in the afternoon. She had travelled to London by an early train for her appointment with her solicitor, and when their discussion was over had looked in a desultory way at skirts in Simpson's, trying one on but deciding that it was too expensive. She never used to consider a good skirt an extravagance; they lasted for years. She would think about it, she told the assistant, and walked along to Fortnum's for lunch. Afterwards, she went into Hatchards and looked at the latest books produced by Louise's former employers. She bought nothing.

The days she spent in London were oases in the desert of what life had now become. On neutral ground, in some gallery or museum, she could make her mind a blank and simply assess visually what she saw before her. She seldom remembered detail, but she was soothed by the impersonality of paintings or sculpture for they were not flesh and blood. Moore's curving lines were pleasing to gaze at, whatever the subject; she sat on a bench in front of one of his groups and thought about nothing. She had found a way to exist.

Moving had helped her. She no longer saw ghosts round every corner, friendly ones though they had been. At first she had feared that her mother's dominating presence would haunt the Lodge House, but it was magically erased by the new building work. The extensions, the complete re-decoration throughout, had expunged images of the thin, hawk-nosed old woman in her high-backed chair endlessly crocheting. In her final months her eyesight had failed but she still crocheted, making large loose shawls for starving Africans when she could no longer do more intricate work.

She had lost both her sons and never complained aloud. When Louise disappeared, she had reacted with anger. She was angry that the girl had somehow put herself in jeopardy and angry that Feringham, once a peaceful market town, could harbour such menace.

When Susan was a girl, white slavery had been a much dreaded peril, and Mabel had fed her tales of revenge wrought by disenchanted servants or nurses who allowed their charges to be wafted away, never to be seen again. Now, other dangers threatened young women. The worst had already happened to Louise, and Susan was no longer vulnerable, except over Malcolm. Why had she been unable to help him discover the best in himself, find his true direction? His failure had to be hers.

When her own little son had died, she had blamed herself. Even when the inquest had decided that he had died by misadventure and the police had stopped behaving as if they thought she had smothered him, guilt had been mixed with her grief, but in those days you pulled yourself together and got on with your life, as her mother had firmly told her. Susan had plunged into her nursing, working hard and with long hours on duty, often harrowed by the suffering she saw, but always returning home at the end of her shift to sleep in her comfortable room, with the house kept quiet by day when she was on night duty.

What she had wanted most was another baby to hold, a soft little form to clasp against her, silken hair to brush her cheek, a petal mouth to smile at her, little chortling laughs. She had not looked beyond this to the growing child, the difficult adolescent. She had married George because he was kind, patently adored her just as Hugh had done, and was attractive in his dark, sturdy way, quite unlike Hugh. He brought her more physical pleasure than Hugh had managed in their short time together, but as the years went on she found that merely agreeable, nothing more, and in the end it became a bore. Once, when she was about fourteen and staying briefly with the Spencers, she had seen Lady Spencer and her husband, Sir Giles, walking through the coppice that formed part of their land and where, in spring, the ground was strewn with bluebells and primroses which gave off a heady scent. The two were arm in arm, and Lady Spencer was listening earnestly to something Sir Giles was saying. Suddenly they stopped and, to her amazement, kissed one another ardently, clasped together there in the woodland, unaware of Susan who had been picking primroses nearby. She had felt her whole body blushing as, intruder that she was upon such a private moment, she shrank back against the nearest tree, crouching as still as a statue until they moved on. They had not seen her.

She had never seen her own parents exchange more than a peck on the cheek, and even now could not imagine them having an intimate life.

When Norah had got into trouble, she and Mother had been of one mind. David's reputation must be protected now that he was dead and could not decide himself what ought to be done.

'It will be my grandchild,' Mother had said, just once, and had added, 'No matter.'

It was she who, after the decision was made, had discovered the name of a doctor from Lady Spencer, who had many sources of information.

Once it was dealt with, they had not discussed it again.

Malcolm had been a pretty little baby, with his quiff of dark hair and his large blue eyes. Small strong fists had clutched Susan's finger; sturdy legs had thrust against her as he sucked hungrily at his bottle.

He had never snuggled close in quite the same way as little Harry had done. It wasn't in his power, at first, to detach himself, but as he grew bigger he would push away from her, disengage himself, hold his head back and stare at her as if to say, 'What made you do it? Why me?' and she would have to charm him back into accepting her.

It was still like that, she thought, as she travelled home in the train after her day in London, except when he was in trouble and then he turned to her at once.

She had made up her mind that this must stop.

While Louise was living at home, Susan had worried only intermittently about Malcolm in Australia. That had been a happy time, though she had wished that Louise would enjoy more of a social life. Feringham's Choral Society seemed a strange choice of activity to Susan. Sometimes Louise joined in the dinner parties her mother gave, but more often she elected to eat in her room, saying she must work on a manuscript. Now and then, if Susan had been shopping in London, she and George had met Louise after work, taken her out to an early meal and then to a theatre, all three driving home afterwards, for George would take his car up on those days. They would stop at the station on the way back to collect Louise's Mini.

Since her disappearance, Susan and George had almost stopped going out at night, except for occasional evenings spent at the Cartwrights', or perhaps a charity event they felt obliged to attend. When Norah began looking after Mrs Warrington, George had sometimes suggested a night in town and he had even secured seats for *Phantom of the Opera* for Susan's birthday; both alleged that they enjoyed these excursions, but they would have been just as content staying at home. It made each of them feel, however, that they were attempting a normal life.

Every summer they took the car to France or Italy, staying in small hotels in out-of-the-way places, visiting châteaux and galleries and tasting the wine. Neither expected too much from the other, and these expeditions were a gentle success, resting them both and providing a change of scene.

Norah took holidays, too; continuing the custom begun

when she started to earn a good salary, she went off on some cultural tour, shepherded by a knowledgeable guide around Tuscany, or to Verona for the opera, or to Vienna or Salzburg. She set off alone but always seemed to find someone congenial to talk to and received Christmas cards even now from acquaintances met on such trips. She spent a lot on these journeys, and Susan told George she thought they were a gross extravagance.

'Darling, you think nothing of tripping round the Louvre or the Uffizi. Why shouldn't Norah do it too? She'll enjoy it all quite as much as you, and she'll learn more, since she starts off without your knowledge.'

'Yes, you're right. I'm a meanie,' said Susan. 'I still can't forget that shabby little girl with her hair tied in bunches and not an "H" to her name.'

'Think of Michael Caine,' advised George. 'He's done all right for an evacuee.'

'But the voice,' Susan objected.

'He can talk just like your old dad if he wants to,' said George. 'Or like me, if you prefer. Anyway, Norah owes her polish to you. You got her to join the ATS and start her climb.'

'Yes,' Susan agreed. 'She'd have stayed on in that factory otherwise, working a lathe or whatever it was that she did.'

It had not been straightforward, since Norah was already doing war work in the factory, but medical advice that she should be employed out of doors had made the change possible.

Susan still sometimes imagined that when she returned from one of her days in London, Louise would have come back. There she would be, her mother dreamed, sitting by the fire with George while Norah made up a bed for her in the little spare room and filled a hot-water bottle, found her a nightdress and cooked her a meal. She would look just the same, with her fair hair brushed straight or held in a plait. She would have escaped unscathed from bondage in some dreadful bordello, avoiding a fate worse than death because her innocence would have led the madam to employ her as a book-keeper or in some other harmless guise; or she would have been married to a Middle Eastern potentate who had respected her and treated her kindly, finally, in response to her pleas, allowing her to escape. In wilder scripts she would have been involved in espionage ever since she began working in London, and had been wafted off behind the Iron Curtain on a mission of such secrecy that no reassuring cover story to explain her absence had been devised. She had been caught and imprisoned and only now was released.

These fantasies were a comfort, and after indulging one it was an anti-climax to come home and find George and Norah alone. He would always hear her car and come out to close the garage door after her, carry her parcels when there were some, and ask how her day had gone.

Tonight George told her about Marsh's visit, reminding her of the young sergeant who had spent so much time with them twelve years before. He and Norah had discussed whether to tell her or not, and had decided that they must in case she ran across Marsh herself and was unprepared.

'They're not starting it all up again, are they?' she asked.
'No.'

'Though maybe they'd find out something, if they did,' she said. 'If they went round talking to everyone they interviewed then.'

George thought it likely that Marsh would do exactly that. Some had moved from the area, like Tim Francis. His ex-wife, who had remarried, still lived in Feringham; she worked in one of the banks. The children must be growing up, he supposed – no, there had been a baby who would still be only about thirteen.

'I don't think anything new will turn up now,' he told Susan. How could it?

Unless, even after all this time, her body were discovered.

Susan had not seen Malcolm for some weeks, nor heard from him. When he was silent, she felt it was always the lull before the storm and would only be ended with a plea for help. Occasionally, when her anxiety became too great to bear, she went to his workshop to see him.

He always seemed pleased to see her, would stop whatever he was doing, switch off the radio, kiss her warmly and lead her into the office where he would make her a cup of Lapsang Souchong tea, which he kept especially for her. There was always a lemon, too. He was admirably organised there, with his sink and his shower and his cordless telephone, and his paperwork so orderly that none of it was in view. It did not occur to her that a great muddle lay inside the drawers of his desk, a confusion of final demands and even a writ. She would see his superficial tidiness as evidence of ability never developed and tell herself, yet again, that all he needed was to find the right opportunity and he would be a success.

The day after her trip to London and Marsh's visit to Selbury, she went to the workshop. The doors were closed and a paper attached stated that he was with a customer and would be back at four o'clock.

The drive over had taken her nearly an hour. Susan decided to look round the shops and visit the abbey. She often did that when she came to Malchester, sitting quietly in a pew being soothed, as in an art gallery, by the beauty of the ancient building, the long fluted columns and high vaulted roof, with perhaps the organist practising and great rolling chords echoing round her.

She wished she could have retained the unquestioning childhood belief that had been fed into her along with porridge and cod-liver oil and malt. Father and Mother had regularly gone to church, and when she was five she joined them, though at that age she was not expected to sit through the sermon; taking her out gave Mother an excuse to leave too. School had continued the indoctrination, with prayers night and morning read by the headmistress who stood before the assembled girls in her gown, the rest of the staff on either side.

All that conviction had been destroyed in the war, though for years she had gone through the motions, still attending Matins on Sundays because she could not face explaining her defection to her mother. Now, she went because it was expected of her. Sometimes she wondered if the vicar was there only for the same reason.

In the abbey she was able to accept that Louise was dead. Here, she could think of her without pain, know that whatever torment her last hours had brought was over and nothing worse lay ahead. The building itself somehow made these thoughts possible. Susan would imagine the ancient masons toiling with no modern aids, hauling every stone into place, chipping away as they carved the decorations. So much that was wonderful had been achieved in the name of Christianity – so many fine buildings and such marvellous music – but there had been so much slaughter, too, such lack of toleration. Life was a lonely journey, and people needed a goal, a cause to believe in. There had always been gods of one sort or another to praise or placate; now people worshipped their status, their car, a political party, football, or some crusade such as opposing blood sports. Susan herself no longer had any aim beyond cherishing her garden.

She dozed a little, sitting there, while a clutch of late tourists walked round talking together in reverent whispers and a sacristan in his long black gown padded by. It was quite warm; the place was efficiently heated.

After a while she roused herself, left the abbey and went to a nearby café for tea. There were still two old-fashioned tea shops in the centre of Malchester, where other towns now offered only Wimpy bars and the like. Here, the Cobweb was thriving and today it was warm and busy. Susan sat with her tea studying the other customers. What sort of homes were they returning to? How many had faced or were facing tragedy, or had it yet to come? She often had such thoughts now, and would walk along a street looking at the passers-by and imagining them all weighed down by some dire form of stress. Once, in a rare moment of communication, she had told

George this and he had tried to comfort her, telling her that in the end most people adjusted to their pain though it might never be healed. She must not, he adjured, go round believing that everyone's heart was breaking.

Since that conversation he had started devising surprise treats. He would suddenly say they were going to Paris for the weekend, or would bring her a present, a piece of porcelain he had found in an antique shop and hoped she would like, or a plant for the garden. On other days, he would produce a special bottle of some good wine for dinner, or suggest an extra glass of sherry. She went along with his efforts, pretending to be cheerful.

If only Malcolm could be successful and, if possible, happy, she thought she could throw off this black cloud. As it was, like water dripping on a stone, the anxiety wore her down.

When she returned to the workshop he was still out, although it was nearly five o'clock. The note was still attached to the door. There was no point in waiting; he might not come back that night.

What did it matter what work he did, as long as he made an honest living? She knew he did not sell dud cars; look how hard he worked on them, taking a long time to move them because he would not sell unless he was satisfied with their condition. If she gave up believing in him, who else would? She had to trust him, though sometimes he made that very difficult.

She had never been able to forget that long-ago night when he had been at Selbury House unknown to her. Since his recent return from Australia, although supposedly living in Cornton, he often turned up without warning and of course he had a key. Restless because of a bad dream, she had gone down to the kitchen to make herself a cup of tea, moving very softly so as not to disturb George and leaving their bedroom in darkness.

He had stirred slightly when she left, but he had not woken; he was a sound sleeper. She had tiptoed along the passage to the head of the stairs, not a great distance, and as she reached for the light switch she heard a faint sound. She snapped on the light and caught a movement from the corner of her eye: a dark figure stood outside the door of Louise's room, one hand on the knob, and she thought that the sound she had heard was the door closing.

As she stared, almost giving a shriek of fright, the figure had moved towards her, gliding smoothly, and she saw that it was Malcolm. She was trembling as he reached her and he put his arm round her.

'What a fright I gave you! Sorry,' he said. He held her arm and went down the stairs with her, set her in a chair and put on the kettle. 'I thought I'd crept in without waking anyone,' he added. 'I had a late run out to Oxford with a fare and decided to drop off here instead of going all the way back to Cornton tonight.'

'Oh yes,' said Susan. 'I see. Lucky Daddy hadn't put the bolts across.' She always referred to George like this to Malcolm and Louise.

While Malcolm was in Australia, George had always bolted every outer door at bedtime. Since Malcolm's return, he had twice had to come down to let Malcolm in when he had suddenly decided to spend the night, so the front door was now left on the Yale.

'Yes,' said Malcolm, smiling.

While they both had tea, he told her about several amusing fares he had had. Then they went upstairs again. She watched him go past Louise's door to his own room, further along the landing and on the other side.

Why had he been outside her door, with his hand on the knob? Again and again she had pictured the scene and it was always the same, the stationary figure, frozen, it seemed, and the hand on the knob. Had she really heard him closing the door?

Brothers could innocently enter their sisters' rooms, but such visits were not usual when the siblings were in their twenties and it was the middle of the night. Adopted brothers and sisters, reaching adult years, might, however, regard themselves as outside the bounds of incest, and it was true; technically they were.

She had never mentioned the incident to a soul, and over the years she had tried, without success, to forget it.

Two days afterwards, Louise had vanished.

As she drove home it began to rain, not hard, but in a misty drizzle. Susan turned on the wipers and stared past their hypnotising swish at the oncoming traffic. Lights were on now, and she peered ahead, anxious about cyclists difficult to see in the shadows. She had always had excellent, rather long sight, and disliked having to wear spectacles for driving; it was less easy, now, to judge distance in the darkness.

The car heater sent comforting waves of warmth round her legs and she began to look forward to reaching home, for she was tired. Anxiety was very exhausting. Would Norah be in, or would she be enjoying the social round she seemed to be developing? Perhaps Myra was entertaining tonight; it wasn't her French class evening. Susan pretended to herself to be glad when she and George were left alone. Norah always left the dinner ready, either a casserole in the oven or something to grill, or to heat in the microwave which George had bought during Norah's last holiday. Susan had lost all interest in cooking, which she had once enjoyed, and in Norah's absence George often made the few preparations necessary and loaded the dishwasher afterwards.

Mother had been dreadful, refusing to install one or allow her to have it done when Norah began looking after her.

'A machine costs money,' she had declared. 'And I've heard they're expensive to run. Besides, there are only two of us to wash up for.'

But there were often more, when Mother's surviving friends, some mere sprigs of eighty, came over. She soon resumed her lunch parties and the bridge afternoons she had enjoyed for most of her life, and then tea and sandwiches were produced by Norah. Susan pointed this out.

'Never mind. Let her see to it,' Mrs Warrington had said. 'It's what she was brought up to, and if it wasn't for us she'd have been in service all her life.'

It wasn't true. Resident domestic help had almost disappeared after the war, and Norah would have found her level in time, whatever she did.

It would be nice if she were at home tonight. Susan craved some cosseting, and Norah would provide it. Her wish was granted, for as she drove in, Norah heard the car and came out to greet her, just as George always did. He was out tonight, at a PCC meeting, Susan suddenly remembered. Of course Norah would not have gone out too, leaving her alone. They never did that.

'Have you had a nice afternoon?' Norah asked, taking a Jaeger bag from Susan when she had shut the garage doors. 'Had a good spend?' Susan occasionally went on a shopping spree and would then clear out her cupboards to make room for her new acquisitions, but this had happened less often lately. Norah suspected the reason was an economy drive.

'I bought George a new sweater,' said Susan. 'That old maroon one he wears is so shabby. I got one for myself, too,' she added.

Would it be black or beige? Susan wore too much black, Norah thought. It looked chic on younger women but depressing on the old unless they had high colouring themselves, or wore a bright scarf. Beige had suited Susan until ten years ago but now her fair hair was almost white and her face, when she masked her threadlike broken veins with make-up, seemed to tone in so that she looked beige all over. Norah resolved to buy her a rose-coloured sweater for Christmas.

'Good,' she said now. 'The Scouts are having a jumble sale next weekend. I said we'd find something for them.' Susan's throw-outs were notorious snips at sales in the village.

'It's good to be home,' said Susan as she entered the house. She slid her coat off and let it drop on to a chair in the hall. Norah would take it upstairs later, when she drew the curtains and turned down the beds.

'Did you see Malcolm?' Norah asked.

'No. Why should I have done that?' Susan was instantly on the defensive. She had told no one where she was going.

'Well, you've been to Malchester,' said Norah. There was no branch of Jaeger's in Feringham. 'So it's natural that you'd look in on him. He wasn't there?'

'No. He was out on some business or other. There was a note on the door,' Susan said.

'You didn't go round to the house in case he went straight home?'

'No. I thought Brenda might not like it,' Susan said.

Thank goodness she'd had that much sense, Norah reflected.

'You could always telephone,' she suggested.

'Yes. Perhaps I will,' Susan said.

'George went off early,' Norah told her now. 'The vicar wanted to talk to him about old Mr Bernard's funeral. There's some problem about where he's to be buried. He'd fancied a place near the yew tree but he may not be able to have it, since there's so little space.'

'I hope the vicar gives him a drink,' said Susan.

'He will. George took a bottle along,' said Norah. 'You go and have one yourself while I see about dinner. George said he'd have his later, when he gets back.'

'Then he'll have indigestion, since the meeting is sure to go on for hours,' Susan said. 'Eating late doesn't agree with him.'

'I know, but he didn't want to have lamb chops at six, either,' said Norah, going off to the kitchen.

Susan went into the drawing-room and crossed to the drinks tray, where she poured herself a glass of dry sherry and then went to sit in front of the fire. George would be having a whisky at the vicarage; he'd need it; he was in for an arduous evening.

When had Norah started to call them by their Christian names? It had gone on for years, of course, and Mother had been shocked when she first noticed. George had told her not to be stuffy. He had always stood up to Mother, who had enjoyed sparring with him, but in this instance she had waspishly commented, 'Familiarity breeds contempt. You'll be sorry.'

But familiarity between Norah and David had developed a long time before that, and they had undoubtedly addressed one another by their given names: indeed, to the family, Norah had always been Norah.

Had they expected too much from Louise? Sometimes Susan wondered about that. Helen Cartwright had a theory that parents expected their children to succeed where they had failed as well as to emulate their successes. Put like that, it seemed a tall order and likely to daunt even the most able. Helen had made her statement when Susan had lowered her guard enough to admit to despair about Malcolm's inability to lead a normal life.

'By normal, you mean conventional, don't you? Wife and two children, job in town?' Helen said.

'Well – yes. I suppose I do.'

'I felt the same,' Helen had confessed. One of her daughters had become a television producer who showed no signs of marrying; the other was a zoologist who, at the time of this conversation preferred baboons to people and was exploring in some distant jungle. Subsequently she had married and produced children who were brought up with few rules but seemed very bright and happy. The producer daughter, now in her late thirties, had expressed the desire for a child and seemed likely to accomplish her wish without settling down with its father; indeed, Helen feared that the man would be selected for no other reason than good health and appearance and then dismissed. Her son had dropped out of university to pursue the hippie trail to the Himalayas. Some years later he had returned and was now a financial expert in the City. He lived in St John's Wood and keenly followed cricket, hoping that one of his two sons would play in a Test Match. 'Don't expect too much,' Helen had advised, from her own experience. 'He's got problems to sort out.'

'Lots of adoptions work out very well.' Susan, stung, had been on the defensive.

'I know. Probably most of them do, but my point is that all parents have these sorts of worries, and brothers and sisters are often jealous of one another. Malcolm may resent Louise because she's really your child. Does he harbour a grudge against his real mother for giving him up?'

'He's very fond of Louise,' Susan had declared. 'When they were small, they quarrelled a lot, but children do. Yours often did. That passed as they grew up.'

But it had been succeeded by something she pretended she had not noticed. He hung round Louise, teased her verbally but with an undercurrent of something more than mischief; it was almost malice. She had been relieved when he got married.

After he went to Australia and Louise came home, she had picked up old threads of friendship in the area and had sometimes played tennis or squash or swam. There was no pool at Selbury House but friends had pools and courts, and kept open house at weekends. On summer Sundays any young people who were around made the most of what was offered. The various mothers baked and roasted, froze and thawed, catered lavishly and spared no effort to provide for them. George had had the hard court laid, and Susan persuaded Norah to come down for frequent weekends at that time of year, for she was always a help when it was their turn to be the hosts, but Louise had never wanted to go to late parties, nor to give them.

Years later, when Norah was a permanent part of the household, Susan wondered what she had done at Christmas in the past. At the time, she had never thought about it. Of course, there was plenty going on in London, concerts and church services, and she must have made friends at work. Since Louise's disappearance, Christmas had become a time of anguish and for the last few years she and George had gone to Portugal, where they had found a quiet hotel which laid no particular emphasis on seasonal merrymaking. Norah, left behind, did not lack for invitations from her new friends in the village; in addition to Myra, she seemed on intimate terms with two families in the new houses, often babysitting for one and apparently spending hours with a boy from the other, trying to play computer games. Occasionally Susan felt resentment towards these people, incomers, who had a stake in Norah's life. Still, it seemed to amuse her and meant that she would not want to leave them. Sometimes, though it shocked her to acknowledge the thought, Susan felt that she would miss George less than Norah if either were to die before she did.

She wouldn't be too sorry to die, herself. When she allowed herself to reflect that her mother had lived to be over ninety and that she might have to exist for another twenty years, Susan felt real dread. Even Norah might not survive her, let alone George, and Malcolm would put her into a home where she would sit drooling in a chair all day, exposed to non-stop television with the volume on at full blast. The fact that her mother had never drooled for one day in her life, except possibly as an infant, did nothing to dispel this nightmare prospect.

If anything happened to George, she would look for an acceptable place where she might end her days in reasonable comfort, protected from the worst humiliations meted out to the old. Though she had eaten into her capital through rescuing Malcolm, what was left of it plus the money the sale of the Lodge House would bring should be enough to pay for such an arrangement. If not, there was always an alternative: you could give up and finish it yourself, if you had the means. She might have to do that, one day, if she could, faced with only Malcolm to take care of her.

But he would, wouldn't he? Didn't he love her? Hadn't he always turned to her when he was troubled? Or was it just for the money he knew she would find for him?

She had already accepted the answer.

6

Richard

Detective Superintendent Marsh instructed a young, ambitious detective constable to track down Richard Blacker, Louise Vaughan's sometime lover, according to her brother Malcolm. He would have to pursue the search in spare moments since the case was dormant.

Whitlock began on the telephone, first ringing various advertising agencies he found listed in the Yellow Pages. It was going to be a tedious task. He looked at the big boxed notices and dialled a few, but none had a Richard Blacker working for them. Then his gaze turned to the ordinary smaller entries and a name stood out: Blacker, R., with an address in West London. Could it be as simple as this? Was this the Blacker who had known Louise?

He telephoned the number and said he was a solicitor seeking a firm who had handled work for a deceased client. The client had manufactured an ingenious type of clothes-peg. The agent's name had been Blacker, and he lived in Essex. Unfortunately the client's records were incomplete, but it was thought that money had been owed to the agent and the executors wished to settle the debt.

'I don't think that's our Mr Blacker,' said the telephone voice. 'He lives in Oldington – has done for years. That's not in Essex.' She did not say where it was.

'Robert Blacker, would that be?' asked Detective Constable Whitlock smoothly.

'Oh no. Our Mr Blacker is Richard, like in Dick Whittington,' said the girl.

'Sorry. I must have got the wrong address,' Whitlock said.

He was very pleased with the result of this short interview and, in a gazetteer, soon located an Oldington in the Thames Valley, between High Wycombe and Reading. Directory Inquiries gave him R. Blacker's telephone number, and, when prodded, the name of his house.

'Let's hope it's the right Blacker,' said Marsh, when Whitlock reported the results of this swift bit of sleuthing. 'We'll follow it up and see. You go over to Oldington and mosey around a bit, find out the set-up and if there's a wife and kiddies – all that. And if it's a second wife or what. Then we'll decide what to do.'

Whitlock was pleased at the prospect of a day in the country. Oldington was about twenty-five miles from Feringham, reached, once he left the motorway, along narrow winding lanes edged with tall hedges that almost met overhead. He passed two horsewomen wearing hard hats and padded jackets, their mounts, one grey and one chestnut, jogging along the tunnel-like way at some considerable risk, he thought. But roads were originally made for horses and he liked to see them, though an alarmed animal hitting a car could damage itself and the vehicle severely. Whitlock, in his red Mazda, edged past, and the women nodded at him in thanks for slackening his speed. That was the life, he thought: fresh air and exercise. This was a welcome break from trying to find stolen cars and interviewing shoplifters.

He soon found Blacker's house, which lay in a valley between beech woods in an unspoilt piece of countryside.

'Nice area,' he observed over half a pint in the pub. 'Not much building going on.'

'No. There's big landowners here,' said the publican. 'They keep the speculators out.'

'Oh,' said Whitlock, nodding wisely.

'Just passing through, are you?'

'That's right.'

'We're not on the way to anywhere,' remarked the publican, though walkers and wayfarers often came to his inn.

'No. I'm going to Reading,' Whitlock volunteered. 'But I've time to kill before my appointment so I thought I'd go the long way round. The wife and I do a bit of rambling at weekends and I know there's lots of footpaths about here. It might be worth our coming over.' Whitlock was not married.

'Oh, it would be,' agreed the landlord. 'Thirsty work, rambling.' Too often the rucksacked groups that came this way were self-sufficient, laden with cardboard cartons of fruit juice and plastic-wrapped sandwiches. They even, sometimes, ate them in his garden at his picnic tables.

'I noticed a pretty house – Martin's, I think it's called,' mentioned Whitlock. 'What would a place like that fetch these days?'

'You're talking about a cool four or five hundred thousand,' said the landlord. 'But the fellow that lives there isn't likely to move. He's owned the place for years. He's in publicity of some sort. They have a lot of people down at weekends and he sometimes brings them in. All on expenses, you can be sure.'

'Not married, then?'

'Oh, he's married all right. Got two girls and a boy,' said the landlord. 'Pony mad, the girls are. This is a great area for horse-riding.'

'I met two ladies on the road, on horses,' Whitlock said.

'You should meet the hunt,' said the landlord. 'That's a pretty sight. Blocks the lanes up something awful.'

'I can imagine,' Whitlock said. 'Been here long yourself?'

'Six months,' said the man.

'Ah,' said Whitlock, who had picked up this useful response from Marsh, who often used it. He had better not show too much interest in Blacker, so he stated that he wouldn't mind moving into one of the smaller cottages if his number came up on the pools.

'You do that, mate,' said the landlord.

Some other people came in then, and his steak and chips arrived, served with broccoli from the freezer. Whitlock took his plate to a corner table and listened to the talk round him as the bar filled up. He heard nothing useful. Where did these people come from? There were young men in smart suits, business people doubtless working in the towns around; how could they spare the time out of their offices? They weren't all discussing deals. There were some older people, too, mostly grey-haired couples; the retired, presumably.

Later, he parked his Mazda at the entrance to a footpath and walked up a hill to a position where he could look down on Martin's. So late in the year, with the trees bare of leaves, he could see it clearly. It was an old house built of mellowed brick, with a tiled roof, and with various plants, none of them now in bloom, growing up the walls. A swimming-pool covered with a green tarpaulin stood a little apart, sheltered by a high wall. Lattice windows, all tightly closed, sparkled brightly, reflecting the winter sunlight. Whitlock could see the burglar alarm attached to the house. It was a secluded place; such houses, in their rural isolation, were an invitation to thieves who sped along the motorway, did a place and were gone again with scant chance of being caught. Those jobs were carried out by experts who would reconnoitre first, just as he had done. A few questions in the village shop or at the post office might establish if Mrs Blacker was likely to be at home, for instance, unless the people there were more discreet than the publican who had freely talked about his customers. He was new to the trade; experienced innkeepers were more wary. Many of these large places needed two salaries to meet the mortgage, but Blacker had owned his long enough to have bought it relatively cheaply. He contemplated going up the drive, pretending to sell double-glazing, but that would exceed his brief and he could not support such a statement with any documentation. He settled for taking some photographs of the house before dusk fell; then he'd hang about, see if lights came on and whether there were visitors. He sat in his car near the gates to Martin's, and was rewarded by seeing a large blue Audi turn into the drive at five o'clock. After a shorter day than usual in the office, Richard Blacker had come home.

On his next day off, Marsh visited Blacker's London office. He had no appointment and Blacker's secretary was reluctant to admit him, so Marsh made it official.

Soon afterwards he was being ushered, with some deference, into a large room which occupied most of the second floor of an elegant Georgian house overlooking a small garden north of Hyde Park.

The secretary, aged about thirty, was attractive, fair and slim. She was much the same physical type as Louise Vaughan, Marsh noted, tabulating the information away in a file in his mind, to decide later if the relationship should be investigated in case it was continued outside the office. A man – or woman, come to that – who had played away from home once might do so again.

'Would you bring some coffee, please, Sarah?' Blacker requested before she closed the door.

'Not for me, thank you,' Marsh said curtly, and Blacker made a gesture to the woman before asking her to see that they were not disturbed.

'What's this all about, Superintendent?' he inquired when they were alone.

'You knew Louise Vaughan,' Marsh stated, and had the satisfaction of seeing Blacker turn quite pale, grip the arms of his chair, and stare at him in stupefaction. So this was the right Blacker.

His quarry had pulled himself together.

'Yes, I did,' he answered, wetting his lips, trying to keep his voice from shaking. In the face of such a confident assertion, it was useless to deny acquaintance. 'What about it?'

'You never came forward when she disappeared.'

'No. I hadn't seen her for over a year,' said Blacker.

'You had an affair with her,' said Marsh.

'I – yes. Yes, I did.' Wherever the superintendent had got his information, it was sound. Lying could only lead to trouble, but if he was frank, once the reason for this interview was known, his confidence might be respected. Richard Blacker had never had cause to tangle with the police and did not mean to do so now. 'I hope that admission need go no further,' he suggested nervously.

'Who broke it off?' snapped Marsh. He had taken a dislike to Blacker, and for no good reason since so far the man was cooperating, looked intelligent and pleasant, with dark hair greying elegantly, a well-tailored suit worn with a pale silk tie, and large brown eyes behind horn-rimmed spectacles.

'She did. She couldn't cope with the need for secrecy,' said Blacker. 'My wife, you see—' he let the sentence trail off, implying that they were both men of the world.

'There was no question of you getting a divorce and marrying her?'

'No. Oh no. Mind you, she thought so for a while, but I promised nothing,' Blacker said. 'I couldn't break up my family. There were the children to consider. They were quite young then. I've got three – a boy and two girls. The eldest is at university and the second girl is doing A levels. My son is younger, just thirteen.'

Marsh calculated that the boy had been born during the year before Louise vanished. Had she known about him? Very likely; women often kept tabs on old flames, let alone former lovers.

'Has your elder daughter got a lover?' Marsh demanded.

'Probably,' said Blacker. 'But what's that got to do with Louise?' Or you, come to that, he thought angrily.

Marsh could see he was beginning to smoulder. Good.

'Only that Louise can't have been much older than your daughter when you started your affair with her,' said Marsh.

'But I was younger, too. It was years ago,' said Blacker. 'God, Superintendent, she's been dead for twelve years.'

'Oh, of course that excuses everything,' said Marsh. 'You were a man of experience, not like the students your daughter mixes with. What if she has an affair with a married tutor?'

'Now look, Superintendent, I don't have to listen to this,' said Blacker. 'I'm extremely busy, but I don't imagine you've come here to read me a lecture on my responsibilities to young women. Has poor Louise been found?'

'What do you think happened to her?' asked Marsh.

'I imagine some pervert or maniac got hold of her and dumped her in a river or quarry or under the concrete of a motorway,' said Blacker. 'It's too terrible to think about. I was badly shocked when I heard, I can tell you.'

'Oh, were you? I'm glad to know it,' Marsh said caustically. 'It's difficult to believe that a competent young woman, such as everyone agrees she was, would find herself, when in her own car, not on foot, in such danger in a town like Feringham, and so long ago, when we heard less about such cases.'

'What are you getting at, Superintendent?'

'Suppose she met someone she knew? Someone she trusted? She'd let him into her car, wouldn't she? Even drive off into a quiet street where they could talk?'

'I suppose so. It's possible.'

'Was it really Louise who ended your affair or had you become bored with it?' Marsh asked. 'Had she pestered you to get a divorce? Was she pestering you again and generally being a nuisance – more of a nuisance than ever since you'd now got a son to carry on your name?'

'What are you implying?' Blacker's face had flushed. He shuffled some papers on his desk.

'You might have been meeting again,' Marsh suggested. 'She might have wanted to renew the relationship. You might have decided to put a stop to it, once and for all. You'd know about her regular singing nights if you'd been seeing her again. Where were you the night she disappeared, Mr Blacker?'

'I'm not sure. At home, probably,' said Blacker. 'How can I possibly remember after all this time?'

'I should have thought it would have been like it was when President Kennedy was killed,' said Marsh. 'People can still remember where they were when they heard that news. Your former mistress had disappeared in mysterious circumstances and the case made headlines for quite some time. I don't think anyone concerned would forget the date or what they had been doing at the time.'

Blacker doodled on his blotting paper. Upside down, Marsh could see that he had drawn a gallows. What should he infer from that?

'No – well, I was at my flat in London,' Blacker admitted. 'I keep a place in town for when I have to entertain clients and am likely to be late. My real home is in Oldington, but I expect you already know that. I don't want to drive down there after a night out and have your chaps after me to test my breath.' He attempted a light laugh as he uttered this sally. 'It's just a tiny flat,' he added. 'Quite near here, as a matter of fact.'

Convenient for entertaining mistresses, Marsh thought sourly.

'Were you alone?'

'Of course I was,' said Blacker.

'Not with a lady?'

'What do you think I am, Superintendent?'

'Your wife might have joined you for an evening out,' Marsh stated.

'She couldn't. She can't come up often, she's tied up with the children, and she was especially then, when they were small,' said Blacker.

'I see,' said Marsh.

'If you're going on with these questions, I'm going to call my solicitor,' said Blacker, recovering some of his normal self-possession. 'Where was Louise found?'

'She hasn't been found, Mr Blacker. I wonder if you can suggest some likely place for us to search?'

'I know nothing about it,' said Blacker stormily. 'I was very upset at the time. I still am, when I think about it, which now you're forcing me to do. She was a lovely girl, very sweet and fresh – rather unworldly in some ways.' For the first time in their conversation a genuine emotion – or it seemed to Marsh that it might be genuine – sounded in his voice. 'I would have liked to marry her,' he added. 'But it just wasn't on. Those situations don't work out easily. It's so hard on the children. And my wife's a wonderful woman – a perfect mother. The home and family mean everything to both of us; they're what I work for. A different sort of girl would have been content to let things run on as they were.'

'And miss her chance of marriage and children?'

'She'd make up for it with her career,' said Blacker.

'But Louise wasn't personally ambitious, was she? She had an interesting job but not anything very lucrative. It wasn't like a high-flying career in the City.'

'She was bright enough to switch.'

'But she preferred her books, didn't she? Her wildlife and natural history?'

'At that stage, yes,' Blacker agreed. 'But later she'd have seen the light and changed.'

'Yes – to compensate, when she saw she had little else going for her,' said Marsh. 'Well, Mr Blacker, her body hasn't been found but I have returned to Feringham. I was involved with the case as a young man. Now I'm in charge of the CID in that division and I am curious about all those concerned.'

'One of them told you about me. Who?'

'That's irrelevant,' said Marsh.

'Not to me, it isn't,' Blacker said. 'We were very discreet. No one knew.'

'People always know,' said Marsh, pitying Louise who had kept faith and told no one his identity, for if she had confided in a girl-friend, surely that girl would have spoken up at the time? Though one or two had hinted at an unhappy romance, no one had named the man. 'Someone did, anyway. Your wife may have suspected something but preferred not to have a showdown.'

'I hope you're not going to tell her now,' said Blacker anxiously. His pulse was racing. What about his blood pressure?

'Not unless I have to,' Marsh replied. 'Now, is there anything helpful you can tell me? Anything that might bear on the case? What about her relationship with her parents?'

Blacker relaxed in his chair as the talk took this safer direction.

'She was devoted to them, but they stifled her. She was living in London to assert her independence, as young women do.'

'But she went back to live at home. Was that after you broke up?'

'Yes. They'd pleaded with her to return, and we both thought it would make things easier. The break, I mean,' said Blacker. 'She was quite unhappy,' he confessed. 'She may have felt she needed their support to see her through a bad few weeks. But it's possible that, when she'd got over it, she felt oppressed. They'd want to know where she was, who she was seeing, that sort of thing. Parents do,' he added wryly.

'So if she was meeting someone else she might keep it from them?'

'It would depend,' said Blacker. 'They were older parents, weren't they? They'd been married a while before she was born. That might have made them over-protective. Later motherhood wasn't as common then as it is now.'

'The mother had been widowed in the war. She had another child that died,' said Marsh.

'Louise never told me that,' said Blacker. 'There was an older brother. He was adopted.'

'Did she talk about him? How did they get on?'

'She didn't like him. In a way, I think she was afraid of him,' said Blacker. 'He tormented her when they were children – pulled her hair, that sort of thing. Kids can be terrible. She felt bad about not liking him – thought it reflected on her, as if she was in some way jealous of him, which she wasn't, or so she said. The mother seemed to dote on him.'

'Ah.'

'He got married. Then that went wrong and he came back to live at home. She was still living in London then.'

'But she went home later. He had gone to Australia by then,' said Marsh.

'So he had. I'd forgotten.'

'And she died soon after he returned,' said Marsh slowly.

The two men looked at one another across the desk. It was a long, brooding gaze.

'Coincidence,' said Blacker at last.

'He was living in Cornton. That's at least thirty miles

away,' said Marsh. 'He was driving a taxi and had taken a fare to Heathrow that night. It would have been checked out.'

But had it been? He remembered little about the brother then, except that he had accompanied several of the search parties. Hundreds of officers had been working on the case but their reports would be on file. He couldn't sanction going through them yet; not without some evidence of one kind or another. He took a card from his wallet.

'There's where to reach me, if anything occurs to you,' he said. 'We talked to her flatmates at the time, and her colleagues at work, but they could tell us nothing useful.'

'She could be as close as a clam,' Blacker told him. 'But someone knew about me. Otherwise you wouldn't be here.'

How had Malcolm known about the affair? Marsh wondered about that as he left the building.

7

Malcolm

Marsh went round to Brenda's house the following Monday evening.

Malcolm was out.

'May I come in a minute?' Marsh requested, having identified himself, and Brenda, looking puzzled, stood back to admit him.

The house was very small with, he guessed, only two bedrooms. The living-room contained a plain dining-table and chairs in a pale wood. The walls were painted off-white with a pinkish tinge, and there were pink silk-covered cushions on the sofa which was upholstered in fabric matching the walls. Everything looked modern, new, and expensive, but might well be low-price from a discount warehouse.

'Your house,' he stated.

'Yes. Malcolm's been living here a while,' she said. 'How may I help you? Why do you want him?' His debts, she thought; there had been telephone calls from angry creditors wanting to know when he planned to settle. They must have been worried to track him down at her address and she did not like that; she had worked hard to establish her own business and she did not want her reputation tarnished by association with someone who might be about to go bankrupt, as he must unless he paid his dues.

'How long have you known him?' asked Marsh.

'A few months. Why? Nothing's happened, has it?' She knew a moment of stabbing anxiety and in the next second recognised that it was not dread of some accident he might have had, but of her own involvement if he was in trouble.

'Not to my knowledge,' Marsh replied. He went on to explain his interest in Louise Vaughan.

'Oh, I see. That was dreadful. Poor girl,' said Brenda. 'He was fond of her. He said it broke him up. He couldn't understand how such a thing could happen in a place like Feringham.'

'Such things can happen anywhere,' said Marsh. 'Does he talk about her much?'

'No. In fact, I didn't know about her until we went to see his parents. He wanted to warn me in case I asked who it was in a photograph or if they mentioned her at all. It happened before I came to this area. Didn't you have any idea of who had done it?'

'Not a one,' said Marsh. 'No leads at all. All the usual dubious characters were investigated but there was no reason to suspect any of them.' He did not mention Tom Francis and the tough time the police had given him. It had had to happen; routine procedure was to eliminate possible perpetrators close to base before a wider net was cast even if, in the process, the trail to the real villain grew cold.

'She was never found, Malcolm said.'

'That's right,' said Marsh. 'It happens, though not very often, I'm pleased to say.'

'She might turn up one day. Her – her body, I mean.'

'Yes. Some years ago a missing woman's body was found when a lake was dragged during a search for someone else who'd gone missing,' Marsh informed her.

'So that one was tidied up?'

'It was.'

'That could happen again.'

'Yes.'

'Malcolm wasn't living in Selbury then. He was just back from Australia and had a flat in Cornton.'

'Yes.'

Why had she told him that? She had answered a question he hadn't asked. Was it to reassure herself?

'I can't tell you where he is now,' she stated. 'Maybe selling a car.'

She would not suggest that he might be in a bar with people he thought of as his cronies, but who only hung round him because he was an easy touch for free drinks. He said it was a good way to pick up business. Much of his trade was with youngsters; they were the ones who bought used cars now, or women, Brenda thought wryly, for so many men had cars as part of their jobs. Some women did, too, she had to admit, and she ran her small Citroën on her company account.

'How's he doing?' asked Marsh.

'You'll have to ask him,' she said. 'We're not in business together. We're just friends.' She smiled at Marsh, a stocky man with dark hair receding above a creased forehead. It must be sad to lose your hair; she wouldn't like hers to fall out. With this reflection she tossed her auburn curls, which she wore tied back in the office but which now tumbled unrestricted about her shoulders.

The gesture unsettled Marsh. She was a good-looking lady. How had a failure like Malcolm Vaughan managed to make it with her?

'Forgive me – you've a mortgage?' he asked.

'Yes.'

'Does Malcolm Vaughan pay it?'

'Whatever gave you that idea?' She laughed harshly. 'Certainly not.'

So Malcolm had lied. What he had done once, he could do again.

'Tell him I called, will you?' Marsh asked her.

'Do you want him to come and see you?'

'No. I'll find him myself, another time,' said Marsh. 'There's no hurry.'

When he had gone, Brenda felt uneasy. Why this revived interest after so long? The poor girl had been dead, if not officially buried, for twelve years; the police were not going to discover new clues now, unless they found her body.

Malcolm couldn't have known anything more about it than he'd told her. He'd been driving a taxi then, a temporary arrangement till he started up some business of his own, he'd said, and he had taken a fare to Heathrow that night. You would remember something like that, she supposed: whatever you were doing while your sister was murdered.

She shivered. Murder! That wasn't an everyday thing at all, not something everyone had to cope with like work and marriage and money and sex.

There had been his marriage. Malcolm had told her nothing about it except that they had been too young to know what they were doing and were not right for one another, which was true of a good few couples. She had been sympathetic; her own husband had walked out on her, preferring someone else. But suppose Malcolm had knocked Gwynneth about? It wasn't impossible; he could be quite aggressive and she had sometimes found it exciting, but he'd gone too far once or twice and she had stopped him.

What if she failed, some time? What if he really beat her up?

He had a very jealous nature: she knew that. One night when they were out together a man she knew had chatted her up while Malcolm bought their drinks. Seeing the man put his arm around her, Malcolm had been furious; he had smouldered at her and squared up to the man, who had laughed and backed off. She'd been annoyed; she wasn't Malcolm's property. He'd taken quite a time to simmer down, and subsequently she had noticed that his face would redden if she exchanged more than a few words with another man; he would start to speak aggressively and would move close to her, touch her, act the owner. She hadn't liked it and she had told him so.

What if he was jealous of his sister in some way? There could be dozens of reasons. For one thing, she was the real child of their parents, and for another she seemed to have been good at most things, where he had clearly failed to make his mark. In any case, jealousy need not be rational; often it was quite unjustified.

This was ridiculous. He'd had nothing to do with the death of his sister; such an idea was quite impossible and he had had an alibi for the time in question. She was letting that policeman's interest get to her and give her silly notions. All the same, when Malcolm at last came in, it was still on her mind.

By that time, she had begun preparing a meal for herself. Usually they ate together, often out, but her budget did not run to many restaurant meals. If Malcolm paid, it made up for the fact that he contributed nothing to the mortgage and very little to the housekeeping, so she had no qualms about letting him settle the bill, always charged to one or other of his credit cards. He had this grand way with him which at first she had rather enjoyed, as if he had a bottomless bank balance. It was the way to get on; she had begun her own business with an assumed air of confidence which now, since she was succeeding, had become natural. She had an increasing register of firms for whom she found employees; she took trouble to suit both parties and her name was good with staff and companies, but her continuing success depended on keeping everything going and she employed only one other woman, also divorced and with two school-aged children. Brenda allowed her to work flexible hours so that she was able to collect the children after school, and during the holidays let her go, engaging a temporary helper for that period. As a result, she had a loyal and contented assistant but was very busy herself. She had recently embarked on talks with local firms about improving arrangements for working mothers, either by introducing child-care facilities or fitting in with school hours; it had to be done, for there was a shortage of skilled staff in the area where new businesses were opening all the time, and a vast supply of potential workers was restricted by such problems. Brenda herself did not like the idea of young children wandering around the town waiting for their mothers to return; some could be trusted to let themselves in, find something to eat, turn on the ubiquitous baby-sitter, the television, and remain in reasonable safety on their own. Others got bored and wandered out in search of something to do, and those were the ones at risk from other people, whether older youngsters leading them astray, or worse.

Brenda hoped to change things, and she meant her business to expand. If Malcolm had problems, whether debts or connected with his sister, she could, by association, be affected.

She'd have to think about it seriously.

Malcolm, when he arrived, had brought a bottle of burgundy.

'What's for dinner?' he cried, bursting into the kitchen exhaling whisky fumes.

'Well, I'm having chicken,' said Brenda. She had taken a chicken breast out of the freezer and was preparing it with the dregs of some white white left over in an almost empty bottle and a few grapes out of the fruit bowl.

'Surely there's some for me too?' Malcolm halted, his face falling into sulky lines.

'There was only one piece left,' said Brenda. 'And I didn't know your plans.' Then she relented. 'There's a lasagne in the freezer,' she said. Thank goodness for the microwave which came to the rescue at such moments.

'That'll do,' said Malcolm, genial again. He opened the bottle and poured two glasses of wine.

'You can lay the table,' Brenda told him.

'Done,' said Malcolm.

He was in a good mood; perhaps he had sold a car. This was how he had been when they first got together, full of charm and easy to please, but with a tough streak which appealed to her. She had not held out against him very long, for living without sex was frustrating. Brenda did not subscribe to the view that any partner was better than none, but when she learned that Malcolm's flat lease had expired – a less than accurate description of his accommodation problem – she was ready to suggest he should move in for a while. Now she was going to tell him to move on.

Malcolm had sold the Jaguar that afternoon. He whistled as he set the table and he even scrubbed a potato to add to his lasagne.

'A policeman was here today, asking about you,' Brenda reported when they were sitting at the table. His lasagne steamed beside the large potato and a pile of green beans.

'A policeman? Why?' Malcolm looked immediately alarmed.

'Why should you worry? Your conscience is clear, isn't

it?' said Brenda, in a teasing tone. 'Or have you been up to something I don't know about?'

'It's not a joking matter. What did he want?' Malcolm leaned across the table and grabbed her wrist, squeezing it painfully. 'Tell me,' he said. His face had gone that ugly shade of red and he was glaring at her, his eyes turned to hard blue pebbles.

'Let go my arm,' said Brenda.

'Not till you explain.' He gripped it harder and as she tried to wrench free, between them they knocked over one of the glasses of wine.

'Oh, hell,' said Brenda. 'Now look what you've done!'

'Leave it.' Still Malcolm held her wrist. 'Why did a policeman want me?'

'I'm not telling you until you let me go,' said Brenda. She picked up her knife and made as if to stab his hand. Before she could do so, he released her.

'Bitch,' he said.

Brenda was trembling. She stood up and fetched a cloth to wipe up the spilled wine. It had spread into a wide pool but it had not dripped on to the carpet. She mopped at it carefully, not wanting him to see that she was frightened and was very near to tears.

'It was Superintendent Marsh,' she said. 'He was asking about your sister.'

'Oh, that.' Malcolm sat back. 'Why couldn't you say so?' He tried to speak calmly; giving way to panic might lead to other revelations.

'What else could it be about?' she demanded. 'Is there another reason for the police to be interested in you?' There was no teasing in her voice now.

'Of course not. How could there be?' he blustered.

But there must be something; why else would he be so upset?

'He said he'd find you sometime,' Brenda said. 'It can't be urgent.'

Malcolm had resumed his meal.

'That's up to him,' he said, affecting calm.

Why had he reacted so vehemently? Had he been up to some trickery at work, fiddling his book-keeping, dodging the VAT? Brenda had parried Marsh's question but she knew his business was not doing well; she had gone round to the workshop recently to collect her own car, which he was servicing to save her a garage bill, and while he was just finishing what he was doing to it, she had gone into his office to wait. Curious, she had opened a drawer of his desk and had seen the bills and threatening letters.

She had said nothing, going into his washroom to prink in the mirror, and flushing the lavatory so that he would not suspect her of prying. She didn't think the police served writs; those were civil actions and private detectives did it for their clients.

'Well, I've told you, anyway,' she said. She cleared away her half-eaten chicken, all appetite now gone. What should she do? She couldn't turn him out tonight, so late; that would be too harsh. Besides, he was so touchy, he might blow up and get really violent. For the first time she felt afraid of him and she went upstairs before the *News at Ten*.

This was no way to live. He had to go, and soon.

She contemplated locking the bedroom door, but he would be capable of knocking it down if she did. Stories she had heard from other women came into her mind to reinforce her fears. Her own former husband had not been violent, only unfaithful; in fact he was rather a gentle sort of person, too quiet for her, and his escapade into adultery had surprised her by its boldness.

Malcolm did not come upstairs. She lay cringing in the big bed, fearful that he would lumber in wanting sex, but he had had a lot to drink and might find the wish exceeded the performance, as someone had remarked. It had happened before and he got angry every time.

After a while she heard sounds from below and then the front door banged. A few moments later his car started up outside; there was no mistaking the Porsche as it roared away. Brenda went downstairs and locked the house, pushing bolts across and putting up the chain so that he could not return. Let him spend the night in his workshop; he'd done it often enough before he moved in with her; he had a folding bed and sleeping-bag.

Malcolm had been briefly frightened himself when he held Brenda's arm so fiercely and felt hate and rage welling up within him. This was how he had felt when he met Louise that last night. Brenda had made him very angry with her taunting talk of the policeman's visit. What were they up to? What did they know? He'd told them about Richard Blacker; that should have given them something to think about, a line of inquiry to follow. Wasn't that how they phrased it?

He'd often hurt Louise. He'd enjoyed it, grown excited when he saw that look of fear on her face. It had been the same with Gwynneth, and with other women, but tonight was the first time he'd seen Brenda with the same expression. Making women fearful gave him a sense of power, but he liked it, too, when they smiled at him, were impressed by the good manners and unbounded charm he could turn on so easily. He despised them for their gullibility.

He drove away from Brenda's house because he did not know how to play the next scene. To recover his self-confidence, he began explaining to himself that she had provoked him, leading him on, not telling him quickly what Marsh wanted, just as Gwynneth made him lose his temper when she looked at him with those large woebegone eyes spilling tears. A man liked a bit of spirit, and Brenda had plenty; meeting her, he had been instantly attracted, and when he discovered that she owned her own house and was living alone he made haste to let her know his feelings. She was a looker and available, and she posed a challenge. Malcolm thought he could have any woman he fancied; he had been successful enough to bolster this conceit, but he had never been capable of sustaining a relationship.

Look at Louise. What made her so po-faced about it? They were not related by blood, after all. If she expected preferential treatment from George and Susan because she was their own child, then she couldn't suddenly decide that getting together with him was against nature. Those were the words she had used, trying to fend him off, struggling as he tussled with her.

Well, he had got what he was after, not that it was anything so great, but it meant he had won, had beaten her.

Susan never suspected a thing. Even when she had caught him on the landing, she'd never given it a thought.

That generation was so bloody ignorant, or people like George and Susan were, insulated by money and possessions from what went on in the real world. All her life Susan had been sheltered, living in that one large house for nearly the whole of it. She hadn't a clue.

With Louise out of the way, he'd expected her to turn to him all the more, and in a way she had. There was no one else in the running now, unless a ghost could be a rival. There would be her money, too, when she and George were dead. With that he could set up elsewhere, start again with adequate finance at last, open a leisure centre or a sports club; that was the coming thing, swimming-pools and gyms. In his mind he anticipated inheriting at least a million pounds.

Malcolm now owed over fifty thousand pounds on unpaid bills, his mortgage, and interest to money-lenders he had used to keep some of his creditors quiet. His bookie's account, seven hundred, was the least of his worries. He owed over a thousand pounds to a filling station. He used a lot of petrol, driving about as he did, picking up cars.

He decided to go for a drive, alarm Brenda by staying out for a couple of hours. She'd be glad enough, after that, when he returned.

He drove over to Cornton where he went into The Bear and Ragged Staff, getting there just before it closed. He downed three drinks in rapid time, then drove around the town. It was too early to go home. No police car came up behind him as he weaved his way back to Malchester, and luckily no hapless third party crossed his dangerous path. By the time he reached Brenda's house his belligerent mood had gone and he was almost maudlin, ready to beg her forgiveness. Very occasionally he had done this with other women, not deliberately as a tactic but because it happened naturally. They had always come round, cradling him in their arms, acting the mother, but he hadn't tried it yet with Brenda.

He didn't want to break with her. Where was he to go? He'd be on his own again, and he had no money to rent a flat. Even he couldn't be expected to find someone else to move in with overnight. What a pity it was too late to buy her some flowers. Still, he'd do that tomorrow, an enormous bouquet, the best Bloomers could provide.

When he reached her house and blundered his way out of the car, he had difficulty opening the gate, focusing on it carefully, elaborately raising the latch, pushing. He met resistance, some obstacle that blocked the path. Malcolm leaned down and felt the hard shape of a suitcase. There was a second beside it, and a heap of carrier bags.

The bitch! The trollop! Malcolm called Brenda every name he knew, aloud, kicking at the bundles, as he took in the fact that she had packed up his things and left them on the path.

Upstairs, sitting with her hand on the telephone ready to call the police if he made a scene, Brenda listened to him swearing. Instead of returning to bed after she locked up, she had rushed round the house collecting everything that she could find of his, stuffing them into his cases and into plastic carriers, heaving them out on to the path as quickly as she could before he could come back. Then she had locked up again.

The swearing stopped. She heard the car start up

again. He hadn't loaded his cases; there hadn't been time. But he'd gone; that was enough for now.

In the morning, very early, she ordered a taxi, and when it arrived she paid the driver to deliver Malcolm's possessions at his workshop, and to dump them on the forecourt if he was not there.

She thought he would be. Where else could he go? Even Malcolm wouldn't have run back to his mother in the night.

But he had.

It was after one o'clock in the morning when Malcolm arrived at the Lodge House. It was his true home, wasn't it?

There was a bed in the spare room; it should by right be his except that the room was too small for anyone other than a child. He might demand to live at home, see that Norah moved. But what if she really was his mother? What then? How could she be punished?

He drove out to Selbury in a mood that swung from maudlin misery to obsessive rage as he thought about the twists of chance that had ordered his existence. Some primitive sense of self-preservation kept him hugging the kerb and travelling at a steady pace, only speeding up when he came into the village. Luck, also, kept police cars off the roads that he was using. He was about to blow the horn when he turned in at the Lodge House gates, just as he always did arriving there in daylight, when the darkness of the house reminded him of the time. Well, he'd got his key. He'd let himself in as he had so often done at the big house. He cut the engine and hauled himself out of the driver's seat; then, his bladder bursting, he urinated extravagantly against the wall beside the front door. There was more to the action than simply physical relief; the gesture made a territorial statement. Then he selected the appropriate key from the bunch which included those to the workshop and Brenda's place.

Norah, not yet asleep, heard the door open and at once knew who it must be, even as she picked up the stout stick she kept in her bedroom in case of intruders. She put on her dressing-gown and bedroom slippers and stepped out on to the landing, knocking on George's door and opening it, turning on his light.

'George,' she called softly. 'There's someone in the house. I think it's Malcolm.'

She did not wait for him to answer but went quickly down the stairs, her stick at the ready, just in case. Thieves could catch them out, because neither she nor George would ever suspect a nocturnal visitor of being anyone but Malcolm, so conditioned were they to his sudden unwelcome appearances.

He was in the drawing-room, pouring himself a large whisky from the decanter on the drinks tray.

'Well, what's happened now?' Norah demanded, dismayed to find that she was trembling. She must be getting old.

'I need a bed for the night,' said Malcolm. 'So naturally I came home.'

'Turned you out, has she?' Norah could not refrain from straight talk, but she managed not to add that she was not surprised. 'What's wrong with a hotel?'

'Costs money,' Malcolm said. 'And I've a cash-flow problem at the moment. Besides, where should a fellow go but to his mother?' He drained his glass and filled it again.

'Keep your voice down,' Norah said. 'Let Susan sleep, if you've any feeling for her at all. You've brought enough worry to her, as if she hadn't plenty to cope with already.'

'I said my mother should help me,' said Malcolm and he lurched towards her, an odd look in his face. 'My real mother,' he added.

'Don't be silly,' Norah said. 'How can she help you? We don't know where she is.'

'Don't we?' Malcolm advanced further. 'What about you? You're my mother. You had a baby and he was adopted. You're my real mother.'

As he said this, he advanced further and Norah shrank away from him, horror on her face.

'Don't say such things,' she gasped.

'Good of the Vaughans, wasn't it?' he continued, snarling now. 'Rescued you, didn't they, taking me in when they were wanting a son?'

Norah regained control.

'You don't know what you're talking about,' she said. Would George never come? 'I had no son.'

'No, because you gave him away,' said Malcolm.

'God help you if you think that,' said George, coming into the room and moving close to Norah. 'Your mother's name was on your birth certificate; you know that. Jane Frost. Father unknown.'

'It's easy to give yourself a false name, registering a birth,' said Malcolm.

'She was a farmer's daughter,' George answered. 'You were born in Yorkshire. You can try to find her if you want to. There are societies to help you.' Poor woman, he briefly thought. They'd been told she came of good country stock, a healthy girl, and probably the father was some local married man; anyway, she wasn't saying. If Malcolm traced her now, he would truly be a chicken come home to roost.

'Lies, all lies,' said Malcolm. 'Norah had a baby. I'm him. It all adds up – why she's kept so close to you all these years. Doesn't make sense otherwise.'

Norah had recovered, shock replaced by icy rage.

'I got pregnant,' she told him. 'I had an abortion. It was during the war, years before you were born. I was seventeen years old.'

'It's easy for you to say that,' Malcolm sneered. 'You can't prove it.'

'I'm not in the habit of lying,' Norah remarked. 'Who have you cast as your father in this fantasy of yours?'

'I don't know.' Malcolm's laggard imagination had not carried him that far. He looked at George and opened his mouth.

'No, Malcolm,' George intervened. 'I am not your father, but you have been my son in every way except biologically. You've had every opportunity in life, help when you've been in trouble; too much, perhaps, for your own good. You've made Susan ill with worry about you when she's had quite enough to bear already. I'm not going to allow you to disturb her now. I'm going to drive you back to Malchester, as you're obviously unfit to drive yourself, and I wouldn't wish you on that young woman in your present condition so I'll take you to your workshop. Give me your keys.'

He held out his hand and, faced with his authority, Malcolm crumpled. Like an automaton, he handed them over.

Norah, looking at George for the first time since he had entered the room, saw that he had put on trousers and a sweater. How sensible of him.

If Susan had heard them, she would have been downstairs by now; with luck she would not waken; she often took a pill.

'I'll follow and bring you back,' she said.

'Thanks,' said George, who had known that this was how she would react. A few things in life were certainties. 'A note for Susan, maybe? Just in case she wakes and comes downstairs? We're helping a motorist in trouble, perhaps?'

She nodded.

'Put on something warm,' George told her. 'I'll drop Malcolm and meet you at the Baptist Church.'

They would be gone some time; best part of two hours if the expedition went without a hitch. Norah watched George march Malcolm out of the house and then she went upstairs to dress. Before leaving, she listened outside Susan's door; all was quiet.

She left the note on the kitchen table. If Susan woke she sometimes made herself a cup of tea or a milky drink, refusing to have a kettle or a thermos in her room. She said that walking about the house settled her, and in the summer she would go into the garden, sitting in the stillness sniffing the jasmine or the night-scented stock and other plants she grew for their sweet smell. Poor Susan; she was one of the walking wounded.

But aren't we all, thought Norah fiercely, even Malcolm. She was glad that it was George who was tackling the Porsche, not her; she backed her own car quietly out of the garage and set off in pursuit.

She had to wait some time for George.

She parked, as arranged, outside the red brick Victorian church round the corner from the workshop. Posters exhorting her to put her trust in the Lord and fear no man and to walk hand in hand with Jesus frowned down at her from framed billboards beside the gate. Much good that did you if a gang of muggers went for you, she thought. The world had always been a savage place and turning the other cheek only invited fresh attack. What chance had Louise had, the night she was abducted? A good course of self-defence, taught to every schoolgirl, might save some, but not if they were outnumbered by an evil mob.

George would be talking to Malcolm, she supposed, trying to win something positive from this disastrous incident. Or perhaps Malcolm had finally passed out and George was putting him to bed; she knew there was a camp-bed in the office. Susan was greatly troubled by thinking that he might sometimes have to use it.

Norah had a chronic dread that one day he would carry out some act so grave that no one would be able to protect him from the consequences. Maybe it would be the best thing: a spell inside Brixton or Wandsworth might pull him up, make him take a grip on himself, and at least it would keep him out of circulation for a time. But Susan would take it all on herself, see it as her failure, want to go prison-visiting.

She had been sitting there making herself thoroughly depressed by this line of thought for about ten minutes when a police patrol car drove slowly past her, stopped a short distance ahead and then reversed towards her. A youthful uniformed officer got out and approached.

Oh dear, thought Norah, winding down her window, ready to be ingratiating though she was committing no crime. Still, older women did not customarily park in urban streets in the small hours of the morning.

'Good evening, madam. Anything wrong?' asked the officer, shining his torch into her eyes and making her blink.

'No, not at all. I'm waiting for someone,' Norah answered.

At her age, she couldn't be a prostitute waiting for a punter, could she? The young officer pondered it, eyeing her, a woman of sixty, give or take a few years, with bright brown eyes and an alert face innocent of make-up. Still, you never knew.

'And who would that be?' Police Constable Perry inquired.

'My employer,' said Norah curtly. 'My name is Norah Tyler and I am housekeeper to Mr and Mrs Vaughan at the Lodge House, Selbury.'

Selbury. That was thirty miles away or more.

'I see, madam,' said the constable equably while he wondered what her employer was doing while she waited. 'May I see your driving licence, please?'

'I'm sorry, I haven't got it with me,' Norah answered.

'And where is your – er – employer?' Perry doggedly pressed on.

'Mr Vaughan has just driven his son home after a visit,' Norah said. 'He – the son – wasn't feeling very well.'

'Mr Vaughan junior does not live in the Baptist Church,' said Perry with some confidence.

'No, but we agreed this would be a good place for me to wait, near a light and where I would not be harassed,' said Norah firmly.

Enlightenment dawned on the constable.

'Would it be Mr Vaughan junior who runs the used-car business in Sebastopol Road?'

'That's correct,' said Norah.

'Hm. And he's unwell?'

'Yes, but it's nothing serious.' Norah did not want to prejudice the constable. 'Nothing that need concern you. I'm sure you've more important things to see to.'

'I'll just ask you to give me your full name and address,' said Perry, nettled by this remark. 'And you must take your driving licence and certificate of insurance to a police station within seven days.'

'If you say so,' Norah replied. 'But what offence am I committing? There's no parking restriction here.'

George came round the corner to see Norah standing on the pavement, breathing into a breathalyser.

Luckily she had been at home that evening and had had only a glass of sherry before dinner and one glass of light white wine; had she been to Myra's, she might have had a gin and much more wine. George had certainly drunk two glasses of wine, maybe a third; would there have been time for that to clear his bloodstream? It would be just like life for one of them to be clobbered for protecting Malcolm.

Perry had not meant to get in so deep over this, once he recognised that Norah was, apparently, harmless. After all, she didn't look like a car thief, and he could soon check out the vehicle which she had said was hers. But you had to stay in charge of the situation or lose face, and she had needled him. Besides, finding such a person in such a spot at such an hour was, to say the least, unusual.

Norah cast George a desperate glance as she exhaled into the machine. Perry carefully inspected the result.

'Good evening, officer.' George spoke calmly. 'Miss Tyler is waiting for me. I don't think the car is causing an obstruction, is it?'

'No, sir,' said Perry, now heartily wishing himself elsewhere for Norah's test showed her well below the limit.

'I hadn't got my licence,' Norah said.

'Well, I've got mine,' said George, taking his wallet from his jacket pocket. He had automatically picked it up before leaving; money might be needed before the night was over.

The constable scrutinised George's licence, a blameless document bearing no endorsement. 'Detective Superintendent Marsh, at Feringham, knows me well,' he added. 'And Miss Tyler, too. I'm sure he'll vouch for us when you make your report.'

'That won't be necessary, sir,' said Perry, daunted by the name of Marsh, whose area included this division. 'I'm sure everything is in order.'

'Do you still want me to bring my licence round?' Norah asked in dulcet tones.

'No,' said Perry, giving in. 'Not under the circumstances.'

What circumstances, wondered Norah: their acquaintance with the superintendent?

'Well, if that's all, then we'll be off,' said George briskly, holding the driver's door open so that Norah could resume her seat. 'Good night, officer.'

'Good night, sir,' said Perry, backing off as George walked round the car to the passenger's side.

'Let him go first,' warned George as the policeman strode back to his car, swaggering slightly to make himself seem the victor. 'He'll want to get away without making a worse idiot of himself, but if we do the least little thing wrong he'll be on to us like a hawk.'

'Have you no confidence in me, George?' asked Norah. 'I, who drove three-ton lorries in the service of His Majesty?'

'I've got two hundred per cent confidence in you, my dear,' said George. 'But none in our luck holding out until we get home. I won't offer to drive in case there's one of that young fellow's pals lined up to ambush us. We know you're in the clear, and I may not be.'

Their route lay away from the abbey and the old part of the town, not enough of which, people thought, had been protected from planners who tore down old warehouses and shops, and built fortressed towns to enclose new stores and supermarkets and covered malls. They went down residential streets, past sleeping houses veiled in darkness punctuated by tall streetlamps. The night was fine and clear with only a few wispy clouds occasionally crossing the sliver of moon, and, as they progressed into the country, dark trees stretched black skeletonic branches in silhouette against the sky. When the headlights touched them, boughs and hedges turned brown or grey, with the faded winter green of grass verges beneath. Their journey was uneventful; no police car pounced on them from a side road.

'What took you so long?' Norah asked at last.

'I had to clean him up,' said George. 'He was being sick. I couldn't leave him to choke on that. Difficult to explain to Susan. Or to the coroner.'

'I see,' said Norah.

'It's never going to go away,' said George.

'You mean Malcolm?'

'Yes. The worry of him. We can't wash our hands of him.'

'You can only do so much,' said Norah, as she had said to George on countless occasions, and even to Susan too.

'He's capable of doing something really dreadful.' George echoed Norah's thought. 'There's so much latent violence there, and his thinking is so warped. If he hadn't been so drunk tonight, who knows what he might have done?'

'Where did he get the idea that I was his mother?' Norah asked. It had been in her mind since he had made the accusation. 'How did he know I'd had a child?'

She had told George herself, in a weak moment after they became lovers over twenty years ago, when he took her out one evening in London. Often before, they'd been to a theatre together; this time they went back to her flat, and it set the pattern for their rare meetings afterwards, always when Susan was busy with something to do with her mother or the children. She had not told him who the father was; Norah still protected David, as his mother and sister had done. Why else was the child aborted?

If Susan had adopted him – or her – things might have been so different; Malcolm might never have entered the family. But the other Malcolm, Susan's brother, was still alive then; he was to have produced the heirs.

She had told George that the father was someone she had met and fallen for when she was young and silly; she knew Susan would never have betrayed her brother's secret, even to George.

'A random shot,' he had said, seeing no point in adding what he still thought: that it was a pity she hadn't had her child, for it might have inherited her spirit and, if adopted, have been a blessing to its new family.

'He must be very disturbed about his antecedents,' Norah said. 'Maybe he ought to find out all about them. Face his past.'

'He might have heard some talk in the village.' George was still beavering away at the source of Malcolm's allegation. 'There must have been some, after all.'

'I doubt it,' Norah said. 'I was in the factory then, though I still lived at Selbury. It was all over and done with before there was time for people to suspect anything. Susan and her mother saw to that, and I'm absolutely certain they would not have told a soul.'

'What a time you must have had,' George said. 'Poor little kid. Only seventeen.' He reached out and patted her knee with easy familiarity, wondering as he did so if they would ever go to bed together again. Neither could be said to be filled with ardour now, but some human closeness would be rather pleasant. He sighed a little, recognising that they were excellent friends.

Norah spared a hand from the steering-wheel to press his as it lay on her thigh. She was very fond of George.

What a ridiculous pair we would seem to anyone observing us, she thought; what an extraordinary way we have spent the best part of the night.

They were very quiet when they returned to the Lodge House, but Susan heard them.

She had woken as Norah drove away, mildly puzzled by the sound but soon settling back again. For some time after hearing the car start up outside she lay warm in bed, drowsy with sedative, seeking sleep. The radio that helped Norah during bouts of insomnia was no aid to Susan; she preferred silence. She cast her mind into the past, something she now did more and more, trying to evade the present, lying there half-dozing in the clean square room with its print curtains, its button-back chair and some of her mother's good furniture, pretending that she was a child and Mabel would come in with her hot water. Those brass cans and sets of washstand china — bowls and jugs and carafes — were collectors' items now. So much had changed, and not always for the better; Norah, for example, could not be expected to do all that once Mabel had done for Susan. Shopping, she thought, turning her mind in a less personal direction; no supermarkets then, but Mr Dobbs himself sitting in the kitchen writing down the order and delivering requirements several times a week. Now it was Sainsbury's for what could not be obtained from Mr Dobbs' latest successor in the village, where Susan still felt obliged to deal. There had been other sorts of shopping: trips to London with her mother, to Debenham and Freebody's, and Harrods where they went for gloves apart from other things; you rested your elbow on the counter while an assistant fitted on the glove, having first dusted it inside with talc and stretched the fingers with a type of tong. No one bought gloves like that now; indeed, people rarely wore gloves at all except in cold weather, and even royal personages were to be seen with their hands in their pockets.

No one does things for other people now, Susan lamented; service has become a dirty word. We put our own petrol in our cars; machines perform functions once carried out by humans and thousands are out of work. Thousands more are isolated because they are denied trivial daily encounters, and at night people sit at home, often alone, watching television instead of going out because city streets are dangerous and it is difficult to park.

We help each other here, though, she accepted; or rather, George and Norah both help me. With the clarity of small-hour perception, she saw that she did little, if she ever had, for them.

This realisation shocked her into total wakefulness and she had to get up. That was another tiresomeness of being older; if you woke in the night, sooner or later you had to visit the bathroom. Afterwards she went downstairs, very quietly so that she would not disturb the others, not listening to the part of her mind which told her that the car she had heard was no passer-by but had left from here. She would make a drink and maybe take another pill; it wouldn't matter if she slept late in the morning; she had no appointment.

She saw Norah's note and, reading it, understood that they had both gone out, leaving her alone.

Susan didn't like that. She put the kettle on and paced about in her long quilted satin dressing-gown with the warm lining. How had they got involved in a Good Samaritan act? It must have been someone from Selbury House who was in difficulties, and bossy Norah had dragged George into a rescue operation instead of leaving it to other people. Norah always had to be involved; she could never leave well alone. Cross, Susan found a cup and saucer, then a tiny teapot; let Norah clear it all away in the morning: that would show her. Only by degrees did Susan allow herself to deduce that the stranded motorist had been Malcolm and that they were taking him home, for it was the only solution that made sense. George would have made a different plan for a stranger.

What was wrong? Was Malcolm hurt?

She wrote various scenarios in her mind, sitting there at the table, glad of the warmth from the Aga, waiting for their return. She drank a cup of tea, and then another; finally, she admitted to herself the folly of her vigil, brooding like an avenging angel ready to expose whatever deception George had devised to save her pain. She would leave it till the morning, trap them with questions at breakfast, find out what Malcolm had been doing. She had a right to know; she was his mother.

Only she wasn't.

What would her own little Harry have been like if he had lived? She often wondered that, and it was easy to endow him with every virtue. He might have grown up confident and boastful, like her elder brother, or more like his father. She had scarcely known Hugh except as a charming, romantic figure who made her feel good because he was handsome and had excellent manners. In truth, what had they in common? He was a friend of the Spencers and it was there, playing tennis one summer's day a year before war was declared, that she had met him. They had met again at various dances and more tennis parties, and after that, as a Territorial officer, he had been called up. There had been many hasty marriages in the war, people snatching at what they thought was love from dread of what lay ahead, although everyone thought the war would be over in months.

Susan cleared away her tea-things to leave no trace of her recent presence in the kitchen. Then she went back to bed where the electric blanket had kept it warm and snug.

How ignorant we were, she thought, and remembered a visit she and George had made to Hugh's grave not so very long ago. It was George who had been the more overtly upset as they toured the long lines of symmetrical tombstones in the vast cemetery, a beautiful and peaceful place. Were they truly Hugh's bones under that particular patch of soil? An enemy soldier had doubtless given him his first swift burial, a man no better and no worse than Hugh but one opposed to him by a mere accident of birth. If he had lived, he might have returned from the war physically or mentally maimed, and how would she have coped with that? Or, if he had escaped all wounds, would their marriage have become an uneasy truce between two polite people preserving a façade, as was so common in their generation? Younger couples were not prepared to settle for so little and shopped about optimistically for other partners, often ending up no happier.

She did not want to know if George had ever been unfaithful. If so, he had been discreet. Their secure life together mattered to them both and they were bound by troubles shared.

While Susan's thoughts ran thus, Norah had turned the Golf in at the gate and driven into the garage. She cut the engine and the pair of them sat there for a moment, silent, collecting themselves. They got out of the car together and she waited for George while he closed the garage; then they entered the house together, very quietly, closing the door with barely a sound. George poured himself a stiff tot of whisky and Norah put a mug of milk to heat up in the microwave, so neither of them touched the kettle to discover from its warmth that it had been boiled quite recently. Norah's note was still on the table; Susan could not have wakened.

They stepped softly up the carpeted stairs past her door, parting outside George's, where he leaned across and lightly kissed Norah's soft, familiar lips. If Susan had witnessed that tiny moment, she would have been astounded and quite uncomprehending; the idea that George might feel anything other than a comradely affection for Norah, born of their long acquaintance, would never have occurred to her.

Glad they were back, sure they had resolved Malcolm's immediate problem in the wisest way and that it would be time enough for her to learn about it in the morning, she snuggled down under her duvet and, eventually, drifted off to sleep.

After parting from George and Norah, Police Constable Perry continued his patrol through the town. Officers usually went in pairs at night, but his station was short-handed with two men off sick and another hurt in a fracas with drunken hooligans at the weekend, so he was alone. He had been right to question the woman. She could have been waiting for an accomplice who was involved in some felony in the area, or, more probably, in view of her age and appearance, she could have been having mechanical trouble with her vehicle. Their interview had got out of hand because of her manner, and it did not do to lose face.

Perry knew Malcolm Vaughan both by sight and by repute. One of Perry's colleagues had bought a Vauxhall Astra from him and it had been a success, fairly priced and in excellent order. Driving through the centre of Malchester, Perry brooded. He stopped two youths who were walking along the street and demanded to know where they had been and where they were going. They had been visiting friends, said the youths, and were on their way home. It was credible; they were not drunk. Perry told them to watch it and sent them on their way, feeling frustrated. It would have been good to find someone flouting the law, bring off a coup, restore his morale and earn a commendation from his sergeant.

It was odd that old Vaughan had taken his son back to the workshop, seeing that he was ill. Why hadn't he been put to bed at home or taken back to wherever he lived? Surely he did not reside at his business premises?

Perry completed a circuit of the shopping area where break-ins were easy because most upper floors, once flats, were now offices and deserted at night. As people retreated, crime advanced in city centres, and Perry was too young to remember a time when there were plenty of people about such streets after the working day was over. He turned off and went round a housing estate, emerging again near the Baptist Church but facing the opposite way so that it was easy to turn into Sebastopol Road and draw up outside Vaughan's Reliable Cars.

A number of vehicles were parked on the forecourt; Perry got out of his Escort and walked towards them. There was an old Triumph Vitesse, a blue Metro and a Maestro as well as a Porsche. All, except the Porsche, bore price tags. Perry touched the Porsche's bonnet. It felt cool, but the engine might still be warm. He circled it critically but could see nothing wrong, shining his torch on the tyres, which were good. The car bore a valid tax disc. He supposed the man Vaughan had trade plates to use if he took a car he was selling on the road, to cover its licence. He went up to the workshop, an unlovely concrete building with galvanised folding doors, which he tried. They were firmly locked. Perry walked round to the pedestrian door let into a side wall; it had a Yale lock and was secure. There was a window beside it, a blind drawn down obscuring the glass. No light showed, and there was silence.

Perry banged hard on the door, reasoning that if Vaughan were inside and ill, an inquiry as to whether he needed help was only his duty.

There was no reply to his knock, so he thumped again, then went to the window and shone his torch on the blind, trying to peer past it, but he saw nothing. He rapped on the pane.

'Police,' he cried. 'Open up!'

After repeating this command several times and rapping again on the glass, a light went on and he heard bumps and bangs from within, then a groan. The blind went up with a snap and a man stood at the window, gazing out in a bemused way and blinking in the light from Perry's torch. Perry turned the beam towards his own uniformed chest and made gestures towards the door. After what seemed to him a very long time, and was, indeed, several minutes, it was opened, and Malcolm stood revealed, fully dressed apart from shoes and his tie.

'What's the matter?' he asked. He had sobered up considerably after his unpleasant interval in the washroom before George departed, but his head was throbbing and there was a familiar sour taste in his mouth. What did this bloody copper want? Had one of his cars been stolen? That was all he needed now.

'Are you all right, Mr Vaughan? I thought you might be ill,' said Perry. 'Seeing that you're still on the premises.'

How had the fellow known he was there? He hadn't left the light on. Malcolm was too fuddled to work out that he had been deliberately roused, only that something didn't quite fit.

'I'm quite all right, thank you,' he answered crossly.

'I'm entitled to spend the night here if I wish. There's no law against it.'

Perry hoped there might turn out to be some bylaw by which he could, on a future occasion, trap the man. He would leave the statement unchallenged now.

'I'll say good night, then,' he remarked, doused his torch and went back to his car. If he couldn't catch Vaughan over sleeping on the premises against some archaic rule or other, he'd watch out for him on the road; his breath had smelled horrible and the cause of his so-called illness was plain. His father had brought him back here because he was not fit to drive himself. It was an odd destination, though; the son must have a flat or a house somewhere, or at least a room. Perry would have to find out.

He cheered up at the prospect of discovering something which might not be quite how it ought to be, and the night was further enlivened when he was called to a break-in on the far side of the town, where he caught one of the miscreants trying to get away over a wall. Perry was young and fit, an advantage in a chase. He was elated with success when he took his captive into the station and charged him.

Malcolm had been in a stupor when the policeman woke him and now he had little memory of how he came to be spending the night in his office. Someone had put up the camp-bed and had found the sleeping bag, laying it over him. Someone had removed his shoes and his tie. Could it have been George? He seemed to remember a male voice, icy with anger that was being controlled by iron effort, directing him to move here, do this, do that, but it could have been a voice from the past.

He made himself some strong coffee and laced it with brandy. The hair of the dog, he thought, swallowing. The clock on the wall showed half-past three. What a time to be having a brush with the law, and what an extraordinary hour to be here. Why wasn't he tucked up warmly with Brenda in her comfortable bed? And why had that damned copper come nosing round?

Slowly, fuzzily, the night's events began to come back to him. Brenda had locked him out. Then he'd gone home to his parents. Confused images of Norah confronting him, then George, came into his mind. They'd turned him out, too; that was it. George had brought him here. The drink Malcolm had swallowed rose in his throat as he remembered just making it to the lavatory, George pushing his head over the pan. He did not recall George sponging his face with cold water and helping him on to the bed, covering him over, finally leaving.

Sitting alone in his office chair, Malcolm was conscious of silence around him. A distant lorry changed gear, the sound a welcome break in the absence of noise. How could he bear to stay here until morning?

His radio stood on the desk. He switched it on and twiddled the knobs until he found speech, then lumbered back to his bed, lying there with the voice droning on in a foreign tongue until he lapsed into sleep again.

Next morning he showered and shaved and felt better, but he had no clean clothes to wear. Never mind. Brenda would have come to her senses by now and be ready to apologise for her conduct the night before. He'd pop round to give her the chance to do so before she went to the office.

He was searching for his keys, which George must have used both to drive the Porsche and to get into the office, when he heard a car draw up outside. He went out to find a taxi parked on the forecourt, the driver depositing two suitcases and a pile of carrier bags: his belongings.

Malcolm tipped the driver the last pound he had in his pocket, thanking him in a grand manner as though the man had done him a favour, then heaved the baggage inside. He was very angry.

So she'd done it. Damn her! Now he was really alone. Well, it wasn't the first time, but such periods had to be kept as brief as possible. Meanwhile, he couldn't stay here; it was uncomfortable and far too oppressive at night. He'd soon find another woman, and until he did, he'd check into a hotel. No need to pay with money; he'd use one of his plastic cards. Or perhaps not: there were other ways to evade the reckoning.

Malcolm found his keys in the top drawer of his desk among the pile of threatening letters and unpaid bills. He wondered if George had seen what they were, not that it made any difference; there would be no help from him. If only he could get himself straight, Malcolm thought for the umpteenth time; that was all he needed, just to have his debts cleared and the slate wiped clean, then make a fresh start without the fates turning against him, as, in the end, they always did.

Now, at last, he remembered why he had gone to the

Lodge House and what he had said to Norah. Was she really speaking the truth when she denied being his mother? There was only her word for the fact that she was so young when she was pregnant. Of course she would give out that story, but somewhere in among her things there would be papers to prove what had really happened. She could have given a false name when she registered his birth; she could have agreed to the tale that she had had an abortion to maintain the fiction. All he had to do was get her out of the way and go through her possessions. Women were tremendous hoarders; look at all the stuff his grandmother had kept, piled into drawers and boxes. It had been transported from the big house when she moved to the Lodge House; she had refused to destroy a thing. After her death Susan had had a colossal bonfire. She might not have burnt everything, however; there might be a diary or some other document which would prove the truth of his theory. Somewhere at the Lodge House there would be information he could use. The word blackmail did not come into Malcolm's mind as he slowly worked things out, but the prospect of money did; knowledge was money; people did not like old scandals being raked up and would pay to keep things quiet. When Norah was pregnant, abortion was illegal and so she would have had the child; he was sure he would find some way to prove it if he went through the papers he was certain to find at the Lodge House.

He'd go and search. He would have to find a time when they were all out, a day when Susan was at a lecture and George at a meeting. He could deal with Norah alone. In his scheming, he did not define what method of dealing he would employ, but she was not a large woman and he was strong. He would not allow her to stand in the way of his getting the evidence he had convinced himself existed. He forgot that even in nightdress and dressing-gown she had outfaced him during the night. He could lock her up, bind her and gag her, while he hunted for what he required. He could pose as a thief, wear a stocking mask and leave her tied up until George or Susan came home to release her. He had never liked her; now he would have his revenge.

He needed some breakfast. By rights he should be at Brenda's, drinking freshly perked coffee and eating toast and marmalade, though it was true he didn't fancy food at the moment. He made himself more instant coffee and poured in a further slug of brandy, and he was drinking it when a thin man in a fawn suit came to the door and served him a writ, another one, for an outstanding debt. This was from a finance company he had turned to when he had to keep other creditors quiet.

The money raised by selling the Jaguar had instantly gone to a solicitor who had succeeded in delaying two summonses. He had to lay hands on some more real money, in cash; not promises.

The Vaughans should provide it. They would pay anything to preserve their precious reputation. A few thousand would stave off the immediate crisis. Malcolm ignored the fortune which Susan had already invested in his various ventures and the pay-off to Gwynneth as, in his mind, he endowed her with a bottomless purse and resolved to act without delay. He could not wait for an opportunity to present itself; he would create one.

He set off in the Porsche to book himself into the Manor Hotel, newly opened on the outskirts of Malchester, one he had not yet visited, so no one there knew him. As he entered he saw on a board the names of two firms holding conventions there, and he said he came from one of them, a late entry, and that was why his room had not been booked in advance. He used all his charm on the blonde receptionist in her trim uniform and accepted a room on the ground floor, registering with a false name and address.

He would need the room for only a matter of days. He would soon be in funds again and able to rent a flat while he started a new business. Used cars were a busted flush now; he would cash in on those he had got and avoid laying out on others, then set up something else though at the moment he had not decided quite what that would be. Still, there were always needs to be met and this time he would pick just the right opening. Malcolm was quite used to starting off in a new direction, and the resolve to do so always improved his spirits; by concentrating on the future, he could forget past failures.

He had run out of cash and was unable to tip the porter who brought his bags to his room. He patted his pockets and shrugged, and promised to see the man later.

He would have to get some money at once. Would anyone take a cheque? He could not try the hotel, for he was not Malcolm Vaughan here.

He had given his name as Edward Tyler.

★ ★ ★

Susan had drowsed off towards dawn, and she began to dream.

She saw Hugh, still young and handsome, not dead at all but walking along a country lane, wearing his uniform. In her dream she knew he was going to post a letter, and it was to tell her that he had been killed.

'But you haven't,' she struggled to say, in the fearful dream compulsion of an action devoutly desired but impossible to perform. 'I can see you, Hugh. It was all a mistake and you're still alive.' But as she said the words her feet seemed to be immured in the ground and she could not make him hear her. Now, though, he must learn that their baby had not survived and he would blame her for that. Yet Hugh had died before the baby was born. Past and present were confused in her dream, and there was joy because after all Hugh had been spared; she must waste no time in spreading the news. George must be told, and that would be sad for him because it meant that their marriage was null and void. In her dream, her paralysis at last came to an end and she ran to catch Hugh before he mailed the letter while George stood waving sadly in the background. She was, however, her present age in the dream, with her blonde hair almost white and faint brown specks already beginning to show on the backs of her sinewy hands, while Hugh was as young as when she last saw him and unscarred by any wounds. Now a schoolgirl Norah appeared, wheeling a pram in which sat a laughing infant whom she knew as Harry, although he had died before he could sit up. For a moment, in the dream, she questioned his identity: was it really Harry or could it be Malcolm? No, it was Harry;

and beside the pram walked a fair-haired little girl: Louise. The fact that Louise was born years after Harry died was of no account in this happy scenario.

Suddenly it began to rain and the figures dissolved, Harry vanishing into a hole in the ground and the others dispersing like smoke, yet their disappearance was not distressing. She had been with them and it was bliss.

She woke feeling rested and content, more peaceful than for years, and was able to recapture calmly what had seemed so real. There was Hugh, young and strong, and the smiling child, and Norah before her fall from grace; horror had been banished and innocence restored. All recollection of Norah and George's nocturnal adventures had gone and Susan came down to breakfast smiling and happy until, seeing the others heavy-eyed and gulping down strong coffee, she remembered.

Would they tell her what had happened or would she be forced to ask?

George rose and kissed her cheek; it was soft and cool.

'Slept well, did you?' he asked.

'Yes,' said Susan, thus making it impossible to admit that she had heard them moving about in the night. 'I had the most wonderful dream.'

'Oh? What was that?' George had sat down again and picked up *The Times*, which he always read at the breakfast table. He peered at her over his half-glasses, giving her his full attention.

How old he looked, compared with Hugh in her dream. How lined he was, with deep furrows creasing his cheeks. His thick eyebrows were almost white. He was a kind, good man, and she felt thankful that she was not compelled to desert him for the situation provoked in her dream in order to return to Hugh, as she had chosen then.

If she told him about it, the memory might vanish; if she kept silent, the dream might return another night.

'I can't really remember now,' she said. 'Just that it was sunny and warm and no one was dead.'

'Perhaps it was all about heaven, then,' George suggested.

'Yes,' she agreed. 'Perhaps it was.'

Later that day Detective Constable Whitlock, who had been sent to Malchester on another inquiry, went round to Vaughan's Reliable Cars to find out how Malcolm had known about Louise's affair with Richard Blacker.

The place was locked up, with no sign of its proprietor, which, thought Whitlock, was tough on anyone wanting to buy a car. He took a look at those on view and decided his own Mazda had been a most judicious purchase.

While he was strolling about, feeling that Malcolm Vaughan was sure to turn up soon for work, the man himself was just settling in at the hotel where, to fill time before attempting to make new friends among the businessmen who were in their conference rooms, he had decided to have a sauna, which he saw was available, then a swim in the hotel's indoor pool. He found his swimming-trunks in one of the bags Brenda had packed, brightly patterned ones he had bought in Rhodes where he had gone with some girl whose name he could no longer remember.

The hotel's pool was part of a leisure complex used as a sports club by local people as well as hotel guests. When Malcolm went in, two elderly women and a grey-haired man were sedately swimming steady lengths, while in the gym women of varied ages, wearing leotards, laboured away on treadmills and stationary bicycles. Malcolm marched out of the changing room and dived into the pool between the two women swimmers; he made a considerable splash and a large displacement of water. He scraped the tiled floor of the pool, which was shallow and where diving was forbidden as stated on notices clearly visible to anyone entering the enclosure, but as he had gone extremely flat he did not damage himself except for stinging the whole of his chest and stomach. He swam angrily up and down. He was a strong swimmer and used a powerful crawl, breathing heavily, making a big wash and occupying the centre of the pool.

The three other older, regular swimmers, who normally progressed in silence, concentrating on maintaining their rhythm and counting their accomplished lengths, exchanged irritated glances as they drew level with each other, and formed an avoiding column in file to continue with their exercise. Such things happened sometimes. Inconsiderate hotel guests ignored the rights of others in the pool.

Malcolm behaved as if they were not there. He swam up and down until he tired, which was soon for he was far from fit and quickly became out of breath. He left the water, patting his chest, sleeking down the wet pelt of hair that covered it, trudging off towards the changing rooms. The three other swimmers adjusted their positions and carried on. They could all keep going indefinitely.

Malcolm felt refreshed and ready to give of his best when, afterwards, he met the conference delegates in the bar. Soon he interested one of them in buying a used car for his wife. He had led the conversation round to cars by asking what the various delegates drove. One company supplied their executives with Sierras or Granadas, according to status; the second ran mainly Montegos, with a few Rovers for the higher operatives. Malcolm found a man from the Montego range who expressed interest in something for his son, just down from university. That afternoon, when they broke for the day, the two potential customers met him at the workshop and he took them for spins in the Maestro and the Vitesse, hoping to sell them both, but the men were only amusing themselves and Malcolm was left with no sale.

He was about to follow them back to the hotel where he could charge a good meal to his account and look for new faces in the bar, perhaps even an available woman with a place of her own, when Detective Constable Whitlock arrived for a second attempt at catching him on the premises.

At first Malcolm thought his call was connected with the uniformed officer's visit during the night.

'I'm not sleeping here now,' he said, 'if that's why you've come, though there's nothing to stop me, if I've a mind to.'

'No, I'm sure there isn't,' agreed Whitlock, baffled at this line of talk. 'You've been living here for a while, have you?' he asked, trying to tune in.

'Only last night,' said Malcolm. 'I told that copper so. I'd decided to move from where I was and hadn't had time to make other arrangements. I'm fixed up now.'

'So where are you staying?' said Whitlock, for he might need to know.

Malcolm named the hotel, forgetting that he was registered there as Edward Tyler. 'I'm only there for a night or two,' he added. 'Just till I find a new place of my own. You can always contact me through my people, they live in Selbury.' This was supposed to reassure Whitlock as to his impeccable standing.

'I know that, Mr Vaughan,' said Whitlock. 'It's a family matter I want to discuss.'

'Oh?'

'About your sister,' said Whitlock.

'But I talked to someone the other day about her,' said Malcolm. 'That's all over and done with now and I mentioned then that I couldn't help.'

'Oh, but you did, Mr Vaughan,' said Whitlock. 'You told Detective Superintendent Marsh about Richard Blacker and we've traced him.'

'So?' Malcolm waited. What had they dug up? He had only mentioned Blacker to get the police off his own back.

'He confirmed what you said but denied seeing her that night,' said Whitlock, not adding that Blacker had no alibi.

'She might have gone to him afterwards,' Malcolm suggested. 'It's possible.'

'After what?'

'After she – after whatever happened to her,' he added, and went on more confidently, 'After she was attacked.'

'So she was attacked. You're sure of that?' Whitlock said carefully.

'Well, wasn't she? It's the only explanation,' said Malcolm. 'And she got away from the area. Or was taken.'

'You're suggesting she wasn't killed in Feringham, but was able to get to London?'

'Well, there was no blood in her car, was there? Or so it was said at the time,' Malcolm declared.

'How would she get to London without her car, unless someone took her?' asked Whitlock.

'There's a train,' said Malcolm. 'She used it every day to get to work. It's possible.'

'But she had no money. Her handbag was in the car.'

'A lift, then. She hitched.'

'But why? Why should she want to get away? Wouldn't she want to go home, if she'd been assaulted?'

'Maybe she didn't want to face them. They fussed over her all the time, as if she was made of china,' said Malcolm, and there was bitterness in his tone even twelve years later.

'If that's so, why didn't whoever gave her a lift come forward?'

'Well, would you, if you were the last person to see her alive?'

'Yes, if I had nothing to do with her death,' said Whitlock.

'Maybe he was the bloke who did for her,' Malcolm suggested.

'Will you tell me about your own trip to Heathrow that night?' Whitlock invited.

'Oh, I can't remember the details now,' said Malcolm

irritably. 'I told the police at the time. I was living in Cornton then, and I had to pick up these Americans at the Star Hotel and take them to catch a plane. It was about nine at night – their flight, I mean.'

They would have had to be there long before takeoff. Malcolm would have had plenty of time to get over to Feringham after dropping them and meet his sister when her rehearsal was over.

'How long does it take to drive from Heathrow to Cornton?' Whitlock wondered aloud. 'Or rather, how long did it take then, before the M25 was built?'

'Less than two hours,' Malcolm said. 'Though you'd need to allow that in case of delays.'

'So you could have dropped them and driven to Feringham by nine or nine-fifteen. The choir practice ended at around ten-fifteen that night.'

'What are you getting at?' Blood rushed into Malcolm's face as he spoke.

'You could have met your sister. You could have been the man who attacked her,' said Whitlock.

Malcolm's face was almost purple. Veins bulged on his temples and his slightly protuberant blue eyes glared at Whitlock who recognised, then, his potential for violence. Whitlock's nose for the hunt sharpened.

'Is that what happened?' he asked, very quietly.

A pulse worked in Malcolm's jaw and he clenched his fists to prevent himself from lashing out at the man.

'What a suggestion,' he said, almost hissing the words. 'Why should I want to hurt my sister?'

'But she wasn't really your sister, was she? You might have felt something about her that wasn't in the least brotherly,' Whitlock pressed him. 'As you weren't true kin, it wouldn't have been incest.' He used the word bluntly.

'There was nothing like that,' said Malcolm, his tone flat as he bit back the expletives he felt like uttering. 'She – we didn't get on all that well,' he added.

'You never said that at the time,' Whitlock pounced.

'No – well, I wasn't going to say anything bad about her, was I?' said Malcolm. 'After all, she was dead, or so everyone seemed to think.'

'Suppose you did meet,' said Whitlock. 'Suppose you saw her by chance that night.' He decided to leave for the moment the point that Malcolm could have travelled to Feringham on purpose to see her away from their parents. He would have known about the choir and where to find her. 'Suppose you quarrelled and she ran off?'

'Well?'

'Did you run after her?'

'What do you mean, did I? This is all your idea. It isn't what happened,' said Malcolm.

But as he made the denial, Whitlock knew he had hit his target. He could see the iron effect Malcolm, not a man notable for his self-control, was putting into keeping his temper. It was not a natural reaction to what was being alleged.

'Did you catch her, Mr Vaughan?' he said softly. 'I think you should let me know.' For an instant he wondered about cautioning Vaughan, then let it go. The moment might pass and he had no evidence. That could come later.

But Malcolm was holding on.

'I never saw her that night,' he said.

'I think you did,' said Whitlock. He waited, but Vaughan said no more. 'You quarrelled and she ran off, leaving her car. You moved it later.' That would account for the seat being pushed back to accommodate longer legs than Louise's.

'You've got a vivid imagination,' Malcolm replied. 'You should try writing a thriller. You'd do well.' He stared at Whitlock, swaying a little, determined to outface him.

'Truth's often stranger than fiction,' said Whitlock tritely. 'And I mean to get at the truth of this, but it's waited a long time and it can wait longer yet.'

He must tell Marsh about it, see if Vaughan could be brought in and given as much of a hard time as was possible now, under PACE. If he was feeling inner guilt, he might confess, but there was not a shred of evidence to use against him, nor any new light on where to search for some.

'I'll be speaking to you about this again,' he said, and left. The question about Blacker could wait; this had priority.

Afterwards, Malcolm sat at his desk in a turmoil. If he told the truth, he would not be believed, any more than he would have been at the time. Only two people knew what had really happened that night and one of them was dead. Protection lay in silence.

He would have to leave. That detective had been like a terrier with a rat, determined to shake something out of him, the merest admission on which to build a case, however circumstantial it might be, and he would be able to do it for want of proof to the contrary. Malcolm had no illusions about the police; they would fit him up if they chose.

He had intended to seek some proof, at the Lodge House, that there was a connection between him and Norah, force her to pay him, if not his due, certainly money for keeping quiet. His intention, then, had been to stave off court action over his debts; now there was more from which he must escape, and it was urgent. He must act without delay.

Canada, he thought: it was far away, required no entry visa, the language was the same and he could soon be absorbed into the country, losing his pursuers. Unless Louise's body was found, they would have no grounds for attempting to extradite him, and she had lain hidden so long that only a fluke would deliver her up to them now. He must raise all the cash he could at once, which meant selling the cars he still had, cutting his losses, making what he could out of them without wasting time looking for profit. And he would go to the Lodge House to see what he could achieve there. They wouldn't want a scandal to break over their greying heads.

He went back to the hotel where his possessions were stashed away in his comfortable room. A good dinner would restore him, give him the strength he would need for what lay ahead, and he'd let his new friends there know he was going to Canada very soon and he would undertake commissions. Then he'd make a plan for tackling the three at the Lodge House. He needed to know the truth about Norah and the child she had had, still convinced that she had lied, perhaps about dates, and that he was that infant, for it explained everything, her links with the Vaughans, her authoritarian manner. She'd been so strict on her visits, always defending Louise against him, and making him stand in the corner for lying when he denied taking a pound from his grandmother's purse. The fact that he was guilty did nothing to mitigate Malcolm's sense of resentment, as strong now as it had been then, when he was twelve.

Women, he thought: too many of them had been around in his life, messing things up. First his mother, conceiving him carelessly and then not standing by what she had done but selling him to the highest bidder; then Susan, and her mother who was ruthless when Susan was always conciliatory; then Louise, who was George's pet and who would not submit. He had almost forgotten Gwynneth, his wife, and the women between until Brenda, the latest, had failed him.

There would be women in Canada, bold frontierswomen used to an outdoor life, thought Malcolm, who hated that sort of existence himself, or business women needing a man to run things. Either type would suit him. Cheered by this positive thinking, he had a good evening at the hotel. The delegates were, in the main, used to all sorts and listened with tolerance to his tales of success in Australia, and he generously stood unlimited drinks all round, charging them to his account.

In the morning he used guile.

He went to his office and dialled the Lodge House. When George answered the telephone, he did a trick he had been shown by an Australian con man; he put two fingers into his mouth, between his teeth, to affect his articulation, and he pitched his voice into a Cockney timbre, such as he had sometimes attempted in jest, lowering the tone to make it sound deeper. He said he was speaking for Superintendent Marsh, who had something important he wished to show Mr Vaughan, something that had come to light out of their area but near the railway embankment just outside Reading. Would Mr Vaughan meet the superintendent at Sonning, where a police car would convey him the rest of the way? Malcolm was pleased with himself for using that word; the police always used words like convey and proceed. The superintendent further suggested, Malcolm went on, that at this moment in time it might be best not to mention the purpose of his journey to Mrs Vaughan but to make some excuse.

George's voice was level and calm as he replied that yes, that would be quite all right, he would set off at once and be there in about an hour.

Malcolm chortled with glee at the ease of this deception. He thinks they've found Louise, he congratulated himself; it would be at least two hours before George realised that it was a hoax, and longer before he returned to the Lodge. Malcolm left the Porsche, so clearly identifiable, on the forecourt and got into the Metro, not clipping on the trade plates which would be an instant giveaway. He drove towards Selbury planning how to get Susan, if she happened to be at home, out of the house so that he could search through the drawers at his ease. He'd dig up some sort of dirt, for sure, enough to make them finance his departure. They'd be glad to see him go, he thought bitterly, just as they were when they sent him off to Australia. Well, they need not think they had seen the last of him; he'd be back when things died down, or he'd find a way to go on bleeding them from a distance.

Driving on, he remembered stories he had been told about various confidence tricks successfully played by men he had met in prison. People were gullible, he had learned; they wanted to believe messages relayed in a confident manner or persons who appeared at the door well dressed and carrying credentials which at first glance appeared to be genuine.

George and Malcolm passed on the road, but George barely noticed the Metro going the other way; Malcolm, however, had been looking out for the Volvo. George was gazing straight ahead, concentrating on the road and his mission. Malcolm laughed aloud.

Two miles from Selbury, he stopped at a callbox and waited there for twenty minutes. It was agony to waste time, but he must let enough elapse to make his next story credible. By now George had been gone from the house for about forty minutes.

Malcolm dialled the Lodge House again, and this time Susan answered. He put on an American accent, pitching the tone higher this time, and said he was sorry to trouble her but her husband had been involved in a road accident near Henley-on-Thames and was on his way to hospital in Oxford.

'Which hospital?' snapped Susan, her voice almost a scream. 'The John Radcliffe?'

Malcolm had not foreseen the complication of several Oxford hospitals. The one she mentioned would do for his purpose.

'Yes,' he agreed, and added, 'He's not badly injured.' He had never wanted to hurt Susan. 'A broken leg, and some cuts,' he elaborated. 'I was just passing by and he asked me to call you.'

Susan's voice was still shrill with fright as she thanked him. He hung up before she could ask any more questions. Then he drove on to Selbury and parked in the village square where he could watch who emerged from the road that led to Selbury House and the Lodge. No one would recognise him in the Metro. There was an old cloth cap in the glove compartment, one he had used when taking the car to a prospective customer a few days before; he put it on and crouched down behind the wheel as if he was having a snooze.

Ten minutes later Norah's Golf, not Susan's car, paused at the road junction, then pulled out and headed off towards the Oxford road. The two women were in the car; of course, Norah would never allow Susan to set off after George alone. Now the coast was clear at the Lodge; he would have plenty of time to ferret about and find what he could, steal Susan's jewellery and any money that was lying around, leave the impression that they had been deceived by some outside thief, not their son taking only what was his own.

By the time he reached the Lodge House he had forgotten that his original aim had been blackmail of a sort. He had forgotten, too, Mrs Gibson, who had come in daily to clean for his grandmother and now came twice a week to help Norah, for even Susan did not expect her to undertake every domestic task.

Malcolm parked his car in the garage, whose doors were

open. Susan's Opel was not in sight; it was, in fact, being serviced, but Malcolm did not wonder about it for long as he closed the doors so that no casual caller or passer-by could notice the Metro. Then he let himself in with his key.

Mrs Gibson had heard his approach and was in the hall as he entered, one hand on the vacuum cleaner which she was about to use in the drawing-room.

'Oh Malcolm, why didn't you get here sooner?' she exclaimed. 'Your poor mother – you've just missed her. She's gone off to the hospital. It's a terrible thing, your father has been in a car smash.'

'Oh,' said Malcolm. He was astonished to see her. 'I've come to collect some papers they've left for me,' he said, thinking furiously. 'It's important or I'd come back another time. I wonder if they've left them ready. I'll just have a look. Then I'll go after them,' he added. That was a good touch: Mrs Gibson would expect it.

'Right,' said Mrs Gibson.

She would not query his presence, but she would tell George and Susan later that he had been to the house. If she did that, they would know the identity of the hoaxer, especially when things were missing. He would have to see about this complication but he put it to the back of his mind while he dealt with what was, at the moment, his main task.

'I'll make you some coffee,' said Mrs Gibson, abandoning the sweeper and padding off towards the kitchen. She was old, now, and shapeless, her body a wedge above sturdy legs in warm tights. He had known her for most of his life. While she was out of the way, he went to Susan's desk in the drawing-room and looked inside. It was tidy, quite unlike his own; a few bills, all paid, were held in a clip. Envelopes and headed writing-paper were stacked in pigeon holes; there were files to do with her charity work and her art interests in the drawers, but no diary, no evidence from the past. In the bottom drawer was a file full of cuttings about Louise's disappearance and an envelope.

'Found it, dear?' asked Mrs Gibson, returning with a cup of coffee and two custard creams.

'No. Perhaps she went off in such a hurry that there wasn't time to leave it out,' Malcolm said. 'I'll just make sure.'

Inside the envelope was a copy of Susan's will. Malcolm read it carefully after Mrs Gibson had left the room, murmuring that she would leave him in peace and get on elsewhere.

It was dated the previous week. He saw that only when he had read, with disbelief, its provisions, and turned to the signatures on the final page. The witnesses were the vicar and his wife.

Susan had carried out one of the most positive acts of her life and had virtually deleted him as her heir. Everything was to go to George, with no trusts or restrictions of any description. If they died together, or he died first, the beneficiaries were his sister's children. Apart from that, and a legacy to Mrs Gibson, five thousand pounds were to go to Norah Tyler, and a further five thousand to Malcolm.

Five miserable grand! Why, she would be leaving hundreds of thousands! The Lodge House alone must be worth two hundred thousand or more.

The truth was that, by helping him so much over the years, Susan had depleted her capital to such an extent that apart from the house there was not a great deal for George to inherit.

Malcolm closed the drawers of the desk. He went upstairs to Susan's bedroom, and was taking the jewellery out of her red leather case – her engagement ring from Hugh – she always wore George's – her mother's rings, two of them very valuable, one set with diamonds and sapphires and the other a large square emerald surrounded with diamonds; her diamond drop earrings; several brooches and clips – when Mrs Gibson, carrying the sweeper, came into the room and stood staring in amazement at what he was doing.

'Why, whatever are you up to, Malcolm?' she exclaimed, and before she could say any more he had rounded on her and caught her by the neck, shaking her, squeezing the life out of her. Her horrified eyes stared at him above her purpling face as she made little choking sounds which soon ceased as her gaze went blank. She was dead.

As he strangled her, Malcolm cursed her, calling her a silly, interfering cow and many worse epithets, not consciously intending to kill her, merely wanting to silence her and protect himself and, at the same time, hurt someone for what had been done to him by denying him, as he saw it, his due inheritance.

When he let her go, he flung her across Susan's bed like a stuffed doll and she fell limp, her head to one side, her arms spread out.

He was shaking. He took some deep breaths to steady himself, then put the jewellery in his pocket, wrapping it first in some handkerchiefs of Susan's. He had time now; no one else would interrupt, and he looked in the bedside cabinet to see if there was anything useful there, in the end tipping the drawers on to the floor. There was a volume of poems by Walter de la Mare in one, and as it fell a faded envelope that might have been marking a place dropped out. It was an old letter addressed to Mrs Hugh Graham, and Malcolm couldn't think who that was at first; then he remembered that it had been Susan's first married name.

There was a letter inside the envelope. It was very short:

Dear Sue,
You'll only receive this letter if I don't come back some night or other. If that happens, please see that Norah is taken care of. She's a darling girl and she thinks she loves me, so she'll be sad, but there's no commitment between us and I'm not sure if she'll feel the same when she's older. Besides, what would mother say?
Lots of love,
David.

The letter bore a date in August 1943. Two weeks later, David had been reported missing, believed dead.

She'd had it off with David, then, the filthy slut! But did that mean that he was David's son? If so, he truly was a Vaughan. For a moment Malcolm felt quite dizzy, until he took in the date and saw that it was seven years earlier than the one on his own birth certificate. The letter didn't mention a baby, but surely David knew about it? Surely that was what was meant about taking care of Norah?

Malcolm did not work out that David would probably have worded his letter differently if he had known that Norah was pregnant. All he knew was that what he had imagined was untrue: Norah was not his mother. The baby Norah should have had had been got rid of so that it would not bring disgrace to the respectable Vaughans.

Malcolm put the letter in his pocket, along with the things he had stolen. Then he looked at the body of Mrs Gibson.

He would have to conceal the fact that she had been strangled, and any trace of his presence in the house. He hadn't worn gloves; his fingerprints would be all over this room.

Hurrying now, for George might already have discovered that he had been lured out on a false trail, and Susan and Norah would soon make a similar deduction, Malcolm ran downstairs and out to the shed where petrol for the mower was always stored. He brought the can into the house and poured the contents over the floor in the hall and up the carpeted staircase. Then he lit some crumpled paper and flung it down to start up the blaze. He had used fire before to vent his rage; now it fulfilled a more useful function.

It was only twelve o'clock as he drove away.

PART THREE

1

Carol

Carol Foster read about it on Thursday in the *Daily Mirror*, which Eric's mother bought every morning from the newsagent's on the corner. It was on the kitchen dresser when Carol called in after work to collect Joanna and William. Her mother-in-law always picked them up from school, took them home with her and gave them tea, amusing them until Carol arrived, when she, too, would be given tea and a slice of home-made cake to tide her over until she and Eric had their meal together later.

BODY IN BLAZE, she saw, in banner headlines, and below, in large black print: DOOMED FAMILY LOSE HOME IN FUNERAL PYRE. She did not pay attention, for she seldom bothered with news of any sort; there was plenty going on in the world which she could not influence and which she preferred to ignore. What concerned her was the destruction of the environment and how it would affect succeeding generations, more particularly her own children. One day, she hoped, they might be able to move into the country, but property was expensive everywhere and especially outside the town; here there were the conveniences of urban living: good schools, buses, a leisure centre with a splendid swimming-pool, and work for her within easy reach of home. Eric ran a car, an elderly Citroën, cherished because he saw no prospect of ever affording a replacement, and he had the permanent drain on his finances of supporting his first wife, Frances, and their daughters who were now in their teens.

'I never liked that Frances,' her mother-in-law had confided, some time after she and Eric were married. 'Gave herself too many airs, she did. Eric's better off with you.'

Carol knew that Frances had locked Eric out of the house one night and never allowed him back, and for no apparent reason; she had simply tired of the married state. They had divorced discreetly, without rancour, on the grounds of desertion by Eric of Frances, and ever since that time Eric had paid her mortgage and an allowance, regularly increasing, for the girls.

'Terrible thing, that,' said Ethel Foster, seeing Carol glancing at the paper. 'As if they hadn't had enough to put up with, poor things. I remember that case well.'

'What case was that?' asked Carol, adding, 'More tea, Mother?'

Hearing that she was an orphan, Ethel had insisted that she be thus addressed when Eric announced that they were getting married. Ever since that day she had made Carol feel truly loved, seeing her through the births of both children, their subsequent mumps and chicken-pox and other mild disasters, and Carol loved her in return.

'Please, dear.'

Carol poured out more tea for Mrs Foster and a second cup for herself. The children were sitting in front of the television set watching *Neighbours*, like almost every other child in the land. Carol thought it a wholesome programme; she had called it the Enid Blyton of the soaps to Eric, who, unlike his mother, understood exactly what she meant. During its span, she and Ethel had a chance for a quiet chat. She enjoyed these interludes, when she felt safe and sheltered in the small semi-detached house where Eric had grown up. Ethel had lived there nearly all her married life and throughout her widowhood, and Carol knew she had a secret dread of being forced to leave it through old age or some infirmity.

'I doubt if you'd remember it,' Ethel was saying, 'It'd be before you came back to England. They lost their daughter years ago. Murdered.' She lowered her voice to say this, nodding towards the children who were engrossed in the doings of Charlene.

'Read it, dear,' said Ethel, frowning, with a finger to her lips. Murder was not a topic for her grandchildren's ears.

Carol kicked off her shoes, sank into the dilapidated armchair beside Mrs Foster's blazing coal fire and tucked her feet up under her, taking a bite of chocolate cake as she did so. Mrs Foster regarded her with sharp, affectionate interest as she read the front-page outline, then, putting her cake down on the worn velour of the chair-arm, turned the page to follow the more detailed story within. She was an odd, quiet girl and had seemed a little lost at first when she joined their family, but it had been a lucky day for Eric when he met her in the library; she suited him, and he adored her.

'Well, they're all right, at least,' Carol said at last.

'Who, dear?'

'The – the parents. The Vaughans.' Carol was surprised to hear her own voice sound so steady in her ears.

'Yes. What a thing to do – lure them away by hoax telephone calls and then rob the place. That poor woman, though, the cleaning lady. I don't suppose he expected to find her there.'

'No, I suppose not.'

This was not brilliant deduction on the part of Ethel, merely an echo of Detective Superintendent Marsh's words at a hasty press conference held on the night of the crime.

'He'll have cased the place, known they had plenty of stuff after moving out of such a big house,' went on Ethel, who like many kindly people enjoyed following lurid and gruesome crimes at second hand and regularly watched police series on television. 'Someone local, it was, you mark my words, or someone who'd made a study of their habits.'

'Just as long as they weren't hurt themselves,' said Carol. She had been quite shocked, Ethel noticed with surprise; her face had turned quite pale. But then she had a tender heart; she salvaged wounded birds attacked by cats and had kept a lost hedgehog through a winter's hibernation.

'The woman would have recognised him, you see,'

Ethel went on. 'Could have described him, if he'd let her go.'

'Yes.' Carol unfolded her legs. 'May I have another cup of tea?'

'Of course, dear. You don't have to ask,' said Ethel comfortably. She loved these sessions, her little gossip with her daughter-in-law, the children stretched out on the floor on their stomachs, eyes glued to the screen. After they had gone, she always missed them; the house felt lonely and cold, even though in fact it was always warm and snug.

Carol and Eric lived twenty minutes walk away, in a modern house on an estate being built as they were married; Eric had taken out a large mortgage to obtain it, but Carol too was working then, in the office behind the scenes at Boots. She had carried on until six weeks before Joanna was born and, as soon as the baby was four months old, she had found evening work in a hotel nearby, serving drinks and snacks in the bar. Ethel had known that Carol hated it, though she never complained. It was the only way she saw then to bring in some income. After William was born, she took in typing and translating for an agency; it seemed that she was very good at French, which was a surprise, but she talked so little about the past.

She told them that her parents had been killed in a road accident when she was very young. At that time they had lived in the south. After this, she had gone to live with her only relative, her mother's sister in Australia. When her aunt died, Carol had decided to return to England. She had had various jobs, she explained, moving about the country, wanting to learn about it; then she had met Eric.

Carol had thought it out carefully, devising it in such a way that she could not be caught out easily, and hard to check unless anyone grew suspicious. She'd used it to account for why she had no official papers – no National Health card, none of the documents necessary for a normal life. She had done temporary work for several years, work which was paid in cash. Then she'd found a way to confirm her new identity.

'Terrible, that, to lose their daughter. Never to know about her,' Ethel said. 'Murdered, of course, that Louise.'

'Yes,' said Carol faintly.

It was true. Louise had been done to death, but by her own hand, and here she sat, twelve years later, reborn as Carol, owner of official marriage lines.

On the way home Carol bought two papers for herself, all that were available as they passed the newsagent's on the way to the bus-stop. She bought the children sweets to keep them quiet; she had never bought them comics. Had she read any as a girl? She didn't think so; pony books were what she had liked at ten. Suddenly, crystal-clear, she remembered her father reading the *Eagle*, which he had ordered for Malcolm, and saying to her mother that it was a pity the boy wouldn't read it as it was fun.

The memory pierced her with an agony that was like an arrow wound.

Such things rarely happened now, but sometimes a chance word, some phrase overheard, brought back the days of childhood as if they were only yesterday. Most of the time she successfully blanked out the past, except occasionally in dreams. She had her new life with Eric and the children. Meeting him had been the turning point, for he had offered her a future, and he must never learn how she had deceived him. All she wanted was here, in Tetterton, two hundred miles away from Selbury. Never mind that she had been the one to leave, while Malcolm, the outsider who had caused her flight, had remained.

She kept her emotions in check in the bus, listening to the children, joining in their conversation. Later she would read the papers carefully, savour every detail they disclosed about her parents and their present circumstances. Now she knew they were both alive; she had often wondered if one of them had died. How they must have suffered when she ran away! At the time she had known they would grieve, but since she had had children of her own, she had understood more personally the pain she had inflicted on them; the worst thing that could happen to her would be for harm to befall either Joanna or William.

She could have escaped from the claustrophobic trap she felt her parents weaving round her by a different means; she could have gone to work abroad, in Paris or Geneva, say; or even in America. People did that sort of thing to get away from mothers who wanted them to make safe marriages and repeat the pattern. She'd gone a bit mad, she realised now, flipping when Malcolm got into her car that night in Feringham. But after what he'd done to her, she lost her head completely.

You don't scream when your adopted brother gets into

your car. You don't run through the streets yelling 'Rape!' even if that's what he did to you only a few nights previously. And you don't tell your parents about it, because your mother might not believe you, and if your father did, he would be furious enough to kill Malcolm. Besides, she had felt so guilty; she should have been able to protect herself, not let it happen, only Malcolm was so strong and she had felt unable to call out. He'd known that, banked on it, his hand over her mouth as they struggled in the silence of the night. It had all been over very quickly; he couldn't have had much pleasure from it, but he had destroyed her, and that, she thought much later, was really what he meant to do. He hated her.

During the subsequent nights she had scarcely slept and at the choral society practice was barely aware of what was going on around her. No one seemed to notice; she supposed she looked much as usual, and one of the delights of singing was that it took you right out of yourself so that you thought about nothing else. She had managed her job without making any serious mistakes; obviously someone else had finished editing the books that she was working on, and the series had been completed by a colleague for she had seen the resulting publications in the library and had felt a pang of envy.

Thank God she hadn't got pregnant. She went on feeling soiled for years; in fact she'd never fully recovered her self-esteem though things were easier as Carol, who was another person.

She bathed the children and they came downstairs in their dressing-gowns to wait for Eric's return. He would be late tonight, for there was a training session at the store. Eric was head of the furnishing department at a big branch of a nationwide department store in Flintham, twenty miles away. When they met, he was an accounts clerk in a china works; then, due to a takeover, he lost his job and had to start again. He had crawled slowly up the ladder in the store, learning new ways, coping with new sorts of colleagues, determined to succeed, and she admired him. It was all so different from anything she had known before and that made it easier to forget Louise. She trusted Eric, and his mother, and she supposed they trusted her, which made her all the more resolved never to fail them, or her children.

She had a good job now, herself, as secretary to the managing director of a plastics firm, the sort of job that Norah had. Carol had not thought about her for years. She must have retired by now and probably was living in a retirement flat in Eastbourne or some other coastal town. That had been her plan.

The children had sandwiches and milky drinks for supper. While they ate their meal in front of the fire – a gas one, there were no open fires in this house – Carol put the casserole she had prepared that morning in the oven, spread the papers on the table and read through their reports of the killing in Selbury. She remembered Mrs Gibson, a plump middle-aged woman who had cleaned for her grandmother. Of course the old lady must be dead; she would have been ninety-four or so by now. They'd sold the big house, it appeared, and were living in the Lodge. It must seem very small. Why had that happened? Had they lost their money? She couldn't imagine her mother enjoying lowered status in the county.

In one of the papers there was an old photograph of her when she was Louise, with her straight blonde hair framing her thin face. She looked very young and solemn.

Carol had dark hair worn in pre-Raphaelite curls, a style that had come in not so long after she ran away. At first she had dyed it black, but gradually she had lightened it to a nondescript brown and perhaps by now it would have faded anyway. She rinsed it regularly, hiding the bottles of colouring from Eric, just as she hid so much from him.

There would be more in the papers tomorrow. She bundled today's together, folded them and took them upstairs to hide beneath her sweaters in a drawer.

She was just dishing up the vegetables when Eric came in, looking tired. He had been learning a new computerised system for operation in the store; supposed to make things easier, it was, in fact, quite complicated and susceptible to human error. Once he had mastered it, it would be his task to train new entrants to his department.

As always when he came home, his heart gave a little lift of happiness: here she was, his lovely, strange, secretive girl whom he could never hope to understand completely, but then how could any human totally understand another? He loved the homely scene, the children, clean and smelling sweet of soap and Johnson's baby powder, playing some childish game and waiting to wrap themselves around him with adoring hugs. They loved him now but they might not always feel the same; his older daughters had once seemed to think him wonderful, but now he thought he simply had their toleration.

Since his promotion to head of department money had

been easier, and they could afford to do things outside the home. Carol took the children swimming once a week, and she went to evening classes on a Thursday, studying the History of Art, which she found absorbing. She had also joined Tetterton's Choral Society, a long-established choir which performed at Christmas and at Easter. She liked that, and always returned from practice looking happy. Eric was out two nights a week as well; on Tuesdays he went to German lessons and on Fridays he helped at a youth club. On the few evenings they spent together they got on very well. Eric was kind, and had been badly hurt by his first wife's rejection. Carol was grateful for his gentleness and the shelter of his name; she tried to be all that a good wife should, so that he might never regret their marriage. She could never make amends for cheating him, but she could be loyal. What she felt for him was a deep and calm affection, peaceful after the pain of her affair with Richard and the terror Malcolm had inflicted on her. Eric was never angry; he was sometimes rather quiet and would go off for a solitary weekend walk or even before breakfast in the morning, but that was because he had things on his mind, not because he was angry with her or the children. He worried a lot: about money and the children's future; about his older daughters over whom he had so little influence and whom he saw only once a month when they spent Sunday afternoon with him and his new family. These were difficult times; Carol feared that the girls would be bored and then they would cease to come at all.

They were nice girls. She had suggested various expeditions as her own two grew older, trips to the country to watch wildlife or look for rare flowers. Eric was amazed at how much she knew about these things and her ability to discover where to see them. They went for walks beside canals and rivers, and once had a rare weekend on a barge, a big success, with the older girls cheerfully helping with the cooking and glad to operate the locks. The weather had been glorious and they had seen all sorts of waterside creatures. In the evening Carol had read them *The Wind in the Willows*, and William had spent the next day vainly looking for Mole and Ratty. For a girl who had grown up in Australia, she knew an extraordinary amount about English natural history.

Carol felt nervous about the old photograph of her that appeared in the press. There were likely to be more, unless some other case stole the headlines. Would anyone think she looked like Louise Vaughan?

'Oh, do I?' she planned to say, if someone mentioned it. 'How peculiar.'

But no one did. Only Eric, some days after the first reports, reading the latest instalment and a résumé of Louise's disappearance, had wondered who the photograph of the missing young woman with her fair, straight hair, reminded him of, failing to glance across the room at his small daughter whose own fair, straight hair, at that moment was caught back in a single plait.

Carol carried on with her established routine.

Mornings were busy, with the children to get up and ready for school after Eric had finished in the bathroom. She made sure he had plenty of time to shave and prepare for the day and saw him off, in his dark suit with his spotless shirt and a restrained tie, well before she and the children had to go. She had always risen early, so that was no new challenge for her, and she made preparations for the evening meal before leaving the house. Long ago she had left Selbury House at seven to catch her train to London; her father had followed an hour later, travelling first class. When she first returned to live at home he had said it would be nice if they travelled together, but she had refused to let him pay the difference on her fare and she didn't like watching his discomfort as their train filled at stations along the line. So she had said she must go earlier and he had taken the hint.

Poor Daddy. She really loved him, and Mummy too, but they had made her feel too precious. It was easy to understand but it had laid a burden on her, and had provoked Malcolm's jealousy. Norah, on her visits, had noticed a lot and understood more than she let on. She had saved Carol, when she was Louise, from some of Malcolm's torments and she would certainly have believed what Malcolm had done that dreadful night. Carol had thought about going to see her in the flat in Pimlico, telling her about it, seeking her help, but what could Norah do? Telling their parents would only cause worse trouble, and it was impossible to involve the police; the scandal and the shame would be unbearable.

She had been so feeble. She saw it now. She should never have come home, but it had been a simple solution to her problem over Richard, making the break easier. That was when she should have struck a blow for independence and gone abroad instead of taking the easy way, and if Malcolm had been around she might have done things differently, but he had been safely in Australia. Besides, she enjoyed her job and did not want to give it up; seeing the series through was interesting and she liked liaising with the authors and the artists.

She had had no plan, that night, jumping out of the car in terror and running down the street. In fact, she had not thought at all when Malcolm suddenly opened the passenger door and got in beside her, laying his hand on her leg. She'd braked and leaped out, regardless of whether any other car was coming up behind, but in fact the traffic lights where she had stopped were at the junction of four residential streets, busy by day but quiet at night, and by chance there was no one about. It seemed, from later reports in the press, that she had not been noticed. She realised afterwards that he had known the route that she would take and had lain in wait for her at this spot. If the lights had not been red, she would not have stopped, but he'd have chased her, waylaid her in the country, maybe overpowered her once again.

If her car door had been locked, she would have been safe, but the passenger's side was faulty. He knew that.

She'd run and run through the steady rain that was falling, dashing down an alley when she heard Malcolm start up the car to follow her.

The alley – a narrow footpath between two rows of houses – emerged quite near the station. She had not been reasoning at all when she rushed towards it, but as she ran into the booking hall, she realised that this could be a safe place because there would be staff about.

But the station was deserted. At that hour, the booking

office was closed and if you caught a late train you paid the guard, if there was one, or at the other end.

She had hidden in the ladies' room, which was unlocked, bolting herself into a lavatory. There was less vandalism then; today even such a sanctuary would have been denied her. She did not know how long she crouched there in the darkness, afraid to turn the light on, hardly breathing, expecting at any moment to hear footsteps in pursuit. At last, after what felt like hours but was more likely thirty minutes, she thought it would be safe to telephone her father from the station call-box, tell some tale about her car being stolen and ask him to come and fetch her.

Nervously, peering about lest Malcolm was lurking in the shadows, she approached the red cubicle which smelled of stale tobacco smoke and worse, only to find that the instrument had been pulled from its fixture and she could not make the call. If she walked to another box, Malcolm could be waiting for her somewhere in the streets of Feringham. She stood there, helpless, wondering what to do. Then she heard a train approaching.

There was a scarf in her raincoat pocket. She put it over her wet hair and tied it under her chin. Then she walked to the end of the platform where the last coach would draw in, hiding against the buildings, hoping the driver would not notice her.

No one left the train as she dashed across and got into the empty last coach.

She had not thought then of disappearing; in fact she had not thought of anything except avoiding Malcolm. She had no money, and no plan for when she reached the terminus. Shivering, she put her hands in her pockets, shrinking into the corner. What would she say if a guard came along? Would she be arrested?

She was trembling, and she shook and shivered through the first half of the journey. The train stopped at quiet stations. No one entered her coach. When she reached London she would explain to the ticket collector that she had lost her handbag. She would suggest they telephoned her father who would guarantee her fare; then she would return on the next train, even if she had missed the last one and might have to wait until morning. Her father would meet her. When that happened she would decide how to explain her flight. He and her mother must already be wondering where she was, since she was never so late home after the choral society meeting. She might have to explain her actions, but she'd somehow do it, even if it made her sound as if she'd lost her wits. She had, she told herself; of course, she had.

Then she saw the purse. It was tucked down the side of the seat facing her, where, unnoticed, it had fallen from its owner's capacious bucket-bag. It took her nearly ten minutes to overcome her scruples enough to pick it up and open it. Inside was some change and nearly fifty pounds in notes, as well as an Access card and a driver's licence. It also contained a rail season ticket between London and a station two stops beyond Feringham. The owner of the ticket might not have needed to show it, either because she was well known to the collector or because the station was, like Feringham, imperfectly manned, and had possibly still not discovered the loss of the purse. The train had started back without it being noticed; at this hour, no one would look through the coaches.

If I leave it here, someone else may steal it, Louise reasoned. I can take it, use the ticket to get off the platform, borrow some money for the night and return it to its owner when I've decided what to do.

She laid the purse back on the seat opposite, staring at it, her talisman to freedom. Should she use it? Was fate dictating what she ought to do?

As the train drew in to the terminus, she picked up the purse and removed the ticket. Showing it at the barrier, she walked through unchallenged and went straight to the station hotel, which had an entrance from the platform. She had often used its first-floor cloakroom in the past, and she went there now, though without a comb or make-up, while she decided what should happen next.

She never once considered going round to Richard's flat, asking for help or, at the least, shelter for the night. She did think of taking a taxi to some friends, then dismissed the idea. Something strange had happened to her; she was letting events manipulate her, not her own free will.

The name on the driver's licence was Carol Mount. That was who was sheltering in the ladies' cloakroom in the station hotel, washing, smoothing her hair, doing what she could to freshen up. Instinct, though, told her to lie low, not make herself conspicuous by wanting a late meal or occupying a seat in the lounge. She had a lot of money; fifty pounds in 1976 was more than enough to pay for a room for the night and have a great deal over, but she had no luggage and, if a search were made for her, the desk clerk might remember her if questioned.

She moved off down the corridor and tried a few doors. All the rooms were locked, but eventually she found one that yielded, opening into a housemaid's cupboard. Fatalistic now — if she was caught, she would say who she was and plead loss of memory — she went inside and closed the door. There she spent the night, curled up on the floor, chilly, sleeping a little now and then. When first light came she went back to the cloakroom and, eventually, left the hotel unchallenged.

Even then she could have gone to the office, somehow resumed normality, but instead she crossed London by tube and went to Euston station. There, she had some food and wondered where to go. It must be somewhere north, to Scotland, maybe?

There weren't enough people in Scotland. She had been to the Highlands with her parents, on a touring holiday years ago. Malcolm was with them, bored and bad-tempered, and it had not been a successful experiment. By a loch they'd hired a boat; Malcolm had tried to push her overboard. She wouldn't think about him; she'd go somewhere where he'd never been.

In the end she walked along the road to King's Cross and caught a train to Leeds, which was large and might offer anonymity. York, more interesting to her, would be smaller, more Louise's choice; Carol Mount was setting off for Leeds.

Though she had intended to repay the money she had used to the real Carol Mount, whose address was on her driving licence, she had never done so. She owed her everything, in fact: her name; her fresh start; her liberty, for that was what, despite the insecurity and the fear that haunted her during the first months, she had ultimately gained.

Every day, now, she bought the papers to read about the Selbury case. It soon faded from the front pages because its real interest lay not in the murder of an elderly cleaning woman but in its link with her own disappearance, where there had been the inference of a sexual crime. Violence sold newspapers; so did sex, and a combination of the two was both common and compelling. Mrs Gibson was no sex object, though one reporter did a piece about her husband, an invalid suffering from a chronic bronchial condition, and the fact that their only child, a daughter, lived in Minnesota. *Neighbours rally round grieving widower*, ran the text, and, reading it, Carol could imagine what was going on in the village that seemed, now, to be light years away.

Her parents would be besieged by the press. She wondered if they still thought about her. Perhaps they did; she hoped so. It would be sad to be totally forgotten. How could they ever forgive her for what she had done, for the grief and pain she had caused them, if they found out about it? They could never understand; she did not understand herself, completely, only that after a time it seemed impossible to undo the deception and she had no wish to do so.

At the office, Carol did her usual work. She dealt with all the normal things. She had done well, she supposed, to get this really quite good job with very little to offer as credentials. What had the real Carol Mount done? Had she a degree, or been computer trained? The real one was a little older than Louise; she had realised that when she worked her age out from her driving licence.

At first, arriving off the train in Leeds, Carol had secured casual work as a waitress in a cheap café. She had found a room to rent, walking the streets where vacancies in boarding-houses were advertised, picking one at last. She stayed for a month in a small room at the back, sharing the bathroom with the other tenants, going then to Sheffield. She felt it was vital to keep moving while the papers were full of the investigation into her disappearance. She picked up work successfully, answering advertisements. It might not be so easy now, with high unemployment, but she had not been over-choosy. Her fear was that if she took on something permanent she would need papers, and as she had none she devised the story about coming from Australia. She knew a bit about the place, for her mother had been interested in the country when Malcolm went there, though his letters did little to satisfy her curiosity. Carol, in the evenings, read about it in the public library.

Somehow the weeks and then the months slipped by. She contemplated going to the DHSS, making herself official, even signing on, but that would be the way to get caught out. They would check on her. If she truly was who she alleged, a woman born in England who had, as an infant, gone to Australia, her birth would be registered in England and she would have a certificate to prove it. Without a birth certificate, she could not prove her identity; with one, she would be safe.

She had read *The Day of the Jackal*, learned how the

assassin equipped himself with false identities from studying tombstones and applying for the certificates of those born near his own birth date but dead as infants. She even went to graveyards, studying dates and names, wondering if she could do the same. But you needed more: you needed to know the mother's name and the place of birth. She found that out by asking on the telephone.

She had Carol Mount's identity. Carol was four years older than herself. She knew Carol Mount's address.

It took her a long time to find the courage, but at last she did it, convincing herself that all she had to lose was the cost of the telephone call.

She had been working as a cleaner for a while. It was hard work, but she enjoyed it because it could be mindless and it was entirely free from hazard, as cleaners were paid in cash and stamped their own cards, or didn't, as the case might be. She answered advertisements in shop windows, and soon was going out five days a week to various houses in an up-market residential area. She told her employers that she was a single mother – divorced – with a child at school. It was easy to lie once you began, she had discovered; the first time was the hardest. She invented Billy, her little boy aged six. Her employers were impressed by her neat demeanour, though not all of them admired her wildly waving hair. She spoke nicely, in a soft voice without any sort of accent, and she wore a navy skirt and sweater. Carol had done some shopping at an Oxfam shop after her first purchases of washing things and a change of underwear. She liked being in the large, comfortable houses, and two of her employers were often out when she was working.

She used the telephone at one such house to make her call to Carol Mount, for if she used a call-box the fact would be obvious when the telephone was answered. Pollsters did not use call-boxes, and that was what she would purport to be.

She knew that Carol Mount went out to work for she had owned a season ticket. Therefore, it must be an evening call, and she might not catch her in the first time.

She took to babysitting for the Boxes, telling them that her mother would always sit with Billy if they wanted her. The Boxes, a prosperous couple with two lively children, liked dining out; they gave dinner parties, too. Carol came and washed up several times, for now that she had invented her mother, she was stuck with her. She did not mind the work; it kept her busy and she was well paid; in fact, looking back, that time was very therapeutic for she was working physically hard.

Carol Mount did not answer the telephone the first time the imposter using her name tried to speak to her. The second time, just as she was about to dial, one of the children in the house woke and came wandering downstairs in search of company.

Ten days later Louise, now Carol, made a third attempt. Her quarry must still live at that address, or directory inquiries would not have been able to provide the number.

This time a woman answered.

Using a brisk voice, the new Carol said she was speaking for a research organisation conducting a survey into the movements of people away from their birthplaces. Would Carol Mount, whose name had been selected at random from the electoral roll, mind disclosing where she was born and on what date, and how long she had lived at her present address? Would she mind also revealing her mother's maiden name and some details about her and her father?

Carol Mount did not mind at all. She gave the answers readily and said it was an interesting project.

From the digs where she was now living, her usurper wrote the following day to the Registrar of Births and Deaths in the area where Carol had been born, easily discovering the correct address from the telephone directory in the library, where volumes covering the whole country were available. She enclosed a postal order for the fee.

Not long afterwards she received a copy of the real Carol's certificate. Now she was equipped, and legal, but she was apprehensive until she realised that what she had done would only be detected if someone grew suspicious, and that wouldn't happen.

What about a passport? She didn't need one at the moment, but who could tell about the future?

Someone checking up on her, if she were to become suspect for another reason, could detect the fraud, but they would have no cause to do so for she would make certain that, apart from this major deception, she would not defy the law.

She worked for Mrs Box for several months; then she left and moved to Manchester, where at last she equipped herself with proper documents, unchallenged.

She moved away again. The more you moved, the less likely you were to be traceable in the event of any query.

She had been in Tetterton for a year, in her first permanent job, when she met Eric in the library, where she always spent a lot of time.

If she were to meet her parents now, would they even recognise her? She'd sometimes imagined, when money was short, or she was ill, or when she was in cold, uncomfortable digs, going back and pleading for their forgiveness, but she had always managed, thanks to Carol Mount's original bounty, and she got a sort of satisfaction out of having done so. It was strange, however, to recollect that once she had been an editor, commissioning work; now she was content to have limited authority. What mattered was the money she contributed to the family budget and she was lucky to be in an airy office overlooking the canal, with agreeable colleagues. She'd hated the night-time bar job she had done after Joanna was born; she'd got so tired and she had loathed the smoky atmosphere and the occasional sexual overtures made by customers. Some women liked it and thought that they were failing if they did not attract flirtatious back-chat and attention. Sexual harassment, people called it now. Carol had developed a chilly manner and a glacial smile. The manager had asked her to try to be a bit more friendly, there's a love, but she had not been able to comply. She was efficient, and he did not want to fire her; he kept her in the background when he could, making up the buffet meals.

She never complained to Eric, but he did not like her working there; however, there was nothing else she could find in the evenings, the only time that she was free. Eric's mother was still working herself then, and couldn't be expected to retire to mind the children; she had her own security to think about and must qualify for a full pension. Most of the time Carol deferred to Eric, who was never assertive or unfair, but just occasionally she held out for something whose importance to her he could not always understand.

'I must do my bit,' she insisted when he said he did not want her to take on evening work. 'I must make a contribution to the budget. We all cost you such a lot.'

'But you're my family,' he protested. It was almost as though she considered herself and the children burdens who had nothing to do with him.

Carol, in fact, hated the feeling of having not a penny of her own but what he gave her, and, because she had cheated him by not telling him the truth about herself, she felt a weight of guilt which was slightly eased by effort. Working gave her back some self-respect.

They had been married in the register office, with Eric's mother and father there, and a few friends, mostly his, but several of Carol's colleagues came to the buffet lunch they had afterwards at Eric's flat. Carol wore a navy dress with white trimmings, and a wide-brimmed white straw hat; Eric wore his best suit. That morning, when she got up in the spare bedroom at her friend June's where she had spent the night before, she had thought about her mother and father and of the very different wedding her mother would have chosen for her, given the chance. Then she put them from her mind, she hoped for ever. She had given up her own bedsitting-room and moved her possessions into Eric's flat, where she had spent only rare nights before the wedding. Observing the conventions mattered to both of them, but for different reasons. Eric wanted no breath of gossip or scandal because he aimed to give Frances no cause to twist things round and imply that he was unfit to have access to his daughters. Carol, who had believed that she could never face a sexual relationship again, was anxious to be beyond reproach wherever possible because of all the secrets she was hiding.

Both of them meant to keep their vows, and they had succeeded. Carol, to her surprise, was even happy. It had been a lucky accident that had caused her to knock into Eric accidentally in the library, pushing back her chair as he was passing with a pile of books. When he saw her there a few nights later, he had smiled tentatively and said, 'Good evening.' Then one evening they had gone off for coffee together after leaving the library. Two weeks later they had supper at a new wine bar in the town. Next it was a concert; then a cinema; and at last a day out in the country one weekend when his children were away and he couldn't see them.

He had explained his circumstances, making it clear that he was no catch.

'But you've got a good, safe job,' she said. 'We can't all be Einstein.'

He had laughed at that, and as she got to know him better, she had enjoyed finding ways to make it happen again. His worried face would lighten and his large grey eyes would twinkle; she saw that he could be fun. She'd almost forgotten how to laugh herself, busy being Carol, living from day to day, looking ahead only to paying the rent and subsisting.

He introduced her, at last, to his daughters and, not accustomed to the company of children, she treated them as contemporaries, playing games she remembered from her own childhood, introducing them to Scrabble, which she bought for them. They were too old for the children's version and she and Eric introduced deviations from the adult game which made it easier for them to score. Much laughter arose over this as Hazel invented words she said were the names of exotic beasts and Rowena put in the names of her hamster and its progeny, which it had an unfortunate habit of eating.

Carol still got on well with the girls. She had never felt possessive about Eric and had no grounds for resenting them and their earlier life together. For him, she felt a gentle affection and a wealth of gratitude; her deep emotions only came to life after the children were born, and the intense, primitive love she felt for first Joanna, then for William, her fictional Billy brought to life, was unlike any feeling she had ever known. It obliterated the unresolved trauma of her past and gave her life new meaning. Now she had more for which to be grateful to Eric, and her affection for him deepened. Theirs was, by any standards, a successful, happy marriage.

Sometimes at night, even now, she would start awake with sudden terror that she had talked in her sleep, used some name or expression or in some other manner given herself away. She would lie, heart thumping, listening to Eric's even breathing – he never snored – calming herself, remembering that her offence had been against her parents, not against him, except for her deception. She had no black past to conceal, no terrible crime, only the theft of Carol Mount's money and name. And the fact of her desertion.

She had had to sell her gold watch in those early days when she had needed money, but she kept the locket she had worn. It had been mentioned in the description of her in the papers; if she tried to sell it, an alert jeweller might identify it. She had it still, an aquamarine set in pearls, once her paternal grandmother's. She had worn it since her marriage, but now she kept it in a drawer in case it figured in the new reports from Selbury.

When Eric lost his job, things had been hard for them. At first he could find nothing, and he stayed at home caring for the children while Carol gave up her translating and went back to full-time work. She soon found an office job, one which paid quite well, and then Eric's father died, suddenly, of a heart attack. That was a bad time, but they got over it, pulling together as true partners should. Eric found an opening at the department store; it wasn't the sort of job he had had before but there were prospects. He took it on, made a success in various departments, and finally he was awarded his own small empire.

'You deserve it,' Carol said, celebrating with a bottle of sparkling wine she had bought at Marks.

They'd talked about a holiday in France, but so far they had only been as far as Scarborough, where they rented a self-catering cottage near the beach. The children loved it there, and Carol thought it perfect for them at their present ages. She found North Yorkshire very beautiful, with its unspoilt countryside and the wide, light skies.

She could safely get a passport, if they really did decide to go to France. She had the necessary certification. The sooner the better really, before everything went on to computers and it might be simple to run checks, find that another Carol Mount already had one.

Lately, she had become interested in ecological disasters, shocked by Chernobyl and realising that her children would be threatened if the rain forests were destroyed, the ozone layer filled with holes, the seas contaminated. She read a lot about these things and even spoke of joining Greenpeace. Eric was faintly amused by the passion she showed about withering greenery and soil erosion; wistfully, he wished she would display the same intensity in their more intimate moments. Still, she was always loving and tender, and that was all that really mattered. She had never mentioned past lovers but of course there had been one, at least. At first she had been nervous and tentative; he knew she had been hurt by some unhappy experience and he did not probe. He hadn't told her all that had happened in his marriage, nor about his other romance with a girl called Phyllis. That was in the past. What mattered was the present and they did not need to talk to be happy together. Their whole way of life was proof enough.

Sometimes he wondered at the complete absence of any Australian accent in Carol's speech, but then her aunt had been English, and she had been back in England for several years before they met. She once said that her aunt had not cared for Australian vowel sounds and had sent her to elocution classes.

He accepted everything she told him as the truth, and

she had learned that it is frighteningly easy to deceive, especially where there is both love and trust.

Her routine, since the new crime in Selbury, was to read the paper in the lavatory at work, putting the lid down on the toilet seat and sitting there to study the reports in privacy. Conditions for the female staff were very good, with a large cloakroom containing roller towels that worked and a rack of paper ones as well. There were big mirrors all along the wall behind the basins, and copious hot water. People changed there, even washed and dried their hair, for there was a power point, before going out on evening dates. The factory workers, too, were well catered for, with still more spacious facilities for their far larger numbers. Carol knew that some of her office colleagues, and many of the machinists, went home to poky rooms in grimy streets, much less pleasant than their work environment; for years this had been her own experience. She knew that many children, too, must find their modern school with its bright classrooms and big gym and playing-field a sharp contrast to their homes.

People came and went outside as she read the various accounts of events in Selbury. She was dimly aware of movement and voices; someone tried the door. Carol took no notice and read on. The reporters, referring to her disappearance twelve years before, made capital out of the fact that lightning had, it seemed, struck twice, though this time in another form. Reference to Greek tragedy was made, and finally she read of Norah's involvement.

Miss Norah Tyler, 62, housekeeper to the Vaughans, accompanied Mrs Susan Vaughan, 70, on her journey to, as she thought, her gravely injured husband's bedside, ran one text. There were pictures of her parents, even one of Norah, looking much as she had always done, but none of the dead woman; her fate was lost in the bigger story.

So Norah had been absorbed into the family. When had that happened? Carol digested the information and drew comfort from it, for Norah would support her parents now. She was a shrewd woman who saw through cant, and Carol had always admired her.

Photographs of the burnt-out Lodge House made it look bigger than she remembered it when her grandmother was living there, supported by the larger house with its home-grown vegetables and other resources. When had Norah thrown up her job? Was it after the disappearance of Louise? Carol felt guilty at that thought. What other repercussions had there been from her flight?

You did something, took some drastic action, and at the time your first thought was only of what it meant to you, not of how it would affect a host of other people. Even at the time, her own immediate problems of survival had overshadowed her awareness of the pain her parents must be suffering.

What about Malcolm? At last she deliberately let herself remember him. Where was he in all this latest furore? He was not mentioned in the papers. Had he been sent abroad again? Surely even her mother would finally tire of making excuses for him? Perhaps he had found some other wretched girl to marry.

Carol had once passed the scene of a bad fire when she was living in Leeds. A house near her lodgings had gone up in flames one night, the occupants escaping thanks to the prompt arrival of the fire brigade. For days the area had smelled of smoke, an acrid odour quite unlike the scent of autumn bonfires which she remembered with nostalgia. Now that bitter smell would be lingering around her parents' house. All their possessions would have been destroyed, and with a pang she knew that meant their photographs of her, the albums crammed with snapshots of her life, her small biography. Louise had been truly killed at last, all traces gone.

What would they do about clothes, tax returns, papers, all the bureaucratic clutter of modern life, the things that she had slowly acquired in her renaissance?

She shed some tears, sitting there in the small cubicle, and when at last she emerged, choosing a moment when she was sure there was no one in the outer cloakroom, she took time to pat her face with paper towels wrung out in cold water, and to put on lipstick. She looked at her hair in the mirror; she might have to add some grey streaks soon, to mark the extra years she was supposed to have lived.

When she was pregnant with Joanna the doctor in charge of her expressed surprise at her recorded age, saying he would have thought her several years younger. Luckily she had been officially young enough to avoid extensive tests, but she would doubtless be a freak with a late menopause. It was too soon to start worrying about that, and maybe no one but Eric would notice. And his mother. Not much escaped her sharp eye. Still, even she wouldn't be here for ever. At this thought Carol felt a pang. She depended on Ethel; so did they all. Ethel had truly been a mother to her.

She had deprived her own parents of their grandchildren. After they were born, she had wanted to send photographs to them, had even contemplated doing so, but had pulled herself back from making such a stupid, self-indulgent gesture which might bring ruin to them all. They did not know that she was still alive; they did not know their grandchildren existed; the idea of them, if they had one, would be like the ghost child in that Barrie play – *Dear Brutus*, that was it.

She kept the relevant newsprint pages, throwing the rest away in the waste-bin before returning to her office.

Each day Ethel, too, had read the latest instalment and was eager to discuss it.

'Shows money can't buy happiness,' she tritely said. 'I suppose they're well insured and can rebuild, but it won't bring that poor woman back to life.'

'They'll have to live somewhere in the meantime,' Carol said. She had been wondering about that. Where would they go? Their friends all had large houses. Maybe someone like the Cartwrights would take them in, if they were still alive.

'They won't be homeless on the streets, sent to bed and breakfasts by the council,' said Ethel.

George and Susan had spent the hours immediately after the fire at the Vicarage, which was close by, while Norah made some arrangements. The vicar and his wife, both kind, good people, had three children and only a small modern vicarage, the old one having been sold for enormous sums to a company director who travelled to

London and back each day in his huge Mercedes.

'We can't possibly stay,' Susan whispered, while their hosts pondered which child to move from its room in order to house their homeless parishioners, and worried about the inadequacies of their single bathroom.

'I'll think of something,' Norah had said, and had booked them a room at The Crown in Feringham. It would do for the moment, until a more permanent plan could be devised. Meanwhile, she accepted Myra's offer of her tiny spare bedroom for herself for as long as it was required.

Next, she rang Malcolm's workshop and, as he was out, left a message on the answerphone telling him what had happened and that they were all safe, and his parents would be at The Crown from that evening. She rang Brenda, too, at her office, in case Malcolm went straight home from wherever he was. Brenda, told about the fire, expressed shocked dismay but told Norah bluntly that Malcolm and she were no longer living together.

'My decision,' she added, to make the position perfectly clear.

There was a lot to do. The police took statements about their movements during the day and the telephone calls that had sent them all out. The address of the insurance company had to be traced, since no one remembered it perfectly, for it must be notified. Luckily all three had had their money and bank cards with them, the two women taking their handbags on their trip to Oxford and George with his wallet in his pocket, so there was no problem over the actual cash needed at once to buy toilet things and some clothes. Norah dealt with this, going off to see what she could get at Boots and Marks and Spencer to tide them over, the same priorities Louise had discovered twelve years before when she, too, had only the clothes she was wearing.

There was no word from Malcolm until Thursday, the day after the fire, when he came to see them at The Crown.

'You took your time,' said George.

'I've been away,' said Malcolm. He had driven to Coventry, well away from his home area, where he had sold the Metro for cash. He thought about selling the jewellery there, but it was unlikely that any dependable firm would pay him the large sums it was worth in cash, and to demand it might arouse suspicion. If he tried to open a bank account under a false name and pay in cheques from such sales, he might be caught out on an identity check. That had happened to him in Australia.

The jewellery was his insurance for the future. If he could get it out of the country, he could use it to make a fresh start. Meanwhile he had two other cars to dispose of, and they could soon be turned into money. This gave him assurance, facing George's reproof.

'I knew you were safe. Your message said so,' he replied. 'So I didn't worry.'

'So I see,' said George grimly. 'I suppose it didn't occur to you that we could have done with some help? That we had to find somewhere to stay? That Susan was very shocked? She'd been told I was hurt in a road accident. That was a lie to get her out of the house.'

'I read that in the paper,' said Malcolm, who had turned with interest to the reports of the incident.

'You haven't even asked how she is,' said George.

'Well, she must be all right or she'd be in hospital,' Malcolm said. 'She'd got Norah to see her through, hadn't she? Good old Norah.' He said this with a sneer.

'Yes, she had Norah, thank goodness,' said George, who was still shaken himself though he tried to conceal it from this boorish, ungrateful man who bore his name. I'm getting too old for this sort of thing, George told himself.

'So you'll be staying here for a bit?'

'Yes.'

'Lucky you didn't lose one of the cars,' Malcolm said. 'Though I could have sold you one of mine at a special price. I'll go up and see Susan, then. Which is her room?'

The interview had been taking place in the hotel lounge, to which George had descended when the desk clerk rang to say that Malcolm was there.

'You won't,' said George. 'She's resting. I'll tell her you came round.'

He looked at Malcolm closely. The younger man's eyes were glittering. He had looked like that once before and George had no difficulty in remembering when it was: just after Louise had disappeared.

'How did you know none of the cars was damaged?' he asked.

'It said so in the papers, or on the news,' Malcolm answered glibly.

He'd made a slip but it wouldn't matter.

'Well, if I can't see Susan, I'll be off,' he said. 'I've a customer to attend to.'

He was going back to his own hotel. On the way, he

stopped at a florist's and spent twenty pounds of his profit from the Metro on ordering a huge bouquet of flowers to be sent round to Susan at The Crown, with a message which said: *From your loving son Malcolm.*

When Susan received it, she burst into tears, for hadn't she only just virtually cut him out of her will?

Malcolm himself had a swim when he reached his new base. The activity of the last twenty-four hours had stimulated him and he felt elated and energetic. He tried chatting up one of the leisure club attendants in her white shirt and short pleated skirt, but she, in training, had been warned about people like him; besides, she was going out with one of the under-managers and was no longer available.

Detective Superintendent Marsh had a weird sense of *déjà vu* as he drove out to Selbury following news that a body had been found in the smouldering remnants of the Lodge House.

He spoke to the chief fire officer in charge of the men who had put out the blaze and who had managed to save part of the building. An old man who walked round the village every day, exercising himself and a dog that was mostly collie and keeping both of them out of his wife's way, had seen smoke and flames behind one of the windows and had rushed in to the nearest house to make an emergency call, so the first fire engine had arrived very soon after the blaze took hold. The surviving structure had been saturated with water from the hoses and everything inside was very badly damaged; little would be salvaged. Mrs Gibson had been found on a sodden bed and at first it was thought that she had been overcome by smoke, but she lay on her back, stretched out like a victim of crucifixion. People who died in fires were usually found collapsed close to doors or windows where they had fought to escape; they did not lie down to die unless asphyxiated in their sleep. Until the results of the post mortem were revealed, judgement as to the manner of death must be reserved, but whoever had set the fire was guilty at least of manslaughter.

There was no doubt that it was arson. A petrol can was found in the hall and the way the fire had caught made it certain. A likely reading of events indicated that the fire had been started to disguise the killing and the fact of the burglary, for it was obvious that the cupboards and drawers in the room where the woman was found had been ransacked.

When he reached Sonning, sent there by the bogus telephone call, George had discovered no police car waiting to meet him. He had waited only half an hour before driving on to a call-box to telephone Marsh, for this was the sort of appointment which would be punctually kept. It was soon clear that the message had not come from Marsh's office and a malicious prank was suspected; nothing more. George had turned back for home whilst meanwhile Susan and Norah were on their way to Oxford.

When they arrived at the hospital, it was some time before they were convinced that George had not, in fact, been admitted. He might have been still in the Casualty department. Various calls and checks were made.

While this was going on, Norah had decided to call

the Lodge House. If there had been a mistake in identity, George might be home by now. He had been distinctly cagey about his mysterious errand, saying it was to do with the council, but if so, why had he not explained, and why had he looked as if he had received a blow to the solar plexus?

When she dialled, the line went dead. She tried several times with no better result; then she rang the operator who confirmed that the telephone seemed to be out of order and volunteered to check, then call her back.

Norah did not wait for that; she rang the local police. If George had had an accident, surely they would know?

It was some time before the truth filtered through to the two women and meanwhile they waited at the hospital, for there was no point in going home only to find that George had been sent to some other place, one more suited to his injuries. Various appalling possibilities ran through both their minds as they sat there trying to preserve some calm. Eventually, when the local police could tell them nothing beyond saying that they were unaware of an accident involving George Vaughan, or his car, whose number Norah had given them, she telephoned Detective Superintendent Marsh.

She learned that he was out of the office, already, as it transpired, at the scene of the fire, but when Norah explained why she was calling, a sergeant came on the line and told her that Mr Vaughan was safe and was with the superintendent at Selbury where there had been an incident. Pressed, the sergeant admitted that there had been a fire at the Lodge House, but Mr Vaughan was not involved as he had been the victim of a hoax call which had lured him away from the village. The sergeant did not mention that though he was safe, a body had been found.

Obviously they had been tricked, too. Norah and Susan drove home relieved but sombre, unaware of how serious the fire had been. It seemed they had all been dispersed to leave the coast clear for an arsonist.

Both women remembered Malcolm setting fire to the hay in the pony shed years ago, and the episode of the games pavilion at his school, but neither mentioned this to the other.

George had returned from his bogus mission expecting to find Susan and Norah at home. It was a day when Susan had had no plan for a lecture or other distraction, and had said she was going to sweep up the last of the fallen leaves.

He arrived in the village to find the road cordoned off near the Lodge House and three fire-engines and their teams engaged in trying to extinguish a blazing inferno. He knew total terror, thinking the two women were trapped inside, and when there were murmurs about someone being found upstairs he felt sick with dread. It was a mention from one of her acquaintances among the spectators who had swiftly gathered that made him realise, with shamed relief, that the victim must be poor Mrs Gibson. He asked if there was a car in the garage and learned that it was empty. So the two had gone out: where?

A police officer eventually brought a message that they were on their way back from Oxford.

Whatever had they been doing in Oxford? They'd had no plans to go there; they preferred shopping in Malchester for what could not be bought nearer home, unless they went to London. And why should the police know what they were doing?

Until he saw them, he could not know the answers. He waited for them at the end of the road, anxious to prevent Susan from seeing the wreckage of her home until she could be prepared for the shock, and as they approached, the vicar was walking to meet them, ready with his offer of sanctuary.

Later, Norah was with George when he spoke to the first reporters to visit the scene, saying very little. When they parted, he to take Susan over to The Crown at Feringham, she for Myra's flat, he said, 'They're sure to rake all that up again about Louise. You'll see.'

She did not contradict him. She knew that it was true.

2

Malcolm

Malcolm made his plans fast. After leaving George at The Crown – he had driven over in the Porsche which he had picked up from the workshop when he returned by train from Coventry – he took the Vitesse to an area of Malchester where there was a pub frequented by men with whom, before now, he had done deals. He had picked up bargains there, and he had sold cars which had proved hard to shift. He had also provided one or two for undertakings about which it was prudent to ask no questions.

He sold the Vitesse for a wad of exceedingly tattered notes from a man who knew he could make at least two hundred more by selling it on. Then he took the Maestro to a used car lot on the edge of town where again he sold at a loss.

Now he had only the Porsche left. He'd sell that near Heathrow.

He had dinner at his hotel, and some drinks in the bar

later. A new group of businessmen had checked in for another conference and there were fresh faces to talk to; Malcolm swopped stories with them and bought rounds of drinks in his usual free-handed manner, and went to his room only when the last of them left the bar. He had a bath and shaved: appearances were important and he had a long night ahead of him. Then he packed his bags and, when the hotel was quiet, heaved them over the windowsill on to the lawn outside, then followed himself. He had earlier parked the Porsche as close as he could to the end of the block containing his ground-floor room.

The night staff never heard him move from the lawn to the tarmac to reach his car. He padded to and fro with his load of belongings, taking only what was essential; the rest he left behind, and he rumpled the bedclothes so that it might be some time before anyone realised he had gone. The hotel was soundproofed and the night porter, dozing behind the desk, did not hear him drive away. Malcolm did not switch on his lights until he was clear of the gates. Then he set off for Heathrow.

He checked in at a hotel near the airport. The place was accustomed to people arriving round the clock and found nothing unusual about his request for a room in the early hours of Friday morning. He paid cash in advance, saying he simply wanted to sleep for a few hours after driving up from Plymouth, before catching a plane later on.

He lay on the bed and slept for three hours, after which he went off to sell the Porsche. It was a wrench but it had to be done, and again he was forced to accept a lower price than he might have got in a different way, but he now had several thousand pounds in cash; enough to get him across the Atlantic and launched into a new life.

The post mortem report on Mrs Gibson was through by Thursday morning and it confirmed that this was a case of murder. There was no smoke in her lungs and there was firm evidence of strangulation, with bruising on her neck indicating that the assailant was probably right-handed. Door-to-door inquiries in Selbury, begun on Wednesday and completed the following day, yielded reports of two people who had noticed a blue Metro in the village square on Wednesday morning. There had been a man in the driver's seat. He was there during the time one witness was in the post office mailing a letter to her cousin in Zimbabwe, and was still there while she had a conversation with two friends she met in the grocer's shop. She remembered it clearly because the talk, about the possible closure of the school in the village, had been important.

'With all the building here, you'd think we could keep our own school,' the witness had stated. Pressed by the interviewing detective constable, she had not been able to describe the man.

Neither of the witnesses had ever met Malcolm; they could not have named him even if they had had a good look at him, and neither was paying particular attention. Both said the car was not among those they might have recognised as being regularly parked in the square while their drivers visited the shops.

The priority, now, was to trace the Metro and find the driver, in order to eliminate him from the inquiry. Nobody else seemed to have seen anything that could be construed as suspicious. No one had seen any caller arrive at the Lodge House.

The firemen reported that the front door had been closed and locked on the Yale but the back door was unlocked. Mrs Gibson would have been going in and out, taking rubbish to the dustbin and putting the mat out while she mopped the floor. With everyone out, she would have locked it before she left by the front door.

At that stage no one suggested that the visitor might have been Malcolm Vaughan. Those in the village who knew him would not expect to see him behind the wheel of a Metro, for he always drove sporty, even flash cars. Those who knew his taste for a blaze kept quiet out of dread of what might be exposed if they spoke.

Detective Constable Whitlock had been working on various cases concerning petty theft, trying to avoid bringing charges in a shoplifting case where the goods the store detective declared had not been paid for cost less than a pound – two small tins of baked beans. Meanwhile he turned over in his mind the fragments of information about Louise Vaughan's disappearance which had surfaced during his recent interview with her brother. The scenario Malcolm Vaughan had postulated about someone getting into her car and so alarming her that she had leaped out and run off had convinced him that Vaughan knew much more, but now the investigation into the fire at Selbury and Mrs Gibson's death, to which he had been assigned, took precedence over hypotheses about the missing young woman, however intriguing. But the cases were linked by location. It might be simply coincidence, but was there any such thing? Could it not be defined as fate?

When mention was made of a blue Metro, something nagged at the back of Whitlock's mind; some such car he had noticed not too long ago, but he could not immediately call to mind where it was. However, irrespective of that, Malcolm Vaughan must be interviewed as routine and told what had happened at his parents' home.

A constable from Malchester was sent round to the workshop. The place was deserted when he called on Wednesday, the day of the crime, at about five o'clock in the evening. Outside on the forecourt a Porsche, a Maestro and a Vitesse were parked. A note was made to find Vaughan later; he might have already heard about the fire and be on his way to his parents' side.

Police Constable Perry, who had subjected Norah and George to what could be called harassment, or alternatively extreme attention to duty, heard about the blue Metro in which the CID were interested as soon as he came on shift. By this time efforts to trace local blue Metros were being made and officers were instructed to stop any they saw and question their drivers about where they had been at the time of the incident. Perry had been driving around looking for trouble for some time before he remembered that there was a blue Metro outside Malcolm Vaughan's place on Monday night.

He drove past the workshop and saw that the Metro had gone: so Vaughan must have sold it. He'd sold the Vitesse and the Maestro as well, it appeared, and, as there were no lights and no one answered when Perry banged on the door, had no doubt driven off in his Porsche to wherever he was spending the night.

Perry saw no need for haste in reporting Vaughan's past ownership of a blue Metro. It could not be the one in question. Coming off duty early on Friday morning, he mentioned the matter, information that was thought important enough to be sent through at once to the Incident Room in Feringham.

Whitlock, who had been put on the case partly because every available man was needed for the preliminary inquiries and partly because Marsh himself made sure that he was on it, since he already had knowledge of some of the history of those concerned, was in the Incident Room when the information came through. He remembered himself, then, that he too had seen the car. Perhaps Vaughan had sold it to the thief.

He also remembered where Vaughan had told him that he was staying, and saw that he had not yet been interviewed regarding the crime; not that he could be considered a suspect, for he would not steal from his parents or murder their daily woman. Or would he?

Marsh had been home for only a few hours' sleep and on Friday, when he came in, he was told that Detective Sergeant Newton was proposing to question Vaughan about the Metro to find out who had bought it, as its connection with the crime must be established or dismissed. Marsh found Whitlock hovering, anxious to speak to him.

'I know where Vaughan is,' he said. 'He's got some explaining to do.'

Marsh looked at the young man's thin, sharp-featured face, his eager expression.

'You think he knew more about his sister's disappearance than we gave credence to at the time, don't you?' he said.

'He used the words, "She might have gone back to him afterwards", referring to Blacker,' Whitlock reminded him. 'And I asked him after what, and he suggested she'd been attacked and had then run away. He didn't like it at all when I suggested that he could have been the attacker. I told him I'd be speaking to him again. That was on Tuesday evening. Is there anything in from Australia yet?' After his interview with Vaughan, Whitlock had asked if a check could be run in Australia; it was unlikely that a result would be through so soon, he thought, but Marsh surprised him.

'Funny you should ask,' he said. 'Our pals down under turned him up right away. He did two years for fraud. Got out and came straight back to England. No money, of course.'

'Fraud,' said Whitlock slowly. 'What if he's in debt now?'

'Yes. I'll see what the banks will tell us. Probably nothing, but we'll soon know if he owes money around.'

'There might be stuff in his office. Bills and so on,' said Whitlock hopefully.

'I think it might justify a search warrant,' said Marsh. 'Meanwhile, Detective Sergeant Newton is keen to pick up Vaughan to interview him, and as you know where he's staying, you'd better go with him.'

Whitlock's face lit up.

'Even if he's not our man, he's got questions to answer,' he said happily.

'Yes,' agreed Marsh.

At the moment they had no concrete evidence to connect Malcolm Vaughan with the latest events at Selbury, only their own suspicions and the circumstantial link of his having had a blue Metro for sale.

Whitlock and Detective Sergeant Newton set off for the Manor Hotel. The journey took forty minutes and when they arrived it was to find that there was no record of a Malcolm Vaughan staying there.

Whitlock described their man, adding that he might have checked in on Monday. Then he mentioned the Porsche which he knew Vaughan drove.

'We get so many,' said the reception clerk. 'We've got conferences all the time. But it sounds rather like Mr Tyler; he had a Porsche. He didn't check out with the rest of his group. I wonder if he's up yet.' The hotel, being new, used plastic cards instead of keys to admit guests to rooms, so there was no instant check on possible absence. 'I'll ring his room,' she said, and did so.

'Don't tell him who we are,' Detective Sergeant Newton instructed. 'Just say he's wanted in the lobby.'

'I hope he's in no trouble,' said the girl, but of course he was if the police were after him and if he had booked in under a bogus name.

'He's not if he really is Mr Tyler,' said Whitlock.

He was not altogether surprised to learn that there was

no reply from the room, and further inquiries revealed that Mr Tyler was not in the restaurant having breakfast.

The hotel had a note of his car's registration number, accurately filled in on Mr Edward Tyler's form. A check soon proved that this was, indeed, Malcolm Vaughan's Porsche. It no longer stood outside in the parking area. After this, the two men were let into room number fourteen, which had a *Please do not disturb* sign hanging on the door.

The empty room, with the unwanted trappings abandoned and the hastily dishevelled bed, confirmed the identity of the guest, and, in effect, his guilt.

'Don't touch a thing,' said Newton, including the under-manager who had let them in with Whitlock in this instruction.

'But what's happened?' asked the young man. 'What's he done?'

'Left here without paying, for starters,' Newton replied and turned to Whitlock.

'Bag everything,' he said, and to the under-manager, 'I'm afraid you can't use this room till it's been gone over for prints.'

'Well, as he hadn't checked out, no one else will have been booked in,' said the under-manager. 'What chance have we got of getting our money?'

'Not a lot, I'd say,' answered Whitlock.

'He didn't work for that firm, did he? He said he was with them.'

Whitlock shook his head.

Now there would be a man-hunt. He and Newton began to set it in motion.

* * *

Marsh telephoned Norah Tyler that morning.

Myra answered the telephone, and handed the handset over to Norah, mouthing 'The police.' Myra, in an exotic silk kimono acquired on a trip to Hong Kong, was sitting at her kitchen table smoking a cigarette, an activity from which Norah was resolved to wean her while she lodged in the flat. Norah herself, in the tweed skirt and dark sweater she had worn on the journey to Oxford two days before, had been clearing the breakfast dishes.

'Yes, Mr Marsh, I'll be here,' she said, after listening to her caller. 'I'll expect you in about half an hour, then.' She replaced the instrument and looked across at Myra whose expression betrayed extreme interest. 'Something's happened,' Norah said. 'He sounded very serious. I hope it's nothing dreadful to do with George or Susan.'

'Why should it be? You worry too much,' said Myra, who, by escaping from her native Estonia in 1939 ahead of the Russian invasion had also avoided the later German one and saw no point in anticipating further catastrophe, despite recent events in the village.

'The shock might have been too much for one of them,' said Norah, fretting.

'If anything had happened to either one, the other would have got hold of you, fast enough,' said Myra. 'They can't manage without you. You know that.'

'I've known them a long time,' said Norah.

Myra had often told her that they took advantage of her and that she should escape, that she wasn't too old to start her own business, as Myra herself had done, and have some rewarding years before age forced her to curtail her activities.

'Forget the dishes,' she said. 'The little girl you found for me comes today, remember? We must leave her something to do. She can start by washing-up.'

'Oh, does she? I'd forgotten,' said Norah, thus indicating that she was more upset by what had happened on Wednesday than had, at the time, appeared. Norah never forgot arrangements she had made.

'The Orams are delighted with Mrs Jennings,' said Myra, referring to the couple who lived in the largest flat in the house. 'You've a genius for finding these cleaning ladies.'

'It's not genius. It's contacts,' said Norah. 'But you're right about the dishes. Daisy should do them as it's in her contract.'

Norah had suggested an agreement between Myra and her new, youthful employee, to avoid misunderstandings and for the protection of both. Myra had wanted to make certain that the girl would wash up on mornings after she, Myra, had had people to dinner. She often had friends in for extravagant meals.

'You go and get tidy for your policeman, if he's coming to see you,' said Myra. 'And don't worry. They may have found out who did those terrible things. That poor Mrs Gibson, it's really dreadful. If you're anxious about George and Susan, why not ring them up?'

Norah would not do that. It was still early and they might be sleeping late. She took herself off to the sitting-room to make sure it was tidy enough for the forthcoming interview. She was a great one for plumping up cushions and tidying round when visitors were expected, a habit that Susan found irritating because the Lodge House was rarely in need of such extra attentions since it was always so well maintained. George, speaking very solemnly, had told his wife that Norah had not got Susan's inner sense of security in social situations, since she acquired her polish through experience and not by osmosis.

Now, finicking about, Norah worried that Daisy, when she arrived, might overhear what Marsh had to say for the flat was very small, and she also hoped that Myra, who was incurably curious, would put on some clothes before he came.

Daisy's parents ran the village post office, which also sold stationery and sweets; she was waiting to start her nursing training and wanted work meanwhile. She was very punctual, and Norah heard her and Myra discussing the day's tasks which included cleaning the silver. Over the years, Myra had bought quite a lot as an investment and she used it all the time. The thief would have found plenty to take if he'd called here.

Marsh arrived twenty-five minutes after his call, and Norah let him in. She was apprehensive about what she was going to hear, and began to talk as she showed him into the sitting-room.

'It's an awful mess, isn't it? The Lodge, I mean,' she said. She had been to look at the damage the previous day, when George had met someone from his insurance company at the site, and had found her eyes prickling with tears at the thought of Mrs Gibson perishing in that appalling blaze. She had been so loyal both to Mrs

Warrington and to Susan and George, and though she was getting stiff and slow, she had remained a wonderfully thorough worker of whom Norah was fond. Coming up to the Lodge House got her out of the claustrophobic atmosphere of her home and the claims of her husband who, unable to do much for himself, had become rather demanding. What would happen to him now? Would his daughter whisk him away to Minnesota, or would he end up parked in an old people's home? A neighbour had taken him in while the daughter made plans to come over, which she had said she would do when she heard what had happened. George had wanted to pay her fare, but Norah had advised him to wait and see what her circumstances appeared to be before making such an offer. Mrs Gibson had always implied that her son-in-law was a prospering merchant, and certainly the daughter sent generous presents to her parents. The old man's future was not Norah's problem, but she knew that George would make it his.

Marsh had scarcely taken his seat on the sofa when Daisy came in with two freshly made cups of coffee neatly arranged on a tray with sugar and cream.

Marsh, who had been up for hours, was grateful, and he appreciated the excellence of the brew. Myra always ground her own and bought beans newly roasted every week.

'I'm afraid there's something extremely tricky to be faced,' he told Norah, having agreed that the house was a shambles although much of the original structure had been saved. 'I need your help,' he continued. 'The Vaughans will have to be told that there's a call out for their son. We think he may know something about what happened and he seems to have disappeared.'

'Malcolm? Oh no!' Norah stared at him, setting down her cup, but her protest was a reflex for she felt no surprise, rather a confirmation of her deepest dread. Malcolm had come to the Lodge House on Monday night in a very disturbed frame of mind. He would have known where to find the jewellery. He would have known how to get Susan and George out of the way and he could have disguised his voice so that they did not recognise him when he made the hoax calls; she remembered him adopting various accents in some game or other years before. If Mrs Gibson had seen him, when the things were later missed she would have said he had been at the house, so she had been silenced, and as a final typical touch he had resorted to fire.

The thought made her feel quite sick, but she knew that Malcolm was capable of committing such a crime.

'Well, we can't be certain yet,' said Marsh. 'But he's got some explaining to do. He had a blue Metro for sale, and one was seen in the square on Wednesday before the incident, with a man sitting in it, wearing a cap. And we believe that he's badly in debt.' Even now an experienced detective sergeant and a detective constable were at the workshop inspecting the files.

Marsh told Norah that Malcolm had been staying at the new hotel and had skipped, leaving his large bill unpaid, and that he had booked in under a false name. He did not tell her that Vaughan had used her name; an odd quirk, that. Plenty of prints that were probably his had been found in his room and would be matched with those in his office before obtaining confirmation from Australia, if he were not arrested first. Any found at the scene of the fire, however, could be explained away by a clever barrister as being lawfully there.

'But to kill Mrs Gibson,' Norah said, still reluctant to accept that. 'The robbery – yes, I can believe that, dreadful as it is. I can believe he made the fake phone calls, too. He would know how easy it would be to lure Susan away if she thought George had had an accident.'

'And he would know you'd go with her.'

'Yes. But to get George to leave – to deceive him – that wouldn't have been so easy.'

'Mr Vaughan thought it was something to do with Louise. He thought we'd found her. That was the impression he got from the call which he believed came from me.'

'Was that what happened? Oh, how cruel!' No wonder George had been evasive about the message.

'I'm afraid so,' said Marsh. 'And there's more. Miss Tyler, it's beginning to look as if he may have known something about his sister's disappearance.'

'What?' Now Norah really was shocked.

'Well, you know that since I've been back in the area I've been ferreting about a bit. I've had a bright young detective doing some legwork for me, asking questions. It's not been official, you understand, but simply because I don't like unfinished business. Vaughan mentioned an affair his sister had had with a man named Blacker. Did you know about it?'

Norah shook her head.

'I had an idea there was someone and it ended in tears,'

she said. 'No details. Louise kept very quiet about it, but I sometimes saw her in London and I picked up a few hints.'

'He was married – the usual story,' said Marsh. 'But her brother knew about it and he made some odd remarks when my young officer went to talk to him. He suggested that on the night she disappeared, Louise had been attacked and ran away, perhaps to this Blacker. But Blacker never saw her that night. I'm fairly sure of that, though it hasn't been proved.'

'But Malcolm didn't – he wouldn't – he couldn't—?' Norah's voice trailed off as she stared in horror at the detective superintendent. Then, more robustly, she asked, 'Well, what did he do with her, then?'

'We'll find out, when we arrest him,' said Marsh. 'But her parents will have to be prepared for some shocks.'

'Oh.' Norah twisted her hands in her lap. 'And I'm to do the preparing?'

'Well, if you could tell them that we're looking for Malcolm in connection with the robbery. Just to help us with our inquiries,' said Marsh. 'I can't let them find out from the press or some other way. Not after what they've been through already.'

'You just want to talk to him to eliminate him. Isn't that how it's put?' said Norah.

'That's it,' said Marsh. 'We don't add, "Or not, as the case may be."'

But he'd done it; he'd killed Mrs Gibson and started the fire, and both of them knew it.

★ ★ ★

Malcolm was too late for the ten o'clock Air Canada flight to Toronto. He had gone straight to the airport in a taxi after concluding the deal over the Porsche.

British Airways had a flight leaving at three-fifteen, fully booked in the economy class but with a first-class seat available. Malcolm hesitated. It meant hanging about at the airport, leaving time for something to go wrong. Should he flit quickly across the Channel, then fly on?

He must make up his mind. There was no reason for anyone to suspect him of the crime in Selbury; all the police could do was talk to him because he was related to the family.

But he wasn't. He was a separate individual, one who did not know who he really was.

Standing there on the busy concourse, his bags beside him, Malcolm knew himself to be rootless and alone, and an emotion he had known before but never identified by name swept over him: sheer, blind fear. He must get out, and quickly, and he must not risk too many customs checks. He asked about flights to Montreal and found there was a first-class seat on the British Airways eleven-fifteen departure. He could catch the shuttle from there to Toronto, said the helpful girl, if it would be worth his while to save the time involved, very little in the long run and he would have to hurry or he'd miss that.

Malcolm dared not risk trying to pay by credit card, for he owed on all his accounts. Hating to part with it, he counted out the cash and took his ticket, then set off to catch the bus to Terminal Four. The girl had said she would let the departure desk know that he was on his way.

He checked in his cases straight away, using his charm

on the clerk, agreeing that he had packed them both himself, paying without protest the extra due because they were overweight. Then he went through passport control, the point of no return, and immediately felt safe. He had made it. He had no hand luggage, not even a razor in a toilet-bag to put through the machine. Everything was in his cases, the jewellery dropped into socks and packed inside his shoes.

He'd need a shave before landing. Maybe the hostess would be able to find him a razor. It might be wise, ultimately, to grow a beard, just for a time, but arriving with a day's growth would be no disguise, merely untidy.

A striking-looking man, tall and well-built, his pockets full of banknotes, Malcolm went off to the bar. He'd find someone there to talk to.

Norah did not care for her errand.

She found Susan fretty and restless, hating her enforced stay at The Crown, which was a pleasant enough place with some genuine beams among the later additions, and a friendly staff.

'We can't stay here, Norah,' she said, when Norah knocked on the door of their large room on the first floor and had been admitted by George.

'No. Well, Helen Cartwright has been trying to get hold of you, but without the phone it hasn't been easy. She found me via Myra,' Norah said. 'She's in Scotland just now, with her daughter, but she says you can go to the house and stay there for as long as you like. She wants you to ring her. I've got the number.'

'Oh, bless her,' said Susan. 'I'll do it at once.'

'Before you do, there's something else,' Norah said, and cast a glance at George, who could see that she had more on her mind than Helen Cartwright's kind invitation.

'It can wait while I ring Helen,' Susan declared, springing up from the chair where she had been sitting. 'What's the number?'

'Susan – George – please sit down,' Norah said, standing in the middle of the big room which contained two small armchairs and a desk as well as the two beds. The room had been made up while George and Susan were having breakfast and everything was tidy, but the pair had no belongings to spread about, only what they had been wearing at the time of the fire and the things Norah had bought to tide them over. 'I'm here as a messenger not only for Helen but also for the police. I've got something horrible to tell you,' she continued.

'Nothing can be more horrible than what's happened already,' said Susan. 'No one else can be dead, unless poor old Gibson's died of shock. Is that what it is?'

'No,' said Norah. 'No one else is dead. It isn't that.'

'Well, I can see you're determined to tell us before you let me ring Helen, so get on with it, there's a dear,' said Susan, and sat down again in her chair.

George pulled up the stool in front of the dressing-table and sat on that, leaving the other chair for Norah. She took it, for her knees felt weak. She was not going to tell them about Marsh's suspicion that Malcolm might have been involved in Louise's death; that could come later, and she would warn George first. She looked at his haggard face. How would he cope with what he was about to learn? What if all this proved too much for him and he had a stroke or a heart attack? Such things happened.

But not to George. He was needed too much. He would find the strength from somewhere. She turned her mind away from these grim possibilities to give them her message.

'It's Malcolm,' she said, and plunged. 'The police think he may have done the robbery.' It therefore followed that they suspected he had killed Mrs Gibson too; there was no need for her to spell that out.

'What?' Susan, her face already pale under its network of fine thread veins, went whiter still and her eyes looked enormous, shadowed by deep hollows beneath them. She put a hand to her mouth and whispered, 'No, I won't believe it.'

'They've probably got it all wrong and he'll be able to tell them where he was on Wednesday,' Norah said hastily. 'But he had a blue Metro for sale and it's gone. So has Malcolm,' she added. 'He was staying at the Manor Hotel and he isn't there now.' She decided not to mention his unpaid bill.

'He's not at the workshop.' George's remark was a statement, not a question. He was remembering that Malcolm had known no cars had been damaged in the fire, knowledge he should not have possessed.

'No, and there aren't any cars there, either,' said Norah.

'But that means nothing,' said Susan. 'He's off somewhere on business, probably buying something else if he's sold what he had. And he'll have the Porsche with him. He won't sell that.'

'You're telling us that the police think he made those bogus calls to lure us out,' George said slowly. 'It didn't sound like his voice.'

'No, but he could probably disguise it,' said Norah. 'Don't you remember how he used to mimic accents when he was a boy? There's more,' she went on, speaking quickly while her courage lasted. 'He was in prison in Australia,' she told them. 'For fraud.'

'How do you know?' The swiftness of Susan's response startled Norah.

'Mr Marsh told me,' she said. 'They did a check.'

'But why? Why should they do that?'

Norah shrugged. How could she answer?

'It must be to do with Louise,' George said. 'They've been looking at her case again, haven't they, Norah? Marsh wasn't just making contact. He's been poking about in the past. But why ask about Malcolm? He was miles away at the time. He can't have known anything about it.'

At this Susan suddenly burst into a torrent of hysterical tears and began to mutter incoherently. Disconnected words escaped between her sobs. 'Her room – he wouldn't – no. It's impossible,' they heard.

George put his arms round her and stroked her hair, soothing her as one would a child. Norah got up and fetched a glass of water from the bathroom. After a while Susan grew calmer but she would not explain her words. She would never tell anyone what she had seen that night in Selbury House, and the hideous fear with which she had been filled at the time, and ever since when she let herself think about it.

'He's not violent,' was what she said.

But he could be, and they all knew it, and if it could be proved that he had killed Mrs Gibson, then he would be sent to prison for a great many years.

And quite right too, thought two of them, while the third blamed herself for past, unidentified sins of omission.

Malcolm's flight had been called and he was sitting in the lounge at his departure channel when the police found him.

He had been battering the ears of a new acquaintance with details of the insurance business he claimed to be running in Toronto, believing it all himself as he spoke, and he had not noticed the three men who came in, glanced quickly round and then went up to the clerk who would check the boarding cards as the passengers filed out to the aircraft.

They were being called forward in groups, with the first-class passengers left till last, and the three men waited quietly until Malcolm handed over his card for inspection. Then they closed in on him. Few of the other passengers realised that anything was amiss, so neatly was it done. One of the three was Whitlock, who knew him by sight; the others were Detective Sergeant Newton and Detective Inspector Blake.

Malcolm struggled, but they put an armlock on him, soon followed by handcuffs, and he was borne away. He began to protest and bluster, but stopped when he felt the pain in his arm, and when the locks snapped he knew that he was beaten.

They found wads of banknotes distributed among his various pockets, and more in his cases, together with Susan's jewellery. Airport police, in response to a message, had intercepted his baggage before it was loaded on to the plane.

Carol read about it in the paper the following day.

How could he be so evil!

But he was: she knew it. Back into her mind came the memory she had successfully banished for many years, the sight of his red, vengeful face. There was no love in his attack upon her. People said rape was a crime of violence and she knew it was true; Malcolm hated women and he was bitterly jealous of her.

This might kill her mother.

Carol could not get it out of her mind, and Ethel's keen interest in the case kept it alive as a topic between them.

'Imagine! Their own son!' she exclaimed. 'Well, not really, of course, as he was adopted. How ungrateful.' She went on to tell Carol of other adopted children she knew who had turned out very well, one girl becoming a doctor to the amazement of her adoptive parents whose ambitions for her had been more modest. 'I suppose cuckoos in nests, some of them are,' she sighed. 'As if they hadn't had enough to bear, losing their daughter like that all those years ago. It's too bad.'

'Yes,' agreed Carol. 'It is.'

It died out of the news after the first reports of Malcolm being remanded in custody, charged with the robbery and with murdering Mrs Gibson. Now, until his trial, it was *sub judice* and the reporters could not air their theories about how and why it had happened. All that would come after the trial and the sentence. Ethel thought he would get off with manslaughter, if he had a clever lawyer.

Even she at last dropped the subject as another case arose to catch her interest. Carol had been avid for details about her family; she bought several daily papers while it was in the news, and she began having dreams in which she saw her mother weeping and wringing her hands, and her own image, ghostlike, in the background. If she hadn't run away Malcolm might never have done this and Mrs Gibson might be still alive. But if she hadn't run away, she would not have had her lovely children.

She made huge efforts to put it all out of her mind until the trial, which might not take place for a year or more, Ethel said; she knew about these things, declaring that it would take the police months to prepare the case and the defence more months to get theirs ready.

'They'll dream up extenuating circumstances,' she said. 'Plead provocation to get him off. As if that poor cleaning lady ever harmed him. Probably she let him in. They forget about the victims at a time like this. Even the police do. All they think of is getting their man.'

Even allowing for her racy way of putting things, Carol thought that Ethel's comments were justified; sentencing seemed to be a lottery, with some judges allowing men who had killed or attacked children or women to get off with short terms in gaol.

Carol lost weight. Eric had noticed her poor appetite. He worried. She must be overdoing things. Perhaps the

Christmas break would put her right. Like most of the country, her firm closed down for the full holiday period until after the New Year. He began to talk about the summer holiday. What about France this year? She'd like that, wouldn't she, since she spoke such good French?

With difficulty, even after all this time, Carol remembered that officially she had never been to France, but had learned the language at the good school she went to in Australia and by having lessons with a French woman who was a friend of her aunt's.

Why not, she thought, and said she'd get some brochures.

They had a happy Christmas. Later, Eric often thought of that. Joanna and William loved their well-filled stockings and their other toys, and Ethel came to spend the day. There was a plump turkey and Christmas pudding, with ice-cream for the children. The weather was fine and dry and on Christmas Day they took the car out of town to the hills and went for a long and healthy walk. During the week that followed, he took the children swimming while Carol went to the sales.

She began to look better and happier, and her choir gave their concert, singing *The Messiah* in a large hall. Eric took Joanna along to listen, while Ethel stayed with William who was too young to sit through it.

The New Year came and went and the Fosters' lives went on in the normal way. Only Carol still had nightmares. She knew that she would do so until Malcolm's trial was over.

3

The Company

He would not confess to Louise's murder, nor to anything else.

They asked him endless questions, after charging him with the robbery and with killing Mrs Gibson. He sat mulishly silent while they suggested he account for the presence of Susan Vaughan's jewellery in his luggage. She had refused to identify it because to do so would condemn Malcolm, but George had no such scruples, and there were photographs taken for insurance purposes.

The Metro had been traced to the dealer in Coventry. Malcolm's prints were in it, and by painstaking effort forensic scientists found on a pair of his trousers a thread from the dead woman's sweater. Though saturated by the firemen, the garment was in good enough condition for the comparison to be made. Methodically the police built up their case.

They had automatically notified the airports on that

final Friday morning, and when Malcolm, who had had to travel under his own name because of his passport, had checked in at Heathrow, there he was, logged on the computer. If the team from Feringham had not arrived in time to arrest him, other officers would have detained him, but Whitlock was delighted to have brought him in.

The Porsche was found at the used car sales place near Heathrow.

When Malcolm's belongings were checked at the police station, a faded envelope was found in one of his pockets. The name of the addressee mystified Marsh until he looked inside and saw the letter from Susan's brother David to his sister. When it was shown to her, she admitted that it had been tucked into a volume of poetry he had given her; she had once liked reading poetry, she explained to Marsh, who had brought it to her at the Cartwrights', where she and George were on an indefinite visit.

'Why did he take the letter?' she asked George.

George himself had received an enormous shock at the revelation that David had been Norah's partner in her early tragic love affair. Why had she never told him? Why hadn't Susan explained?

At last George told Susan that Malcolm had had some idea that Norah was his mother.

'That's too easy,' she replied. 'Stupid boy.' She was silent. Then she added, 'How we failed him. Or rather, I did.'

'You didn't, my dear. You did more for him than he had any right to expect. Too much, perhaps. It was he who failed, not just us but himself, his true parents –

everyone.' And Louise, he thought, but did not dare to utter. What about her? What had he done to her?

'But I never really loved him,' Susan said. 'That was why I tried so hard. I'd used him to replace Harry, you see, and you can't replace one person with another. They have to make their own mark with you, individually.'

The relief of making this confession was enormous. As Susan spoke, she felt a sudden extraordinary release. George did not at first realise the significance of what had happened to her. He thought that she would want to visit Malcolm in prison, but she expressed no such wish. She seemed to have put him completely from her in a curious divorcement.

George went to see Malcolm, for he could not totally abandon the man whom he had brought up as his son. Their interview, however, was not a good experience for him.

'Come to gloat, have you?' said Malcolm, who had at first considered refusing to see George but his solicitor advised against such conduct. 'Must make you feel great, seeing me here, considering that you're responsible.'

'Oh, Malcolm,' said George, nearly in despair. 'Why must you always blame other people for your own mistakes? You've done a dreadful thing.'

'I'd a right to that stuff,' said Malcolm. 'It was to set me up in Canada.'

'You'd no right to what wasn't yours, and what had Mrs Gibson ever done to hurt you? You killed her.'

'She shouldn't have been there,' said Malcolm sulkily. 'She got in the way.'

He made no such admission of guilt to the police,

staying stubbornly mute when interrogated until at last his solicitor pointed out that by confessing to theft and manslaughter he might avoid conviction for murder and so escape a life sentence.

When he was interviewed about Louise, he did utter. He was asked how he knew about Richard Blacker and he said he had seen her with the man in London, more than once. He did not reveal that he was obsessed by her in a way he did not understand and had followed her, spying on her, long before his marriage and his sojourn in Australia. His absence had not cured him. He consistently denied having seen her on the night she disappeared, declaring that the words Whitlock had found significant were just a throwaway suggestion. After this lapse of time it was useless to look for anyone who might have seen him in Feringham that night, just as trying to trace the people he had taken to Heathrow had proved impossible.

'It's because there were none,' said Marsh. 'I know it. He knows it. We all know it.'

'He may crack after he's sentenced,' suggested Whitlock.

George took Susan to Switzerland for Christmas. They stayed in a comfortable hotel among mountain peaks which had failed to attract their usual depth of snow, so that bare rock was exposed and skiers had to travel some distance to find a piste. They walked around the town and on the lower slopes, and the pure air did them good. When they came home, they had made a plan for the future, and the Lodge House, still awaiting repair, was put up for sale.

Susan could not bear to live there again, nor to face the rebuilding programme. A developer bought the land and applied for permission to knock down what was left of the place and build four maisonettes on the site, allegedly for young couples, but Norah said she was sure they would work out too expensive for most. She told the developer that if the scheme went ahead, she would be interested in acquiring one of the units. Perhaps she could afford one.

The Cartwrights had friends with a holiday house in Cornwall. It was comfortable and well heated, and they willingly agreed to let it to George and Susan until they should need it themselves later in the year. George and Susan both assumed that Norah would go down there with them, but she said that the time had come for a change and that she was going to start a business offering a domestic cleaning service to local householders. She had already found help for various people in the past; now she would employ staff herself, fitting the cleaner to the job, offering both sides the support of contracts and rules. As part of a team you were less easy to exploit than an individual, and the same applied to the householder who need not pander to too idiosyncratic an employee lest she leave. It was the coming thing, Norah explained.

This was her final chance to break away. If she did not take it, she would find herself supporting Susan through the rest of her life. She had done that for long enough.

She went to Cornwall for a visit, and George said that

they had decided to look for somewhere permanent in the area. New surroundings were benefiting Susan; she liked the sea and the clifftop walks they took in fine weather, and she did not mind the strong wind, which he found a little trying. He never went out without his new tweed hat. There was a Fine Arts group Susan could join and it welcomed husbands if they were interested; George said that he might try it. He had resigned from the council and was relieved to be free of his various duties though he knew he would eventually take on others. He might get a boat, he said; he had liked sailing and had done a lot as a boy, when he had lived not so very far from here. They had seen his sister several times and he was blossoming, Norah saw, at being permitted a life of his own again.

'You'll come and stay,' he told Norah.

'Oh yes,' she said. But they both knew that her visits would be rare and might even cease in time.

'Do you think they'll rake up Louise's death when Malcolm comes to trial?' George asked her. 'What does your police chum say?'

Norah had seen quite a lot of Detective Superintendent Marsh. She sometimes wondered if he was compensation to her for the child she had never had; he was about the same age as it would have been by now.

'Malcolm won't confess,' she said. 'Won't discuss it except to say that he never saw her that night. Without evidence, they can do nothing, even though they're convinced he knows something about it.'

'Susan thinks so, too,' said George. 'She won't tell me why. Something must have happened to make her so certain. Maybe he said something which gave him away. I don't ask her about it. It's better left, except that if we could find her we could give her a proper funeral.'

'It might lay your poor ghost,' said Norah. 'Malcolm might confess when he's been in prison a while. He'll have to see psychiatrists and so on, David says.'

'David?'

'David Marsh.'

'So he's David too. How strange,' said George, and added, 'I never knew, you know. Susan never told me.' He wondered who she had been protecting. 'Poor Norah.'

'Poor David Vaughan. I adored him,' Norah said. It did not hurt now. 'It would never have done, you know,' she added, mimicking old Mrs Warrington's regal tone.

How ruthless the old woman had been, George was thinking. But she'd paid for it when her elder son was lost at Monte Cassino.

'I'm sorry about it now,' Norah said, answering the question George had not asked. 'But I was very young and panic-stricken. One forgets how awful it was then, to get caught like that. He might have been a lovely man by now.'

'Or a lovely woman?' suggested George.

'Yes,' she agreed. 'Funny – I'd never thought of that.'

The Tetterton Choral Society's Christmas concert had been a big success, with every ticket sold. Now they were rehearsing Schubert's *Mass in G* for Easter.

Carol forgot past, present and future while she sang. Your voice joined with those around you, blending or in counterpoint, making a melodious whole, and while she sang she lost her sense of isolation. She travelled into town on the bus and often got a lift back from another member of the choir. Eric could not drive her over because he could not leave the children, and she could not drive herself because this was one area where she had decided not to take a chance. On marrying, she would have had to surrender her old driving licence to obtain a new one in her married name and the licensing authorities might detect the fraud. She told Eric that she could not drive.

There had been plans for her to learn; she could apply, now, for a provisional licence in her married name, but she had not done so, saying that there wasn't time, that she was happy as things were but she'd do it one day.

'I thought everyone drove in Australia. All that outback,' Eric once remarked, and she had smiled at him and patted his hand.

'My aunt didn't,' she declared. 'And we lived in town.'

Easter was early that year and the winter had been very mild. Spring arrived weeks sooner than was usual, even in the north. On a mild night Carol set out for the final rehearsal before the concert, which was to be a week before Easter.

As usual, Eric gave her the money for a taxi back. Each week she returned it to him, grateful for his thoughtfulness but determined not to waste it when she could take the bus if there was no lift available. That night a group of singers went to a pub near the rehearsal hall after the practice ended, but Carol said she must go home and that she would catch the bus. Another woman, not the one who often dropped her on her way, said that she must get home too and would take Carol as far as Milton Road.

They parted on a corner, and Carol, with a little more than half a mile to walk, took a short cut down a footpath between a school playing-field and a wall backing on to a row of houses.

He came over the playing-field fence, running up behind her on silent feet, his arm closing round her throat from behind, stifling her scream. She tried to bend forward, buckling her knees to make him lose his balance, and she tried to jam her elbow backwards into him, but she had no time before her strength gave out.

Eric began to listen for her ten minutes before her usual time. He always did that, putting on the kettle for a cup of tea, looking at the children to make sure they were asleep, so that he could ask about her day and reassure her that they did not need her while she answered him. When she was five minutes late, he went to the gate to look for her. After ten minutes he rang the woman who often brought her back to learn from her husband that she had not yet returned either, so he then relaxed. Twenty minutes later, he rang again, and this time was told that Carol had come straight home, brought back by a different person, Mary Bly. After a little delay, Mary's telephone number was provided and Eric immediately called her.

She had dropped Carol at the corner of Milton Road nearly an hour before.

Eric rang the police at once. It did not take them long to find her.

Carol's death made headline news.

UNKNOWN RAPIST STALKS SOPRANO, said one paper. A veteran reporter mentioned the similarity between this crime and the presumed murder of Louise Vaughan more than twelve years before, the difference being that in her case no body had been found. Both victims had been on their way home from a choral society meeting when they met their fate. It turned out later that they had been of similar build, but one was only in her twenties while Carol was over forty. One victim was fair, the other dark. Much later came the information that Carol's hair was dyed, perhaps to hide the fact that she was prematurely grey, one reporter hazarded, giving her piece the heading SECRET VANITY OF MURDER VICTIM. This journalist had caught Ethel unprepared and asked her if she knew that Carol dyed her hair. Ethel's spontaneous denial was all the eager writer needed to devise her new slant on the story.

After that, Ethel was more cautious, saying nothing.

Norah read about the murder in *The Independent*, which was delivered daily to the cottage in Selbury which she had rented for a year while its owners were abroad. During that time the Lodge House site would be developed and she would make a long-term plan. She had begun her cleaning business in time to catch the spring enthusiasm for thorough operations, and had bought equipment which her team of workers, growing steadily, would take with them to their clients. One of Norah's customers was Brenda, who had hired her to maintain both her house and the office.

The Independent did not give much space to what had happened in Tetterton but later, when she went to Feringham, Norah saw headlines in the tabloids which were much more graphic and she bought one out of what she recognised as a sick sort of curiosity.

Later, she talked to Marsh about it; her team cleaned his wifeless house now and she often saw him.

'It might have been a copybook,' he told her. 'Mention of what happened to Louise might have sparked off someone, but I think the choir angle is coincidence. Carol Foster should not have taken that short cut along the footpath, late at night, alone. And ideally the friend should have dropped her at her door. I expect she'll regret that for ever.'

'Will they catch this one?'

'Who knows? There will be clues this time,' said Marsh, not putting into words the reason: because there was a body. 'There may have been other attacks on women in the area, or there may be more, and if they can't get a line on anyone, they can blood-test all the men in the district. Expensive, but it gets results.' He hesitated, then added, 'As she was raped, there would be evidence of the assailant's genetic fingerprint, you see.'

'Oh yes. That new discovery. I remember,' Norah said.

'It's been used already several times, successfully,' said Marsh. 'It's going to make it much easier to convict rapists in future – and other attackers, too, if the victims have been able to scratch them, draw blood even, leaving traces.'

'And it will exonerate the innocent,' said Norah.
'That too, of course,' said Marsh.

Carol was buried on a bright day at the end of April. The inquest on her had been opened and adjourned, the coroner eventually allowing the funeral to be held. Eric wanted a grave to visit, and a week later he went there alone, with a bunch of tulips picked from the garden. He stood gazing at the patched turf fitted in over the new mound.

In her drawer, sorting through her clothes before sending them to Oxfam, he had found a pile of newspaper cuttings referring to the recent case of arson and murder in Selbury, for which crime Malcolm Vaughan, the adopted son of the house, was awaiting trial. He read about the disappearance of Louise twelve years before.

Eric was alone in the house. His mother had taken the children to the cinema to see *The Lady and the Tramp*, leaving him free to deal with a task that would be more difficult the longer he delayed.

He took the pile of cuttings down to the sitting-room and sat there reading them carefully. Afterwards, he burned them. Then he completed his packing up, putting all her clothes into bags, setting aside a tiny pile of other items – the ring that he had given her, her watch, and a pretty locket that he had not seen her wear for weeks.

Afterwards, he went to the library and, in old newspapers, read about the original case when Louise Vaughan had disappeared. Then he saw the resemblance between his own daughter and the young Louise; he learned about Louise's work in publishing and the type of books she helped produce. In one photograph she wore a locket round her neck.

'Why?' asked Eric, aloud, staring down at the quiet earth beneath which, in her simple coffin, she lay.

Could it ever be proved? There were tests, these days, and the parents were both alive. It might be done.

He thought about them, but what good would it do them now to discover what she had done? And why had she done it? She hadn't wanted even him to know.

She was Carol, beloved wife and mother, and he would put that on her tombstone. Let her keep the secrets she had not wished to share.

He gave Joanna the locket.

'I think that possibly it may have been your grandmother's,' he said.

'I wish that we had more of them,' said Joanna in reply.

'More of what?'

'Grandmothers and grandfathers,' she replied.

There was no answer he could give.

A CASE TO
ANSWER

1

She was invisible.

For a long time Charlotte did not realise what had happened, for the onset was gradual. Approaching pedestrians headed straight towards her when she walked along the street, not deflecting from her path, so that she was forced to step aside, even sometimes apologising, though no one answered. She must also be inaudible, she reflected.

There were moments, such as at the check-out in the supermarket, or against the grille in the post office, when she was perceived, but usually the cashier or the clerk made no eye contact with her. After all, it wasn't necessary for the transaction; why should they bother? And it wasn't as if the post office staff in Granbury had known her before her transformation, for she had moved there only after Rupert's death and, small and dumpy, unremarkable in every way, she was patently a person of no consequence.

Until Jerry called.

He came one evening after dark, ringing the doorbell hard. Charlotte had been listening to the radio and she thought it was the milkman, wanting to be paid. Even he never looked at her, merely taking the money, and asking if she required the usual at the weekend. But instead of him, a young man stood on the doorstep. He looked straight at her out of large eyes whose colour, though the porch light shone down upon him, Charlotte could not see. A new helper for the roundsman, she supposed.

'Are you from the milkman?' she said, and smiled.

'No,' said the caller. 'I'm a young offender. Thank you for smiling,' and he held out a plastic identity card of what she later thought might be dubious authenticity.

'Oh,' said Charlotte, unaware that she had done so, and only briefly startled. 'I never buy anything at the door,' she told him firmly. Such youths had rung her bell in the past, but never one with such a pleasant, open countenance. 'I hope you'll mend your ways,' she said, and added, 'You shouldn't be calling on people after dark. You could alarm someone.' Of a nervous disposition, she nearly added.

'I suppose that's true,' said Jerry. 'Well, thanks,' and, hefting his shabby satchel stuffed with unattractive merchandise on to his shoulder, he turned away and walked down the short path to the gate.

Charlotte was still smiling as she closed the door. What was his crime, she wondered: simple theft, shoplifting, perhaps? Rupert would have given him short shrift, probably even reporting his visit to the police, declaring that such pedlars might be testing to see if houses were unoccupied so that they, or accomplices, could break in. Surely that nice young man wasn't on such a mission?

The thought worried her as she returned to her radio programme and her tapestry. Rupert had died six months ago, suddenly, of a heart attack, and after only two years of marriage, she had become a widow for the second time.

That old bat – well, she wasn't so old – was on the ball about the darkness, Jerry thought, walking down the road, for that was when, unnoticed, you could sometimes find a door or window unlocked and slip inside to help yourself to anything available; there was always something lying around even if you found no cash – a radio or an easily detached video recorder. Jerry enjoyed the excitement of such raids; he wasn't into drugs or nicking cars. He'd done several opportunist operations like this with Pete. It was Pete's scam; Jerry did the sweet-talking at the door while Pete went round the back and sneaked inside to take whatever he could find. The woman had seemed all right; a bit more talk and he'd have got her to buy a few things from him. Still, he'd soon find someone else to dazzle with his sales pitch; Jerry's artless expression and steadfast gaze had got him out of many a past scrape.

While Jerry was knocking on doors and doing his best to sell dusters to whoever answered, Pete was testing for easy entry. Pete was small, slim and agile, and he nipped quickly round the rear of houses while Jerry was busy switching on the charm. They'd mocked up a licence and bought a few dusters and dishcloths at a warehouse sale. As a decoy, Jerry was a useful partner.

Pete, sticking close to the wall of the house, then sliding past the garage, was round at the back before the door was opened. There was no way of knowing, in advance, how many people were at home, so he was alert for movement indoors. Watching the houses was not part of his and Jerry's routine, for that could attract attention; you had to take your chance, nip in fast while the householder was at the door, kept busy by Jerry and his patter.

These recently built houses were less easy to approach unseen than the older, individual ones with well-planted gardens offering cover to prowlers, and unless Jerry, at the front, had a sale, any snitch had to be swift. A security light came on as he tried the back door; it was unlocked, and he stepped inside; the exterior light illuminated the kitchen as Pete glanced quickly round. Two pans were draining by the sink but there was no purse or handbag visible, nothing to be quickly taken, and then he heard footsteps. Jerry had failed to detain whoever had opened the front door. Pete did not wait; he fled as swiftly and silently as he had come, but he'd remember this house, maybe visit it again. A good few folk locked their back doors at dusk, but not, it seemed, whoever lived here.

He was luckier further down the road, collecting a watch and a transistor radio left ready for the taking. Neither was missed until the following day.

The railway station at Becktham had recently been modernised, its ironwork painted vivid red and blue, even a coffee bar established on the up-line to London. Trains carried commuters back and forth, running frequently at peak times and maintaining a good service throughout the day; a number of Granbury's regular travellers found it worth driving the extra miles to use this route rather than the nearer station at Nettington, where the car park was filled to capacity soon after nine o'clock when the first cheap fares operated. Charlotte Frost had forgotten about the young offender when, one morning some weeks later, she inserted her Fiat between a Discovery Range Rover and a blue Honda; she had planned to catch the 9.05, but thought she might not manage it when she arrived at the booking-office, for a large man in a dark suit who was making a complicated booking with his credit card seemed impervious to the fact that there were other passengers queuing up behind him. Buying his season ticket, Charlotte deduced, mildly irritated by the delay but content to catch the train due fifteen minutes later, for she had no morning appointment and was planning to visit an art exhibition before meeting Lorna. She decided that the man was insensitive, pompous and boring; he was entitled to receive whatever attention he required, but his was an intricate transaction; couldn't he have arrived earlier? Standing behind him, her exact fare ready, she wondered about his life. Was his wife bullied into meekness or was he a lamb at home? He was clearly prosperous; was he a city magnate or a lawyer? While she pondered, rapid footsteps pounded up behind her and a breathless woman, streaked blonde hair in some disorder, saw the hold-up ahead, came to an enforced halt behind Charlotte, and stood shifting from foot to foot. She was not merely impatient; she was frantic. The man still stood there, slowly conducting his negotiations while the new arrival chafed.

'The train will be coming. I've got to get to work,' she told the air, or Charlotte.

'Go ahead of me. It doesn't matter if I miss this one,' said Charlotte, standing back.

'Oh, thank you,' gasped the woman, barely looking at Charlotte as she took her place.

At this point the man's business was concluded and he moved ponderously on. The distressed blonde bought her ticket in seconds, speeding off as the train's arrival was announced, and Charlotte's good deed was rewarded, for the clerk produced hers promptly and she, too, was in time to board it. Taking her seat – there was still space, though the train would fill up at the next stop – she wondered briefly about the distraught woman who, like the man, had not allowed enough time to catch her train. Perhaps she had had to take children to school, or the washing-machine had flooded, or some other domestic disaster had delayed her. Charlotte would never know.

She travelled up to London in a different carriage, but, glancing out of the window when the train stopped at Denfield, twenty minutes into the journey, she saw the woman hurry along the platform, still in a rush.

Charlotte enjoyed the exhibition and afterwards took the Underground to South Kensington, where she was to meet Lorna, her stepdaughter, who was a partner in a residential letting agency based nearby. In the cloakroom at the restaurant where they were to meet, Charlotte, who had arrived first, added cautious dabs of blusher to her pale face; she was determined that Lorna should deliver a good report to her brother: they, after all, had lost their father, while she was an interloper, marrying him after the death of their mother, whom Charlotte had never met.

Charlotte had known Rupert slightly for several years; she

had worked for a charity which the company he ran had sponsored, not only financially, but also by providing training and work experience. Meeting at a fund-raising function, each had felt the other to be an old friend, when they were really little more than acquaintances, but Rupert, now widowed, had walked her to her car after the event, and somehow or other they had arranged to meet for dinner the following week. He had collected her from the house where she had lived since soon after her husband's death. One thing had led to another, and because he was now the chairman of his company, Rupert had insisted that they marry. To be openly lovers, he had said, would provoke gossip, and living together without marrying would be even worse. Also, he wanted to give her the security marriage to him would offer. In fact, he loved her, and it had been easy for her, after her first astonishment, to love him in return. Their two years together had been happy, though for Charlotte they were demanding for her new role involved many duties. Rupert's house was large; its grounds were occasionally used for village events; and there were the visits of his children and grandchildren. In addition, there was the garden, which delighted Charlotte, but it took up time and energy. She adapted as rapidly as possible, doing all she could to make friends with his family; then, abruptly, one fine summer's day, everything changed when Rupert collapsed and died at a meeting in London.

Lorna had suggested that they meet today. After their father's death, his children had rearranged Charlotte's life. By the terms of his will, apart from the pension she inherited, she was to continue living at White Lodge, which was left to his children, for as long as she wished, but if she were to move she was to be re-housed, rent-free, in a style befitting her status as his widow. Felix, Rupert's son, soon told her that White Lodge must be sold as it was much too big for her on her own, which was true, and, bustled briskly along by him, she was speedily installed in a three-bedroomed modern house in Vicarage Fields, a small development in the grounds of the former vicarage in Granbury.

Charlotte could not object; it was appropriate and comfortable, but it was not hers: after her death it would revert to Rupert's family.

Granbury's vicar, whose territory now included three other churches, lived in a modern house in one of the other parishes.

Charlotte's son Tim, who was in the navy and serving overseas when Rupert died, thought she should have asked for a cash settlement and bought somewhere of her own. She still had money left after paying off the mortgage from the sale of her house when she remarried, but she had gone along with her stepchildren's arrangements because events had been too rapid for her to think things through calmly. In any case, her capital, in a building society account, had not appreciated as much as house prices. White Lodge was soon sold; probate was not long delayed and it had all happened very quickly.

Number Five, Vicarage Fields, was comfortable, warm and freshly decorated. It was furnished with pieces Charlotte had kept from her former home, and a few new things swiftly bought from John Lewis. Though Lorna urged her to take anything she wanted from White Lodge, Charlotte asked for nothing; she did not want bad blood between herself and Rupert's children lest in future they disputed her right to any items.

Now, buffeted by the speed of her metamorphosis, she felt

herself to be in limbo, invisible, without status, and without even her own identity, for she had a new name, one which had been hers for only two years.

What did Lorna want, she wondered, entering the restaurant, following the waiter to the table which the younger woman had booked. It was an Italian trattoria, and she did not seem to be invisible to the waiter who showed her to her seat; Italians, she reflected, were fond of their families and respected their grandparents.

Lorna, arriving at the restaurant in a rush, gave her a fleeting kiss, summoned the waiter to order a bottle of the house white wine, and dutifully asked about Charlotte's family. Tim was still aboard his ship somewhere in the Mediterranean while Victoria, his wife, and their children were carrying on their lives ashore in Dorset. Jane was working for a publisher in New York.

Jane hadn't liked Felix. Charlotte had been aware of that, early on, but the two had rarely met and she could see no reason for the hostility. Felix, dark and saturnine, not much resembling his father, had an arrogant manner which Charlotte did not care for, but she attributed it to a sense of insecurity, for though he seemed successful in his career, it did not match his father's. In New York, Jane was living with a man she had met through her work; a writer, Ben, a lot older than she was, separated from his wife but not divorced. Charlotte had never met him; photographs showed a thin, pleasant face, and Jane expressed herself as very happy.

Lorna was relieved to learn that all was well with Charlotte's family; if any one of them were having a crisis, either domestically or to do with their work, she would have felt inhibited about asking for Charlotte's help, the reason for today's invitation.

Over fruit salad for Lorna, and zabaglione for Charlotte – she was touched that Lorna remembered how much she liked it and insisted that she have it – this was revealed.

'Felix and Zoe have broken up,' Lorna said abruptly. 'Zoe's gone off with some photographer she met through work.' Zoe, Felix's wife, was a journalist working for a women's magazine. 'The kids are in a mess,' she added. 'Imogen's pregnant and has run away from school. She was missing for a while, but she turned up at Zoe's mother's, and Nicholas can't be found.'

'Oh dear,' Charlotte said, inadequately. Imogen and Nicholas were twins, aged just eighteen. She'd sent them fifty pounds each on their birthday several weeks ago. Imogen had sent a card, thanking her, but she had yet to hear from Nicholas.

'The thing is,' said Lorna, plunging on, 'with Zoe having bunked off – she's in Los Angeles with her photographer who's on an assignment there – I wondered if you'd have Imogen to stay for a while, till she sorts herself out a bit.'

'Oh,' repeated Charlotte, now thoroughly dismayed.

'She's always liked you,' Lorna tried, as a lure.

Charlotte and Imogen had seldom met, but Charlotte knew that Rupert had thought the plain, plump girl was overshadowed by her elegant, hyperactive mother and her handsome twin.

'I suppose this pregnancy is a desperate gesture,' she said.

Lorna was aware, not for the first time, of Charlotte's sharp perception.

'Yes,' she said. 'I think so. But Zoe hasn't come back. Says

Imogen must decide for herself what to do, and she's got to fulfil her contract.'

'So she has been told?'

'Yes.'

'What does Felix have to say about it?'

'He's hit the roof. Furious,' said Lorna. 'And he's furious with Nicholas, too, but he says he'll turn up when he's out of money.'

'When do you want Imogen to come to Granbury?' she asked, making an effort not to sound as reluctant as she felt.

'So you'll have her, then?' Lorna's face lit up in relief.

'For a while,' Charlotte said. 'She'll be bored with me,' she added, on a more hopeful note.

'She needs a bit of looking after,' Lorna said, feeling rather sheepish now that her objective had been achieved.

'Where is she?' asked Charlotte. Imogen was a pupil at a boarding school in Sussex and Nicholas was at a sixth-form college in Oxford.

'She's with Zoe's mother, but she can't stay there. Zoe's mother's going on a Baltic cruise on Saturday,' Lorna said. 'Imogen can't stay in the flat alone in the state she's in.'

Maybe not, thought Charlotte grimly, but she can return to it when her grandmother's cruise is over.

She asked when that would be, and Lorna seemed vague.

'Oh – two weeks or so, I suppose,' she said. 'Imogen will know.'

Charlotte told herself that Rupert would want her to care for his granddaughter in her hour of need, and what if it were one of her own grandchildren in this extremity? Wouldn't she expect someone, in the family or outside it, to rescue her?

The fact that her own grandchildren were still under ten was irrelevant.

'When do you want her to come?' she asked again.

'Could you take her back with you today?' Lorna asked. 'After you've done whatever you've planned this afternoon?'

Today was only Thursday.

'I suppose the grandmother has things to do. Packing and so on,' Charlotte said. She had been wondering why she had been asked to lunch in London when all this could have been settled on the telephone.

'Precisely,' Lorna said.

'Why can't Felix have her?' After all, she was his daughter. And Lorna was her aunt.

'Well, you know he's away a lot,' said Lorna. 'He's abroad now.' Felix was a director of a company with interests in West Africa and spent a lot of his time travelling. 'Besides,' she added, 'he's so angry. He needs time to cool down. He'll telephone, of course.' She'd make him. There was no need to tell Charlotte that Felix, too, had been playing away from home. 'He's always been so disappointed because Nicholas got the looks and poor Imogen is so ordinary,' Lorna went on. 'He had this notion, like all fathers, I suppose, of a pretty little adoring daughter.'

'I've never thought her ugly,' Charlotte defended Imogen. 'Nor did Rupert.'

'No – well – she was very upset when he died,' Lorna said. 'That probably didn't help her state of mind.'

It didn't help me, either, Charlotte thought.

'I'm sure she was very fond of your mother,' she said aloud. Poor girl: she'd been through quite a lot before this break-up of her parents.

'Yes,' agreed Lorna. 'I can't have her at the moment,' she added. 'I've got a lot of work on just now and Brian's in the middle of a big case.' Lorna's husband, Brian, was a solicitor specialising in company law.

When their father remarried, and so quickly, she and Felix had been amazed and even shocked. At first they resented Charlotte. After all, their father could have afforded a housekeeper, they reflected, reckoning that they could provide him with all the affection he might need, and unwilling to acknowledge that he might want a sexual relationship. Though Brian had disagreed, they and Zoe had decided that Charlotte had caught him when he was vulnerable. Lorna's attitude had altered during the brief marriage when she saw its success, and when she realised that Charlotte did not want to usurp her mother's role. She was quiet, undemanding, dependable and self-effacing, and Lorna trusted her to do her best for Imogen in the short term.

'Does Imogen know about this plan?' Charlotte asked. 'What if she won't agree?'

'She has agreed,' said Lorna. There was no need to describe Imogen's hysterical reaction to the idea, but after she had calmed down she had seen that there was no better alternative.

'What about the young man involved?' Charlotte asked.

'She won't say a word,' Lorna replied. 'Nicholas may know who he is. Some boy at the school, I suppose.'

What a pickle, Charlotte thought, agreeing to meet Imogen at Marylebone. The grandmother would despatch her there in a taxi; only the train they would catch need be decided. It had all been well thought out. She had been skilfully manipulated into a position from which she could not extract herself without seeming to be very disobliging.

* * *

She reached Marylebone well before the time of the train she had selected as convenient; always well organised, she had a timetable in her handbag. Emerging from the Underground, she saw that Imogen was already standing below the departure indicator board, her shoulders slumped, as though beneath the burden of her long straight hair, a large holdall at her feet. She wore a navy fleece jacket and baggy tracksuit trousers. Remaining invisible for a few minutes more, Charlotte studied her as she approached. She looked lost and dejected, and she was very young. Poor unhappy girl, I must make her feel welcome, Charlotte told herself, advancing. She's having a bad time now and there is worse to come, whatever she decides to do about her present predicament.

'Hullo, Imogen,' she called, as she approached, and the girl turned a pale, mutinous face towards her.

The woman with the mane of tangled hair who had been so desperate at the ticket office that morning got into their carriage when they stopped at Denfield on the way back. Still in a rush, she sat down across the aisle from Charlotte, who was in the gangway seat of a set of three, with Imogen, separated by a vacant seat, next to the window, staring out. The woman did not notice Charlotte. Invisible again, thought Charlotte, who throughout her lunch with Lorna had been looked in the eye across the table but whose gaze Imogen had steadily avoided after first greeting her with a sullen 'Hi.'

The woman left the train ahead of them, but Imogen, even with her holdall, was close behind her, not waiting for

Charlotte as she ascended the stairs and crossed the bridge over the track.

'You wait here with your bag while I get the car,' Charlotte told her when at last she halted, looking indecisive, outside the station buildings. The girl had dozed off during the journey, drooping against the window, scarcely stirring. Charlotte, who had brought a book, read it with determination if not wholehearted comprehension. She did not view the days or weeks ahead with optimism. Lorna had declared, before they parted, that it was up to Charlotte to get Imogen's story out of her and talk her through the choices that were before her.

'After all, you're not related. You can be objective,' Lorna had said. 'There's not a lot of time in hand,' she added.

Meaning if the girl was to have an abortion, Charlotte thought.

'Any decision has to be hers,' was her reply.

'Of course,' Lorna had agreed.

Now, as if she had not heard Charlotte's instruction, Imogen trudged along behind her with her bag, and heaved it into the boot of Charlotte's Fiat. The woman with the hair was ahead of them, still walking down the parking lot, but as Charlotte started the engine she drove past them, rather too fast, in an old red Metro.

Her working day was a short one, Charlotte reflected; she had spent the journey gazing out of the window and she, like Imogen, was a troubled soul.

2

That evening Lorna telephoned her brother Felix, now in Germany.

'It was OK,' she said. 'Charlotte was only too pleased to help. Imogen will be safe with her. I'll call her soon and see if they've had a good talk, and you should ring, too.'

'Wretched girl,' said Felix. 'She's done this just to get at me. And Zoe, I suppose.'

'I doubt it,' said Lorna. 'The running away from school, maybe, but not the pregnancy bit, but she'd have been sacked anyway, when they found out. That's probably pure accident.'

'Or impure,' said Felix. 'I thought girls knew it all these days – safe sex, morning-after pill and all that.'

'They do, in theory,' said Lorna. 'It's the hormone bit that's unpredictable.' And peer pressure, and other unforeseen things, uncomfortable ones like emotions.

'Do you think she'll get rid of it?'

'How do I know?' Lorna replied. 'If she talks to Charlotte, I'm sure all the pros and cons will be fully aired. Charlotte is very sensible.'

'And she owes us,' Felix said.

'Oh, come on, Felix. She made Dad very happy and she's taken nothing that was ours.'

'The house,' said Felix. 'There's nearly three hundred thousand tied up in that house, bringing nothing in, and she's only sixty-five.'

'It'll hold its value – even appreciate,' Lorna said. 'And she's going to see to its upkeep herself. You're just thinking of the settlement you'll have to give Zoe.'

'It had crossed my mind,' said Felix.

Lorna did not remind him that she owned half of Charlotte's house.

'What about Nicholas?' she asked. 'Have you tracked him down?'

'No. I've left messages with his flatmates,' said Felix. 'But he hasn't rung back.'

'I hope he hasn't run off somewhere, too,' said Lorna.

'No. The flatmate was so cagey that I think he knows where he is,' said Felix.

'Did you leave a message about Imogen with the flatmate?'

'No. We don't want her foolishness broadcast all over the place,' said Felix. 'I just said I needed to speak to him urgently.'

'Well, he'll ring eventually,' Lorna soothed. 'You could let him know where Imogen is,' she added.

'I'll go down to Granbury when Charlotte's had a chance to talk to her,' Felix decided. 'Make her see some sense.'

'That's up to you. I thought you were going to go to LA to try to win Zoe back,' said Lorna.

'I thought about it,' he answered. 'But what good will it do, if she's made her mind up?'

'Can it do harm?' asked Lorna. 'At least it shows you want her back.'

'But do I?' Felix said, in bitter tones. 'If I persuaded her, she might take off again.'

They could go on talking in circles like this all night.

'Look, I've got to go now,' Lorna said. 'Think it over and talk to me again.' And you might say thanks, seeing that I've sorted out your daughter, however temporary the solution, she thought.

Felix, hurt and angry, did not want to end the conversation. 'I suppose you've got things to do,' he said.

'Something like that. People to feed and so on,' said Lorna, whose husband was even now preparing dinner for the family.

'Don't give me that,' said Felix. 'I know Brian's the cook in your house.' But he laughed as he said it.

'Take care,' said Lorna, and hung up.

After her good lunch, a snack was all Charlotte wanted for her supper, but she had a pregnant mother in her care. Nourishing fare must be offered.

It had not taken her long, after she married Rupert, to get used to catering again for others than just herself, even though it was some time since her own family had left home, and now, just as easily, she had resumed the solitary's pattern of minimum supplies. There were no remains of a leg of lamb or roast chicken in the fridge to fall back on, but there were fresh vegetables, eggs and cheese. She suggested an omelette, and Imogen, who had not said a word since they met, merely obediently following her like a silent shadow, nodded.

Despite her resolution to be patient, Charlotte was exasperated.

'Imogen, I realise that you are very unhappy and going through a bad patch in your life, but you haven't lost the power of speech, have you? I know you to be normally well-mannered. Please show me that you haven't changed and reply so that I can hear you.'

'Yes, I'd like an omelette, please,' said Imogen. Then she burst into tears, and rushed upstairs.

Charlotte, who was tired after her day in London and the unexpected way in which it had ended, sank down at the kitchen table in defeat. She would not follow the girl. Let her cry or sulk or both, and if she were hungry, eventually she would reappear. She had put Imogen in the nicer of the two spare bedrooms, where a bed was already made up, as it always was in case, however unlikely it might be, an unexpected guest arrived. Imogen had dumped her bag and then, after Charlotte had taken clean towels for her from the airing cupboard, had gone across to the bathroom, but had soon emerged and followed Charlotte downstairs.

I can only do so much for her, Charlotte decided, and poured herself a whisky. Must I take her omelette up to her, she wondered, while she ate a cheese sandwich. After she had finished it, with no sign of Imogen reappearing, she decided that she should, so she whipped one up, adding parsley and tomatoes, made some toast and laid it all on a tray which she carried upstairs. She knocked on Imogen's door and said, 'I've brought your supper up.'

There was no reply, and during the few seconds before she decided to try the door, she wondered what she would do if it was locked and Imogen refused to open it, imagining slit wrists and overdoses, so it was a relief when it yielded to her hand.

Imogen was lying on top of the bedspread, fully dressed but without her heavy trainers, which were neatly placed below the window. Her face was tear-stained and she was fast asleep, a deep, exhausted, natural sleep. There was no glass of water or paracetamol packet at her side.

Charlotte took the duvet off the other bed and draped it over her. Then she drew the curtains against the night and tiptoed out, closing the door quietly, taking the tray with her.

Pete, returning to Vicarage Fields on a further opportunist expedition, had seen a number of lights on at Number Five, which he had marked down on his earlier visit with Jerry as a likely target. Figures passed to and fro, two women, and at last the lights went out, but he decided to leave that one tonight and try another time. He turned back out of the close and into the High Street, off which it led, continuing until he came to Meadow Lane and into Church Street.

Meadow Lane was a quiet road with a few old cottages which had been renovated and were now much sought after by couples moving out of London. Charlotte would have liked one of these pretty houses with their established gardens, and Apple Cottage had been for sale when she moved, but at a far higher price than Number Five, Vicarage Fields. She had seen for herself that this ruled it out before Felix had explained that a modern house cost far less in upkeep; with an old place, he said, you were always having to find money for repairs. There was no argument.

Pete remembered that there had been a very elderly man at one of these houses; Jerry had said the man had spoken to him firmly, advising him to go to the Job Centre and look for real work. He'd gone and done it, got a job, though not through the Job Centre, and he'd said he wouldn't go out nicking any more. Stupid twit, thought Pete. On his previous visit, he had been able to get to the rear of this cottage under the cover of various bushes and shrubs while Jerry sweet-talked the old man, but the back door had been locked. However, Pete had seen that there was no burglar alarm, and that there was a window with a half-light which looked easy to force; he had decided to try it one night. With luck he could reach inside and open the latch. Now was as good a time as any.

He walked up the road with his usual loping stride. Pete did not swagger, as Jerry often did; he was thin but muscular, appearing to pose no threat but in fact wiry and strong. People remembered Jerry, but they overlooked Pete. Reaching the cottage, which was some distance from the nearest street light, an advantage for anyone seeking unlawful entry, Pete opened the gate and went across the short front lawn to the side of the house, which was in darkness. Though his eyes had adjusted, he stumbled at first, almost tripping over the stone border to a flower bed, but immediately a bright security light blazed, and he ducked into the shelter of a large bush. Nothing happened, and he moved cautiously on; cats could set those things off, he reminded himself as he edged round to his target. Another light came on, and Pete swore under his breath. The place was wired up like Fort Knox. He moved close against the wall, calculating that this would remove him from the orbit of the sensor and that the light would soon go out. The window he was aiming for was only a few yards away and he inched towards it, stretching up with his knife to force it open. Pete had done plenty of breaking and entering in his young life, and this should be an easy one. He balanced on the sill, reaching in for the catch of the main window which, after a struggle, he managed to unfasten. Soon he was crawling across the drainer by the sink, lowering himself on to the floor. He felt his way to the back door and opened it: a getaway route was vital, in case the householder should wake up. All this time the outside light was illuminating the interior, but now, abruptly, it went off, and Pete switched on the torch he carried, revealing a pine table, pine fitments round the walls, an electric cooker and a large refrigerator. Hoping to find cash, he opened a few drawers, but saw only cutlery and rolls of plastic bags, foil, J-cloths in a pack, and, in one, a stack of tea towels. He moved on to the kitchen door, opened it, and crossed the stone-flagged hall, entering a large room where there were two armchairs in faded blue linen covers and an oval oak dining-table with four wheel-back chairs set round it. Two matching chairs stood against the wall, and there was a flat-topped desk in one corner. Pete hurried over to pull out drawers, looking for cash, a pension book, credit cards – anything of value.

A slight sound made him turn at the same moment that Howard Smythe, a retired naval captain, eighty-six years old, turned the main light on as he entered the room, and, holding aloft a golf club, demanded to know what he was doing.

Pete's pencil torch was too slim to serve as a weapon, and he looked round for one, grabbing a heavy paperweight and advancing towards the old man who was blocking his way out. Pete flung it at him and Howard Smythe was forced to duck. Pete pushed past him while he was off balance, but the old man did not fall. He hooked Pete round the ankle with his number four iron and had the satisfaction of seeing the boy trip, crashing to the ground.

Pete was young, with quick reflexes, but Howard Smythe was tall. He stood over him, golf club at the ready, well aware that a householder, in such circumstances, must not use inappropriate force, even in self-defence, or he would be the one to be arrested.

'You miserable little wretch,' he said, as Pete, his face pressed against the thick Indian carpet, tried to struggle to his feet. 'Lie down,' he added, and, still wielding the golf club, pushed him hard between the shoulder-blades with his slippered foot. 'Now crawl,' he ordered, and made Pete move on hands and knees across the room until Howard could reach the telephone, which was on the desk.

The police took fifteen minutes to arrive. They found that the back door was open and by then both captive and capturer were feeling the draught which blew across the hall and into the sitting-room. Captain Smythe, in his ancient Jaeger dressing gown, was sitting in a large wheel-back chair which he had placed across the intruder's legs. Every time Pete, still lying face downwards on the floor, started to wriggle free, a sharp tap on the shoulder from the golf club caused him to subside.

'It was a good sight,' said PC Dawkins, first on the scene, after he had charged his prisoner at Nettington Police Station. 'The little toe-rag hadn't had time to take anything. Kept complaining that he'd got his face full of fluff off the carpet, if you please.'

Charlotte, though tucked away in Vicarage Fields, heard the siren of the first police car that hurried to the scene; sounds carried strangely, and when the church bells rang she could hear them clearly, their peals funnelling across a gap between trees and buildings. Oh dear, she thought: trouble somewhere. She sat propped up in bed, spectacles on, reading a short story by Carol Shields. Short stories were just right for reading in bed, she found; you could finish one and then compose yourself for sleep. Tonight, however, after she closed the book, her mind began to dwell on the presence and the problems of her uninvited guest. At some point they would have to discuss Imogen's plans, if she had any, and if her visit lasted more than just a few days she should see the doctor.

Eventually, Charlotte went to sleep, and did not wake when Imogen, in the early hours, crept downstairs and made herself a hearty fry-up. Charlotte only discovered that the girl had done this in the morning. Imogen had washed up the plates and cutlery she had used and left them to drain, but the last two eggs had gone, much of the milk, the end of a loaf and the two remaining bananas.

She must be feeling better, Charlotte decided, taking bread out of the freezer, and putting on the kettle for her coffee. What was she going to do about her? When would Imogen deign to appear downstairs? And if she did, what then? She couldn't simply hang about all day doing nothing. If she were younger, useful or interesting tasks could be devised; Charlotte remembered school holidays with her own children and the activities that had occupied them – tennis, swimming, going to museums. But that was a long time ago, and Imogen was not a child.

At this point in her thoughts, the telephone rang. It was Nicholas.

'I think you've got my sister there,' he said. 'I'd like to speak to her.'

There were no preliminaries, no lead in to the conversation, so Charlotte wasted no time either.

'I'll see if she's awake,' she said. 'Just hold on, Nicholas.'

Irritated by his belligerent tone but relieved that at least he had now surfaced, she went upstairs and tapped on Imogen's door, then opened it.

'It's Nicholas on the telephone,' she said, addressing the bed, where a humped bundle under the duvet was all that could be seen. 'I'll tell him you're coming to talk to him, Imogen.'

There was a grunt, and then some mumbled words.

'What did you say?' asked Charlotte.

'I said, haven't you got a cordless?' Imogen growled. They were virtually the first words she had uttered within Charlotte's hearing.

'No, I haven't,' Charlotte snapped. 'But you can take it in my bedroom, to be more private. It's just across the landing,' and she went from the room, leaving the door open and going down the stairs.

'She's on her way,' she said to Nicholas.

'Thanks,' he managed.

'Where are you, Nicholas?' she asked.

'Nowhere important,' he replied, and at that moment Imogen's voice cut in on the other instrument. Charlotte replaced hers firmly. She could dial 1471 after they had finished their conversation, and learn the number he had called from. It might be necessary to tell Felix that his son had made a move; she'd think about that.

How had Nicholas, reported to be missing, known where his sister was?

3

Half an hour later, Imogen left the house.

After talking to her brother, she sprang into action. Charlotte heard her running a bath, and while she was in the bathroom Charlotte dialled to discover Nicholas's number. By its length, she knew the call had come from a mobile phone, so she was none the wiser as to where he was. Soon, Imogen appeared, dressed in clean jeans and a white sweater under the heavy fleece jacket she had worn on the journey yesterday. She had washed her dark hair, which hung damply round her shoulders.

Charlotte offered her the hair-drier, but Imogen said no, it would be all right, thanks. She had to go out and she didn't have time.

Charlotte managed not to ask where she was going.

'When will you be back?' she enquired, instead.

'I don't know,' said Imogen. 'Maybe I'll phone you.'

'Please do. I need to know about meals,' Charlotte said. 'Do you know my number?'

Imogen didn't, and Charlotte wrote it down on a piece of paper.

'Thanks,' Imogen said, still not looking Charlotte in the eye.

'Have you got any money? Or a phone card?'

'I've got a mobile,' said Imogen, patting her jacket pocket. 'It wasn't turned on. That's why Nick had to ring you,' she added, grudgingly, rightly interpreting Charlotte's expression.

Everyone except Charlotte seemed to have one these days.

'Enjoy your walk,' was all she said, as the front door closed behind the girl.

Wherever she went from Vicarage Fields, Imogen would have to go into the High Street, but unless Charlotte followed her, there was no means of finding out which way she turned after that. I'm not her keeper, Charlotte told herself; but she was. Imogen had seemed animated at last, however. Making contact with her brother had brought her to life. Perhaps she was going to meet him somewhere now, but she hadn't taken her luggage, such as it was, so she must mean to return. Charlotte went upstairs into the spare bedroom where the girl had spent the night, expecting to find the bed unmade and discarded clothes flung about the room, but it was scrupulously neat: the bedspread was tidily arranged, tucked up under the pillows; the only sign of occupation was the plain wooden-backed hairbrush and a black comb placed neatly parallel on the dressing-table. In the bathroom, the same high standards prevailed: Imogen's peach-coloured towel hung on a hook, away from Charlotte's green one, which was over the heated rail. Her sponge bag was on the windowsill, with her wet pink and white striped flannel folded on top of it. She hadn't even hung it on the side of the bath. This was the behaviour of a well-trained schoolgirl, and Charlotte felt tears stinging her eyes. What was going on in Imogen's head?

When Lorna telephoned half an hour later to see how things were, Charlotte reported that Imogen had slept well, was being no trouble, and had just gone out for a walk. She did not add that the girl had had no breakfast, but since she had eaten a large meal during the night, Charlotte thought that was of no consequence.

Imogen had to find the church. She was going to meet Nicholas, but he would not come to the house because of Charlotte's presence, so they had had to choose a meeting-place which both could easily find. Wherever you were, you could always find the church, he had said. Nicholas had a car – Imogen had not yet passed her test – and they could go off in that for a bit, decide what to do next.

She hadn't asked Charlotte for directions because that would have revealed where she was going, but if she didn't come within sight of the church as she walked along, anyone she met would know where it was. Imogen had seen nothing of Granbury when they arrived the previous evening, for by then it was getting dark. She had never been there before; it was about twenty miles from White Lodge, her grandparents' house, which she had often visited, particularly before the death of her grandmother and several times after her grandfather had married Charlotte. His death had been a great shock to her; Imogen had loved him, and he had always indulged her. With him, she had never felt herself to be ugly, as she did with everyone else, and especially her brother, who had all the looks, as she had often heard people comment when she was younger. She turned right out of Vicarage Fields into the High Street, walking past several houses, a post office with a telephone box outside it, and, set back from a small parking area, a butcher's and a general store. After passing a row of terraced houses, she came to a side road. Meadow Lane, said a sign, and she decided to go that way. She had walked only a short distance down it – there was no footpath – when a police car overtook her; it slowed down, stopping just ahead of her, and a uniformed officer got out of it, walking towards her, putting his cap on.

Imogen halted. He couldn't be after her; her brief vanishing trick was over. Going missing wasn't a crime.

'Excuse me, miss,' said the officer, very politely. He was young and fair-headed. 'Do you live in Granbury?'

'I'm visiting,' said Imogen cautiously.

'There was a break-in at a house down this road last night,' said the officer. 'We caught the offender but we think he had an accomplice. Did you see or hear anything suspicious?'

'No,' said Imogen. 'I went to bed early and slept all night,' she declared, not altogether truthfully, since she had woken feeling hungry and had raided the fridge during the night. 'I'm staying with my step-grandmother,' she added. 'In Vicarage Fields.' It sounded very respectable.

The officer seemed satisfied.

Did he think she might be the accomplice? Imogen felt affronted at the mere notion of being a suspect and she would not stoop low enough to ask the policeman where the church was. She wondered which house the thief had chosen. In the dull grey light of a chilly morning she glanced at the trim façades, the tidy gardens and spruce boundary fences. Some bore names painted on decorative pottery plaques. She saw Apple Cottage and Candlemakers. One gate-post had Rose Cottage etched in Roman capitals on a dark brown varnished board, and as she paused to glance at it, a man came round the side of the house and walked towards the gate. Embarrassed at being caught staring, she moved on, but he called out, 'Good morning,' and she hesitated.

'Good morning,' she replied, uncertainly.

'Not that it is,' he said. 'It may rain.'

He was very tall and very old, Imogen observed as he came towards his open gateway. He would know where the church was. She asked him.

'I'm going there,' he said. 'It's down this way – not far.' She saw then that he was carrying a small bunch of tiny daffodils. 'I'm taking these to my wife. She's buried in the graveyard. Aren't they lovely? These small ones come out before the main crop, you know.'

Imogen didn't, but she nodded, and the old man walked round behind her so that he was on the traffic side of the road. Her grandfather had done that, she remembered. When he died, he wasn't nearly as old as this man.

'I met a policeman,' she said. 'He told me someone's house was broken into during the night.'

'It was mine,' said the old man. 'But no one was hurt and the thief didn't manage to get away with anything. That's something to be thankful for. Wouldn't you agree?'

'Yes,' said Imogen. 'Certainly. The policeman said he'd been arrested. He thought there might have been an accomplice.'

'I don't think so,' said Howard Smythe. 'If there had been, he'd have tried to help his friend.' A second youth, entering the house and using force, might have been too much for him.

'Would he? Wouldn't he have just run off and saved himself? People let each other down all the time,' said Imogen. 'But it was smart of the police to catch him.'

'Yes,' said Howard Smythe, not revealing what had really happened. 'There's the church,' he added, pointing with the hand that held the flowers. 'It's very old,' he told her. 'Parts of it date back to the thirteenth century.'

They walked the rest of the way together, and once through the church gates, he raised his hat to her.

'I go this way,' he said, stepping off the path and on to the damp grass. 'The church isn't locked,' he added. 'Goodbye.'

'Goodbye,' said Imogen, and walked on, oddly moved by this encounter. What a nice old man, and he seemed quite calm even though his house had been broken into.

Imogen did not realise how unusual it was for the church to be unlocked; most churches were no longer open to passers-by because of theft and vandalism, but St Mary's, Granbury, was an exception; experimentally, under a new vicar, it was accessible for most of every day. Imogen lifted the latch on the heavy old oak door and opened it, expecting it to creak, but it moved silently. She stepped inside, closing the door behind her. The damp interior felt chilly, and she shivered, looking round her. A worn blue carpet stretched along the aisle, and the original pews had been replaced with chairs. Nicholas hadn't arrived; she knew that, for if he had, his Peugeot would have been outside. Restless, she prowled around, peering at the memorial slabs set into the wall. There were several generations of one family, starting with Sir Alfred Rowan and his lady; their descendants and their siblings were remembered, some killed in various wars. How dreadful, but that wouldn't happen now, Imogen thought vaguely, and then she saw a small tablet recording the death of another Rowan, lost in the Gulf War. She blinked and looked away, wandering between the choir stalls to the altar, which was draped in a purple frontal. There were no flowers. It was Lent, but that did not register with Imogen, although she quite enjoyed the services in the school chapel which she was obliged to attend during term-time. She liked singing hymns and sitting quietly, with no one hassling her. Thinking of this, she slumped into a choir stall and gazed at a restored painting on the wall, a coat of arms, wondering what its symbols signified. She was still sitting there when the church door opened and Nicholas came in.

He did not see her at first as he looked around. His bright presence seemed to light up the whole building. Nicholas had dark golden wavy hair, worn slightly long to just below his ears; he had deep blue eyes and was over six feet tall. Imogen sat still for a few moments, watching him as he glanced around impatiently. He paid no heed to the memorial tablets that had caught her attention, walking halfway down the aisle and then stopping in frustration, gazing about him.

She moved then, and he saw her, and she ran towards him so that they met at the chancel where they hugged.

'Hmm – you smell nice,' she said, inhaling his aftershave.

She smelled faintly of Charlotte's Crabtree and Evelyn soap and the shampoo she had used that morning, a clean and unseductive smell.

They sat down together in the front row of chairs, and Imogen began to cry.

'What are we going to do?' she wailed.

'Same as everyone else. Get on with it,' said Nicholas robustly. 'Lots of people's parents split up and they survive.'

'You must mind. You disappeared,' Imogen said. She pulled a crumpled tissue from her pocket and feebly blew her nose.

'Ugh – that's disgusting. Haven't you got a clean one?'

Nicholas asked her. Imogen was usually fastidious, which made her current predicament all the more disturbing.

She shook her head.

'I'll get some more at Charlotte's,' she said. 'She's got loads. Where have you been, Nick?'

'I holed up with a friend,' Nicholas replied. He'd been with Phoebe.

'But why? Why did you vanish?'

'I wanted to give them something to think about that wasn't you, silly,' he answered. 'What did they think I'd done?' he added, curious.

'Granny thought you'd gone abroad, like blokes ran away to sea in her young days,' said Imogen, and she giggled. 'She's got a thing about the sea – she's off on another cruise.'

'Got a thing about a sailor, more likely,' Nicholas said. 'Harking back to her navy days.' Their grandmother had been a cypher officer in the WRNS during the war. 'Did it work?'

'Did what work?'

'My diversionary tactics.'

'Not really. Dad's just furious with both of us,' she said.

'Well – can you wonder? What a pair we are,' he said, and they both began laughing.

Imogen was feeling better. When Nick was around, things were never quite as bad as she had thought at first.

'We haven't brought Mum back,' she said, speaking sadly. 'And Granny's fed up with Mum – her own daughter. She won't talk about it. Just says it's most regrettable and it's lucky we're not little children.' She mimicked their grandmother's clipped tones, making him laugh again. 'Wouldn't you think she'd want to stand by me?' she added. 'Mum, I mean.'

'Not really,' said her brother. 'She'd probably tell you what an idiot you'd been, not to take more care. Can you imagine Mum getting caught like that? What did she say, anyway?'

'Just what you've said,' Imogen told him, and burst into tears once more. 'It was on the phone,' she said. 'It was horrible.'

Nicholas produced a spotless white linen handkerchief from his pocket. It was perfectly pressed and laundered. He gave it to her, and she mopped her face, then glared at him.

'You've got that slag doing your washing,' she accused. 'Phoebe. What a name.'

'It's a very nice name and she's not a slag, she's a good woman,' Nicholas declared. 'She knows I like things nice.'

Phoebe lived in Oxford; she was twenty-three and a single mother with two small children. Nicholas had met her some months ago when the wheel came off her pushchair in Tesco's. He hadn't been able to fix it on the spot, so he'd driven her and her children back to their flat, which turned out to be not far from where he shared a house with five other students. He'd managed to mend the pushchair, and a few evenings later, bored, he'd called round to see whether the repair had lasted. He'd stayed overnight. Phoebe had wanted him to move in, but he had enough wit to see where that might lead; she received occasional maintenance from the father of her children – they had not married – and she had support from social security, which could have been jeopardised if anyone suspected that she had a permanent lodger. Besides, he liked his freedom.

'I'll bet she's not the only one you're on with,' Imogen said, sulkily.

'You're wrong, but that's not what we're here to talk about,' said Nicholas. 'Who's got you into this pickle? I'll sort him out in no time.'

But she wouldn't tell him, nor would she tell him what she planned to do.

'You can't have meant it to happen,' he said, challenging her.

'Maybe I did,' she said.

They were still sitting there when the church door opened and the old man who had walked to it with Imogen entered. He removed his hat, closed the door, then came slowly down the aisle towards them.

Howard Smythe had heard the young man's car draw up outside the church, and had seen him walk rapidly up the path and enter the building. When, after an interval, no one reappeared, he decided to make sure all was well before he went home. Now he saw that the girl had been crying.

'Is everything all right?' he asked, looking from one of them to the other.

'He's my brother,' Imogen said.

'Oh – I see.' Could it be true? They were not the least bit alike.

Nicholas stood up and held out his hand.

'Nicholas Frost,' he said. 'Imogen and I are twins, but, as you see, dissimilar.'

'But close, no doubt,' said Captain Smythe. 'You don't live in Granbury, do you? Howard Smythe,' he added, shaking the young man's hand.

He hadn't seen either of them before today, and he had lived in Granbury for thirty years, since retiring there with Helen, who had died ten years ago. Even so, the pair could be residents, for the population had grown and its composition had altered profoundly. The girl, however, had not known where the church was; that must mean they were strangers.

'No, we don't, but Imogen is staying with our step-grandmother,' said Nicholas. 'I'm at Oxford,' he added, hoping Howard would imagine him to be a member of one of the older colleges.

'Who is your step-grandmother?' he asked. 'Perhaps I know her?'

But he didn't. They told him that she had been living in Granbury for only a few months, since soon after their grandfather's death, but they did not mention their own parents' troubles. Howard Smythe nodded.

'I'll get on home, then,' he said. 'Goodbye,' and he left them to it.

They drove past him as he reached his own gate. Nicholas tooted the horn, and Imogen waved. Howard hoped she had cheered up so that this Charlotte Frost, of whom he'd never heard, would not have to deal with tears.

'Don't let's go back to Charlotte's,' Imogen begged, as Nicholas paused at the High Street junction.

'You've got to, some time,' Nicholas said. 'Until something better turns up, that is.'

'Like what? Can't I come to your place?'

'And crash out in a sleeping bag on my floor?' he said. 'It's a house of blokes, Immy. You wouldn't go for it, not in your condition. Besides, they'd set the police on us, for all we know. Charlotte would. She's quite prim.'

'We could just take off.'

'That won't put things right,' he said. 'You've got to have

a plan. Which way's her house? It's all right – I won't dump you there now.'

'You go to the left here,' said Imogen.

'We'll go the other way, then,' he said. 'Let's suss out Nettington.'

He pulled into the main road and set off to the market town six miles away, accelerating as soon as he passed the decontrolled sign. The car was quite lively; he could get up a good speed. He'd bought it with money his grandfather had left him. Imogen's legacy was in a National Savings account. Driving along, he put on a tape, so that they could listen to music and not be forced to talk or think.

Nettington's main street had a number of shops interspersed with estate agents' and solicitors' offices; they went into a shoe shop and Imogen tried on some boots, but neither had enough money to pay for them. Imogen had not brought her purse, and Nicholas, who had his bank card, knew his balance was low. He'd need petrol, and they'd better get something to eat; he'd had no breakfast. They decided to go on to Becktham, where Imogen had arrived on the train the previous day; it might be larger, with perhaps a cinema where they could spend the afternoon.

In the outskirts, Nicholas saw a chip shop, and he stopped.

'Let's get some fish and chips,' he said. 'We can ask if there's a cinema or anything interesting to do. It seems a bit of a dump.'

'I didn't see much of it last night,' said Imogen. 'I don't know where the station is.'

'Well, we don't need it – we're not catching a train today,' Nicholas said. He pulled in to the kerb and parked behind a lorry outside the chip shop. 'You stay there and mind the car,' he instructed.

In the chip shop, a youth much his own age was behind the counter, and a middle-aged woman was tipping sliced potatoes into the frier. A burly man with a shaved head and an elderly woman in a long brown raincoat were ahead of Nicholas, and he waited patiently for his turn. The youth was efficient, packing up the orders and taking the money with a smile.

'Where are you off to now?' he asked the man.

'Manchester,' said the man. 'Want to come, Jerry?'

'I might do, one day,' Jerry answered. 'I might just take you at your word,' and he handed the man his bundle. 'Cheers.'

'Cheers,' said the man, and left the shop, climbing into the lorry.

Jerry was now serving the woman. She wanted a small portion of cod and chips.

'How's your mum?' she asked him.

'She's good,' said Jerry.

'Likes that job, does she?'

'Seems to. Sounds a bit dull to me. Making out accounts all day.'

'Has to be done,' said the woman who was frying the chips. She turned away from the frier to the counter. 'Can I help you?' she asked Nicholas.

When he came out of the shop, the lorry had gone and there was no other vehicle near them.

'Let's eat here,' he said. He had seen a litter-bin attached to a wall nearby. They could get rid of the rubbish after they'd eaten and then decide what to do. He didn't like mess in his car.

It occurred to neither of them that Imogen should telephone Charlotte to say she would not be back for a while, and, in Granbury, Charlotte, annoyed by Imogen's prolonged and silent absence, but not yet worried, and needing to cater for her guest, pinned a note on the door saying that she would be home in half an hour. It was an invitation to burglars, she knew, but Imogen had left without a key to the house, and if she returned before Charlotte, would not be able to get in.

Do her good to have to wait outside in the cold, Charlotte thought sourly. It wasn't raining, but it was distinctly raw and chilly. She would not be long; the village shops could provide enough for the next twenty-four hours, and tomorrow she would go into Nettington for a proper stock-up. Imogen might be persuaded to come too. On the other hand, if she continued to sulk, it might be better to leave her behind.

First things first. Wrapped up well in her dark green padded jacket, she set off into the High Street, turning right towards the general store which Imogen had passed earlier. Two women with pushchairs came towards her, not moving into single file to let her pass, but Charlotte had already stepped into the road, for she knew they had not seen her. A man with a border collie was not far behind them, and once again she moved off the path. He did not look at her. People avoided eye contact these days, even in Granbury. The shop sold newspapers – Charlotte's was delivered every day by a schoolboy – sweets, and basic groceries. Charlotte bought butter, Flora – for all she knew, Imogen eschewed butter, though she had used some in her nocturnal fry-up – eggs, a sliced loaf – the shop sold no other kind – and biscuits. She might make a cake. During her brief marriage to Rupert, he had enjoyed her baking, and a chocolate cake might sweeten Imogen. Invisibly, she moved past the shelves, stocking up her basket, and was surprised when a tall old man, who had entered the shop behind her, stood aside to let her pass. So she was not invisible to him.

'Thank you,' she said.

The old man had come to pay his paper bill.

'You shouldn't have bothered today, Captain Smythe, after what happened,' said Beatrice Evans, who ran the shop with her husband. 'It could have waited.'

'News travels fast, Mrs Evans,' Howard Smythe replied. 'As a matter of fact, I wanted to get out.' Calm though he thought he was after the incident, and used to far worse experiences during the war, among them having twice had his ship torpedoed, Howard Smythe felt restless, and he had been further disturbed by the distress of the young woman in the church. It had not been a good day and the walk had tired him.

'You were tied up and robbed, I heard,' she said. 'Surely you should be taking things quietly?'

'I wasn't robbed and I wasn't tied up,' Captain Smythe replied. 'The thief was caught before anything like that could happen.'

He paid and left the shop, pausing to lift his hat to Charlotte, who was now waiting near the counter.

Mrs Evans seldom looked at Charlotte when she bought things at the shop, merely focusing on the items, the money and the till, but today she did.

'Captain Smythe's house was broken into in the night,' she said. 'I'd heard he was hurt and all his war medals were taken.'

'How dreadful,' said Charlotte. 'But he said it wasn't

like that,' she pointed out. Mrs Evans had sounded almost disappointed. 'Where does he live?' She had seen the old man before. There was a track across some fields to the river, and Charlotte sometimes walked down there. The tall old man had walked there a few weeks ago, and he had been in church on Christmas Day. Charlotte went to church only then, and for funerals and weddings.

'In Rose Cottage. That's in Meadow Lane,' said Mrs Evans. 'He's lived there for ever such a long time – before we came here.'

Charlotte had assumed that the Evanses were incomers, like herself and a good percentage of Granbury's residents. Mr Evans had a real Welsh lilt to his voice, and he took notice of her in the shop, but she bought very little there, going once a week to the supermarket in Nettington where there was so much choice and delicious bread. If it hadn't been for want of time, because Imogen might return, she would have gone there today, but it was wrong not to use the general store more; village shops deserved to be supported.

She resisted the temptation to question Mrs Evans about the robbery. Gossip should not be encouraged, and, in any case, Mrs Evans had not known the true story. Charlotte left the shop and went on up the road to the butcher, who also sold vegetables and fruit. Captain Smythe was just leaving as she arrived, emerging with a single chop. He nodded and lifted his hat, and Charlotte smiled. Then she plunged.

'I'm sorry to hear what happened,' she said. 'Mrs Evans told me, after you'd gone.'

'She exaggerates,' he said.

'Well, even so, it must have been—' Charlotte had been going to say terrifying, but that might seem extreme to an old man who no doubt had a distinguished war record. Mrs Evans had mentioned medals. 'Alarming,' she decided on.

'I was angry,' Captain Smythe told her. 'The wretched little youth has probably never done an honest day's work in his life. I didn't see why he should help himself to my possessions.'

'You caught him,' Charlotte realised. 'Well done!'

'Luckily I woke and heard him,' Howard said. To his surprise, although he had turned down the offer of a visit from Victim Support, it was quite a relief to talk about it. 'I threatened him with a golf club,' and he laughed, a croaky sound, as though he did not laugh a lot.

'Did you? Did you clobber him?' Charlotte asked.

'No. He surrendered fairly quickly,' said Howard Smythe. 'He didn't seem to be armed,' he added.

'Well, you didn't know that, did you?' she said. 'He might have had a knife.'

'True.'

'Which way do you go home?' An awkward thought had come to Charlotte: she remembered the young offender who had called at her door a few nights ago. Could he have been responsible for this? 'I wondered if you'd like a cup of coffee,' she went on. If he accepted, she could ask him to describe his burglar. Surely that nice young man hadn't been responsible for the break-in? 'I live just round the corner, in Vicarage Fields,' she added.

Captain Smythe thought it would be rather agreeable to be given a cup of coffee by this pleasant woman.

'Thank you. How kind,' he said.

'I've just got to buy a chicken and some vegetables,' she said. 'I won't be long.'

He waited for her, and they walked to Vicarage Fields

together. There was no sign of Imogen. She unpinned the note from the door.

'My step-granddaughter is staying with me,' she explained. 'She went out today without a key. I left this message in case she returned before I did.'

Captain Smythe peered at her. There couldn't be two wandering step-granddaughters in Granbury today.

'Has she a twin brother?' he asked.

Charlotte made proper coffee in a pot. Once he was settled in a large armchair in her sitting-room, Captain Smythe had turned rather pale. He must be at least eighty, Charlotte thought, and however lightly he chose to regard it, he had had a shocking experience during the night and doubtless not much sleep afterwards. While he drank his first cup, he told her about meeting Imogen that morning, and of her brother's arrival at the church.

'I didn't know the young man was her brother,' he said. 'I felt I must ensure she was safe before I came away.' He did not mention the tears.

'I'm so glad you did,' Charlotte answered. 'And I'm relieved to know they're together, because however late she decides to return, or even if she doesn't, he'll look after her, now he's appeared on the scene. They're both rather upset,' she felt obliged to explain. 'Their parents have just separated.' There was no need to enlarge.

'I'm so sorry,' Captain Smythe replied. 'Such things are very sad.'

'Have you a family?' Charlotte asked.

Sitting there, facing her, Howard Smythe felt strangely

soothed. In Granbury there had been several women whom he had known for years, who had known Helen, and whose dead husbands he had known, and they all had concern for him, left on his own. After her death they had invited him round to meals and popped in with cakes, flowers, and invitations at Christmas. But all were dead now, or had moved away to live near their families, or were so frail that it was he, though older than all of them, who made duty visits to them. Now he was in the company of a woman young enough to be his daughter and one who, unlike his own daughter, maintained a comfortable house and was neat in her ways. Howard's daughter was an academic; she taught economics at a university in the north of England and had six children whom she had neglected while she pursued her career. It hadn't seemed to harm them, though they were often unwashed, unfed, according to Helen, and frequently left to fend for themselves with the older ones minding the younger. All had turned out well, and all led conventional lives, two becoming teachers, one an engineer, one a chef, and the other two were accountants. All had found work overseas. 'To get away from their mother,' Helen had said, sad not to see her grandchildren. Their father, a history tutor, had been bludgeoned by his wife into entering politics, but had abandoned the struggle at fifty, worn out, struck down by a heart attack.

Howard delivered a brief sanitised account of all this to Charlotte. He explained that he had a computer, and communicated by e-mail with his grandchildren. If in England, they visited him, and he had stayed with a grandson in New Zealand and a granddaughter in Canada.

'And your daughter?' Charlotte asked.

'She comes sometimes.' When prodded by one of her

children, or by her conscience, or if she wanted to pose as a caring child. 'My aim is to cause no trouble,' he declared.

'Mine, too,' said Charlotte, and filled him in briefly on her own background. 'About your burglary,' she said. 'You saw the thief? You said you captured him, in fact?'

'I certainly saw him,' said Howard. 'A miserable little runt of a fellow,' he added.

'Oh!' No one could have described Charlotte's caller in those terms. 'I was afraid it might have been a young offender who called selling dusters,' she explained. 'He was such an engaging lad. I was hoping he'd learned his lesson.'

'I know the lad you mean,' said Howard. 'He called on me, too.'

They worked out that they had probably both received visits on the same evening, about three weeks ago, with Howard's an hour after Charlotte's. So the youth had paid no heed to her advice not to call so late. Howard revealed that the police suspected his burglar had had an accomplice.

'The nice lad,' Charlotte said.

'I think my thief was alone,' Howard said. 'An accomplice would have come to his aid.'

'Not necessarily. He might have preferred to save his own skin,' said Charlotte.

As it was now one o'clock, she insisted on making some sandwiches. It was after three when he left, and even then, handing him his chop, which she had kept in the refrigerator during his visit, she was anxious, watching him walk away, tall, thin, and upright, one of the last of his kind.

4

Felix listened to Charlotte's clear voice on the telephone as she told him that Nicholas and Imogen had met in the village earlier that day, and they had gone off somewhere together. She expected them back at any time. This was a euphemistic description of her opinion, yet it was true; she had no idea when they would turn up, if ever, so to say 'any time' was fair enough.

Charlotte was always so controlled and courteous; she was totally unlike Felix's mother, who had been an amateur painter, thin and beautiful, and a brilliant hostess. She must have found his father dull; Felix knew she had had lovers, and this consoled him when he did the same, but just as his father had never known about them, he was confident that neither had Zoe learned about his. When she took off with Daniel, her latest, he could not believe that she was serious; none of his affairs, not even his current one, had, as he saw it, threatened the stability of their marriage. Surely she could have got over the fever in the blood and continued with a life in which she had her independence. His fury at the behaviour of his children was a reaction to his anger against her; Charlotte,

'The Wise One', as he and Zoe had referred to her behind her back, was, he suspected, aware of this. Charlotte had brought a new dimension into his father's life, and even knowing that the short time they had spent together had been happy, Felix continued to resent her, and he resented the financial drain on his father's estate. It was base to feel like this; he knew it. She could have claimed much more than the free tenancy of the modest house.

'You'll keep me up to date,' he said now. 'Make Imogen see sense,' and, having done his duty by telephoning, with the bonus of being spared a conversation with his daughter, he rang off before she could suggest that he should come and remove her. How had things come to this, he thought, despairingly: how could so much hope and trust end in bitterness and hatred?

What did he mean by sense? A termination? Charlotte did not know what would be the best decision; in any case, it was Imogen's to make, not hers, but she would point out the options, including having the baby adopted, a solution which rarely seemed to be considered nowadays. With more babies available for adoption, draconian fertility treatment, with its limited success rate, might, in many cases, be avoided. Charlotte fretted about children not knowing who their fathers were, or even their mothers, thinking of donor eggs. Such choices had not been available in her day. She had become pregnant with Tim soon after marriage, but there had been a gap of several years before Jane was born, with two miscarriages after that. It hadn't all been plain sailing.

After their sandwich lunch, she had left Captain Smythe in the sitting-room while she cleared away, and when she returned he was sound asleep, his mouth a little open, a gentle snore escaping now and then. She'd sat down with her book, and, sure that he would be embarrassed at dropping off in the presence of a stranger, as soon as she noticed that he was stirring, she had gone to make some tea, returning with a pot and cups and saucers on a tray.

'I believe I had a little nap,' he confessed.

'Did you? Well, I'm sure you needed it after the disturbed night you had,' she said. 'Milk and sugar?'

Departing, he had said, 'If you're worried about those twins, do telephone.'

He had discovered that she was scarcely on nodding terms with the neighbours on both sides; the couples were out at work all day, and some children she had noticed were young teenagers, all at school. Uprooted from her past, she had no friends.

Imogen and Nicholas sat in the car listening to tapes while they ate their fish and chips. Imogen savoured hers, finishing every last morsel.

'Course, you're eating for two, now, aren't you?' Nicholas said. 'What are you going to do about the brat? Have it?'

'Why not? I'd cope,' she said. 'Dad and Mum would have to help, if it was a fact in front of them.'

'And yelling its head off,' said Nicholas. 'Do you think Mum will go all cooey and granny-like?'

'Not really. She wasn't all that maternal,' said Imogen.

Nicholas had to agree.

'Only when we were sweet little things, being admired,' he said. 'It was really always Mum and Dad, exclusive.'

They remembered their parents, young and handsome, dashing out to parties, or the theatre.

'Dad wanted to move to White Lodge after Granddad died,' Nicholas said. 'He fancied being a country squire. That was why he was so keen for Charlotte to clear out straight away. I think he hoped Mum would like all the county bit. Being important. All that status stuff.'

'But we've got a lovely house already,' Imogen said. 'And she loves her job. It makes her independent.'

'She'd retire one day. Maybe Dad thought he'd persuade her to do charity stuff instead, like Granny and Charlotte.'

'They didn't do it in a fine lady sort of way,' said Imogen. 'Granny grew into it, you could say, over the years, and Charlotte just did her best to carry on, but low key, sort of.'

'You like Charlotte, don't you?' he asked.

'Mm. She's always been nice. She's being nice to me now, and I've been being a pain,' said Imogen.

'She knew Dad wanted her out of White Lodge. He was miffed at having to pay for her new house.'

'They sold White Lodge. They could have sold The Elms,' said Imogen.

'But they were splitting up. Maybe Dad thought moving would save their marriage, only it was too late. Mum had decided to bunk off.'

'What's Daniel got that Dad hasn't?' Imogen asked.

'Perhaps he's better in bed,' said Nicholas.

Imogen ignored this.

'Dad's got more money,' she said.

'Maybe, but the business hasn't been going so well,' said Nicholas. 'Some merger hasn't been a success. And he's going to have to give Mum a mega settlement. He used some of the money from White Lodge to pay off the mortgage on The Elms. He told me that. He's going to need the money from Charlotte's house before he's through.'

'But Mum dumped him.'

'That's how it works,' said Nicholas.

'It's not fair.'

'What is? It's not fair that you're in this mess,' said Nicholas. 'But anyway, Dad was screwing around first, so you can't blame Mum.'

'Was he?' Imogen sounded shocked.

'He's been having it off with Amanda for years,' said Nicholas. Amanda was Felix's personal assistant. 'Anyway, what about you?'

'I don't want to talk about it,' said Imogen.

'Well – you'll have to some time, but you needn't now,' said Nicholas. He began gathering up the paper trays and the wrapping from their meal. 'I'll chuck these,' he said. 'Then we'll get moving.'

He walked the short distance down the road to the bin, and had just thrown away their rubbish when the young man from the chip shop emerged on to the pavement.

Nicholas gave him a friendly grin and said, 'Hi.'

'Hi,' said Jerry, recognising him. 'You still here, then? Too late for more chips – we're closed till five o'clock.'

'No – we're just leaving,' said Nicholas. 'We ate them in the car. What's there to do in this place, anyway?'

'Not a lot,' said Jerry. 'I'm going home to my mum's. Might watch a video. She's at work. You can come if you like,' he offered. 'That your bird?' he added, glancing at Imogen, who was watching them.

'My sister,' said Nicholas, startled by this sudden invitation.

'Oh, right. Well, do you want to?'

'Why not? Yes, thanks. We're visiting our step-grandmother and it's best if we don't go home just yet. Is it far?'

'No,' said Jerry. 'Less than a mile. Shall I get in the back? I walked here.'

'Help yourself.'

Nicholas tipped the driver's seat forward and Jerry climbed in.

'Hi,' he said to Imogen, and put on the smile that had charmed Charlotte and a great many more people of all ages. It was working already on this pair.

'Hi,' said Imogen, smiling back.

Nicholas was relieved at having a plan for the afternoon, one which would enable him to postpone returning Imogen to Charlotte; and Jerry, who had not been with Pete the previous night but who had heard of his arrest, was happy to have company to take his mind off what his friend had done.

Pete had come into the chip shop just before it closed yesterday. He'd bought some chips, then said he was going out that night. He wanted Jerry to come along when he finished his evening shift. Jerry had given up the door-to-door selling, breaking up their partnership. He said he'd met a householder who had smiled at him, and it had made him feel bad about conning her. Besides, now he'd got the chip shop job, he wanted to keep out of trouble. One term in prison was enough for him; his mother had been ashamed of him and he intended to make it up to her. Pete had said he had gone soft. He'd marked down several targets in Granbury, houses where entry looked easy, and he meant to try them. He needed wheels; Jerry's mother had a car and he could borrow it, if he talked her up enough.

But Jerry wouldn't do it. Pete waited for him to finish work and walked home with him, trying to make him change his mind, but Jerry was firm. He'd passed his test before he went to prison, but his mother's car was insured so that only she could drive it; she'd said if he kept out of trouble for three months, she might consider getting cover for him and letting him use it so that he could get practice. Then he might get a driving job.

At the chip shop they knew about his record but were giving him a chance. If no one would employ him, how could he reform, they reasoned. Jerry didn't mind the work; he was getting to know the regular customers and he enjoyed chatting to them, but between shifts, it was boring. He had been arrested after going on a spree to London with some friends; they'd been round several stores and got away with some good stuff, in Jerry's case a wool jacket, worn under his big anorak, a Walkman, trainers. Then, on the tube, Jerry, euphoric with success, had lifted a purse from a woman's unzipped shoulder-bag.

Not an experienced pickpocket, he'd been seen by an off-duty police officer who was on the train. Jerry, wearing the concealed wool jacket and without a receipt, with the other items in his pockets, and the purse, was desperate to escape. He had punched the policeman and broken his nose, but the arrest was made with the help of another passenger who had been called as a witness to Jerry's violence. There were no mitigating circumstances, and Jerry received a two-year sentence, getting out after a year because of his good behaviour. Pete, whom he knew from school, was also in the young offenders' centre, serving a sentence for robbery.

Last night, Jerry's mother's car had been stolen. As usual, she'd parked it in the road outside their small semi-detached house. His mother worked at several jobs; her main one was with a lighting equipment firm which had just moved from Becktham to Denfield, two stops up the line by rail, and this week the firm was doing short days because building work in the new premises was not complete; she also put in three nights a week as barmaid at a pub close to where they lived, and on Fridays she did night duty at an old people's residential home. When she found her car had gone, she was hysterical. She ran to the station, telling Jerry to report it; she'd miss her train today, for sure.

He hadn't reported it. He'd known who'd taken it. The spare key, kept on a hook in the kitchen, had gone. Pete had helped himself the day before and when Jerry went round to his house to demand the return of the car, he learned on the way there that Pete had been arrested in Granbury. If Pete hadn't got himself nicked, he'd have brought the car back and no one would have been any the wiser. And if Jerry had gone with him, he might not have been caught and the car would have been there this morning. Because of that, it could be Jerry's fault that the car was missing. It was probably parked in Granbury. He'd go and look for it when the chip shop closed after his evening shift; he'd get there somehow, hitch a lift, even walk.

If he could persuade them to stay long enough, his new friends might save his mum a taxi fare by giving her a lift to the residential home tonight. She'd be impressed because they were a classy pair – students, probably – and she'd be glad he'd got such respectable friends. He led them into his house, quickly shoving some magazines under a cushion in the living-room, which wasn't too untidy considering his mum had rushed off in such a state this morning.

Hospitably, he offered them drinks – there was a can of lager in the old, slightly rusty fridge in the kitchen, and some orange juice. Nicholas asked for orange juice but Imogen said she'd like the lager, if Jerry – he had told them his name – didn't want it. Nicholas frowned at her.

'Should you be drinking?' he asked her.

'Should I be living, you mean,' Imogen growled. 'One lager's not going to hurt it, surely.'

Jerry caught on quickly.

'You expecting? That's nice,' he said.

'You're the first person who's said that,' said Imogen.

'Kids are all right,' said Jerry. 'Specially little kids, before they start turning into monsters. How about we split the lager? It might cheer you up.' He found a glass and poured her half the tin, poured Nicholas some juice from the cardboard carton into another, and prepared to drink the rest of the lager from the tin. Then he gestured to his guests to sit down on the large, comfortable sofa, and turned on the television. There was a gardening programme on one channel and horse-racing on another. Jerry found a *Star Wars* video and put it on, then sank into an armchair with his drink. Easy together, spared the need to talk, they were content. Nicholas and Jerry concentrated on the film, while Imogen glanced curiously around. The three-piece suite looked almost new but the room was shabby, needing doing up; however, that wasn't what was odd about it. She realised that she couldn't see a single book, nor a photograph; there were several china ornaments on the mantelpiece, and some flower prints on the walls, which were a dirty, washed-out blue. A rubber plant stood in a pot in a corner, and there was a pot of yellow chrysanthemums on the windowsill. Although dingy and characterless, it was a cosy room. She returned her attention to the film, but soon their peace was broken by the telephone. It was Jerry's mother, ringing from her office to find out if her car had been recovered.

Nicholas and Imogen heard his side of the conversation.

'No, Mum. Nothing yet,' he said. 'You'll have to take a taxi tonight, and get one back. I know, but tomorrow's Saturday. Something may turn up,' he encouraged her. 'Cheers. See you,' and he replaced the handset. Then, turning to the others, he told them that his mother's car had been stolen during the night.

'She's at work,' he said. 'In Denfield. When she gets back, she'll be off in an hour to do night duty at an old people's home. It's ten miles away. There isn't a bus. She'll have to get a taxi.'

He had turned the sound down on the television while he was on the telephone; *Star Wars* was continuing to unfold in silence.

'How did she get to work today, if she couldn't drive?' asked Nicholas.

'She goes by train. There's not much parking at the other end, and her office is right by the station. She's been doing short hours this week as they're not properly open yet at this new place. She's not fixed up with a season ticket in case she decides to drive but she's nervous about the rush hour. She's a very nervous person,' he said.

'That's awful about her car,' said Imogen. 'I suppose a taxi would be quite expensive. We could give her a lift, Nick, and then go and face Charlotte.'

'That your gran?'

'Yes.'

'Mine died,' said Jerry.

'So did ours,' said Imogen. 'Charlotte married our grandfather after that. Now he's dead, too.'

'Don't you like this new gran of yours?' asked Jerry.

'She's all right,' said Imogen. 'But where she lives is a dump. There's nothing to do, and I'm stuck there for ever.'

'You're not. I'll rescue you somehow,' said Nicholas.

'Where is this place?' asked Jerry.

'Granbury. Do you know it?' said Nicholas.

'Granbury?' Jerry could hardly believe it. 'You mean she lives in Granbury?'

'Yes. She's been there since just before Christmas,' said Imogen.

She had felt it was wrong that Charlotte had had to move so soon, but her father had said it was her own wish. If she'd stayed at White Lodge for Christmas, which she could have done as the new people – it had sold instantly – didn't move in until the middle of January, they could all have spent it with her, had a real family time as they'd done before, and maybe Dad and Mum would have made up and stayed together.

'Could you take me there now?' Jerry demanded.

'What? To Granbury?' Nicholas was startled.

'Yes. You've got to go there anyway, haven't you, back to your gran?'

'Yes, but what about your mother?'

'I've had an idea about her car,' said Jerry. 'If I'm right, she won't need a lift and I'll be able to get back for opening time at the chip shop.'

'You mean you might know who'd taken it? Someone from Granbury?' asked Nicholas.

'Someone with no wheels who wanted to visit a friend in Granbury,' said Jerry.

Brother and sister exchanged glances.

'It's a friend of yours, isn't it?' said Nicholas.

'Maybe,' said Jerry, poker-faced.

'It'd be good if you're right,' said Imogen. 'I mean, not about your friend taking the car, but if you could get it back.'

'Let's find out, then,' said Nicholas. 'If the car's not there, we can bring you back and decide what to do about your mother.'

It was a long shot that if Pete had taken the car and left it somewhere in Granbury, it was still there, but if the police had found it abandoned, Jerry guessed they'd have traced the owner by this time and come knocking at his mother's door. If that happened, they might even connect him with the burglary. He and Pete had borrowed his mother's car more than once, unknown to her, when she was working in the bar at The Bugle, which was just a short walk from the house; she never took the car there. It meant she could have a few drinks during the evening, which she needed to keep her going.

'Right,' said Jerry. 'Let's go.'

They put on their jackets – the boys had flung theirs down on the floor in a corner of the room but Imogen's was neatly draped over the banisters in the hall – and piled out into Nicholas's car. Setting off down the road, they began to sing along with the tape he put on, Imogen joining in, briefly happy, but as they approached Granbury, Jerry fell silent and began to look about him.

'Where does this guy live?' asked Nicholas.

'I'm not sure,' Jerry prevaricated. They had called at so many houses in Granbury and neighbouring villages, sometimes finding people out, sometimes with Jerry gaining entry doing his patter and Pete often successful in getting in at the back and grabbing loot. 'It may be near the church,' he tried. That was a quiet area, and there were several houses in the narrow lanes which were surrounded by shrubs and bushes offering concealment to the approaching thief. Pete had thought it promising territory. It was where the tall old man lived who'd advised Jerry to get a job.

'Well, let's start down there,' said Nicholas. 'What sort of car is it?'

'It's a Metro. Red,' said Jerry, peering out.

But he saw it before they reached the church. It was among other cars in a small parking area outside the butcher's. Pete must have left it centrally so that he could leg it back from several possible targets. He shivered, unnoticed by the pair in the front.

Imogen had also seen it.

'There's a red Metro,' she called out.

Nicholas jammed on his brakes, almost causing a following car to crash into him.

'Sorry, sorry,' he said, moving on. 'I'll stop in a tick.' He went up the road, turned and came back, indicating as he turned into the small bay outside the butcher's. 'Is it the right car?'

It was.

'Have you got the key?'

Jerry hadn't, for Pete had the spare and his mother had the other, on a ring with her doorkey.

'Yes,' he said quickly. Once, in Nettington, they'd been in a hurry to get away, after a householder had given chase; Pete had reached the car first and had had to wait while Jerry, with the key, had caught up with him. After that, they'd left it tucked into the exhaust pipe for the first one back to seize. Would Pete have done that last night? Though he was alone, he might not have kept it on him in case he was caught and linked with car theft. If the key wasn't there, Jerry would have to hot-wire it. 'Just drop me,' he said. 'And thanks a lot.' He hopped out of the car and went round the back of it, stooping down and fumbling. The key was in the pipe. 'Just checking,' he called out, and gave a thumbs-up sign to Nicholas and Imogen as he unlocked the Metro. What luck that no one else had nicked the car after Pete's escapade, but it was probably pretty late when he left it. Jerry's heart was high as he drove away. He wasn't covered by insurance, but he had a valid licence. He must concentrate on getting back to Becktham safely.

Nicholas and Imogen waved as he left. The butcher, who had noticed the car outside, was busy serving someone and never saw it go.

5

'You'll come in with me, won't you, Nick?'

Nicholas had no desire to face Charlotte, but he couldn't leave his twin to meet her possible wrath unsupported.

'You can rely on me,' he said bracingly, parking outside Charlotte's house, which he had never seen before. 'I'll take the blame for whisking you away.'

Belatedly, it had dawned on the pair that Imogen's unexplained absence for the entire day might have caused Charlotte some inconvenience, even worried her, but Nicholas had always managed to deflect trouble by the use of charm; he was confident it would work now, and anyway, if Charlotte had been worried, she would be too relieved at Imogen's return to be angry.

He was, to some extent, correct in this assumption. She was in her sitting-room trying to do the crossword in the paper when she heard the car arrive. Concentration had been difficult for months, ever since Rupert's death, but she had been through bereavement before and knew it was a reaction which, in time, would ease. As well as grief, however, she felt that she had lost her identity. The last few years had brought so many changes: unexpected happiness, but the need for swift adjustment to fit in with Rupert's ways had involved the suppression of her own. Then, abruptly, he was gone and she was transplanted to a place where she had no roots or associations, and no friends. If, when she married, she had let her own house instead of selling it, she could have returned there and resumed her previous existence, but at the time it had made sense to sell, pay off her outstanding mortgage and have the rest to draw upon, so that she was not wholly dependent on Rupert; however the same result could have been achieved by letting. It was easy to be wise afterwards; she had an income from the pension Rupert's arrangements had included, and, with no rent to pay, there were financial advantages in her present situation. It couldn't continue, though, for it meant she had obligations to his family and they would call on her, as now with Imogen, to help them out. She ought to want to help them, she supposed, and as Rupert's widow it was, to some extent, her duty, but not to be manipulated and made to feel beholden. Once this business with Imogen was over, she must structure her life more effectively, take up a hobby, join an educational class, improve her garden, but most important, she must insist on paying a fair rent. Also, she could try to make a friend of Captain Smythe. He was so old that he would not misconstrue her motives, and he might be lonely. She would like to hear about his life, his war experiences; old men like him had endured all sorts of rigours, survived perils undreamt of by a modern generation. They were the sort of men who should be role models for the young, not pop stars and footballers.

She had been half-listening for Imogen's return, or for the telephone to ring. Now, with the twins approaching up the path, she refrained from rushing to the door to let them in. She must conceal anger and anxiety, though she was feeling both. She was standing in the hall behind the door by the time the bell rang, but she did not open it at once. When she did, Nicholas was smiling warmly – ingratiatingly, was how she later thought of it – while Imogen looked defiant.

'Ah, there you are,' she said calmly. 'Nicholas, how nice to see you. Come along in.'

There was no scolding, no recriminations. She held the door wide and, like recalcitrant ten-year-olds, they trooped across the threshold.

Imogen had been ready to withstand reproofs; now she did not know how to react, but Nicholas slid into his performance. He bent to kiss Charlotte on both cheeks.

'I hope you weren't worried when Imogen was out for so long,' he said. 'But she was with me all the time.'

'I wasn't to know that, though, was I, Nicholas?' she said sharply. The fact that she did, thanks to Captain Smythe, need not be disclosed, or not yet. 'It would have been thoughtful to have telephoned. You had the number, after all. I had no idea if you would be in for lunch, Imogen,' she said. 'Are you staying to supper, Nicholas?'

His sister sent him an imploring look; she did not want to be left alone with Charlotte, facing a possible dressing-down or at least an inquisition.

'Yes, please,' he said, without enthusiasm. 'If there's enough.'

There would be; Charlotte was an excellent cook and provider; but he didn't need a ticking-off for irresponsibility, nor did he wish to take part in a discussion about Imogen's situation, which he feared would be inevitable.

But he underestimated Charlotte.

'You'll want a wash,' she told them both. 'I've made a chicken casserole and we can eat at any time. And you're welcome to stay the night, Nicholas, if you'd like to.'

'Thanks, but I must get back,' he said, though he was almost tempted. Charlotte had a way of making you feel welcome, warm and soothed, even in this boring house, not much bigger than Jerry's, where they had spent the afternoon, though in better shape and furnished with more taste.

Charlotte's casserole was ready and was keeping hot in a low oven. She had only to cook some rice and the frozen peas. The brother and sister went meekly upstairs to freshen up; they took their time, consulting together, or plotting, Charlotte supposed. When they reappeared, she offered them elderflower cordial or fruit juice; Nicholas was driving, and Imogen was pregnant, so, as she reminded them, rather meanly she thought, they could not share the bottle of wine she had opened.

They both drank orange juice and asked if they could dilute it with tonic water to give it zip.

'I met an interesting man today,' she said, making conversation during the meal, and described her encounter with Captain Smythe. 'I think you met him, too, Imogen, on your way to the church.'

'Yes – yes, I did.' Imogen addressed her plate.

'I don't suppose he told you his house was burgled during the night,' said Charlotte. 'Nothing was taken, because he heard the burglar and caught him.'

Now she had caught the attention of her audience.

'He did say something about it,' mumbled Imogen. 'He said his wife was in the churchyard. He seemed pretty old,' she added.

'He was lucky the burglar didn't beat him up,' said Nicholas.

'Yes, he was, but he's very tall and he said the burglar was quite small,' said Charlotte. 'Besides, Captain Smythe is a brave man, and the burglar was a coward. The police told Captain Smythe that there have been a series of burglaries around the district recently with people calling at doors, selling things, while their accomplices go round the back and, if they can get in quickly, take anything they can find while the householder has been occupied at the door.' They preyed upon the old and solitary, it seemed, which implied that they were watching target houses. She decided not to tell them that both she and Captain Smythe had had a young offender calling after dark. Captain Smythe had also had a well-dressed woman purporting to be from the county council at his door, but he had insisted on telephoning her office to confirm that she was genuine, and when he asked for her identification, she had made an excuse and gone away. At the time, he had reported this to the police, and they had taken details over the telephone, but he had heard no more.

'They caught this guy? The one who broke into the old man's house?' Nicholas wanted to be sure. 'They didn't let him out on bail?' A very uncomfortable thought had struck him as he remembered Jerry's accurate deduction about where his mother's stolen car might be. But Jerry couldn't have been the burglar; Charlotte had said he was small. Could he have been some mate of Jerry's, though? Had Jerry even lent him the car without his mother's knowledge? It was possible.

'No, he hasn't been released. Or not yet, anyway,' Charlotte answered. 'At least, I don't think so. I suppose he could be out by now, if he was in the magistrate's court today. But he might have been remanded in custody.' Rupert had been a magistrate, so she knew something about how such things worked; strictly speaking, the thief hadn't been violent, so he might get bail.

'Better be careful, Charlotte. Don't let anyone in who you don't know,' Nicholas warned.

'I won't,' she promised.

He left when the meal was over. Imogen walked out to the car with him, but he did not mention his theory about Jerry's mother's car to her. She had enough to worry about, and it wasn't as if Jerry lived in Granbury.

Imogen, after he had gone, was trying not to cry as she went to help Charlotte with the washing-up. Poor girl, thought Charlotte. She needs her mother, not me. She'd gladly hug her and try to comfort her, but Imogen had constructed a barricade of invisible prickly barbed wire around herself. How could Charlotte break through it? She must try.

'Nicholas looks well,' she said, as she put the glasses away.

'He's all right,' said Imogen.

'I know you're both very upset about your parents,' said Charlotte, deciding that Imogen would probably dash up to bed if she didn't tackle her now. She might run off anyway. 'It happens, though,' she went on. 'People do separate and it's always sad, but it's sad for the couple, too. They don't make such decisions lightly.'

'Mum met this guy. She took off. It's as simple as that,' said Imogen. 'She can't care about me at all.' Her voice became a wail.

Charlotte had her chance. She put an arm round Imogen's shoulder and tried to draw her close, but Imogen resisted. Tears began to flow, however, which had to be a good sign.

'She didn't know you were pregnant when she left,' said

Charlotte. 'You hadn't told her, had you?' Perhaps Imogen herself hadn't known then.

'She knows now, and she hasn't come back,' sobbed Imogen.

'But she will, in time,' said Charlotte. 'If you have the baby, then she'll come when it's born, I'm sure.' But would she? Zoe, in the grip of either a steamy sexual passion or a burst of romantic love, even both, might be as insane and selfish as many lovers were.

'And if I don't have it, will she come then?' demanded Imogen.

'I don't know, Imogen. How can I tell?'

'None of this would have happened if Granddad hadn't died,' wailed Imogen, still sobbing. She took a tissue from the box on the worktop and blew her nose.

'You don't know that,' said Charlotte gently. 'He wasn't Zoe's father, after all. He couldn't have prevented her.'

'Everything went wrong after that, though,' said Imogen. 'Dad got cross and he wanted you to leave White Lodge, and then you did, and it was cruel to you, and then Mum was always angry and so was he. It was horrid.'

'Let's go and sit down,' said Charlotte, leading Imogen out of the kitchen and across the hall to the sitting-room; she seized the box of tissues as they went. 'Now,' she said, guiding Imogen to the sofa and gently pushing her down so that she folded up in the place where Captain Smythe had had his nap. 'When someone you love dies, it's always very sad, and they leave a big gap in your life. But your grandfather wasn't young, and he died very suddenly. He didn't suffer. That's a comfort.' She was touched at the sympathy for her which Imogen, in her outburst, had revealed. 'Your grandfather was very fond of you,' she went on. 'He was proud of you. You're a clever girl.' Imogen had gained ten GCSEs, all As except for a B for history, at the girls' day school she had attended, but then, in a move Rupert had not approved of, Zoe had had a whim to send her to a boys' public school which took girls for A levels. It would develop her, Zoe had said, broaden her horizons. It seemed that she had been only too right about that. If the boy's identity was known — for surely the baby's father must also be at the school — he would be expelled, and Imogen's permanent departure must be assumed, one way or another. For all Charlotte knew, though she had run away from the place, she might already have been expelled.

It was no good scolding her. They were all supposed to know so much about safe sex, the morning-after pill, and the mechanics of the act, but was love mentioned in the talks they heard, or, more important, lust? What about loneliness and the need for human contact, an embrace, some sympathy? A few steps along such paths and basic physical desire could banish any shreds of self-control, just as alcohol could overcome inhibition. The inexperienced were not aware of this.

'It's possible that your mother and father haven't been getting along for quite a while,' she suggested. Lorna had declared that their separation was an accident waiting to happen, with Felix using money to stave off a final break.

'They haven't,' Imogen admitted. 'They had some awful fights. It scared me.'

'I expect it did,' said Charlotte. 'They may be happier apart. Zoe will be coming back after this job she's doing ends.'

'She won't. She's going to leave the magazine. Daniel — that's her bloke — is transferring to some outfit over there and she'll either do the same or find another job in California,' said Imogen.

It was the longest speech she had uttered since they met the day before, and surely that was progress, but Lorna had not seemed to know these details, so how had Imogen learned them? Or were they guesses? It didn't matter now; that could be discovered later.

'I see,' she said. 'Well, you'll be able to visit them in America. That would be rather fun.' But would the baby be a welcome guest? Zoe couldn't have expected to become a grandmother quite so early in her life.

Imogen didn't answer this.

'You're going to have to see a doctor fairly soon, Imogen. You know that, don't you? There's a very nice woman doctor in the practice here. What you discuss is entirely confidential. You can talk things through with her – and with me, too, if it will help.'

'You mean, get rid of it,' said Imogen bluntly. 'That's what everyone will want. Then go on as if nothing's happened.'

'It wouldn't be as easy as that, but after a while it would fade,' said Charlotte. 'It's not your only choice. You could have it adopted, or you could keep it. But you can't put off a decision for very long. I suggest I make an appointment for you with the doctor for Monday or Tuesday. Will you keep it, if I do?'

Imogen had still not looked Charlotte squarely in the eye. Now, gazing at her own jean-clad knees, she grunted an agreement.

That was something accomplished, Charlotte thought. It was enough for now. There was a wildlife programme on the television, and she proposed that they should watch it. After it was over, Imogen went up to bed.

'Goodnight, Charlotte. Thanks,' she managed, as she left the room.

In Becktham, Jerry's mother, Angela Hunt, had returned from Denfield to find her car in its usual place outside her house.

She walked all round it and could see no sign of damage. Almost dizzy with relief, she fumbled in her handbag for her keys, found them, and got in. Her memory of the mileage on the clock was vague, but as far as she could recall, it hadn't altered all that much. She turned on the ignition and saw the petrol gauge rise to show almost full; the day before it had been nearly empty. The thief, or the police, must have put some in the tank. Thoroughly cheered, she locked the car again and went into the house, throwing her bulky shoulder-bag down on the sofa and going through to the kitchen to put the kettle on.

That morning, seeing from her window that the car was missing, she'd left without breakfast or even a cup of tea, running up the road to try to catch her train. Luckily for her, it was ten minutes late, a legitimate excuse the other end, but next week, when the office would be running normally, she would have to catch the ten past eight. Because her office was so central, and taking into account the rush hour – particularly bad, she knew, in school terms – the train was quicker, but she hadn't yet compared the costs. If she were to go by car, there would be the problem of finding somewhere to park in Denfield, and she might not find a residential street with unrestricted parking space close enough to the office. Leaving it in a pay area would be too expensive. She'd have to do some calculations, and she should walk to Becktham station; parking there was adding to her outgoings. One of her problems was that she never worked things out enough in advance, muddling through, finding out her misjudgements after the event. She'd discussed some of this with Heather, the stock controller at the office, whose own routine had been helped by the move, for she lived in Denfield and now caught a bus to the office. Angela could park at her house and do the same, she had suggested. It was worth investigating, Angela decided, putting a tea bag in a mug and adding boiling water.

Because there were no breakfast things waiting to be washed, she noticed the glass, rinsed and upended on the drainer, where Imogen had left it, but gave no thought to it, though she frowned when, on the coffee table in the sitting-room, she saw an empty lager tin and a second glass, which, on inspection, had held orange juice. Maybe Jerry had given the police drinks when they brought the car back.

She changed quickly into the black trousers and tank top she wore at The Gables and stuffed her blue overall into her large bag. She was thankful that Jerry was holding down the chip shop job, and because he was there in the evenings, had given up the door-to-door selling he'd been doing with that other lad, Pete Dixon. Angela knew it was supposed to be authentic employment for those trying to go straight, but she wanted him to drop his old associates for fear of being tempted to further wrong-doing. It had been so dreadful when he was arrested, and worse when he was sentenced; it was a sentence for her, too – a single mother who had failed, a stereotype who'd fitted the pattern spelled out to her when, pregnant at the age of seventeen, she'd elected to keep the baby.

It had been very hard. She'd intended, when Jerry was

old enough, to study – get a degree and a high-powered career – but all she'd managed was a business course, and her computer skills were limited. With her different jobs, she paid the rent, fed them, and ran the car, and now Jerry was contributing a little.

'You need a love life. Someone rich,' Heather had told her.

'Chance would be a fine thing,' Angela had replied.

'Maybe one of the old dears at The Gables will leave you a fortune,' Heather had suggested optimistically.

'I wish,' said Angela, laughing.

Over the years there'd been a few men – none rich, but some she'd been really fond of, and apart from the sex, which had varied as a pleasure, the closeness, someone to cuddle up to, had been such a comfort. She'd been very careful not to fall pregnant again, and that had upset Mike, who'd been around for three years, though not all the time, and who was wonderful with Jerry. He'd wanted to have a child with her.

'And then you'd go off and leave me with it,' she had said.

None of them would commit, not even Mike. Soon after that discussion they had broken up. He'd found someone else and married her, and that really hurt.

She'd gone to singles clubs and had a few one-night stands while Jerry was in prison, but she hadn't brought anyone home for a long time. Now it was just her and Jerry, and she had to keep him straight. He'd got the job at the chip shop because she knew Val and Bobby Redmond, who owned it. They were customers at The Bugle on Sunday nights when the chip shop wasn't open. They knew about his record, but they'd lost a son of their own in a road accident when he was twelve; he would have been nineteen now, like Jerry, and they wanted to give another lad an opportunity.

'Just one chance,' they had warned.

It had been enough for Angela to weave a fantasy about Jerry doing so well that Val and Bobby opened another shop and made him manager.

Why not? If you didn't keep on hoping, you might as well give up.

She drove past the chip shop on her way to The Gables but she didn't stop. For one thing, she hadn't time, and for another, she didn't want Jerry, or his employers, to think that she was checking up on him.

She'd left a note on his bed.

'Great about the car. Well done, the fuzz,' she'd written.

It never crossed her mind to wonder how the thief had stolen it without breaking the lock.

6

Charlotte had had a troubled dream, in which she was running across a field chasing Imogen, who was carrying a bundle and heading for the river. It was a relief to discover that it was a nightmare, and infanticide was not on today's programme. It was still early, but she had been waking at five or half-past ever since Rupert died. During the dark winter days she had usually gone downstairs and made a cup of tea, taking it back to bed and sometimes dozing off, listening to the World Service on the radio or trying to read. Often she would think back over the last few years and months, wondering how so much could have happened in so short a time, when before she married Rupert her life had been comparatively uneventful. She had been a widow for twenty-six years. After David died, she had returned to teaching – her career when they met and during the first part of their marriage. David was a research scientist, working for a pharmaceutical firm. She had returned, part-time, to her profession when Tom and Jane were both at grammar school, and had settled to longer hours when David's short but harrowing illness had struck. She had compassionate leave during those dreadful months; afterwards, she went back to teaching, quietly, as was her way, making no fuss. She took early retirement when it was forcibly suggested to her because younger, less experienced teachers could be employed more cheaply. Implicit was the fact, also, that her successful methods of teaching children to read were out of date. The fact that all the children in her care could read by the age of seven, often earlier, was not thought relevant.

Disenchanted, she had found the position with the charity and this had led to her brief second marriage. It wasn't like her first; she hadn't expected that it would be; there were no fireworks and no excitement, but she had loved Rupert warmly, and he was reliably there, unlike David, who had so often worked long hours, and, as his career progressed, had had to attend conferences in places as remote as New Zealand and Panama. They'd talked of how she would go with him when the children were old enough to be left. That day had never come. Now, it seemed as though all this had happened to another person.

Who am I? Where do I belong, thought Charlotte, and, unable to find a consoling answer, got out of bed.

She'd have to shop properly today. Unless Imogen refused point blank, she'd take her into Nettington, round Waitrose, where she might reveal what food she'd favour for the next part of her visit. And Charlotte decided to ring Felix up; she would invite him to lunch tomorrow.

When Angela returned from The Gables, she always went straight to bed. Jerry was usually still asleep. Even before he started at the chip shop, he seldom rose before eleven, and now, most days, he got up just in time for work. There was nothing to get up for, he reasoned, unless there was work to be done in the garden; he enjoyed that. He could listen to the radio or his Walkman in bed, and sometimes he would read – Tom Clancy, Stephen King – exciting books. He lived from day to day, rarely looking further ahead; what was the point?

He'd met up again with some former school friends. A few of them thought it cool that he'd been inside, but Jerry didn't want to repeat the experience, and he told them so. When he was out with Pete, he couldn't go drinking with them in the evenings, and now he'd got the job, he wasn't free until the chip shop shut and sometimes, then, he went to visit Tracy. Two lads he knew played football at weekends, and Jerry had briefly thought he might take it up. He'd played a lot in the young offenders' unit; he'd enjoyed it, but back at home, it was easy to slip into idleness.

This Saturday, waking late, he thought about the brother and sister he'd met the day before. Twins, though you'd never think it. Fancy the girl expecting! She didn't seem too thrilled about it, but maybe she was having a hard time from her family, and the grandmother. The brother was all right – lucky guy, with that car, able to get around. Jerry reflected that it would be years before he'd be able to have one. He liked cars; he'd quite like to be a mechanic and it would be useful to be able to fix cars that broke down, like his mum's did sometimes. He mused about it, wondering how you found a job like that, without any training. Then he began thinking about Pete. Would he have been bailed?

He might go and find out, ask his mum. There'd be time before work. Pete was a mate; it'd been bad luck that he'd got caught, and even with a good brief he'd go down because there was no doubt about his guilt. Jerry, though reformed, gave no thought to the victims of Pete's thefts. However, with a mission planned, he rose. He went off to shower, although, as usual, he'd showered when he came home from work last night. In spite of wearing a starched white cap and overall, he always felt he smelled of fat and fish. He'd grown accustomed to prison smells while he was inside, and to the noise, but already, three months after his release, he'd got used to fresh air, being able to shower when he liked, and to his privacy, although sometimes that palled. He'd liked the company, yesterday, when those two came back with him. He should have asked them where their gran lived, then they could have met up again. Never having had a grandmother himself, Jerry like the idea of someone else's; he pictured a bent old lady, maybe with a zimmer, white hair framing a wrinkled face, like those old souls at The Gables – though some of them were lively enough, and a few still drove. Jerry wouldn't mind working there himself, in a handyman sort of way, maybe, but he guessed, with his record, they wouldn't think of giving him a job. He'd have to stay at the chip shop for the moment, and it wasn't bad, though it was hard work at busy times, and the cleaning up had to be meticulously done. He liked chatting to the customers.

Jerry took trouble over shaving, and slicked down his brown hair. He'd let it grow a bit since leaving prison, but Val at the chip shop had said he mustn't let it get too long or else he'd have to put it in a net, like hers; now each strand was about an inch long, brushed forward over his forehead. He smiled at himself in the mirror. A nice smile could get you almost anywhere, as he had proved, but it was surprising how few people had the habit. Lots of folk went round looking as miserable as sin – Imogen, for instance. What sort of name was that, for goodness' sake? She'd a reason, though; she wasn't exactly jumping for joy about the baby. Jerry wondered about its father, just as he wondered about his own. He had asked his mother about him a few times, but she never wanted to discuss it. She'd snap at him and say there was no need to puzzle his head over such things. Sometimes he wondered if his mother even knew who it was, but she must have done, unless she'd been a proper slag, and he didn't want to believe that, or unless she'd been raped. It would be terrible to be the result of such a thing. If he had a grandmother, she might tell him. It said *father unknown* on his birth certificate. He looked quite like his mother, except that he had brown eyes and hers were blue. Her hair wasn't really blonde; it was naturally much the same colour as his.

He was glad he looked like her. He'd caused her a lot of worry and he regretted that. It was thanks to the smiling woman in Granbury that, just in time, he'd pulled out of the scam with Pete. Otherwise he might also be on remand today. He hoped Pete wouldn't grass him up for previous things they'd done. Though it was always Pete who did the entering and actual nicking, Jerry had been an accomplice and they had got a lot of useful stuff – mainly cash and credit cards, but also radios, bits of jewellery and watches, which they sold around the pubs.

He made his mother a cup of tea before he left the house, and took it in to her. She was still asleep, but she stirred slightly, one bare arm emerging from under the dark blue duvet, which was patterned with stars. She turned her head and peered up at him, muttering his name drowsily.

'Brought you some tea, Mum. Then you can go back to

sleep,' he said, and heard her murmured thanks as he went out. She might be asleep again before she had time to drink it, but she did like a cup any time she hadn't to get up early.

Whistling, virtuous, Jerry strode off down the road and walked for nearly a mile before he came to Pete's house, where he rang the doorbell.

It was a different sort of place from his, a pebble-dashed post-war former council house. Pete's was also semi-detached, but it was much bigger and had a garage; there was a lawn at the front with neat flower beds round the edge and beneath the bay window. At the back there was another patch of grass with more flower beds and a small pond, and two apple trees. Jerry thought both house and garden wonderful, but Pete spent as little time there as he could. He found his parents boring. Pete stole for excitement as much as for profit.

It was a neighbour of the Dixons who had told Jerry about Pete's arrest; now his mother came to the door and Jerry saw at once that she had been crying.

'I'm surprised you dare show your face here, Jerry,' she said, wearily. She didn't sound angry; simply sad.

'I came to ask if Pete got sent down, Mrs Dixon,' Jerry said, awkwardly, embarrassed by her distress. 'I'm sorry about what happened.'

'You were there, too, weren't you? But you ran off and got away,' she accused.

'No,' said Jerry, put out by this unjust allegation. 'I've got a job at the chippy. I was there till ten and then I went straight home.'

'And your mother can confirm it, I suppose,' said Mrs Dixon, in a tone he didn't like.

'Yes,' said Jerry. 'Anyway, I've given all that up.'

Pete's mother gave a sniff of disbelief.

'Is Pete here? Did he get bail?' asked Jerry.

'No. He's remanded in custody for a week. He might get bail then,' she said. 'But if he does, you'll keep away from him if you know what's good for you, Jerry Hunt.'

'He did ought to have bail,' said Jerry. 'Didn't hurt anyone, did he?'

'Of course not. He's not violent, not our Pete,' said Mrs Dixon.

That's all you know, Jerry thought. In prison Pete had been handy with his fists and it wasn't because he was little and people went for him. He had a vicious temper when he was roused. That was what frightened Jerry now; he might drop Jerry in it, and so might Mrs Dixon. But Pete might be expecting the police to find the car; that would connect Jerry with the crime without his grassing.

'Where did he go? Where did he get caught?' he asked. He meant, at whose house.

'As if you didn't know,' said Mrs Dixon.

He'd better not push his luck.

'I don't,' he said. 'I wasn't there. I'm sorry he got nicked. Goodbye, Mrs Dixon,' he said, and this time did not risk his smile.

He walked back into town and to the chip shop, leaving Mrs Dixon wondering if his denial could possibly be the truth.

Imogen refused to go to Waitrose with Charlotte. She wasn't rude, just slightly surly, and Charlotte decided that it was probably better to leave her at home than try to persuade her to change her mind. In any case, she could not insist; Imogen could scarcely be dragged screaming into the car.

'I won't be long,' she said. 'What will you do?'

Imogen had appeared downstairs at eight o'clock, asking if she could take some coffee up to her room and Charlotte had told her what she intended, explaining that she must go into Nettington early as Waitrose's car park soon filled up on Saturdays.

'I don't know,' said Imogen. 'Nothing much. I expect I'll still be in bed when you get back.'

'Is Nick coming over? Do you plan to meet him?'

'We didn't fix anything,' said Imogen.

'Well, if you go out, please leave me a note saying when you expect to be back,' said Charlotte. Judging by yesterday's events, impulse could dictate the day. 'And please telephone if you'll be late. Have you any money?'

She had two pounds.

Charlotte gave her a twenty-pound note.

'It'll cover a taxi if you wander off somewhere and get lost,' she said. 'And I'll find you a front door key.' She had a spare one.

'Oh, thanks,' said Imogen, and at last she smiled. What a change, thought Charlotte, as the pale, discontented face lightened up.

'I'll leave the key on the kitchen table,' Charlotte said.

'Right,' said Imogen. She definitely looked brighter at this prospect of some freedom and fixed herself a tray with cereal and coffee, which she took upstairs.

When she had gone, Charlotte, convinced that Felix ought to come and see his daughter, telephoned him, but all she got was his answerphone. Bleakly, she left a message inviting him to lunch the next day, but she was sure that he wouldn't reply till it was too late to accept, even if he received the message in time to do so. He was acting irresponsibly; he hadn't even made sure that Imogen had some cash.

Charlotte sighed, recalling her own years of bringing up Tim and Jane alone, her financial worries when they were growing up, her fears for their safety. They'd done well; Jane, in New York, had a successful career which she enjoyed, and Tim's naval promotions seemed to be following upon one another in a satisfactory way. Captain Smythe might be interested in hearing about this. If Felix wouldn't come to Sunday lunch, perhaps he would like to come instead.

She set off on her shopping trip, determined not to hurry. While she was in Nettington, she'd buy a lottery ticket; she'd done this before, fantasising that if she won, she'd wave goodbye to Felix as her benefactor and buy a house of her own, but where? Not in the Plymouth area, where Tim's was; Victoria wouldn't want her mother-in-law on the doorstep, even if she were to be a useful babysitter. Her own parents lived only thirty miles away and were very supportive during Tim's absences at sea. Charlotte could go back to the market town where she had lived throughout her first widowhood, but even during her brief absence, things had changed there; people she had known had moved, and some had died. She might slot back into her former niche; at least some of the tradespeople would be the same, but they wouldn't know her as Charlotte Frost; to them, she was Mrs Paterson, and she had taught some of them, and their children, at school.

She could revert to her previous name.

Such an idea was startling. In a sense it would mean the abandonment of her second marriage, a rejection of Rupert and his calm but genuine love. The idea, however, once acknowledged, was intriguing.

But she wouldn't win the lottery: that was certain; and both her husbands would have teased her for even trying. All the same, she'd take a ticket. She put on her crimson cashmere-lined jacket; perhaps, if she wore it more, she would be less invisible to other people, but she hadn't felt like wearing anything brighter than her dark green padded jacket or her grey overcoat since Rupert's death. He had given her the jacket for her birthday in November, saying he liked to see her in rich colours. A little cheered, because it suited her, she went off, glad to escape from the house and her new responsibility. Imogen, if she decided to get up, would have to amuse herself, but starting on Monday, a more disciplined regime must begin.

It was a raw day; the spring-like weather of the week before, when people had joked that here was summer, had ended. In the supermarket, Charlotte tried to plan ahead and think of what might tempt Imogen's appetite; in the early stages of pregnancy, she could be feeling queasy. Inspecting the fresh fruit, choosing apples, Charlotte thought that she should be encouraged to study; surely the school would forward her work? Charlotte did not know if the school was aware of her predicament; maybe that was a bomb yet to explode and when it did, she would certainly be expelled. She had been due to take A levels in the summer and, depending on when her baby was due, she could do them, if necessary from a sixth-form college like her brother. It must be arranged and Felix should have thought of it already, even if Zoe was in such a state of besottedness that it precluded her considering the interests of her daughter. Charlotte, who had taught young children, might not be able to help her with her work, but, if Imogen were to stay on in Granbury, there would be other retired teachers in the area, or even working ones, who might be prepared to coach her privately. But she wasn't staying on; this was a temporary solution.

Cheered by such positive thinking, Charlotte extravagantly put some imported peaches into her trolley and two bunches of daffodils which were still in bud but would come out in a day or two. In the newsagent's, where she went to buy her lottery ticket and had to wait in line to pay, she glanced at the tabloid newspapers. On the front page, international news was ignored in favour of a celebrity sexual scandal that had been exposed, but on the front of the *Nettington News*, stacked nearby, in a boxed picture at the side, Charlotte recognised Captain Smythe. PENSIONER FIGHTS OFF ATTACKER appeared in bold script beside it. Charlotte bought the paper.

When she returned home, the house was empty. Imogen had left a note on the kitchen table saying she had gone to meet a friend and would be back around six o'clock.

Friend? What friend? This was the first Charlotte had heard of Imogen having friends in the area. But perhaps the friend wasn't local: perhaps it was the father of her baby, come to seek her out, even to stand by her. However tragic the whole business was, that, at least, would be some comfort to the wretched girl, Charlotte told herself as she put away her shopping. She arranged the daffodils, some in a vase in the sitting-room and the rest in another on the kitchen windowsill; then she went out to survey her small garden. She'd been here so short a time, too late to put in any bulbs; there was just a patch of grass, much scuffed, from where the previous owners' small children had played. Felix had told her, bracingly, that she was such a good gardener, she would soon sort it out and that she would enjoy doing it.

'We should have got someone to come and plant it up for her,' Lorna had said.

'Why waste more money on her?' Felix said. 'She's not old, she likes gardening, and she's got nothing else to do. It'll be therapeutic.'

This attitude would have horrified their father, but Lorna did not argue. Felix and Zoe's lives were in a mess and he could think of little else, convinced that Zoe would take him for his last penny if she could. Anyway, Charlotte wasn't destitute; she could afford to pay a gardener for a few hours.

Unaware of this discussion, Charlotte sighed, looking at the bare wooden fencing, up which no single climber – no rose, no clematis, no jasmine – had been trained. The patch of grass had too many bare patches to be called a lawn; it needed to be sown or laid with turf. Laying turf would mean a swift improvement, but she must make it interesting by breaking it up with flower beds and perhaps a winding path. Standing there, she wondered about shape: where would roses look good? Should she have an arch and trellis? Would Imogen be interested in such a project? It was unlikely, but Charlotte would mention it; it would be something impersonal that they could talk about. She went back into the house and made herself a cup of coffee. She'd forgotten about the paper, which lay unread on the kitchen table. Picking it up, she took it and her coffee into the sitting-room where she put on her spectacles and began to read what it had to say about Captain Smythe's experience.

Late on Thursday night, she read, *pensioner Howard Smythe,*

86, was roused by a noise downstairs. Armed only with a golf club, the former sailor bravely tackled an intruder who was ransacking his desk, and took him captive until the police arrived to make an arrest. As a result of this incident, a man aged 19 is now in custody. Howard Smythe, a former Royal Navy captain, brushed off suggestions that he was a hero.

At least it stated that he had been in the navy; why start by labelling him a pensioner? It wasn't an occupation, yet that was how retired people were described whenever they were the subject of media reports. Charlotte would be so defined, she supposed, if some mischance – or even a lottery win – befell her – twice-widowed pensioner, probably, or even invisible pensioner widow, Mrs Frost, not retired teacher. And Imogen would be a pregnant teenager, not a student.

Angered by the report, which seemed to diminish Captain Smythe, Charlotte put on an old anorak and her boots and went into the garden once again, where she began arranging clothes pegs to mark out possible future flower beds. She was on the point of digging out trial edges when Captain Smythe himself appeared round the side of the house.

'I rang the bell. Perhaps you didn't hear,' he said. 'I came to thank you for your kindness yesterday. Your neighbour said you were in the garden.'

'Oh—' Charlotte was surprised, unaware that either neighbour had noticed her existence.

'A helpful young man,' said Howard Smythe. 'He'd just come back from shopping.'

Charlotte had occasionally seen a couple leaving early in the morning and returning, the man at about seven and the woman some time later. The man drove a large black car and the woman a small blue one. She'd seen no children there, though there were some on her other side.

'I don't really know them, I'm afraid,' she said. 'I haven't been here long.'

But it was long enough to have exchanged casual greetings with the couple. She could have taken the initative, but she wouldn't have recognised them if either of them had been in Waitrose earlier, as probably they were, if the man had just been shopping.

'Things have changed in Granbury,' said Howard Smythe. 'These young people come and go – they move into larger houses – they get to know one another through having children at the school, or they meet in one of the pubs. It was very different when my wife and I first came here, thirty years ago. Then a lot of the people living in the older cottages, like ours, were retired; all those folk, except myself, have died off and now city slickers and whiz-kids have bought them on enormous mortgages and modernised them into gems.'

At this, Charlotte laughed.

'You've seen a lot of changes,' she observed.

'Too many,' he replied. 'I've lived too long.'

She wouldn't contradict him. Perhaps he had, but he seemed reasonably fit and little the worse for his experience with the burglar.

'Come in and have some sherry,' she said. 'Imogen is out, heaven knows where, so we won't be setting her a decadent example.'

'I don't think sherry at noon is decadent,' he answered, following her into the house through the back door. 'I think it's civilised.'

Again, she laughed, kicking off her boots. She took off her

old coat and hung it on a hook nearby, and Howard hung his beside it. It had been good to hear her laugh. She washed her hands at the sink and then took two sherry glasses from a cupboard, putting them on a tray with a bottle of Gonzalez Byass Fino.

'Young people don't drink sherry,' he remarked. 'Or very seldom. Had you noticed?'

'Not really, but you're right, now that I think about it,' she replied, leading the way to the sitting-room.

Howard instantly noticed the local paper. He picked it up and began to read the piece about the break-in.

'I've been to Nettington. I saw the photograph and felt I had to buy it,' Charlotte said. 'I'm sorry.'

'Don't apologise,' he answered. 'I hadn't seen it. Best to be warned. Some young fellow with a camera came sniffing round yesterday.'

Charlotte told him how she felt about his being described as a pensioner.

'At least it did say you'd been in the navy,' she added.

'Yes. When you retire, you lose your identity as well as a slice of your income,' he commented. 'Why not say retired bus driver, retired clerk – whatever it may be.'

'Why not?' agreed Charlotte, pouring out the sherry.

Captain Smythe, however, would never be invisible. He was too tall, and he looked much too distinguished.

Imogen had gone to Becktham.

Not long after Charlotte went off on her shopping trip, she'd got up, resolved to leave the house herself before Charlotte's return. She couldn't face their being alone together; Charlotte was being kind to her, and she was behaving like a prat, but she couldn't bring herself to break the chain of graceless conduct which she had constructed. Yesterday, in Jerry's house, it had been good. He knew nothing of her and Nicholas's history, so he took them both at face value, as they did him. He was just an ordinary bloke with a duff job at the moment – he couldn't want to spend his entire life frying fish and chips – but it was work for now; obviously he hadn't had the comfortable upbringing that she and Nicholas had shared until everything had fallen apart.

Imogen had been glad to leave her girls' day school, but she hadn't wanted to be sent away; that was how she'd seen it, when packed off to what she considered was a remote spot in the country. She'd hoped to go with Nick to his sixth-form college, but their mother believed in separating them; they couldn't always be together, so after primary school, they were sent in different directions, but, like mercury, when near enough they coalesced. Imogen had known none of the other girls at her new school, and she found the boys an alien tribe. She embarked upon her two years there in a spirit of having to endure. No one was unkind to her, but no one was particularly friendly. Imogen knew that much of the problem was her own fault; she was shy and awkward, which, when she tried to be more forthcoming, made her snap at people, sounding harsh and hostile. She was good at maths and physics, and had thought about becoming a doctor, but her mother had laughed and said she'd never stick the training. Nick had said her best plan was to get good A levels and take it from there, prove Mum wrong; academically she'd done well until this present term, and she'd even performed in the school play, as Lady Capulet in a curtailed version of *Romeo and Juliet*.

She'd enjoyed that, forgetting herself while pretending to be the distraught mother of Juliet, who was played by a very pretty girl. Imogen's grandfather had died a few days after the final performance. He hadn't been there; at the funeral, Charlotte had said they would have liked to come, but they hadn't known about it. In other words, Mum hadn't given them the chance, but she hadn't come, either, nor Dad. They both wanted to be rid of her. Even now, at this crisis in her life, they didn't want to know, farming her out on Charlotte, who, when you thought about it, had no responsibility for her.

So far, Imogen had managed to avoid a serious talk with her, but she wouldn't be able to do it indefinitely. Today, though, she could dodge it by going out. She'd tell Charlotte that she had gone to see a friend. It would be the truth. Jerry was a friend. She didn't know his surname, so she couldn't find his telephone number in the directory to ring and ask him if it was all right, but she knew where he lived and where the chip shop was. He'd probably be working this morning. She'd go on the bus, or if there was no bus, hitch a lift.

7

It was after twelve o'clock when Imogen reached Becktham. The bus left Granbury from opposite the butcher's, where last night Jerry had found his mother's car, and went through Nettington, where it stopped in the market square. Imogen shrank into her seat, head down, while it paused, in case Charlotte passed and saw her. The journey took forty minutes, and the route did not pass the chip shop, so Imogen had to ask the way; however, when she reached it, there was Jerry behind the counter, busy serving. The shop was full; Imogen joined the queue and watched him joking with the customers in an easy, friendly way, which she envied. He wasn't cheeky or familiar, but he seemed to know some of them, regulars, she supposed, and asked one man about his dog, which was tied up outside and had an ear infection. Football prospects were discussed with someone else. None of this chat slowed up his preparation of the orders. By the time she reached the counter, Imogen was smiling; she could see that he was having a benign effect on everyone.

'Oh, hi,' he said, recognising her.

Imogen didn't want to get him into trouble by interrupting him while he was at work, so she bought some chips.

'I've escaped,' she said.

'So I see.'

'I thought we might meet when you finish,' she said, while he was wrapping them.

'Nick's not here?'

'No.'

'You can't be hanging about waiting. Can you find your way to my place?'

'Yes.'

'Mum's out.' She did a stint at The Bugle alternate Saturdays and some Sundays. 'There's a spare front door key under a little stone owl in the back garden. Go in and make yourself at home. Make some tea – whatever.'

She beamed at him, paying for her chips. Not everyone was an enemy.

'Right,' she said. 'Thanks. See you.'

'Cheers,' he answered, and turned to the next customer.

His employers, Val and Bobby, busy too, had barely noticed this exchange.

Imogen left the chip shop with her package, stopping at a newsagent's on the corner to buy a tin of Coca-Cola and a KitKat. Then she went on up the street, crossed over, turned up the wrong road but realised her mistake and worked her way back until she came to the house where she had spent the previous afternoon. She walked confidently round to the rear garden, not wanting to arouse suspicions in any watching neighbour by seeming hesitant. The plot was much longer than Charlotte's; this former council house was built when all such estates had space for tenants to grow vegetables to feed the family. Here, there was a lot of grass, but it had been cut, and there were several mature apple trees at the end, set in a patch of freshly-dug soil. Twigs stuck in the ground indicated that seed had been sown in rows, and flower beds, with wallflowers and polyanthus in bloom, punctuated the part nearer the house. Jerry's mother clearly loved her garden.

Imogen soon saw the owl, not far from a rotary washing line on which hung two pairs of jeans – Jerry's, presumably – a pink nightdress, three tee-shirts and some other washing. Imogen lifted the owl and found the key, then went round to the front door and let herself in. It was quite exciting, and it was great that Jerry trusted her.

She took her chips into the kitchen and ate them there, to avoid filling the sitting-room with their smell. Then she made herself a cup of coffee; the jar of instant was standing on the worktop so she did not have to search his mother's cupboards. There was a mug on the drainer, and milk in the fridge. With her drink and her KitKat, Imogen settled down to watch television. It would be a little while till Jerry came.

Angela Hunt left The Bugle early. She enjoyed her stints at the bar; Heather at work had asked her why she took on so many jobs, and Angela never gave her the true answer, which was that while Jerry was inside she had to keep busy or, she feared, lose her reason, and also it was difficult to make ends meet on her wages. Travelling to the young offenders' institution where he had served most of his sentence was expensive; she had to run the car to make the journey, which otherwise would have taken much longer and cost a lot in rail and bus or taxi fares, but because the Metro was old, it needed constant repairs and would soon require a new set of tyres. Before his arrest, Jerry had learned to drive unofficially, with other boys who borrowed their parents' cars with or without permission, and at a garage where he sometimes did odd jobs, cleaning cars and the premises. She'd paid for him to have lessons after his release, and he'd passed his test; if he were to be caught driving some car he wasn't entitled to, at least she could make sure he was licensed. She'd thought he'd kept straight so far, though he'd been mysterious about the evening work he'd been doing until recently. It was just casual, he'd said, a bit of this and that. He'd given her money towards his keep, and a nice little clock radio which she'd got by her bed. When he produced a video recorder, she had been worried, but he said it was one he'd bought cheap in a pub. Then Bobby and Val said they needed help in the chip shop, as their last regular assistant had walked out, and Angela had been eager to volunteer him for the post, but she told them of his past; she didn't want to mislead them, though no one at her office knew about his sentence.

Today she'd got a bad headache and was feeling dreadful, so Norman, the landlord at The Bugle, had sent her home. Angela had protested; she wanted to finish her shift; absenteeism was not in her nature. Norman knew this, but he was a good employer who appreciated her; she was reliable, was friendly enough with customers but never overstepped the mark, and if other staff failed to turn up, or were off sick, she would always fill in if she could. She was glad of the extra money. Friday night, when she went to The Gables, was the only time she could never come.

Now, seeing her white face, Norman wondered if working alternate Saturdays, after her night on duty, was too much for her. Perhaps she should phase them out, or give up The Gables, but she seemed to like that job. Last night one of the residents had died suddenly and her shift had been more demanding than usual; she confessed this when he noticed how unwell she looked and saw her swallowing paracetamol.

'Off you go,' he told her. 'Get your head down. Get some sleep.'

She'd given in, relieved to do as he said, putting on her coat and walking up the road, back to her house.

When she opened the door, she heard the television straight away. Jerry must be home, but he wasn't due till some time after two, when the shop shut. He'd lost the job, got the sack. Her heart sank, and bile rose in her throat as she moved towards the living-room, still in her smart black coat.

'Jerry, what's happened?' she demanded, entering, then stared, amazed, as an unknown, pale, plump girl sprang to her feet and stood at bay, like a frightened animal, backing away from her.

'Jerry's not here. He said I could wait for him,' she gabbled. 'I'm Imogen.'

As she stood up, the television remote control had fallen to the floor; a sports programme was in progress on the screen. Angela bent down, picked up the handset and clicked it off. Her head and stomach reeled. It was a migraine; she got them sometimes, particularly after periods of stress.

'Oh,' she said, and then, seeing the sheer terror on the girl's face, 'It's all right, I'm not going to eat you. You're a friend of Jerry's, I suppose.'

'Yes,' said Imogen, whose heart was pounding. 'He said

he'd be back before you. He told me where to find the key, and to make myself at home, so I did.'

'That's OK,' Angela said. 'I had a shock, that's all. I didn't expect anyone to be here. Let's calm down.' She took a breath. 'I came home early, I've got a headache,' she explained. Fright was giving way to relief, because Jerry hadn't got the sack after all, and, moreover, he seemed to have acquired a new girlfriend.

'Oh, I'm sorry,' Imogen was saying. 'Can I get you anything? Shall I make you some tea?'

A cup of tea might chase down the paracetamol, or it might make her sick, but either way, it would be worth trying.

'Tea might be good,' she said.

'You sit down, and I'll make it,' Imogen urged her, and she smiled at Angela, who was not so far gone that she failed to notice how the girl's face lit up, giving her a charm that until now she had appeared to lack.

'That would be wonderful,' she said. 'Thanks.'

'Let me take your coat,' said Imogen, turning into a nurse, and she helped Angela remove it. Seeing no handy hook in the hall, she draped it carefully over the banisters at the foot of the stairs as she passed on her way to the kitchen.

Angela sank down on the sofa, her head throbbing, grateful to submit. She shut her eyes, opening them only when she sensed Imogen approaching with a tray. She had not just dunked a tea bag in a mug but had found a small teapot and made proper tea, with a cup and saucer, and milk in a small jug. She'd put some sugar in an eggcup.

'Oh, that looks good,' said Angela, as Imogen put the tray down, finding space for it among the magazines on the coffee table. She had already tidied them from their normal scattered state into two neat piles, Angela vaguely noticed. 'Aren't you going to have a cup?' she asked.

'No, thanks,' said Imogen. 'I had some coffee earlier. Jerry said to help myself,' she added.

'That's all right,' said Angela. 'Good.'

'Shall I pour it for you?' Imogen offered.

'Please,' said Angela.

Imogen did so, without spilling any.

'How much milk?' she asked, jug poised over the filled cup.

'Just a splash,' said Angela, immediately putting Imogen into a different social slot than her own. She sipped some tea.

'Have you anything to take? Paracetamol, or something? Can I fetch them for you?'

'It's all right – I took a couple before I came home. This'll wash them down,' said Angela. 'How long have you known Jerry?'

'We only met yesterday,' said Imogen. 'Me and my brother. We bought some chips and then Jerry asked us back here. He was very upset because your car had been stolen.'

'Yes – but the police were wonderful. They got it back for me – no damage had been done to it,' said Angela. 'And they'd even put some petrol in the tank. Wasn't that good of them? A nice surprise.'

Imogen was just about to say that it was Jerry who had returned it, when she stopped herself. He must have had a reason for keeping quiet about his part in its recovery but that was strange. And how had he known where to look for it? Perhaps he had some dodgy friends, and guessed they might have borrowed it. What for, though? To get home? Or to do a robbery? Much later than her brother, Imogen made the possible connection with Captain Smythe's burglary, but decided that these must be two separate incidents. Crime happened. The world was a cruel place.

'It must have been,' she said, and swiftly changed the subject. 'Your garden's lovely,' she volunteered. 'I noticed it when I picked the key up from under the owl.'

'Jerry does it,' Angela told her. 'He's got it all into shape. I'd let it go, rather, while he was away. He was working in another part of the country,' she explained, before the girl could ask awkward questions. 'What did you say your name was?'

'Imogen.'

'That's pretty,' said Angela. 'Unusual.'

'It's OK,' said Imogen, who didn't like it. Why couldn't she have been called Sarah or Catherine?

They had run out of conversation. Angela felt too fragile to make an effort.

'I think I'll go up to bed,' she said. 'You wait for Jerry. He shouldn't be too long now.'

'Shall I tell him not to disturb you? You might go to sleep.'

'Yes – yes, please,' said Angela. 'Thank you, Imogen.' She put the cup and saucer back on the tray.

'I'll clear that up,' said Imogen. 'You go along, Mrs – er – I'm sorry, I don't know your surname.'

'It's Hunt,' said Angela, and something stopped her from telling this very well-mannered young woman to call her by her first name.

'I put your coat over the banisters,' said Imogen. 'I didn't know where you kept it.'

'I'll take it up with me,' said Angela.

The girl was very quiet, moving about downstairs. Angela, as she drew her bedroom curtains, could not hear a sound from below. She took off most of her clothes and slid into bed. She'd kept the painkillers down; a few hours' sleep and she would recover.

Apart from the money, she enjoyed the social side of her job at The Bugle, the banter with the customers and the sense of being part of a team behind the bar. With staggered weekend shifts, there had been time to visit Jerry, and she had stayed with this routine since his release. She wanted to keep the structure of her own life secure, for there was no guarantee that he would keep out of trouble; alone at home, she brooded, blaming herself and her deficiencies for his misdeeds, and worrying about the future.

The girl, Imogen, was good news; she was well spoken and neat. So many youngsters were decent enough, though they were painted as potential troublemakers in the papers and on television. Plenty that she met were bright and civil, though there were a good few of the other sort, of course. That friend of Jerry's, Pete Dixon, had been in and out of trouble for even longer than Jerry, she'd heard, and now he'd been arrested for an offence in Granbury, breaking and entering a house and attacking some old man who'd turned the tables and nicked him. Well, at least Jerry hadn't been there. She'd been watching television when he returned from the chip shop on Thursday evening and they'd both gone up to bed around half-past ten; she'd have heard him if he had gone out again.

Having such a nice girlfriend would help to settle him down. She hoped this thing, whatever it was, with Imogen – very new, obviously – would last; she'd enjoy having the girl around the place. Comforted by these reflections, and tired out, Angela fell asleep.

Jerry returned to find Imogen reading one of his mother's magazines. She hadn't put the television on again for fear of disturbing Mrs Hunt, and she hastened to intercept him, finger to lips.

'Your mother's back. She's in bed – she's got a headache. We mustn't wake her,' she said.

'Oh!' Jerry looked startled, and Imogen gave a sudden giggle.

'It's all right. She was cool about me being here,' she said. 'I explained. She said you did the garden. It's marvellous. So tidy.'

'I like gardening,' he confessed. 'It's satisfying.'

She wondered whether to challenge him about his mother's car, and decided not to at the moment. He'd have his reasons for bending the truth.

Imogen went back to Granbury on the bus.

Jerry walked her to the stop. His mother was still asleep, and he then confessed that he wasn't supposed to drive the car because he wasn't insured. His mother had a one-driver-only policy and hadn't yet included him as a named driver.

'She thinks because I'm under twenty-five it would cost a lot,' he said. 'But it wouldn't, because her car's not worth much. It's a way of keeping me down.'

'She thinks the police brought her car back,' Imogen said. 'I didn't tell her it was you.'

'Shit – thanks,' said Jerry. 'Mum thinks I reported it

missing, but I had to sort it. I didn't want to drop a mate in it, did I? Not if I could fix it.'

'No, I suppose not,' said Imogen, but doubtfully.

'He'd just borrowed it,' said Jerry. 'He won't do it again. My mate.'

'I hope not,' said Imogen. 'It must have been awkward for her, though.'

'Not as awkward as if a real villain had taken it and smashed it up,' said Jerry.

She could not think of what to say to that, so she made no comment. Jerry waited till the bus came, then, as he gave her a quick light kiss on the lips, her heart seemed suddenly to lift. It wasn't like the heavy, thrusting snogging which hitherto had been her experience, to be endured because this was LIFE.

'I'll ask Charlotte if you can come to lunch tomorrow,' she said. She'd given him her telephone number at Charlotte's, and she had his. 'I'm sure it will be all right. We could go for a walk or something, after. If you'd like to, that is.' She knew the chip shop didn't open on a Sunday.

'That'd be great,' he said, and meant it.

Charlotte, determined that Imogen should have a proper diet at least some of the time, had bought a leg of lamb on her shopping trip that morning. After Captain Smythe had gone, she made an apple pie in preparation for tomorrow's lunch, hoping Felix, if he were back in the country, would accept her invitation, and a sponge cake in case anyone arrived for tea. Imogen would eventually return, and it was good to be feeding someone other than herself. She prepared a fish pie for supper; it would heat up quickly when required. Perhaps it would be possible to persuade Imogen to talk about the future after they had eaten, unless she went out again with her mysterious friend. If it wasn't whoever was responsible for her condition, who was it?

Still hoping that Felix might be coaxed to come over, Charlotte left another message on his answerphone; he couldn't duck his responsibilities for ever. She didn't know how to get hold of Zoe; a transatlantic call to her might at least relieve Charlotte's feelings, if it achieved nothing else. A further talk with Lorna was indicated, but she should try to get somewhere with Imogen first.

Imogen arrived back soon after five; she let herself in and came straight through to the kitchen. Charlotte had just taken her apple pie, and some jam tarts made with the pastry remains, out of the oven. The sponge cake halves sat on wire trays, cooling.

'What a lovely smell!' cried Imogen, inhaling the warm aroma of Charlotte's baking. 'Mm. Can I have one?' and she reached out for a jam tart.

'Careful, they're very hot. You'll burn yourself,' warned Charlotte, carried back to when her own children were small – not young adults like Imogen – wanting to lick the bowl, as they called it, spooning out the scrapings. She prised a tart out of its tin with a knife and put it on a plate. 'There,' she said. 'Give it a minute or two. Would you like some tea?'

'Yes, please,' said Imogen, sitting down at the table, still in her fleece jacket.

Charlotte did not spoil her mood by suggesting she should take it off. The girl looked entirely different; she was bubbly and glowing. This change confirmed Charlotte's suspicion that she had met the father of her child – her boyfriend.

Perhaps he had not wanted to know about it earlier, hence her misery, and now he was facing up to what had happened. It was hardly likely that they would plan a wedding; shotgun marriages had gone out of vogue. The outcome might depend on who he was, and on his background; he must be a pupil at the school. He couldn't be a member of the staff, surely?

Charlotte shut her mind to the problem. Live for the moment, she told herself; Imogen is happy now; let's have a good evening together, if we can.

Felix Frost had picked up Charlotte's messages. Surely she could cope with Imogen for a few days without support, he said to his sister Lorna on the telephone.

'For Christ's sake, she's got nothing else to do,' he complained.

'You should listen to yourself,' said Lorna, who had six people coming to dinner that night. 'This is your daughter we're discussing.'

But Imogen was not his daughter, and knowing nothing about the man who was her father had become harder to endure with every year.

'Zoe should be dealing with this,' he said.

'You mean it's women's work? She's ratted on it, certainly, but we didn't know about it till she'd left the country,' answered Lorna.

'I can't think why the damn school couldn't keep her till the end of term. It's not as if the brat's due next week,' Felix said.

'They didn't chuck her out. She left,' his sister reminded him. 'But once they do hear about it, they'll refuse to have her back. And there's the boy concerned. This could be a major scandal for the school if the press get on to it.'

Felix, wrapped up in his own concerns, which included the possible bankruptcy of his company, hadn't thought of this.

'I suppose we must be thankful for small mercies,' he said.

'They may not be so small. She's a twin. They run in families. What if she has twins?' said Lorna ruthlessly. 'Why don't you go down to Granbury and have a showdown?'

'Maybe I will,' he said. 'If she gets rid of it, she could go back to school and no harm done.' If he could find the fees for another term. He might have to pay anyway, as she'd left without warning.

'Oh, Felix,' sighed his sister, hanging up.

Felix had not yet commited himself to any programme for Sunday. Some better way to spend it than going to Granbury might crop up, but he wasn't in the mood to take himself off to a gallery or museum. It might have to be bloody saintly Charlotte, but he wouldn't ring her now. He'd wait until the morning.

'Did you like helping your mother in the kitchen when you were a child?' Charlotte asked Imogen, after she had eaten a second jam tart and drunk two cups of tea.

'We never did. Mum isn't a great cook,' said Imogen. 'She scarcely gave up work after we were born, even though there were two of us. We had a daily nanny and then lots of au pairs. Some of them were all right,' she added. 'Mum's a good journalist, you know.'

Charlotte wasn't sure that she did know. By the time she

and Rupert met, Zoe had been on the staff of a fashion magazine for several years and she knew very little about her step-daughter's previous career.

'It must be interesting work,' she said, carefully.

'I suppose. She's met all sorts of people,' Imogen said. 'That's how she met this Daniel she's gone off with. They've been on several shoots together.'

'Oh,' said Charlotte. 'And have you met him?'

'Yeah, once. He was at home when I came for half term,' she said. 'Mum had forgotten.'

'So you went home on your own and he was there?' guessed Charlotte.

'Yeah.' Imogen drew patterns among the crumbs on her plate with a finger. 'Dad was abroad,' she went on. 'They were quite surprised to see me.'

Charlotte found that easy to believe. Had the girl caught them *in flagrante*?

'I don't suppose Zoe had really forgotten it was your half term,' she said. 'Perhaps she got the dates confused.'

'She was confused all right,' said Imogen. 'Daniel was cool, though. He said she should have remembered. I quite liked him, after a bit.'

Clever Daniel, contriving to beguile her.

'Well, that's good, then, if he's going to be around,' said Charlotte.

'He won't be. He's got a contract in the States and Mum's staying there with him,' Imogen said. 'I told you that.'

'Are you sure? Surely she'll have to come back and see about things?'

Imogen shrugged, and Charlotte judged that it was time to change the subject.

– 104 –

'Why don't you go upstairs and have a wash, and then we'll think about supper,' she said.

Imogen meekly rose.

'I asked a friend to lunch tomorrow. I hope that's OK,' she said.

'Perfectly,' said Charlotte.

'Jerry's his name,' said Imogen, and Charlotte heard her whistling as she went upstairs.

It was some time before Imogen reappeared. In the interval, she had had a bath and she was arrayed in a spotless white polo top and well-pressed black trousers; her face, innocent of make-up, shone. She had very good skin.

'How nice you look, Imogen,' Charlotte said, meaning it, and Imogen blushed.

'No one's said that to me before,' she mumbled.

'I'm sure they have, dear. You've forgotten,' Charlotte said. What about this boy? The one who'd made her pregnant, this Jerry? Or was he someone else? Or had something really dreadful happened, rape in fact, to cause her pregnancy?

'You said Granddad liked me,' Imogen conceded. 'At least, I think so.'

'Yes, he did. He was very fond of you,' said Charlotte, grasping at this reassuring certainty. 'You can be sure of that.' She hesitated. 'Did you have anything of his – any special thing – as a keepsake, after he died?'

'No,' said Imogen. 'He left me some money, though. Nick bought his car with his.'

'What about you? What did you spend yours on?'

'It's in the bank,' said Imogen. 'I might get a car, too,

when I've passed my test. I failed, the first time,' she confessed.

'Well, you'll have to take it again, won't you?' Charlotte said. 'Perhaps we could arrange some lessons, while you're here.' Being pregnant needn't stop her driving; it would give her something to do.

'That'd be great,' said Imogen, then, as Charlotte put the fish pie in the oven to cook through, she said, 'Fish pie – great. I love it.'

Did she know no other word of commendation?

'Your grandfather liked it, too,' said Charlotte. 'And he'd want you to have something special as a memento. I've got just the thing,' and she went out of the room.

Left alone, Imogen began to set the table. Her mind was comfortably unworried; she had had an interesting, unusual day, spending time in Jerry's house and meeting his mother. It was so unlike her own home, a five-bedroomed postwar house in Surrey, set in nearly an acre of garden, mostly lawn and woodland, among other houses of a similar nature, many of them larger, all well separated from one another by shrubs and trees. There was no village nearer than two miles away; the station from which her parents travelled up to London was a fifteen-minute drive. It was a comfortable house, furnished in the best of taste, and she had a lovely room, with, recently installed, her own shower and lavatory. Now it would be sold, the money split between her parents, and where would home be?

Still sanguine after her day, Imogen thought she might be able to live here with Charlotte, who was kind, and didn't ask too many questions, for the present, anyway.

At this point in her thoughts, Charlotte returned.

'Your grandfather gave me this,' she said. 'It had been his mother's. I think he'd like you to have it. He never gave it to your grandmother; perhaps he always meant it to come to you eventually.' He would have known that Lorna, his daughter, would not have worn it; she went in for chunky, dramatic, modern jewellery. She handed Imogen a small tooled leather box, faded with age.

Imogen took it from her silently, and opened it. Inside was a chased gold locket on a chain.

'There are two photographs in it. They're of your great-grandparents,' Charlotte said. 'It's quite difficult to open. See if you can do it.'

Still without speaking, Imogen tried to prise apart the two halves of the locket; then, seeing a slight indentation, she inserted a fingernail into the tiny hollow and the hinge moved. There were the two faces, the whiskered man with a lofty brow and large eyes, and the round-faced woman in her high-necked lacy dress.

'Your grandfather had meant to change the photographs inside,' she said. She'd dodged the issue; she hadn't wanted to put in theirs, as he had suggested. She had worn the locket, however.

Imogen looked up at Charlotte.

'It's lovely, thank you,' she said. 'But I'm not a bit like either of them, am I?'

'Not yet. They must have been in their sixties when those photographs were taken,' Charlotte said.

'You see, Felix isn't my father. We're test-tube babies, Nick and me. We don't know who our father is,' said Imogen.

'Oh, my dear child!' Charlotte exclaimed. She had no idea if this was true. 'How do you know?' she asked.

'Something I overheard. Mum and Dad were arguing. Mum said something about Dad being useless and not even being able to give her a child,' she said, and her large eyes began to fill with tears.

8

'They must have wanted you very much,' Charlotte said, deciding that it was no good contradicting Imogen when she did not know the facts herself. She'd read a certain amount about the subject; you couldn't miss it, these days, and she had noticed several pairs of twins and even one set of triplets on her trips to Nettington, when once seeing twins was a rarity. It was possible.

'Well, they don't now,' said Imogen. She had got it all worked out. 'Mum might have had a lover. It could be that,' she said. 'But anyway, it's put Dad off us – me more than Nick, because I'm a disappointment. And it's set Mum and Dad against one another.'

'I can't disprove what you're saying, Imogen, because I simply don't know the truth. You haven't asked your parents to tell you, have you?'

'No.'

'Well, I suggest you do, when you get a chance,' said Charlotte. Whatever the answer, Zoe must be the twins' mother, even if they were the result of an adulterous affair, but at the moment, saying so would be no comfort to Imogen.

'Your grandfather certainly regarded you as his granddaughter. You must believe that. And I'm extremely fond of you, Imogen. I'm just sad because you're going through a bad time at the moment.'

'I'd no right to take it out on you, and I've been doing that,' said Imogen. 'I'm sorry. Here you are, stuck with me.'

'And you with me, which can't be too much fun,' said Charlotte. 'Let's forget all that and have a truce.' Tentatively, for she had never been demonstrative, Charlotte put her arms out, and the girl embraced her in a bearlike hug, from which eventually Charlotte, touched but embarrassed, drew back. 'The fish pie's ready. I can smell it,' she declared.

After supper, Charlotte managed to get Imogen to play rummy. She kept cards and a few board games in preparation for visits from Tim's children, though so far they had been over only once, for a day, when Victoria brought them to see the house. Victoria's dismay at her changed situation had been patent; she remembered Charlotte's earlier house, before she married Rupert, where she had lived for years. It wasn't large, but it had character, and it contained a lifetime's acquisition of furniture and trappings, some of which were now to be seen in Number Five, Vicarage Fields. Charlotte had been determined that her daughter-in-law should send a good report to Tim; he must not be given cause to worry and she had been resolutely cheerful during the visit. Her brief marriage to Rupert had not alienated Tim and Victoria; she was never the grandmother first called on for support, as Victoria's own parents were nearly always available, but she had been a backstop, and she had seen quite a lot of the children when they were very small.

While Tim was based in Portsmouth they had visited White Lodge several times, swimming in the pool and running free in the large garden, but, abruptly, everything had changed.

Victoria felt very sorry for her, facing such sudden changes; the years with Rupert had undeniably been happy, and she had moved up the social ladder. Victoria, a service wife and daughter – her father had been in the army – was very conscious of hierarchical significance and saw that her mother-in-law, because of where she lived, had now dropped lower down the scale. Several times she had invited Charlotte to stay, but Charlotte had only ever come down for a day – a long drive for a short visit.

On Saturday evening, Victoria telephoned; there was news of Tim, whose ship had been patrolling in the eastern Mediterranean, and she mentioned that the children's school holidays would soon begin. Perhaps Charlotte would like to come for Easter?

'I've got Imogen staying for the moment,' Charlotte said. 'Imogen Frost. Rupert's granddaughter,' she explained, in case Victoria were confused. 'Her mother's in America and she's here for a visit.' She glanced at Imogen, who was studying her cards, as she said this. 'No, I'm not sure for how long. Shall I ring you in a few days' time? It's very kind of you, Victoria.'

With more civil exchanges, they ended their conversation. Victoria, if she were to be in touch with Tim soon, could tell him that his mother had some company.

'That was my daughter-in-law,' said Charlotte.

Imogen remembered her from Rupert's funeral, a composed, quiet but confident woman; she was much younger than Zoe but she was the conventional sort of mother Imogen wished that she had. It was difficult to think of Victoria having lovers; Zoe had had several before this last one, Nicholas asserted, and reminded Imogen of various men who had been about the place, particularly when Felix was overseas.

'She wanted you to visit, didn't she? And you said you couldn't because of me,' Imogen said now.

'She did invite me, yes,' Charlotte agreed.

'You could go. I'd be all right here on my own. I am eighteen,' said Imogen.

And pregnant, to boot, thought Charlotte, refusing even to contemplate what might happen if her back were turned.

'She asked me for Easter,' she said. 'If you're still here then, there will be other times.'

'But her children are your real grandchildren, and you haven't any others, have you?'

'We could both go to see them, for a day, if you're still here in a week or two,' said Charlotte. 'Some sea air would be good for you. For both of us, perhaps.'

She felt suddenly immensely tired. It was part of bereavement; she knew that, a huge fatigue which seemed to linger so that you felt it would never ease, and then, very gradually, it lifted. This time, she hadn't yet reached that stage. They finished their game, and though it wasn't late, Charlotte said she was going up to bed.

'You can stay up and watch television, if you want to,' she said. 'But you won't go out again tonight, will you, Imogen?'

'No, of course not,' Imogen replied. 'Don't you trust me, Charlotte?'

'Of course I do, my dear,' said Charlotte, but it wasn't altogether true. What if this boyfriend Jerry suddenly turned up and swept her off to some nightclub? There must be clubs in the area, decadent places where the young took drugs. Or Nicholas, who was probably no more reliable, might reappear and do the same.

She had to take a chance. Charlotte went upstairs.

Imogen did think of going out again, but where to? Her only friend was Jerry, and he lived miles away; there were probably no buses after ten o'clock, just as it was at home, and anyway, with the chip shop closed, he might be out clubbing or in a pub. Granbury was a dull sort of place, full of commuters leaving early in the morning and coming back at night, quite late. She'd seen the neighbours going off, and noticed how quiet it was when she went to meet Nicholas the day before. Any children in Vicarage Fields would be at school by then; she'd seen the primary school when driving round with Nick. What a dead and alive dump for Charlotte to end up in; there didn't even seem to be any oldies for her to socialise with, except for that really ancient man who'd escorted Imogen to the church and been burgled. Imogen banished a pang of anxiety about Jerry's possible indirect link to this incident and fell to contemplating her own situation. What a mess she had made of everything! She and Nick had gone to separate single-sex schools, but in the same area, and she hadn't wanted to change; her school had had its failings and she'd never been one of a group of girls all hanging out together, but most people had been decent enough and beyond some minor teasing, she'd got by. Besides, she had a huge asset in her good-looking brother whom her schoolmates clamoured to meet; invitations to The Elms had been prized, and were extended when it amused Zoe to offer them. Because of Nick, and because she was good at maths and physics, she had earned respect, and she was expected to do well academically. Then Mum had had this idea that she ought to mix around a bit and meet more boys. Imogen thought the truth was that she wanted to get her out of the house, and now she knew why: so that Mum could go ahead with her own little schemes, have it off with Daniel or anyone else she fancied without a schoolgirl coming home each night. Other girls who went to the same school as Imogen and lived in the neighbourhood had managed an outside social life, partly in each other's houses, or, as they grew older, meeting in the local town, but somehow Imogen didn't fit in with any of this. She and Nick both loved swimming, however, and went to the local pool in the winter when their own outdoor one was covered up against the weather. While Nick was around, Imogen's other problems didn't matter, but then, at sixteen, they were parted.

Imogen had hated the school to which she was sent as a boarder. She had a room to herself, which was something, but she knew no one. Never good at making friends, though more at ease if Nicholas was with her, she met overtures with suspicion, and her brusque response alienated both girls and boys, though she learned to get along, on a superficial level, with a few of them. There were new rules and mores to absorb, and she had to learn the layout of the building and the grounds. She had struggled through her first sixth-form year, working hard and revelling in the swimming; there was a huge indoor pool, available all year round, and in the water she was happy, but out of it, she felt herself to be a misfit. There were occasional taunts because she was overweight, but most of the other youngsters who enjoyed the pool admired her ability, though some envied it and were jealous when she won races and competitions.

Things had gone seriously wrong after Christmas. Mum had taken off to New York, and Nicholas had come to see her at school only once in all the time she'd been there; if he had come more often, his visits would have improved her standing, as had been the case before. He should have found it easier now he had a car, but he'd met this Phoebe and become entrapped, as Imogen saw it. Well, he'd made the effort to get to Granbury, now that she was in a lot of trouble. That was something.

Her flight from the school had been hushed up. Pupils should not run away, but she had set the scene for her abrupt departure by scratching from a house swimming competition. She told the PE teacher that she felt unwell, but, defiantly, she told the other members of the team that she was pregnant.

'Why cancel? You could still swim,' said Daphne, also in the team, when she had recovered from the immediate shock of Imogen's revelation.

'It might not be good for the baby,' Imogen had said.

'It would solve your problem, then, wouldn't it?' said Daphne. Fancy getting caught like that, she'd said later to her friends. 'Probably thought it was safe the first time, or standing up, or some such crap.'

Daphne had a boyfriend at home; the boys at school were all too young and inexperienced to interest her, and she and her cronies spent some time wondering who had been Imogen's partner in folly. In the end they decided it must be the assistant groundsman, a drop-out from a local comprehensive who might fancy her as a bit of posh.

'Posh – Imogen?' said someone.

'To him,' qualified the speaker.

'He'll get the sack,' said someone else.

One girl, who in fact was having a furtive affair with the assistant groundsman, conducted in the shed where the tennis nets and other equipment were stored, kept silent to preserve herself. She thought it might be a boy from the town.

Imogen fled before she had to face further questions and exposure. Her safe arrival at her grandmother's was a relief to the staff; the girls who knew about her pregnancy kept quiet about it, except amongst themselves, but her grandmother, arriving days later in a silver-grey Jaguar to collect her belongings, and angry, was less discreet. Imogen had refused to come with her, and the housemistress had had to organise the packing. Where, wondered the housemistress, were the fruits of all the talks on human biology, covering sexual mechanics and contraception? She had a difficult interview with Imogen's grandmother, a well-preserved seventy-year-old who looked as if she might have had a racy past, and advised that, with special arrangements, Imogen's A level exams might still be taken, a message Zoe's mother neglected to pass on.

Imogen, lying in bed in Charlotte's spare room, thought about the immature groping boys who, at discos in the school, had kissed her wetly, slobbering and thrusting their aggressive tongues down her throat as they tried to fumble her, and felt disgust, but she was not going to reveal the truth. Let them wonder.

The morning was again fine and sunny. Charlotte went into her garden and once again surveyed the dismal plot. In this continuing good weather, the faint urge of the day before to do something about it persisted. Roses, she thought; scented ones, climbers to hide the raw fencing on either side, and shrubs around the patch of so-called lawn.

Imogen, from her bedroom window, saw Charlotte out there. Absorbed by her own troubles though she was, Imogen nevertheless recognised the despairing droop of Charlotte's shoulders.

A wave of sympathetic pity swamped Imogen. Charlotte was another of her father's victims, forced out of White Lodge at short notice and parked in this dump – well, it wasn't a dump by most people's standards and the house was a palace compared with Jerry's, but after White Lodge it was a positive hovel, and it wasn't even hers. She was there by Dad and Lorna's gracious favour. Granddad would have been furious. Why hadn't he taken better care of her in his will? Imogen wondered what he'd actually said; Dad was capable of having turned it around to suit himself. She'd thought wives had the right to stay in the family house after the husband died. Unaware that Charlotte had contributed to the haste of her own departure, Imogen condemned her father utterly, and thought that Lorna might have done more to see that Charlotte was treated properly.

She'd settle down here eventually and be all right, Imogen decided. What she needed was friends and outside interests. She hadn't had outside interests at White Lodge; running it and looking after Granddad had, as far as Imogen knew, kept her fully occupied, but maybe she'd done other things before they married; she'd been a widow for a very long time. It was rather a pity they'd married, really, since it had lasted such a short time and now she was a widow once again. Kindly planning for Charlotte's future, Imogen washed and dressed, and went down to find her still in the garden.

Charlotte did not comment on her early rising as they greeted one another.

'I was trying to decide what to do about all this,' she said, gesturing at the bleak scene around them. 'I've made some marks where beds might look good.'

'Won't you need some help?'

'Probably. I might be able to find a man – a jobbing gardener.' Captain Smythe might know of someone; perhaps he had help.

'You can get firms to come in and do it all, can't you?' said Imogen.

'Landscape gardeners, you mean? Yes, but I think they're very expensive,' said Charlotte.

'Jerry wouldn't be,' Imogen said. 'He'd need a fair wage, of course, but he wouldn't want to fleece you.'

'Jerry? He's a gardener? A horticulturist?'

'No, but he knows a lot about it and his mother's garden is as neat as anything,' Imogen declared.

'This same Jerry who's coming to lunch?' Charlotte needed to be sure.

'Yes. He works in a fish and chip shop, but he gets lots of time off when the shop's shut,' said Imogen, in her enthusiasm ignoring any difficulties about his travelling to Granbury when he had no transport. 'He doesn't work on Sundays, and the chip shop's shut on Mondays,' she continued.

'Well, let's see what he thinks about it,' Charlotte temporised. It was good to see Imogen looking animated, but this information about Jerry eliminated him as the father of her expected child. The fact that Imogen had met his mother was in his favour.

'He's nice. You'll like him,' Imogen assured her. 'He's not a frightening sort of bloke.'

'Do you find most – er – blokes frightening?' Charlotte asked.

'Some – yeah,' said Imogen. 'They're big and noisy and they want to make you drunk,' she said. 'I'll go and put the kettle on, shall I?' and she went into the house.

Charlotte would not probe further now. She followed slowly. Goodness knows what had happened to the girl, but this new friend, Jerry, could be welcomed without reservation. Plenty of students worked in fast-food shops; why not Jerry?

After breakfast she tried Felix again, but the only reply was from the answerphone.

'Imogen, I've tried to get hold of your father to ask him down to lunch,' she said. 'However, he seems to be away. I'm going to invite Captain Smythe.'

'Good idea,' said Imogen.

Charlotte thought he would be a help in the entertaining of Jerry from the chip shop, background otherwise unknown. She found his number in the telephone book and caught him just as he was setting off for church. He was happy to accept.

Imogen helped her to lay the table in the dining-room. Charlotte still had the cutlery and crockery from before her second marriage, and some Swedish glassware; these and other things not needed at White Lodge, but not sold, had been stored there in the loft. She had some good claret; Tim and Victoria had sent her a case of wine as a house-warming present. There was also Coca-Cola, which Charlotte had bought on her trip yesterday, but no lager, which Imogen, remembering the tin they had shared at his house, suggested Jerry might prefer.

'Too bad. We have none,' Charlotte observed.

'He won't mind,' Imogen said airily, and, sure that she could do no more to help, went upstairs to have a bath and wash her hair before the guests arrived.

She really likes this Jerry, Charlotte thought. That was good, but what about the father of her baby? What was to happen? Since Thursday, they had drifted along in a state of limbo, deferring looking to the future, not facing facts. It must stop tomorrow. Tomorrow an appointment with the doctor must be made, and a serious discussion must follow.

When Imogen returned, her hair still slightly damp, she was wearing a long black skirt and a clean red sweater reaching to her hips. Her pregnancy had not begun to show; it must still be in its very early stages. What a pity it had been discovered before the school term ended. Depending on the decision that she made, it might have all blown over with no fuss, but, of course, there was the boy involved.

Captain Smythe arrived before Jerry. He was carrying a Waitrose plastic bag; inside was a bottle of sherry.

'A contribution,' he said. He had wondered what to bring. If you took wine, the hostess might feel it should be used at once, but it needed to settle and it might be inappropriate for the chosen meal.

'Thank you,' she said. 'You've met Imogen,' she reminded him.

'How nice to see you again, Imogen,' he said, bowing slightly.

'How are you, Captain Smythe?' Imogen asked. 'I hope you've recovered from what happened.'

'I'm none the worse,' he said. A veteran of the Murmansk and Atlantic convoys in the war, Captain Smythe had many times met extreme peril, but then he had been in his youthful prime; now, the loss of physical strength and mobility was what he found hard to bear.

'What time did you tell Jerry to come?' Charlotte asked Imogen.

'I didn't. I just said lunch. He'll know one-ish,' said Imogen with confidence. After all, he worked in a chip shop which catered for that meal.

'Jerry is our other guest,' Charlotte explained. 'Imogen says he's a keen gardener. She thinks he might be able to help me.'

'Excellent,' said Howard Smythe.

'We were looking at the garden this morning,' Charlotte said. 'It's desperate. There's nothing there.'

'I can give you some slips and seedlings, and other plants,' said Howard. 'My garden is well stocked and it will do the perennials good to split them up.'

'Oh, thank you,' said Charlotte.

'You'll have to plan it first, of course,' said Howard. 'Shall we have another look at it now? It's such a fine day, it won't be cold out.'

They trooped out through the French window on to the rough patio outside and surveyed the scene.

'A blank canvas,' said Howard. 'It takes five years to make a garden, I always say, but there are these instant gardeners nowadays who do it in a trice.'

'Perhaps there can be a compromise,' said Charlotte.

They were discussing possibilities when the doorbell rang. Imogen sped to answer it.

'I don't know her friend Jerry,' Charlotte warned. 'Imogen's only just met him. He's working in a chip shop in Becktham.'

'That's in his favour,' Howard Smythe remarked. 'He's not a layabout.'

'I imagine he's a student,' Charlotte said.

Imogen, at this moment, was leading Jerry out into the garden, telling him it was a mess which needed making over.

Charlotte saw a youth dressed in well-pressed dark jeans and spotless trainers, and a dark green sweatshirt. She'd seen him somewhere before, but where? It took her a little while to remember, but Howard recognised him straight away.

'This is my step-grandmother, Mrs Frost,' Imogen was saying. 'And this is Captain Smythe,' she introduced, with pride.

'How do you do,' said Captain Smythe, holding out his hand.

Mesmerised, Jerry shook it. He had very nearly decided to turn back when he located Vicarage Fields and realised that he had been there with Pete, but it looked different in daylight and maybe this would be a house where no one was at home when they called. Imogen was a nice kid and down on her luck, and she was just a friend, no more. Besides, his mother liked her. Hitherto always ready to take a chance, he'd do so now; however, he was confronted simultaneously with the woman who had smiled so warmly and the old guy who had turned him away but who later Pete had robbed.

Not a coward, Jerry steeled himself.

'Pleased to meet you,' he said, returning the old man's steady gaze squarely, for after all, he had taken his advice and got a job, an honest one.

The grandmother was smiling once again.

'Come along in, Jerry,' she said, and offered him some sherry.

9

After this, Charlotte marvelled that the lunch went off so well.

Neither she nor Howard Smythe was aware that the other had met Jerry in different circumstances; each was determined to hide the knowledge from the other and from Imogen, until the time for disclosure was appropriate. Charlotte carved the lamb, Captain Smythe poured the wine and Jerry made sure that everyone was able to reach the vegetables, which were served in Denby dishes on the table. Howard automatically poured wine for the two young people; there were wine glasses set at each place, and they were adult; it was automatic.

He did not know Imogen was pregnant. She did not refuse the wine. Charlotte, in her own pregnancies, had not given up moderate social drinking except when suffering from sickness in the early months with Jane. In those days, people were less prescriptive and also much less hypochondriacal; the claret might be good for Imogen; wasn't it full of iron? Wine had not figured much in Jerry's life thus far, but he could see there was no beer so, in the spirit of adventure, he tried it, having accepted, also, the pre-lunch sherry he was offered. His mum liked sherry, but her choice was rich brown in colour and very sweet, not like cat's piss, which Jerry thought his glass of fino resembled.

'Are you driving, Jerry?' Charlotte had asked him before the wine was poured, and he said no, he'd hitched a ride over as the bus took for ever, and he'd hitch one back.

'Tell us about your job in the chip shop, Jerry,' Howard Smythe invited, when everyone was settled, with mint sauce or redcurrant jelly – both, in Jerry's case.

'This is so good,' said Jerry, before answering the question. 'Mrs Frost, you beat them television chefs, you really do.'

Imogen hastened to endorse this commendation.

'You are brilliant, Charlotte,' she said. 'When we went to White Lodge, you always put on a great meal. Better than Gran ever did. Even Mum agreed with that. Granddad was lucky to get you.'

Some explanation was needed.

'Rupert – Imogen's grandfather – and I were only married for two years before he died, very suddenly,' Charlotte said.

'What a bummer,' Jerry said.

'They were good years,' Charlotte stated quietly, and it was true. There had been several holidays abroad, and they had been friends as well as tender lovers – again, a new experience for her. But if they hadn't married, her life would not have been turned topsy-turvy twice in a short period of time. Pressing her to marry him, Rupert had thought he was conferring material benefits on her and raising her social status; so he was, but briefly, and she needed neither.

'Dad and Lorna made her feel she couldn't stay on at White Lodge – that was their house – a lovely old house in the country, with a swimming pool and all that — and so she's here,' said Imogen, her colour high, her eyes bright.

Perhaps the wine was a mistake, thought Charlotte.

'It doesn't matter, Imogen,' she said. 'I chose to go quickly and your father found this house for me.'

Both the men were listening intently to this story, but while Jerry couldn't hear enough of it, Howard was embarrassed for Charlotte; these revelations must be painful for her. He returned to the subject he had tried to introduce.

'The chip shop, Jerry,' he prompted. 'Please tell us how you found the job and what it's like.'

He fixed the young man with a blue gaze before which mightier men than Jerry would ever be had quailed, and Jerry, remembering that this was the old bloke who'd nicked Pete, did as he was told.

'My mum found it for me,' he artlessly explained, without disclosing why he was not in work already, which two members of his audience already knew. 'She's got lots of jobs herself,' he went on. 'Well — three. One's in a pub, The Bugle, in Becktham, and my bosses in the chip shop drink there sometimes. Not often, because they're working most nights, but they go in at weekends. They mentioned that they had a vacancy.'

'Their fish and chips are very good,' Imogen contributed. 'Nick and I had some on Friday. That's how we met Jerry. And I've met his mother,' she added, for though Charlotte knew this, Captain Smythe didn't.

It sounded admirable, even respectable.

'We get all sorts in the chip shop,' Jerry volunteered. 'On Tuesdays — that's pension day — we have special prices for pensioners. You should see the old dears lining up. It's great for them, means they get a square meal cheap. You get to know them after a bit – there's one with a dog that's in a right mess, he leaves it tied up outside because they aren't allowed in. Hygiene, you see. And then there's Nell, who's on the game – she has a regular on Wednesdays at twelve, and she comes in for chicken and chips at half-eleven. She keeps it hot and they have it after.' He paused in his narrative, not for dramatic effect but to get on with his meal.

Howard and Charlotte exchanged glances. The old man's mouth was twitching, and Charlotte dabbed at hers with her napkin, hiding her smile. Even Imogen gave a snort of laughter, quickly suppressed.

'Who else is a regular?' she asked, and Jerry told them about the schoolchildren who came in in the evening, and the sales representatives, and the lorry drivers. He needed very little prompting to keep talking, and he seemed to know individually a great many of the regular customers and their stories.

'How have you found out so much about them, Jerry?' Charlotte enquired.

'I just ask them about themselves while I'm putting up the order,' Jerry said. 'People like to talk. Lots of them are lonely – and that's not just the old folk.'

He was being a success. Imogen listened, happy and proud. He might come from a different background but he fitted in. Howard wondered if he had genuinely reformed, and if so, whether it would last. If not, he had the makings of a prize con man – which, of course, he was already. Both Howard and Charlotte, well aware that thieves, and even those who had shown violence, often got little more than a reproof these days, were wondering what offence had led to his incarceration.

The apple pie was consumed completely; Jerry had a large second helping and Imogen a smaller one. After Howard Smythe had finished with a tiny slice of cheese, Imogen announced that she and Jerry would clear away and do the washing-up.

'We'll bring you coffee,' she said. Charlotte had already left the tray prepared. 'If we can't find where things live, we'll stack them neatly.'

'Thank you, Imogen,' said Charlotte.

She and Howard moved into the sitting-room.

'Well,' he said, when the young people were out of earshot.

'Well, indeed,' said Charlotte. She was wondering what to tell him.

'That was an excellent meal. Thank you,' he said. 'A treat.'

'I had thought Imogen's father might come,' said Charlotte. 'He's been conspicuous by his absence, so far.'

'Is the girl in some sort of trouble?' Howard asked, and Charlotte nodded.

'The oldest kind,' she said.

'How very unfortunate,' the old man observed. 'She's only a child.'

'She's just eighteen,' said Charlotte. 'But immature.'

'And now she's taken up with this youth. Hm.' Howard hesitated. She had to know.

But she forestalled him.

'I've met him before,' she said. 'He's the one who rang my bell one evening.'

'Yes,' said Howard. 'Mine too. Perhaps we should discuss this later, privately.'

At this point Imogen arrived with the coffee. She set the tray on a small table in front of Charlotte, and went out. They heard the kitchen door close.

'He said he was a young offender,' Charlotte said. 'When he called, I mean. He seemed so nice. Did he admit it to you, too?'

'He did,' said Howard. 'He's clearly a lovable rogue, as the saying is.' He'd met a few in his time.

'Imogen doesn't know about it,' Charlotte said. 'I'm sure she doesn't. They met by chance on Friday. He could have reformed.'

'Yes. Perhaps he has,' said Howard. 'Some do.'

'He still came today. He must have recognised the house. And us. He didn't run away. He can't have had anything to do with your burglary,' said Charlotte.

'He could have known the culprit. They may have been together when Jerry called on us originally. Reconnoitring,' said Howard.

'But that was about three weeks ago. At least, that was when Jerry came here.'

'Two weeks, certainly,' said Howard. 'Perhaps it was longer. It doesn't let him off the hook of being implicated.'

'Oh dear,' sighed Charlotte. 'Do I warn Imogen?'

'Not immediately,' Howard advised. 'It might make him seem all the more appealing and in need of her friendship. And I doubt if he'll steal the silver from under her nose.'

'I could let him do the garden,' Charlotte said. 'It would give him a chance to prove he's genuinely trying to keep out of trouble, and it might make a difference to Imogen.'

'How long is she staying?'

'I don't know. Her parents – her father is my stepson, as

you know – have parted and they seem to have washed their hands of her. Her mother is in America.'

'And her present predicament?'

'We haven't discussed it in any depth,' said Charlotte. 'Not yet.'

Sounds from the garden now indicated that the washing-up was done and the washers were outside, conferring about its condition.

'Why don't you all come back with me and look at my garden,' Howard suggested. 'I can show you various plants which can be split up to give you a start. We can see if Jerry really does know what he's talking about. You obviously think we should give him the benefit of the doubt about having turned over a new leaf until proved wrong.' Howard didn't sound convinced that this was a good idea.

'I do,' said Charlotte. She stood up. 'It's a lovely afternoon and it will do the young people good to have some exercise. I'd love to see your garden.'

Howard thought it a great pity that he was so old. If he were twenty years younger, he might have considered aiming to become her third husband; she was kind and restful, and extremely capable. But would he be offering her more than a post as an unpaid housekeeper, albeit with an affectionate employer?

Twenty years ago, probably. Not now. And thirty years ago, a widow in reduced circumstances could be offered a position as a resident housekeeper, but today, in such a case, all sorts of wrong assumptions could be made by outsiders, and tiresome legalities might be necessary.

* * *

They walked in pairs along the road, past where Jerry had found his mother's car, and turned down Meadow Lane towards the church. They met other people out enjoying the sudden warm spring weather, some with children, some with dogs, some with both. Each group seemed absorbed in its own affairs and no one greeted them. Howard Smythe told Charlotte that he recognised no one, not even from attending church.

Imogen and Jerry, walking faster, were ahead.

'Your gran's all right,' said Jerry. 'I expect she's sad, your granddad having died.'

'She must be, I suppose. I haven't seen her cry,' said Imogen. 'Not even at the funeral.' Imogen herself had wept copiously.

'That generation – her and the captain – they're brought up not to cry,' said Jerry. 'It's good. I don't like it when women cry.'

His mother's tears had overflowed when he got into trouble, and that had happened more than once before he went to prison, but on the earlier occasions he'd got off with community service, which was a doddle. Sweeping roads, he'd seen chances for opportunist theft and had taken them, sometimes even when still on the job, but usually returning at another time. He was wondering whether to tell Imogen about his earlier meeting with Mrs Frost, who seemed to have said nothing. Perhaps she hadn't recognised him. It was possible. He decided, for the present, to keep quiet.

He almost gave himself away by stopping at Captain Smythe's gate, but Imogen forestalled him.

'This is it,' she said. 'I asked him where the church was on Friday, when I was meeting Nick there. Churches are good places to meet because you can always find them. Captain Smythe said it's not kept locked.'

In his previous life, Jerry would have stored away this useful information. Churches contained valuables, even collecting boxes. Now he told himself to forget it. They waited for the other pair to catch them up. Captain Smythe opened the gate and ushered them through, then showed them round his rosebeds, all lightly pruned.

'I don't cut them back hard,' he said. 'It's not necessary with these continual flowering ones. I cut out the weak growth and the flower heads.'

Jerry marvelled at the long lawn, almost free of moss, and the trimmed shrubs. Early daffodils and crocuses bloomed, and under some trees there was a sheet of fading snowdrops.

'Do you do it all yourself?' he asked.

'A man comes once a year to trim the hedges,' said Howard. 'And I get someone in occasionally to help me tidy up. Otherwise I manage. It's an interest.' He led Jerry down the garden, intending to ask him what plants he could recognise but also, as he had arranged with Charlotte on the way here, to let him know that they had both recognised him. They would allow him time to tell Imogen about his past himself, and Mrs Frost might consider employing him to lay out her garden, but both of them would be keeping a careful eye on him.

'You'd be on probation,' he said sternly, after delivering this decision.

'I am already,' Jerry answered cheekily.

'You understand me,' Howard said.

'Yes – sorry, sir,' said Jerry, inspired to use this respectful term.

'And you will tell Imogen, in your own time,' Howard repeated.

'Yes. Poor kid, she's got troubles too,' said Jerry.

'She has. You'll respect her,' Howard said.

'Course,' said Jerry, adding, 'Sir.'

'The burglar who broke in here last Friday. Pete Dixon. Do you know him?'

The question took Jerry by surprise. His instinct was to deny it, but the old man might see through him.

'Yes, I do,' he said. 'And I did go round with him, on the sell, when I called on you and Mrs Frost. But she was nice, and smiled at me, and you were all right, too, sir. I never done the stealing, I just rang the doorbell and kept the person talking, while Pete went round the back. Often he couldn't get in,' he added, and went on, 'I decided to chuck it, because of you and Mrs Frost, and for my mum's sake, and then she got me the other job. You told me to get a job. Well, I did,' and he turned on his irresistible smile. 'Sir.'

'So you had nothing to do with the break-in here?'

'No, sir. Not at all,' said Jerry. 'Sir.'

'If you take advantage of Mrs Frost, or of Imogen, I'll see the police throw the book at you,' said Captain Smythe.

Jerry believed him.

Charlotte and Imogen had discovered the pond. They had walked through an archway in a clipped yew hedge into an enclosed area, and there it lay before them. It was about twenty feet across at its widest point and perhaps twice as long, irregularly shaped, and was fed by a spring which flowed from it into a rivulet joining a stream beyond Captain Smythe's boundary.

'How lovely,' Charlotte exclaimed. 'What a surprise!'

She spoke as Jerry and Howard Smythe came round a further corner of the hedge, arriving at the far side of the pond.

'We used to get a lot of flooding down here,' said Howard. 'I had the pond enlarged to prevent it. All's well unless the stream gets blocked. Eventually it connects up with the river. Sometimes it does overflow.'

The grass around the area was very lush, and water-garden plants — reeds and rushes, mainly, and clumps of iris — flourished round the edges. Water lilies covered part of the surface and a small wooden jetty on stout stakes jutted out into the water at one side.

Jerry stared, entranced. Charlotte, watching him, saw that he was genuinely spellbound by its tranquil charm.

'If you had a little bridge, it would be a miniature Monet,' she said. 'It's lovely. Are there any fish?' She moved on to the small jetty to peer into the depths.

'No,' said Howard. 'There were some carp. My daughter gave me a pair one year. She thought they might breed, but instead they vanished. They're quite valuable. Someone may have removed them.' A workman, he had thought at the time, not sorry to have lost the fish. 'I didn't like them much,' he confessed. 'I thought they had a baleful look.'

'How can fish look baleful?' asked Jerry.

'Oh, they do,' Charlotte confirmed. 'Not just carp. On fishmongers' slabs they do.'

'There were carp in the pond at White Lodge,' said Imogen. 'Granddad liked them. He used to feed them.'

'Well, all the fish I meet are dead fillets. Cod and haddock,'

Jerry said. 'Would you like a water feature in your garden, Mrs Frost? You needn't have any fish in it, but a little fountain would be nice. We could do it.'

'Let's not be too ambitious, Jerry,' Charlotte said.

'I am going to help you, then?' he said eagerly. 'I can start tomorrow. The shop's shut on Mondays.'

'Is that all right?' Imogen looked equally enthusiastic.

Captain Smythe and Charlotte exchanged glances. It seemed to have been decided. The young people were going to seek each other out anyway; Imogen, when she heard about Jerry's record, would doubtless disregard it. At least, if he were working here, Charlotte would know where they were and that would spare her worry. Captain Smythe, on the other hand, thought she might be inviting trouble, and he determined, if this went ahead, to keep an eye on things.

He saw them off at his gate. The trio walked along together, talking animatedly. Jerry was gesturing, making plans for the garden and telling Charlotte that Captain Smythe could spare plenty of specimens.

'Not just cuttings,' he explained. 'Things that have self-seeded or that need splitting up, like phlox and Michaelmas daisies.'

'We must discuss rates of pay, Jerry,' Charlotte said. 'I shall consult Captain Smythe about what would be fair.'

'Yeah – right, Mrs Frost,' said Jerry.

'How will you get here?'

'I'll hitch,' said Jerry. 'It's OK – I'll get a lift eventually. The bus takes too long.' And costs, he thought.

It wouldn't be easy to come over during the week, when he had only a few hours off in the daytime. Still, he could do a lot in two whole days each week.

Charlotte hoped this would work out, but whatever happened, Imogen must see the doctor as soon as an appointment could be arranged. She must face up to her situation.

She was going to have to do it rather sooner than expected. As they walked along Vicarage Fields towards Number Five, Charlotte noticed a car outside her house. There were other cars parked in the road, but this was a large Mercedes. She and Imogen simultaneously recognised it.

'It's Dad,' said Imogen.

Charlotte took a deep breath.

'Yes.'

'He's a bit late for lunch,' said Imogen.

'I'll be off, then,' Jerry said, hastily. 'Thanks for the lunch, Mrs Frost, and I'll be over tomorrow about the garden, as early as I can get here. Cheers, Imogen,' and he hurried away.

'I'm delighted that your father's come,' said Charlotte firmly, walking towards the car.

There was no one in it.

'He'll have a key. He'll have let himself in,' said Imogen.

She was right.

10

Charlotte was outraged at Felix's effrontery, while acknowledging that perhaps he had some right to enter what was, in fact, his house. Trying to suppress her anger, she opened the door and beckoned Imogen inside.

Felix was sitting on the sofa reading the paper, a glass of wine beside him.

'Make yourself comfortable, why don't you?' Imogen almost snarled the words.

Felix slowly laid the paper down, took off his half-glasses and, without haste, rose to his feet. Not inconsequentially, Charlotte realised that neither of his children looked the least like him, though Nicholas was as tall, and as slimly built. Felix was much darker; he was, she noticed, very thin, surely much thinner than at their last meeting, when he had handed her the keys to this house. He wore a dark green shirt, tieless, under a darker green v-necked sweater, and black cord trousers with expensive-looking loafer shoes.

'Sorry I'm too late for lunch,' he said smoothly.

'Have you eaten?' Charlotte, too, spoke sharply. 'There's some lamb left. I see you found the wine.' They hadn't quite finished the bottle, but she knew he was capable of searching for and opening another if they had.

'I've had lunch, thank you, Charlotte,' Felix said, sitting down again. 'You seem to have had a full table without me.'

Charlotte realised that he had deduced this because Imogen and Jerry had not put the wine glasses away, and the coffee tray, though with only two cups and saucers on it, was still waiting to be dealt with.

'We had friends in, yes,' she said. 'As you hadn't said if you were coming and I couldn't get through to speak to you in person.' Because he had let himself in, he hadn't seen Jerry; at least he need not be explained.

'You look well, Charlotte. Been for a walk, have we?'

Charlotte and Imogen were both waiting for him to speak to his daughter, or even to notice that she was there.

'Imogen is here, standing beside me, Felix,' Charlotte said. 'A greeting would be in order, don't you think?'

'Oh, Christ. Are we going to be in a mood?' said Felix wearily, rubbing his hand across his forehead. He sank back upon the sofa.

'It's all right. You don't have to recognise me. I'm not your child. Father unknown, that's it, isn't it?' said Imogen, and rushed out of the room.

'Christ,' said Felix again. 'What have I done now?'

'It's what you haven't done,' said Charlotte. She was still standing, while he reclined, and now she gripped the back of a chair to give her support. 'You've just completely ignored her, and you've handed her and your parental responsibility over to me.'

'Now come, Charlotte. Haven't you a duty to us? Can't we expect you, as our father's widow, to fulfil your obligations?'

'Hasn't Imogen a right to your support? She thinks you're not her father. Could that possibly be true?' Charlotte demanded.

For the first time, reluctantly, Felix saw what had made his father want to marry Charlotte; she wasn't just a capable woman who could rise to most occasions; she was passionate. He didn't like the thought, and banished it.

'What's given her that idea?' he asked, warily.

'She heard you say so, when you and Zoe were quarrelling.'

'Zoe had some affairs in the past,' said Felix.

'But no test tubes? That's what she suspects, because she's a twin. Fertility treatment sometimes results in multiple births,' said Charlotte.

'Twins are hardly multiple, are they?' Felix snapped.

Charlotte ignored this.

'You could have tests, if there's some doubt,' she said shortly. 'But anyway, to all intents and purposes you are her father and you have a duty towards her.'

'Well, I'm here, aren't I?' he snapped. 'Fetch her down and let's have it out with her.'

'I won't do that,' Charlotte said. 'I won't have you upsetting her.'

'What about her upsetting us? Me and Zoe?' he demanded.

'Zoe and me,' Charlotte, ever the pedant schoolteacher, corrected him, and then went on, 'Oh, never mind. You upset her first, breaking up and not telling her about it. You upset both of them, but Nicholas has always had more confidence than Imogen. It worried Rupert.'

'Granddad's pet, eh?'

'It's a good thing she was someone's pet,' said Charlotte. 'And for the moment, she's mine. She'll see a doctor next week and if necessary a counsellor, to help her decide what's best. That is, unless you've come to take her home.'

'I haven't, as you well know,' said Felix. 'What's best is that she gets rid of it, and sharpish.'

'She may not agree,' said Charlotte. 'I'll back her up, whatever choice she makes. If she does have a termination, there could be a huge emotional problem.'

'She'd get over it.' Felix was dismissive.

'She'd never totally forget it,' Charlotte said. 'And what about her mother? Where does Zoe stand in all this?'

'She can't think of anything except her big romance,' Felix said. 'This Daniel.'

'Imogen seems to like him,' Charlotte said. 'And Zoe must be worried about her.'

'She's confident that you'll sort it. Do what's best,' said Felix grudgingly. 'So's Lorna.'

'What about your business worries?'

'What about them?'

'You don't deny you've got them?'

'Lorna told you, I suppose.'

'I believe it's been reported in the business columns, but I rarely read them,' said Charlotte, who intended to do so in future if Felix's company were to be mentioned.

'It's bad. The receivers are coming in,' said Felix, dropping some of his aggression. 'We're just holding on.' He wouldn't tell her about the possibility, still uncertain, of a management buy-out. He needed every penny he could raise, and now Zoe was determined on a divorce which was an additional and superfluous complication.

'I'm sorry,' Charlotte said, realising that for Felix to admit it to her, the situation must be very serious.

'Yes – well, it's not your fault,' he managed to allow.

'It's not Imogen's either. Felix, whether you're her biological father or not, you are her legal father, as much as if you had adopted her, and you can't just walk away from her without discussing her problems.'

'Can't I, though?' he challenged her. 'Just you watch me,' and he stood up. 'Goodbye, Charlotte. I expect you to get in touch with me when the silly little bitch has come to her senses. And meanwhile –' he pulled his wallet from his pocket and plucked out several banknotes which he dropped, fluttering, to the ground. 'These will help towards her keep.'

Charlotte was too astonished to react before he marched from the house. He banged the door behind him, and she heard his car start up, leaving with much exaggerated acceleration. She bent to gather up the money. He hadn't counted it, simply pulling out a wad, in a gesture: there were four twenties and a fifty-pound note.

If he needed petrol on his homeward way, he'd always got his credit card, if it was still worth anything, she supposed.

Imogen entered the room while she stood there, holding the money.

'I think you ought to change the locks,' she said.

'How much of that did you hear?' Charlotte asked her.

'Enough,' said Imogen. 'You were great.' She flung her arms around Charlotte and hugged her. 'Thanks.' She had clearly been crying, but there were no tears now. 'I'm right, aren't I? There is something strange about us. Our birth. Nick and me.'

'There may not be,' Charlotte temporised. But Felix had not denied the possibility. 'Your mother could have had an affair. It happens. As it's worrying you, you should ask her, when you get a chance.' Imogen's need to understand her own heredity would increase, now that she was pregnant. Perhaps, if confronted with the problem, Zoe would be able to reassure her.

'And when will that be?'

Charlotte shrugged.

'Maybe sooner than you think,' she said. 'Eventually she'll have to come back and see to matters over here.' Then she added, slyly, 'At least you know who your baby's father is.'

Imogen turned away.

'If I have it,' she said.

The moment of intimacy had gone. Charlotte handed her the money.

'Felix left this for you,' she said. 'Put it somewhere safe, and let's make a plan about the garden so that we've got something positive to talk about to Jerry in the morning. And I think you're right about the locks. I'll ring a locksmith first thing.'

But she forgot.

Nicholas telephoned that evening. Charlotte sent Imogen upstairs to talk to him on the bedroom extension; she had no wish to catch even a fragment of their conversation.

Jerry took some time to get back to Becktham. He was unlucky over lifts, with a dearth of commercial vans, and he was ignored by suspicious Sunday motorists who wouldn't take a chance, but eventually a man driving a shabby transit stopped for him. He was going to a store he'd got in Becktham and asked Jerry, as a return for a free ride, if he'd help offload some stuff he'd got in the back. Jerry was agreeable, only wondering when they unloaded it – a job lot of china, bits of furniture and several television sets – if they were stolen goods. The man said he'd bought everything at a boot sale. More likely he'd tried to flog it, Jerry thought, but he lent a hand and then sloped off, remembering the address for possible future contact.

His mother was at home, much recovered. She'd had a lazy day, but she'd cleaned the house up a bit. She didn't want that nice Imogen to think her a slut, even if she was one. Jerry told her about the old guy's garden and the plans for Charlotte's.

'It'll be great, Mum. I can be there all day tomorrow, and then Sunday and Monday next weekend. If it stays fine and I stick at it, I'll get a lot done. Imogen can help with the light stuff.' That wouldn't hurt her; it would do her good to be in the fresh air.

'Why only the light stuff?' asked Angela. 'She's a fit, strong girl. She can dig as well as you.'

Of course, she didn't know about the baby. She'd better not, or not yet.

'Very true,' he said, and found a pad of paper.

He spent some time that evening sketching out possible designs for Charlotte's garden, not to scale, for he'd taken no measurements, but by guesswork.

'You did learn something in that prison, didn't you?' his mother said, with satisfaction.

'Found my vocation, maybe,' Jerry answered.

Nicholas's term was ending and he hadn't decided what to do in the vacation. The Elms, their family house in Surrey, was up for sale, but he could still go there, since even if it went quickly, which was likely, it would be some weeks before the sale was completed. However, his father was based there and Nicholas had no wish, just now, to spend time with him. He needed funds. Over the weekend he had combed advertisements in the local papers, and he had found a job as a waiter at one of the hotels. He would stay on in his house, where the rent had been paid in advance; even though hand-to-mouth, he would manage. He had offers from two universities, depending on his A level results. He must do well in those exams; after that, there were other choices. If necessary he could take a year out and earn some serious money; maybe he should, to stand by Imogen if she went ahead and had the kid. What a mess she'd made of things.

Felix had rung him up on Sunday night. He'd gone to Granbury, only to find Charlotte and Imogen were out and he had to wait for their return.

'Did they know you were coming?' asked Nicholas.

'Charlotte invited me for lunch,' said Felix.

'Did you accept?'

'I hadn't spoken to her. I imagined the invitation stood,' said Felix.

'Well, what time did you get there?'

'Around half-past three. Maybe nearer four.'

'Four o'clock! Dad, you know Charlotte and Granddad always had lunch at one, or, at the latest, one-fifteen.'

'And that's another thing,' said Felix, refusing to be wrong-footed. 'Has Imogen spoken to you about this whim she's got, questioning your birth?' If she hadn't, she or Charlotte soon would. He'd better get in first.

'Our birth? What do you mean?'

'She thinks you might be test-tube babies, just because you're twins, and not identical.'

'Shit – does she?'

'She does,' said Felix, in a weary tone.

'Well, are we?' Nicholas demanded. 'All you have to do is say no, if we're not.'

'There was no reasoning with her,' Felix said. 'She ran out of the room before I could reply. Talk to her, Nick. Try to make her see sense about an abortion, there's a good chap. Must go. Talk to you soon.'

He rang off, and Nicholas, replacing his receiver, realised that Felix had dodged the question. And what a question! Nicholas didn't like Imogen's theory one bit. He thought about it, feeling rather sick. Surely it couldn't be true? All that stuff about test tubes was creepy, and weren't he and Imogen too old for it to have been possible in their case? Hadn't it got fashionable quite recently? He didn't know a lot about it. Certainly neither he nor Imogen resembled Felix, or their mother, come to that. Perhaps they were adopted, but wouldn't they have discovered this from their birth certificates? Nicholas couldn't remember ever needing his; he'd had a passport all his life, renewed without providing one. Perhaps he should ask for it, confront their father. If they weren't the products of straightforward sex, they had been deceived. He'd always got on well enough with Felix, for Nicholas, whilst not excelling in any particular direction, was an achiever, playing in school football teams and doing well academically. But so was Imogen; she had always had better results at school than Nicholas, and she was an outstanding swimmer, though not good at games, but their parents had never given her credit for her successes. In fairness to herself, and for the future, she ought to do her A level exams next term. He'd have to speak to Charlotte about it, and about this test-tube business.

Meanwhile, though, he was going round to Phoebe's place. She might know a bit about test-tube babies.

Phoebe knew about blue and brown eyes, the Mendelian theory. She explained it to him, and gave him a run-down on fertility treatment. Nicholas hadn't bothered much about her IQ. Their relationship had been intensely physical, and he had genuinely tried to help her, even getting quite fond of her little kids, a boy of two and another of four months. He felt pleased when he managed to shut them up when they were bawling, but they were messy. He tried to avoid all that, but Phoebe as a person was so clean; she washed herself, her children, and their clothes remorselessly. Nicholas, a bit of a dandy, appreciated that; it contrasted agreeably with the sluttishness of some other girls he knew. But Phoebe wasn't a girl; she was a woman. He liked that. Hearing her talk knowledgeably, he thought he could do worse than stick with her for a while.

In bed with her in her flat in a drab council building, he wondered if she'd thought of taking in ironing as a way of adding to her meagre income. His mother used an ironing service, had done for years. There might be money in it in Oxford.

Charlotte rang Granbury's Health Centre as soon as it opened on Monday morning. There was a slot when Imogen could see the woman doctor at half-past twelve. This was lucky; Charlotte had expected her to be booked up all day, and possibly on Tuesday, too.

She told Imogen that she must keep the appointment, and, sulky again, the girl agreed. She had been very cheerful when Jerry arrived. He'd got a lift from a neighbour, a plumber, who was a customer at the chip shop and went out of his way to drop him off half a mile from the village. Charlotte had been up for some time; Imogen was woken by their voices.

Charlotte had decided, overnight, that the scrubby patch of grass she had inherited must be replaced. Cut regularly, it would look good; taking up the old turf and levelling the ground would keep Jerry occupied while she faced up to things with Imogen, and Imogen might be reasonably content while he was there; he was young company for her. If she hadn't known about his past, Charlotte would have taken him for what he seemed, a pleasant lad, but she would be careful; she wouldn't leave money or valuables, such as her watch, lying around, though he must know that if anything were to disappear, he would be the immediate suspect.

She had a spade and a rake, and some other basic tools which Felix had permitted her to take from White Lodge, remarking that their value at the auction he was planning for the better things from the house would be negligible. Jerry set to work. He'd brought a spirit level, anticipating the need for one. He began stacking up the turf to be discarded; it would rot down and form topsoil. Imogen had come downstairs as soon as she heard his voice; she was dressed in what she slept in, a long tee-shirt with a flower motif across her chest.

'Hi,' she said.

Jerry said, 'If you're coming out, you'll catch your death like that. Put some clothes on.'

'Right – I'll be out later,' Imogen promised, and meekly went upstairs.

One up to Jerry, Charlotte thought. She walked down the garden to ask him not to stop Imogen keeping her doctor's appointment.

'She has told you she's pregnant?' She needed to be sure.

'Yes. Poor kid,' said Jerry in paternal tones.

'She won't talk about it at all,' said Charlotte.

'She hasn't told me who the bloke is, if that's what you're getting at,' said Jerry. 'Maybe she doesn't know.'

Charlotte looked at him, shocked.

'It's possible, but I don't like to think of such a situation,' she said.

'There's that drug now. I forget its name – begins with R,' said Jerry. 'The girl doesn't remember anything about it. The rape drug, they call it. It's slipped into a drink. Dead easy.'

That was an answer Charlotte hadn't thought of; it might be the right one, and would explain a lot about Imogen's attitude.

'She must see the doctor, anyhow,' she said. 'She may tell her what happened.'

'Doesn't make much difference, does it? She's still going to have a kid, whoever the guy is.'

Charlotte would not discuss with him the possibility of another choice.

'The father has a responsibility,' she said primly.

'Ah – but girls like babies, don't they?' Jerry said. 'Gives them something of their own, someone to love, who loves them back.'

'Someone who gives them sleepless nights and exhausts them,' Charlotte replied tartly.

'Yeah – well – worth it in the end, innit?' Jerry said. 'I never had no dad. Don't know who he was. My mum won't tell me.

She managed, and she didn't have a gran like you to help her.' She'd died before he was born.

But Charlotte wasn't Imogen's grandmother and she didn't want to help her with the baby. However, if Jerry's mother had had a family to help her, he might have kept out of trouble, she reflected.

She left him to his labours and went indoors.

Imogen brought an armful of clothing with her when she came downstairs again, dressed, and asked if she might wash it.

'Put it in the machine and I'll turn it on later, when you've finished your breakfast,' said Charlotte, and she reminded Imogen about the appointment.

Imogen went silent.

'You must go, Imogen. You must be medically checked. There are dates to calculate – matters to discuss.'

'I don't see why. I'm perfectly well. I'm not even being sick,' said Imogen.

That might be a treat in store.

'I'm responsible for you, Imogen. You have to see the doctor,' Charlotte said.

'Typical teacher,' Imogen said rudely. 'Bossy,' and, with a piece of toast in her hand, she went into the garden to help Jerry. He soon had her raking the revealed subsoil, levelling it by eye as best she could.

If Imogen mentioned the appointment to Jerry, he might make her see the sense of it. Jailbird though he was, he appeared to have a good effect on her.

Charlotte drove Imogen to the surgery, which was at the further end of the village, down a turning on the road to Nettington. Imogen had protested that she would walk there.

'You don't trust me,' she said.

'I think you might have trouble finding the way, and I'm giving you my support, Imogen,' Charlotte replied.

'Well, I can walk back,' Imogen said.

'I'll see you in, and then I'll wait for you in the car,' said Charlotte. 'I'll bring the paper and do the crossword.'

The surgery was in a modern block added to an older complex where there was a community hall and library. Charlotte had not consulted a doctor since she moved into the village, but she had registered with the practice. She had some sleeping pills which were prescribed after Rupert's death, but, fearful of dependency, she seldom took one; when they were gone, she might ask for more, as a precaution, but a new doctor might not want to give them to her. That could wait, however.

As it was such a lovely day, it was no penalty to abandon the warm waiting-room with its upright chairs and old magazines, and sit in the car with the window down. The receptionist had taken Imogen's details, and the fact that she was a visitor, smiling at her kindly. Even so, this must be intimidating for her, Charlotte thought. Worse was to come, whichever way she decided.

She had not locked the house up when she left, though she had considered it. At eleven, she had made a mug of instant coffee for herself and offered one to Jerry, who had chosen tea, and so had Imogen. The two of them had sat on cushions on the so-called patio – a few paving slabs outside the French window – while they drank it. They were chatting and Charlotte wondered what they found to talk about together.

In fact, Imogen had asked Jerry how he came to be so keen on gardening, and he had taken the plunge; before Charlotte could ask him if he'd done it, as agreed, he told her about his prison sentence.

Imogen didn't react with shock, and she didn't ask him what he'd done, so he told her it was a bit of thieving, not mentioning his earlier conviction when he was with a group of youths who had beaten up a shopkeeper when they raided a small grocery store in a Midlands village. Jerry had been on other raids with this group, but because he was only fifteen he had got off with probation that time, though the ringleaders had been sent to prison; however, he was tainted by association and he had a record. His mother, aware that he had fallen into bad company, had resolved that they must move to a new area, and so they came to Becktham where he had done two years at school, scraping a few undistinguished GCSE passes. After that he had worked in a supermarket, stacking shelves, until, bored, he got into more trouble. This time, after his arrest, he had been sent down.

Imogen emerged from the surgery after little more than half an hour. She was smiling.

'Everything's fine,' she told Charlotte. 'The doctor was very nice. I'm to go back when I've thought about things a bit.'

'And when is the baby due?' asked Charlotte, knowing that if there was to be a termination, delay was not a good idea.

'October some time,' Imogen said airily. 'I don't want to think about it now.'

Charlotte could not force her to speak. They drove home in silence, to find that Jerry had finished lifting the turf. He'd marked out prospective beds and a curving path.

'We'll need to order that new lawn, Mrs F.,' he said, when they returned. 'I've measured up what we'll need, and I took the liberty of ringing up a couple of places listed in the Yellow Pages, to get quotes. One guy could deliver today.'

'Oh, Jerry!' One of these youngsters, but unfortunately the wrong one, had a sense of urgency. 'Explain it to me. Then we'll order them.'

11

Charlotte felt she was being rushed. She telephoned the turf supplier Jerry had mentioned, and some others, but in the end she settled for the original one which he had found; Jerry would be there when the load arrived and could stack it, ready to start laying it the following Sunday.

By the time all this was accomplished, dusk was falling, but Jerry toiled on, starting to roll out the new grass. Charlotte paid him at a rate of six pounds an hour, which was a pound more than Howard Smythe had advised when she telephoned to consult him.

'I'm sure the chip shop doesn't pay as much,' he told her. 'The boy's unskilled, and only nineteen. He'd be lucky to get four pounds stacking shelves in a supermarket.'

'What do you pay the man you employ?' Charlotte challenged.

'Ten pounds an hour,' confessed Howard. 'But he's a mature man, a knowledgeable gardener.'

'Jerry has been working hard,' Charlotte replied. 'He's done an amazing amount in a day.'

'And you've fed him, I expect,' Howard guessed.

She had, of course. She and Imogen had enjoyed his company as they ate cold roast lamb and baked potatoes. Imogen had raked up stones and marked out the edges of future flower beds, and when Jerry began laying the grass, she helped, crawling about on hands and knees, copying how he did it. Jerry asked for the lights to be on at the back of the house so that he could continue working; one of Imogen's tasks was to move within range of the external halogen light's sensor each time it went out, making it come on again.

When Charlotte went to tell him he must stop, all the turf was down.

'I'll fill in the joins and design the beds next time,' he promised. 'It would be good if you could water it, though, unless it rains. There may be some rough bits, but I'll soon neaten those up.'

Charlotte believed him as she agreed to carry out his instructions. She'd buy some plants, too, a few shrubs to begin with, as he'd otherwise have little left to do the next weekend.

While he washed at the kitchen sink, Imogen said, 'Do you think we could drive him home? It may take him ages to get a lift.'

'Oh!' Charlotte hadn't thought of that. Equally, even though the area was small, she had never expected him to remove the old grass and lay the new turf in a day. It had been achieved because he had found a firm able to deliver promptly and by the time it arrived, he had prepared the ground. He certainly did not lack initiative. 'You're right,' she said. 'We must.'

Jerry protested. Someone would pick him up in the end, he said. Then he had another thought. If he accepted, Mrs

Frost could meet his mother who was sure to be impressed, and she might agree to arrange car insurance for him so that he could drive over at the weekend. It was worth a try. After a further amount of protesting, he gave in and they all piled into the car.

Jerry sat in the back. He had thoroughly enjoyed the day's work; transforming what had been a tip into a presentable plot was satisfying, and Mrs Frost had been grateful. A reference from her, in due course, would help him on his newfound upward path. The money, too, was good; if he offered to pay for the extra car insurance, his mother would find it difficult to refuse.

When they reached Becktham, Jerry directed Charlotte into his road and as she stopped, he said, 'Please come in and meet my mum, Mrs Frost.'

'No, Jerry, we must get back,' Charlotte said.

'Oh, please, Charlotte,' Imogen implored, already getting out of the car.

'It's late – your mother won't want visitors now,' Charlotte said.

'It's not a night for her evening job,' Jerry insisted. 'She'll be glad to see you.'

And he was right, she was. Angela had not drawn her sitting-room curtains and she had seen the car draw up outside, behind her Metro. By the light of the streetlamp, she saw Imogen emerge, and was out of the door in seconds, hurrying down the path.

Charlotte had to comply. As soon as they were in the house, she realised she had seen Jerry's mother before, but it was a little while before she remembered where.

For her part, Angela had never looked at her benefactor

at Becktham station's ticket office; she had no connection to make.

There was no point in reminding her of the incident; one should not draw attention to one's good deeds. Charlotte remembered how she had thought the woman a troubled soul, and no wonder, with Jerry's record.

Angela was offering coffee. Imogen was astonished when Charlotte, intrigued now, accepted, thinking that it would be as well to learn what she could about this family as Imogen had already made friends with them.

'I'm Angela Hunt,' she had said, greeting them and holding out a warm, dry hand.

'Charlotte Frost,' said Charlotte. 'I think you know my step-granddaughter.'

'Indeed I do,' said Angela. 'She looked after me so nicely on Saturday when I wasn't feeling very well. Made me tea and bundled me off to bed. She's lovely,' and she smiled at Imogen who had turned pink with pleasure.

Imogen helped her now with the coffee, while Jerry took Charlotte into the sitting-room and guided her towards an armchair. Noticing the pristine large sofa and its matching chairs, she recalled the television advertisements which advised that you could buy now and pay nothing for a year, or even longer. What happened when the money was required? Perhaps you undertook another job.

Jerry drew the curtains.

'Mum ought to pull them when it gets dark,' he said. 'I'm always telling her. People can see in, and that. Gives them ideas. Or can.'

Charlotte refrained from commenting that he, if anyone, should know. He perched on the edge of the other chair and strove for something to say.

'Mum and Imogen got on brilliantly the other day,' he said. 'But she doesn't know about Imogen's trouble. That's for Immy to tell, isn't it?'

Immy. Charlotte had never heard her called that; the diminutive indicated that he really liked her.

'Yes,' she said.

'My mum works in Denfield. She goes on the train,' he said.

'Oh,' said Charlotte, who already knew this.

'Her firm's just moved from Becktham so she has a bit of a journey to make now,' he said. 'But she goes by train because of the parking.'

'I see,' said Charlotte.

'She's a great mum and I don't want to worry her no more,' said Jerry, fixing Charlotte with his most sincere expression.

'I'm sure you don't, Jerry,' she said. 'And if you go on working as hard as you did today, I'm sure she'll be proud of you.' How sanctimonious I sound, she thought, but what can I say to the boy? It's up to him, after all.

Angela and Imogen soon appeared, Imogen carrying the tray and Angela a plate of biscuits. Charlotte banished thoughts about supper, accepting a cup of excellent freshly brewed coffee and a Rich Tea biscuit.

'Jerry tells me your firm has moved,' she prompted, and Angela launched into an explanation of the various journey choices before her. Charlotte, seeing her less harassed now than at their earlier encounter, realised that she was a pretty woman, in a rather faded way, and probably still under forty.

'Jerry worked miracles today,' she said, when Angela ran out of steam. 'He took up a patch of so-called lawn and almost finished laying a new one. It just needs a bit of tidying up, doesn't it, Jerry?'

'Yeah – then a few shrubs and stuff around the place. We'll have it looking good in a few weeks,' Jerry said.

'Jerry's got green fingers,' said Angela. 'He only has to look at a plant and it grows.'

'Perhaps you should take it up professionally, Jerry,' said Charlotte. 'Do a horticultural course.'

'That's a brilliant idea. You could enquire,' Angela said. There were all sorts of courses you could do. She beamed. Things were looking up.

Going home, Imogen said that it had been a good suggestion, but wouldn't it cost? Even if Jerry were accepted, he might have to pay, and he wouldn't be earning.

'There could be a solution,' Charlotte said. 'We could find out what the possibilities are.' Thoughts of Kew, or the gardens on Tresco, ran through her mind. 'His mother must have had a hard time,' she said.

'And she's still having it. All those jobs,' said Imogen. 'She looked dire the other day. Greenish-grey.'

'She likes you,' said Charlotte.

'I like her, too,' said Imogen.

'There's enough chicken casserole for supper,' Charlotte said. 'I wonder what those two will have.'

In Angela's view the chip shop ought to open on a Monday, but Bobby and Val liked to have a proper break.

'We could have had some nice fish and chips tonight,'

Angela was grumbling. Fully recovered, and having had a cheese sandwich for lunch, she was hungry.

'Let's have pizzas,' Jerry said. 'I'll pay.' He'd been at Charlotte's for ten hours and she had paid him sixty pounds, not docking time taken for lunch.

After this it was easy to ask his mother about the car insurance; she capitulated swiftly.

'I was going to walk to the station anyway,' she admitted. 'It'd save the car park fee. So you could go over to Granbury for a couple of hours in the afternoon. Only don't be late for the chip shop. That's a solid job – once the garden's done, the one with Mrs Frost will finish. I'll fix it up tomorrow, Jerry.'

'You won't forget? With work, and that?'

'No,' she promised. 'I'll do it first thing when I get to the office.'

'So I know it'll be OK to take the car in the afternoon?'

Sighing, she agreed.

Their pizzas soon arrived, brought by a youth on a motorbike, a boy Jerry knew. There was some badinage on the doorstep as he paid; then the courier sped off with much revving of his exhaust.

'She's a nice lady, Mrs Frost,' said Angela. 'Widow, is she?'

'Yeah.' Jerry related what he knew about Charlotte's history. 'Immy's sorry for her – said her dad – Immy's dad – more or less turned her out of the house because he wanted to sell it. He turned up yesterday in a bloody great Mercedes.'

'Why's Imogen staying with her gran?'

'Oh – some family trouble,' Jerry said airily.

'What's the father like?'

'I didn't stay to find out,' said Jerry. 'His car was parked outside when we got back from a walk in the afternoon.'

A walk, he said. But Imogen had told Angela that they had gone to look at Captain Smythe's garden, and she had revealed that Captain Smythe had caught a burglar in his house on Thursday night. Angela had not heard about this incident, and Imogen did not name the offender. Well, it wasn't Jerry; he had been safely in bed on Thursday night.

'Seen Pete lately?' Angela asked, and Jerry, cheese stringing from his mouth, shook his head.

She was not sure if that was true; later, in bed, she thought about her son and worried, eventually managing to console herself with the reflection that he had made friends with a nice respectable girl, and she'd now met the girl's grandmother. While Jerry worked in Mrs Frost's garden, and also in the chip shop, he was with people who could only influence him for good. She wondered if he fancied Imogen; that Imogen might fancy him went without saying, for he was a lovely-looking boy with that warm smile, and nice ways when he chose to use them. He was a good son who had fallen into bad company; that Pete, she thought, brushing aside Jerry's earlier misdemeanours committed without Pete's aid. A short film strip ran through her mind as she grew drowsy: Imogen, slimmed down a little and with her hair arranged in a flattering top-knot, wearing gleaming white satin and a shower of tulle, and Jerry in a morning suit, outside Becktham parish church. She was beside them, dressed to kill, and holding the arm of a handsome middle-aged man with greying hair: Imogen's father, owner of the Merc.

Basking in this vivid fantasy, Angela slept.

* * *

Jerry turned up in Granbury the next day, soon after half-past two. There was no one at home, and Mrs Frost's car was not in the garage. That was a disappointment, but Jerry spent his two hours neatening up the turf. The garden tools were kept in the garage and, though closed, it was unlocked – sheer folly, Jerry thought as he wheeled out the hose and connected it up. After he had carved out two new flower beds and forked them over, he gave the new turf a good watering. Then it was time to go. He couldn't leave a note; he had neither pen nor paper. They'd see what he'd done and would understand, and he'd telephone. He was, after all, due another twelve pounds, and Mrs Frost wasn't one to cheat.

Imogen came home just as he was leaving.

Charlotte had wasted no time in planning for her, and she had been out for a driving lesson, returning in the driving school's dual-control car to be dropped at the door by her instructor.

'Can I come back with you, Jerry?' she asked, when she saw he had the car.

'I've got to go to work,' he said. 'I'll be there till nearly ten o'clock. You'd be better here. Mrs F. will be back soon, won't she? Where's she gone?'

'Shopping. We ate everything yesterday,' said Imogen.

'Mum fixed the car insurance for me, so I did a couple of hours,' said Jerry. 'I'll be over tomorrow. Cheers,' and he leaped into the Metro, driving off with a flourish that impressed Imogen but not her instructor, who had been making a few notes before he, too, left the close.

She'd see Jerry the next day. It wasn't long to wait.

Charlotte, when she returned with washing powder and further food supplies, was pleased to find more work done in the garden, and Imogen with pink cheeks, looking happy. The driving lesson had gone quite well, too.

Jerry came over again the next day. He was eager to start planting. All three of them spent time standing on boards he had rescued from a skip and brought with him to lay across the new turf as they discussed what should go where. Charlotte could see that if she let him have his head, costs might become exorbitant.

'Why don't I ring up Captain Smythe and ask him if you can go down there and collect whatever he can spare; then we can buy other things later?' she suggested.

Jerry accepted this proposal, and she telephoned Captain Smythe who said they were welcome to come round straight away. Jerry whisked Imogen off with him in the red Metro; there wasn't much time before he must go back to Becktham but he could make a start.

In the end, he left Imogen at Rose Cottage with Captain Smythe, the two of them digging up various plants, keeping damp soil around their roots and putting them in plastic bags in boxes. They would be all right for several days.

His enthusiasm was infectious. After he left, Imogen and Captain Smythe spent a pleasant, peaceful hour together, jointly digging up and dividing irises and rooted shoots of jasmine and other shrubs, none of it strenuous, and Captain Smythe thought Imogen too fit and strong a girl to be at risk of a miscarriage from a bit of digging. That, if it were to happen, would be a solution to her problem, but not necessarily the right one.

They did not talk much, limiting their conversation to the work in hand.

Charlotte, meanwhile, with Imogen out of the house, and aware that the term was almost over, had telephoned her school to ask if there were any possibility of her work being sent to her. The house-mistress, eventually located, thought there would not be a problem. All her subjects could be worked on at home and references sought in libraries. A study plan might be set up; involved staff would certainly cooperate.

That was a big hurdle passed, Charlotte thought. Relieved, she decided to iron Imogen's washing, and took the pressed garments into her room to put away. She opened a drawer where Imogen had put underclothes and tights, and to her astonishment saw an opened pack of sanitary pads. Two or three were left, and there was an unopened pack beside them.

A pregnant girl would not be using pads.

Imogen had seen the doctor only yesterday.

She closed the drawer and put the freshly-ironed clothing on the bed.

As the afternoon passed, Charlotte realised that Jerry must have gone back to Becktham. Unless she had done another disappearing trick, Imogen might be still at Rose Cottage so Charlotte walked down there. What was she to make of her discovery? Imogen might have the pads in case she miscarried, or perhaps her period had come on late, and she had never been pregnant at all, the victim of a false alarm, but why not say so, if that were the case? Thoroughly confused,

Charlotte arrived at Rose Cottage, walking round the house to the garden. Imogen's trainers were neatly placed by the back door, beside the captain's ancient, shining brogues, and alongside several wooden trays containing plants in plastic bags or pots. She continued down the garden and found the two of them standing on the little jetty surveying the pond. It seemed a pity to disturb them, though they appeared not to be talking; restful silence was a blessing. This part of the garden was well screened on all sides by trees and shrubs, a miniature forest glade. As if he sensed her presence, Howard Smythe turned and saw her; he said something to Imogen and came towards her. Imogen's jeans were tucked into a pair of old black wellingtons; later she told Charlotte that these had been Mrs Smythe's and the old man had kept them thinking they might come in handy. Charlotte wondered if he had retained other relics of his wife; people sometimes did, unable to bear the process of discarding once precious possessions. Felix had taken charge of Rupert's things; she neither knew nor cared if he would use the suits and shirts. She was the item that had been superfluous and she had been cast out promptly.

Left, however, with responsibilities which were not hers: this young woman now approaching, flushed and happy, apparently having banished all thought of her predicament. But was there a predicament at all? And if not, why had Imogen invented one? Whatever the answer, it looked as though the serious talk that must take place between her and the girl required a different script, and should not be undertaken in a hurry.

She called out to them. As Howard walked towards her, he stooped a little. Charlotte had never noticed that before; he had seemed to hold himself so straight and upright, as though on parade, but the experience of the break-in must exact some price; perhaps he was having a delayed reaction.

'We've boxed up lots of plants,' said Imogen.

'If I come down in the morning with the car, we could collect them and save time for Jerry when he arrives to do the planting,' Charlotte suggested.

'I wish I could bring them up for you, but I don't drive now,' said Captain Smythe. 'My sight's not what it was.' He had incipient glaucoma, but he was not going to tell them that.

Charlotte had wondered whether he still drove; loss of the car would have affected his independence. Now she knew, she could offer to give him a lift when she was going shopping. The thought warmed her; it would be good to have his company.

Back at the house, Imogen exchanged the boots for her trainers, and she and Charlotte set off home before it got too dark for them to see their way.

Imogen had devised a plan; it had occurred to her that afternoon, when Jerry had once again given her a soft, friendly, parting kiss before he drove away.

12

If Imogen isn't pregnant, there's no hurry to make plans, Charlotte thought, in bed that night. Even so, she must be tackled. No wonder there was no sign of morning sickness, not that every pregnant woman suffered from it. At least she'd seen the doctor, so if she had miscarried, there were no problems.

Circumstantial evidence doesn't prove a case; the presence of pads in Imogen's drawer was not conclusive. However, Charlotte was reluctant to reveal that she had found them, in case the girl, in a prickly mood, accused her of prying. Perhaps she should defer action until the next batch of ironing needed to be put away. However, she told Imogen that the school was going to send her work on.

'You must be occupied,' said Charlotte. 'You can still help Jerry when he's here. You've worked hard and done well at school; there's no reason why you shouldn't take your exams.' If she wasn't pregnant, perhaps she could return to school next term; there would be no grounds for her exclusion. However, that was looking too far ahead. Slyly, she added, 'If you're going to have a baby to look after, the more qualifications you can get, the better.'

'That's true,' Imogen said, almost meekly. 'I suppose there are crèches at some colleges.'

'I believe so,' Charlotte answered, somewhat unnerved.

I should have tackled her then, she thought later, challenged her, asked her for dates, for facts.

Another driving lesson took up time the next morning. While Imogen was out, Charlotte took the car down to Rose Cottage to collect the plants. Captain Smythe helped her load them into the Fiat. She felt an urge to tell him about her suspicions, but refrained; he was old, and a man, and she didn't know him very well. He might be embarrassed. There wasn't really anyone with whom she could discuss the theory; the doctor would respect patient confidentiality and disclose nothing. Charlotte realised that throughout most of her adult life she had walked away from confrontation; in her first marriage she had accepted her husband's preoccupation with his work and that her role was to manage an efficient household, not to worry him about trifles. He had not lived long enough to be in conflict with his children over their academic and professional choices; she had been involved with their decisions, discussing all their options, aware that their father might have opposed Tim's wish to join the navy and could have tried to direct them both towards careers of his selection. She'd even married Rupert rather than hold out for a part-time relationship which, these days, would have been appropriate for many in their situation and might, she thought now, with hindsight, have been just as happy and had a far less damaging aftermath.

She wouldn't have had this troubled, naughty girl to deal with, for naughty she was, if she had dreamed up a deception just to cause distress. Parents split up all too frequently these days but it wasn't as grim a fate as the death of either one, and it wasn't an abandonment. What had Imogen hoped to achieve? To draw attention to herself?

Was her real concern the question of her own heredity?

In the small hours, Charlotte fell into a troubled sleep and woke next morning feeling unrefreshed.

The break-in at Rose Cottage and the arrest of Pete Dixon was a satisfactory result for the police. Unfortunately they hadn't caught him in possession of stolen goods, to link him up with other burglaries; there were none at his address when it was searched, so no doubt he got rid immediately of what he stole, but with his record he was likely to go down for several months, if not a year or two, which would take him out of circulation for a while. Since his arrest no more similar crimes had been reported in the area where there had been a series, usually involving a distraction by a second youth selling makeshift articles at the door, so, although this incident had followed a different *modus operandi*, taking place during the night, there may have been a connection. Pete, however, had not mentioned an accomplice and no pointers towards one had occurred. With plenty of unsolved crimes to be resolved, and the paperwork for those and others piling up, no one was going to put in time looking for a second perpetrator unless there were strong indications of involvement.

Pete was likely to be remanded for a further week, though he might get bail. The case would be heard in full when the prosecution was prepared.

Jerry hadn't spent much time thinking about his former partner. Pete had been unlucky, getting caught; that was all. Captain Smythe was a tough old guy and very far from helpless, as he had proved; Pete must have expected to be in and out in minutes, undetected. He'd not go down for long, Jerry decided optimistically, planning to ask Mrs Frost how he could find out about this garden training business.

Nicholas came over that morning. He turned up without warning, just as Imogen returned from her driving lesson. Two packages of her folders and books from school had already arrived, and Charlotte had said she could work in the dining-room. Nicholas's arrival was a distraction, but he approved as the big padded bags were undone and the contents stacked on the table.

He was full of new plans. He and Phoebe were setting up an ironing business; it was his idea, and he was buying her a fancy iron and ironing board. They would collect and deliver – that was Nicholas's role, and he would do the billing. Fliers would be run off on his computer.

'What about your exams?' said Charlotte, hearing this.

'I'll have plenty of time to work. Phoebe will be doing all the ironing,' Nicholas answered. 'I've got my job as a waiter, too. I'll be all right for money if it takes off, and it will, I'm sure. People hate ironing.'

Charlotte rather liked it; it was satisfying, and quite soothing, and you could listen to the radio.

'It sounds a good idea,' she said, wondering about Phoebe.

'You'll end up marrying that woman,' said Imogen darkly. 'She's got two kids,' she told Charlotte.

'Well, you'll have one, too, before long,' said Nicholas airily. 'I hope that won't wreck your chances.'

Here was Charlotte's opportunity to launch forth, saying, 'Oh, and by the way, are you really pregnant?' while she had a witness and possible support, but she let it go.

'Come and see the garden,' Imogen said, leading Nicholas out there. 'Jerry's done it.'

He was impressed.

'And all from a meeting in a chip shop,' was his comment.

He stayed to lunch, but he had gone by the time Jerry arrived.

Imogen had to get through the rest of the day and tomorrow before she could put her plan into action. To help time pass, she decided she might as well get on with some school work, and after Jerry left she settled down to revision. It was only two weeks since her abrupt departure from the school; she had not missed a great deal. Tomorrow she would have been in Granbury a week, yet it felt as if she had been there for ever.

Nicholas had determined to have a show-down with Felix and if necessary demand a blood test to determine their paternity. What worried him was that Imogen had blue eyes; his and Felix's, and their mother's, were brown. According to Phoebe's explanation, this supported Imogen's theory. The only other possibility seemed to be that he and she were not related, and that she was some foundling sharing the same birthday and taken in by Felix and Zoe; hardly likely.

Jerry was not due again until Saturday, when during his afternoon break he was to meet Charlotte and Imogen at the garden centre on the edge of Nettington, which was the best locally for shrubs and roses. He had prepared beds for what they would buy then, and for Captain Smythe's contributions, a few of which he had already planted; the rest could wait until Sunday, when he would put in everything.

Imogen's driving lesson went well on Thursday, and she did school work that afternoon. On Friday morning the instructor said she should put in for her test.

'But you won't be here, Imogen. Your grandmother will be home – you'll be with her again, or your father,' Charlotte said. 'You should apply in their area.'

'You want to get rid of me,' said Imogen, and the ugly, sulky look she had worn for the first few days of her visit returned.

'I don't, but this is a temporary arrangement,' Charlotte said, somewhat desperately, though really, if it were a faked pregnancy and she went back to school next term, she might as well spend the holidays, and Easter, in Granbury. 'Let's talk to the instructor on Monday,' she temporised. 'Let's see what he says about how long you'll have to wait.'

They left it. Imogen went upstairs to wash her hair and have a bath. After supper she settled in the dining-room with her revision, but at nine o'clock, saying she was tired, she went up to bed. Charlotte stayed in the sitting-room, with the television on. She did not hear Imogen leave the house.

Imogen had practised shutting the front door without a sound, using her key in the lock. She had rung the taxi on her mobile phone. At half-past nine, it was waiting for her at the corner of Vicarage Fields.

* * *

Jerry had enjoyed his evening at the chip shop. That afternoon, he'd given his mother's car a thorough wash and polish. It took him over an hour, and afterwards, noticing one of the tyres looked a little soft, he drove to the nearest service station to check them. Then he watched television until it was time to go back to the chip shop. Once the weekend was over, he'd have finished Mrs Frost's garden; it hadn't taken all that long to do. Someone less conscientious than he might have spun it out a bit, taken more time, and Imogen had helped, which had reduced the size of the task. She'd worked hard. What a funny girl she was, weird, not like other girls Jerry knew, kind of innocent, really. It was strange to think of her having a kid, but then again, plenty of girls her age or younger did, every day, and looked after them well, very often. Some had come visiting at the prison, bringing their little mites with them. The kids would be all spruced up and smart, the dads quite proud. It was good to have kids while you were young yourself.

He put out a tray for his mother's snack when she came in, with a salmon paste sandwich and a cup ready for her coffee. She'd get a proper supper at the residential home, but she'd need something to get her going after the office. She seemed to be managing to catch the train, though on Wednesday she'd been late and he'd driven her to the station. He always heard her moving about in the morning and sometimes got up to make tea, even when he later went back to bed himself. He wished she could meet some nice guy who'd look after her, make her life easier, but at the same time he'd resent an intruder; they were cosy, him and his mum, with never a cross word, and she'd been brilliant about his trouble. He was glad he'd met Mrs Frost with her smile, and her instruction that he must mend his ways, before he ended up in the nick again.

Fridays were always busy at the chip shop. During the day a brisk wind had sprung up, and the night was chilly. A group of lads, some of them known to Jerry, came in at nine on their way from one pub to another; they were rowdy and slightly drunk, but not too far gone. Val hoped the chips they bought would sober them up. Bobby hoped none of them was driving, and Jerry told him that all the lads were local, from Becktham; they'd have come on foot. Clearing up took some time; Jerry hurried home, eager to return to the warmth of the house.

His mother had cleared up her tray, which was quite a surprise. Jerry went into the sitting-room and put on the television, leaning back to enjoy the can of beer he'd bought on his way home.

Upstairs, in his bed, Imogen waited, shivering.

The taxi had dropped her on the corner of his road. On the way over, the driver, a middle-aged man with grey hair curling on to his collar, commented on the spell of fine weather they'd been having, and then the amount of traffic on the road – not a lot, for a Friday – to which Imogen replied in monosyllables; discouraged, he became silent, but he, a father of two teenaged daughters and a younger son, watched her in the mirror and saw that she was sitting perched forward as far as the seat-belt would allow, not at all relaxed. She didn't seem drunk, as girls needing cabs at night sometimes were, though rarely as early as this, nor was she visibly distressed; there were no tears. She leaped from his cab the moment it stopped, impatiently asking how much it was and thrusting a twenty-pound note into his hand, not waiting for her change. In her fleece jacket, her dark trousers and trainers, she ran up the road.

She had brought a small torch which she'd found in Charlotte's kitchen where it stood on a shelf beside a larger one. Using it sparingly, anxious again about curious neighbours, she went round to the back of the Hunts' house and found the owl. The key was there; her main fear had been that it would not have been replaced. She let herself in. A light was on in the hall. Going through to the kitchen, Imogen went into the garden through the back door, which she left ajar while she replaced the key, for suppose Jerry needed it when he got home? Then, seeing the tray used for Angela's snack, she quickly washed up the few things it had held. There was no time to waste; making sure the house was secure, carrying her trainers lest she leave marks on the carpet, she went swiftly upstairs. She knew which was Angela's room; there were two other bedrooms and Jerry's was easily identified. In the dark, Imogen drew the curtains; if he noticed, he might think his mother had drawn them before she went out. After that, unable to postpone the moment any longer, she undressed quickly, folded up her clothes and laid them neatly on top of her shoes in a corner where they would not be visible when he entered and turned on the light.

Taking a deep breath, Imogen got into Jerry's cold bed and pulled the duvet up round her neck. She lay there, gasping, while her heartbeat steadied; slowly she became aware of various smells, partly soap – Jerry always seemed very clean, except after hard work in the garden and then he smelled rather nice, if sweaty – and other strange, not unpleasant smells. She tried to breathe evenly. There was nothing to be afraid of, for Jerry wasn't like other boys she had encountered; he was friendly and kind. He wouldn't hurt her, or only as much as couldn't be helped. Imogen, though lacking experience, was not totally ignorant.

By the time she heard him come in, her uncontrollable nervous shuddering had settled into plain shivers. She thought he would come upstairs at once, but he didn't; she was aware of him moving around downstairs and she heard the television come on. It didn't matter, now, how long it was before he came up to bed, for Angela would be out all night at her job in the home. Imogen had thought no further ahead than this.

At last the television went off. Its faint sound had almost sent her into a doze, but now she began to shiver again as Jerry came upstairs. He didn't come into the room straight away, going into the bathroom first, where she heard him loudly urinating. He hadn't closed the door, and she heard the shower start. Jerry had shed his clothes on the bathroom floor, as he did every night, and stepped straight under it. He wouldn't smell fishy, Imogen thought, pleased; that might have been a bit of a turn-off. When he did come in, whistling, naked, she was right under the duvet, her face covered, and he did not see her when he switched on the bedside light. He only discovered her presence when he slid under the covers himself.

'Shit!' he cried, and he leaped from the bed, dragging most of the duvet off her to hold in front of himself.

This was not what Imogen had envisaged, though her planning had been unable to carry her far beyond the moment when he got into bed beside her. Warmth, and a cuddle, gentle kisses, and then something which he would know how to do and which she might not enjoy but which would, with luck, make her pregnant. She might be able to persuade him to do it again when the chance came along, to make sure. Blokes always wanted it; she knew that. You didn't have to be in love. Imogen, after telling the doctor she was worried about being overweight, which was true, had decided that the best way out of her false predicament was to make it genuine.

She crouched under what she could of the duvet, gazing up at him, terrified, he began to realise, as his own first shock abated.

'Shit – what are you doing here?' he asked her.

'I thought you might like it,' she said. She was trembling uncontrollably.

'You're pregnant by some crap bloke, and you're missing it, and you thought I'd do? Is that it?' he demanded. In spite of his anger, or because of it, he felt a physical response which made him clutch the duvet more firmly against his wayward member.

'No – no, Jerry! I thought you liked me,' Imogen said, and she began to cry.

'Oh – shit. Tears,' Jerry muttered. 'I never came on to you,' he said. Would it be so wrong, though? Here she was, readily available, and he could always do with some sex, not that he fancied her. 'What if I'd brought someone back with me and we'd found you here?' he said, for he sometimes did bring a girl back on a Friday, knowing the coast was clear. There was Tracy, whom he knew from school, and Shirley, who frequented The Swan, where he sometimes went after work.

'Well, you haven't,' she pointed out.

His anger had frightened her, but now she relaxed a little.

'You're as cold as ice. How long have you been here?' he said.

'Not very long. I came in a taxi. I knew where the key was.'

'And you want sex?'

'Yes,' she mumbled.

'Well, then,' said Jerry. 'Why not?' and he slid in beside her, pulling the duvet over them both. A quick fuck and then he'd take her home.

He didn't kiss her. He tried to force her tightly clenched legs apart with his knee and at first met resistance, though she did not struggle nor try to push him away. Taking a deep breath, she separated her thighs, and in the light from the lamp Jerry saw that she was still crying, while her face was set in the same determined expression she wore when she was carting turf or rolling it out, though she didn't weep then.

'For Christ's sake, Imogen, do you want it or don't you?' he demanded, rolling off her, and then, suddenly, he understood. 'You haven't done it, have you? Not ever? You're a bloody virgin, aren't you, and you aren't pregnant at all.'

Downstairs, the telephone rang. Both of them ignored it.

13

They ended up cuddled together under the duvet.

Jerry, for safety, pulled on some boxer shorts and a tee-shirt, and he looked away while Imogen put on a blue shirt which he pulled from a drawer and threw to her.

'Now,' he said. 'What's this all about?'

So she told him that it had got out of hand. She was upset because her parents had split up, and she thought if she stirred things, they would unite in the crisis and be reconciled. Also, she hated her school where, she said, no one liked her and the boys either ignored her, or wanted to snog not her, particularly, just any willing girl. Jerry thought she had probably got things wrong about that.

'You were unhappy so you decided to make everyone else unhappy too,' he said sagely. 'But why add me to the list?'

'I didn't want to make you unhappy,' she said.

'Well, if I'd got you pregnant, you would have. Hadn't you thought of that?'

'But no one would have known it was yours. They'd have thought it was the other bloke.'

'What other bloke? The one who doesn't exist?'

'Yes.'

'But it would have been my kid,' said Jerry, who never had unprotected sex but who might have with Imogen, thinking her pregnant already. Whew! 'Don't they teach you nothing at your school?' he said, despairingly.

'I wouldn't have asked anything from you. You wouldn't have known,' she said.

'But if it's my kid, don't I have a right to know? To be a dad to it?' Jerry asked.

'Maybe. But I don't know about my dad,' she said, and, amid more tears, she revealed her doubts about her own paternity.

Jerry was out of his depth.

'You need to talk to Nicholas,' he said. 'He must sort you out.' He kissed her gently, as he had before; then, feeling her soft body, warm now, close against him, almost moved further; after all, he had condoms nearby and she had to start some day, so why not with him? But he thought of Mrs Frost. She would not approve; she would say he had taken advantage of Imogen, and it would have been true. Besides, once started, she might get keen and become clingy and demanding. It happened with girls.

'We must get you home before Mrs F. finds out you've gone,' he said. In the morning, he'd get hold of Nicholas. Imogen could tell him the telephone number and address. It wouldn't be right to discuss what had happened with Mrs Frost, but someone ought to know how mixed up Imogen was.

Charlotte had discovered that Imogen had left the house.

She was late going up to bed herself. When she woke after

falling asleep in front of the television, she had shaken up the cushions and turned off the sitting-room light. In the hall, she paused. The cloakroom door was ajar, and she always kept it closed. Imogen could not have been in there after their meal; she had gone up to bed so early. Besides, she had never left it open during the week she had been in the house. Something made Charlotte not simply close it, but put on the light and look inside. Even then, she did not at first realise what else was wrong; then she saw that Imogen's fleece jacket was not on its peg.

That meant nothing; though normally it hung here, she could have taken it up to her room.

Charlotte went quickly upstairs and softly, so as not to disturb her, opened the door of Imogen's room. There was a shape in the bed, but it was the old trick. A pillow had been placed lengthwise to make it look as if the bed was occupied.

Charlotte sat down abruptly, her heart thumping. Where had she gone? All sorts of ideas ran through her mind. She couldn't be meeting her lover because he didn't exist; she wasn't pregnant – at least, it seemed unlikely. Had she left a note? Recovering herself enough to switch on the light, Charlotte looked round the room but saw no sign of a note. Everything was orderly; the girl was so neat. Her holdall was there; she had not packed her things.

Perhaps she had been unable to sleep and had gone for a walk. Maybe she had looked in on Charlotte to say she was going out, and, seeing her dozing, had decided not to disturb her. Briefly satisfied with this explanation, Charlotte looked about downstairs in case a note had been left there, or even in Charlotte's room, but there was nothing.

The cloakroom door might have been left open so that any possible noise it could make being closed was avoided.

The best course was to remain calm and hope she would soon reappear. Charlotte made some coffee and drank it, watching the clock. Imogen might have gone to a club, or even a pub. Perhaps she hadn't mentioned it lest Charlotte forbid her to go. Young people were often unpredictable. Wherever she had gone, it was nearly midnight and surely she would come home before long?

But she didn't.

Could she have planned to meet Jerry? They got on so well, and it seemed that there was no other boy in the background. She might have arranged to meet him after the chip shop closed, though if that were the case, why not say so? Because she, Charlotte, might disapprove?

At what point should she ring the police? Wouldn't they simply say it was too early to worry and to ring again if Imogen didn't turn up the next day? And she couldn't ring Felix so soon to say she was missing.

It was much too late to disturb Captain Smythe and ask his advice.

If she went to bed herself, Imogen would probably be safely back in her room in the morning.

Imogen was. It was Charlotte who was missing the following day.

Charlotte had undressed and made ready for bed. Then, propped up on pillows, she had tried to read, listening for Imogen's return, but she was unable to settle and sleep was impossible. Finally she gave up, deciding to look for Imogen around the village. Perhaps she *had* been sleepless – there must be a lot on her conscience – and had gone for a walk. As she'd arranged the pillow in her bed to resemble a sleeping form, she must have thought that Charlotte might look in, but there was no way of knowing when she had gone out. Before Charlotte left the house, she dialled the Hunts' number; they were Imogen's only friends, apart from herself and Captain Smythe. She just might be with them.

There was no reply. Mrs Hunt had several evening jobs; she must be at one of them and Jerry was probably out on the town, after his stint at the shop. It was possible that Imogen was with him, in some club or other. He might have picked her up, having arranged it with her earlier. Charlotte did not know if Mrs Hunt would need the car to get to whatever work she would be doing tonight.

Hoping that this was the answer, Charlotte, nevertheless, put on trousers and a thick sweater, her padded jacket, and strong shoes, then set off for the village areas where she had been with Imogen. If she had gone for a walk, she might have had an accident – fallen and hurt herself, even been hit by a car. If she did not find her, Charlotte would ring the hospitals, then the police, and try to contact Imogen's father.

Granbury seemed to have settled down for the night. No cars passed while Charlotte was on the main road, and the parking area outside the few shops was deserted. She hesitated, wondering whether to go straight on towards Nettleton; then she decided to go down Meadow Lane, a more likely route if Imogen were simply out for a walk. She had taken her big torch, not noticing that the smaller one was missing, and she used it as she walked down the narrow lane where there were no street lights. All the houses were dark. Imogen wouldn't have gone to Captain Smythe's for a sympathetic chat, but she might have gone into the church. Charlotte tried its door, which was locked now.

If Imogen had done the same, maybe guiltily wanting to sort out the confused tangle she must have in her head, and aware that it was open during the day, what would she have done next, finding it closed? Walked round the church to the east end? Tried other doors, if there were any? Charlotte followed this course. There was a side door, but it was locked. She shone her torch over the graves, some marked with flowers, and went carefully round them till she came to the wall at the end of the churchyard, where there was a stone stile. Charlotte climbed it, and followed the path on the further side as it crossed a field. This way led down to the river; she had been along it several times before and though she had not brought Imogen here, the girl, pursuing the route which Charlotte had embarked upon, might have found it herself.

The night was very cold. Charlotte pulled a scarf from her coat pocket and tied it over her head, hesitating, wondering whether to turn back. She had not expected to be out long and had left no note explaining where she was; Imogen, however, if she returned first, would not realise she had gone out so she would not be alarmed, but if she had come this way and got lost, or worse, Charlotte might find her. She crossed another stile, shining the torch ahead. There were rustles in the field, and a sleepy heifer loomed towards her. Several of her sisters came sidling up, their eyes gleaming in the darkness. Charlotte kept on. They were mild, bemused creatures and would not hurt her. At last she reached a stile in the post and rail fence which ran through the hedge at the end of this field, beyond which lay the river. She would walk along the bank to the bridge, and work her way back to the village from there. She was tired now, and discouraged. If Imogen had suffered some misfortune while walking through the night, she could have used that mobile phone of hers to summon help, providing she had it with her, but Charlotte's fear was not of a simple accident; Imogen was emotionally upset and she might have decided on drastic action.

The path here ran close to the river's edge, curving sharply at a bend. Charlotte shone the torch ahead, briefly looking up, calling Imogen's name. She heard a faint sound which could have been one of the heifers lowing softly, or might have been something else, and turned, failing to watch where she was stepping. She put a foot in a hole, stumbling and toppling sideways, dropping the torch which rolled away from her as she slipped again, this time on some mud. All sense of direction lost in the sudden darkness, and her balance gone, Charlotte fell backwards into the river.

14

Jerry had rung for a taxi while Imogen was dressing. She kept his blue shirt on, pulling her sweater over it.

When she went downstairs, he was wearing clothes he had taken from a pile in the kitchen waiting to be ironed.

'You'll hate me now,' she said. 'You won't want to come and do the garden.'

'I'll finish it,' he said. For his own satisfaction, and for the money he would earn, he would complete it; besides, Mrs Frost would be a good referee for him when the work was done. 'I can't let Mrs F. down,' he went on. 'And I don't hate you.' He was sorry for Imogen; he was even flattered that she had cast him in the role of prospective father of her child. 'Here's the taxi.'

He went with her. He was afraid, if he didn't see her into Mrs Frost's house, that she might take off again and get herself into more trouble, which might involve him. They sat in the back of the cab, Imogen curled up, arms crossed over her body, giving occasional shuddering sighs. The pair were otherwise silent, and the driver formed quite the wrong impression of what was going on.

In Granbury, Jerry asked the driver to wait at the end of the close while he walked with Imogen along the road. She stopped him some way from the door.

'Don't come any further,' she said, and she thrust at him the rest of the money she had with her. It was quite a lot.

'For the taxi,' she said. 'Sorry.'

Jerry's hand closed over the notes. Maybe he needn't finish the garden after all; he didn't like leaving a job half done, but putting plants in was easy enough. Mrs F. and Imogen could finish that. As he hurried back to the cab, he heaved a huge sigh of relief. She really was a nutter and he was better out of it.

Imogen saw no significance in the hall light still being on when she entered the house. She put the torch back on the shelf, then crept upstairs and into her room. She was cold again. Shock and shame swept over her as she pulled off her clothes. Jerry's shirt came off with her sweater and she bundled both into a drawer, then put on the long tee-shirt in which she slept and got into bed, where she lay shivering, reliving what had happened.

Jerry had been very kind. She knew it, and lying against him, tucked up together, warm beneath the duvet, had been, for a few brief minutes, wonderful, but how could she ever look him in the face again?

It was a very long time before, at last, she dropped into a troubled, restless sleep, finally submerging into a series of frightening dreams which she could not remember when, at twenty past nine, she woke up.

The house was quiet. On all the previous mornings,

Charlotte, though not noisy, could be heard moving about but today there was nothing. Maybe she'd gone shopping. Imogen decided to have a bath; she was still cold, and she felt dirty, soiled by her own lies, as she told herself when lying in the water. Today she must confess the truth to Charlotte, and wait for her punishment.

She couldn't be sent back to school, or not yet, as the term was over, and she wouldn't look as far ahead as next term.

She drowsed a little in the bath, then freshened it with hot water before washing her hair, sinking down with the long strands floating around her. It was half-past ten when she finally got out of the water, dried herself, wrapped a towel round her head and got dressed, putting on some of the clean clothes which kind Charlotte had ironed. Then she went downstairs.

The blind was still drawn in the kitchen, which was strange. Imogen pulled it up; she felt thirsty, though not particularly hungry, and she put the kettle on and found a mug and the jar of instant coffee. There was milk in the refrigerator. The house around her was still silent and while the kettle boiled, Imogen went into the other downstairs rooms, where the curtains were still drawn. Charlotte must be sleeping in, and why not? Imogen's mother often did; just because Charlotte hadn't done so on any of the other mornings during Imogen's stay didn't mean she couldn't now. Imogen pulled the curtains back, and because Charlotte would often have the kitchen radio on, usually tuned to Classic FM, she turned it on now, keeping the volume low so as not to disturb Charlotte. That was more normal.

The coffee cleared her head, and she made herself some

toast, then drank another cup, her mind a blank. She could avoid Jerry by not going to the garden centre this afternoon, though Charlotte would think it strange. Perhaps Nicholas would come over. If she told him the truth, he might tell Charlotte for her.

At that thought, she cheered up, and went out into the garden.

It was raw and cold; the fine weather of the previous few days had gone but it wasn't wet. Looking up at Charlotte's window, she saw the curtains were still drawn and felt guilty. Because of her, Charlotte's routine had been disturbed and now she was tired out, but this unusual behaviour meant that Imogen could postpone revealing her deception. Virtuously, she went into the dining-room and pulled out her books to attempt some work; however, she began to wonder if Charlotte might be ill when, by half-past twelve, she had still not appeared. Imogen hadn't heard her going to the bathroom, but she could have done that while Imogen herself was having breakfast. She had better go and see if she should take Charlotte some lunch.

There was no reply to Imogen's gentle knock on Charlotte's door. She opened it carefully and looked in. The room was in darkness. Imogen called Charlotte's name softly; then, when there was no reply, she felt a surge of panic. Charlotte had died — she had had a heart attack during the night and had been lying upstairs dead all this time. Almost sick with fright, Imogen turned on the light, prepared to discover a lifeless body, but the room was empty.

She took some deep breaths, walking forward, staring. The bed had been slept in; the duvet was thrown back, the pillows dented, but there was no Charlotte. Slowly, Imogen took in the fact that Charlotte's nightdress lay on the bed. She must have dressed and gone out somewhere.

Imogen raced downstairs to see if the car had gone, but it was in the garage.

Where could she be? Perhaps something had happened to her son – an accident at sea – some emergency – but wouldn't she have left a note? She'd left one when she went shopping. Panicking now, Imogen ran all round the house looking for a message. There was none in the kitchen or any of the downstairs rooms, nor was there in Charlotte's bedroom.

Charlotte must have been taken ill and been whisked off to hospital in an ambulance, and she was so bad that she hadn't been able to get up to call Imogen to help her, or to leave a message. Or had she called, and when there was no answer because the house was empty, decided that Imogen was so deeply asleep that she hadn't heard? Even then, she'd have had to be very bad not to have asked the ambulance people to wake her.

Imogen went all round the house looking for anywhere that Charlotte could possibly be, but there was nothing to explain her absence. What was she to do? Should she call the police? If she did, would she have to tell them that she had left the house herself?

In the end, Imogen rang her brother.

Nicholas's advice was to telephone Captain Smythe. Perhaps he had been taken ill, telephoned Charlotte and she had gone down there.

'She'd have taken the car,' said Imogen. 'And she'd have left a note.'

'Well, try him, and if he hasn't got a better idea, ring the police,' said Nicholas. 'Or the hospitals. Or both. Anyway, didn't you hear her go out?'

'No,' said Imogen.

'I'm surprised she didn't wake you and tell you where she was going, or at least leave a note,' said Nicholas, feeling cross with Charlotte for such thoughtlessness. 'Look, I'm busy now. I've got to pick up some washing – we've got going already with our ironing service – ring me back in a bit.'

Imogen knew that Charlotte might not wake a girl she thought was pregnant.

'Leave your phone on,' she pleaded, but he had rung off.

A chance to tell him what had really happened had gone, but he had told her what to do. Imogen looked up Captain Smythe's telephone number and dialled it.

He took a long time to answer the telephone, and then he had trouble understanding what Imogen was saying, for she burst into tears, becoming almost hysterical.

'I'll come over at once,' he said. 'Try to calm down, Imogen.'

He had heard the telephone as he came in from the garden, hurrying when it went on ringing. He had been walking around looking for signs of spring and finding plenty of shoots appearing. Each year he expected never to see another, yet round the months went again, and soon it would be April. Methodically, he locked the house and set off towards the village. He still walked briskly, but it was uphill until he reached the High Street and he was always a little short of breath when he reached the top. At best, it would take him ten minutes to reach Charlotte's house.

He refused to speculate about what had happened until he

got there and could persuade Imogen to give a rational account of what seemed to be Charlotte's disappearance during the night. She might have returned by the time he arrived.

Imogen was watching for him, and opened the door as he came up the path. Her face was white and she looked terrified.

'Oh, thank you for coming, Captain Smythe,' she said, in a gabble.

'Let's sit down, Imogen, and you tell me calmly what has happened,' he said, ushering her in front of him into the house.

Imogen explained that she hadn't come downstairs herself until after half-past ten, and it was only then that she realised Charlotte must have slept in because the curtains were still drawn. Much later, when Charlotte still hadn't appeared, she had gone to her room to discover it was empty.

'There was no note? And you heard nothing during the night?'

'No.'

'You're sure about the note? You've looked in every possible place?'

'Yes.'

He had to take her word for it. She wasn't a child.

'The car's here,' she said.

'I see.' Howard pondered for what seemed to Imogen an age but was only seconds. During their brief acquaintance, Charlotte had seemed calm and controlled, but who knew what she was really feeling, recently bereaved, and with this troubled and possibly troublesome girl now thrust upon her, not to mention the tearaway youth, Jerry, at large in her garden? 'What is missing?' he asked. 'Has she taken a coat? Boots? What was she wearing?'

'She was dressed,' said Imogen. 'Her nightdress was on the bed, just tossed down, not folded or anything.'

Howard understood her. Charlotte was tidy, a nightdress folder rather than a bundler.

'Let's see what coat she had on. There was that nice red one, and she had a green padded one,' said Howard. 'Let's see if either of those is missing.'

They established that the padded jacket was not in the downstairs cloakroom, where it was normally kept, and, just to make sure, Imogen went upstairs to look in Charlotte's cupboard in case she had hung it there for a change, but no. Her strong shoes were missing, as far as Imogen could tell.

'Perhaps she couldn't sleep and went out for a walk, and had some sort of accident,' said Howard. 'That's the most likely explanation.' People did that sort of thing, occasionally. 'You didn't hear her?'

'No.' It had been nearly two o'clock by the time Imogen returned herself. She did not mention that. 'Perhaps we should go and look for her?' she suggested.

'We don't know where to start,' said Howard. 'First I'll ring the hospitals, and then, if we don't find her, we'll call the police.'

It was what Nicholas had suggested.

'Make some tea, Imogen, while I telephone,' said Howard, who had had no lunch and nor, presumably, had the girl. It would give her something to do.

The two local hospitals took a little while to check their records, but neither had admitted a possible accident victim called Charlotte Frost in the past twenty-four hours, and neither had an unidentified woman in any ward.

Captain Smythe had some difficulty in explaining to the police that this was a genuine case of a disappearance, not someone who had gone off on a whim.

Or was it? Had she flipped and vanished? She had not taken her handbag, nor her spectacles. Both were in her bedroom, into which, feeling himself a gross intruder, Howard had gone in Imogen's wake. It was only when he asked to speak to the detective constable who had come out to Rose Cottage after the break-in that he persuaded them to take his concern seriously, and he was told an officer would call round.

He had a real sense of foreboding. Charlotte was not in hospital, but if she had gone walking during the night, she might have been hit by a car and fallen into a ditch.

'Do you think someone's kidnapped her?' Imogen said, as she assembled bread and cheese.

'No,' said Howard. 'I think she went for a walk and had some mishap.' He feared she lay out of sight, hurt and unconscious; last night had been cold and she could be suffering from exposure.

'She took a torch,' Imogen said suddenly, looking up at the shelf from which she had taken the small one. She had been in such a state when she put it back that she hadn't noticed the larger one was missing. 'There were two kept there – a big one and a smaller one.'

She seemed very sure.

When WPC Cornish arrived twenty minutes later and heard what they had to tell her, the fact that Charlotte had taken no money or spare clothing, nor the car, convinced her that Mrs Frost had either met with an accident or, though she did not say it, gone out with the intent to commit suicide.

Both Howard and Imogen picked up the implication.

'She wouldn't,' said Imogen, bursting into tears, for she, with her presence, rude and ungrateful, and a liar, would have been the direct cause, the last straw.

'There was no note,' said Howard.

'She might have posted one,' said the officer.

Jerry had not gone straight home. He got the taxi to drop him off near Becktham station and from there he went to the bungalow where Tracy lived. He tapped on her window, and she let him in as she had done many times before. He'd slip out the same way in the morning, no one the wiser.

His mother was already back when finally he returned; she had sensed that the house was empty and it wasn't the first time. She would ask no questions, simply hoping he was with a girl. He was a grown man. Perhaps he was with Imogen, though if so, Mrs Frost might be none too pleased. Tired after her night shift, she went to bed and did not wake when he came back to shower and change for work. By now he had put Imogen out of his mind, but as the chip shop closed for the afternoon, he remembered that he was due at the garden centre. Mrs F. could do with his advice, even if he didn't do the planting, and it was all money. The best thing was to go on as if nothing had happened. After all, it was the truth. Imogen might well be embarrassed at seeing him, but he'd be easy with her so that she'd think no more about it. On reflection, and as he didn't know Nicholas's mobile phone number, he'd leave the business about the baby. It was nothing to do with him, after all.

His mother, wearing a pink quilted dressing-gown, had been in the kitchen eating a cheese sandwich when he went home, and she was expecting him to take the car. She was going back to bed, she said.

'I've promised to see this job through for Mrs Frost,' he told her. 'We're picking up some plants this afternoon and I'll put the lot in tomorrow. An old guy she knows has given her some other stuff.'

'That's all right,' said Angela. 'Just don't be late for the shop.'

'I won't be,' Jerry promised.

But when he reached the garden centre on the outskirts of Nettington there was no sign of Mrs Frost's Fiat. Jerry, who had arrived on the dot of when they had arranged to meet, locked his mother's car and wandered off to look for climbing roses. Even if Mrs F. didn't recognise the car among the others parked outside, she'd realise that he was there ahead of her. Or them. He supposed that Imogen would come with Mrs Frost. He selected several pot-grown specimens, loading them into a trolley; Mrs Frost would accept his advice on what to grow, he felt sure. When she still had not arrived after he had been there twenty minutes, he was annoyed. She knew his time was limited; he had been punctual, so why wasn't she?

She hadn't expected him to come and pick her up, had she? Jerry was sure they'd arranged to meet at the garden centre. All the same, maybe he'd better go back by way of Granbury in case there had been a misunderstanding, though soon he'd run out of time. He abandoned his laden trolley near a pile of paving stones; someone else could put the plants away. Then he went back to the car and drove to Granbury.

Turning into Vicarage Fields, he saw a police car outside Number Five.

Jerry drove straight past. Now what had that mad girl gone and done?

15

There was no need for anyone to know that she had been out so late, nor was there any need to lie, for no one suspected her absence. Imogen said that she had not heard Charlotte leave the house, which was true. She related how she had gone to bed early leaving Charlotte watching television – also true. She truthfully described her surprise when Charlotte was not up at her usual time, and the gradual growth of her unease.

'We were going to the garden centre today, to buy some plants,' she said. 'Charlotte has been getting the garden sorted.' She did not mention Jerry. The less said about him the better, for he was the only person who could give her away, though if he did, people might wonder about him, since he had a record, and there was the question of his mother's car being parked overnight in Granbury when Captain Smythe was burgled. For both their sakes, the less said the better, but if Captain Smythe told the police that Jerry was due to meet them, no one could imagine that the arrangement was connected in any way with Charlotte's disappearance.

'I can't understand why she went out, apparently in the

middle of the night, without leaving any sort of message,' Captain Smythe declared.

But Imogen could. It took her rather a long time to work it out. If Charlotte had not committed suicide – it was unthinkable that she might have done – she could have looked into Imogen's room and, finding her gone, set out to search for her.

But why had she not returned? Wouldn't she give up eventually and come home, if only to report Imogen's absence?

That afternoon, Charlotte was found by a man and his two small sons who had started to play pooh-sticks on the bridge over the river and had seen her body caught in reeds near the bank.

The nightmare began then. Imogen stuck to her story; if she confessed to leaving the house, she would have to say where she had gone.

Howard Smythe had explained his presence in the house as a friend and fellow resident in Granbury.

'Mrs Frost has a son and daughter,' he told Sergeant Beddoes, who had come to break the news that the body of a woman answering Charlotte's description had been found but had not yet been positively identified. To spare Imogen, he volunteered.

'Perhaps it isn't her,' said Imogen wildly. Charlotte couldn't be dead. It wasn't possible.

'The sooner we find out for sure, the better,' Howard stated. The chance of its being someone else was too remote to be seriously entertained, and this was one fact that could swiftly be established.

Beddoes agreed. The body had not yet been moved from the river bank, where life had been pronounced extinct by the police surgeon; a forensic pathologist was at the scene, for foul play could not be ruled out until after a full examination of the site, as well as of the body. It was a short walk from the nearest road, across the bridge and along the path. Captain Smythe could go there; it would be quicker than waiting for the body to be taken to the mortuary.

He went off in a police car, promising Imogen that he would return as soon as possible, but suggesting that meanwhile she telephone her father.

WPC Cornish, left at the house with Imogen, urged her to take this advice, and Imogen, still snuffling weepily, dialled Felix's number, but the answerphone was the only response. She hung up.

'Why didn't you leave a message?' Rachel Cornish asked.

'He doesn't care. He'll be no help,' sniffed Imogen. 'He sent me here to Charlotte to get me out of the way.'

'Why so?' asked Rachel Cornish.

But Imogen decided not to tell her the whole truth.

'He's split up with my mum. There were problems,' she said.

Rachel Cornish had established that the missing woman was not Imogen's real grandmother.

'Where do Mrs Frost's son and daughter live?' she asked.

'Her son's in the navy and her daughter is in America.'

If the body was that of Charlotte Frost, they would be her next of kin and must be informed.

'Do you know their addresses?' Rachel asked.

But Imogen didn't even know what Charlotte's surname had been before she married Rupert. Dry-eyed now, she lapsed into a silence which the police officer, who was prepared to make some allowance for shock, nevertheless deemed sulky. She tried a few calming overtures, commenting on the garden, saying it was neat, realising that the lawn had been freshly laid and sparsely planted beds awaited filling. She had seen the boxes of plants from Rose Cottage waiting on the path beside the garage.

'Your grandmother must be a keen gardener,' said Rachel, not using the past tense because, technically, it did not yet apply.

A shrug was Imogen's response. Then she said, 'She's not my real grandmother.'

'You were staying with her. That means she was – is – fond of you,' Rachel said, falsely, for it did not follow.

'She had to have me,' Imogen said. 'They made her – Dad and my aunt.'

Rachel decided not to pursue this contentious line. If the girl was always as ungracious as this, Mrs Frost must have found her a difficult guest.

'How about some tea?' she asked briskly.

'I'm not bothered,' said Imogen, adding, in a surly tone, 'You have some if you want.'

Anything to escape for a few minutes from this tiresome girl, thought Rachel, going into the kitchen, which was tidy, with no unwashed dishes on the drainer. From Imogen's sullen behaviour, she would have expected lack of domestic ability, but all was as orderly as if the grandmother had just popped out of the room. She put the kettle on to boil and found the teapot, setting out some mugs. When the old man came back, he might appreciate a cup. He wouldn't be away much more than an hour, if that; there'd be the walk along the bank to the scene, but it wasn't far, and he seemed fit enough. Once there, identification would be a matter of seconds rather than minutes, unless the dead woman's face had been disfigured. She could not have been in the water long enough for it to have had much effect. Old Captain Smythe had doubtless seen many drowned bodies during his wartime service; he would not disintegrate at the sight of one more. Returning to the sitting-room, she picked up the colour supplement from the previous weekend's *Sunday Times* and began reading it.

To Imogen, the wait seemed endless, but while it lasted she could tell herself that Charlotte would walk in at any minute; the woman in the river must be someone else. Sitting here in silence with that cow of a policewoman callously reading a magazine was almost unendurable. She put on the television. On Saturday afternoon there was always sport to watch; several choices, usually.

'Completely heartless,' reported Rachel Cornish later.

Howard looked rather grey when he returned. He was glad of the officer's tea, and could have done with a dash of brandy in it.

'I'm afraid there's no doubt,' he said to Imogen. 'Charlotte is dead, my dear.'

Imogen did not react at all. There were no tears and no hysterics, but she, also, drank a cup of Rachel's tea.

She was calm enough to give her father's name and address, but it was Charlotte's relatives who must be found before news of her fate leaked out.

Howard Smythe, who carried a card with his daughter's address on it in his wallet, suggested that she probably had something in her handbag which might reveal her next of kin, and sure enough, there was an engagement diary in her bag.

— 201 —

It gave her son Tim's address in Dorset, and her daughter's in New York. Now the police machinery could grind into action, routine dictating how they would be told about their mother.

'Her son's at sea,' Howard said.

During his naval career, it had sometimes been his lot to give men and women serving under his command bad news, and it was never easy. Tim Paterson would be given compassionate leave to return home as soon as it could be arranged. He told Imogen this, but it drew no response. The girl was in a state of shock, and the sooner her own family came to care for her, the better.

'Why don't you ring your brother up and see if he'll come over?' suggested Howard.

'You've got a brother?' Rachel Cornish pounced.

'Yes, she has. A twin,' said Howard. 'Nicholas Frost. He lives in Oxford.'

'Her father isn't answering his phone,' said Rachel. 'But now that his stepmother has been identified, he will be informed.'

'She's close to her brother,' said Howard. 'He's got a car, and it isn't far. I'm sure he'll come over if he can.'

Imogen thought it would be wonderful if Nicholas were to turn up.

'I wish you wouldn't talk about me as if I wasn't here,' was, however, what she said.

Eventually Howard persuaded her to give the police officer her brother's mobile telephone number, but there was no answer. However, a message asking him to call his sister as soon as possible was accepted.

He would have to be located.

'Tell us his address,' said Sergeant Beddoes.

Imogen gave him Nicholas's address, but she did not know Phoebe's, nor her telephone number, and that afternoon Nicholas was at her flat, dealing with enquiries for their ironing service. The telephone was in his car and it was some time before he received the news.

As routine, the police called at Charlotte's neighbours asking if they had heard anything unusual during the night. When had they last seen Mrs Frost?

Charlotte would have been surprised to know how many of her neighbours had noticed her; the couple on one side with the children, and the pair who went off to work so early, knew her well by sight, and had observed the work being done in the garden. Jerry had been seen laying turf; a woman opposite had even witnessed its arrival and could name the supplier. Mrs Frost seemed quite reserved, everyone said; she had not been there long and there had been no social contact. Imogen's presence had been noted; she had helped the young man who was doing the garden work and one neighbour had seen them kiss.

The woman opposite, whom Charlotte could not have described if she had been asked, and who was married to an air steward who was on a flight to Australia, had seen Imogen enter the house early on Saturday morning. It must have been getting on for two, she said; she had been unable to sleep and had come downstairs to make some tea. Looking out of her window, she had noticed the hall light on in Mrs Frost's house much later than was usual, and then she had seen the girl – she thought it was the girl, not Mrs Frost –

open the front door and slip inside. She could not swear to which upstairs lights were on, if any; the curtains were lined and fitted well, and though chinks might be visible, she was not aware of any showing at that hour.

She had not waited at the window, going back to bed and falling asleep quite quickly. The girl had probably been out clubbing, she said tolerantly.

Slowly details of life at Number Five, as observed from outside, were disclosed as more enquiries were made at other houses in the close. Because it was the weekend, people were at home and several had seen Jerry arriving; two were sure he drove an old red Metro.

'Who was this man who was working in the garden?' Imogen was asked eventually.

'What man?' asked Imogen.

'The man who laid the turf. A young man. Your neighbours have described him,' Rachel Cornish said impatiently.

'I don't know. Someone Charlotte found,' said Imogen.

But Howard, who had refused to leave Imogen on her own with just a police presence in the house until he had handed over responsibility for her to some member of her family, even if it were to be only Nicholas, knew his name was Jerry and that he lived in Becktham.

'He's a friend of yours, isn't he?' he said to her. That was how Charlotte had come to employ him. 'You must know his other name, Imogen.'

She said she didn't. In her world, only first names counted.

Rachel Cornish noted that she had lied about not knowing who the gardener was. Now, why had she done that?

Howard wondered why Imogen was being so obstructive. Shock, he supposed. The fact that Jerry had a record did not mean he was involved in any way with Charlotte's accident – for it was an accident: it had to be. He kept his counsel about that.

He wanted to go home. Seeing Charlotte's pale, sodden corpse had been most distressing; he grieved for her, and he was weary. All the same, he owed it to Charlotte, if not the girl herself, to do what he could for her. While WPC Cornish was conferring with Sergeant Beddoes in the kitchen, and Imogen was apparently watching television, he went into Charlotte's dining-room, looked in the sideboard where, among her small stock of wine, he found glasses and some brandy, and poured himself a tot, which he drank. Feeling better, he followed the officers into the kitchen.

'Imogen has had a bad shock,' he told them. 'It's natural that the sudden death of someone she was fond of should upset her.'

'But she's not upset,' said Rachel Cornish. 'She's watching television.'

'She's frightened,' Howard said, and he left them, returning to the unhappy girl he now thought of as his charge.

'She's acting guilty,' said Rachel Cornish.

'Guilty of what?' asked Beddoes.

'I don't know. She's hiding something. She said she didn't know the gardener but Captain Smythe said they're friends.'

At this point PC Daniels, who had been carrying out door-to-door enquiries in Vicarage Fields, came in with the information about Imogen's excursion in the night.

Imogen would have to tell them where she'd been. Beddoes went to ask her.

But she refused to say.

* * *

Howard was startled when he heard. Nevertheless, something was explained.

'Mrs Frost must have discovered that Imogen had gone out without telling her, and went to look for her,' he said. 'She'd be worried. After all, the girl is pregnant.'

'Pregnant?' Beddoes glanced at WPC Cornish. 'Did you know?' She shook her head.

'Who's the father?' she asked, not that it made much difference.

'Imogen won't say,' said Howard, wishing that he had not been the one to tell them. Still, perhaps they would now make some allowance for her present conduct. 'It's obvious what happened,' he went on. 'Mrs Frost found her room empty and went to look for her. During her search she somehow slipped and fell into the river.'

Charlotte must have gone that way because she feared the girl might have done something stupid, but it was Charlotte who had acted foolishly.

'What if Mrs Frost found Imogen meeting some young man down by the river, and they had an argument?' Rachel said to Beddoes, after Captain Smythe had left the room. 'That girl comes from a dysfunctional family. She's dysfunctional. She could have killed her grandmother.'

'Yes, she could,' said Beddoes.

Imogen had walked away from everyone and was in the garden. She had put on Charlotte's wellington boots and, glad that Jerry hadn't finished doing it, was putting in more of the plants from Rose Cottage. Howard Smythe went out to see how she was getting on.

Her face was tear-stained, and muddy marks showed where she had wiped her hand across her eyes.

'They might as well go in,' she said. 'Else they'll die.'

'Quite right,' he said. Physical labour was an excellent remedy for grief, anxiety, almost anything.

'I don't know what they are or where they're meant for,' she said. 'But it doesn't matter now. Dad can sell the house and cash in.'

'Your father owns the house?'

'Yeah. He calls it Charlotte's grace and favour residence,' said Imogen. 'He'll be mighty glad to cash it in.'

'Hm.' Howard had not known about this arrangement.

'I expect someone will snap it up quite quickly,' Imogen said, fiercely digging out a hole in which to put some roots of phlox.

'I expect so,' Howard said.

'So he won't be sorry about Charlotte.' Imogen brandished a slip of winter jasmine. 'Where shall I put this?'

'Against the fence, perhaps,' Howard suggested.

'He's not really my father, I'm glad to say,' said Imogen.

'Isn't he?'

'Nick and I think we're test-tube babies. Or else Mum had a fling. She's always having them,' said Imogen. 'We're not a bit like either of them, but we're not adopted.'

'If it's worrying you, you'd better talk to them about it,' Howard advised.

'Nick tried with Dad. He wouldn't give a straight answer,' said Imogen.

'This viburnum slip would look good in the corner at the end of the plot,' Howard said. 'It will grow quite tall and it has pale pink flowers throughout the winter.'

'Oh, all right,' said Imogen, and went off to the corner of the garden with her spade.

Howard thought of asking her where she had gone last night, but what difference would it make if she told him? She went out without Charlotte's knowledge and her absence was discovered. That had to be the sequence of events. He was tired and he was distressed. He wanted to go home, but he had lived a life devoted to his duty and his ways would never change. In silence, he handed her the few remaining plants, and watched her put them in. The light was going when they were called into the house because Detective Inspector Fleming had come to talk to Imogen.

They were still talking when Lorna arrived.

Charlotte's daughter-in-law, Victoria Paterson, had telephoned her after a police officer had arrived at her house to tell her about Charlotte's death. Victoria could e-mail the ship, and this she did; then, while waiting to hear from Tim, who would telephone as soon as possible, she knew, she called Jane, her sister-in-law, in America.

Officialdom had not yet reached Jane with the news. Victoria told her all she knew herself, which was not a lot. It seemed to be a ghastly accident which had happened during the night.

'Shall I go over there, Jane?' asked Victoria, who wanted to stay put until she had heard from Tim. 'That girl's there. Imogen. Rupert's granddaughter. The spot of bother, Tim called her, because she's in one.'

'Oh – yes. Poor kid. How dreadful for her, on her own with this,' said Jane, who was still trying to absorb the news that her mother was dead. 'I'll come over as soon as I can fix a flight.' But however fast she moved, she could not be in England until the next day. 'Get Lorna,' she said. 'She'll see to Imogen. It was Lorna who got Mum to take her in. That family can't walk away from this. Mum was their father's widow, after all. Felix is useless at the moment. Apart from Zoe taking off, his business is in trouble.' She'd heard this from her mother the last time they spoke on the telephone. Jane had meant to call this weekend to see how things were going. Now it was too late.

'Ben's there?' Victoria asked. 'You're not on your own?'

'Yes. It's all right,' said Jane. 'He'll fix things for me at the office if I can't get hold of anyone.'

'Do you need to come right away?' asked Victoria. 'There's nothing you can do for Charlotte, is there? Not now. Not for a few days. There has to be an inquiry,' she explained.

'I'll come. It may take Tim a day or two, and someone must hold the vultures off. I'll telephone when I know my flight.'

'I'll meet you if I can, or I'll organise someone,' Victoria said. 'Be in touch. I'm sorry, Jane.'

'Yes. I know.' Jane's voice cracked. 'See you soon,' she said. 'Get Lorna,' she repeated. 'And don't let her wangle out of this.'

'I won't,' Victoria promised.

On a Saturday afternoon, Lorna was not at home but her husband was. Shocked by Victoria's news, he promised to find Lorna, who had gone to show some clients round a property to let but who had a mobile phone, and something would be done about Imogen.

'Wretched girl,' he said. 'Causing so much grief.'

Replacing the receiver, he feared that they would have to take her in until her maternal grandmother returned from her cruise. She couldn't be left alone in Charlotte's house during the police investigation of a suicide. For what else could it be, happening in the night? Mature widows did not go walking round the fields and byways in the dark simply for exercise. Charlotte had become unbalanced – not altogether surprising in her situation, except that she had always seemed so calm and level-headed, but those were the very people who hid inner turmoil.

He traced his wife immediately, and she said that she would go to Granbury as soon as she had finished with her clients.

16

Imogen did not like the questions she was being asked.

'Were you on good terms with your grandmother?' Detective Inspector Fleming wanted to know.

'She's not my grandmother. She married my grandfather,' Imogen said, yet again.

The interview was taking place in Charlotte's dining-room. Imogen's school folders were stacked at one side of the table, and she was sitting opposite the officer, a lean, dark man with greying sideburns. With him was a detective sergeant, a fatter, younger man with cropped hair, acne scars and a scratch across his face.

'Were you on good terms with Mrs Frost?' asked Fleming patiently.

'Yes. She was very good to me,' said Imogen curtly.

'In what way?'

'She was kind. She took me in when my own family had no time for me. She ironed my clothes. I wasn't very nice to her,' Imogen said.

'In what way were you not nice?'

'I was rude and ungrateful.'

'Rude enough and ungrateful enough to make her want to get away from you?'

'She never said so. Anyway, she could turn me out. It's her house. Well, not exactly.'

'How do you mean, not exactly?'

'It belongs to my father. And my aunt. They let her live here. They have to. It was in my grandfather's will,' said Imogen.

'So she leased it?'

'She doesn't pay rent,' said Imogen.

'She was having the garden made over. Who was doing the work?'

'Just a guy.'

'What guy?'

'A guy she knew.'

'His name?'

Imogen shrugged.

'You must know his name.'

'I forget,' said Imogen.

A huge sense of unreality was swamping her. This could not be happening. Charlotte couldn't be dead. It was all a dreadful dream and she couldn't be sitting here discussing her relationship with Charlotte with this weedy, skinny man who was trying to look trendy with his sideboards.

'Why were you staying here with your – with Mrs Frost?'

'I told you. She took me in because my own family wouldn't. My dad and mum have split up and my mum's in America with her boyfriend.' Imogen burst into tears as she spoke.

It brought the interview to a halt.

'We'll continue this at the station,' Fleming decided.

The sergeant thought the interview should have been done

there anyway, since Fleming was taking such a hostile stance.

While they were conferring, the telephone had rung twice and had been answered in the sitting-room. Now Rachel Cornish came in to report that Imogen's aunt was on her way to Granbury, and Charlotte's daughter would arrive from America as soon as she could get a flight.

'A word,' said Fleming to the woman officer. 'Keep Imogen company for a few moments,' he told Detective Sergeant Morris, leaving his colleague to deal with Imogen's tears, and he left the room, drawing Rachel Cornish into the hall where they could not be overheard by the pair in the dining-room or by Howard Smythe, who was in the sitting-room. 'What do you make of that young lady?' he enquired.

Rachel Cornish told him.

Howard Smythe, meanwhile, who would not desert the girl, weary though he was, drew encouragement from the news that her aunt was coming. He could honourably leave after this saviour arrived. The police, also, were relieved; if Imogen were to be left alone overnight, an officer would have to stay with her, lest she, like Mrs Frost, do something stupid, but meanwhile she could be taken to the police station to make a formal statement.

Rachel Cornish had told Fleming that in her opinion Imogen knew more than she was saying.

'She met some boy last night. Maybe Charlotte flushed them out,' she had said.

'Hm. The father of the kid,' Fleming suggested.

'Or this gardener. One of the neighbours saw them having a snog,' said Rachel.

'You don't like her, do you?' Fleming asked.

'Not a lot,' said Rachel.

Detective Sergeant Morris, in spite of his unappealing appearance, was more tolerant. Left alone with Imogen, he spoke gently to her.

'You've had a nasty shock,' he observed.

Imogen did not answer. She sat staring at the window, not wanting to look at Morris's stubby hands, with their short, blunt fingers, resting on the table opposite her.

'This has to be done. All these questions,' he said. 'We have to find out what Mrs Frost was doing down there by the river. How she came to leave the house.' He paused. 'You were out on a date, weren't you?'

Imogen did not answer.

'She heard you go out and followed you.'

Still Imogen said nothing.

'You were seen coming back. One of the neighbours saw you.' Morris's tone was silky.

Imogen stiffened in her chair. If this was true, the neighbour couldn't have seen Jerry because he hadn't come right down the road with her.

'If you haven't got anything to hide, why don't you explain?' asked Morris, reasonably enough.

But Imogen had a lot she wanted to conceal.

Lorna arrived to find that the only person in her stepmother's house was a distinguished-looking, tall, thin, elderly man.

She wasn't sure what she had expected: a weeping Imogen being cared for by a neighbour, or by a policewoman, perhaps.

Howard had been listening for her car ever since the police had left the house with Imogen. He had suggested to Detective Inspector Fleming that surely her statement could be taken in the morning, after her aunt had arrived and she had had a night's sleep, but Fleming had said it was best to get it over. In fact, he wanted to question Imogen while she was still overwrought and unsupported. The post-mortem was already in progress, not held over till the next day or even Monday, as could happen in such circumstances.

There was no evidence, yet, to suggest that Charlotte's death had been anything other than an accident, but the girl's behaviour had been suspicious and, in his opinion, not consistent with genuine grief. An experienced officer, and a cynic, he knew that there were often dark compelling forces behind apparent calm.

If suicide were ruled out, what was a respectable widow in her sixties doing at night by the river bank? Where had the plain, uncooperative and pregnant granddaughter been at the relevant time? When had Mrs Frost left the house? And whom had Imogen met, other than her grandmother? Used to dealing with splintered and extended families, the detail of Charlotte's being a relative only by marriage did not hinder Fleming's speculations. And who was the father of Imogen's expected child? Was he involved?

'You must be Imogen's aunt,' said Howard, opening the door before she had time to ring the bell.

'Yes. Lorna Price,' said Lorna.

'Howard Smythe,' said Howard, ushering her in. 'I am – was – a friend of Charlotte's. When they left, I stayed until you arrived, to explain.'

'When they left? Who's left? Has Imogen gone off again?'

'Imogen is at the police station in Nettington,' he said. 'Fleming – the man in charge – insisted that she go there without waiting for you to arrive.'

'But why?'

'Won't you come in, Mrs Price, and I will try to explain. I don't really understand why the police couldn't leave it until the morning,' said Howard.

He stood back to let her precede him into Charlotte's sitting-room. All was orderly; the bossy policewoman had washed up the mugs used for the tea that had been consumed, but Howard had tidied up the cushions and the newspapers. Everything was shipshape.

He gave Lorna a brief account of what had happened, as he knew it.

'But surely Charlotte's death was an accident? Or do they think she killed herself?' Lorna, driving to Granbury, had had time to wonder about this.

'They don't know. They'll know more after the post-mortem, I imagine,' Howard said. 'I don't think she did,' he added.

'Surely even Imogen couldn't drive her to such desperate straits,' said Lorna, not sure herself if she meant the remark to be a joke.

'One can't tell what makes a person snap,' said Howard gravely. 'I agree that Imogen was not likely to have been the final straw, but Charlotte had had a difficult time, nevertheless, with the brief marriage to your father, then his death, then her move to an area where she knew no one. I met her in the butcher's shop,' he added. It was less than two weeks ago.

He explained that Imogen had, it seemed, left the house on Friday night after telling Charlotte she was going to bed.

'She won't say where she went. The police think that Charlotte went to look for her.'

'That's probably correct,' said Lorna. 'Why won't she say where she was?'

'They think she was meeting someone. Some young man.'

'The father?'

'It's a reasonable supposition,' said Howard.

'Do they think Charlotte found them by the river and there was a row?'

'They haven't said so, but I suspect that is their theory,' Howard said.

'But if Imogen had seen Charlotte fall into the river, she'd have got her out,' said Lorna. 'She's an excellent swimmer. And the young man would have helped, surely?'

'One would imagine so,' said Howard. He added, 'Imogen was extremely upset when she found that Charlotte was missing. She rang me up – that's how I came to be here. It was about twelve-thirty. She'd thought that Charlotte was having a late morning, but that was unusual, I gather.'

'I really didn't know her well enough to say,' said Lorna, somewhat sheepishly. 'I didn't see a lot of her, after she married my father. But when I did go to White Lodge – his house – she was always up and about early.'

His house, she had said, Howard noted.

'Her daughter is coming over as soon as she can get a flight,' he said. Presumably this woman knew that her stepmother had a daughter in America. 'And her son will come as soon as it can be arranged.' He spoke sternly. That family had not cared a jot about their father's widow. 'We can't do much for Charlotte now,' he added. 'But Imogen needs help. That's why you've come, isn't it? Should you go to the police station and try to get her home? She could be interviewed tomorrow.'

He was right.

'Where's Nicholas in all this?' she asked. 'Does he know about it?'

'He wasn't answering his telephone,' said Howard. 'Nor was Imogen's father,' he could not resist adding.

'No – well, Felix is difficult to get hold of at the moment.' Lorna rose. 'Thank you so much, Mr Smythe, for helping out,' she said coolly. 'Will you make sure the house is locked before you leave? I have a key to let myself in when I return.'

With Imogen, I hope, thought Howard grimly. He had been going to ask her if she would drop him off at Rose Cottage on her way to Nettington, though it would mean a small detour. Now, nothing would make him do so, but he had been feeling slightly faint and he knew he would be wiser not to walk.

It was less than a mile, but he would ring up for a taxi after Mrs Price left. He often used them.

Lorna, rescuing Imogen, was missing an evening dining with friends in Richmond. There had been no option about going to Granbury; Brian had unenthusiastically offered to go with her, but he still had work to do on a big case he was handling; he could put in several hours before he had to leave for the dinner engagement, and it hadn't seemed necessary for both of them to deal with the immediate situation. They agreed that Charlotte's own children would have to take over as soon as they arrived. Meanwhile, since Imogen's parents were neglecting her, someone must do something for her, even if it meant Lorna bringing her back with her to London until Felix could be made to see that he really must take care of his daughter.

At Nettington police station she was not allowed to see her niece immediately, so she made a fuss.

'What is happening?' she demanded. 'Surely Imogen has told you what she knows about Mrs Frost's movements? She was found hours ago, I believe – it can't be taking all this time.'

'Someone will come and see you shortly,' said the desk sergeant, urging her to take a seat, and Lorna waited, fuming at the delay, then gradually beginning to feel anxious. If what Mr Smythe had said was right, there could be reason for concern.

By the time she was taken into the interview room where Imogen, with a white and tear-stained face, sat at a table, she was ready to consider any theory, and seeing her, Imogen started to weep again, but she was not sobbing in hysteria. Silent tears coursed down her cheeks in a seemingly endless stream and Lorna, angry though she was – for at the best, Imogen had been stupid – went to her and hugged her.

Imogen responded by clinging to her and now the tears became great gulping sobs.

'You've been bullying her. How dare you – a pregnant eighteen-year-old girl,' stormed Lorna, glaring at Fleming and Morris. 'Perhaps she should see a doctor.' Lorna held Imogen away from her and looked at her keenly.

'I'm all right,' said Imogen. 'I just want to get out of here.' She took a deep shuddering breath. 'They seem to think I pushed Charlotte into the river.'

'Do you?' Lorna turned to challenge the two detectives.

– 219 –

'Not as such. Not yet,' said Fleming. 'But Imogen won't tell us where she went last night.'

'She will tomorrow,' Lorna promised. 'She's exhausted. Can't you see that? She's not fit to be questioned. I'm taking her home.'

Fleming had been taking a chance, trying to push Imogen into an admission, if not of guilt concerning Charlotte's death, at least of revealing where she had been and with whom. He let them go, promising to be in touch the next day.

By then the post-mortem results would be through.

When they were in the car, Imogen could not stop shaking. She was shuddering and trembling, seriously shocked, as Lorna realised, putting the car heater on full blast.

Finding the police station had been rather a matter of luck; as she came into Nettington she had seen a patrol car entering the town and had followed it, hoping those in it were going back to base, which they were. Now she was not sure of the route back to Granbury and Imogen was in no state to direct her, but she saw a signpost at a junction just in time to avoid going the wrong way, and eventually they returned to Vicarage Fields.

There was no question of taking Imogen back to London yet. The girl had to be put to bed as soon as possible; moreover, that foxy-faced detective would be wanting to talk to her in the morning.

Imogen's teeth were still chattering as she stumbled into the house after Lorna.

'Now come along,' said Lorna. Thank goodness the house was warm. Thank goodness, also, that there was a gas fire in the sitting-room. Lorna bundled Imogen on to the sofa, then ran upstairs to fetch blankets or a duvet. The room she went into was Imogen's and she pulled the duvet off one of the beds, running down with it and wrapping the girl up in it. Then she lit the fire, and after that, put the kettle on. A hot drink would help, but, as Imogen went on shivering, she decided that she must call the doctor.

First she made the tea, adding sugar.

'Now Imogen, you must drink some,' she said. 'Come along, dear. I know it's dreadful. Poor Charlotte. But you must try to calm down.'

She held the mug to Imogen's lips, coaxing her to sip, and the girl managed to swallow some of the tea. Her shaking slowly eased a little, and her icy hands felt warmer, but when Lorna judged she could leave her long enough to telephone, she was still trembling.

Lorna took Charlotte's telephone book into the kitchen, closing the door. She looked under D for doctor; if Charlotte had not listed her GP there, she would have to go through the whole book, but there it was: the village health centre was listed. Lorna dialled the number, but as it was a Saturday, and getting late now, she had to call the duty doctor.

She explained the situation as quickly as she could.

'The girl's very shocked. She's pregnant. No, I can't bring her anywhere. She must be put to bed and kept warm,' said Lorna firmly.

Some instinct told her that it might be useful if a doctor could testify that Imogen was in no state for further questioning, and, indeed, should not have been subjected to the cross-examination she had just endured.

The call made, she went upstairs to see if Charlotte had

a hot-water bottle, and found a blue rubber one hanging on the bathroom door.

Imogen had drunk the tea and was looking marginally pinker when her aunt returned.

'Thank you,' she managed, as Lorna helped her to undress, put on the long tee-shirt in which she slept, and get into bed.

'The doctor's coming soon,' Lorna told her. 'He may give you something to calm you down. I'm going to ring up Brian now, to explain what's been happening and that I will be staying here tonight.'

She did not notice Imogen's swift look of alarm, but she did pick up her trainers and her coat and take them downstairs. She couldn't flit far without a pair of shoes.

Lorna left the bedroom door ajar, too.

17

Jerry, busy in the chip shop on Saturday evening, was annoyed at having wasted his afternoon, and he was worried because of the police car parked in Vicarage Fields. Imogen hadn't gone and swallowed pills or something crazy, had she? She'd been in quite a state when he took her back, shivering like a shaken jelly. He was thankful that at least he'd made sure she got home. After that, anything that happened was down to her, but what was she thinking of, pretending to be pregnant when she'd never even done it?

'Why would a girl say she's pregnant when she's not?' he asked his mother, over a late Sunday breakfast. He was dressed, but Angela was still in her pink dressing-gown.

Angela was surprised by the question. She pondered for a moment.

'To get her bloke to marry her?' she suggested.

He hadn't thought of that, but it couldn't be Imogen's reason as there was no bloke involved.

'Maybe,' he said. 'Any other ideas?'

'To get attention?'

That was more like it. Imogen was certainly getting plenty,

sent to her grandmother in disgrace, and with Mrs Frost fussing over her like a hen with a chick.

'Why do you want to know?' his mother asked.

'Oh – nothing special,' Jerry said. His mother didn't know about Imogen's pretence.

'She might do it to get a flat,' Angela said. 'Pregnant girls can get them. But I should think they'd check. Wait till it showed or even till she'd had the baby. I don't really know.' It hadn't worked like that for her; the system came in later. She'd spent some time in a hostel with other pregnant girls, then in a mother-and-baby home run by a charity and that had been good; there was company and support. It must be scary, as it had been for her when she had to leave, being in a flat on your own with an infant when not much more than a child yourself.

'Are you going over to Granbury today?' she asked. 'You met them at the garden centre yesterday, didn't you? Did they buy a lot of stuff?' The more plants Mrs Frost bought, the more lawful work there would be for Jerry, putting them in.

'No,' he said. 'Mrs Frost must have changed her plans. She didn't turn up.'

'Oh! But you were there?'

'Yeah. Waited about, didn't I, wasting time and petrol.'

'And she didn't let you know?'

'No.'

'Well, I am surprised. I wouldn't have thought that nice lady would be like that.'

'Nor would I,' said Jerry.

'Maybe she's ill,' Angela suggested. 'Are you going to ring them up to find out why they weren't there?'

'No,' said Jerry. 'I've got better things to do.'

Like what, his mother almost said.

'I might paint the lounge,' Jerry said. 'You know it needs doing.'

It did, but Angela was surprised at this sudden proposition.

'All right,' she said meekly. He might change his mind if she said this wasn't a convenient time.

'Get dressed, Mum, and we'll go to B&Q to choose the paint,' said Jerry.

They'd just returned, and Jerry, with the furniture piled into the centre of the room, had begun filling in the cracks around the window frames, when Nicholas arrived.

'What's been going on?' he demanded.

Jerry, in an old tee-shirt and jeans, looked up from his pot of filler as Nicholas came bursting into the sitting-room ahead of Angela, who had answered the door. She had no idea who this white-faced angry young man could be and was terrified that he was some former prisoner with a grudge against Jerry. He'd stormed past her at the door, saying, 'I want a word with Jerry.'

Jerry also turned pale and put down his tin.

'Who are you?' Angela was quavering in the background.

'I'm Imogen's brother and I want to know what's been going on,' Nicholas said. 'I suppose you do know Imogen, do you, Mrs – er –?' he turned to glare at Angela.

'Yes, of course. How is she?' Angela relaxed, all smiles now.

'Practically in prison,' Nicholas answered. 'Haven't you heard?'

Mother and son looked at him in bewilderment, but Jerry felt the start of panic.

'In prison?' he repeated.

'Charlotte's dead. They found her in the river yesterday, and the idiot police seem to think Imogen put her there on Friday night.'

'Oh no!' Jerry exclaimed.

'My Christ!' said Angela, sitting down. 'Oh, that nice lady!'

'Yes, she was. Imogen would never hurt her,' said Nicholas.

'But what's happened? Why do they think Imogen—?' Angela could not finish and Jerry was so startled that like his mother, he had to sit down.

Nicholas had calmed down slightly.

'I only heard about it this morning,' he said. The previous evening, he had been at his waiter's job until nearly midnight and he hadn't checked his messages. His father, traced eventually by Lorna's husband to a hotel in Belgium where he was hoping to raise money for his own financial rescue, had got through to him on the telephone, telling him that Charlotte had had some accident and Imogen was in a mess; would he go and sort it out? Nicholas had telephoned the house in Granbury and got no answer, so he had driven straight to Rose Cottage, hoping that Captain Smythe might be able to explain.

Howard had done his best. Nicholas now knew as much as he did, including that Imogen had been seen returning to the house sometime after midnight on Friday night and discovered Charlotte to be missing on Saturday at around midday.

'Do you know where she was?' Nicholas now asked Jerry.

– 226 –

'She hasn't any other friends that I can think of, except the guy who's landed her with a kid, if he's around.'

Jerry had some choices. Imogen was weird, but it seemed she hadn't said she was with him, for if she had, the police would have already been to question him, and she couldn't have pushed Mrs Frost into the river. She wasn't as far out of it as that. Besides, when could she have done it?

'Why did Mrs F. go to the river?' he asked, reasonably enough.

'No one knows, unless she meant to jump in,' said Nicholas. 'The police think she was looking for Imogen, who'd gone out somewhere. They think Imogen met someone by the river – some bloke – and Charlotte found them and there was a row, and she fell in or was pushed. At least, that seems to be the general idea.'

He'd gone from Captain Smythe's house to the police station, where he had found his aunt, Lorna. She told him that Imogen was being questioned and that Brian, her husband, was with her in his legal capacity. Though not a criminal lawyer – his field was financial litigation – he had decided that if she were being aggressively questioned, as seemed likely, she must have a solicitor present. He would be at least as effective as someone plucked at random from those available, and he'd managed to learn some of the post-mortem findings.

'I know who the gardener is,' Nicholas had said. 'I'll go and see him. Maybe he can tell us something.'

Captain Smythe had known his name was Jerry, but no more.

Nicholas did not know his surname, either, but he knew where he lived.

* * *

'But this is dreadful,' Angela said. She had taken in the fact that Imogen was pregnant. 'The poor girl.' Then she remembered Jerry's earlier question and warning bells began ringing in her head. Jerry couldn't be responsible, however; he'd only just met the girl: or had he? 'Was it you, Jerry?' she accused.

'What? Oh – shit, no,' said Jerry. 'I only met her a week ago, or less. And you,' he said to Nicholas. This was what came of being nice to people, welcoming them into your home. He forgot that Nicholas had driven him to search for his mother's missing car.

'That's true, Mrs – er –' said Nicholas. 'What is your surname?' he enquired, much calmer now. It was obvious that though Jerry had been at Charlotte's, working in the garden, as Captain Smythe had revealed, neither mother nor son knew anything about Charlotte's death. His news had shocked them both.

'Hunt's our name,' said Angela.

'Mrs Hunt,' Nicholas repeated. 'Well, I'm sorry if I alarmed you but Imogen is in a lot of trouble and I need to find out what's been happening. You've been doing the garden, haven't you, Jerry?' He'd get this fact confirmed.

'That's right.'

Nicholas was remembering his suspicions about Jerry's knowledge of where his mother's missing car might be found. Jerry might not be whiter than white, but unless he was a maniac, he couldn't have killed Charlotte. Why should he want to do such a thing?

Jerry was thinking that he might well have been tempted to push Imogen into the river had they been near it on Friday night but not her grandmother, who had all her marbles. Now he knew why Mrs Frost wasn't at the garden centre yesterday, and why the police car had been outside her house. She was already dead.

'But what happened? Could she have killed herself?' Angela asked.

'I don't know. Who knows why people do things?' said Nicholas. 'But she could swim – she used the pool at my grandfather's house while they were married. And Imogen's an excellent swimmer. Really first class. She'd have hauled Charlotte out if she'd fallen in, but Charlotte should have been able to save herself, anyway. Captain Smythe said the river isn't very deep.'

'Why can't Imogen just tell them where she was?' asked Angela.

'I've no idea,' said Nicholas.

So she really wasn't saying. Jerry hoped she'd stick to that. He must keep out of this. Earlier, he'd wanted to get hold of Nicholas to tell him that Imogen wasn't pregnant, but he would not do it now. The less he claimed to know, the better. Even so, why wasn't she telling?

Jerry did not realise that Imogen's silence was due to shame.

'The only part that seems clear is that Imogen went out during the night – a neighbour saw her coming back – and the police think Charlotte discovered she was not in the house and went looking for her. They think she found her near the river and there was some sort of row and Charlotte ended up in the water. Then Imogen came home and reported her missing next day. Lorna – my aunt – seems to think this is what the police have decided happened. When they started to search for Charlotte, they realised she'd gone out because her boots and coat had gone, and a torch. She didn't take the car.'

'It's difficult to get the police to change their minds, once they've decided something,' Jerry said feelingly. 'It's all about collaring people. Never mind if they're innocent. Have they found the torch?'

'I don't know. What does it matter?'

'If someone did push her, they might have nicked it,' Jerry said.

'I suppose they might,' Nicholas allowed. 'And I suppose the police will have thought of that.'

'You can't be sure what they'll be thinking – not if they're thinking Imogen had something to do with it,' said Jerry. Imogen had been in no state to do anything that night except get herself into bed.

'Poor girl,' said Angela again. 'And pregnant, too. I wonder if it could have been the father, though why should he do such a thing?'

'I can't see Charlotte and him having a prearranged meeting by the river,' Nicholas said. 'My uncle is sure it was an accident, but even so, it needs explaining.'

'When is her baby due?' Angela asked. She avoided Jerry's gaze as she spoke.

'Oh – I don't know.' Phoebe had asked the same question. 'In seven or eight months, I suppose,' Nicholas hazarded.

'You're sure she is pregnant?' Angela asked.

'Well, of course. She ran away from school before they found out.'

'Did she like that school?'

'No. She hated it.'

'Well, maybe she just said she was pregnant to get away. Or

to get attention,' Angela said carelessly, and when Nicholas stared at her incredulously, she said, 'Girls do strange, silly things, sometimes.'

'I can't believe she'd do that,' Nicholas said at last. 'Can you, Jerry?'

Jerry simply shrugged.

Imogen sat mutely in the interview room at the police station. Beside her was her uncle by marriage, Brian Price.

She and Lorna had arrived at ten o'clock that morning, as requested by Detective Inspector Fleming the previous evening. Lorna, not wanting to share with Imogen in the twin spare room, had spent the night in the third bedroom, which was small but warm and comfortable. Charlotte's room was off bounds for now. The relief doctor who had come to see Imogen was a middle-aged man who accepted what he was told by Lorna and was unafraid of prescribing a mild sedative for a shocked pregnant young woman. He had gently palpated her abdomen and asked her if she was in pain. Imogen muttered 'No,' and was silent when he asked her when her baby was due.

'There's no point in trying to talk to her now,' he had told Lorna. 'She's in no state to answer questions.'

'I was afraid all this might bring on a miscarriage,' Lorna said. But if it did, would that be such a bad thing? It would solve one problem.

'I don't think there's any risk of that,' said the doctor. 'How many weeks is she saying she's pregnant?'

That was the nearest he could go, bearing in mind patient confidentiality, to casting doubt on the veracity of the girl's condition. Imogen had been wearing a long cotton tee-shirt. He had not inspected her above the waist, and she was a plump girl, so he could not be certain, but she had no obvious signs of an established pregnancy.

'I'm not sure. Two or three months?' Lorna guessed. 'She won't talk about it. Or anything,' she added.

'She's in shock. That's the immediate problem,' said the doctor. 'I'm sure you'll get her to your own doctor as soon as possible – or her own,' he added, remembering that this was the aunt, not the mother.

'Of course,' said Lorna. 'Thank you for coming out.'

'Not at all,' said the doctor, anxious to get home.

Imogen had slept for several hours, but this morning she still felt as though she were acting in a play or dreaming; however, Brian's presence beside her was reassuring. She did not know him very well but she liked him; at family gatherings, unlike Felix, he always had time to talk and even seemed interested in what she said, though that was never much.

'I'm here to help you, Imogen,' Brian said. 'What were you doing when you went out on Friday night?'

'Nothing special,' said Imogen.

'Well, where did you go? Did you meet anyone? Is there anyone who can say where you were?'

There was, but she would not bring Jerry into this. No one else must know what had happened. He could have raped her but then, just when she began to wish he would, he hadn't. She'd been awful but he'd been great, even making sure she got safely home, and he was the only person who knew she wasn't pregnant.

'No,' she said.

'Imogen, my dear, you are not helping yourself by this silence. I'm acting as your solicitor now; what you tell me is confidential. I won't reveal it to anyone – not the police – not your aunt – not your parents.'

'I didn't go anywhere in particular,' she said. That was only a tiny lie.

'Had you planned to meet anyone? Your boyfriend?'

'No.' That was true, anyway, and Brian noticed how she said the word with conviction.

'You just went for a walk? At half-past nine at night? On a cold, windy night?'

'Yes.'

'You never thought of telling Charlotte you were going out?'

'She wouldn't have let me go,' said Imogen. 'I didn't think she'd know. She was watching television when I left.' Then she added, 'If she'd respected my privacy and kept out of my room, she wouldn't have known I wasn't there.'

That was probable.

'She was concerned for you,' said Brian, also wishing that Charlotte had been less conscientious, for, after all, Imogen had returned and if Charlotte had simply gone to bed, this tragedy would not have happened. And Felix, his brother-in-law, by abandoning his wayward daughter at a crisis in her life, had set the whole sad business in motion.

At this point, Fleming and Morris came back into the room. Uncle and niece, or solicitor and client, whichever way you chose to define it, had had plenty of time for their confidential consultation.

Brian had seen that Fleming had formed a poor opinion of Imogen, who was looking particularly unattractive this morning. There was an angry spot which she had picked at on her chin; her skin looked sallow and she had shown a truculent defiance towards the detective as she gave minimum details of her movements on Friday night. She was overweight, too, but some of that might be the baby. All she would admit to, when Fleming resumed the questioning he had begun the day before, was to leaving the house around half-past nine or ten, and returning some hours later; she was not sure of the time.

The neighbour had said she came back at about two o'clock in the morning.

'Well, if they say so.' Imogen shrugged.

'That's four and a half hours. Where did you go?'

'I just walked around.'

'For four and a half hours? That's a long time to be walking around,' said Fleming.

Imogen did not answer.

'Plenty of time to see your grandmother leave the house, follow her and have an argument,' said Fleming.

Still Imogen did not reply.

'Mr Fleming, is that a serious suggestion?' Brian asked.

'We only have Imogen's statement that she closed her bedroom door. If she had left it open, or ajar, Mrs Frost would have seen that she was not in the room.'

'Are you implying that my client waited for Mrs Frost to emerge, then set off in pursuit?'

Put like that, it sounded ridiculous and Fleming knew it, but he also knew that there was a whole lot the girl could say if she were pushed hard enough.

'What possible motive could Imogen have had for such behaviour?' Brian asked.

'Who knows what goes on in young women's heads?' Fleming responded.

'You have had the post-mortem report in. Surely the findings indicate an accident?'

The findings indicated sudden heart failure due to shock. Mrs Frost had not drowned. A fright could have caused her to die and then fall in the river.

'The findings offer various interpretations,' Fleming said.

'Imogen, why don't you simply tell us where you were, and whether anyone saw you who can confirm it?' This was Detective Sergeant Morris.

'No one notices you when you're just walking around,' said Imogen.

But someone might. Not everyone was tucked up in bed by midnight, and if she left the house at half-past nine, as she claimed, people would have been about, even in Granbury.

Imogen was eventually allowed to leave, but Morris and a detective constable followed her and Lorna back to Vicarage Fields. They wanted to remove for testing the clothes she had worn on Friday night. Brian remained behind, saying he would join them after he had had a talk with Fleming. The man was like a terrier with a rat; he had taken a dislike to Imogen – and it was understandable, as she had revealed none of her qualities while in his presence. What were her qualities, Brian wondered briefly: academic excellence, sporting prowess, but a disposition that was often sullen. Brian and Lorna had two sons, one in his first job as a systems analyst, the other in his final year at university. The problems daughters could pose might be more serious than those boys manifested, he reflected, but Felix and Zoe had a lot to answer for; particularly

Felix. Perhaps Zoe's flight into other arms was understandable.

He was in the midst of challenging Fleming to explain why he was treating Imogen as a suspect in the matter of Charlotte's obviously accidental death, when the telephone on Fleming's desk rang.

'Right. Bring him up,' Fleming told his caller, then turned to Brian. 'It's Nicholas Frost,' he said. 'Perhaps he can tell us something useful.'

Brian sat back. Perhaps he could.

18

They went through all Imogen's things, though she had not brought much with her to Granbury. Morris stood by while the woman detective did the searching. From time to time he handed her a transparent bag into which she put what she was removing.

In the top drawer of the chest in Imogen's bedroom were the sanitary pads which Charlotte had discovered; one pack had been opened and several pads had been removed. Bundled in another drawer, not neatly folded as were the rest of Imogen's clothes, was a dark sweater, with, as the officer soon discovered when she removed it with her gloved hands, a blue shirt tucked inside it. Imogen moved abruptly when she glimpsed the shirt, then looked away, aware for the first time that it was a football shirt.

They took Imogen's trainers, so that she was left with only a pair of flat-heeled pumps, and they took the soiled washing she had put in the bathroom bin – some underwear and a tee-shirt. Then the detective who had found the pads returned to the bedroom and pulled back the duvet. On the lower sheet was a tiny bloodstain.

She looked at Imogen, who glared at her.

'I'll leave you these,' she said pleasantly, indicating the remainder of the packet. 'You OK?'

'Yes,' said Imogen sourly.

'A word,' said Morris to his colleague, drawing her outside.

Detective Constable Patsy Wilson followed him on to the landing, where they muttered together.

Lorna, meanwhile, was alarmed.

'Imogen – are you bleeding? Are you in pain?' she asked anxiously.

'No – I'm all right. It's nothing,' Imogen answered. 'Just a drop,' she added wildly. Her period, often irregular, had come on that morning.

Morris had returned to the room.

'We'd best get you to hospital,' he said. If she miscarried, and police harassment were to be alleged as the cause, there could be serious trouble.

Imogen saw the plain, cropheaded detective regarding her with an expression of concern; he was ugly, like her, but it didn't mean he wasn't a nice person. Her aunt and the woman detective were also looking anxious, but she sensed that Morris's gaze was truly sympathetic. If she let them take her to hospital, they'd discover that she wasn't really pregnant.

'Can I talk to you in private?' she asked him, and though she tried to speak calmly, the words emerged aggressively.

Morris nodded.

'Let's go downstairs,' he said, aware that being alone in the bedroom with the girl could later lead to accusations even more unjustified than those his boss was planning to level at Imogen.

They went into the garden, where DC Patsy Wilson and Lorna Price could see them from the window. Overhead, the sky was overcast; soon it would rain.

Imogen stood on the new lawn, beside a small senecio shoot she had planted. Gazing at its grey leaves, she confessed.

'I'm not pregnant. I never was,' she said.

'I see,' said Morris. He maintained his calm demeanour. 'And did Mrs Frost find out?'

'What? You think she did and I pushed her in the river to stop her telling?'

'No. As it happens, I don't,' said Morris. Those others might, if they knew. 'Your walking around in the night makes more sense now. You'd told a lie, for some reason, and it got bigger and bigger and you didn't know how to stop it. Is that more or less right?'

It was, except that she had wanted to make it into fact rather than admit to her deception.

'Sort of,' she said.

'So you walked around and meanwhile Mrs Frost found you'd gone out and went looking for you.'

'I suppose she did,' said Imogen.

'Could she have found those pads? Could she have suspected you weren't telling the truth?'

'I don't know. She might have, I suppose. She ironed my washing but she didn't put it away. And I might have had the pads anyway, in case of trouble, even if I had been pregnant,' Imogen said.

Morris saw what could have happened. Mrs Frost had meant to put the washing away and had seen the pads. If she acknowledged her discovery, she would have had to challenge Imogen, and she could have decided to give the girl time to own up herself.

'A doctor saw you last night,' said Morris.

'Yes, but he didn't examine me. Just gave my tummy a bit of a feel. He didn't ask awkward questions. Charlotte took me to the doctor here, and I said I'd come about my weight. The doctor told me to eat more fruit and vegetables, and cut out chips and chocolate,' said Imogen, and at last a hint of a smile crossed her face. 'Will it be all right now?' she asked.

'I'm afraid not,' said Morris. For now there was a motive. If Charlotte had discovered the truth, it could be alleged that Imogen, a girl with serious problems, might have wanted to stop her from revealing it.

'Must you tell them?' Imogen asked him.

He saw that it was almost more than she could do herself; she was like someone who had dug a large pit and jumped in, then could not clamber out unaided.

'Someone has to,' he told her.

'I can't,' she whispered. 'They'll be so angry.'

'Well, you've caused a lot of bother,' he pointed out.

'I know. And now Charlotte's dead.'

'If you tell your aunt, I'll tell Mr Fleming,' he said.

At least he could spare her, but not for ever, the wrath of that bitter man.

She nodded.

'I'll do it now,' she said. 'I haven't got to go back to the police station, have I?'

'Probably,' he said. 'But maybe not right away.'

* * *

'Where's Imogen?' Nicholas looked at the two men, Fleming and his aunt's husband Brian, who were seated facing one another in a small bare room with a table between them.

'She's gone back to Granbury with Lorna,' Brian said.

'Surely she told you everything she knew yesterday,' said Nicholas. 'Why have you been talking to her again? She must be very upset.'

'She is,' said Brian.

'She won't tell us where she was on Friday night, when Mrs Frost went walkabout,' said Fleming.

'Wasn't she the one who went walkabout? Didn't Charlotte go looking for her?'

'It's possible,' said Fleming.

'Of course it's possible. Imogen was bloody stupid to go wandering about in the night, and poor old Charlotte fell into the river and drowned. Rotten luck. Why couldn't she clamber out?'

'She didn't drown, Nicholas,' said Brian. 'It seems she died of shock. Vagal inhibition, it's called, due to the water rushing up her nose. Like the brides in the bath.'

'Who on earth were they? Well – never mind – so she didn't drown, but it was an accident.'

'Of course it was,' said Brian.

'We have to investigate every possibility,' said Fleming. 'Your sister has not been at all cooperative.'

'Well, what do you expect? She's had an awful shock, and she's pregnant.'

'Oh, is she?' Fleming sneered the words. 'I've just had a message from my sergeant,' he continued. 'She's been telling porkies. It seems she isn't – never was.'

Nicholas looked from him to Brian.

– 241 –

'Is this true?' he asked.

'So it seems,' said Brian. Fleming had received the call from Morris a few minutes before Nicholas had arrived.

'She told my sergeant the dreadful truth,' said Fleming.

Nicholas couldn't see what was dreadful about it. It was good news.

'What made her do such a crap thing?' he asked. 'What a prat.'

'We don't know why,' said Brian. Maybe Imogen herself didn't really know.

'She's upset about Mum and Dad,' said Nicholas. 'They've split up,' he told the sly-looking detective.

'People split up all the time. You're not little kids,' said Fleming.

'Nick, this isn't really helping Imogen,' said Brian. 'You had a reason for coming here. What was it?'

'Oh yes!' Nicholas put himself back on track. 'It's the gardener. Charlotte's gardener. I know who he is. Jerry Hunt's his name – lives in Becktham. He works at the chip shop, but not on Sundays. To tell you the truth, I had thought there was something a bit dodgy about him. His mother's car got nicked and he had an idea where it might be, so I took him there, and it was. How did he know?'

'And where was that?'

'Well, it was in Granbury, parked in that area outside the shops.'

'What sort of car was it?' Fleming was enjoying this.

'A red Metro.'

'Just when was this, Nicholas?' Fleming asked. 'Can you tell me the date?'

Nicholas could.

Fleming did not believe in coincidences. He left the room and asked a constable to do some checking.

No red Metro had been reported missing from Becktham on the date in question, but the previous night there had been an attempted burglary at Captain Howard Smythe's house in Granbury. Jerry Hunt had a record, and he'd been banged up with Pete Dixon, charged with the offence. There could be a connection.

Imogen and Lorna were in the sitting-room at Charlotte's house.

While Morris and DC Patsy Wilson were driving back to Nettington with Imogen's clothing, Lorna had rung Brian but their conversation had lasted only seconds. Lorna feared Imogen might be taken in for further questioning but she was going to try to get some explanation out of her first. Meanwhile the girl was upstairs in the bathroom.

She came downstairs eventually. Her face was pale but she was more composed than Lorna had ever seen her.

'It's time we had something to eat,' Lorna said. Even when the world was falling apart, people had to eat. She looked sharply at Imogen. 'I expect it's a relief in a way that you've been found out,' she added.

Imogen nodded. In fact she felt almost purified, washed clean by the shedding of her load of deception.

'I'm sorry,' she mumbled.

It was no good lecturing her.

'Do you know why you did it?'

'Not really. It seemed a good idea,' said Imogen.

'Well, let's not worry about that now,' said Lorna. 'Let's see what Charlotte's got in her freezer.'

She led the way into the kitchen and began poking about in the small refrigerator which Felix had considered large enough for just one lady's needs.

'Dad'll be able to sell the house now,' said Imogen. 'He never wanted Charlotte to have it, did he?'

'He's a bit pressed for cash at the moment, I believe,' said Lorna. 'But Charlotte was your grandfather's widow. She had to be looked after.'

'What Dad did was awful. Turfing her out of White Lodge with Granddad barely dead and not giving her a chance to decide where she wanted to be.'

Lorna had found a frozen cottage pie large enough for two which Charlotte had recently bought at Waitrose. She peered at the packet, trying to read it without her glasses which were in her handbag in the other room.

'I wonder how long this will take.' She slipped the sleeve off the dish and put it in the microwave. 'I'll give it ten minutes,' she decided. 'But I'd better get my specs and make sure.'

'I'll get them.' Imogen was eager to be helpful.

'Thanks. They're in my bag. It's on the chair.'

Imogen rushed to get it, stumbling against the table as she went. Lorna sighed. She was like a clumsy puppy. Something must be done about her; she'd have to see a shrink or other sort of counsellor. She took her bag from Imogen and found her glasses, setting them on her nose and scrutinising the instructions on the packet.

'There's some lettuce,' Imogen said. 'I'll get it, shall I?'

'Oh, yes. Good idea.'

'What will happen now?' Imogen asked.

'I don't know,' said Lorna. This wasn't the end of it, by

any means; Charlotte's death must still be explained to the satisfaction of Detective Inspector Fleming.

'Will I get into trouble?'

'What do you expect? You know where the knives and forks and things are, Imogen. Find some, will you?'

'With the police, I meant.'

'I can't answer that. You still haven't said where you were on Friday night.'

'Wandering about. That's all,' said Imogen.

It might just possibly be true, Lorna thought, searching back through memory to her own teenage years.

Detective Inspector Fleming had separated Nicholas from his uncle. Impatient, but reluctant to leave the police station while the situation regarding Imogen was unresolved, Brian was in one room while Nicholas was in another. Each had been brought a cup of tea which neither wanted.

After an interval, Fleming entered the room in which Nicholas sat fretting.

The policeman was smiling.

'Well, Nicholas, your information about Jerry Hunt has been useful,' he said. 'And perhaps you can clear up some other problems for me.'

'Like what?'

'Your father owns Mrs Frost's house. He'll get his cash back if he sells it now?'

'I suppose so. Him and Lorna. My aunt.'

'And with your parents splitting up, he's short of cash?'

'Yeah – I suppose.' Nicholas sensed danger in the question.

'Imogen would know this?'

'Probably. Yes – she would.'

'So Mrs Frost's death would free up some money which would come in useful for your dad.'

Now it wasn't a question, simply a statement. Fleming, whose own marriage had recently ended with the selling of the couple's mortgaged house and his wife's acquisition of the larger part of the resulting funds, now lived in a stark flat in a new block in Nettington while his wife and their two children had moved in with the man who had supplanted him.

Nicholas made no comment. He couldn't see why the detective inspector was so interested in his parents' finances. Fleming, however, had not finished with him.

'Fond of football, is she? Your sister?' he asked. 'Follows a team?'

'What?'

'Plenty of women are keen fans. Chelsea or Arsenal would be her favourites, I'd guess,' Fleming said.

'She barely knows the first thing about it,' Nicholas replied. 'It may surprise you to know that more people go to art galleries than to football matches.'

The arrogant young bugger.

'Your sister does that, then? Goes to art galleries?' he snapped.

'I don't know. Maybe. If it's easy,' said Nicholas. He couldn't see Imogen making much effort but their racy maternal grandmother had taken both of them to the Tate, though primarily to have lunch and enjoy the Whistler murals. 'She's keen on tennis. Follows that,' he added helpfully.

'So she's not an Everton supporter?'

'No. What's given you that idea?'

'She had an Everton shirt in her possession,' Fleming said. 'And as she isn't pregnant after all, the obvious answer doesn't spring to mind.'

'There could be a boyfriend, though,' said Nicholas.

'Oh yes.' Fleming was willing to admit that.

'Or there was one,' Nicholas said. 'For her to get herself into this tangle over.'

Fleming was now intent on finding out who owned the shirt, unmistakeably that of an Everton supporter. He could start by picking up Jerry Hunt and asking him about the break-in at Captain Smythe's. Had he been driving his mother's car that night? A red Metro's ownership had been traced to Angela Hunt, who lived at the same address as Jerry. Nicholas had even noticed the number of the house. He would be a good witness against his sister and Jerry Hunt, if it turned out that in some way they had conspired to bring about the death of Charlotte Frost.

There was a financial motive now. Imogen, undeniably a naive girl, not very streetwise, and concerned about her father's money problems, had seen that selling the house could be the solution. Jerry Hunt might not be involved, but they were acquainted.

There were some questions to be answered. Now he must speak to the girl again, but before her brother had a chance to talk to her.

19

Jerry was getting on well with his refurbishing of the sitting-room when a plain-clothes police officer rang the bell that afternoon. With his radio on and his back to the window as he painted the rear wall, he did not hear her, nor did he see her coming up the path, and his mother, opening the door to DC Patsy Wilson, did not recognise her for what she was.

Patsy, smiling pleasantly, produced her warrant card, and Angela's heart began to pound. She immediately thought Jerry must be in trouble again, but then she remembered poor Mrs Frost. Jerry had known her; it was natural that the police would want to talk to him about her.

'Jerry in?' asked Patsy.

'Yes. He's doing some painting for me,' said Angela. The sitting-room door was shut and Jerry's music could be heard in the hallway.

'It's you I want a word with, Mrs Hunt,' said Patsy. First, anyway, she thought. Fleming had been crafty sending her and not a man. Jerry might have got the wind-up if a male detective had arrived. Two officers could not be spared; Morris had got others out tracing taxi drivers after a tip-off during door-to-door enquiries that a taxi had been seen waiting for a fare on the corner of Vicarage Fields, its engine running, round about half-past nine on Friday night.

As she walked up the path, Patsy had observed the industrious scene within.

Angela led her through to the kitchen.

'Yes?' she said. 'It's about that Mrs Frost, is it?'

'No,' said Patsy innocently. 'It's about when your car was stolen, Mrs Hunt.'

'Oh! Wasn't I lucky to get it back so soon, and quite undamaged. It was ever so kind of you to bring it back,' said Angela. 'I wonder where you found it? You never did tell me.'

Beyond blinking slightly, Patsy did not betray surprise.

'Let's see, when exactly did you report it missing?' she said calmly. She had intended to ask Mrs Hunt where she had been on the night of the break-in at Captain Smythe's, and if she was not using the car herself, to enquire whether Jerry could have borrowed it and if she knew where he might have gone, but here she was, giving spontaneous information.

'It was missing on the Friday morning,' she said. 'That's not last Friday – the one before. Jerry said he'd report it – I hadn't time – I had to rush off to catch the train to work but I was going to need it to get to my evening job. There it was, when I came back from Denfield,' she added. 'And with the tank filled up.'

Patsy took down the details of Angela Hunt's jobs and made sure she had the dates and times correct. She didn't even have to work round to ask about Jerry's contact with Mrs Frost for Angela asked her if there was any news about what had happened.

'Poor lady, whatever was she doing down by the river?' she said.

'You've heard about it, then?'

'Yes. Nicholas came to see us. He and his sister – Mrs Frost was their grandma – are friends of Jerry's.'

'I see.'

'Mrs Frost came here once. She and Imogen gave Jerry a lift home. She was ever so nice,' said Angela. 'Jerry's been helping her in her garden.'

'Has he?'

'Yes. He works in the chip shop here, but he loves gardening,' said Angela.

Patsy made movements indicating that she was about to leave.

'Does Jerry follow any particular football team?' she asked, as if she'd just thought ot it.

'Everton,' Angela said promptly. 'He got keen –' She was about to say, when he was in prison, but, although the police would know he had a record, she thought better of it. 'A year or so ago,' she ended sedately.

'I'm a Manchester United fan myself,' said Patsy.

She went away without seeing Jerry at all. She'd got what she came for, and more.

Detective Sergeant Morris had not told Fleming about his taxi-tracing project.

The inspector had got it into his head that Imogen knew more than she was saying – which was true – and it was accepted procedure not to take an apparently accidental death at face value; alternative scenarios had to be investigated thoroughly to satisfy the coroner, and when you had a member of the deceased's circle acting strangely, questions must be asked. Nevertheless, often the simplest explanation turned out to be the right one.

Fleming had unearthed a motive. Because of his marriage break-up, the girl's father needed money. Fleming could sympathise with this predicament. When he asked Brian Price who would benefit from Mrs Frost's death, he learned that Price's wife and her brother owned the dead woman's house, for which she paid no rent. It followed that now the property would be released, capital could be realised, and the father's financial problems solved. What he had not learned was why Imogen had pretended to be pregnant, but Morris intended to discover that.

When Patsy Wilson returned from her visit to Becktham, he intercepted her before she could report the results of her enquiries to Fleming. He needed to know them first.

'It probably is Jerry Hunt's shirt,' she said.

'Doesn't prove the pair of them pushed her in the river,' Morris said.

'No,' said Patsy Wilson. 'It may prove that they're an item. But Jerry is involved with the burglary in Granbury. He's going to have to explain how he knew where his mother's car was, and why he didn't report it missing, as she thought he had.'

'Sounds as if Jerry's in trouble either way,' said Morris. 'What's Fleming doing now?' He didn't want to see the man himself; Fleming might order him to arrest Imogen and before then he wanted another chance to talk to her.

'He's not let Nicholas Frost leave yet. Doesn't want those twins getting together and cooking up a story, but the uncle will soon start kicking up a fuss.'

— 251 —

'Hm.' Fleming, always a difficult man, had grown very bitter since his marriage break-up; his irascible temper had become more unpredictable and he had always leaned towards seeking evidence to fit his theories, instead of the other way about. Now, in his eagerness to make swift arrests, he had become more stubborn and intractable. If he'd cast Imogen as a scapegoat and could find enough circumstantial evidence, he was capable of charging her. 'I'm going to see Imogen,' Morris told his colleague. 'At the house, with the aunt there. She's got to have a chance to save herself.'

'Fleming'll bring the Hunts' car in,' Patsy said. 'There may be evidence to link Jerry Hunt with the Granbury break-in, and there were those thefts before, with a lad calling at the door selling stuff while his mate went round the back. Jerry and the lad Captain Smythe collared, Pete Dixon, were in the nick together. That fits.'

'Yes,' Morris agreed. 'Well, Jerry Hunt can look after himself. Imogen Frost needs a bit of help.'

He left before Fleming could discover he was in the station and prevent him from attempting to provide it.

Lorna opened the door to him.

'Ah—' This was the detective who had somehow got through to Imogen and found out about her faked pregnancy. 'Come in,' Lorna said.

'I'd like a word with Imogen,' said Morris.

'She's in here.' Lorna led the way into the sitting-room, where the television was on, turned to a sports programme.

Imogen was curled up on the sofa, almost dozing. She looked up as Morris entered, and he saw fear in her expression but it changed when she recognised him. Imogen smiled. Lorna was astonished: this was a rare phenomenon. 'I'll leave you to it,' Lorna said, and did so, going into the dining-room with the Sunday paper which had been delivered that morning.

Imogen turned the sound down. A football match was on the screen.

'Like football, do you?' Morris asked.

Imogen shrugged.

'Not really. It's all that's on today,' she said.

'Mm. That's Tottenham playing Leicester,' Morris said. 'The Worthington final.'

'Oh.'

'Doesn't interest you?'

'No.'

'What about the boyfriend? Is he keen?'

'What boyfriend?'

'Well, I thought you had one,' Morris said.

'You mean, because of what I said?'

'Yes.'

'There's no baby and there's no boyfriend,' Imogen said.

'So how did you come to have an Everton shirt in your possession?'

Imogen stared at him, not understanding.

'There was an Everton shirt in your drawer,' said Morris.

'Oh!' Imogen went pink. Then she rallied. 'I didn't know that's what it was,' she said. 'I borrowed it from someone.'

'I see,' said Morris. 'Well, I think you borrowed it from Jerry Hunt. He's an Everton supporter.'

'What if I did?' Now Imogen looked defiant.

'Imogen, I'm not here to trap you.' Morris spoke gently. 'You and Jerry made friends. There's nothing wrong in that. So you borrowed his shirt. Why turn it into a mystery?'

'Jerry's got nothing to do with this,' said Imogen. 'He's just a friend Nick and I met by chance, buying fish and chips from where he works. It ended with him coming to work in Charlotte's garden. That's all.'

'And in the course of your friendship he lent you his shirt?'

'Yes. He knew I hadn't brought much stuff with me,' she invented.

'And when was this? Which day?'

'The day I went there and met his mother,' Imogen was inspired to say. 'It was about a week ago. That's right. It was on Saturday. The next day Jerry came to lunch and made the plan about the garden.'

'You're fond of Jerry.'

'I told you, we're friends.'

'He hasn't been to see you since Mrs Frost died.'

'He doesn't know about it,' Imogen retorted. 'She's only been dead a day,' she said, and the tears began again.

'He does know. Nicholas has told him,' Morris said.

'Nick? Where is he?'

'At the moment he's at the police station with your uncle,' Morris said. 'I'm sure he'll be here soon, once Mr Fleming has finished talking to him.'

'But Nick can't know anything about it either. We couldn't get him on the phone.'

'In the end your father told him,' said Morris. 'Nicholas thought Jerry might know something useful.'

'Why should he?' Now Imogen was frightened. It seemed that Nick had somehow blundered in, involving Jerry.

'Only because he'd been working in the garden. No one knew who the gardener was, except that his name was Jerry.

You weren't saying anything. All this has happened very fast, Imogen, and you haven't made things easy for yourself.'

She and Jerry had been seen kissing. More than just the movement of a shirt might have passed between them.

'What's going to happen to me now?' Imogen asked. 'You don't think I killed Charlotte, do you?'

'No, I don't,' said Morris. 'But unless you can prove you were somewhere else, Mr Fleming will find it difficult to agree with me. Ring me, when you decide to tell the truth, Imogen,' he said, and gave her his card. 'Every little lie leads to a bigger one, you know.'

Soon after Morris left, Nicholas and Brian arrived in their separate cars. They muttered together outside the house, and then came walking up the path.

Lorna let them in, but Imogen hung back as Nicholas followed his uncle into the sitting-room which suddenly seemed very full of people, and came over to give her a hug.

'It'll be all right, Imogen,' he said. 'It must have been awful for you, with that smarmy copper making snide remarks.'

Brian sank down in an armchair. A cautious man, by nature and profession, he did not hasten to endorse Nicholas's comment, though he agreed with his description of Fleming.

'He has a duty to eliminate all possibility of foul play,' he said portentously.

'What evidence is there to support such an idea?' asked Lorna.

'Nothing. It's all in his head, but if Imogen could prove that she was nowhere near the river because she was somewhere else, it would help.'

Three faces turned to look at Imogen.

'I was just walking around,' she insisted. Then she took a deep breath.

'I'd got into a mess and I was wondering how to get out of it,' she said, studying the carpet. There was a muddy mark on it; that was from where Sergeant Morris had stood after being in the garden when she told him the truth. The big lie had already been admitted; some of the smaller ones might not have to be revealed.

Lorna knew that her explanation might be true. The girl might even have got as far as the river and been contemplating drastic action on her own account, except that she was such a good swimmer that she'd have failed.

'Did Charlotte find you? Did you have a talk?' she said, not adding, ending in an argument.

'No.' Imogen denied it fiercely. 'How could I know she'd go poking into my room and be stupid enough to follow me?' she said, at last showing some emotion.

'We'd left you in her care, Imogen, and she thought you were pregnant,' Lorna said.

'Well, I should have been in my father and mother's care,' said Imogen. 'Why didn't they come when I needed them?'

'Is that what this is all about, Imogen?' Brian asked her. 'Did you think that if you were in trouble – in other words, pregnant – they would get together again?'

'I thought it might work,' Imogen said sadly. 'If they really are our parents. Dad, anyway.'

'What do you mean?' Brian asked.

'Imogen's got this idea that we came out of test tubes,' said Nicholas. 'She thinks we've got an unknown father and that's why Dad doesn't like her – at least she thinks he doesn't. I'm sure he does.' As he spoke, Nicholas longed to be back in Phoebe's shabby flat, with her steadily ironing at one side of the living-room while her children watched cartoons on television, and where the only tears were theirs. Phoebe was magically calm.

'Why don't you speak to your father about it, if it's on your mind?' said Brian, avoiding his wife's gaze as she marginally shook her head.

'We did, when he came over here, but he didn't give us a straight answer,' Nicholas said.

'You didn't come from test tubes,' Lorna said. 'I promise you that.'

This conversation was making Nicholas feel uncomfortable.

'I've got to go,' he said. 'I'm on duty in the restaurant this evening.'

'Can I come with you? Would Phoebe put me up?' said Imogen. She turned to Lorna. 'You've been so kind, considering I'm not really your niece at all. I know you've got to get back home. I've wrecked your day.'

Not just our day: the next weeks, quite probably, even months, if that pigheaded inspector didn't change his attitude, thought Brian, who intended to get hold of Felix and, however grave his misfortunes, make him come back to face his responsibilities.

'No.' That wouldn't do at all, Lorna decided. 'I'll stay overnight again,' she said. 'I can go up to the office in the morning.' Imogen could come too. If the police knew where to find her, they couldn't object.

But before either Brian or Nicholas had left, Charlotte's daughter Jane arrived, offering a different solution.

* * *

She came from Heathrow airport in a taxi. Tim would probably arrive on Monday, Victoria had said, when Jane had telephoned her sister-in-law from New York before she left. As their mother was, in fact, dead, the urgency was less acute than if she were critically ill, and though no ship in the Mediterranean was ever far from land, there were logistic problems.

In the taxi, Jane had wondered whether she would be able to get into her mother's house but if Lorna had gone, a neighbour might have a key. Victoria had said that Lorna was there with Imogen. Seeing lights on and cars outside, Jane was glad she would be able to gain entry, but she wanted the Frosts out. This was still, technically, her mother's house. When their father died, the Frosts had behaved in a callous, mercenary fashion, bundling his widow unceremoniously out of White Lodge, then instantly putting it up for sale. Tim and Victoria had been indignant, and so was Jane, when she understood the perfidy of Charlotte's step-family. Until her possessions had been removed from Granbury, her memory must be respected and Jane meant to see that everything was dealt with properly.

There was the problem of Imogen, too, she realised, when she was led in to the sitting-room and saw the twins there, with their aunt and uncle. Charlotte had mentioned her arrival the last time they had spoken on the telephone: last Sunday. Of course Imogen was still here, but no doubt they'd soon remove her. A week ago Jane had spoken to her mother, and heard the reason for Imogen's visit; now Charlotte was dead.

Jane was very tired, but she was not going to let those Frosts be witness to her distress. Not a tear should escape her eyes in front of them, she resolved.

They were all hanging back, even Lorna, who at their only previous meetings – the wedding and Rupert's funeral – had seemed extremely poised; Jane deduced that they were more embarrassed than sad. Then Lorna took control and offered tea.

It seemed a good idea. Tea-drinking gave you time to think, and it could even make you feel better.

She had never been in this house which for so few months had been her mother's home. Suddenly tears threatened, and abruptly she said that she would like a wash after the journey.

'Imogen will take you up to the bathroom,' Lorna said severely, and Imogen, in silence, led the way.

Jane followed her upstairs, and Imogen pointed to the bathroom.

Once safely locked inside, Jane gave way to tears, burying her face in a large, peach-coloured fluffy towel hanging on the rail and which she imagined was her mother's. She spent some time in the bathroom and Imogen, reluctant to return to the troubled group downstairs, waited anxiously for her in her own room, with the door ajar. When Jane emerged at last, she asked which was her mother's room, and Imogen pointed silently to its door. Jane went inside, fumbling for the light.

Downstairs, the others were unnerved, and Nicholas decided to leave. He didn't want to lose his waiter's job. He bounded up the stairs calling softly to his sister, and she met him on the landing, gesturing to show where Jane had gone.

'It'll be all right,' he said, giving her a hug.

But would it? What had she really done? Where had she really been? Suppose she and Charlotte had met on their nocturnal walk, or even gone on it together, and for some reason Charlotte had slipped into the river, surely Imogen would not have walked away? Had Charlotte found out she wasn't pregnant and fear of the truth coming out had made Imogen do something dreadful?

That man Fleming thought this and money needed by Felix provided a motive. Nicholas couldn't believe that Imogen would do anything so outrageous, but her pretence pregnancy had been pretty wild.

They couldn't talk about it now, nor about Jerry's possible involvement in the burglary at Captain Smythe's. He drove back to Oxford and his job. And Phoebe.

When Jane came out of Charlotte's room, Imogen managed to say, 'I'm so sorry. Charlotte was very kind to me and my grandfather really loved her.'

'Thank you for that, Imogen,' said Jane, calm now. 'You've had a bad time, too. This must be shocking for you.'

'Yes,' said Imogen. Then she added, 'I must tell you quickly, before they do – I'm not pregnant. I never was. I don't really know why I pretended to be.'

'You must have had a reason,' Jane said. 'Maybe we can work it out later. Let's get the next bit over,' and she went downstairs, into what she thought of as the lion's den, although she swiftly found that neither Lorna nor her husband were in a fierce mood. They plied her with tea and biscuits, and explained that the police were still making extensive enquiries into the circumstances of Charlotte's death.

'But it was an accident, wasn't it?' said Jane.

They had to fill in the details, explain about Charlotte's late walk and that Imogen had been out of the house.

'It's all my fault,' said Imogen. 'If I hadn't gone out, she wouldn't have, either. But she shouldn't have gone looking in my room,' she added, still defiant.

Jane's head had cleared and she tuned in to the conversation with the sharpness that sometimes comes with extreme fatigue.

'Why did my mother have to look after Imogen at all?' she asked. 'Why couldn't she go home?'

Charlotte, when she spoke to Jane on the telephone, had been afraid of Imogen overhearing the conversation; she had said very little, simply that the girl was pregnant and had run away from school while Zoe was in California and Felix away on business. Now Lorna repeated this, and explained that Zoe's mother, with whom she had stayed at first, had gone on a cruise.

'I'm going to get hold of Felix and see that he comes over,' Brian said now. 'He is needed here.' There was no need to tell Jane about Detective Inspector Fleming's suspicions; she would find out for herself, soon enough.

'Jane, I'll stay here tonight,' said Lorna. 'Imogen will probably have to talk to the police again tomorrow as there are some points to be cleared up. I can go to the office in the morning.'

'But there's no need for that, since it's difficult for you,' said Jane. 'I'm here now. My mother was looking after Imogen. I'll take over. This is still her house, I take it, until at least the funeral?'

That barbed remark went home.

'Of course,' said Lorna, and then, 'Would you, Jane? Just for a short time? It would be simpler.'

'I can see that,' said Jane. 'My mother's car is in the garage, I suppose? Imogen and I can use it. We shall need to get about. She can show me the way.'

Brian and Lorna left ten minutes later, having written down every relevant telephone number they could think of, and after they had gone, Jane looked at her watch.

'Look at the time, Imogen. You must want your supper, and I want lunch. Let's ring up for a pizza. It must be possible. Where are the Yellow Pages?'

20

Jerry had finished painting the ceiling and two walls of his mother's sitting-room. Angela was wondering whether papering them would have made a nice change, though it was a messier and longer job, and was discussing it with him when the doorbell rang again.

She hadn't told Jerry about the visit from DC Patsy Wilson. He'd had his radio on so loud that he hadn't heard her, and after the policewoman had gone, Angela realised that she still didn't know where the Metro had been found; DC Wilson hadn't said. She hadn't said a lot, really; she'd seemed only to want to verify the date when it went missing, and then she'd said it hadn't been reported after all. Something was wrong; the detective must have made a mistake. Angela had a feeling that the date coincided with Pete Dixon being caught trying to rob someone's house in Granbury. Jerry had stopped going out at nights with Pete some time before that date. He couldn't have been involved, but maybe Pete had stolen her car and Jerry guessed it and had got it back. She wouldn't mention it, or not just yet.

This time the callers were two male detectives. They wanted

to take a look inside her car, and they wanted to ask Jerry a few questions.

Under the matting in the boot of Angela's car they found a gold chain-link bracelet. It must have slipped down there after Pete had stolen it on one of their excursions, Jerry thought, his stomach lurching with sick fear. Its owner could identify it.

He was taken in for questioning.

At the police station, Fleming was delighted. While he was working on one case, a sudden death in Granbury, a thief acquainted with the girl he suspected of knowing more than she had said about that incident had been nicked. The case against Pete Dixon was watertight; he had been apprehended in the act by the besieged householder, a man of exemplary character. For all Fleming knew, deprived by Pete's arrest of his usual partner in crime, Jerry Hunt could have enlisted Imogen as an assistant and that was why she was being so cagey about her whereabouts on Friday night. Maybe she wasn't pushing her grandma in the river; maybe she was out thieving.

He floated this idea to Morris.

'She's no need to steal. She comes from a comfortable background,' Morris said.

'Does it for kicks, maybe. Likes a bit of rough with young Jerry Hunt.'

Fleming was getting a buzz out of this.

'Would you be so sure that she's mixed up in something if she was a pretty girl?' asked Morris, all his life the butt of animosity and even suspicion because he was an ugly man who had been an unattractive child. Added to her plain looks, Imogen had a brusque, off-putting manner; she made a negative impression.

'Plenty of pretty girls are crooked,' Fleming said. 'We'll go and interview young Jerry Hunt and see what he can tell us.'

Jerry had had to leave his paint roller and his gear in mid-task. He had not been allowed even to clear up.

'It's all right. You'll soon be back,' his mother had said, as he was driven off, but as soon as he had gone she burst into a torrent of tears. He'd promised, and she'd believed him. She still believed in him.

Neither could have known that, as a form of insurance, Pete had deliberately dropped the bracelet, one of no great value, which he had kept back from an earlier burglary, in the Metro before he went to rob Captain Smythe. If he were caught, either on this occasion or another, and he wanted to bring Jerry down, it would be easy.

'Look in the car,' was all he would have to say. He hadn't done it yet, but he might.

'I drove the car a few times with Pete,' Jerry admitted now. 'That's all. I never did the thieving.' This was true. All he did was ring the doorbell and chat up whoever answered. Eventually, desperate to save himself, he described how meeting Captain Smythe and Mrs Frost, both of whom had told him he should change his ways, had convinced him he must break his association with Pete Dixon. Mrs Frost had even given him a job.

'What do you know about her death? Mrs Frost's?' demanded Fleming, pushing his thin, angry face towards Jerry's round, ingenuous one.

'Nothing. Only that she is dead.'

'How did you hear about it?' A local radio broadcast had reported the discovery of a woman's body in the river but she had not been named.

'Nicholas Frost told me.'

'Ah – so you do know the family?'

'Yes. I worked for Mrs Frost, in her garden,' Jerry said. He'd best stick to the truth as much as possible.

'Where were you on Friday night?'

What a bit of luck that after he'd dropped Imogen off, he'd visited Tracy. She fancied him rotten and she'd say he'd been there, he was sure. Besides, it was true.

'With a girl,' he said.

'What girl?'

'A girl I went to school with.'

In the end he gave her name. He couldn't say he'd been with Imogen first.

While Jane and Imogen were waiting for their pizzas, Captain Smythe telephoned. Jane answered the telephone. It might be Ben ringing from New York, or her brother Tim.

'Jane Paterson speaking,' she said.

'You're Charlotte's daughter.' The male voice was deep and steady.

'Yes.'

'My name's Smythe. Howard Smythe. I'm – I was a friend of your mother's,' he said. 'Can I be of any help? Is Imogen all right?'

'Sort of,' said Jane.

'Are her parents there?'

'No. Her aunt and uncle were, Lorna and Brian, and Nicholas, her brother, but they've gone now. We're on our own. I haven't been here long,' said Jane.

'You've come from New York?'

'That's right.'

'I live in the village. I don't want to intrude, but would you like me to come round?' he offered.

'That sounds a very good idea. May I just have a word with Imogen?' said Jane. Here was a link with her mother. She covered the mouthpiece with her hand and said, 'It's a Howard Smythe. Friend of Mum's. Sounds nice. Shall he come round, he says?'

Imogen nodded vigorously.

'Yes, please. We'd like that,' Jane told him.

'I will be there in about fifteen minutes,' Howard said.

'He's pretty old,' warned Imogen. 'He was Charlotte's friend, but they hadn't known each other long.'

She told Jane that he had caught a burglar in his house.

'Sounds a great guy,' said Jane.

'I'll have to tell him about the baby.'

'The non-baby,' Jane said. 'There wasn't one. Don't give it an existence it never had. Will he drink wine or something stronger?'

'I think he might like something stronger,' Imogen said.

'Let's see what Mum's got beside wine,' said Jane.

They found brandy, and a bottle of Famous Grouse.

'Mum enjoyed a nip now and then,' Jane said. 'And so do I. Drink can be a friend, but it can also be an enemy.'

'I know. I don't drink much,' Imogen said.

'You stick to that. All the same, a glass of wine with your pizza won't hurt you. It might make you sleep,' said Jane.

'You're being so nice to me,' said Imogen. 'And if it hadn't been for me, Charlotte would be alive.'

'We won't even think about that now,' said Jane, but probably it was true. 'For all you know, she might have had a car accident next week, or been stricken by a dreadful illness. From what my sister-in-law told me on the telephone – I rang her from Heathrow – she can't have known much about it.' Punctilious, anxious to keep Charlotte's family fully informed, for his wife's had much to answer for, Brian had telephoned Victoria about the post-mortem results.

Howard carried a torch to light him on his way. It had rained during the afternoon but it had stopped now; however, there were puddles on the road. He walked carefully; it would be easy to slip and at his age a fall could be seriously damaging. Less resilient with every year, he still felt tired and he was worried about Imogen. Nicholas, calling that morning, had said that the police had been harassing her, as he put it.

'She's a difficult girl,' he had said. 'Thinks the world's against her.'

'Well, you're not, and nor am I, and nor was Charlotte,' Howard had replied. 'Better get that into her head, if you can.'

Imogen opened Charlotte's door to Captain Smythe.

'Ah – Imogen,' he said. 'How are you?'

'All right,' she said. 'Let me take your coat.'

He shrugged off his oiled jacket and gave it to her, with his old tweed hat, and she hung them up beside Charlotte's raincoat in the cloakroom. Then she led him into the sitting-room where Jane waited. They had decided that this was how they would do it, rather formally.

'This is Jane. A sort of aunt,' said Imogen. 'Captain Smythe,' she added, in a mumble.

Jane held out her hand, and as Howard took it, looking at her, small and neat, with brown hair and arching brows over deep blue eyes, he said, 'You are very like your mother.'

'So they say,' said Jane.

'You've got here very quickly.'

She had, securing a last-minute standby seat on a flight that had been delayed.

'It was necessary,' she said. 'My brother will be here soon. I haven't seen the police yet. I know there will be formalities – an inquest – all that.'

'I'm afraid so. I'm so very sorry,' Howard said. 'Charlotte was a new friend and I was looking forward to seeing more of her. She was a kind and charming woman.'

'I'm glad that she had met you,' said Jane. 'She was very lonely. She was bundled here by the Frosts.' Saying this, Jane frowned.

'It's true,' said Imogen. 'And Dad resented her being here, rent-free.'

'She intended to insist on paying,' Jane revealed. 'She knew the arrangement would cause bad feelings, but there wasn't time to make a different plan when White Lodge was sold so quickly. She meant to look into things with a solicitor and see what could be done to regain her independence.'

'Granddad would have been very angry if he'd known what they'd done,' said Imogen.

'She did have a pension,' Jane pointed out. 'From his estate, I mean.'

'I should hope so,' said Imogen.

And she had her own, as well as the state pension.

'She wasn't badly off,' said Jane. It was time to change the subject. 'Won't you have a drink, Captain Smythe? What would you like?'

She moved like Charlotte, he noticed, purposefully and economically, as she poured them both considerable whiskies. Without asking her, she gave Imogen a glass of white wine. He wondered what her father had been like.

'I expect the Frosts will want to sell the house as soon as they can,' Jane continued. 'Sorry, Imogen, but it's the truth. However, for the time being, I regard it as my mother's. I shall stay here for as long as it's necessary, and I'll look after Imogen, too, as my mother did, till some member of her family takes over.'

'They'd made good friends, your mother and Imogen,' Howard said. 'Hadn't you, Imogen?'

'I was a trouble,' said Imogen. 'Captain Smythe, I have to tell you, I'm not pregnant. I made it up.'

'Really, my dear? That was a silly thing to do, wasn't it? Couldn't you have found another way of telling your parents how unhappy you were?'

'They wouldn't listen,' Imogen said. Then, 'You don't seem shocked.'

'It takes a lot to shock me, Imogen,' he answered. 'Charlotte's death has shocked me – and shocked you. And Jane, and her brother. Even your family.'

'They'll be glad in the end,' said Imogen. 'It solves Dad's problems.'

'Oh no, Imogen,' Captain Smythe replied. 'You're wrong.' It was such a waste, he thought; here was this bitter, angry girl who might have been the catalyst for these events, but it was her family's denial of her that had involved Charlotte, who, it now appeared, they had treated shabbily. 'What is the present situation?' he asked.

'The police think I pushed Charlotte in the river,' said Imogen. 'I did cause her death, by going out that night.'

'Imogen, my mother wasn't very sensible to go roaming off in the dark over fields – she went across fields, didn't she? The river path was in a field, wasn't it?' said Jane.

'She took a torch,' said Imogen.

'Well, I'm glad to hear it, but really, unless she had some reason to think you'd gone down to the river, why didn't she stick to the roads or call the police?'

'Perhaps she thought I was going to jump in, because of being pregnant,' Imogen said.

'All the more reason to call the police. They might not have come if she'd just said you'd gone out – they can't go looking for every girl who's simply out late – but if they knew there was a particular reason to be anxious about you, they might have taken it seriously. Though I suppose they couldn't do a lot in the dark. What a pity she didn't just go back to bed and wait till morning to look for you,' she added.

'Imogen, you must be mistaken, surely,' said Howard Smythe. 'Have they suggested you were there when Charlotte fell into the river?'

'Sort off,' said Imogen. Oddly, she did not feel like crying now. She felt grown-up and sensible. 'There was something about Charlotte not drowning. Like the brides in the bath, someone said. I don't understand that part.'

Howard did.

'There was a man who went in for serial marriage, as it's called today. This was years ago – in my childhood. He insured them heavily and then each one drowned in the bath. It was suggested that he caught hold of their feet and tipped them up, causing the water to rush up their noses so that they died from sudden heart failure. You must have been told to hold your nose when jumping into water, Imogen. It's a crucial precaution – you can do it like this,' and, separating his thumb from his fingers, he put his hand under his nose, the soft skin against his nostrils. 'It's important if you have to abandon ship.'

'And they think something like that happened to my mother? But if she'd been pushed in, it wouldn't have, would it?' Jane said. She would have struggled, fought against the water or her assailant, taken time to die. She shuddered.

'It's difficult to say,' said Howard. 'It would depend on how she fell.' He hesitated. 'If you want to go there, Jane, we could tomorrow, when it's light. Perhaps we could work it out.'

'It's true about holding your nose,' said Imogen. 'I had a swimming instructor when I was very young who was paranoid about it, making us do it whenever we were jumping off the diving board or even the side of the pool.'

The doorbell rang.

'That'll be our pizzas,' said Imogen.

But it wasn't. The pizza courier, who came from Nettington, was having trouble finding Vicarage Fields and it was the driver of the taxi Howard, fearing weakness on his part or further rain, had ordered for his return before he left his house.

Imogen opened the door to him.

'Well, hullo,' the driver said. 'You're OK then? I was worried about you the other night. I've called for Captain Smythe,' he added.

He was the man who had taken Imogen to Becktham on Friday.

21

Imogen shot away from the front door into the house.

'It's not the pizzas – it's a taxi for you, Captain Smythe.'

'Oh – thank you,' said Howard. He looked at Jane somewhat sheepishly. 'I walked up, but I ordered a taxi back for two reasons – one, to stop one of you from feeling you should escort an old man, and two, because the lane is dark and if I slip and fall, I could be a nuisance and might even cause someone else to have an accident.'

'I'd have driven you,' said Jane. 'Mother's car is here.'

'You've had a long journey,' he said. And a drink or two, he did not add. However innocent of causing any accident, a driver could be breathalysed and hounded by the law. 'I no longer drive,' he told Jane.

Imogen had fetched his coat. The driver, she saw with relief, had returned to his car.

'I'll telephone in the morning,' he said, putting on his coat. Imogen handed him his hat, and he patted her shoulder. 'You have got friends, my dear,' he said.

'Thank you for coming,' Jane said, heartened by his visit.

The taxi driver had driven Captain Smythe many times,

usually for short journeys round the area but also to meet some of his grandchildren for lunch in various places.

'That young girl all right, is she?' he asked now, as they moved off down Vicarage Fields to join the main road. Here was the spot where he had picked her up on Friday night.

'Under the circumstances, not too bad.' Howard was surprised by the question. 'You've heard about it, then?'

Now it was the driver's turn to be surprised.

'About what?' he asked.

'Her grandmother – step-grandmother – had a fatal accident. She was found in the river yesterday,' Howard told him.

'I did hear there'd been a drowning,' said the driver. 'Very sad. I didn't know who it was.'

'Why did you ask about Imogen?'

'I drove her to Becktham on Friday night,' the driver said, negotiating the turning into Meadow Lane.

Howard stayed entirely calm.

'Oh yes,' he said, as if he knew about the trip.

'Picked her up on the corner. She was in a bit of a state and I was anxious. Young girls, you know.' He did not mention Imogen's generous tip.

'Quite,' said Howard. Nicholas had said that Jerry lived in Becktham. The fog of subterfuge was clearing, and if Imogen had been in Becktham on Friday night, she couldn't have been down by the river. 'Was it you who brought her back?' he tried.

'No. Maybe she got a lift. Or a local cab,' said the driver, drawing up outside Rose Cottage. 'It's all happening in Granbury, then,' he added. 'I'm sorry about the girl's grandmother. That's bad. All right, sir, yourself, are you, after the burglary?'

'None the worse,' said Howard.

'Glad you caught the little monster,' said the driver.

But Pete hadn't been a monster. He was a greedy, undisciplined, lazy boy, the sort that, if he were directed down a route with purpose, might be turned around.

Howard paid the driver, bidding him goodnight. In the morning he would have to decide what to do with his new knowledge – whether to confront Imogen and give her a chance to speak up before telling the police, for of course it cleared her. She was unlikely to have gone down to the river after a trip to Becktham. If she wasn't pregnant after all, the situation was very different and there could have been something between her and Jerry.

He would sleep on it. In wartime, snap decisions must be made, but this was not one of those occasions. Things might look different in the morning.

Jerry had been cautioned and questioned.

He denied involvement in the burglary at Captain Smythe's house and disclaimed knowledge of the bracelet discovered in the Metro, but he agreed that he had not reported his mother's car missing because he suspected that Pete might have taken it. Pete was already on remand awaiting trial and there was no way he was going to get off since Captain Smythe had caught him.

'I did go round with Pete, selling dusters and that.' Jerry had admitted this already. 'I didn't have nothing to do with the stealing. I just talked on the doorstep.'

'But you knew what Peter was doing. You shared in the profits,' said Detective Sergeant Beddoes, the officer who had charged Pete. He was conducting the interview but because of Jerry's connection with the Frosts, Fleming had decided to be present.

'Pete wanted to borrow Mum's car. I said no,' said Jerry. 'He could have taken the spare key when he came to our house. I guessed that was what had happened and I found the car and brought it back. No harm done. I didn't want to waste your time,' he added, winningly.

'Don't waste your smiles on me, Jerry,' Fleming snapped. 'I'm not a gullible pensioner you can charm, nor a silly young girl like Imogen Frost.'

'Imogen's got nothing to do with this,' Jerry said.

'No?'

'Captain Smythe's place was done before she ever got down here,' said Jerry. 'I met her next day, in the chip shop. Her and her brother.'

This could be checked. Beddoes knew – as the whole CID team did – that Fleming had taken a dislike to Imogen Frost and had convinced himself that she was the active cause of her grandmother's death. Fleming was a good detective and he had solved many awkward cases, largely through perseverance, but he was stubborn, and he wanted convictions. There was no single piece of substantiated evidence to connect Imogen with the river death, nor a motive that would stand up in court, but there could be grief along the way – and for Fleming as well as the targeted girl. If he went too far, there could be a complaint and it wouldn't be the first time he had overstepped the limits with a witness. Beddoes and his colleagues were sure that Mrs Frost's death was due to misadventure. There was no crime to investigate: only suicide or accident. But theft was different. Jerry had a record; he was the confidence trickster who had kept victims talking while Pete took the stuff.

In the end they locked him up for the night. He could be charged in the morning.

Jane had not noticed Imogen's reaction to the taxi driver. The pizzas arrived soon after he left, the courier apologising for the delay.

They needed warming up. Jane put them in the oven, then said she'd have a shower and change her clothes before they ate.

'I'll sleep in Mum's room,' she said.

'I'll find some clean sheets,' said Imogen.

'Don't worry, Imogen. That's OK. It's my mother's bed, not some stranger's. I'll just feel at home.'

Jane hurried, however, not wanting to steep herself in grief, and she wanted to call Ben, who would be wondering about her. Wrapped in the towel she thought was Charlotte's but which had been used by Lorna, she rang him from the telephone in the bedroom. They had a short talk. She explained that she hadn't yet spoken to the police but there were unresolved problems concerning Imogen, who had been out of the house when Charlotte went for her midnight walk. Before she left America, Jane had been convinced that Charlotte had not taken her own life; that would not be her way, unless she had had a total breakdown, which no one had suggested. Now she was still more certain. She promised to ring Ben again when Imogen, whose timetable was five hours ahead of theirs, had gone to bed.

There would be a great deal to sort out in the morning,

but Tim would soon arrive, perhaps even tomorrow, and lend a hand.

'The good news is, I didn't let those Frosts walk all over me,' she said, not telling Ben that an encounter with Felix was yet to come. Lorna had been quite nice, she conceded, though swift to accept Jane's offer to take temporary charge of Imogen.

She dressed in clean clothes and went downstairs, where Imogen had laid the table in the dining-room. The salad that Charlotte had bought on her last shopping expedition had kept fresh in its sealed bag in the fridge, and there was the wine Jane had already opened. Imogen had even found table napkins, and candles, which she lit when she heard Jane on the stairs.

'Oh, Imogen, that does look nice,' said Jane.

Imogen glowed.

'I know you're sad, but Charlotte would want you to feel it's home,' she said.

'You're right,' said Jane, pouring the wine. She took a gulp. 'The garden's looking good,' she said. 'I didn't expect that.'

Of course, she didn't know about Jerry.

'Charlotte had some help,' Imogen said. 'A friend of mine and Nick's. He did most of it this week.'

'Oh?'

'And Captain Smythe gave us a lot of plants. We were going to get some more yesterday.' They were to have met Jerry at the garden centre yesterday. What had he done? He wouldn't have known about Charlotte. Had he gone there, as arranged?

'Mum had said it was a mess,' Jane said. 'Some moth-eaten lawn clawed up by dogs and cats. Or children, possibly.'

'We put down new turf,' said Imogen.

'I expect she was pleased.'

'Yes.' Imogen was glad she had put in the plants. 'Captain Smythe was burgled, the night I got here,' she said. 'He caught the thief and hung on to him till the police arrived. He's a great old bloke.'

'He seems to be. What sort of captain was he?'

'He was in the navy.'

'Was he? Tim would like to meet him.'

'Well, he will, when he gets here,' said Imogen. 'How long will you stay?'

'I don't know. Between us, if we can, till everything's settled.'

'You mean the funeral? Perhaps she can be buried near Captain Smythe's wife, in the graveyard here,' said Imogen.

'Perhaps,' said Jane.

After Rupert's death, Charlotte had said she wanted to be cremated. Should she look in her mother's desk for a will? Had she made a new one after Rupert died? It might be complicated, if she hadn't. There was no point in worrying about that now, but it would be a good idea to find a solicitor who wasn't Brian, a Frost connection. Captain Smythe could advise them.

There were some pears which needed eating. Jane and Imogen had one each for their dessert, and Jane told Imogen about the flight and a man who sat next to her on the plane and talked about planting a vineyard in Lancashire.

'I told him it might not be his best choice because of the climate,' said Jane. 'Too little warm sun. He was possessed of a dream. Not a bad thing, in fact.' Had Imogen a dream? Hers at that age had been to get good exam results, a degree, and an interesting career, with maybe marriage and a family along the way. She'd achieved the first three of these ambitions; marriage and a family had eluded her, but her relationship with Ben was mutually sustaining and, she believed, would last.

'Jerry has a dream of being a proper gardener. A horticulturist,' said Imogen. 'Charlotte thought we could help him find out how to do it.'

'He'll have to do that for himself now, won't he?' Jane said. 'It won't be difficult. The internet, for starters, you could suggest.'

But Imogen did not expect to see Jerry again.

They watched television later; it saved talking. Neither took in much of what was on, and, when they went to bed, alone in their rooms, both wept bitterly, one from grief, the other from fear and remorse. After Jane had dried her tears and spoken on the telephone to Ben, she propped open her bedroom door and put a chair across the landing at the top of the stairs, just in case Imogen decided to go walking in the night again. With any luck, she would hear her either falling over or removing the obstruction.

Jane woke next morning to a tap on the half-open door.

It had taken her some time to go to sleep, lying in her mother's bed wondering what Charlotte's thoughts had been as she lay here. There were two books on the bedside table, short stories by Carol Shields and Alice Munro. Jane had given her both of them; when she was in England for Rupert's funeral she had recommended the authors to Charlotte. There was a marker in the Carol Shields; this must have been the last of her mother's reading. How lonely she must have felt, uprooted from all that was familiar, forced to readjust again. Jane and Ben had tried to persuade her to visit them, and she had agreed to come when Jane could take time off to be with her. Victoria had been concerned about her, wishing she would visit them more often, but Jane knew her diffident mother had been anxious to avoid being thought pushy and interfering; perhaps she had erred too much the other way. At least she'd met that nice old man, Captain Smythe, through whom she might have made other new friends; Jane did not realise that he was also isolated.

She had been deeply asleep when the knock came, and struggled back to consciousness, trying to remember where she was, without Ben beside her, and why she was being disturbed in the middle of the night.

But it was morning here. She was in England in her dead mother's bed, and responsible for a disturbed, unhappy girl.

'Yes – what –?' she called out groggily, blinking, pulling herself into the present.

The door opened and Imogen came in, carrying a tray.

'I know it's night for you, but it's nine o'clock here and we're going to meet Captain Smythe,' she said. Though no time had been arranged, Imogen wanted to be out of the house before the police came for her again, as she feared they would.

'Oh – that's sweet of you, Imogen. How lovely,' said Jane, heaving herself up as Imogen set the tray down on the dressing-table stool and carried it over.

'I thought you'd want coffee but I can easily make tea, if you'd rather,' said Imogen anxiously. 'Here's the paper.' She had *The Times* tucked under her arm. 'There's just toast. Would you like an egg?'

'Coffee's fine. I won't be long,' said Jane. 'Thanks, Imogen.'

A few minutes later the sound of the vacuum cleaner could be heard as Imogen set about clearing up after yesterday's incursion of visitors. Poor kid, she was certainly doing all she could to be a ray of sunshine now, but she bore a lot of responsibility for the tragedy that had taken place.

'I do blame her,' Jane had said to Ben, last night. 'But it wasn't sensible of Mum to go off like that in search of her. And now Imogen says the police think she may have pushed Mum into the river.'

'Do you think so?'

'No. She's troubled and disturbed. But she was fond of Mum. She can't really believe what's happened and nor can I.'

'I wish I could be there with you,' said Ben.

'So do I. But Tim is coming. Meanwhile, I mean to rout the Frosts – except for Imogen.' Ben knew what she felt about their treatment of her mother.

'You do that,' Ben encouraged. As she had the wayward Imogen to keep an eye on, she wasn't alone, and this elderly acquaintance of her mother's, Captain Smythe, was good news.

Howard Smythe telephoned just as Jane, carrying her tray, came downstairs. They arranged to meet almost immediately, as soon as Jane and Imogen could get to Rose Cottage. They would come by car, Jane said, aware that as he had used a taxi the night before, he was perhaps more fragile than he appeared.

They had just left when Detective Inspector Fleming called them on the telephone.

* * *

Howard intended to challenge Imogen. He was sure the police would interview her again today, and Jane would have to talk to them about the inquest. Probably it would be opened the next day, or on Wednesday, he thought, and even though it would be adjourned to a later date, by then the investigating officer would hope to be able to satisfy the coroner as to whether it was an accident or something more sinister.

There had been cases where, because an involved person had an unfortunate manner, was brusque or surly, or even simply ugly, an impression of guilt could be created and the investigation became geared, not to discovering the truth, but towards finding evidence to support the prejudice. It would be dreadful if for this reason Imogen were considered to be under suspicion. Such people often gave a poor account of themselves under cross-examination, alienating juries. Now, though, there was a taxi driver who could reveal where she had gone.

Imogen sat in the back of Charlotte's car as Jane, directed by Howard Smythe, drove the short distance round the lanes to the nearest point where they could leave it before crossing a stile and walking to the narrow footbridge. There was a police car by the verge, and as they drew closer to the bridge they saw a lone constable on duty beside tapes marking off an area a hundred yards or so further along the bank.

None of them spoke. Imogen hung back while Captain Smythe, with a word to Jane, led the way. Straight and tall, he walked across and paused to let them catch up. The path was narrow, and they had to go in single file. This was where Charlotte had come that night, but had she approached from the road, as they had done, or across the fields? Could the answer ever be discovered?

The constable stood forward alertly as they came towards him.

'I'm sorry, sir. I'm afraid you can't come any further,' he said.

'Officer, this lady is Mrs Frost's daughter,' Howard said.

'Oh. Well, even so, Scenes of Crime may be coming back,' the constable replied.

'But there was no crime, officer,' said Howard gently. 'It was an accident.'

'That may be so, sir, but I have my orders,' said the policeman.

'And you must obey them,' Howard said.

He looked past the man, aware from walks here himself that some way beyond where the constable was standing the path curved, and the bank was steeper, cut away. There would have been nothing for Charlotte to clutch at if she had slipped there, and the current could have moved her body to the spot where, caught up in reeds and grasses, it seemed that it had come to rest. However, she had had a torch.

'Has the torch been found?' he asked.

'I can't answer that,' said the constable. After all, he was uniform, not CID.

'It could have fallen in the river or it could have rolled away,' said Howard. 'Be good enough to glance up and down in the grass beside the path further away from us, Constable, where it bends, and also in the water. We'll wait here.'

Faced with Howard's quiet authority, and seeing no chance that he might contaminate the crime scene, if that was what it was, any more than those who had trampled it when removing the body from the water, the constable did as he was bid, while Jane thought that surely the area would already have been carefully examined and the torch found, if it was there.

The constable saw it, some distance from where he had been standing, half-hidden in the grass, a heavy, black rubber torch. His boredom fled; here was evidence. After the rain, his own footsteps had left marks on the path, but there were others, not wholly obliterated, by a pothole close to the edge above the river, where the bank was high and steep above the water. He called the station straight away, gesturing, thumb up, to Howard as he did so.

Howard glanced at the two women.

'I think this means that Charlotte entered the water further along than this roped-off area. You'll be able to come back later, Jane, after the significance of what the constable has found is assessed and the police have gone. We would be wise to leave the scene before reinforcements arrive.'

22

Felix had returned to England late the night before. His answering machine was filled with urgent messages, some about business and others concerning Imogen. Zoe had tried to get him; who, she asked, was looking after Imogen now that Charlotte was dead?

Bit late to start worrying about that, thought Felix, listening to Brian telling him that Jane had taken on this role. He wondered who had told Zoe about Charlotte; he hadn't.

Brian's final message mentioned, in no uncertain terms, that Imogen was in a dicey situation.

Bloody girl, thought Felix. The stupid little cow had never done him credit. He'd given her his name, brought her up as his, and no one knew who her real father was. Nicholas was different; he was a boy any man could be proud of and it had not been difficult for Felix to convince himself that he was his real son. Perhaps their real father had been a stupid, shiftless idiot, like Imogen. Thinking that was less painful than imagining him to be an accomplished lover. Felix had tortured himself with such speculation.

He would have to go Granbury and sort out this mess.

Surely even Imogen couldn't have been crazy enough to push Charlotte in the river? But you couldn't be certain. What about criminal genes? Who knew what she had inherited? A promiscuous disposition, evidently. He would like to know what the two of them were doing, roaming round the countryside in the middle of the night. Charlotte must have been behaving very irresponsibly towards the girl. There was no denying that with her off the scene, his financial situation would be much improved; the house would be easy to sell, and he might persuade Lorna to let him use her share of the capital, short term. Though Brian wouldn't approve; he'd advised Felix against going ahead with a merger that had proved a sad mistake, leading to his company's present trouble, and now Zoe had escaped.

Felix had very little feeling left for Zoe. She had been happy when the twins were born, and had seemed fulfilled, but once their baby stage was over – even Imogen had been no plainer than many other babies – she had begun to distance herself from Felix. Perhaps she was also haunted by that unnamed man, wanting him again. Living comfortably, both busy with their careers, they had seemed to have an enviable life, but in fact it was, increasingly, a sham. His mother had sensed the truth, but she had died, and all too soon, Rupert married Charlotte.

Felix telephoned Brian at seven o'clock on Monday morning, and he did not enjoy hearing what Brian had to tell him, nor did he thank his brother-in-law for his efforts to protect Imogen's interests.

'You'd better get over there, Felix,' Brian told him. 'And be careful with Inspector Fleming. He's developed an antipathy to Imogen and she hasn't helped herself by refusing to say where she went on Friday night. See if you can get her to tell you, and keep cool with Fleming.'

Fat chance of either result, Brian thought, as the conversation ended, leaving Felix more angry and astounded about Imogen pretending to be pregnant than any other detail.

Felix showered and shaved. Next, he made telephone calls and sent some e-mail messages. He had secured a loan of several hundred thousand pounds, but at high interest; perhaps bankruptcy would have been a wiser action, for after an interval he could start again, but to do so meant conceding defeat and he was too stubborn to do that. He put on a dark grey suit and a pale blue shirt and tie. Let Fleming see that he was a man of consequence. Then he got into his Mercedes and set off towards Nettington.

He had picked quite the wrong image to impress Fleming. Jeans and a sweater, and a show of parental emotion, might have pierced the inspector's hostile armour; not city slicker presentation; and Fleming, foiled by getting no reply when he telephoned to warn Imogen that a police car would shortly call for her, was about to leave for Granbury to look for her when Felix arrived.

As it was, Felix's interruption meant that Fleming was still at the station when the constable on the river bank rang in to report the discovery of the torch.

'Why didn't someone calculate that the body would have been carried by the current?' Fleming barked at Morris, when the significance of the find and of the nearby scuff marks was made plain.

Because you didn't think it relevant, and you didn't order the search to be extended along the bank, thought Morris, who yesterday had raised both these points and been shouted down for his pains.

'You've gone soft on that silly girl,' Fleming had said. 'She's a liar. She could have got up to anything.'

Now it was raining, and vital marks could be expunged. Morris went off with protective sheeting to preserve what could be saved, if anything. Let the girl's father and Fleming join battle, as clearly they were about to do, while he looked for evidence in Imogen's defence.

'What is going on?' demanded Felix, looming over Fleming. 'Where is Imogen?'

'You tell me,' said Fleming. 'I've just telephoned the house to say we want her in here, and there's no reply. I'm on my way to get her.'

'If they're not answering the phone, you won't find her, will you?' Felix snapped.

'That sort of attitude isn't going to help,' said Fleming.

'You've been harassing a young girl. One who's had a shock,' said Felix, who though furious with Imogen had picked up on some of the points Brian had made.

'She's lied and wasted police time,' said Fleming.

'She's entitled to legal representation if you're questioning her,' said Felix.

'And she had it,' Fleming replied.

'My brother-in-law isn't available now. Another solicitor must be found. Whoever is available,' said Felix. 'She'll qualify for legal aid.' Felix could not pay legal fees.

'You seem to agree that she has a case to answer.'

'You are putting her in that position.'

'She's done it herself, by refusing to answer questions and by proving herself a liar over saying she was pregnant.'

'That's not the point,' said Felix.

'Oh yes, it is. Mrs Frost may have discovered that it was a lie and Imogen wanted to stop her from talking.'

Brian had warned Felix that once the groundwork of a prosecution theory had been laid, tiny circumstantial straws and bits of grit could be added to build up the edifice, blinding those constructing it to other possibilities, so that opposing facts and theories were never aired, let alone discussed, and Imogen's own conduct, with her not immediately appealing appearance, as he put it in an attempt at tact, her brusque manner and her refusal to talk were the cement that bound the whole. Now Felix saw a man obsessed with a theory, worrying it like a dog with a bone. Fleming had made up his mind and would not look for other explanations.

'She'd better be found,' Felix muttered.

Both men thought she might be doing something stupid. In fact she and Jane were in the kitchen at Rose Cottage, having coffee with Howard Smythe.

'You haven't seen the police yet, have you?' Howard asked Jane. 'Apart from the constable we met just now, I mean.'

'I don't suppose they've realised I've arrived,' Jane said. 'I suppose I can't put it off much longer. I ought to call them.'

'Ring from here,' said Howard. 'And while you're gone, Imogen can stay with me – if that will suit you, Imogen?'

Imogen nodded.

'They'll want me, as well. That creep Fleming will third-degree me and start twisting everything I say,' she muttered.

'Aren't you exaggerating, Imogen?' said Howard. 'The problem seems to be that you won't say anything.'

Imogen had the grace to smile, though in a shamefaced way.

'There's no need for you to go over there unless they ask you to,' said Jane. 'And I doubt if they'll think of looking for you here.' She didn't want to leave the girl alone, and Howard's was a good suggestion. The two got along, Jane saw, and the wise old man was skilled at handling people; the constable on the river bank had instantly done as he had been asked.

'Will you find the way?' asked Imogen.

'Once I get to Nettington, anyone will tell me where the police station is,' said Jane. Howard gave her some directions, Imogen lent Jane her mobile phone, and Howard wrote down his telephone number.

Jane felt apprehensive, driving off, after telephoning to say that she was on her way. What would she hear? Had her mother struggled and suffered or had Brian been correct when he said that death came suddenly?

She passed Felix on the road, but neither recognised the other's car.

Fleming had planned to grill young Imogen this morning, but he had barely parted from her father when news came that a taxi driver who had taken her to Becktham on Friday evening had been traced.

Fleming would not let this information alter his construct of what he was convinced was a crime. Imogen could have gone to Becktham and come back in time to lure Charlotte Frost from the house to the river.

Meanwhile, a resident of Becktham, a youth with whom

Imogen was on very friendly terms, since they had been witnessed kissing, was conveniently locked up in one of his cells. Questioning Jerry Hunt about his relationship with Imogen might produce interesting results.

But Jerry wouldn't say a word: only that of course he knew her, working as he did in her grandmother's garden.

After Jane had left for Nettington, Imogen asked Howard what would happen when she arrived at the police station.

'The formalities will be explained,' he said. 'And she may want to see her mother. It's natural. When someone dies suddenly, it can be difficult to believe unless you see them. It happened a lot like that in the war, when ships were sunk and relatives received telegrams, and there was no funeral.'

'She'd never been to the house,' she said. 'Jane hadn't, I mean. She was never there with Charlotte, and I was. It's so unfair.'

'Life is, Imogen. You know that,' Howard answered. 'The police will explain about the inquest – there will have to be one, I feel sure. Afterwards, they will be able to arrange the funeral.' He thought about sailors dying of their wounds, their bodies buried at sea, and sighed.

'I hope her brother comes soon. I'm no help – I'm just a nuisance,' said Imogen.

'I'm sure you're not being a nuisance now, Imogen, and you are company for her. That's good. You may have been the last person to see Charlotte alive. That will mean something to Jane and her brother.'

'You don't think I pushed her into the river, do you?' asked Imogen.

'You know I don't,' he answered. 'But why don't you tell Mr Fleming that you went to Becktham on Friday night?'

Imogen's face turned ashen as she stared at him.

'How do you know?' She spoke in a whisper.

At least she hadn't denied it.

'The taxi driver who brought me back last night drove you there. He recognised you.'

'Yes – I knew that, when he came to the door,' she said. Then she got angry. 'He had no right to tell you,' she stormed. 'It's my business.'

'He was worried about you. He thought you were upset, that night,' said Howard. 'You went to see Jerry, didn't you?'

Imogen remained silent, and Howard sighed again.

'Imogen, I'm not trying to trap you. I'm trying to help you but you are doing nothing to help yourself,' he said.

'Jerry was out,' Imogen said. 'And his mother.' It wasn't a lie; they were, when she arrived.

'So you came home?'

'After a bit.'

'In a taxi?'

Imogen debated whether to say she had hitched a lift, but that would provoke a heavy lecture about the risks of hitching. In the end, she stayed silent, an answer in itself.

'I see,' said Howard, and he fell silent too, meditating on what line to take next.

Imogen broke the silence.

'But for me, Charlotte wouldn't be dead,' she said.

'Charlotte was unwise to go over the fields at night, alone, searching for you, if that was what she was doing,' said Howard. 'But she had had a difficult time herself latterly, and she may not have been thinking very sensibly. She'd been married to your grandfather for only a short time, hadn't she? She'd had to adapt to that, and then he died and almost at once she moved here. That's right, isn't it?'

'Yes.'

'It must all have been very distressing and difficult for her,' he said. 'Your coming to stay must have been a mixed blessing. I could see she was fond of you, but to have a girl to stay who was causing her own family a lot of worry must have been a strain.'

'Do you mean I was the last straw and she committed suicide?'

'No. I don't think someone like Charlotte would take such a step. She would know it would cause a lot of sorrow and make other people feel guilty.' Unless she really had snapped, he thought, and had a breakdown. Desperate people did not always show outward signs of acute distress.

'What must I do?' said Imogen.

'I think you should tell Fleming what you've told me – that you went to see Jerry but he was out, and so after a while you came back,' he said.

Unless Jerry told, no one would know that she knew where the key to his house was kept, and that she'd used it.

Imogen didn't know that Jerry had been arrested.

'Must I go and tell Fleming now?' she said.

'I think he'll be busy with Jane. Probably he'll want to see you anyway but he doesn't know you're here. Let's wait a bit and see what happens,' Howard said.

He wondered how to keep her occupied, but Imogen, restless, got up and walked about his study, where they had been sitting after Jane's departure, peering at photographs displayed on shelves and on his desk. Most were of ships and sailors, and she asked about them. They ended up sitting beside one another at his desk, looking at his albums which contained photographs of ships' companies, and of Malta and other places where he had been based after the war.

'All this makes what I've done seem so petty,' she said.

'The navy was my profession,' he replied. 'And I was more than eighteen years old when the war began.' But eighteen-year-olds had gone to sea, and had flown Spitfires. And been killed.

'What will happen? Will I go to prison?' she asked.

'I doubt it.'

'Felix will kill me.'

'I don't think he'll go quite that far, Imogen, but he has every right to be extremely angry.'

'If they don't lock me up, I could go to Africa and help starving children. That would get me out of everybody's hair.'

She could, if she could be trusted to behave sensibly and think of others, not herself. On the other hand, as she was so given to fantasy, perhaps a career in the theatre might be more appropriate.

'You could begin by apologising,' he suggested.

Felix, arriving at Vicarage Fields, found the house empty, and again he let himself in.

He walked through the ground-floor rooms, feeling the radiators, which were agreeably warm to his touch, and looking out, he saw the tidy garden with the new lawn laid, beds freshly dug, and a few small plants bravely standing up against the weather.

That was an improvement. It would add to the value of the house.

He walked all round, inspecting it with a vendor's eye. The room Imogen was using was extremely neat; no clothes were strewn about; it barely looked occupied. He was denied the satisfaction of anger at untidiness as he gave a snort of frustration and shut the door. Charlotte's room was less orderly. The duvet had been drawn up and the pillows plumped, but the bedspread was folded back over the end of the bed, and a pair of black trousers lay across a chair. A make-up bag was open on the dressing-table on which were a wooden-backed hairbrush and a bottle of paracetamol tablets. A suitcase, not yet properly unpacked but unzipped, was on the floor. He lifted the lid and looked inside. The contents were disturbed, where Jane had rummaged for things she wanted straight away. He picked up a sweater and sniffed it, then shoved it back again. He had no interest in Jane. The room itself, like the rest of the house, had been decorated before Charlotte moved in; Lorna had insisted on that, saying the least they could do was make sure everything was fresh and clean.

He might give the estate agent through whom it had been bought a call, advise that it would soon be up for sale again. Fortunately, as it was his and Lorna's house, there would be no need to wait for probate. He'd hustle the police, make them get on with things.

Though there was still the problem of what to do with Imogen.

Felix had left the police station after he and Fleming had been interrupted by another officer wanting to speak to him. Fleming had left the room, clearly annoyed, and soon Felix had decided to waste no more time waiting for his return.

The discovery of the torch by the river had prompted the possibility that the body had entered the water higher up the river than had been assumed. A good detective doesn't make assumptions; he seeks facts, but Fleming knew that facts could sometimes prove assumptions. He wanted to expedite the resolution of this case; delay cost time and money, and he took pride in his reputation for decisive action.

Now there was the possibility that the wretched girl had been in Becktham at the time of the fatality.

The post-mortem report could not be totally precise about the time of death. Fleming, prejudiced against Imogen from their first meeting, had not read the scenes-of-crime reports carefully enough to absorb details about the deceased's coat trapping air, so helping to keep her body near the surface of the water. Absence of any suicide note, and the girl's behaviour, had convinced him that she had much to answer for – and she had. He would not be deflected.

If she went to Becktham, she must have been to visit Jerry Hunt.

He sent for the youth. What would he have to say about that night?

But Jerry denied all knowledge of her visit. He'd already said that after work he had been to visit Tracy, where he spent the night.

Fleming, having been spared by Felix's impatience a resumption of their interview, was not pleased when he was told that Charlotte's daughter was in the station.

Morris brought the message.

'You'll want to see her yourself,' he told his boss.

'Bring her up,' Fleming said, resigned, preparing to switch his approach to that of kindly officer concerned for grieving relative. Would she weep? He hoped not; women's tears disgusted him.

But Jane was one who wept in private.

Detective Sergeant Morris had taken her to Fleming's office, and he had no difficulty in expressing sympathy.

'It must have been such a shock,' he said. 'I'm very sorry.'

'It's such a waste,' said Jane. 'She could have had good years ahead of her.'

'Yes.'

'I'm sure Imogen had nothing to do with it,' Jane stated. 'Except that she's been very silly.'

'That young lady thinks the world's against her,' said the sergeant.

'My mother wasn't. Nor was her grandfather.'

'Well, neither of them are here to help her now, are they?' said the sergeant, and while Jane was closeted with Fleming, he went himself to see the taxi driver who had taken a young girl from Granbury to Becktham on Friday night.

'I saw her again last night,' said the driver, who was about to go to Heathrow to meet a customer. 'When I went to collect a fare from Vicarage Fields.' He told Morris how Imogen had fled into the house like a startled rabbit when she opened the door to him. 'Up to something that other evening, in my opinion. Or she'd had a row with the boyfriend. She was very nervous.' He told Morris that his passenger last night had been a regular customer, the valiant Captain Smythe who had apprehended a burglar.

His statement might save Imogen from a worse fate than a row with the boyfriend. If Fleming got as far as charging her, persuading him to retract without strong evidence in Imogen's defence would involve the inspector swallowing his pride. Morris knew that Fleming had telephoned Mrs Frost's house earlier and had no answer, but he also knew that Jane and Imogen had been with Captain Smythe when the torch was found. Without mentioning his mission, he set off for Granbury and Rose Cottage.

Nicholas had also telephoned Charlotte's house, and he had tried Imogen's mobile phone, with no reply from either. Anxious about his sister, he had spoken to Brian.

He had spent the night with Phoebe, arriving late after his shift in the restaurant, and she had been asleep. He had snuggled in beside her warm body, wanting to wake her but respecting her need for rest; she worked hard with the children, and now the ironing, which had taken off in an amazing way. He had left flyers in shops and cafés and had been surprised at how successful it had been so soon. In the morning, both of them were woken early by the arrival on their bed of Toby, Phoebe's elder son, wanting cuddles before the baby started asserting his demands. Nicholas thought Toby a great little guy and was good-natured about this daily custom. He didn't remember such domestic happiness in his youth; he and Imogen had not been encouraged to burst into their parents' bedroom in this way. It had been a cold upbringing; he saw that now.

Once the day was under way, with the baby washed and fed, Phoebe asked him what was happening to his sister, so Nicholas, trying to discover, had made the calls.

'You should go and find her. Spirit her away,' said Phoebe,

when he reported what Brian had said. 'Hide her here. They'd never think to look.'

Imogen had suggested it and he had turned her down.

'She's not an easy girl,' he warned.

'She's not a killer, though, is she?' countered Phoebe. 'I expect she thought your mum and dad would get back together if she made a stir.'

'That's about it, I'd say,' Nicholas admitted. He hated speculative sentimental talk. 'She doesn't help herself,' he added. 'She gets people's backs up.'

'If she'd really been pregnant, she'd have something to worry about,' said Phoebe. 'She's not the maternal type, from what you say, which I always was. Hadn't you better go over there and find out what's going on?'

Phoebe thought Nicholas was worth hanging on to, if she could do it; he was kind and undemanding, and generous with what funds he had, but he was so young that he would eventually want to leave her. She didn't look too far into the future; he'd help with the ironing business, which had been his idea, and he was already thinking that a house-cleaning service would be a good scheme, if they could get the workers. Perhaps Imogen could be the first one. Poor kid, she must be scared if the police had got it in for her. She could doss down on the sofa for a bit.

Nicholas kissed Phoebe briskly and said, 'Goodbye, lads,' to the children. Then he set off on his errand. He might just make it there and back in time for midday duty in the restaurant. If he could find Imogen.

23

Morris walked up the path at Rose Cottage and rang the bell.

After a little delay, during which time he heard some movement in the house, Captain Smythe opened the door.

Morris produced his warrant card. He and Captain Smythe had never met.

'I wonder if Imogen Frost is here,' said Morris. He looked the old man in the eye. 'For her own good, I need to find her.'

Imogen had mentioned the nice sergeant and Howard had at first thought she meant Beddoes, but when she named Morris, and described him – a shortish man, stout, and balding – he had known it was another man, and here he was.

Hearing the bell, Imogen had panicked.

'It's probably a salesman, or someone making a charity collection,' Howard had said, accustomed to such callers. The collector could not be turned away but there was a notice attached to the doorpost stating WE DO NOT BUY OR SELL AT THIS DOOR. It discouraged some, though it had not prevented Jerry from ringing the bell.

'I'll hide,' said Imogen, and fled from the room.

Now Howard led the sergeant into the sitting-room.

'Come in, Sergeant Morris,' he said, loudly enough for Imogen, who had dashed into the kitchen, to hear.

Morris followed him into the sitting-room.

'Sit down, sergeant,' said Howard, adding, 'Well?'

'I was wondering if you could tell me where Imogen Frost is,' said Morris. 'Miss Paterson is at the police station and there's no one at the house. When last heard of, she was with yourself and Miss Paterson down by the river.'

'Hm – yes,' said Howard.

'A taxi driver has been found who can testify to taking her to Becktham on Friday night,' said Morris. 'He dropped her on the corner of the road where Jerry Hunt, the gardener, lives with his mother. No prizes for guessing where she was going.'

'You want her to admit it,' Howard said.

'Coming from her, voluntarily, it would be well received,' said Morris. 'Then there's the little matter of a shirt. An Everton shirt. She's said that she's not interested in football, but Jerry Hunt's an Everton supporter. I wonder how she came to have this shirt?'

Howard would like to know the answer, too.

'Hunt's in custody,' Morris told him. 'On a different matter.'

This was news to Howard. He nodded sadly.

'What does he say about Friday?' he asked.

'Says he never saw her. Says he spent the night with a girlfriend. A different one,' said Morris. 'The girl's confirmed it.'

'What's he being charged with?'

'He hasn't been charged yet. He's suspected of involvement in thefts from the area, in partnership with Pete Dixon, who broke in here.'

'Oh dear,' said Howard. 'I thought he'd decided to go straight.'

'I believe he had,' said Morris. 'The evidence – a bracelet found in his mother's car – links him to an earlier offence.'

'That would have been when the days were shorter,' Howard said. 'They called on older people, I believe, one of them at the door while the other slipped round the back. Mrs Frost and I had each had Hunt calling at our doors, and perhaps his friend was trying his luck about breaking in, but they took nothing then.'

'It gave Dixon an opportunity to scout round your place, and come back later,' Morris remarked. 'He may have used Hunt's mother's car that night, and Hunt may have known about it.'

'I see. That could imply a connection.'

'Yes.'

'Sergeant, if you'll excuse me for a moment, I'll just fetch something from the kitchen,' Howard said, and he left the room.

Morris understood him perfectly, waiting for him to return with Imogen.

But he didn't. He came hurrying back, pale and out of breath, at last revealing that he was, indeed, an old man and one not in the very best of health.

'She's gone,' he said. 'Oh, the silly child! She was in the kitchen, out of the way until she knew who was at the door. When she realised it was the police, she must have run off.'

* * *

Nicholas found his father at Charlotte's house.

When he saw the Mercedes outside, he almost turned away, but then he thought of Imogen at the mercy of their father. Or their non-father. He had no key, but he rang the bell, pressing it hard. It buzzed throughout the house, and after a few minutes Felix appeared.

'Oh, it's you,' he said, ungraciously.

'"Hi", or "good to see you" would be nice,' said Nicholas, realising with a shock how rarely he received such greetings from Felix. Imogen must have had a poor reception still more frequently.

'I've a lot on my mind,' said Felix. 'That damned policeman is an idiot.'

'If you mean Fleming, yes, he is,' said Nicholas, adding, sweetly, 'Aren't you going to ask me in?'

'Oh, come in, then,' Felix growled.

'I'm pleased to see you, too,' said Nicholas, and suddenly his brain seemed to soar as he walked into the house and he said, 'You and Mum have done all this damage. Charlotte's death and now whatever Imogen's got up to.'

'Imogen caused Charlotte's death,' snapped Felix.

'Indirectly, yes, because you and Lorna made Charlotte have her to stay when she'd been a prat,' said Nicholas. He stood facing Felix, tall, angry, young and fit, a challenge to the defeated middle-aged man whose name he bore. 'And you hustled Charlotte out of White Lodge without giving her time to think about where she'd like to live. Granddad would have been furious.'

'Don't speak to me like that,' Felix roared at him. 'How dare you?'

'You can't bully me. You treated Imogen like shit but I must say you were always decent enough to me,' said Nicholas, his rage abating slightly and turning to elation as he saw Felix on the point of disintegration. Stand up to bullies and they crumple, he thought defiantly.

'Imogen wanted for nothing. Neither of you did.'

'You – or Mum – dragged her away from a school where she was doing well and had earned respect even if she hadn't many friends,' he said, in full flow now. 'It's a wonder she didn't get herself really pregnant – perhaps it's a pity, except for the kid. Though it could do worse,' he added, thinking of Phoebe. Maybe having a kid would bring the maternal out in Imogen, but it hadn't in their mother: or not for Imogen.

'You don't know what you're saying.' Felix tried to gain control.

'Yes, I do. I'm telling you that you and Mum are selfish parents, and you've both neglected Imogen emotionally.' He hated using such a word, but now he'd begun on this, he'd see it through, wherever it was going. 'Why did you have us, anyway, if you hate kids so much? Or did Mum have an affair and got pregnant, and you went along with it? You never gave an answer when I said you couldn't be our real father.'

At this, Felix suddenly subsided totally. He slumped into an armchair, rubbing his hand across his forehead.

'I'm not your real father,' he said. 'I'm infertile – not impotent, in case you think they're the same thing,' he added, with regained asperity. 'Zoe wanted children. People had children. It's what you did – you got married, got the house, maybe the dog, then the children, but in our case they didn't come. I didn't know it was my fault till later. Zoe was obsessed by it – I don't know if it really was this craving women get. There's no doubt they do – and some men – we met them when we had tests, heartbroken, some of them. Pitiful. Zoe wasn't like that. Maybe she thought she was failing in one of life's challenges.' He paused, then said, 'Nicholas, for God's sake sit down. Stop looming over me.'

Nicholas had never heard Felix speak in such a bleak, subdued tone. He sat down on the sofa, waiting for what was to follow, for he would not let Felix stop now, even if he wanted to.

'We found out it was me. Zoe didn't want clinical intervention then – it was only just beginning, what you called test-tube stuff, and sometimes there were lots of babies – five or six. As by then we knew I was to blame, I agreed that she could deal with it the way she wanted. So she went to Crete and met someone. She told me recently that there were several men. All I knew was that it had worked.'

For the first time in his life, Nicholas felt sorry for Felix.

'She didn't love the guy. Guys. It was a one-night stand,' he said. 'Or they were.'

'Maybe they – or one of them – was better in bed than me,' said Felix bitterly. 'I loved her a lot, Nicholas. You must understand that. I wanted her to be happy. I thought it would be all right because, as you say, it was casual – there was no relationship – not like her and Daniel now. They're colleagues, too. In a way.'

They were. That was how they'd met.

'So who was our father? He must have had brown eyes,' said Nicholas.

'Maybe he was Greek. Before she took off with Daniel I tried to get her to tell me. I'd spent years tormenting myself, imagining someone fair, like you, or some ugly chap like

Imogen. She said there'd been a Swede, a German and a Greek. If that was true, maybe you've got two different fathers.'

'Is that possible?'

'I don't know and I haven't tried to find out. But on two consecutive nights – or the same day, in the afternoon, another at night – who's to say?'

'What about AIDS? Weren't you afraid of that?'

'It was before the AIDS scare started. But there could have been other diseases, of course. I expect she picked carefully. She'd look for healthy specimens. And she was very attractive. Still is. She'd have had no problem finding someone. I keep wondering about him – who he was – what you've inherited.'

'You still love her, don't you?' Nicholas said.

'To tell you the truth, I don't know,' Felix said. 'I love what she was – beautiful and clever. Everyone thought I was a lucky guy and so did I.'

'Was she a trophy?' Nicholas asked. 'A prize?'

'In a way, I suppose.'

'But so were you. You had a successful father with a lovely house in the country, a good job and prospects.'

They'd known each other at university, though they hadn't got together then, meeting again on a skiing holiday.

'It wasn't enough. I wasn't enough,' said Felix. 'More money wasn't enough. And the company's in trouble.'

Nicholas was embarrassed now.

'Sorry,' he said. 'But we haven't sorted Imogen. Where is she? With the police?'

'No – or not when I left that self-satisfied inspector this morning. He got called away and I hadn't time to hang about. I'd better get back.' He'd got details to tie up about the loan.

'Not till we know about Imogen,' said Nick, who had to get back too, though only to the restaurant.

'Wretched girl,' said Felix.

'And not your daughter, but she's your responsibility, and whatever else, she is my sister,' Nicholas said. 'I want to know where she is. I'll try her mobile.' He pulled his from his pocket and punched in her code, but it didn't ring. 'Shit,' he said. 'She's not switched on.'

'No, she's not,' said Felix. 'And there's no need for that language.'

'Well, we've got to find her.'

'Jane isn't here either. Probably they've gone shopping,' said Felix. 'They may need food.'

'I'll see if the car's there,' said Nicholas. When he arrived, he'd seen that the garage door was shut. Now he left the room and went outside, returning promptly. 'It's out.'

'Well that's all right, then,' Felix said. 'Jane'll look after her.'

'Dad – Felix –' He was going to stop calling him Dad. 'You can't just expect Jane to take that on. Why should she? She's no relation. You know Imogen's screwed up – we have to find her and save her from being accused of Charlotte's murder.'

'That isn't going to happen.' But Brian had thought it might. 'What are you suggesting? That we sit tight here until she turns up?'

'Yeah – why not?' But Nicholas saw his restaurant shift time rapidly approaching. He heaved a sigh, then pulled out his mobile once again and dialled the number. He'd have to say that he was sick and couldn't make it. 'Oh well, if I lose that job, there's always another,' he said aloud.

Felix didn't even know he had a job. Nicholas told him about it, and about Phoebe and the ironing, and his idea for the cleaning service. It was perhaps the most significant conversation they had ever had. By the end of it, Jane and Imogen had not returned.

'We don't know what time they went out,' Felix said. He was impatient now.

'You can't leave. Not till we know the score,' said Nicholas, his own employment bridge perhaps already burnt. Then he had an idea. 'I wonder if they've gone to see the old man.'

'What old man?'

'Captain Smythe. He lives down near the church. He's great – he caught a burglar and sat on him till the police came.' That reminded Nicholas of Jerry and the suspicious manner in which he had known just where to look for his mother's stolen car. 'He was a friend of Charlotte's and he knew Imogen.'

'No harm in trying,' Felix said. 'Give him a ring.'

But there was no reply from Howard Smythe's number.

After Howard told him Imogen had gone, Morris went straight into the kitchen and out of the back door.

He didn't think she could have got upstairs without their hearing, for Captain Smythe had left the sitting-room door open; she had probably run off even before they embarked on their brief talk which had been largely engineered for her benefit, but he asked Howard to have a look round the house. Morris went down the garden, which was large and full of bushy shrubs and places where a child would love to hide, but though everyone seemed to be thinking of Imogen as a child, she was a young woman and she was unlikely to be crouched behind a laurustinus. He remembered how he had felt at much her age: grotesque, he had been called, a nerd, and worse. His face had been spotty, and as he started to shave, though it was unnecessary except to keep up with his classmates, the spots he scraped became infected, growing even bigger. He was picked upon and bullied, and he was blamed for pranks and other mischief at school. Because he was plain and ugly, people thought he had a plain and ugly soul, and when his mother went off with another man, leaving him and his small sister with their father, he, aged nine, was sure it was because of him. If he had been a fine handsome lad, she might have stayed. He understood Imogen; she thought everything bad that happened was her fault and she had no confidence. Morris's world had changed when his father remarried and his new wife's son, older than he, took him along to Judo classes. This led eventually to his joining the police, where a tough appearance was, at times, an asset. Now he had a wife who loved him; she had been let down by smooth, better-looking men, and she knew his worth. His acne had cleared up, though it had left some scars; Imogen had beautiful pale skin, and, with a weight loss and some guidance, could look good. There was hope for her, with a change of attitude.

Where would he have gone, in the situation she was in today? Captain Smythe had hoped she would step forward, volunteering that she had been to Becktham. Why be secretive about it now? If she had overheard their conversation, she would have learned of Jerry's alleged connection with Pete

Dixon, and that might have shattered some of her illusions. Maybe this had made her lose her nerve. She had plenty of that, misguided though it was, maintaining her pretence for so long. Walking swiftly through the garden, casting round, Morris came to the pond. He stared down at it, moving to the little jetty. After the rain, its surface was slippery. Imogen could have slid from it into the water, copying Charlotte's fate, and it was possible to drown in just a few inches. This quiet pool might be deep; he'd have to call out men to search for her. With sticks and probes they could discover whether she was here. He pulled out his phone to call for this support but then he glanced up at the hedge on the far side of the pool, and saw broken twigs. Someone had gone through this way, and recently. A stream linked the pond to the field beyond; it must join up with the river.

A constable was still down there, at the spot where Charlotte's body had been found, but there were other places where a suicide, a desperate girl intent on a final gesture, could make the attempt.

24

Imogen was not in the house. Howard Smythe had known he would not find her there but the sergeant's decision that it should be checked had been correct, and he, as the younger man, was the one to speed down the garden.

Howard looked in cupboards and under the high, old-fashioned beds, but the rooms were empty. Holding on to the banister rail, he went downstairs again and made sure Imogen was not skulking in the cloakroom, where there was a big press full of coats and boots. Then he put a jacket on and went into the garden. He was out of earshot when Nicholas tried to get him on the telephone.

Morris had gone over the hedge, further along than where it seemed clear that Imogen had crossed, but as Howard approached, he clambered back.

'She went this way,' he said. 'See where she's caught her jersey on the wire.' The hawthorn hedge had strands of barbed wire running through it. Morris had picked a different place to go through, so as to leave the evidence untouched. 'I thought at first she might have tried the pond.'

Howard was somewhat out of breath. He stood on the

jetty looking down into the depths, but the lilies seemed undisturbed; there were no torn or broken leaves. The pond was more than three feet deep, enough for a repeat of Charlotte's fatal fall, and if Imogen had slid over the jetty's edge there need not be much trace, but a young woman's reflexes would cause her to struggle for survival. This was, however, a girl who ran away from problems.

'I don't think she's down there,' Howard told Morris.

'She might have gone to the river,' Morris said. 'I've got support coming out to search for her.' He was afraid Fleming would be among those now on their way.

'She doesn't know these fields and paths,' said Howard. But she could work out for herself that the small stream running through the field would link up with the river. There were cattle in the further field; would she be familiar enough with country ways to walk through them? He didn't know.

'She's not in sight,' said Morris. 'But I'll go on that way, following the stream. Support will soon be here and they'll spread out further on. There hasn't been time for her to get far.'

'Will they bring dogs?' asked Howard.

'If we don't find her quickly, probably. Or the helicopter.'

'I'll go back,' said Howard. 'Jane Paterson will be coming to collect her.' He was too old to be helpful in the search; trained officers were the ones most likely to find her. 'She hasn't got a coat,' he added. 'It's still in the house.' She'd left it on a chair in the hall. 'She had a black jumper on. Oh – you know that, from the wire. Blue denim jeans, too.'

'Right.' Morris was straddling the fence again, catching his trousers on the wire as he went.

Howard saw him running into the field; for such a heavy,

thickset man, he was swift on his feet, but Imogen, much younger, would be faster. He walked slowly back to the house, circling round the garden as he went, looking into the shed, which Morris might have missed, making sure she wasn't there. He loathed being no longer strong enough to take an active physical part in the search, but his brain was not defective, and he probably knew the locality better than some of the police, who came from Nettington and whose officers might live in other areas. Charlotte might have ventured as far as the river before her fatal last walk, but Imogen's knowledge was likely to be very limited.

Back in the house, he wrote a note for Jane and put it on the kitchen table. Then he pinned a notice to the front door, for she would ring the bell when she returned, telling her that he was out and to go in round the back. Too bad if a burglar came and read it first, but Dixon and Jerry were both off the scene at present. He let Imogen's jacket remain where it was; it was evidence of her presence. Then he left the house.

Imogen had heard very little of the talk between Howard Smythe and Detective Sergeant Morris. As soon as she realised who the caller was, her instinct, as always, was to flee, and she went out by the back door, pausing only to shut it quietly, racing down the garden to the pond. There, she hesitated, glancing round. She saw the shed, but if she hid there, any search would be certain to include it. She ran because that sly inspector thought she had killed Charlotte and he would do his best to prove it, and because the secret of her visit to see Jerry would be exposed. With the taxi driver's evidence, Jerry would never deny that he had seen her; by admitting it, he would prove that she couldn't have been there when Charlotte fell, but such a statement would also prove, lest he be suspected of being implicated, that neither was he.

She broke through the hedge at the bottom of the garden, snapping twigs and branches as she went, and tearing her long black sweater on the wire as she squeezed through the strands. Ahead, the stream ran through the field where some heifers grazed; none took much notice of her, and Imogen made a tentative move to cross their meadow. Then she changed her mind. Pursuit would be in that direction, the obvious one. She must go another way.

Felix and Nicholas were wondering what their next move should be, each separately deploring the waste of precious time that could have been profitably spent, when the telephone rang.

Nicholas answered it.

It was Jane, using, as she told him, Imogen's mobile phone and calling from the car. She had pulled in to a gateway on the way back to Granbury after taking a wrong turn, and had tried first to telephone Captain Smythe to say that she was on her way to collect Imogen; however, there was no reply. Imagining that Imogen might have returned to Vicarage Fields, she had decided to try ringing there.

Nicholas explained that Felix was with him and that they did not know where Imogen was. He had also telephoned the captain, but with no result. It was agreed that they would meet at Rose Cottage, since that was where Jane expected to find Imogen.

'They're probably in the garden,' Jane said calmly. 'It's quite big. They might not hear the phone. I'll go there, once I get back on to the right road.'

'We'll meet you there,' said Nicholas.

He and Felix got into the Mercedes and were soon at Rose Cottage, parked outside the gate where there was a police car drawn up close against the road edge.

'Shit,' said Nicholas. 'Now what's up?'

'I wish you wouldn't use that word so much,' said Felix irritably.

'It's habit,' said Nicholas, getting out of the car as soon as it had stopped.

The gates were open, and on the front door was pinned the note left for Jane. There was nothing written on it to arouse alarm, but the presence of the police car seemed ominous to Nicholas. He ran round to the back door and opened it. On the kitchen table was the other message.

Imogen has run off. The police are searching for her. Suggest you wait here, or, if you go back to Charlotte's house, please leave a message saying you have done so. H.S. Time: 12.30 hours. A ballpoint pen lay beside the note.

Twelve-thirty: it was now getting on for one.

'She's gone off, just like Charlotte did,' said Nicholas, his face white, as Felix came into the house.

'Why on earth—? The stupid, senseless little—'

'Don't you bad-mouth her any more. Haven't you done enough damage as it is?' Nicholas yelled at him. He stood there in the kitchen, briefly irresolute, and if Felix had been a fanciful man, he would have said he was attempting psychic communication with his twin, but Felix did not believe in such notions. 'I'm going to look for her,' he went on. 'You stay here and wait for Jane.' With this instruction, Nicholas rushed off.

Christ! What next? Felix subsided on to a kitchen chair and read Howard's note. Who was this Captain Smythe, anyway? A local hero, evidently. He drummed his fingers on the table. Bloody Imogen and bloody Zoe, and bloody Nicholas as well, a rude, ungrateful boy. Felix was in the mood to blame everyone but himself not just for his personal difficulties but even for his financial crisis. Angry and frustrated, he went into the garden, marching up and down, not heeding his surroundings, totally consumed with rage.

He was still out there, pacing about, when Jane arrived.

'She's still missing,' Felix greeted her. 'I should think you'd like to strangle her. I certainly would.'

'Oh, for heaven's sake—' On their few meetings, Jane had thought Felix a hollow man, not as clever as he liked to think he was, and not someone to be helpful in a crisis. A word of condolence from him, concerning Charlotte, might not have come amiss at this moment, but she would not waste energy on scoring points.

'Mind you, that inspector's got a lot to answer for, treating the girl as if she's a murderer,' Felix went on.

'There I agree with you,' said Jane. 'But seeking to apportion blame is pointless. Imogen has been very silly, but no more. She's hurt herself as much as anyone else.'

'She's caused your mother's death,' said Felix in a pompous tone.

'She hasn't. Mother fell, and as far as I can discover, there is no proof whatsoever that she even went into Imogen's room on Friday night. She may not have known that Imogen had gone out. For some reason – maybe her own unhappiness – she went for a walk after Imogen had gone to bed, not thinking it was necessary to leave a note because she expected to return. It was unwise to leave the road and go so far. No more. Now our concern must be for the living – Imogen. I passed several police cars on the road beside the river. I suppose they're looking for her there.'

'I suppose so.'

'Well, I'm going to wait in the house,' said Jane. 'If she's found, someone may telephone.'

She turned on her heel and left him. She would not join the searchers; she had no idea where to begin.

In the house, after reading Captain Smythe's note, she rang her sister-in-law, to learn that Victoria had gone to Gatwick to meet Tim, and they would come straight to Granbury. Meanwhile her mother was taking care of the children and fielding messages. Victoria had a mobile telephone and her mother gave Jane its number; now they were in touch.

After her morning with Detective Inspector Fleming, and a harrowing visit to the morgue where she had seen her mother's body, Jane needed to visit the lavatory. She went into the hall. This house doubtless had a cloakroom, and she saw a likely door. On her way towards it, she caught sight of Imogen's coat on the chair in the hall where she had left it earlier. Wherever she had gone, she had no coat and it was cold.

Jane, now acquainted, to some extent, with Imogen, had rationalised her anger with the girl. Dysfunctional was a fashionable phrase much used to describe families such as Imogen's; for one reason or another, the girl was very unhappy and had ended in Jane's mother's care. It was probable that but for Imogen, Charlotte would still be alive. However, had it not been for Felix and Zoe's callous treatment of their daughter

– their marriage break-up had clearly had a destructive effect upon her – she would not have been in Charlotte's house. Charlotte had told her on the telephone that Imogen was rather like an ill-trained puppy – after some early hostility, anxious to please, and very immature. Despite her resentment at having been manipulated into having her to stay, Charlotte had been sorry for her. Charlotte had been steamrollered by the Frosts over moving to Granbury without time to think about it, and again over taking in the wayward girl. Blaming Imogen for Charlotte's death was futile. Blame, if it had to be appointed, lay further back along the line, with self-seeking Felix and his wife. Imogen, however foolish, did not deserve to be a second victim.

Jane was exhausted, emotionally wrung out. She went into the sitting-room and sat down in Howard's big leather armchair, hoping Felix would not join her. If she could just hold out, her brother and his wife were on their way; she would not be alone in this much longer. To those Frosts, except for Imogen, it was as though her mother had never existed, as if she were invisible.

She closed her eyes, trying to compose herself, and as she did so, she heard a helicopter flying low overhead. That would be the police, looking for the missing girl. Jane feared another tragedy.

Fleming had gone straight down to the river, where as many uniformed officers as could be spared were fanning out, searching for Imogen. He strode up and down near the bridge, and was peering over it into the murky depths when Morris approached.

'What are you doing here?' he barked, though he knew the message about Imogen's disappearance had come from him.

'She went through the hedge at the back of Captain Smythe's garden,' Morris said, not explaining.

'Guilty as hell,' said Fleming. 'Otherwise why run?'

'Frightened,' Morris answered curtly.

'She'll soon be found,' said Fleming. 'She hasn't had time to get far.'

This was true.

'Wasting police time,' Fleming growled. 'Well, get on with it, Morris. Don't waste any more. And what were you doing out here, anyway?' he repeated.

'We had the statement from the taxi driver. I thought a gentle approach might get Imogen to tell us about it herself.'

'But she saw you coming and ran away,' said Fleming, accurately enough. 'You exceeded your authority.'

Morris hadn't; moreover, it was he who had got Imogen to admit the lie about her pregnancy. He was saved from making a sharp reply by the sight of another figure walking towards the bridge from the road. It was Detective Chief Superintendent Thomas, head of the divisional CID, come in person to see what was going on.

Fleming turned to him, immediately transformed into a respectful subordinate.

It was Thomas who had ordered the helicopter.

Morris faded away as he heard Fleming being told about it. Fleming would consider it an unnecessary expense, but having a dozen or more uniformed officers and every available detective also searching for the girl was not cheap. If Imogen was in or near the river, she, or her body, would very soon be found. Morris turned back the way that he had come.

In Nettington, Jerry, charged with complicity in several burglaries, had come before the magistrates.

They debated whether to send him to prison while he was on remand, or allow him bail. Proof that he had been involved was limited to the discovery of a bracelet in his mother's car, alleged to have been stolen some months earlier.

Ownership of the bracelet was not immediately established. There were no initials on it, and while several gold bracelets had been stolen recently, they were often quite alike and, without initials or some inscription, identification could be difficult. Burgled householders would need to be asked if it was theirs.

Bobby Redmond, Jerry's employer, hearing about his arrest from a sobbing Angela, had gone in person to the court to speak up for him, and the magistrates allowed him to have his say.

'Here is a young man who has turned himself around,' said Bobby. 'His job is waiting for him. I believe he has reformed and if he is detained in prison he will be tempted to slide back into his former ways.'

The magistrates were swayed. The police did not oppose bail, and Jerry was remanded for a week on the understanding that he lived with his mother and continued at the chip shop, where Mr Redmond undertook to be responsible for him.

'I've done this for your mother,' Bobby told him, in the car driving back to Becktham. 'You'd better not let me down.'

Jerry had been lucky in the particular magistrates who had

heard his case. Very little evidence had been produced – his mother's missing car not reported because Jerry feared a friend had borrowed it, and the bracelet. Pete Dixon's prints had been found on the bodywork of the Metro and the boot, but any inside the car had been overlaid by Angela's and Jerry's. Further enquiries might link Jerry to earlier thefts, and if so, he could be questioned again. He admitted finding the car in Granbury, suspecting that Pete had borrowed it, but did not say that Imogen and her brother could testify to that; he did not want his connection with her to be revealed and it did not come up in this preliminary hearing, though there was no guarantee that it might not at his next appearance.

Back at the shop, Jerry, very docile and compliant, went to put on his white coat and hat while Bob telephoned Angela, who had gone to work as usual.

'You must,' Bob had told her. 'You'll do no good in court.'

She might have broken down and even interrupted the proceedings, which would not have helped. The young solicitor acting for Jerry had done a good job and been respectful to the bench. Now Jerry must keep his head down.

Angela was tearfully grateful. Punishing Jerry with imprisonment would mean an undeserved punishment for her. It might still happen, Bob knew, but time enough to face it then.

'I'll finish off the painting,' Jerry said. 'They nicked me when I was doing up our lounge.'

'You do that,' Bob approved, hoping he would not regret supporting the young man.

* * *

By following the hedge that ran along the boundaries of Rose Cottage and the neighbouring houses in Meadow Lane, Imogen had worked her way to the path which Charlotte, on her last walk, had taken from the churchyard through the fields towards the river. Imogen had been to the church on her first day in Granbury and now there was nowhere else to go. Charlotte had been a friend, but she was dead, and dead because of Imogen. Her parents – if they were her parents – hated her and were ashamed of her, and Jane, who was being kind because she was a nice person, like her mother, must hate her too. Nicholas was the only one who was on her side. He might rescue her, but she hadn't got her phone to call him; she'd lent it to Jane.

Wallowing in misery, shame and self-pity, Imogen looked for somewhere in the church to hide from her enemies. That spiteful Detective Inspector Fleming would charge her with murder if he found her, and even if the taxi driver said he'd taken her to Becktham, who would believe her when she said she was nowhere near the river when Charlotte fell in? They could say she had gone there after going back to Granbury. It could have happened like that and no one could prove otherwise, even though there would be no reason for her and Charlotte to have been there in the middle of the night. She'd be found guilty and sent to prison, and when she got out, if ever, she'd be old. She'd never have any sort of career and even Nicholas would give up on her eventually.

The choir stalls, where she'd waited for Nicholas, were too exposed to hide in. The tower would be a good place, and if she couldn't bear it any longer, she could always jump off. That would solve everybody's problems and Nick was the only person who might miss her, but then he could give up worrying about her and have more time for Phoebe. She tried a door which, from its position, must lead up to the belfry and found it locked. So that was out. Another door, leading to the vestry, was also locked. Under the regime of a previous vicar, the altar had been moved forward towards the chancel steps, so there was a space behind it. Imogen went round there and lay down on the floor, curling herself into a ball, arms crossed over her chest, tormenting herself by remembering past hurts and her own part in what had happened here in Granbury.

Howard Smythe, used to its weight and tendency to creak, opened the church door very carefully and pulled it to behind him, leaving it ajar. It made no sound. He stood for a moment on the heavy coir mat inside, then took one step forward, quietly, looking round.

The ancient building was cold and still. He listened. Nothing stirred. Slowly he walked forward down the central aisle, looking to right and left. Since the pews had been replaced with chairs, the chance to crouch down, hiding under the seats, had been removed. Howard knew that the belfry and vestry doors were kept securely locked. He advanced towards the choir stalls, where Imogen had been before, when she met her brother; then he halted.

'Imogen, if you are in here, come out, please. You are not making things any easier by running away, and I'm sure you don't want Jane to be more upset than she is already,' he said, standing in the chancel.

Silence.

'A great many policemen are out looking for you and in the end they'll think of coming here,' he continued. At that moment the helicopter droned overhead, and, raising his voice, he added, 'That helicopter is probably looking for you, too.'

Waiting for a response, he took more steps forward. She might be behind the altar, but if he went to look, she could dodge round the other side and run from the church. He could not run after her.

'Sergeant Morris has traced the taxi driver who took you to Becktham,' he continued. 'This proves you had nothing to do with Charlotte's accident. You must come back and face it, Imogen. There will be another driver who brought you back, no doubt. Jerry Hunt says he never saw you on Friday night. He spent the night with a girlfriend. He's in trouble too. He's been charged with theft.'

He waited again. Feeling tired, he sat down in the choir stalls.

'I'm going to stay here until you are ready to come back to my house,' he said and paused again. After a while he resumed. 'A bracelet has been found in Mrs Hunt's car, and it is alleged that it was stolen when Jerry and a friend of his, the youth I caught in my house, were working a joint scam. Jerry rang the bell and talked nicely to whoever answered, trying to sell them cheap articles while the other lad looked for a way into the house at the back, taking whatever he could find while Jerry kept the householder occupied.'

He paused, sighing, and went on, wondering if, after all, he was addressing only the Almighty, should there exist such a being, which he often doubted.

'Jerry had called on both Charlotte and me,' he said. 'We both advised him to give up his dishonest ways.'

Another pause.

'Some weeks later, after you arrived and he came to lunch, we both recognised him. He knew we'd done so. He worked hard in the garden and we both thought he had genuinely reformed.'

Howard had no more arguments. He waited again. He'd give her another few minutes and then he would look behind the altar, for perhaps he had been wrong and she was, after all, in the river.

There was a faint sound from beyond him, and very slowly, a figure rose up behind the altar. Imogen stood for a moment, not seeing where he was at first, and then she moved slowly towards the seated figure. He stood as she approached.

'He has reformed,' she said.

Jerry had not given her away, but neither had he saved her. She'd better save herself, if she could.

As they walked towards the door, Nicholas came from behind a pillar where he had been standing after entering as silently as Howard Smythe had done, during his soliloquy.

'I knew this was where you'd be, you loon,' he said, hurrying towards her. He hugged her. 'Come on. Dad's hopping mad.'

'Run along, the pair of you,' said Howard. 'I'll follow.'

'Thank you, sir,' Nicholas sounded truly grateful as he took his sister's hand.

Outside the church he pulled out his mobile phone. Jane had told him she was using Imogen's, so he punched in her number, hoping it was still turned on.

It was.

As Howard Smythe shut the church door, the helicopter could be heard, returning. He hoped the twins would reach Rose Cottage before a voice from above could order them to lie down on their faces. Feeling every minute of his age, Howard walked home.

Morris met the twins by the gate of Rose Cottage, where Jane had just had time to warn him that Imogen had been found.

'Go in very quietly,' he told them. 'You father is giving our chief a piece of his mind.'

He had been quite sorry to leave the show himself, as Felix, meeting Detective Chief Superintendent Thomas, who had climbed through the broken fence and entered Captain Smythe's house in company with Fleming, had launched into a fluent complaint about the detective inspector's treatment of his daughter. The opinion he was voicing was not his own, but Jane's, as he declared that there was no proof that Charlotte Frost had known that Imogen had left the house at all.

Fleming would have some explaining to do, thought Morris, quietly delighted.

'I'm taking you back to Phoebe's with me,' Nicholas told her. 'Felix will fix it for you to take your A levels somehow. Maybe you can go back to school next term – the exams finish so soon, it'd only be for a few weeks. You could stick it out. They might make you sleep in the sickroom or something, but that wouldn't be so bad. Felix has had a few shocks, one way and another. He'll do it.' Nicholas would make him.

Morris turned to Imogen.

'Keep cool in there,' he warned. 'Say very little but be ready to apologise.' Then he fixed her with his kind, steady stare. 'Jerry says he didn't see you last Friday, although you went to Becktham in a taxi. He spent the night with a girlfriend.

Do you think it's possible that the bracelet found in the car might be Mrs Hunt's?'

Imogen's eyes widened. She put her hand to her neck, where, under her bulky sweater, the locket Charlotte had given her lay concealed.

'Very probably,' she said. 'Why don't you ask her? It is the most likely explanation, after all.'